THE WINE CLUB

THE WINE CLUB

By Laurie Lisa

SEPTEMBER

1

REGGIE

It all started over a bottle of wine, a twenty-dollar bottle of Meiomi pinot noir, to be precise. Now I blame that particular bottle of wine for a multitude of sins that followed, but on that particular night, I was sitting on my back patio with Audrey, my next-door neighbor and a good friend of mine at the time. She might have even been my best friend, if you excluded the fact that we had a tendency to lie to each other. Well, maybe back then they were more like fibs, or baby lies, such as telling Audrey that she didn't look like she'd gained five pounds when, in fact, it was glaringly obvious that her stomach was overhanging her waistband, or Audrey telling me that of course my husband was still crazy about me after twenty years of marriage when, in fact, he slept on the couch way more often than he did in our marital bed. At that time, the fibs and lies of omission were usually meant to spare the other's feelings. They were acts of goodwill, in a way.

Audrey and I had shared many bottles of wine and secrets over the years because our daughters, Hayley and Marcy, were best friends and tended to join the same clubs and activities. It is a well-known fact that nothing can bring two middle-aged, middle-class, suburban soccer moms closer together than carpooling. And on that particular night, the Saturday of Labor Day weekend, we had forgone our usual jug of Gallo or bottle of Vendange and splurged on the Meiomi because we were celebrating our daughters' latest victory: the pom squad at Mohave High School. We'd had to sweat out the jitters of our daughters as they fretted and practiced all summer long, and then we'd had to endure the agony of the tryouts, sitting on the hard bleachers and clutching each other's hand as Hayley and Marcy sashayed and shimmied across the polished gym floor. It was only today, a full week after tryouts, that we'd heard the results. Our daughters were Mohave Tigerettes! All was right with the world at that moment.

I raised my glass in a toast. "To Hayley and Marcy, the newest Tigerettes."

"Here, here," Audrey said, taking a sip. "And to think that they made the team as sophomores," she marveled. "That's quite an accomplishment."

"All that hard work paid off." I savored the wine on my tongue.

Nothing could dampen our good spirits on that night, not even the heat. In early September in Scottsdale, Arizona, it was still blazing hot with no relief in sight. The overhead misters did little to lessen the suffocating heat, but did we consider moving inside? No. This was where we always sat for our wine drinking pow wows. We had solved many of our problems over a bottle of wine. We had solved many of the *world's* problems over a bottle of wine. It was too bad we couldn't remember those solutions the next morning. Or the problems, for that matter.

"What do you think of the new coach, Reggie?" Audrey arched her perfectly arched brows even higher.

Audrey knew exactly what I thought of the new coach. She and I had whispered viciously about the blonde, buxom knockout throughout the tryouts. Audrey and I could be quite catty about women who were beautiful or had more money than we would ever hope to have. But because I was in such a good mood and wasn't going to have to listen to Hayley's whining about how she would just *die* if she didn't make the team, I decided to play along. "I'm sure the former Mrs. Arizona America will be quite accomplished."

"It's funny how many times Cynthia Stewart, the beauty queen, can work that juicy tidbit into a conversation, isn't it? Most of her sentences start with, 'Back in 2008 when I was the reigning Mrs. Arizona America,' blah, blah blah."

"And she constantly brings up the fact that her perfect daughter Felicity has been the captain of the team for two years running. They're both so perfect that it's sickening."

Audrey laughed. "Why don't you tell me how you really feel, Reggie?"

I smiled fondly at my dear friend. Audrey was a beauty in her own right, with her chestnut hair that hung to her shoulders and eyes the color green that you only see on a newly leafed tree. Although she was on the short side, her figure was perfectly proportioned-- voluptuous, actually. Being tall and on the skinny side, with straight black hair that hung halfway down my back and bangs that were supposed to accentuate my dark brown eyes but were usually too long and hanging over them, I tried not to be jealous of my best friend. But Audrey made it easier by being seemingly unaware of her beauty.

Unfortunately, Marcy had taken after her mother. Unfortunate, that is, for Hayley, who had taken after me. Audrey and I had often joked about our cloned mini-mes. But it pained me that Hayley drew the short end of the stick. I kept telling her that I, too, had been a late bloomer, but that didn't cut it with my daughter, who could still pout like a two-year-old. And it wasn't like I could promise her that she'd eventually grow a good-sized pair. From the looks of things, she was going to be on the tall, lean, flat-chested end of the spectrum, like me. Embarrassingly enough, I had on a couple of occasions wondered if it was possible to be envious of my best friend's daughter's rack.

I took another sip of my wine. Because it was so much more expensive than the wine we usually drank, I felt I owed it to the Meiomi to savor it. "And to make matters even worse, Cynthia is married to some bigwig land developer. She's loaded."

Audrey nodded. "She's got more money than God."

"Nobody ever said life was fair. Some people get all the luck." Not that I meant to complain, not really. My family lived a comfortable, middle-class life. Kent worked hard at his job as a project manager at Honeywell, and while it was a decent salary, it didn't allow for a lot of extras. Like paying our son's college tuition at U of A. Caleb had gotten a partial scholarship and taken out a student loan, but I still felt bad that we couldn't provide him with the chance to get out of college debt-free. I knew that nowadays it was the norm for college graduates to be in hock, but it was still something I wished Kent and I had given our son, and all too soon, our daughter. But every single time we had a little money put away, something came up. Like braces or a busted water heater or a minor fender bender in the parking lot of Big Lots. It was as if any extra Carson cash just went zinging against a fly zapper. *Thwack!* It was history.

Audrey was basically in the same boat. Her husband Paul worked in pharmaceutical sales, but lately, his sales had been lagging, and therefore, his income. Audrey suspected that Paul was just plain bored with his job, and she had wondered if on some days he didn't work at all. Sure, he acted cheerful on the surface, but Audrey was beginning to wonder if her husband was suffering from depression. She didn't voice this to him, though, only to me.

"I have to admit that I'm a little worried about the cost of the outfits. Marcy said they need three, a practice uniform, and one each for home and away games." Audrey fingered the stem of her glass.

This was news to me. "The school doesn't pay for them?"

Audrey shook her head. "Does Red Cross pay you if you donate blood?"

I stared hard at her. "Is it really that bad?"

"I'm just kidding, Reggie. Of course we can scrape up some money for a couple of lousy outfits. They're such skimpy little things. They can't cost much." Audrey laughed.

It was a fake laugh, and I knew she was lying, but that was the thing in those days. It was an unspoken rule that we didn't call each other out on these little untruths, especially if it would embarrass the person who was lying. "I hope they're not *too* skimpy."

Right about then I was thinking: *Well, that's just great.* My daughter might be sashaying in front of hundreds of people with her small tits and ass hanging out. It was one more thing to worry about--as if there weren't enough already. These days, the normal worries for a parent, such as a kid's grades and health and happiness, were not enough. These days, a parent had to worry about all the gun violence that happened in schools and harbor the secret fear that her kid would be in the wrong place at the wrong time. And a parent had to worry about online bullying and sexting and all the other crap that the news was full of. It seemed ludicrous now to think that my biggest worries in high school had been whether or not I'd make the field hockey team and if I'd accidentally get knocked up before graduation. Now I had to worry about my daughter getting drugged and date raped, and then the video appearing on YouTube.

Furthermore, there were the worries of all the influences of social media. The truth of the matter was that Hayley seemed to be spending more and more time on her phone, computer, or tablet, or on the worst days, all three devices at the same time. Now I considered myself to be as well-informed as the next mother, and of course I had read that Snapchat, Facebook, Twitter, and Instagram all led to increased feelings of depression, anxiety, poor body image, and loneliness. But when I tried to bring up the subject with Hayley or suggested that she spend more time reading an honest-to-God book, all I got in response was a weary eye roll and a "You worry too much, Mom. Everyone's on social media." Maybe Haley was right; maybe I did worry too much. But it was my job, wasn't it?

"Skimpy or not, I'm just glad they both made the team." Audrey reached for the wine bottle and poured a splash into each of our glasses.

"I suppose this puts them in a whole new social status, according to the arbitrary hierarchy of Mohave High School." Secretly, I was glad about this. The high school, with over 2,000 students, was one of the academically strongest in the state, but it was known to be cliquish. With all the news reports about bullying, I had been worried about both girls when they started freshman year. They had a nice circle of friends, but it seemed inevitable that they would run into a mean girl here and there. I had pretty much held my breath during those first few weeks of high school, but Hayley seemed to have adjusted just fine. And I figured that if someone was bothering her, she would have told me about it. My daughter and I had always been close. Still were, as far as I was concerned. However, all those worries were water under the bridge now. Hayley was a Mohave Tigerette, which carried some guarantee that she was accepted, maybe even more popular now. Naively, I thought that it meant that she was safe. She had a place where she belonged in the choppy waters of a twenty-first-century high school.

It was already glaringly apparent to me that boys and girls had completely different experiences in high school. Or maybe that was too broad of a statement. The differences I was noticing between my son and daughter could have been caused by the fact that they were polar opposites of each other. Hayley desperately wanted to belong, while Caleb had never given a damn. During his tenure at MHS, he had been studious and withdrawn and had drifted through the years without landing in any certain social niche. He hadn't made waves, and consequently, no waves had threatened to pull him under. Had I thought it was odd when he never wanted to go to a football game--heaven forbid he would actually go out for a team--or a homecoming dance or even on a date, for crying out loud? Hell, yes, I'd thought it was odd. But in my effort to be supportive of his non-participation, I knew I'd stepped over the line and into out and out badgering on more than one occasion.

Caleb kept saying to me, "I'm fine, Mom. I have Donald. One friend is enough for me. I'm happy. Lay off, will you?"

Yes, Donald. I liked Donald just fine, even if he did seem a little *out there* to me with his fascination with all things relating to *Star Wars*. But as long as Caleb was happy, I was happy. Let me tell you, I repeated that mantra to myself a lot. Donald was Caleb's roommate for the second year in a row at U of A in Tucson. Caleb was studying to be a CPA, and Donald was studying to be an RN. All that was fine and good, but why didn't they just come out and say they were lovers? Audrey and I had dissected this subject at great length. Ultimately, Audrey told me that I should respect my son's privacy. Easier said than done.

Audrey snapped her fingers in front of my face. "Earth to Regina. We haven't had enough wine yet for you to go into orbit."

"Sorry." I reached for my wine glass.

"You were thinking about Caleb just then, weren't you? You always get a certain look on your face. That wrinkle on your forehead deepens--no offense--when you think of him. So what if he's gay? Have you seen the latest issue of *People* magazine? Everyone is gay now, or wants to be. It's very *in* to be *out*." Audrey gave her low, throaty chuckle.

"That's just it. Caleb's not out yet. Why in the hell isn't he out?"

"Maybe he is, but just not to you."

"But I'm his mother!"

"That's precisely my point. He's nineteen years old. He's not obligated to tell his mommy everything."

That stung a little bit. I hated when Audrey was right, when she verbalized what I refused to admit. I was about to come back with some retort when the girls slid open the back door and tumbled onto the patio, all breathless and excited. It was good timing on their part. What I would have said next to Audrey probably would not have been very nice. I do that sometimes, speak my mind before I've filtered my thoughts and emotions. It is not one of my finest traits.

"OMG! Felicity just sent out a group text to the team. She's got the greatest ideas for new routines," Hayley gushed.

"She thinks we should all get these white leather boots at Nordstrom." Marcy flashed her phone in front of our eyes so quickly that neither Audrey nor I could get an actual look.

"And she thinks that we should get our hair and makeup done before every game. She says we could all go to her stylist at Pucci Salon." In her excitement, Hayley was bouncing up and down on her stork-like long legs.

"And she wants us to get matching gold rings to show that we're a team--"

"And jackets, Marcy, don't forget the white leather jackets! This is so awesome!" And without waiting for any kind of reply, both girls hurled themselves back through the door, slamming it shut behind them.

"Who are those girls?" I said, staring after them. Our normally sweet, polite girls seemed to have evaporated and been replaced with these down-right *giddy* fifteen-year-olds.

"What girls?" Audrey looked shell-shocked. "All I saw were dollar signs. Do you know how much boots from Nordstrom will cost? Naturally, I'm assuming they won't be on sale. And leather jackets and gold rings and hair and makeup appointments for two basketball games a week . . ." she trailed off dismally.

I was also doing the math in my head, and I didn't like the mounting sum. But maybe we were getting ahead of ourselves. "These are all Felicity's *suggestions*, Audrey. Just because this Felicity is a senior and the captain doesn't mean that everything she says is the way things are going to be, right? Maybe the girls will take a vote on these *suggestions*, and the majority will have the good sense to see that the price of all of this would be exorbitant."

"Or maybe her mother will step in and tell her how unreasonable she's being?" Audrey asked hopefully.

"The former Mrs. Arizona America?" I said, remembering that Cynthia Stewart's hair and makeup had been perfect that afternoon, no doubt compliments of a premier stylist at Pucci Salon, and she'd had a rock on her finger that, if sold, would generate enough money to feed an entire third-world country for a couple of years.

"In other words, we're screwed."

"Let's drink," I said, pouring us each some more wine. Audrey readily complied, and we changed the subject, flitting from one topic to the next, but the conversation kept stalling. It's like neither one of us could escape the elephant in the room, that elephant being in the form of a seventeen-year-old girl with long blonde hair and a flawless complexion and her equally bodacious beauty queen mother. We really were screwed.

"I'm thinking about getting a job," I said to Audrey after our other conversational topics had petered out. It was true. I had been thinking about it a lot lately. There was no longer any reason for Kent to shoulder all the financial burden of the family. In a few short months, Hayley would be getting her driver's license, and while I shuddered at even the thought of that, it was a reality that had to be faced. She would no longer need me to chauffeur her around to her various practices and orthodontist appointments and sleepovers. I would no longer be structuring my days around her schedule. God knows that I had bitched and moaned about that part of motherhood enough times, but now that the end was in sight, I found myself rather sad about it. It was the end of an era, the death of my usefulness, in a way.

I had teared up just a few days before as I dropped her off at school, thinking about how each drop-off was bringing me closer to the end. So I went and treated myself to a Starbucks Hazelnut Mocha Coconut Milk Macchiato. Just when I was beginning to feel better, the thought occurred to me that Hayley was going to need a used automobile of some sort for transportation. Caleb had taken the very old but reliable-in-an-emergency VW Beetle down to Tucson, Kent of course needed the truck for work, and she would only get my older model Honda minivan over my dead body. And I wasn't dead yet. We would need to buy Hayley a car.

"The restaurant business can't have changed that much over the past nineteen years, can it?" I asked Audrey. I had been the manager at five different restaurants before I "retired" to have children, from McDonald's to IHOP to NYPD Pizza to Olive Garden to an upscale family restaurant called Lindy's. Over the years, every time I had thought about going back to work, I had always talked myself out of it when I thought of the long hours and the temperamental work environment that was part and parcel of the business. Consequently, I'd hemmed and hawed and hesitated myself right out of the loop. At forty-four years old, I didn't know if I had the stamina to keep a thriving, lively business going five or six nights a week. Or the patience. And I'd have to learn a whole new skill set with the computer system, probably some new program that I'd never heard of. Yes, I'd had plenty of excuses over the last two decades. And now I was just plain scared to go back to work.

"As far as I know, people still need to eat." Audrey was twirling around her glass of wine like she was some trained wine expert, which she wasn't. Audrey used to be a high school art teacher before her son Jimmy was born. She'd planned on going back to work once her son started kindergarten. What she hadn't planned on was having a son with special needs. Audrey had taken it upon herself to homeschool Jimmy--she had the mistaken, yet understandable idea that Jimmy's problems were all her fault--until she finally came to the conclusion that she wasn't doing her son any favors by keeping him out of the social environment that school offered. He was acting out, and he wasn't progressing as he should. Only last year, she had enrolled Jimmy in a small private school that catered to kids with his special needs. The only problem with the school was that it wasn't cheap.

"I've been thinking about going back to work too, but I feel like I've waited too long. And now all the Scottsdale schools are cutting out the arts and music and PE programs. It's such a shame." Audrey sighed. "I suppose I could always do something freelance, sell a watercolor here or there." Then she gave her signature throaty, sexy chuckle. "There's so much money in art, right? I could make a bundle when I show my work in an Old Town gallery during the Thursday Scottsdale Art Walk. I could start painting cowboys and Apache warriors and Pima basketweavers with their coiled braids. They're what all the tourists want, didn't you know?"

"You could do it, Audrey. You're a good artist." She'd shown me some of her earlier work from time to time, and while I didn't know much about art--okay, I didn't know anything about art--I liked what she had shown me.

"Oh, sure. I'm forty-three years old, and I haven't picked up a paint-brush in years." Audrey sighed again. "Let's change the subject. Better yet, let's get tipsy. We're celebrating, remember? What's the alcohol content in this wine?"

"I hope it's high." I took a long sip of the wine. It was a good wine, Much better than the lower-shelf wines that Audrey and I usually drank, the ones in the ten-dollar and below range, mostly the *very* below range. We were not averse to wine that came in boxes either. Certainly, this wine was good, but still. I didn't know what I'd been expecting, but this pinot noir didn't exactly knock my socks off.

I held my glass up to the light. The color was excellent, a pale ruby. Back when I worked at Lindy's, the family who owned the restaurant, in an attempt to properly train their employees, had given sporadic seminars on food and wine. It had been a long time ago, but maybe I still retained a little knowledge, even though the last time I had picked up an issue of the *Wine Advocate* had been in 2008, even though my taste buds had probably atrophied from gallons of Gallo. "What do you think of this wine?"

Audrey took a sip. "It's delicious."

"What else?"

"It's very pretty." She held up her glass, imitating me. "You know the only thing I'm an expert at when it comes to wine is drinking it. What is it I'm supposed to be looking for?"

"Hmm." I was trying to remember. "The general tasting rules of swirl, sniff, and sip are a start." I swirled my glass and held it up to the light. "Do you see those slender lines of wine slowly dripping down the sides? They're called the legs. They don't really mean much when it comes to a good wine, but they can clue you in on its alcohol content."

I then sniffed the wine, even though I felt slightly silly and pretentious and knew I probably looked more like a rangy bloodhound than any kind of connoisseur. "You're supposed to ask yourself what you smell. Peppers? Tobacco? Blackberries?" Some of those micro seminars at Lindy's were coming back. "Chances are, the more you smell, the better the wine may taste. I think you want the wine to have three aromas of things your nose likes."

Audrey stuck her small nose in the goblet and inhaled deeply. "I smell wine, and that's good enough for me." She drained her glass and reached for the bottle to pour us each another round. She held it up. "Now that's sad. There's only a tiny splash left for each of us."

"I'll go get some more." I went into the kitchen and got a bottle of YellowTail pinot that I had gotten at Fry's for $4.97. While I was opening it, I had an idea. I grabbed two fresh glasses out of the cabinet and returned to the patio table. "Okay, Audrey, let's see if we can tell the difference between this bottle and the Meiomi." I poured us each a taste into the new glasses. "Here goes." I did the swirl, sniff, and sip routine with both my glasses of wine. Audrey copied my every move.

"You know I don't know what I'm doing, don't you?"

"Maybe not, but you act like you know what you're doing. That's good enough for me."

I smiled at her. That was one of the things I loved about Audrey. She would always go with the flow. "So, what do you think about the wines?"

"Honestly, I can't tell the difference." Audrey took another small sip from each glass. "I think I like the cheaper one better. I guess it's just further proof that my palate is unrefined. Big deal. What about you?"

I thought that the Meiomi was definitely better, but I didn't want to hurt Audrey's feelings, so I said, "Same here."

"I always thought that the more expensive the wine, the better it was supposed to be."

"Not necessarily, but I suppose a higher-priced wine does change a person's *perception* of how it should taste. However, some people do know their wines. There was a couple once at Lindy's who complained to the manager because their server brought the wrong *year* of a certain bottle of wine." At the time, I'd thought the older couple had pretended to be snobs about it because they didn't want to pay the two hundred dollars for the supposedly wrong wine. I wasn't alone in that. I'm almost positive that their waiter, a young college guy, spit in their cream of asparagus soup. I was on his side.

Audrey shook her head adamantly. "But most people don't. A lot of people might *pretend* that they know the difference between a bottle of five-hundred-dollar wine and a bottle of Two-Buck Chuck, but I highly doubt that they do. The only thing that really distinguishes the bottles is the label."

"That's just the artist in you talking. But I have to admit that I sometimes buy wine if it has a pretty label."

"Me too. And of course, the price." Audrey immediately looked glum again. "How much do you think this Tigerette squad is going to cost us?"

"Let's not worry about that now." I filled up our wine glasses, and as the dark red wine poured into the cup, I had an idea. Once Audrey and I started in on our second bottle of wine, I always had so-called bright ideas, but I have to say that I thought at the time that this one was brilliant. "Maybe we should start a wine club. What if we could drink wine and make money at the same time?"

At least the suggestion wiped the sourpuss look off Audrey's face. "It would be ideal if we could swirl, sniff, and sip our way to some extra cash, but who are we kidding? We don't know the first thing about wine, other than we like to drink it."

I reached for my phone and started googling. Audrey had a point, and I knew that I sometimes got a little carried away with my bright ideas and didn't always follow through. Not so long ago, I'd had the brilliant idea to refurbish my dark kitchen cabinets, to strip and sand and paint them white. As it stood right now, half of my cabinets were still a dark walnut, and half were in various stages of the stripping process. Every time I walked into my dismal kitchen, those cabinets, lined up in a row, some dark, some bare, reminded me of a meth addict's rotting teeth. So now I just avoided the damn kitchen.

"There's a lot of information online about how to start a wine club, wine tasting party games, that kind of thing." I could feel a grin spreading over my face. "There's a game called *Drunk, Stoned, or Stupid.*"

And there came Audrey's sexy chuckle. "That sounds right up our alley."

I kept scrolling. "Oh, and get this. There's something called OneHope. You get the wines from Napa Valley, have a wine party, and 10% of your proceeds go directly to the 501(c)3 charity of your choice."

"I thought we were the charity."

"Good point. We would want a total for-profit organization, wouldn't we? We're too mercenary to be charitable."

"I don't think it's wrong or particularly uncharitable to want to provide your kid with the required skimpy, flesh-baring costume of a Mohave High School Tigerette." Audrey's face was flushed a pretty pink, something that always happened when she reached a certain point on our wine drinking nights.

I wasn't paying attention to Audrey right then. I kept scrolling; I was on a roll. "We could go to some local wineries in Cottonwood or Jerome and do some wine tasting, ask questions, and then use select bottles from those places."

"This is never going to happen, Reggie. You know that."

Sometimes Audrey could be such a pessimist, even if she was probably right. My Brilliant Ideas While Drinking Wine rarely panned out. But like I said, I was on a roll. "I don't see why not."

"Because the only thing we know about wine is that we like to drink it."

"Just bear with me, okay?" I poured her more wine and continued my search.

Before too long, I heard Audrey start to chuckle again. "You know what would be incredibly funny? What if our hypothetical wine club switched the labels on bottles of wine? Say we bought a couple of cases of Two-Buck Chuck and switched the labels to a fancy bottle of wine like--"

I was already on it. "A bottle of Napa Valley's Screaming Eagle Cabernet Sauvignon, with an average price of $2,776." I looked up, and I'm pretty sure my face was flushed by then, with both the wine and excitement.

Audrey clapped her hands like a little kid. She was finally getting with the program. "Right. So you tell the women that you've assembled for your wine club party that this bottle of wine is that expensive stuff you just said, you pour little tastes, and everyone starts to ooh and ahh. So you open another bottle and talk it up, all the color and the legs and aromas, and then *presto!* You sell the rest of the bottles for the exorbitant price, and you have a net gain of over $2700 per bottle!"

"Or you could make the wine even more special by saying it comes from a vineyard in France. People always think that French wine equals expensive wine." My heart started beating faster at the illicit prospect of it all. Could we really pull something like that off?

"That's good." Audrey nodded vigorously. "But we know even less about French wine than we do American."

I arched my brows and intoned in a phony French accent: "Have I not mentioned my distant cousin who is a vintner for one of the most prestigious wineries in Bordeaux? He and I go way back, w-a-y back, and he sells me rare, select bottles of wine at a discount, which I pass onto select customers. Only a lucky few get incredibly expensive wine at a bargain price. Who could resist?"

Audrey fanned her face with her hand. "My, my, Mrs. Regina Carson, you are a devious soul."

"And I return the compliment to you, Mrs. Maynard.."

That was when we started to grin at each other like drunken fools. But we weren't drunk. At least I wasn't. I realized it was all wine-tipsy talk, but deep inside, I felt a distinct glimmer of possibility. It had been a long time since I'd felt excited about anything, too long. So that in and of itself was something special.

"I suppose our hypothetical wine club would be illegal," Audrey said after I returned from the kitchen with our third bottle of wine, a Barefoot cabernet that was the only thing left, wine-wise, in the house.

I poured new glasses, spilling a little on the glass tabletop. "We would be selling fraudulent wine to unsuspecting people. We'd be conning them out of money. Hell, yeah, it would be illegal. And the people we'd be conning would have to be unsophisticated wine drinkers."

"They'd have to be pretty stupid people in general, wouldn't they?" Audrey's mouth was stained purple, and even that looked good on her.

"Or maybe just vain. I saw this episode of *American Greed* not too long ago, and to pull off a successful con, you'd have to appeal to someone's vanity. And with wine, I think it would have to be a person who craved social status."

"There's no scarcity of vain people in north Scottsdale who are craving social status."

"That's for sure." Audrey and I had dissected the motives and exorbitant spending habits and one-upmanship among the families we knew too many times to count.

Thoughtfully, she said, "I'd really have to dislike someone to con them out of money intentionally."

"Or maybe that person did something hurtful to you, and you just wanted to get even." Right then, I couldn't think of any person I would want to get even with. Oh, there had been slights and hurt feelings over the years with some of the women I was forced to cohabit bleachers and soccer fields with, but nothing major. I didn't particularly like most of those women, so I avoided them.

"Even so, it would be illegal. We could go to jail." Audrey was starting to slur just a tiny bit, and I knew it was going to be one of those nights that I walked her home. She lived next door, but she had once made a wrong turn and ended up in our pool. Once had been enough.

"We'd only go to jail if we got caught." Obviously, I wasn't feeling any pain by that point either.

Audrey took another sip of wine. "It's a good thing our wine club is hypothetical. It's starting to get out of hand."

"We won't even remember this conversation in the morning," I assured her.

But the funny thing was that I did remember, every single word.

2

CYNTHIA

My daughter had a tendency to manipulate me and had been doing so since she uttered her first words. I knew this, yet I didn't seem to be able to stop it. Richard told me that I indulged her, but he said that with fondness, rather than any condemnation. She was the apple of his eye, and I knew it, and Felicity knew it. He adored his only daughter. We both did. Did we give her too much, too soon, as many people have accused us of doing? Probably. But Felicity had always been a good girl, an above-average student, and hadn't given us any trouble up until then, so we both gave her permission to have the sleepover at the guesthouse on our large property. Felicity reminded us that it was a tradition, that the Tigerettes always had this little party right after tryouts and before the season began. But honestly, it didn't take much coaxing from her. Richard and I were like putty in her hands.

Richard's two sons from his first and second marriages were grown men and long gone. I had only met them once, eighteen years ago, on our wedding day in Vegas, and it had been a decidedly uncomfortable meeting. You see, I was only twenty-three years old; Richard was fifty-two. And not only was I young enough to be his daughter, but I was also younger than both Jeffrey and Dirk. They smelled a money-hungry rat and made no bones about letting their feelings be known. Then when they found out I was pregnant right before the ceremony began--the minister had just uttered *Dearly beloved*--the shit really hit the fan. To this day, I can't bear to repeat all the filthy things they said about me. Suffice it to say that they called me every variation of *whore* that exists in the English language.

Then they stormed out of the wedding chapel of the MGM Grand, never to be seen again.

But Richard married me anyway.

Did I marry Richard for his money? I would like to say that the answer to that question is a resounding *no*. And leave it at that.

Richard and I had a few good years together. I was very attracted to him in the beginning. And it wasn't because of his money, although money brings power, and power is a very attractive quality in any person. He was a strongly built man, tall with broad shoulders and that mane of silver hair that he wore slightly too long, as if to prove that he was virile for a man his age. We made a striking couple at the various fundraisers and charity events that we were invited to, and there were a lot in those days. We also traveled extensively, trips to Gstaad to ski and sailing on the Med and wining and dining in France. Life was very, very good.

But when Richard decided to take an early retirement five years ago, things changed. He was only sixty-five, but it was as if he suddenly decided to act like an old man. He didn't want to go out anymore, and he didn't want to travel. As if those things were not bad enough, he reinforced his transformation by declaring that he had become impotent. My handsome, powerful husband could no longer get it up, or maybe he just didn't want to get it up for me. He decided that his time was better spent playing golf and holing up in his study to manage his investment portfolio. He met with a lawyer to revise his will. That made my spine tingle ominously, but I would not lower myself to ask what revisions he had decided to make. More than almost anything, I value my pride.

But back when things were still going well and Richard was proud of me, we were at a fundraiser for Scottsdale Memorial Hospital when a woman approached me during cocktail hour and told me that I would be a perfect candidate to run for Mrs. Arizona America. She was one of the organizers of the pageant, and well, her flattery blew me away. But as flattered as I was, I still felt the need to tell her that I really wasn't qualified for such an honor, that I didn't normally do that sort of thing. I mean, it would have looked undignified for me to accept the offer right away.

It was Richard who stepped in then, scotch and soda in hand, and said, "That sounds like something interesting for you to do, Cynthia."

It was loud in the room, so I whispered what I said next. "Don't you think it sounds kind of silly, a beauty pageant for married women?"

The woman, her name was Geraldine Mitchell, must have had hearing like a dolphin because she got a little snippy then. "I assure you that it is not. The women who enter our pageant are quite accomplished. It is much more than a beauty pageant." She handed me her business card. "Think about it."

"I think you should do it," Richard said as we were herded into the banquet hall for dinner. "You're by far the most gorgeous woman in this room. You could win, hands down."

I continued to demur throughout dinner, but secretly I desperately wanted to enter the beauty pageant. I'd wanted to wear a tiara on my head since I lost out to Mary Wilson for Homecoming Queen senior year at our small high school in Kansas. To this day, I think someone, somewhere along the way, cheated by stuffing the ballot boxes, or something like that. I was much prettier than Mary, but she was more popular than me, despite her average looks and mousy brown hair, probably because she was nice to everyone. In truth, I wasn't very popular at all, and I knew that people called me *stuck up* behind my back. I wasn't stuck up; I was just very pretty. And the kids in my high school should have voted according to the true merits of what a queen stood for--i.e., beauty. But they didn't, and I lost. Jealousy can make people do cruel things. I've seen it happen over and over again.

So later that week, after Richard agreed that I could get a little nip and tuck, I called up Geraldine Mitchell and said I would compete in the pageant. And I worked hard to be a winner. I went to LA Fitness five times a week, I studied current national and local news, I watched old videos of former winners, and I bought the most fabulous Oscar de la Renta dress I could find, a scarlet gown hand-embroidered with tonal sequins and dimensional faille organza petals on a silk-faille base, with a soft tulle illusion neckline. I bought it at Saks for just under $13,000, and it was worth every penny. According to Richard, I glowed when I walked across the stage at the Mesa Arts Center. I could tell how impressed the judges were by the looks on their faces, so I wasn't surprised when they announced the winner: me, naturally.

Consequently, 2008 was one of the best years of my life. I loved going to the opening of shopping centers and speaking before various women's groups and visiting sick people in hospitals. For once in my life, I felt like I was truly accomplishing something. I had worked as a dancer for a private gentlemen's club in Vegas--which is how I met Richard, at the club--before marriage and hadn't worked another job since then, so now I had something worthwhile to occupy my time. Certainly, I was disappointed when I didn't win the Mrs. America title in Vegas a couple of months after my coronation as Mrs. Arizona. I'd had such high hopes for that pageant too, but it wasn't meant to be. First of all, I had recently gotten over the flu and wasn't looking my best, and secondly, I think that my recent illness caused my equilibrium to be off. That was the reason why I tripped over my gorgeous Oscar de la Renta gown in my five-inch stilettos and fell flat on my face in front of hundreds of people. It was a mortifying experience, and Richard had to threaten to sue the pageant to keep that picture out of the paper. But enough about that. I don't like to dwell on my unpleasant memories.

After my reign as Mrs. Arizona ended and I joined "The Formers," as retired queens were called, life seemed pretty dull. Don't get me wrong. I liked being a mother and all that jazz, but there was no *zing* to my days anymore. Then one afternoon as I was waiting in yet another interminable carpool line, the idea came to me like a thunderbolt: I should go back to dancing. Pre-Richard, that's what I did. I danced. My parents--may God rest their souls--might not have had a lot of money, but they somehow managed to get me into every dancing class that our small town offered: jazz, tap, ballet (sort of), modern, you name it. I was always the best one in the class, and I deduced that I had a calling for that particular art form. So as soon as I graduated from high school, I hightailed it to LA with what little money my parents could spare and big dreams. Although Hollywood didn't make many big-budget musicals anymore, I was certain that I could land some dancing role in a feature film or on the stage.

Unfortunately, I discounted the fact that Hollywood was teeming with talented, naive young girls, all with dreams that rivaled mine. What's more, it was a town crowded with a bunch of losers and jerks too. I have always tended to be a trusting soul, and I would be lying if I didn't admit that I got duped a time or two by shady roommates and unscrupulous agents and producers and casting directors. It was a town full of phonies. But I limped along for a year or two. Literally. I was always spraining or overstretching some limb or muscle in an effort to kick or leap higher, in an effort to demonstrate my talent, which seemed like it was not all that impressive in that town. When one casting director suggested that my talents might be better suited for the adult film industry, that was it. I went back to my apartment, packed up, and left. More than almost anything, I value my pride. Plus, if my parents found out I was starring in porn movies, they would most certainly have stopped sending me money.

I landed in Vegas, which wasn't exactly a town full of genuine people either. I realized I was just one more cliched statistic, but I managed to find work here and there. It was amazing what I would do to earn a buck. Not that I was sleazy; I wasn't. I kept my pride and dignity intact most of the time, but there were some hard days and nights. I was seriously thinking about moving on again, without a clue as to where I could go, when I landed the plum job in the private gentlemen's club. It was certainly the best job I'd had since I left Kansas. The working environment was upscale, and so was the clientele. And the money! I could actually afford to buy a steak and a nice bottle of wine every once in a while, along with some decent clothes. I was doing great, comparatively speaking.

I'm sorry, but no. I'm not going to mention the name of that club. It's not important, and it went out of business a long time ago anyway.

Let me get back to my story. One night, Richard walked into the club. I noticed him right away. All the girls did. Now there were a lot of wealthy men who frequented that club. But there was something special about Richard. He had that swagger about him that made him stand out, and he was so much better looking than some of the other old farts. Maybe he was too old for me, but I'd never let that bother me before. I'd dated men of almost every age and race. But now I was ready to settle down and have someone take care of me. I consider myself a feminist as much as the next woman, but sometimes a gal gets tired, you know? And that man was there in the right place at the right time. I batted my lashes at him, and he fell--hook, line, and sinker. We had a whirlwind courtship, as they say, and were married three months later. The timing was perfect. My dancing days were over because my prince had finally arrived and handed me the glass slipper. I took it.

And I'd been pretty happy married to Richard, all things considered. Our marriage, like all marriages, had its ups and downs. There was the time that Richard flew off to Costa Rica for some business trip. I think he was looking at some land to invest in, but I'm not sure. Richard, even from the beginning, didn't share his business dealings with me, which was A-OK in my book, just as long as the money kept rolling in. Anyway, he was supposed to be gone for a week. He came home two months later and said he had decided to work on his golf game. But the funny thing was that he didn't have a tan. And there was the time when he went to South Africa for a week and stayed for four months. Again no tan. But this was the thing: He didn't offer any explanations, I didn't ask, and he always brought me back a very expensive piece of jewelry. From day one, Richard and I had always had an understanding. It was probably the reason our marriage worked so well.

But then five years ago, Richard retired and everything changed. I will be the first to admit that I hadn't taken into account that marrying a much older man means that you eventually will still be in the prime of life, and he's now obsessed with doctor appointments and his cholesterol and glucose levels and long-term health care for senior citizens. It's so aggravating! I kept telling him that seventy wasn't old, but he scowled at me like he resented the fact that his wife was only forty-one. Well, I say that *he* should have taken that into account when he married me. He was the one who supposedly had all the answers. But of course he didn't consider my tender age because Richard is a very, very vain man. I don't fault him for that quality at all, but when I gently suggested that he might think about getting a little nip and tuck himself, you'd think I'd brought him home a case of Depends or something. He locked himself in his study and wouldn't even come out for dinner that night.

This is the truth: Getting old sucks, but it sucks even more for good-looking people. Enough said on that subject.

Anyway, I was in the carpool line one day and decided that I would go back to dancing. Shopping was all well and good to pass the time--and Richard, God bless him, never said a word about how much money I spent--but a gal only needed so many pairs of Jimmy Choos and Louboutins. I'd tried doing charity work over the years, like women in my station tended to do, but going to a soup kitchen and physically being near homeless people was not pleasant for me. For one thing, they are not well-dressed people. Shortly after that sordid experience, I decided that I would much rather write out a check than be in close physical proximity to a person who did not have ready access to a shower.

So as I was sitting in the car that day, I thought that I had pretty much exhausted all the appropriate ways I could spend my time, and then the song came over Sirius radio. It was "Boom Boom" by Eric Clapton, a song

I used to dance to in Vegas, and I thought: *Why not?* I was still in good shape, and that song was some sort of omen.

Richard was not thrilled with the idea, though, not at all. "We agreed that your dancing days were over when you married me." Although his voice was mild, I could tell by his clenched jaw that he was going to start seething soon. Richard was not a fan of reliving my past. As far as Richard was concerned, my life started the night he walked into the gentlemen's club. I guess it was true, in a way.

We were eating dinner at the kitchen counter, salmon steaks that Louisa, our housekeeper/cook, had prepared earlier in the day. "Now, Richard." I was using my sexy baby voice, the one that used to be able to get Richard to do anything I wanted him to do, back in the day. "Hear me out about this." I put some spinach and mandarin orange salad on his plate.

"The suggestion is ludicrous." Richard made a face when he took a bite of the spinach. It was not his favorite. "There is no reason in the world why a wife of mine should be working. If you want more money, I'll increase your allowance."

"I'm not talking about doing it for money, Richard. The fact of the matter is that I'm *bored*." Lately, I had been thinking that boredom should be added to the list of the Seven Deadly Sins. Number eight: Boredom. Nothing good came out of being bored. Boredom was probably why people turned to a life of crime.

"Then take another yoga class, or better yet, take golf lessons. The women's league plays every Tuesday morning."

I was terrible at golf, and he knew it. I had no patience for the game, and being out in the scorching sun for hours at a time would put my skin on the fast track to aging. I'd stick to spray tans, thank you very much. "I was thinking something along the lines of community theater."

Richard didn't even bother to respond to that suggestion.

"Or maybe," I went on, warming up to the subject, "I could open a dance studio. I mean, you could fund it, and I'd run it and teach classes--"

Richard held up his hand to stop me. It was a gesture I despised. "You don't know the first thing about running a business, Cynthia."

I would need Richard for the funding and needed to play my cards exactly right, but still, he was making me mad. "I could learn, Richard. I'm not a complete idiot." I refilled my wine glass and took a deep drink.

Richard went into placating mode, something he was very good at. "Honey, you haven't danced professionally in eighteen years. I'm not saying that you weren't good--" He held up his stupid hand again, causing the words to die in my throat. "But don't you think you've moved *beyond* that stage of your life? And you know very well what I mean."

"I always wanted to be a dancer. Dancing is in my blood," I said stubbornly, and drank more wine. It seemed like I was doing a lot of that lately.

A smile played around the corners of Richard's lips. He knew he was winning. "I remember this one dance you used to do--"

"What dance?" Felicity had chosen that moment to walk into the room. She opened the refrigerator door, searching for her carrots and low-fat yogurt. She was dieting before the Tigerette tryouts, not that she needed to. But she was determined to look her best, and I admired her resolve. Some mothers might worry that their seventeen-year-old daughter was heading toward anorexia, but not me. I was proud of her. She was naturally slim, like me, although she didn't have the boobs yet. I figured that would be a good graduation gift in May before she headed off to college.

"Nothing." Richard beamed at her. "Looking good, sweetpea."

"Thanks, Daddy." Felicity opened a diet Coke and looked to me. "What dance?"

I took another big drink of the pinot grigio. "We were talking about the dance I did in my last off-Broadway musical. Your daddy really liked that dance." The story, as far as our daughter was concerned, was that I had danced in a couple of off-Broadway shows and worked as a personal stylist by day before I got married and retired. It wasn't that I was ashamed of my past--I wasn't--but I was a completely different person now. She didn't need to know more. There was no point.

"You took a lot of dance classes when you were young, didn't you, Mom?"

"I certainly did. I could dance any style of dance." At least this was true.

Felicity appraised me, cocking her head to one side. She looked like Richard when she made that gesture. "Do you think you still could?"

I didn't look at Richard then. "Of course I could. It's like riding a bike. It's not something you forget."

"The reason I'm asking is that Ms. Roberts has to drop out as coach of the Tigerettes. She's pregnant, and because she said I'm a shoo-in for captain again this year, she asked me if I know anyone who could coach the team. I told her I'd keep my ears open. I didn't even think about you, but the team is in desperate need of a coach." She looked me up and down, frowning. "I don't know--"

"I could do it." I'd gotten out of my chair before I even knew what I was doing. That's how excited I was. "I would love to coach the team."

Richard just had to put in his two cents' worth. "I don't know if it's a good idea for you to coach our daughter's team. You might be crowding her space a bit, Cynthia."

Before I could open my mouth to protest, Felicity added, "Yeah, Mom, you'd have to give me some space. I have my own way of doing things, and my way works. That's why we've been the state champion pom squad for the last two years, and I'm planning on winning this year. I know what I'm doing."

I was breathless and could only nod. Those were Felicity's conditions, and I agreed to them.

If I had been allowed a slot on the judging panel at the Tigerette tryouts, I'm sure that everything would have turned out differently. But being the newly appointed Tigerette coach, I had no say in the judging of the contestants. I was supposed to be impartial. It was my first day on the unpaid job, but watching the girls practice before the tryouts began, I could quickly assess who should make the team. My old dance training was kicking in like the natural instinct it was, and I automatically spotted the winners. Chief among them was my daughter, and I am not biased in the least about this. She was by far the best of the group. Her kicks were higher, her moves sharper, her timing impeccable. *Like mother, like daughter,* I was thinking as I felt a rare glow of maternal pride. I gave her a secret wink for good luck, but Felicity either didn't see it, or she was ignoring me. I suspected the latter.

Fifty girls were trying out for the team, a record number according to the two men and two women who comprised the judging panel, a sour and dowdy-looking group if I ever saw one. Just looking at the four of them, I did not understand how they could possibly have the qualifications necessary to pick the team, but I was the new gal on the block, the outsider, so I kept my mouth shut and decided I would "vote" for my choices with a very loud and vocal round of approval when each one of my picks had finished her routine. It went like this: Clap, clap clap. "You go, girl!"

Fist pump, fist pump. Looking back, I don't think this was appreciated by either the judges or the group of nervous mothers watching from the bleachers. Oh, well.

The ten girls who had been on the team the year before were practically guaranteed a spot on this year's team. This included Felicity, who really had no competition to speak of in the other dancers. All the returning group had to do, basically, was not louse up their tryout routines or do any vulgar or sexually explicit dance moves. I am not making this up. It was in the rulebook, and all the girls had been given a lecture about it before I was appointed coach. Looking at the judges on that day, I could figure out where this had come from. In addition to dowdy, they were obviously a conservative group. It was over one hundred degrees outside, and they were all wearing *cardigans* in various hues of gray. And they looked as somber as if they were sitting in the Episcopal Church on Sunday morning, listening to a lecture on moral turpitude. So at the time of tryouts, there couldn't even be an intimation of twerking, let alone crotch grabbing or simulated humping. All that would come later.

Fair or not, if everything went according to plan, that meant there were essentially only two spots left on the team. Two spots and forty girls vying for position. Upon arriving at the gym, I had immediately dismissed the two sophomores trying out as being pom squad material, although their dancing and gymnastics were decent enough. They not only lacked the polish of most of the other girls. They also lacked the sex appeal, especially the tall, skinny one whose smile was so hopeful that it would have broken my heart if I wasn't such a natural-born competitor. The other, shorter one was cute and all, but she also fell short in the sex appeal department. They just didn't have *it,* that indefinable, magical quality that made a dancer a truly great performer.

I do not have time to argue with people who say that those girls out on the gym floor during half-time are not sexual objects, that they're only athletic high school girls who should be looked upon for what they are--*girls.* That's a crock of shit. Not only do high school boys lust after those girls, but also many of those fathers sitting in the bleachers are not harboring nurturing thoughts about those nubile young women. It's a sick fact, but it's true. I stand by that.

I will admit that there was another factor in my dismissal of those two girls. It wasn't because I had never seen them before, and it wasn't because they were not in the popular MHS crowd, and it wasn't because I didn't think they were up to Tigerette standards. Up to that point, Felicity had been the only girl in the history of the Mohave Tigerettes to make the varsity squad as a sophomore. And what's more, she had been made captain that very first year, which is a feat that will probably never be duplicated again. I didn't see anyone coming along in the near future who had Felicity's talent, poise, and yes, sex appeal. It was a record that would be hard to beat. And I didn't want anyone to beat it. That accomplishment proved to everyone that my daughter was very, very special.

The tryouts successfully completed, Felicity and I went home, supremely confident of who would be on this year's squad. Bubbling over with excitement, Felicity decided to eat dinner with Richard and me that evening, and she actually ate an entire piece of chicken and two bites of sweet potato. That's how happy she was. I even let her have a small glass of wine to celebrate. They do it in Europe, and it's no big deal to give your kid a little glass of wine every once in a while in your own home. Besides, when Felicity was happy, Richard was happy, so we had the most jovial meal that we'd had in a long time. Richard even called us his "two lovely girls." I couldn't remember the last time he said I was lovely.

After we finished dinner and stacked our dirty dishes in the sink--Louisa would load them in the dishwasher in the morning--Felicity even agreed to go into our home gym and let me show her a few dance moves I'd been thinking about. Thinking about. When I performed them for her in front of the mirrored wall, I looked a little stiff. I admit that. The graceful moves I had pictured in my head did not transfer quite so gracefully on to that mirror. My unused muscles felt like taut rubber bands.

"This would look better if I had a workout leotard on." In the mirror, my face looked flushed. It must be from the wine, I thought.

"Right." Felicity had crossed her arms. She did not look impressed.

"I'm a little stiff," I said. "I should have warmed up first. Every dancer knows she has to warm up first." I walked to the barre and started to stretch.

"It's okay, Mom. I get the idea."

"Do you think we can use those moves?" I hated that my voice sounded so hopeful.

"They might be a little, I don't know, outdated?" Felicity walked over to the barre and effortlessly executed a perfect arabesque.

"Showoff." I was proud and jealous of her at the same time. Richard and I had supplied her with private dance lessons for years, and it showed. "All I need is a little practice. I'll be back in shape in no time."

"Sure you will."

I wasn't nuts about her tone, but I let it go. I didn't want to spoil the mood.

After Felicity showed off again by rapidly moving through the first through fifth ballet positions, she leaned backwards on the barre and looked at me seriously. "You don't think there's any chance that those two sophomores could make the squad, do you?"

I was done dancing for the night and wanted another glass of wine. Tomorrow I would start my new exercise regimen. I'd be keeping up with those teenagers on the pom squad in a week or two. "Not a chance."

She smiled. "Good."

But again, I wasn't a judge. When the new squad of twelve girls was announced a week later, I was just as surprised as Felicity. "I'm sure that Hayley and Marcy will be hard workers," I soothed. I can't say that I was looking forward to working with such novice dancers--I'd gotten my groove back by then, for the most part--but as the coach, I was going to have to make dancers out of everybody, like it or not.

"This is horrible," Felicity wailed. "There must be some mistake. Ashley and Eva should have made the team, not those two sophomores. They don't know anything about," she looked at me as if she just remembered I was in her presence, "anything."

"Then I guess it's up to you to teach them the ins and outs of being on the squad."

"I guess it is," Felicity said thoughtfully. "I'll have to show them exactly what it means to be a Mohave Tigerette."

By the night of the Tigerette sleepover, the squad had met and practiced three afternoons, and I was having the time of my life. It was almost as good as being the reigning Mrs. Arizona. I'd show up in my black, skin-tight practice leotard, the same one as the girls wore, and I truly did think like I looked like I could pass for one of the teenage Tigerettes. As a matter of fact, the principal, Mr. Rooney, cornered me in the hall one afternoon as I was on my way to practice and told me that very thing: "You look like one of the girls," he said. Of course he then went on to say that perhaps I should consider wearing something more appropriate to my status as a coach, like a pair of shorts and a t-shirt. But he only told me to *consider* changing my attire, and I could tell by the way his eyes roved over my body clad in the curve-fitting leotard that he thought I looked very, very attractive.

I had no intention of changing into something more conservative. I refused to look like all the other ordinary mothers milling around the school, the mothers who weren't allowed into the practice hall because the practices were closed to the general public. At the time, I had no idea that it was my own daughter who had invented and then reinforced this rule. I simply took it as a given. Plus, I happened to think it was a good idea. Each and every performance would be new and exciting, not your average pom squad dribble of shaking your pom-poms and doing some variation of a boring line dance. That was not good enough for the Tigerettes. According to Felicity, every performance would be spectacular. "We want to razzle-dazzle them," was how she put it. "We want to look as professional as Beyonce." The other members of the squad followed her decree without question, as did I.

Felicity was an excellent captain, although I will admit that she was strict. But in an effort to mobilize and train their troops, all good captains have to be strict, do they not? She was also the person with the most experience on the team, and she didn't hesitate to flaunt it. At the beginning of that first practice, I stood in front of the group and proceeded to introduce myself and list my credentials as being a dancer in two off-Broadway shows, which would be followed by a good old-fashioned pep talk, followed by a demonstration of a dance that I had been working on. I had barely begun when Felicity walked up to the front of the room, planted herself next to me, and said, "I can take it from here, Mom."

"But I'm not finished." I flashed a smile to the group. "I'm sure the girls would like to know more about who's coaching them."

"Everybody knows who you are, Mom." She clapped her hands brusquely together. "Let's get to work, Tigerettes!"

"I have a dance prepared," I said through gritted teeth, although the smile remained plastered to my face. I had been working night and day on that routine, and it was really good. I had been a professional dancer, after all.

But I had already lost the attention of the group, and all eyes were focused on Felicity. I took it with a grain of salt. It was my first practice session, and Felicity had two full years of practice under her belt, so perhaps it was better if I was more of an observer that first time. I joined the group and followed Felicity's instructions too, as she went through her routine step by step, by arm movement, by gesture, by when to cock the head, by when to shake the hip. It was a much more complicated dance than the one I had choreographed, and as the class progressed, I was secretly glad that I hadn't shown my deceptively simple little routine to the girls.

Felicity didn't yell or scream when someone made a mistake. She didn't have to. All she needed was to give the offender who had missed a step an icy look that penetrated to her bones. I had never seen that look on her face before, and frankly, it gave me the chills. She threw a few of those my way--I tripped once or twice--but most of them were directed to Hayley and Marcy, the girls she had already dubbed *the newbies.* To be honest, they did seem to be lagging behind the other girls. But Felicity was having none of it. "Get with the program, newbie," she'd bark, or: "I thought you were *supposed* to be a Tigerette." The two girls, each time they were singled out, would blush furiously and mumble *sorry,* to which Felicity would reply, "Sorry doesn't cut it, newbie."

However, at the end of the class, it was smiles all around and echoes of *good job.* Felicity's methods--acting more like a drill sergeant than a captain-- seemed to work. By the end of the class, everyone had pretty much mastered the routine, including the newbies, although they looked drained and exhausted. When Felicity walked over to them, they almost cowered, but she opened up her arms and said, "Come here, you two." She embraced them. The entire group, myself included, was drenched in so much sweat that our leotards clung to us like cellophane, but I felt like there was a collective sigh of relief at that embrace. I know that I was relieved, mentally and physically exhausted, but relieved.

Each time I went to the next two practice sessions, I hoped to have a bigger role to play as the coach, but it didn't happen. Everyone knew who was in charge of the Tigerette kingdom, and it certainly wasn't me. However, I planned to remedy that situation on the night of the sleepover. I was, technically speaking, the hostess of the affair, and I planned to join in, talk with the girls, let them get to know me. I packed a small bag to take over to the guesthouse and set it on the kitchen island while I took the chocolate chip cookies out of the oven. I didn't bake the cookies my-self, Louisa had, but the girls would never know the difference. I also had bags of chips and candy and cases of soda ready to take over. The girls would be arriving any minute, and I was putting the cookies on a plate when Felicity walked in.

"What are you doing?"

"What does it look like I'm doing? I'm getting everything ready for the party. I'm the hostess with the most-est." I was in such a good mood that night. "Why don't you be a doll and help me carry this stuff to the guesthouse?"

"We're in training, Mom. We can't eat all this crap."

"It's a sleepover, you're teenagers, and you are not, as far as I know, training for the Olympics. Of course you can eat this crap." I kept my voice even, but I was really getting fed up with Felicity's attitude.

Felicity spied my overnight bag on the counter. She put her hands on her hips. "You aren't planning on joining us, are you?"

"Yes, I am. I'm the coach."

"Don't you see how *wrong* that is?" Her voice was incredulous.

I had anticipated this response from her. "Someone has to chaperone you guys."

"We don't need a chaperone." When I continued putting all the food in a big box, she said, "I'm going to tell Daddy."

The long and short of it was that I was outnumbered. I might have been able to take my husband and daughter on one at a time, but together they were unbeatable. I was told in no uncertain terms that it was inap-propriate and immature to crash my daughter's sleepover. I was told that I should butt out, and furthermore, that I wasn't needed at the Tigerette practices anymore either.

Felicity's exact words were: "You can't keep up, Mom. There's no reason for you to be there. Go shopping or something, but don't horn in on my pom squad."

"I'm getting sick and tired of your attitude, princess." Oh, I was mad.

"She's right, Cynthia." Richard put a protective hand on his daughter's shoulder. "The pom squad is her thing, not yours. You don't need to go to every single practice."

Not only was I mad, but I was also hurt. I had thought I might be able to make a difference, and now I was back to square one with too much empty time on my hands. My daughter didn't even need me now, although she would apologize profusely to me the next day and hug me like she was a little girl again. Of course I forgave her. She knew what she was doing, and I did not.

So no, I did not go over to the sleepover at the guesthouse that night, nor did I go over to check on them, not even once.

I should have.

3

AUDREY

Honestly, I always had the best of intentions, but by the end of that September, it had gotten so bad that I was afraid to open the mail. Opening those dreaded credit card statements would only confirm my worst suspicions. It was so easy to take out a cash withdrawal here and there and not record the amount, but rather, be relieved that I now had the money to pay for Jimmy's ADHD medication. Or the ready cash to slip my mother, who lived nearby in an assisted living facility, a couple of extra twenties, so she had some gambling money when she was bussed weekly to the local Indian casino. Or the money to buy Paul some new ties because he seemed to have the odd habit of losing them. Or pre-Tigerettes, the money to pay for Marcy's various lessons and clubs. At the times when one credit card had been maxed out, I could simply apply for another and start the process all over again. I didn't think I was a particularly bad person for doing this. It is a known fact that most Americans live on credit. Most Americans *thrive* on credit, which allows them to buy things that they can't afford. Credit provides fuel for the American Dream.

But I wasn't paying for luxuries with all those cash withdrawals. I was paying for necessities. Paul wasn't bringing in much money anymore, and I hated to nag him about it. I had always felt guilty that he had worked at a job he hated for so many years. He had about as much interest in pharmaceutical sales as I did in dissecting frogs. For years he'd dreaded going to work each morning, and when he came home, tieless yet again, he would barely speak to me until he'd had a couple of beers and scrolled through job openings on his computer. It was funny, though. Paul never did get around to applying for another job. It was almost as if hating his job was what he centered his life around.

When I married him seventeen years ago, his dream had been to become a screenwriter. Naturally, I thought that was terribly romantic and was only too happy to follow him to LA after we graduated from ASU. Believe it or not, we had fun being poor back then. I was teaching art in a charter school and wasn't making much to support us, but we made it work. We knew the best and cheapest happy hours all over town, where all the free outdoor concerts and movies played, and we walked or rode our bikes almost everywhere. But Paul never got his screenwriting career off the ground. In LA, you needed to have connections, and he didn't, and Paul had never been the pushy sort, which seemed to be another prerequisite in the movie-making business. Then inevitably, I got pregnant, so we moved back to Scottsdale and settled in. It was time for us to grow up, I supposed, and Paul never attempted to write another screenplay. I still think that's a crying shame.

Anyway, I had been playing the credit card juggling game for close to a year by that point, and I owed money--more than I wanted to admit--on four different cards. Truly, I only used the cards to take out cash when absolutely necessary. But then came the blasted Tigerettes, and all of a sudden, Marcy needed money for something to do with the team on what seemed like a daily basis. That spoiled little Felicity got her way about everything she set her sneaky little heart on, right down to the leather boots, jackets, and gold rings. Oh, and then there had to be matching necklaces and earrings and barrettes. The season hadn't even officially begun--we hadn't even crossed the hair and makeup at Pucci Salon bridge yet--and already I was close to declaring bankruptcy. I mean, not literally. I was still doing the robbing-Peter-to-pay-Paul song and dance, and I was still naive enough to think I could somehow make it all work, despite the astronomical interest rates those credit cards charged for cash withdrawals. However, to this day, I believe that it was the Mohave Tigerettes pom squad that pushed me over the edge.

Something had to be done about the situation, and naturally, I went to my husband about it first. His solution? "Tell her to quit the squad," he said. "Tell her we can't afford it."

"I can't do that!" Despite everything, that would be the last thing I would do to my daughter. She was still riding that first wave of bubbly excitement, even though she came home from the grueling practices sodden and exhausted.

Paul shrugged. "Then what do you want me to do about it?" He looked genuinely perplexed. To him, the Tigerettes pom squad was only another after-school activity, and he just didn't get how important it was to Marcy.

I hated what I was going to say next, yet I said it anyway. That's how desperate I was getting. "Interest rates are still low. Maybe we could take out a second mortgage on the house?"

He looked at me, incredulous. "For a couple of damn pom-poms? Are you out of your mind, Audrey?"

I laughed stiffly and turned away before he could see the look on my face. "Of course I'm kidding, Paul, I'll have a yard sale or something."

"Hey, you." He reached out and pulled me into his arms. He was so much taller than me that I fit under his shoulder. He had to bend down to kiss the top of my head. "You worry too much, babe. Haven't things always worked out for us? Haven't we always gotten by?"

I nodded into his chest. "Yes."

"That's my girl." He released me and gently swatted my behind. "You still have the greatest ass, babe." Then he took another beer out of the refrigerator and went back to his ballgame.

I sighed. It was so typical. My husband was a very sweet man and a good husband and father. When the kids had been babies, he didn't hesitate to help out with diaper changes and night feedings. And up until recently, he had even helped out around the house, loading the dishwasher or making up the beds, little helpful things like that. And even as I'd noticed that he'd become more withdrawn over the last few months, more absent-minded--he came home almost every day without a tie now--he generally seemed to be in a good mood. Or pretended to be. After a couple of beers, of course.

But Paul was truly terrible with money. I had managed the finances in our household ever since we had gotten married, and that suited him just fine. I couldn't really fault him for that, though. Paul had simply not been taught how to budget and manage money, and I lay the blame for that squarely on the heads of his mother and father. Both of his parents had come from old Phoenix money and had inherited sizable trust funds from their respective parents, so to them, money was no object. Anything they had a hankering for, they bought. Anything Paul mentioned that he wanted, they bought. I'm not kidding. Those two people went through money as fast as hungry hogs eating at a slop-filled trough. There were weekly trips to Vegas on a private Cessna 172 and a new Mercedes every other year. Don't get me wrong. They were nice enough people, in their self-centered way, but I will admit that when their plane crashed in a wind-storm coming back from one of those weekly jaunts to Sin City, I harbored the secret hope that they had left us a piece of that pie. No such luck. They'd gone through it all, and then some. In fact, Paul and I had to take out a loan to pay for their funerals. We did it jointly, a two-for-one type of deal. It was cheaper that way.

I guess it is not an understatement to say that I was in a real bind at that point. I worried about money constantly, to the point that I was perhaps not observant enough about what was going on right under my nose. My seven-year-old son Jimmy had always been a handful, so there was nothing new on that front, and my husband was relying more and more on booze to self-medicate his depression. I knew these things, even accepted them, I suppose. But Marcy should have been a different story. I should have paid extra attention to her. She was dealing with a whole new social circle of friends and added responsibility and grueling practices, and I would like to think that she would have confided in me if she started to feel overwhelmed. On the surface, she still acted like the happiest girl in the whole USA. But looking back on it now, I should have probably sensed some change in her the morning after the Tigerette slumber party, however imperceptible it might have been.

To begin with, she looked absolutely awful when she walked in the door at eleven o'clock the morning after the sleepover. She looked like she hadn't slept a wink. I had expected that. Even I knew that the purpose of a slum-ber party was to *not* slumber. But her face looked pale and drawn, almost like she was in shock. Since I had dropped the girls off the night before at the Stewart McMansion, Reggie was the one who brought them home that morning, and I immediately felt like I had missed out on something important. I don't know why I felt like that; I just did. Call it mother's intuition, or whatever. However, I did not handle that initial conversation in a loving, motherly way.

"Have you been *drinking*, Marcy?" I knew that the accusatory tone was unwarranted and out of line. We were standing in the kitchen, and the counter was still cluttered with Paul's empties from the night before. I hadn't gotten around to putting them into the recycling bin yet because the number seemed to be growing on an almost daily basis, and I hated counting them. Right then, there were eleven Bud Light bottles calling attention to my hypocrisy.

Marcy had never been able to lie--I like to think she inherited that from me--so she hung her head and said, "We only had a little bit of wine. Felicity said that Mrs. Stewart said it was okay. The Europeans let their children drink wine."

"Oh, well, if Mrs. *Stewart,* the former Mrs. Arizona America, said it was okay, then I guess it's just fine and dandy to let a fifteen-year-old drink alcohol." My voice dripped with sarcasm, and at first, I didn't even recognize it. Then I did. It was *my* mother's voice.

"You drink wine, Mom." She cast a glance at my empty wine bottle on the counter, another thing I had failed to put in the recycling bin, and I hadn't even noticed it--until now.

"I'm an adult, Marcy. It's legal for me to drink wine. You, on the other hand, are a minor." I felt myself blush. I was starting to think that I was making a mountain out of a molehill. The truth of the matter was that Marcy didn't act drunk or hungover, and she didn't smell like alcohol. Furthermore, I didn't really care all that much if my daughter had a sip of wine under the supervision of an adult in a safe environment. It was better than her getting in a car with a group of kids and driving out in the desert and partying around a bonfire like I'd used to do. Not that I was going to bring that up now.

"I'm sorry, Mom." She yawned.

I decided it was time to change the subject. "So what else did you do?

"The usual." This time Marcy shrugged. Was I boring her, or was she being evasive? I honestly couldn't tell.

"Oh, come on," I cajoled. I was suddenly desperate to have a heart-to-heart with my daughter. I realized I hadn't had a good talk with Marcy since the Tigerette tryouts. "I'll fix you breakfast, and you can tell me all about it." I was already getting out the frying pan.

"That's okay. Louisa fixed us breakfast."

"Who's Louisa?"

"The Stewarts' maid."

"Of course." I was back to sarcasm. However, I wasn't going to be deterred. "How about some toast?"

"I'm not hungry, Mom."

I am not usually a pushy person, but I pushed right then. My daughter was going to talk to me. I was not going to be one of those mothers who did not know what went on in her children's lives. I pulled out a kitchen stool. "Sit down, Marcy. I'd be honored if you gave me two minutes of your time. Then you can go up and take a nap."

Reluctantly, she did so, looking like she'd rather be anywhere than sitting with me. She still had that strange, sick look on her face, and for the first time, I noticed how dark the circles under her green eyes were. And her face looked leaner, something I hadn't noticed before. I knew that the practices were hard on her. She'd already gone through several tubes of Icy Hot. When I casually mentioned one day that I'd like to go and watch one of the practices to see what was going on, Marcy had informed me that they were closed. "Every dance has to be special," she'd explained. I'd asked her whose bright idea that was, and she'd said Felicity. I didn't, as a rule, dislike teenage girls, but the more I heard about this Felicity, the more steamed I got. Marcy, however, insisted that she wasn't being treated unfairly. At the time, I chose to believe her.

I poured myself a cup of coffee and sat down next to her. I pasted a smile on my face. "So tell me all about it. Did you play games, watch movies, talk about guys? Did you post pictures of yourselves on Instagram?" I had already planned on getting on her account to check that, along with Facebook and all other social media sites.

Marcy's eyes flickered, and she looked longingly at the stairs. "Mostly, we talked."

"What did you talk about?" I knew I should let my exhausted daughter go to bed. I knew that. But something was making me grill her. It was out of character for me, and it was out of character for Marcy to be so evasive. Maybe that was why. But I also didn't feel like I could trust either Felicity or Cynthia Stewart just yet. Socially, they were out of my league, and I, too, was in foreign territory.

"What it means to be a Tigerette."

"You're a dancer at basketball games," I pointed out, while I was thinking how dramatic teenage girls could be. I stifled a smile.

Marcy sat up a little straighter. "We're the Top Twelve."

"Top Twelve what?" I took a drink of coffee.

"The top twelve girls in the school."

I sputtered, and the coffee came dangerously close to coming out my nose. "According to whom?" I sat my coffee cup down. "I know. Don't tell me. Felicity." I tried to choose my next words carefully. "So, are you saying that the Top Twelve are the girls who are the most popular or special in some way?"

Marcy's eyes flickered. "I guess you could say that."

I couldn't help myself. "That sounds like a pretty snobbish attitude. Look, honey," I grabbed her hand, "you don't have to be like that. You can still be the nice, sweet person you've always been. If being a Tigerette is going to make you into something that you're not, maybe you should think about quitting--"

Marcy whipped her hand from mine. "It's not like that, Mom. You just don't get it."

"I'm afraid that I'm starting to, and I don't like it," I snapped at her, but she's not the teenager I was getting angry with.

"I don't want to quit!" Marcy wailed. "You can't make me quit! I've already taken the Tigerette oath and everything." She looked at me, her eyes wide, and then they filled with tears and overflowed, and she was sobbing like her heart was breaking.

What could I do? I took her in my arms and started patting her back and rubbing her head. "Shh, sweetie. No one's going to make you quit. You've had a tough couple of weeks and a long night. I should have let you go right up to bed." I felt so guilty at that point. I was being overly suspicious and letting my imagination get the best of me. Marcy was on a high school pom squad, teenage girls were overly dramatic, and Felicity was a spoiled little rich girl trying to make herself feel more important than she was. End of story. Once the season got underway, everything would fall into place, and things would settle down.

After I led Marcy upstairs and tucked her into bed, I checked all her accounts, but there was nothing there. I don't know what I was looking for--teenage girls in their underwear, sexting?--but Marcy certainly hadn't posted anything incriminating. And then I called Reggie, who had gotten basically the same information out of Hayley, who had also broken down into sobs and had to be tucked into bed.

"Maybe they had some kind of initiation ritual that they had to go through last night, something that drained them physically and emotionally?" I suggested. I didn't particularly like the thought of that, but both girls seemed physically unharmed, just exhausted.

"Yeah, like Miss Felicity branded them on their butts with the Tigerette mascot," Reggie said drily.

I shuddered. Should I go upstairs and check? "Don't even say that."

"Right. I'm done putting bad thoughts in our heads. Our girls are where they want to be, and we have to trust them to do the right thing. They're good girls, Audrey. We have to remember that."

"Yes," I agreed, wondering if Stockholm Syndrome was possible in a pom squad. I didn't say anything aloud and quickly dismissed such a bizarre thought. We had to trust our girls.

"Say," Reggie said, "have you given any more thought to the wine club? I've had a couple of ideas over the last three weeks. I think we could make it work."

Because Reggie still seemed to be so hot to trot on the wine club idea, and because Reggie could be a very persuasive person, I had agreed to drive up to Cottonwood and Jerome, just south of Sedona, to check out the wineries the next day. I was not then as gungho as Reggie with the whole idea of hosting parties and selling wine, but like I just said, Reggie could be a very persuasive person when she set her mind to it. Over the years, I had learned that more often than not, it was a better tactic to agree with her rather than argue my point. Because nine times out of ten, Reggie would get her way anyhow. I used to think that it was a good quality of hers, that it showed strength of character. I am not as enamored with that particular personality trait of Reggie Carson's now.

I got up bright and early on that Sunday morning and found myself looking forward to the trip. I could use a little day excursion, a mini escape from my daily life and family and financial worries. And the best part was that we would get to taste some new wine, unencumbered by children and spouses. We had already promised each other than we wouldn't drink so much that we couldn't drive the two hours home. I was a little worried that we wouldn't follow through on that promise, but as Reggie pointed out, "We're not guzzling glass after glass, Audrey. We're only going to *taste* it. It will be an education for us." So I let it go--after I insisted that she drive her car.

But as usual, something unexpected happened. And it wasn't anything good. That seemed to be the story of my life at that particular time. And when I say that, I don't mean to imply that I am a complainer or that I'm a glass-half-empty kind of person. No, I was a typical person of the Sandwich Generation, trying to take care of children, one of whom had special needs, and an irascible mother struggling with the early stages of dementia. I was a person with a mother in an assisted living facility, which is really only another fancy name for a nursing home, and therefore, lived on pins and needles as I dreaded The Call. The Call could take a number of manifestations, anything from "Your mother has fallen again" to "Your mother has been transferred to Osborn Hospital" to "We suspect your mother has suffered a stroke." All it took was for The Gardens' number to flash on my screen, and my mouth went dry, my heart started to race, and I felt sick to my stomach.

That time I got off fairly easy, I suppose. The director, Gail, informed me that my mother had fallen again, or as she put it in her British accent: "I'm afraid, dear, that Margot has taken another tumble."

My mother had fallen several times before, and I was beginning to suspect that she did it for the attention. She had a walker, but she seemed intent on "forgetting" to use it two or three times a week. I took a deep breath to steady my still pounding heart. I knew the drill, and maybe I could still salvage the day in Cottonwood. "Does she seem to be hurt?"

"We do believe we see a bruise forming on her noggin'."

A bruise? That was nothing. I still had hope that I could salvage the trip to taste wine. "I'm sure that if you put some ice on it and give her a Tylenol, she'll be good as new."

"Here at The Gardens, we do like to ensure the safety of all our residents, Audrey dear, and we do think it would be the best if you transported her to the ER at Osborn."

I hesitated a fraction of a second too long. "Do you think that's necessary? What about a few hours of observation before we make that decision?"

"Audrey dear, your mother has asked for me to call you to come and take her to hospital."

It was one of the saving graces of my mother's dementia: She could no longer remember how to use a phone. Thankfully, she could neither dial a number nor answer it when it rang. Before that lapse occurred, during the first year she was at the nursing home, my mother would call at all hours of the day and night, insisting that I take her back home, insisting that she was being held captive against her will, insisting that I was the most horrible, ungrateful daughter in the universe because I had put her in that godforsaken place. Gail told me that it was something that The Gardens called Family Phone Hell. She told me it was only one of the stages of adjustment that the residents went through. It did not make dealing with it any easier.

"Why doesn't the ambulance take her?" I was trying to tamp down my impatience, but it seemed like I was getting at least one call a week about yet another emergency my mother was having. And invariably, they were false alarms. I knew that calling an ambulance would be added to my mother's monthly bill, which seemed exorbitant to me, but that was what insurance was for, wasn't it? I was so sick of hearing her complaints, of hours sitting in the ER, of accompanying her to myriad doctor appointments. Then, of course, that made me feel guilty. It was a vicious cycle.

"Audrey dear," Gail's voice was one of trained, modulated patience, "she is *insisting* that you take her to hospital."

"Oh, God," escaped before I could clamp my lips closed. I knew what that meant. Margot was in one of her most difficult moods. My mother could be such a mean bitch when she wanted to be, alternating between a stony coldness and a foul rage. However, when she really wanted something or needed to get her way, she could act like a charming old lady, a perfect aged angel. "I'm leaving now, Gail."

I hung up the phone and called Reggie to cancel the trip to the wineries. I was already filled with dread, and absurdly, I felt like I wanted to curl into a ball on the couch and have a good cry. I felt like I wanted to bawl like a baby. I was supposed to be the grown daughter who shouldered the responsibility and carried on, the one who did the right thing and kept things running smoothly. Yet once again, because of circumstances beyond my control, I felt like I had been cheated out of something I should have rightfully had.

Did I feel guilty for putting my mother in a nursing home, rather than trying to care for her myself? Yes, because I did feel that in some sense, it was my duty to take care of her. I was her only daughter, the only child she had who lived in the state. My younger brother Aaron had moved up to

Oregon to be purposely far from our mother, and he had four children of his own to care for on a fisherman's salary, which was not an easy task. He couldn't afford the price of an airline ticket, he said. His wife had never gotten along with our mother, he said. Honestly, Aaron was an odd one himself, living a back-to-the-earth existence in northern Oregon, with a reddish-gray beard that reached his belt buckle and a wife who made their children's clothes out of hemp. I hadn't seen him in years, other than an occasional picture, and had never met my nieces and nephews. But I did resent him for not stepping in to help with our mother. I thought he was a coward for escaping his responsibility. I also thought he was one lucky bastard to be so far away from her. More guilt.

And no, I did not feel guilty for putting my mother in a nursing home. When it came time for Mother to leave her home--the one I grew up in--a bungalow in south Scottsdale that she had lived in for years, she really had no choice because she fell and broke her hip. She had recently turned eighty-two, had been a widow for fifteen years, and could no longer take care of the house. It was literally falling down around her. I researched and visited most of the facilities in the area, and The Gardens had a good reputation. But let's face it. No nursing home is perfect. Rather, they're downright depressing places, despite the planned games and outings and white tablecloths on the dining room tables. But some people seem happy enough to be there. They're probably the people who were nice in their pre-nursing home lives. My mother was not one of them. She constantly complained about everything, except the weekly outings to the Indian casino.

When I arrived on that Sunday to take her to the ER, Mother, in a wheelchair, crossed her arms and stared straight ahead. So that's how it was going to play out: stony silence. I was happy about that. I infinitely preferred it to her vitriol. After all these years, I still couldn't quite figure out what I had done to offend her so, other than being born, I guess. She once told me that she'd never wanted to have children, which certainly explained why I was born when she was forty, Aaron when she was forty-two. But let me tell you, knowing from an early age that you are unwanted will play havoc on your self-esteem. It had taken me years to build up my confidence, and even as a grown woman, I had to fight to keep it in her presence.

"Hello, Mother," I kissed her on the cheek. I could barely see the bruise on her forehead, possibly because her flaming red wig was pushed too far forward on her head.

"About time," she muttered.

"But the point is that I'm here," I said firmly, determined to make the best of the situation.

Later, after we had been waiting in the ER for three hours, after I had gone to the cafeteria and gotten her a coffee and a ham and cheese sandwich, after I had convinced the girl at the counter to put the NASCAR race on the small TV--Mother was addicted to NASCAR for some strange reason--she finally turned to me and said, "You bring me out in public looking like a pauper."

I could have pointed out that I was not the one who wanted to bring her to the Osborn ER, but I did not. "You don't look like a pauper, Mother." But then I did look at her. She had on an old faded pink sweater that was unraveling at the elbows and blue sweatpants with some kind of brown stain on the thigh that made me shudder. She did look like a bag lady, and it occurred to me for the first time that I hadn't bought her any new clothes in the year and a half she'd been in the home. A pile of guilt descended.

I reached out and patted her hand. Her eyes glittered. Could that be tears? "I'll take you shopping next week. We'll go to Target."

She stared straight ahead at the TV, but I think I noticed a small smile of triumph. My mother would always be the queen of manipulative bitches.

By the time I got home that night, it was getting dark, and all I wanted was a glass of wine. I deserved it, and then some. I had held my own with Mother, not rising to her repeated barbed baiting, and made it through the day. It hadn't been easy. After we finally left the ER--the doctor pronounced her fit as a fiddle, to which she smiled beatifically, acting like the sweet old lady she was not--we had stopped at Walgreens to refill her cholesterol medication. Then she decided she was feeling faint because she had missed lunch, conveniently forgetting about the ham and cheese sandwich, so we stopped at an IHOP, and I watched her devour a tall stack of New York cheesecake pancakes and a side of bacon. I had thought I was home free at that point, but no. Mother decided that she wanted to stop at Target right there and then, before I "returned her to that living hell."

Let me tell you, that stop was excruciating. Do you know how long it takes an arthritic eighty-three-year-old woman to try on clothes? A lo-o-ong time. But Mother insisted on not only ensconcing herself in a dressing room and trying on practically everything in the Women's section, but she also wanted to try them on in the size she previously wore, which soon proved to be a major hurdle. She insisted she hadn't gained any weight at the nursing home, despite the round the clock food available to her, but that wasn't true. She had grown quite rotund in the middle, and finally, out of desperation and after insisting that I wasn't going to buy her Spanx, I brought her an armful of maternity clothes to try on in the dressing room, roomy shirts and pants with elastic waists. Of course I didn't tell her they were maternity clothes, only that they were the newest style. She must have been getting tired by then because she didn't argue.

All in all, the day had set me back close to $500. By the end of the Target hell, I was intimate friends with the ATM in the front of the store, having made three trips to it as Mother's pile of maternity clothes grew larger. The day had certainly not helped my mounting credit card debt, but I wasn't going to think about that now. I would pour myself a glass of wine and relax in front of the family room TV. The kids were upstairs in their rooms finishing up their homework, and Marcy, my sweet daughter, had fixed them a frozen pizza for dinner, so I finally had some time to myself.

So I deserved a glass of wine, very much so. I had just poured myself a hefty dose of chardonnay when my phone rang. It was Paul. That was strange. I heard the TV on in his den, and I had assumed that he was watching another game and drinking beer, his nightly ritual. I'd even called out a "Honey, I'm home" when I went past his closed door. Had the man gotten so lazy that he was now calling me to bring him drinks? Did he actually think I would *cater* to him? If so, he was out of his mind, and I was going to tell him a thing or two. That was what I thought at the time.

"Really?" My voice was sharp when I answered the phone. "You can't leave your precious ballgame for one second to come to the kitchen?"

"No, I can't--"

"Well, I'm not getting it for you. I've had a horrible day with Mother, and I do not need any more aggravation. Get your own damn beer, and as far as I'm concerned--"

"Please stop talking, Audrey. I can't come out of the den because I'm not in the den. I'm at the police station."

Paul, back in his heyday, had been a big fan of practical jokes. "Very funny."

"Audrey, listen to me. I've been arrested for a DUI. You need to come to the police station and pick me up."

Later, I would find out that he had gone out for a beer run to the local convenience store. He'd had a few drinks during the day, but he didn't think he was drunk. And the store was only three blocks away. He would have walked, but he didn't want to miss any innings of the Diamondbacks playoff game. Everything would have been fine if he hadn't been trying to get the ballgame on the radio while he was backing up. He wasn't drunk. He just wasn't paying attention when he backed into the squad car that had pulled into the parking lot behind him.

But right then, while I was wondering how much this was going to cost us and stifling down a rising panic, I was pissed off at Paul for being so stupid. And I was pissed off that I was leaving a wonderful, soothing glass of chardonnay that would have to wait until I'd bailed my husband out of jail. But at that point, what could I expect?

It had just been one of those days.

OCTOBER

4

REGGIE

I was embarrassed when I found out. More than all the other emotions that went roaring through my bloodstream, I felt embarrassment. But not for the reasons you might think. It was not the fact of it so much as the realization that I had been completely blind to it for so many years. I'd stuck my head in the sand and kept it buried there, probably because I didn't want to know. I realize I'm not the first wife who's gone through such a thing. Fran Drescher comes to mind, as does a distant cousin on my mother's side. When that distant cousin found out, she packed up and moved to Bermuda, as I recall. Maybe it wasn't Bermuda, but it was somewhere warm and tropical. I used to think she had behaved like a coward, but now I think that it was an extreme act of bravery. She left her home, her kids, her old life, and just vanished. I only wish that I had been that brave.

I don't think he wanted to be the one to tell me, but I had pushed him too far. It started innocently enough. Caleb had made a rare visit home on that first weekend in October, and I had enlisted his help in cleaning out the garage. I figured that if Audrey and I did indeed start a wine club, I was going to need room to store the wine. The heat had broken some by then, and it wasn't too unbearable in the two-car attached garage. But it quickly became apparent that it was going to be a bigger job than I had anticipated. Throughout the years, the garage had become a repository for all the broken, discarded, and abandoned items in our household, from old tennis rackets missing strings to bicycles missing wheels to boxes filled with old toys to a rusty freezer that hadn't worked in ten years. We had a fan going, but Caleb and I were drenched in sweat in no time flat.

Still, I tried to keep an upbeat attitude. "Do you remember this?" I lifted the lacrosse stick I had just found buried in the corner.

"That does not bring back pleasant memories." Caleb shuddered dramatically. "It goes in the discard pile."

"Oh, come on. It wasn't that bad."

"Mom, I never made it past third string, and the one game I played in, I got knocked unconscious by the other team's captain when I got in his way. I'd say it was pretty bad."

"You were only out for a second or two," I said, but I put it in the trash pile anyway. I had forgotten all about that incident in Caleb's less than stellar athletic career. Even though he was tall like both Kent and me, he had not inherited one iota of athletic ability. In that regard, he took after Kent. I had been the captain and star player on my field hockey team in both high school and college.

I changed the subject, trying to get a smile back on his thin face. "How's school going?"

"It's going okay." Caleb pushed a box of old wrapping paper out of the way, and we both heard a scurrying sound. "I think this place has mice."

It was my turn to shudder. "I'm going to pretend you didn't say that." I knew as well as the next person that mice are generally harmless creatures, but they still scared the hell out of me. I knew it was unreasonable. I could calmly pound a scorpion to death with a shampoo bottle in the shower, but mice? Forget about it.

"How's Donald?" I asked nonchalantly. I knew how Caleb hated me to pry, but the question was innocent enough. I always asked him about Donald.

"He's having some trouble with organic chemistry this semester, but other than that, he's the same." Caleb wiped a sweaty arm across his forehead, leaving a smear of dirt. He looked like such a little boy at that moment that I wanted to take him in my arms and hold him like I used to when he was upset about something. "Why are you staring at me like that?"

I smiled at him. "You have a smudge of dirt on your forehead." I wasn't about to tell him how I wished he was little again. I felt so silly when longings like that came over me. Here he was, practically a grown man, over six feet tall and long-limbed. He was too skinny, in my opinion, but I supposed that time would eventually help him fill out. And he needed a haircut; his dark hair was hanging in his eyes. He and Hayley had both taken after me in their coloring, rather than Kent, with his fair skin and lashes so blonde they were almost invisible. Kent's hair was blonde too--what he had left of it. It seemed like Kent got up every day with a little more of his forehead showing.

Caleb swiped at his forehead, making the smudge worse. "Better?"

"We're both going to need a shower when we're done here." I busied myself sorting through a box of old fabric that I didn't remember buying. I must have thought I'd get around to making curtains one day, which was funny. I was not what you would call a domestic goddess. Not even close.

"Have you and Donald seen any good movies lately?"

"Not really."

"What do you and Donald do in your spare time? When you're not studying, I mean."

"The usual things, you know?"

"No, I really don't. That's why I'm asking." I was not prying. I was only curious how my son and his lover spent their free time. There was nothing wrong with that.

He shrugged. "You know, the usual stuff."

I tried to hide my exasperation. "How about one example?"

"We go out to eat at Del Taco. Satisfied?"

I should have known by his curt answers that I was getting on his nerves and that he clearly wished he hadn't agreed to this project. He was kicking at boxes now and moving fast to finish the job. But I didn't let it go. "What do you and Donald order when you go to Del Taco? Is the food good there? All these years, and I've never eaten at one."

"Shit, Mom, it's like a Taco Bell. Would you give it a rest?"

"It is not a crime for a mother to want to know what her son and his . . . friend like to do to entertain themselves."

Caleb straightened up from the box he was sorting through. "Why did you say it like that?"

"What are you talking about?" I didn't think I'd said anything out of the ordinary.

"The way you said *friend,* like it was in quotation marks or something."

"Did I? Maybe you misheard me." If Caleb wasn't ready to talk about his relationship with Donald, maybe I should just let it go. I could hear Audrey's voice in my head, telling me it wasn't any of my business. But on the other hand, my son was nineteen years old. He wasn't old enough to drink or to vote, not even legally an adult yet. He still needed my guidance on important matters, didn't he? So in my book, that gave me permission to know what went on in his life--at least some of the time.

"I didn't mishear you, Mom." Caleb spoke with exaggerated patience, but with his hands on his hips and his feet planted apart, he looked ready for a fight. "What's with the interrogation? Why so many questions about Donald?"

I could feel that this was the moment I had been waiting for. Maybe Caleb would finally tell me the truth. It wasn't like I was going to judge him. No, I planned to be fully supportive of his choice. He needed to know that. I smiled at him, trying to put into that smile all the warmth and love I felt toward him, but I was so sweaty and dusty that it might have looked more demented than lovingly maternal. "Well, honey, what would you call Donald?"

He looked me right in the eye. "Donald is my best friend."

"And?" I asked hopefully.

"And what? What is it that you're trying to ask me without asking me?" No exaggerated patience now. He was clearly annoyed.

I cleared my throat. Here it was, the moment of truth. But after years of speculating, the words did not come out easily. Instead, they clumsily tripped off my suddenly very dry tongue. "Are you and Donald lovers?"

"No, Mom, we're not." He didn't look surprised by the question, though.

But I was sure surprised by the answer. I'd been positive that they'd been boyfriends for years now. "Then why don't you date girls?" I managed to sputter out.

"How do you know I don't?"

Well, he had me there. Perhaps I didn't know my son very well at all. But I'd been so sure that he was gay! I guess I needed more verification, so I said, "You're not gay?"

I could see Caleb's jaw moving. It looked like he was grinding his teeth. "No, Mom, I'm not gay."

"Are you sure?" That was the remark that put him over the edge.

"Of course I'm sure, Mom," he exploded. "I'm not the one in this family who's gay." He paused for what seemed like a long time. "Dad is."

"Don't be ridiculous--"

"It's so obvious," he said. For a brief second, it looked like he was blinking back tears, but then he turned on his heel and stomped out of the garage before I could utter another word.

That was one of the longest afternoons of my life. As soon as Caleb left the garage, I sank onto the floor. My knees slowly gave out, and I slithered down the wall like a limp dishrag and landed in a heap, nestled between the old boxes of useless junk. Like I said, the first emotion that rushed through me was embarrassment. If Kent being gay was *so obvious*, as Caleb had said, then why hadn't I, his wife, known? Did everyone else know? Did Audrey? Did people get together and talk about me behind my back, saying things like, "Poor Reggie. She doesn't have a clue. What an idiot." Should I be tested for HIV? That old saying, *the wife is always the last to know*, came to my mind and stuck there, playing over and over like a broken record. Then I cried.

When I stopped crying, I got rip-roaring mad. How could my husband of twenty years have kept something like that from me? How could he do that to me, to our family? And I was mad because everything I had thought to be true about our marriage--and therefore, my life--had been a lie. I thought we'd been pretty happy, that our marriage was a solid one. Granted, we rarely had sex anymore, and I couldn't even remember the last time, but I had thought that happened to all married couples eventually. And it wasn't like Kent went away on business trips and had flings. Kent didn't travel for business. He went golfing on most Saturdays--that's where he was that very afternoon--but surely, he wasn't having sex in the men's locker room with one of his golfing buddies. Or maybe he was.

It was just too hard to wrap my head around all the confusion and betrayal. At one point, I thought that maybe Caleb had made up the whole thing to throw me off the track of his own homosexuality. But then that meant that my son was a liar, and the one thing I knew for a certainty that disastrous afternoon was that Caleb was not a liar. Even as a child, if he broke a dish or snuck candy before dinner or hadn't finished his homework, it would only be a matter of minutes before he confessed. And often he would self-punish, denying himself a television show he had looked forward to watching or a family trip to the McCormick-Stillman

Railroad Park. No, my son was not a liar, which meant it had to be true. But how had he found out?

That was when I found the strength to pick myself up off the floor. I needed to ask Caleb how he knew his father was gay. Had he seen him somewhere with a man? Had Kent actually confided in him? Maybe--and this was hard to think about--Kent had gay porn on his computer, and Caleb had somehow come across it. Or perhaps it was that my son was more observant than I was and had detected some underlying unhappiness in his father. I needed to ask Caleb to elaborate on what he had just told me. I went into the house and went upstairs to his room, but he was gone. His bed was neatly made, looking like he hadn't even been there the night before, and his old gray duffel wasn't on the chair beside the dresser. I reached into the back pocket of my grimy jeans shorts and got out my phone. He'd texted: "I'm sorry, Mom." But that was all. The poor kid. He probably felt so bad about spilling his dad's secret and ruining his mom's life that he thought it was better to leave. Mission accomplished.

I poured myself a glass of chardonnay and decided to take a bath. Normally, I'm a shower person because of its expediency, but I decided that I might as well luxuriate in the tub with wine while I waited for each agonizing minute to pass before Kent came home. Hayley was spending the night at Marcy's after Audrey picked them up from the mall at five o'clock. I was glad for that. I don't think I could have pretended that nothing was wrong while she talked incessantly about the Tigerettes. She had now started to take exceptional note of her appearance, more makeup than before, every hair always in place, and practically a brand new wardrobe which she had funded with money from her savings account. I hadn't wanted her to use all her babysitting and birthday money for new clothes--her old ones were perfectly fine, and the savings were earmarked for college--but she'd pleaded until I had finally buckled under the pressure. In a small way, I suppose that I was happy that Caleb had left by then too. I was alone with my demons. I would face my husband without an audience.

But what was I going to say to Kent? Had he always known he was gay or had it been me who had somehow tainted him against women? I knew that was a long shot, but I think that every woman whose husband has an affair automatically wonders if she has been inadequate in one way or another. I could be a very bossy and demanding person, and maybe I had worn him down over the years. But here was the thing: He was still nice to me. I didn't know if you could call his behavior affectionate or not, though. He'd pick up things from the grocery store for me when I was running short on time, and every so often, he would hold my hand when we were watching something on TV. When I'd had a bad cold that past winter, he had brought me chicken noodle soup in bed for two nights running and kept the vaporizer full of water. Was that still love?

I soaked in the tub until my skin puckered and looked old and wrinkled. And then I felt old and wrinkled. I took a close look in the mirror and saw that my crow's feet had gotten deeper. I slathered on some Neutrogena lotion as if that last-ditch effort could make those wrinkles disappear. I was still in good shape because I tried to get in a run four or five times a week, but I didn't do much about my appearance on a daily basis, preferring athletic wear and Sketchers to dresses and heels. I am not a very feminine woman; I admit that. But that glass of wine must have gone straight to my head because I had the wild thought that a gay man would be more attracted to a woman who was not overly feminine. So maybe, if I played my cards right, I could win him back from the other side, turn him from gay to straight. I think it's safe to say that I was an emotional wreck by then. And I needed more wine.

I thought about rooting around in my drawer for some sexy panties and a bra that I'd bought many years before, but my turn of mind toward the pathetic was starting to scare me. I put on my regular cotton bra and panties and went downstairs and poured another hefty glass of chardonnay. I was trying to get myself under control and started my mind on another futile track, telling myself that I had probably gotten myself all worked up over nothing. It was possible that Caleb had misinterpreted a gesture or an overheard comment of his father's. Maybe I hadn't heard Caleb correctly. Maybe he'd actually said Donald is gay, not *Dad* is gay. That would make a whole lot more sense, all the way around.

But the fragile threads of my hope were still unraveling. I started to think about when I first met Kent. I was working as the bartender at Lindy's that night because the regular guy had called in sick. We all knew that the guy had a drinking problem, and it was going to be up to me to fire him shortly, but on that night, I had taken over his shift. And that was the night that Kent decided to give Lindy's a try. The restaurant wasn't busy, and I spent most of the evening talking to the dashing blonde, blue-eyed young engineer. I'd only gone to community college for a year before I decided that I'd rather work in the restaurant industry, so I was totally impressed by his degree from a college back East. He was new to Arizona, he said. He didn't know many people, he said. Would I like to go out? Let me tell you, there was no hesitation on my part. I was twenty-four years old, and I wanted to have a serious relationship and settle down. Handsome twenty-nine-year-old Kent fit the bill perfectly. I remember another waiter at the restaurant telling me that Kent was *pretty* after he left the restaurant that first night. At the time, I'd taken it as a compliment. He was a pretty man. *I was going to date a pretty man.* I thought I'd hit the jackpot.

But on the day my son told me that my husband was gay, after I'd downed the second glass of chardonnay like I was parched and it was a cool mountain stream, I finally realized that maybe, just maybe, that should have been my first clue. Could it be that *pretty* was a code word for *gay*, and I hadn't known it? Maybe that waiter had been subtly trying to tell me that Kent was more his type than mine. I couldn't remember whether or not that waiter had been gay, but evidently, I wasn't very good at making that kind of distinction. Evidently, I had no gaydar at all. For years, I'd thought my son was gay, but he was not. For years, I had thought my husband was a heterosexual man, but he was not. I had to be the stupidest person on earth. *Goddamnit.* It was a good thing that no one was around to see me at that moment because my face was flaming an alarming shade of red with shame and embarrassment.

I poured another glass of wine and walked into the family room. I was going to flop down on the couch and tell Alexa to play the saddest love songs ever recorded. I was in a George Jones "He Stopped Loving Her Today," or R.E.M. "Everybody Hurts," or basically, anything by Lucinda Williams mood. That's right. I had moved into the self-pity stage by then. I would slowly sip my wine and feel justifiably sorry for myself. I made it halfway through "He Stopped Loving Her Today" before I was on my feet and pacing the floor. I am not a good wallower. Maybe it stems from the fact that my dad was an ex-marine who never quite got over his basic training. I was the only girl with three brothers, but I was expected to swallow hurt and disappointment and "take it like a man," just like my older siblings. I can still hear Dad's booming voice in my head: "You've got to pull yourself up by the bootstraps, Private." I miss that lovely, scary man.

And when I thought about it during my pacing--I'd told Alexa to shut up because the songs were seriously depressing me--I remembered that my dad had not been a big fan of Kent's. That first Thanksgiving when I brought Kent home to meet the family down in Tucson, Dad had not been impressed. I thought then it was because Kent refused to join in the annual family football game. That was a huge red flag for Dad. *Everyone* joined in the game, even my mother, manicured nails and all. He'd looked my future husband up and down and said, "You got a problem with organized sports, Private?" Kent had said, "I prefer golf, sir." Well, that was a pussy sport as far as Dad was concerned. He actually didn't consider golf to be a sport at all. In his view, it was a game. Kent held his ground, though, which wasn't easy to do with Dad. I was very proud of Kent for that.

I finally concluded that I probably had known, on some subconscious level, that my husband was gay. Our sex life had never been anything to write home about, but I had always thought that it was more important that Kent and I genuinely liked each other. We were friends first, and on rare occasions, lovers. I guess what I'm trying to say is that he had never seemed that interested in me sexually. Sure it had hurt my feelings on more than one occasion. I mean, I had never spurned his sexual advances, as meager as they were, and he had told me he was too tired on many, many nights, but I thought that was normal. He was good to me, probably kinder to me than I was to him a lot of the time. He never failed to bring me flowers on my birthday, anniversary, and Valentine's Day. If I sometimes felt like I was missing out on something I couldn't quite put my finger on, I thought I was being overly critical. Every marriage is different, right? And no one truly knows what goes on behind closed doors.

When Kent finally walked in the door a little past seven, I had run myself through the emotional gamut. And drunk the entire bottle of wine. And eaten an entire Entenmann's crumb cake that I had been saving for Sunday breakfast. I was wiped out and felt bloated and a little drunk. In other words, I wasn't gunning for bear, as my dad used to say. I was just sad.

"What's with the garage?" Kent leaned his golf clubs against the pantry door. They were too expensive, he said, to keep in the garage. In a little while, he would nestle them gently into the hallway coat closet.

I had forgotten all about the garage. Caleb and I had done more harm than good. Nothing had been carted away, and all the crap was now strewn haphazardly across the floor. Kent wouldn't have been able to pull in his truck.

"And where's Caleb's car? I thought we'd take him out to dinner tonight."

"Caleb went back to school."

Kent frowned, then he spotted the empty wine bottle. "What's going on here?"

I opened my mouth to speak, but nothing came out. I must have looked like an idiot, just standing there with my mouth open and my eyes blinking furiously. The tears had come up again out of nowhere.

Kent was in front of me in two long steps. "Reggie, what's happened? Are the kids all right?"

I heard the panic in his voice. I tried to nod, but when I looked into his familiar face, I lost it. I lunged at him, burying my face in his still damp golf shirt. "Why?" I sniffled. "Why?"

Kent was having none of that. He pulled me away and gave me a little shake. "Reggie, you're scaring me. You're not acting like yourself. Please tell me what's going on."

I shook my head. The tears were pouring down my cheeks.

He shook me a little harder. "For the love of God, will you tell me what's going on?"

"Why are you gay?" I sniffled. "Why wasn't I enough?"

Kent was a very pale man, but what color there was drained from his face. "Who told you that?"

"Caleb."

"Oh, God." He let go of me and ran a hand over his face. "I think we better sit down, Reggie."

He steered me back into the family room, and I kept expecting him to tell me that it was all a misunderstanding, that Caleb had made a mistake, that everything was going to stay the same. But he didn't say any of those things. After he sat me carefully down on the couch and went and got me a tissue so I could give my nose a good honking blow, he just sat looking at me for what felt like the longest time, his blue eyes so sad that they seemed to turn violet.

"I'm so sorry," he said when he finally spoke. "I'm a coward."

Then slowly, carefully, he told me the story. He had fallen in love with a man he met in an economics class at Connecticut College. His patrician parents had strenuously objected when they found out about his love affair with a man. It had been going on for eight years before they found out,

Kent said, but to appease them, he moved to Arizona in an effort to forget the love affair. He'd wanted to do the right thing, he said, and he wanted to have a family. But the feelings had never gone away.

I interrupted at that point. "Didn't you ever love me?"

Kent seemed genuinely startled by the question. "Of course I love you, Reggie. Please don't doubt that."

I was starting to feel my temper rise. I was devastated by the events of the afternoon, but seriously? Kent had been a coward to keep this from me for twenty years. How could he have lived with himself? "What's this guy's name?" I snapped.

He went into the kitchen and came back with a bottle of red wine--which I was extremely grateful for--before he took a deep breath and continued. "Reed. His name is Reed. About five years ago, he contacted me on Facebook. And, well, things started up again."

I took a big gulp of wine and stared at my husband. He looked miserable. I was happy for that too. "What do you mean, *started up?*"

"We've been corresponding."

Absurdly, that made me feel better about things. If Kent had only been writing letters to this guy, then maybe it wasn't such a big deal. I knew that Kent hadn't made any trips out of town without me in years, so that meant that he wasn't having sex with this Reed character. I felt a little bit of hope. It was a shame it was going to be so temporary. "So you haven't had sex with Reed in over twenty years, right?"

Kent didn't look at me. "He's come into town a few times."

I was deflated all over again. It was my turn to say, "Oh, God."

"About a couple of months ago, I was sitting at the kitchen table. I didn't realize that my last email to Reed was still open on my computer, and I was on the phone. I swear I didn't know Caleb was standing behind me until I looked up. He didn't say a word, just turned and walked away."

"You didn't talk about it with him?" My poor son. I think I felt sorrier for him than I did myself. He'd been living with this secret for two months? I was trying to remember that visit, to recall some change in Caleb, but I couldn't come up with a thing. He was such a quiet kid, and I was obviously, glaringly unobservant.

Kent shook his head. "I was hoping he hadn't seen anything."

It was one thing to hurt me, but it was entirely something else to hurt my son. "You really are a coward." My voice rose a note higher on each word.

"Yes. I'm so sorry, Reggie."

"Sorry? You bet your ass you're sorry. The question is," I took another gulp of wine, "what are we going to do about it?"

"I don't know," Kent's voice came out in a hoarse whisper. "I love you both."

I picked up my wine glass, thinking I ought to throw it in his pale face, but I wasn't only mad at him. I actually felt a tiny bit sorry for him too. He had a sick, miserable expression on his face, worse even than the time his appendix burst. I decided not to waste the wine and took a big drink again. I sat my glass down carefully on the coffee table. "You're going to have to choose, Kent. It's either him or me."

Kent dropped his head into his hands. "Please," he said in that hoarse voice, "I can't do that. I love you both."

It took me a little while to realize that he was sobbing, but I was on a roll then, and unfortunately, I showed no mercy. "I mean it, Kent. You can't have it both ways." Then I unsteadily got to my feet, poured the rest of the wine into my glass, and somehow made it up the stairs to the master bedroom. I thought at the time that I was salvaging my last shred of dignity, but when I woke up the next morning, there were large, sloppy drops of wine stains on the carpet, snaking up the stairs like a trail of blood-red tears, proof of my disgrace.

Kent hadn't followed the trail.

He'd left a note propped against the empty wine bottle on the kitchen counter, probably thinking it was a safe bet I'd see it there. Kent's neat, precise handwriting told me that he wanted a week to think things over, that he was moving to a motel room, that he hoped I would understand. Hell, I didn't understand anything, and it wasn't because I was groggy from all the wine the night before, and it wasn't because I hadn't had my first cup of coffee yet. I simply did not *understand*, not any of it. I just didn't get how a man could live a lie for so long, nor how he could have so totally fooled me for over two decades. I stood staring at the note for a long time, wondering what I was going to tell my kids, wondering if my marriage was truly over.

I finally forced myself to move and made a pot of coffee. The long, depressing day yawned before me, and I had no idea how I was going to fill it. With only two of us in the house now, for whatever period of time that would be, it didn't seem worth it to plan the week's menus and go grocery shopping, which was what I usually did early on a Sunday morning. However, the thought of not cooking brightened my spirits a little. Cooking had never been my forte, and now that Hayley had decided to go on a low carb, high protein diet, a piece of grilled chicken and some carrot sticks seemed to suit her just fine. It was ridiculous, but I went along with it. She was in training, she said, even though she was already rail-thin. So I hid my amusement and bought her the chicken breasts and let her cook them in the George Foreman Grill. Chicken breasts were the least of it in the growing list of expenses that being a Tigerette demanded.

As I was pouring my second cup of coffee, my phone rang. I was glad to see that it was Audrey. I hadn't talked to her much in the past week, only once or twice since she canceled the trip to Cottonwood because she had to take care of her mother and then found out that Paul had gotten a DUI. She said she hadn't wanted to talk about it yet, and I respected her for that, and she asked me not to tell, which of course I wouldn't. However, the whole neighborhood knew about it because of our nosy, elderly neighbor Mrs. Simpson, who had nothing better to do than stare out her living room window and spy on the neighborhood. She was the one who told anyone who would listen that she had seen Paul back out of his driveway right into her trash can, and then without even bothering to pick it up, had taken down the street driving erratically at a very high speed. She was the one who said it had taken hours before he returned home, not in his car but in the passenger side of Audrey's, which could only mean one thing: Paul had gotten a DUI.

"Are you up for a trip to Cottonwood today?" Audrey asked. "Paul's going to be around to keep an eye on the girls, and I desperately need to get out of this house."

I hadn't realized how badly I wanted to get out of my own house until right that moment. "That sounds like a plan. I can be ready in ten minutes."

As I threw on some jeans and one of my better t-shirts, a new thought occurred to me, and with it, a whole new set of worries. What if Kent decided that he chose Reed--and the thought made me seethe--and that our marriage was over? Arizona was a community property state, and I would get half of everything, but that wasn't saying much. I supposed that Kent would feel like it was his duty to give me spousal support, but I doubted that it would be enough for me to keep living in this house. I would need money; I would need a job. I didn't have any time left to mull over the maybe I will/maybe I won't aspects of employment. I needed to find a way to make some money--fast.

It soon became apparent that Audrey was thinking along the same lines. We hadn't even made it out of town before she turned to me, her face creased with worry. "I'm going to tell it to you straight, Reggie. I need to make some money. Paul has decided that he wants to go back to screenwriting, and things are going to be pretty tight for a while."

I let out an involuntary gasp. "Is he out of his mind?" At the stricken look on Audrey's pretty face, I wish I hadn't said it, but at the time, I was beginning to wonder if all men, everywhere, had suddenly and inexplicably lost their minds. "I mean, good for him. He's been complaining about his job for years."

Audrey folded her arms across her ample chest and stared straight ahead. "Right. It's a good thing."

I felt bad then. Once again, I had crossed the line without meaning to. "Look, I'm sorry."

Audrey was still staring straight ahead, but I guess she'd decided to talk to me again. "You don't understand. Paul's job in sales requires that he drive. And he can't drive for six months. You have no idea what we're going through. You have a husband with a good job."

I'd had no intention of telling Audrey what had gone on the night before. Kent's betrayal was still festering beneath my skin, but the words suddenly bubbled forth of their own accord. "Kent is in love with someone else." The words made it a reality, and the stab of pain made me wince. I almost missed the turn onto the freeway.

"Oh, for Pete's sake. What's wrong with him? He has *you*." She paused a beat or two. "Who's the tramp?"

I almost told her the truth then, but I didn't. Back then, we meted out major information in our lives after we had digested it a bit. Eventually, over a bottle of wine, the truth might come out. "Someone from college. They reunited on Facebook."

"Why do people keep doing that?"

It was a rhetorical question. Audrey didn't expect an answer, and I was only too happy not to give her one. We drove on, talking sporadically about the Tigerettes and the kids and the weather, the usual stuff, except for our husbands. As I drove, Audrey googled the best wineries in Cottonwood, and we planned to hit them in order. You have to understand that our idea was very nebulous at that point, very vague. When we arrived, we had a very ill-formed plan, the gist being that we would buy a few bottles of four or five wines that we liked. Beyond that point, we hadn't articulated how we were going to make money by reselling this wine to women in the Valley.

We'd gone to three wineries--Arizona Stronghold Tasting Room, Verde Valley Wine Trail, and Burning Tree Cellars--before we could say out loud that our supposedly excellent idea was as full of holes as a moth-eaten sweater. It was Audrey who looked at me over the top of the car and said, "Why in the world would people want to buy this wine from us at a higher price when they can order it online? For that matter, they could join any number of online wine clubs and get monthly shipments of different types of wine. So why buy it from us?"

"They wouldn't," I said shortly.

Without a word, we got back in the hot car, and instead of heading to the next winery on our list, I headed out of town toward I-17. I felt danger-ously close to tears again. Me, a woman who never cried, had shed more worthless tears in the last twenty-four hours than I had in the last twenty years. I felt like such a fool--about everything.

"Unless . . ." Audrey stopped. "No, we couldn't."

"Just spill it, Audrey." I was in no mood for guessing games.

"We did discuss other options on that first night. Maybe we could make one of those work." She turned to me, her face bright with excitement for the first time that day. "What do you think, Reggie?"

I began to smile.

5

AUDREY

As I recall, the whole thing was Reggie's idea from start to finish. We were on our way home from Cottonwood, and I had pretty much given up on the whole idea of selling wine for profit. We didn't have a clue what we were doing, and with all the options available to people online, it seemed downright silly that they would want to buy wine from us. They could just order it and have a case shipped right to their doors, or better yet, they could get in their cars and go to the local grocery store and purchase it right from the shelf. That's what I'd been doing for years, buying whatever was on sale, usually six bottles at a time to get the ten percent discount. So my mind had already turned to other means of employment and the discouraging fact that I would need to write a new resume. If I still had a copy of the one I had used so many years before, it had probably yellowed with age.

But then Reggie said, "There would have to be something special about the wine we would sell. It would have to be something that people couldn't buy anywhere else."

"Rare wines are expensive," I pointed out.

"I know that." Reggie kept her eyes on the road.

I had thought that Reggie's idea of a wine club had been discouraged by what we saw at the Cottonwood wineries too, so I wondered why she didn't just give it up. That was Reggie for you. She could be so dogmatic and stubborn. "We couldn't even afford to put a down payment on some bottles of rare wine, and furthermore, we would have no guarantee that we would find someone willing to buy it from us at an even higher price. I don't see how it could work."

Reggie let out an exasperated sigh. "You're not following my drift here, Audrey. People would only have to *think* it was expensive. Don't you remember our discussion from the other night?"

Have I mentioned that Reggie could be the most impatient person on earth? However, I didn't remember all that many details from a drunken conversation that had happened weeks before. So I quietly sat as she filled me in on that conversation word for word. It did sound vaguely familiar, but boozy talk was just that: boozy talk. That's what I told her, and then I added, "Besides, that would be illegal."

Reggie acted like she didn't hear me. "Maybe we could set up a company, form an LLC to legitimize things. It wouldn't be too hard to do on LegalZoom."

"It's *illegal.*"

Reggie turned to look at me then, not seeming to notice that she was barreling down on the rear end of a semi. "I don't know that it is. I read an article one time that said that the entire cosmetic industry is something like a sham, that the formula for all cosmetics is basically the same. Yet some women would still prefer to go to a cosmetics counter in Saks and pay quadruple for the Clinique label."

I braced myself as the back of the semi filled the front window. "Watch out for the truck!"

Reggie swerved into the left lane at the last moment and didn't even flinch, nor did she notice the terrified look on my face. She kept talking. "And I know for a fact that the smoke shops in town go and buy their cigarettes from the Indian reservations and resell them for a higher price."

"How would you know that? You don't smoke." My heart was still racing from the close call.

"I went into a shop once to buy some cigars for Kent and his golf buddies." She flinched visibly at the mention of her husband's name. "The guy who ran the shop told me. I'm pretty sure he'd been smoking something other than tobacco, but I think he was telling me the truth."

"Sounds like a reliable source."

Reggie ignored my sarcasm, and the tone of her voice shifted from musing to serious. "You said you needed to make some money. Well, I do too, for reasons I don't want to go into at this time. And I cannot--will not--go back into the restaurant business. I'm too old and cranky."

"You're not too old, but you are on the cranky side." I almost laughed then but stopped at the look on her face. It was determined, but it was more than that. Reggie looked like someone who had just received bad news, and of course, she had. Her husband was in love with another woman. Oh, wait. She hadn't said another woman. She had said *someone else*. There was definitely more to the story than she was telling me, but unlike Reggie, I could be patient. I could wait until she was ready to tell me what was really going on. I'd give it until our next shared bottle of wine.

It wasn't like she knew all the details about the mess my life was in right then either. She knew that Paul had gotten a DUI, but I don't think anyone realizes the full ramifications of that until he or she has gone through it themselves. With an alcohol level of 0.15%, Paul had been arrested for an extreme DUI, first offense. He would have to spend thirty days in jail and pay up to $2780 in fines and fees. Also, there was the required screening and counseling. The story Paul had told me over the phone that first night hadn't included all the sordid details. He had backed into a cop's car in the convenience store parking lot, then become belligerent with the cop because he hadn't wanted to miss the ballgame. He was then put into handcuffs when he wouldn't cooperate. When I got to the jail that night to bail him out, he had a cut on his forehead from hitting his head on the steering wheel, the dried blood streaking his face, and he reeked of alcohol. He hadn't only been drinking beer that day. There had been shots of Jim Beam thrown in here and there.

From my point of view, the worst part of it was Paul's inability to drive. In his line of work, pharmaceutical sales, driving was essential. He spent his day driving from doctor's office to doctor's office all across metropolitan Phoenix. I was terrified of Paul losing his job, so I offered to drive him on his first day back at work. It had been truly horrible. I'd park in front of the office and wait like a chauffeur in the hot, stuffy car while he went inside, only to return minutes later and glumly slump into his seat. "Zip," he had said after every appointment. By the end of the day, we were both soggy and exhausted, but the worst part of it was that I now knew firsthand how the job demoralized Paul.

"I think you should quit," I said to him after we got home, long after both kids were home from school, long after the time I should have started dinner.

"I can't do that. We wouldn't have any income."

"We'll think of something." I tried to sound confident, but I felt my insides turn to jelly as I thought about the mountain of credit card debt I had amassed in the last year.

"I could hire an Uber or a driving service to take me on my rounds. It wouldn't be too bad."

I didn't know if Paul was trying to be noble, or if he secretly wanted me to beg him to quit. If I was the one who talked him into quitting, then at least he wouldn't have to be burdened with that. He was already consumed with guilt about the DUI and the disruption that it was going to cause our family for the coming months. But as worried as I was about having even less money in our financially strapped household, I was worried about Paul even more. Working for so many years at a job that he hated--and obviously wasn't very good at--had taken its toll. He had been depressed and drinking heavily. On the night I picked him up at the station, I was forced to see my husband like the rest of the people in that room saw him: a disheveled drunk.

"We'll think of something," I said to him again, but I couldn't look at him as I stirred the Rice-a-Roni on the stove. The kids were waiting hungrily in the next room, and I was frantically trying to scrape up something for them to eat. And I didn't want Paul to see the fear in my eyes.

"What would I do all day?"

What I wanted to say was: *I don't care, as long as you're not drinking.* What I said was: "You could go back to screenwriting."

Paul came up behind me and put his arms around my waist and laid his head on my shoulder. "I love you so much, Audrey, and I'm so--"

"Please don't say it again. I know, Paul." He had apologized profusely during the last few days, and as much as I appreciated it, his apology wasn't going to feed the family. I was going to have to make some money.

"I'll call tomorrow and give my resignation." And just like that, my husband was unemployed, and we were teetering on the edge of financial ruin.

Reggie had been talking for some time. "So, what do you think?"

Startled, I snapped back to the present. We had turned off the 101 and were heading down Shea Boulevard. I wasn't about to tell her that I hadn't been paying attention and didn't know if she was still talking about the wine club or something else. I decided to be neutral. "Well, the Tigerettes pom squad is a money pit."

"You're telling me!" She turned on Scottsdale Road.

"Say," I began tentatively, still not certain what the topic of conversation was, "has Hayley been acting differently lately?"

"She's suddenly obsessed with her weight. As if the kid needed to diet. She's already too thin as it is."

"Marcy's been dieting too, which isn't that bad of a thing, I guess." I had always struggled to keep my weight under control, and unfortunately, Marcy had inherited my build. Neither of us was like Reggie, who could eat anything she wanted and still stay thin. She said it was because of all the running she did. I'd never been a big fan of exercise, and I'd sooner shave my head than go running. I'd tried a yoga class once, but my boobs kept getting in the way. I took it as a sure sign that it wasn't meant to be.

"She does seem more focused, though. That's a good thing."

"Yes." But I wasn't convinced. The thing that was starting to bother me was that I didn't know exactly what Marcy was focused on--school, Tigerettes, boys, or all those things combined? And I was still bothered by the whole Top Twelve thing. It smacked of snobbishness. It smacked of Felicity. But before I could elaborate on this, we were turning into Reggie's driveway.

She turned to me. "Will you at least think about it?"

"I will." I nodded solemnly, more to appease her than anything. I was already dreading going into the house, knowing that Paul was there, knowing that he hadn't tried to write anything, knowing that he'd spent most of the last four days of his "retirement" trying not to drink too much.

Reggie opened the car door, a big smile on her face. "You really are a good friend, Audrey."

"Ditto." I smiled back.

"Do you want to come over for a quick glass of wine?"

"Maybe later." While I wanted to, I knew that Paul would be waiting. It was getting close to five o'clock, happy hour time, and that was the toughest time of day for him. For years the first thing he had done when he walked in the door after work was pour himself a drink or get a beer out of the refrigerator. On weekends he drank slowly, constantly all day. This was Sunday.

I think I knew even before I opened the door that what would greet me would not be good. I could hear the clanking even before I was fully in the house, and I followed the sound to the kitchen. Paul was standing at the kitchen sink, pouring bottle after bottle of booze down the sink. My first thought was: *Where did all those bottles come from?* We had a few bottles of hard liquor in the house that we kept for parties. But there must have been about twenty bottles of vodka, tequila, and whiskey lined up waiting to be poured, or emptied and laying in the sink. Then I knew. Paul had been hiding them around the house.

He was shirtless and wearing a pair of old tattered cotton shorts. And he was drunk. Staggeringly drunk. He reached for another bottle and almost keeled over. I walked over to him and put my hand on his wrist, and that too caused him to lose his balance. He grabbed onto the counter to keep from falling.

"What are you doing?" I had never seen him like that before, rarely seen him drunk, actually, and the sight sickened and terrified me.

"I need your wine bottles. There cannot be any liquor in this house! If I can't drink, you can't either, Audrey. I mean it." He was panting hard and sweating.

My first thought was: *I am not going to let him throw out perfectly good wine.* I'm ashamed to admit that now, but it's true. But luckily, I didn't have time to say it because he crumpled into my arms then, crying and sobbing. "I'm an alcoholic, Audrey. I need help."

The next week is still a blur in my memory. I honestly don't think I understood the magnitude of Paul's admission. I put him to bed that night and started researching AA meetings and treatment facilities close by. All the while I was doing this, mind you, I was drinking wine. I stayed up late, compiling lists and making notes, so by the time I finally went to bed, I was feeling hopeful. With my help, I was confident that Paul could conquer his addiction. All it took was willpower and the support of a loving wife. Looking back, I think maybe it was the wine that bolstered my high hopes and clouded my vision with rose-colored glasses.

I awoke earlier than Paul and made sure the kids ate breakfast, drove them to school, and even stopped by the dry cleaners to pick up Paul's shirts. He still wasn't up when I got back, though, so I made another pot of coffee and waited. And waited. I hated to waste a perfectly good morning doing nothing, so I opened up my computer to pay some bills. However, one look at the Bank of America credit card statement and my heart started to pound, the egg white omelet I'd had for breakfast rising to the back of my throat. What was I going to do? I'd gotten myself in way over my head. *What was I going to do?*

It was at that moment that I heard Paul's footsteps coming down the stairs. I snapped my computer shut and turned toward the door. I tried to smile, but my mouth was so wobbly that it must have looked like I was a cow chewing its cud. "Good morning, honey," I managed to eke out.

Paul went directly to the coffee machine and poured himself a cup. There was nothing unusual about that; he could barely manage to speak until he had that first infusion of caffeine. But I was glad to see that he'd showered and dressed in jeans and a crisp white shirt. His longish brown hair was neatly combed, and he had shaved. I could smell his cologne from where I sat, the Calvin Klein's Obsession that I had gotten him for Christmas. He looked like his old self, and the thought occurred to me that he might not remember what had happened the night before. In that case, I decided that I wasn't going to bring it up. I would help him monitor his drinking, and we would conquer it together. I had no idea how I would manage that, other than spy on him 24/7, but such is the fickle nature of hope.

Paul downed that first cup of coffee and poured another, and only then did he turn around. But he didn't come over and sit with me at the kitchen table. Rather, he leaned his long body stiffly against the counter, and his blue eyes looked at me over the rim of his cup. He looked so normal, like it was just another day, although I could see his hands were shaking as he lowered his cup and took a deep breath. "Audrey, I'm an alcoholic. There, I just wanted to say it in the sober light of day."

"Oh, honey. It's all right. We're going to get through this together. I did all kinds of research last night and found places close by where you can get help." I reached for the stack of papers I had printed out. "Here, look at these." When he didn't make any move to come to the table, I rose from my chair. If he wasn't going to come to me, I would go to him.

"Oh, Audrey."

His light blue eyes were so sad that I stopped in my tracks. "Why don't we go over these places together, Paul? I'm sure we can find some solution--"

"No."

He didn't let me finish my spiel, and believe me, I had one all planned out. "What do you mean, *no*?"

"I've been doing some research of my own, Audrey, and I need to get away from this place." He put down his coffee cup and opened the refrigerator, pointing at the half-empty wine bottle from the night before. "I don't think I can be around any alcohol right now. I need to go away to a treatment center for a while, and I've found one. It's in Wickenburg, a Christian-run kind of old dude ranch, outdoor work, counseling, that kind of thing. If I can get the court to approve it, I'm going."

Well, I was blindsided. All through our marriage, we had made decisions together. But it was more than that. He'd made such a big show of pointing to my wine bottle--was he accusing me of being a bad influence, or worse?

We had been married so long that he could pretty much read my mind. That's when he set down his cup and took my hands. "It's not your problem, babe. It's mine. I need time to think things through. I hope you understand."

My throat closed up. I could only whisper. "What about the kids?"

"I want to tell the kids the truth. Addiction is nothing to be ashamed of. It's a disease. But I am. Ashamed. It's something else I need to work on."

His mind was made up, and there was nothing I could say or do at that point to change it. Believe me, I tried: tears and begging, more or less. But he wasn't budging. So we spent the next two days making phone calls and meeting with a court-appointed counselor. Selfishly, I hoped the counselor wouldn't approve what I considered to be a drastic measure, but the woman we talked to said the Wickenburg dude ranch, called Fresh Start, was an excellent facility. She highly recommended it and would rush the paperwork.

Four days later, with the kids in tow and Paul's packed suitcase in the trunk, we drove to Wickenburg. Fresh Start looked like nothing more than a dusty old ranch to me, with several weathered buildings that had seen better days. I kept reminding myself that Paul was only going to be in treatment for thirty days, that Wickenburg was only an hour away, and that there would be family counseling sessions somewhere down the road. But there was something about the ranch that made me feel that my husband's absence would be much longer than that. Maybe it was the desolation or the rustic nature of the place. I didn't exactly know what it was, but I felt like I was losing my husband, the man I had known and loved for so long, for good.

It was now solely up to me to "man the fort," as Paul had called it when he hugged me goodbye. And there was no other way to put it: I was in deep shit. I had put the first installment of the payment for Fresh Start on the one credit card I had not maxed out, and I had no idea how I would pay for the rest. So the first thing I did when I got home was grab that half-full bottle of wine out of the refrigerator and walk through the gate and into Reggie's backyard. Not surprisingly, she was already sitting on the patio with her glass of wine.

I sat down, lifted the wine bottle, and without preamble, said, "I'm in."

It was a point of no return.

After that, I rarely stopped to ruminate on the fact that what Reggie and I were about to embark upon was, in all probability, deceptive, fraudulent, illegal, and flat-out wrong. I guess you could say that from that point forward, Reggie and I ignored all of that and developed a kind of symbiotic relationship, one that benefitted us both. Both of our husbands were temporarily out of the picture, we desperately needed money, and the more the plan progressed, the more reasonable it seemed. All we were doing, Reggie told me, was giving women what they wanted, a chance to get out of the house, enjoy each other's company, and drink a new wine. Well, a wine they *thought* was new. But even that didn't matter too much in the long run. What we were doing was giving women a new *experience*. It was really too funny how desperate women could talk themselves into just about anything. In no time at all, I started to believe that we were doing something worthwhile, something beneficial for all of our soon-to-be customers.

The first thing we had to do was come up with a name for our new wine. Drinking a lot of wine that first night, after I had dropped off Paul in the middle of nowhere to recover or find himself, or whatever he thought he was going to do on a dude ranch, we didn't come up with much of anything. We drank, spilled our guts about the sorry turn our lives had taken, and shed a few tears. Then we laughed. A lot. It's amazing how a person can laugh when she's wallowing in hurt and confusion, but we both did. I can't speak for Reggie at this point, but for me, the night was cathartic, a new beginning. It was, you could say, my own Fresh Start.

So Reggie came over the next morning after we dropped the kids off at school, and we sat around my kitchen table drinking coffee and brainstorming ideas. In the light of day, we were much more focused and quickly concluded that we should come up with a French name for our wine. Neither one of us knew French, nor had either of us ever been to France, but those two facts seemed like minor considerations.

Reggie reached for her phone--she was always doing that--and started googling. "People think anything French is classy."

"And expensive."

"Even better."

We narrowed it down to three choices: *éclatant*, which meant brilliant and dazzling; *étoile*, which meant star; and *éphémère*, which meant ephemeral, or transient, fleeting. I voted for Éclatant wine, and Reggie agreed, pointing out that if we needed different wines down the road, if we needed to "branch out the business," we could use the other two. Then we researched French wine areas and decided that we liked the sound of Loire Valley. I don't know if it was because I'd had about a gallon of coffee by then, or if I was starting to feel a little overwhelmed by the project, or if it was a combination of both, but I could feel the beginning of a headache coming on. I went and got a bottle of Advil from the medicine cabinet in the bedroom and returned to the kitchen.

Reggie saw the bottle. "What's wrong?"

"I don't know. Don't you think that maybe we're getting in over our heads here? I know I've said this before, but we don't know anything about French wine. What if people go home and do the same research that we're doing? What if they figure out it's a scam?" I tapped out two tablets and filled a glass with water.

Reggie leaned back in her chair and crossed her arms. "I've thought about that too, Audrey, but we're going to have to count on people having a little bit of faith in us."

It seemed like a very odd thing for her to say. "So, to clarify, we're going to have to count on people having faith in a lie?" I sat back down in my chair, hard.

She uncrossed her arms and leaned on the table. "Look, Audrey, we're not talking mega-millions here, and we're not hurting anyone. We're offering an *experience*, and that's the last time I'm going to remind you. Let's get back to work."

I shut my mouth then, and I think that's the last time I expressed any reservations about the plan. When Reggie put it that way, it didn't sound like we were really doing anything wrong. And as I've reiterated *ad nauseum*, I sorely needed the money. So we went back to work, discussing party ideas, what kind of appetizers we should serve, and what kind of chocolate because chocolate would be essential to the experience, according to Reggie. "What's better than wine and chocolate?" she said emphatically. We talked about how much wine we should give away for free before the women--and it was always going to be a women's only club--would have to start buying it. We discussed presentation versus allowing the women to just talk and comment on the wine. We discussed profit margin.

I made turkey sandwiches for lunch, and yet another idea occurred to me. There was so much to think about, and every time we thought of one thing we should or shouldn't do at our monthly parties, another thought would crop up. It was like an endless train of *what-ifs* and *or we coulds*. At one point, I suggested, "Maybe we should offer a free shuttle service in case the women drink too much? It would be a nice touch."

Reggie shut down that idea fast, and it wasn't the first suggestion of mine she'd vetoed. "If they get too drunk, they can call an Uber. We have to think profit margin here."

I let it go, as I tend to do, even if it hurt my feelings that she shot down most of my ideas. "Should our wine club have a name or something, Reggie? What about Scottsdale Wine Club?"

"Why do we need a name? Women don't name their book clubs. They focus on the book they're reading. In this case, our wine club will focus on the wine we are presenting, starting with Éclatant wine."

I guessed that made sense, and by that time, my head was throbbing with all the ideas we had been throwing out all day. However, I did have one more important question. "How are we going to steam the labels off of the wine bottles?"

Reggie was already typing away and read: "'Hold the wine bottle over the pot of boiling water for 10 to 15 minutes. The steam affects the glue and softens the label. Carefully remove the label with your hands. Results: After 25 minutes of steaming--10 on the back side, 15 on the front, one label peeled off with ready-to-mount perfection.'"

"We have to do that for every bottle? That sounds like a lot of work." I could picture myself standing over a boiling pot, my hair turning to frizz, and my face and hands with second-degree burns.

"Hard work will keep us honest." Reggie laughed.

I joined in. "Well, in that case . . ."

It was after two when Reggie looked at her Fitbit, which she used instead of a watch. "Shit, I have to go. I just remembered I have a dentist appointment." She gathered up her notes. "I think we accomplished a lot today. But there's one more thing. I'm leaving it up to you to design the labels." She looked at me meaningfully before she went out the back sliding doors. "The sooner, the better."

I knew what that look was for. For the last two hours, Reggie kept suggesting that I get my sketch pad and see what I came up with--with her input, of course. I kept hemming and hawing, changing the subject. The truth of the matter was that I didn't want Reggie to see my first feeble attempts at drawing. It had been years since I'd picked up a charcoal pencil or a paintbrush. I didn't know if I could still do it. Maybe my "artistic vision" or "my eye," or whatever you wanted to call it, had atrophied over the years. Maybe it had dried up and disappeared altogether. But I did agree with her that time was of the essence, so I reluctantly went to the top shelf of the hall closet and got down the box where I had stowed my art supplies. There was dust on that box, a thick layer, which only fueled my apprehension. I thought seriously of pouring myself a glass of wine to bolster my confidence, but I still had kids to pick up from school. So I steered clear of the wine rack.

When I first picked up that drawing pencil, it looked like an appendage, an extra-long finger, a strange aberration. I stared at it for a long time, thinking *Éclatant* before a spark of an idea came to me. A lady, an elegant French lady, began to emerge, first in my mind, then on the page. She wasn't a Marie Antoinette type; I didn't think that was a good association for our wine, a woman who was beheaded by a guillotine. Rather, the image began to look more like Audrey Hepburn in a chic Chanel suit. The more I worked on her, the more *très élégante* she became. I would work out the other details after I got her right, the placement of the year, the region, the name, all of it in graceful, sophisticated calligraphy.

Before I knew it, it was almost four-thirty and time to pick up Jimmy from his after-school program. At first, I had felt guilty for enrolling him in a program for special needs kids, like I was trying to pawn off my responsibility as a parent on someone else, like I didn't want to deal with his sometimes volatile nature. Don't get me wrong. I knew he couldn't help it that he had ADHD hyperactivity and Oppositional Defiant Disorder. And I had tried for years--was still trying--to use calm, positive parenting to help him cope. But it hadn't been enough, and we had finally conceded to medication. He was on Vyvanse now, and his situation had improved dramatically. I was also convinced that keeping him busy helped, hence the after-school program. I really couldn't say when the last time he'd thrown a major fit had been, but it seemed like I was always on edge around my son, waiting for it to happen. I often wondered if he sensed that. I often wondered if I was avoiding my own child.

I picked him up without incident, and his teacher gave me a thumbs up, meaning that Jimmy'd had a good day. I gave a small sigh of relief. I had almost kept him home from school that day because I thought he might behave badly, act out because we had just dropped his father off at a rehab center the day before. But I sent him to school anyway, preferring to spend my day planning a wine club rather than dealing with any possible repercussions of my son's reaction to the change in our family dynamic. As I said, I can be accused of avoiding my own child. To make it up to him, and because I had another hour before I needed to pick up Marcy and Hayley from Tigerette practice, I took him to McDonald's, his favorite place, for a Happy Meal. Jimmy wasn't a verbal kid, but I tried to talk to him about the situation. The gist of the one-sided conversation was that he only had two questions: "Does Daddy get to have ice cream there? Can I have a vanilla cone?" I bought him the ice cream.

We arrived early at the school, and I decided to go in. I knew that parents weren't allowed in to watch these so-called top-secret practices, but I thought maybe there was a window or something I could peek into. "Come on, Jimmy, let's go into the big kids' school." He didn't seem thrilled with the idea, so I offered him a bribe. "You can play with my iPad while we wait." That got a big smile.

I found the room, and we waited against the far wall of the hallway. I was the only mother there, and I was surprised. Some of the other moms in the school were still helicopter moms, even though their kids were in high school, but on that day, there weren't any around--until I saw Reggie walking down the hall. "What are you doing here?"

She seemed as surprised as I was. "I thought it was my turn to pick up the girls."

"I thought it was mine."

Reggie laughed. "Like we haven't spent enough time together today. Maybe we need to communicate more?" She winked.

"Let's peek in the window."

"Yeah, let's be naughty. Let's piss off Miss Felicity."

Jimmy was playing on the floor with the iPad, and Reggie and I crossed the hall to the small, narrow window. Out of the corner of my eye, I saw a black leotard-clad figure walk down the hall, and at first, I thought it was one of the Tigerettes, returning from a bathroom break. But as the figure rapidly approached, the Barbie doll figure came into full view, and I realized it was the former Mrs. Arizona herself, Cynthia Stewart. She had on the uniform, but she also carried her big Louis Vuitton bag, every hair perfectly in place. Why wasn't she in the classroom? Wasn't she supposed to be instructing the girls?

Reggie had noticed her too. "The fabulous Mrs. AZ approaches. Quick, we have to get a look before it's too late."

We crammed our faces close to the glass, and I could see bouncing, dancing girls, pom-poms flashing, and I searched for Marcy, who would be one of the shorter girls. They were moving so fast that it took me a second or two to spot her, and then . . .

I gasped at the same time that Reggie sputtered furiously: "What the hell? Are they wearing *diapers*?"

6

CYNTHIA

It was the first time that I had met the two women, Reggie Carson and Audrey Maynard, and to say that we did not get off to a good start would be an understatement. First of all, I was miffed that they were so nosy, peering into the practice room like that, and secondly, I felt like I had been caught red-handed. I was supposed to be the coach of the Tigerettes, and I clearly wasn't doing my job. By that point, I had acquiesced to Felicity's wishes that I remove myself from *her* squad. I only showed up every once in awhile dressed in the black leotard for the sake of appearances. That day, unfortunately, happened to be one of them.

By the time I reached the door, the taller, black-haired one was pulling frantically at the doorknob, while the shorter, auburn-haired woman pounded on the door. "Someone unlock this door!" one of them shouted. Meanwhile, a young boy sitting on the floor across the hall started to wail like a banshee.

I decided to pretend that I was in charge. "What are you two ladies doing? These practices are closed. Everyone will see how hard the girls have been working at the first basketball game of the season."

"Who does Felicity think she is, the head of the CIA?" the tall one sputtered. "This is a high school pom squad, not some top-secret government organization."

"And why are our daughters wearing diapers?" the shorter one asked angrily. She glanced over at the boy. "Jimmy, please stop screaming."

Of course I had no idea what she was talking about, and because the kid was making such a commotion, I thought I had misheard her. "What diapers? Who's wearing diapers?"

"Hayley and Marcy, our daughters."

That's when I knew who they were. "Oh, you're the new girls' mothers."

"Duh," Reggie said. "And why aren't you in there? Aren't you the coach of the squad?"

"I was running an errand." It wasn't exactly a lie. I had stopped and gotten a manicure on my way to the school.

"Is your daughter bullying our daughters?" Audrey had walked over to her son and was gently rubbing his back, and he turned down the volume slightly.

I took offense at that. "Don't be ridiculous. Felicity is the captain of the team." However, I did feel a tiny pinprick of unease. Felicity was strong-willed, and let's face it, downright bossy some of the time. But I did not think she could be accused of being a bully. For one thing, she was way too pretty.

"Take a look." Reggie pointed at the small rectangular window.

They were both glaring at me like I was the bad guy in this situation, and I had no choice but to take a look. Felicity had the music up so loud that none of the girls had heard the commotion in the hallway--and let me tell you, that little boy could *scream*--and they were practicing a routine I had never seen before. In the blur of movement, it took me a few seconds before I spotted two white bottoms. However, I couldn't be sure that the two girls were actually wearing diapers. They could have been wearing very short shorts. I pressed my nose against the glass. Definitely diapers. "I'm sure there's a logical explanation for what's going on in there."

"I can't think of one." Reggie had her hands on her hips--what there were of her hips, really, she was built like a boy--and she was still glaring furiously at me.

Me. Like it was all my fault. Their two daughters had no business being on this elite team in the first place, and if it wasn't for those near-sighted, dowdy judges, they wouldn't be here. They so obviously didn't belong. "Don't you think you're overreacting?"

"How would you feel if it was your daughter wearing diapers?" Audrey had succeeded in calming her bratty kid by bribing him with a Snickers bar that she pulled from her purse.

Well, Felicity wouldn't have allowed it; Felicity was a very strong person. It could be that their daughters--in addition to having no talent--had no backbone either. And that wasn't my fault. I was about to point this out when the music suddenly stopped, and I could hear Felicity saying, "Good job, Tigerettes. Newbies, to the front of the room." My heart sank to my feet when I saw Hayley and Marcy drop to their knees and crawl toward her. Instinctively, I blocked the window. No need for these two women to see *that*.

I cleared my throat. "Practice is almost over. The girls will be out soon."

"The warden is about to release the prisoners," Reggie muttered under her breath, just loud enough for me to hear.

I may not have a lot of maternal instinct, but Felicity was my daughter, and that comment put up my hackles. "What are you implying?"

Audrey looked at both of us, and I don't know, maybe she didn't want a verbal outburst disturbing her crazy kid again, but she must have thought it was better if she changed the subject. "I have something to show you, Reggie." She pulled out another Snickers bar to give to the whimpering kid and a piece of thick drawing paper, which she handed to Reggie. "What do you think?" she asked shyly.

Reggie let out a low admiring whistle. "It's perfect, Audrey. I always knew you were talented, but this is really something."

"It just came to me after you left this afternoon." Audrey smiled happily.

"It's been a productive day, hasn't it?" Reggie hugged her. "We're really on our way."

I'll admit it. I was dying to know what they were talking about. Sure, I was relieved that their attention had suddenly shifted from me and what was going on in Felicity's practice session to something else. That said, I'll also admit that I felt a little jealous. The two women were obviously close friends and seemed to be in on something together. I'd never had a truly close girlfriend. Don't get me wrong. I had a lot of so-called friends, mostly women in my specific socio-economic group, among them plenty of former Mrs. Arizonas. But as far as having someone close to me to confide in and commiserate with? I'd never had that kind of relationship with another woman. It was one of the few drawbacks of being beautiful and rich. Other women were generally jealous of me or intimidated by me. I'd gotten used to it, but seeing the way that Reggie and Audrey acted together on that fateful day, I finally felt like I had missed out on something important.

I couldn't help myself. "What are you looking at?"

"Nothing." Reggie folded the paper and handed it back to Audrey.

Audrey, it was becoming clear, was the nicer of the two. "Um . . . Reggie and I are starting a wine club."

Being a woman who enjoyed her nightly wine, my interest was immediately piqued. "Do you mean a club where people get together and taste different wines? I've heard of those."

"Sort of," Reggie said hesitantly.

"We're going to sell wine from France. Reggie has a distant cousin who is a vintner at one of the most prestigious wineries in the Loire Valley--"

"He sells us the wine at a discount, and we pass on the savings to you--"

"It's called Éclatant, and it's impossible to get anywhere else--"

The two women were talking fast, interrupting each other in their excitement, and all I could think was how lucky they were, and not only because they were doing something so exciting together. After all, there weren't many people who had a cousin who was a vintner in France. I, myself, couldn't tell the difference between a good French wine or an Italian or an Australian or something from Napa Valley. Years ago when Richard and I spent that month in France, he had tried to teach me the finer points of French wine. When I didn't get it, he had said that my palate was not sophisticated enough. Back then, he'd said it fondly, and back then, I'd laughed girlishly, a *silly old me* kind of laugh. I didn't think it would be the same today. I was pretty sure that Richard had given up on me ever being sophisticated enough.

But these two women didn't know that, and I did have a reputation to uphold, so when they finally stopped to catch their breath, I said, "I love good French wine. When Richard and I spent a month in France, the wines were glorious."

A strange look passed between the two women, and they looked uneasy. "Isn't that nice?" Audrey finally said.

"You haven't tasted ours yet," Reggie added mysteriously.

"I would love--"

But before I could finish the sentence, the door to the practice room burst open, and the Tigerettes came spilling out, the scent of female sweat overpowering even the antiseptic smell of the hallway. The last three girls to leave the room were Hayley, Marcy, and Felicity. And I would like it to be noted that Hayley and Marcy were not wearing diapers and that Felicity had an arm draped over each of their shoulders. "Good practice, newbies." And then she noticed me. "Hey, Mom, what are you doing here?"

My smile turned rigid. "Why wouldn't I be here? I'm the coach."

Reggie grabbed Hayley's arm. "Were you wearing a diaper during practice?" It would not be the last time I would see how direct Reggie could be.

Hayley blushed. "What are you talking about? And you know you're not supposed to spy on us at practice."

"I wasn't spying, Hayley. I came to pick you up, and I happened to peek in the window. That is not spying."

"Mom?" It was Marcy, who also blushed at the sight of her mom.

"Marcy, I saw you wearing a diaper," Audrey said. At the sight of his sister, the bratty little boy started to laugh delightedly, uncontrollably.

"Oh, that." Felicity waved her hand in front of her face like she was batting off a pesky fly. "That's just a little initiation thing we do from time to time. It's all part of being a Tigerette." Her hands gripped each of the girls' shoulders. "Isn't it, girls?"

They both nodded, attempting smiles.

"I think something's going on here." Again Reggie's hands were on her nonexistent hips, her warrior pose, we came to call it.

"What do you mean, Mrs. Carson?" Felicity's dark blue eyes were wide, as innocent as can be. It was a look I knew all too well. She certainly used it on Richard and me often enough. Richard, naturally, melted at the sight.

"I saw . . . white . . ." For once, Reggie was at a loss for words.

"It's all harmless fun. It's not like we haze the new girls or anything like that. I would never allow such a thing."

"I don't understand." Audrey was looking back and forth, from Marcy to Hayley, as if begging--or daring--them to tell her something.

"Mom, it's nothing." Marcy glanced at Felicity. "It's all part of being a Tigerette," she parroted. "I'm having fun."

Neither Audrey nor Reggie looked convinced, and quite frankly, neither was I. I had a feeling Felicity was up to something, but I didn't think it was anything bad or harmful. You know that old saying, "kids will be kids?" Well, it's true. Felicity had never been a bad kid, never given us any kind of trouble. Now she could be manipulative and conniving at times, but isn't that the definition of a teenage girl? She was driven, focused, and an excellent team captain. If she was a little strict in her methods, so what?

"So everything is settled here, right?" I said brightly. As the nominal coach, I felt it was my duty to wrap things up neatly.

Felicity, naturally, had a trump card. "Would it be all right with you, Mrs. Carson and Mrs. Maynard, if I started to drive Hayley and Marcy home from practices? It would save you an extra trip a day, and honestly, it's not a problem. I would be delighted to give them rides."

I thought it was a genuinely nice offer on her part, and she extended it with just the right amount of obsequious courtesy. Richard had recently bought her a powder blue Porsche Cayenne for no reason other than Felicity had asked him for one, saying that the white Mercedes--formerly my car--was too old lady-like. He'd taken her to the Porsche dealership that very day. Did I think it was extravagant? No, the thought never crossed my mind.

"Well," Audrey said hesitantly, "I guess that would be all right." She looked at Reggie, who nodded.

"That's great! Why don't we start today?" She started to corral Hayley and Marcy down the hall. "I'll be careful, Moms. Precious cargo, you know?" The three girls giggled before they bolted for the door.

And without another word to me, Reggie and Audrey headed for the door behind the girls. I could hear Reggie saying to Audrey before the door whooshed shut, "Wine on the patio tonight?"

"You bet." Audrey was struggling to tug the boy along.

Not surprisingly, they hadn't asked me to join their wine club, and I suddenly felt very alone.

I most certainly had planned to ask Felicity about the diaper episode. Now I didn't see any harm in girls pulling little, harmless pranks on each other. I was sure that it was all in good fun, and I thought it was rather humorous myself. I was also sure that Felicity had her reasons. In all probability, she was trying to bolster team spirit, form a lasting bond between all the girls, something like that. However, I didn't want word of it to get around, especially not to Mr. Rooney, the school principal, who might have deemed it to be rather inappropriate, just like Audrey and Reggie. I liked the man. He was not especially attractive, not at all like Richard. He looked something like Jon Lovitz, but I enjoyed flirting with him in my skin-tight black leotard on the rare days I dropped in toward the end of practices. I might have even developed a tiny crush on the man. Not that I would ever act upon it. I had been totally faithful to Richard in the eighteen years of our marriage. Well, almost totally faithful.

The conversation with Felicity never happened, and there was a very good reason for that. As soon as I pulled onto my street, I could see that some contraption was parked smack dab in the center of my lovely circular driveway, right in front of the door. At first, I thought it was one of our landscapers' vehicles, one of those beat-up old trucks that most of the Mexican landscapers in Phoenix drive. And I am not racist when I say that. It is a fact. You can drive down almost any road in town on any day of the week and see an old truck with four or five guys crammed into the front seat and lawnmowers and rakes and blowers and cut branches wobbling in the back bed. Like I said, it is a fact.

However, as I pulled into the driveway, I could see that it wasn't that. It was an old Ford truck, but it had an ancient, rusted-out camper perched precariously on the back. I parked behind it and spied the license plate: Kansas. I can say with certainty that it was the closest I ever came to hyperventilating.

Did I say that my parents were dead? I'm positive I never said that. My folks, Sally and Dwight, were alive and well and still living in Marion, Kansas--as far as I knew. We kind of lost touch after they quit sending money and I married Richard. It wasn't like we had a falling out or anything like that. I guess I didn't need them anymore. Don't get me wrong. I am not ashamed of my parents. They were hardworking, honest people. Daddy worked on a farm, and Mom worked as a hairdresser. Naturally, they were both good-looking people, back before all that smoking and drinking and hard work made them look old before their time. So it wasn't like there was any big rift between us. We just didn't have any contact with each other. Somewhere along the way, I might have told Richard that they had passed to the Great Beyond. Whatever. The subject hadn't come up in many, many years.

But it wasn't my parents who popped open the back door of that camper, jumped to the ground, and picked me up in one fell swoop. It was Buck Boyd, my old high school boyfriend. "Lordy, lordy, Cindy Lou, you look good enough to eat."

He, on the other hand, did not. Once the proverbial star quarterback of the Marion High School football team, popular and dashing, he had taken a mighty fall from his glory years. This balding man with the beer belly pressing into my skin-tight black leotard had been voted Homecoming King? By the way, it is another reason I should have been Queen. We were going together; it was so obvious. I know someone rigged the ballot box.

"Put me down, Buck," I said to him then. My voice sounded like he was strangling me, which was exactly how I felt. I couldn't breathe, and it wasn't only because he was squishing me against his beer belly. How had he found me, and what was it going to take to make him go away?

Thankfully, he did deposit me safely on the ground and took a step back. "I swear, Cindy Lou, you're just as pretty as you were in high school. You haven't changed a bit."

That was the thing about Buck. He had always known how to push my buttons. I smiled in spite of the circumstances. "What are you doing here?"

"Just taking a trip across the country, thought I'd stop in and say howdy." He gave his old, broad mischievous smile, but it was now tarnished yellow from years of Skoal.

"How did you find me?" I glanced nervously up at the window of Richard's study, trying to see if he was in there, but I couldn't see a thing through the tinted windows.

"Your folks gave me the last address they had for you, and I took it from there. It ain't hard to find people on the internet these days."

I'd hesitated a long time before I set up a Facebook page precisely for that reason, but after I was crowned Mrs. Arizona, it seemed like something I needed to do. It didn't really matter now. This unwelcome blast from my past was here, and I needed to figure out a way to get rid of him.

"You can find out all kinds of things about people on the internet these days." He looked me up and down in a manner that made me very uncomfortable.

"Is that so?" I cocked my head, trying to act flirtatious, but all the time, my mind was racing before it settled on one remembered fact: Buck had gotten a scholarship to Kansas State to study engineering. Despite the dilapidated camper and his middle-aged appearance now, he had been one smart cookie, probably still was. How much did he know?

"Hey, but I'm here now." Buck nodded toward the door. "Got any cold beer in that great big house of yours?"

I wanted to tell him that I didn't have any beer, to tell him to go away, but I had a feeling that he had some kind of agenda. My years in LA and Vegas had given me a sixth sense about that kind of thing when it came to men. Why else would he go to all the trouble of looking me up? I felt chilled, despite the 100+ degree heat. The truth of the matter was that I was scared. Richard only knew bits and pieces of my past, the highlights, you might say. I aimed to keep it that way. "Sure, Buck, come on in. We'll catch up on old times before you get back on the road."

"Not planning on doing that any time soon."

I'd been starting for the front door, key in hand, but I suddenly whipped around. "What do you mean?"

"I've never been to Scottsdale before, and I think I like it. I might stay a while."

"Hotels start to get expensive around here this time of year." I said it mildly, but that chill inside my skin was dropping to the freezing point.

"No problem. I'm staying right here." He patted the camper.

"Smart thinking. The RV parks are much cheaper." I hurriedly opened the door before he could tell me that he didn't need an RV park, that he was planning on staying parked right in my lovely circular drive.

I could tell as soon as I walked in the door that Richard wasn't there. I didn't feel his presence looming up above in his study, and then I remembered that it was Monday, men's league at the club. He'd grab a bite to eat and a few drinks with his golfing buddies after the game, and I wouldn't see him until close to ten o'clock. At least I could feel relieved about that. It was small consolation.

I led Buck to the kitchen at the back of the house, wondering if I'd made a huge mistake in letting him through the door. My house was impressive architecturally with its vaulted ceilings and marble floors, and with its original artwork, various antiques, and Persian rugs. I hadn't had a clue what I was doing when we bought this massive house, but Richard had, and along with an expensive decorator, they had furnished it to perfection. Unfortunately, Buck seemed to have some knowledge about design as well, and he made appreciative comments as we walked toward the kitchen.

"I'd say you did pretty well for yourself, Cindy Lou," he said after we had settled on the bar stools at the kitchen island, and I had poured him a beer into a frosty glass and a glass of sauvignon blanc for myself.

I refused to comment on that. "Hmm. What about you, Buck? Married, children, job? Weren't you going to be an engineer?"

"Nah. I really couldn't hack it at State. I dropped out after sophomore year and went back to the hometown, got married, had a boy. Same old, same old."

"Oh, who did you marry?" Mind you, I wasn't interested. I was only playing nice until I could figure out some way to get him out of my house and out of my life, once and for all.

"Mary Wilson? You remember her?"

I almost choked on my wine, surprised how the name of my former nemesis could still produce a flash of anger.

"Oh, yeah. She was the one who beat you out of Homecoming Queen, wasn't she?" He drained his glass and pushed it toward me, signaling he wanted another. "If it's any consolation to you, she's no looker now. She got good and fat."

I was standing behind the open refrigerator door and was glad he couldn't see the triumphant smile on my face. It might have been petty of me, but it sure did feel good. I returned to my seat. "Go on."

"We got divorced a few years back. She turned out to be quite a bitch. Took me for everything she could, and she's still hounding me for child support and any other thing she can think of. Somehow, I ended up paying for her last root canal. Don't know how she managed that." He grunted disgustedly. "Bitch."

It was a good opening for me. "I'm happily married, eighteen years now. And I have a daughter, Felicity. As a matter of fact, my husband Richard should be home soon, so if you're done with that beer--"

"What's the big deal if he sees me here? I'm just an old friend, and we ain't doing anything wrong. Yet." He winked at me over the rim of his beer mug.

"What?" I'm sure the fear showed in my eyes.

He reached over and patted my hand. "There, there, Cindy Lou, I'm just toying with you. I mean you no harm."

"That's a relief." I was such a fool.

He asked for another beer, and I was surprised to see that my glass was empty too. The guy had said he meant me no harm, and I was beginning to think that I'd imagined trouble where there was none. Years of looking over your shoulder can do that to you.

"How about some music?" Buck said a few minutes later. "This is starting to feel like a party to me."

I obliged and put on a nineties country station on Pandora, remembering that he had liked that type of music. We talked about high school, and I even asked about my parents after the third glass of wine. We were drinking fast, mind you. I don't think that Buck had been in my house for an hour yet, and I was pouring a fourth glass of wine for me, and he was on his seventh beer. When he asked me to dance, I did. He'd been a decent guy back in high school, and there was no reason to think he still wasn't. It was starting to look--and I was starting to believe--that Buck Boyd had no ulterior motive.

And then Buck asked, "How come you never go home, Cindy Lou, never visit your folks?"

The question caught me completely off guard. "This . . . this is my home."

Buck took a casual sip of beer, acting like he had all the time in the world. "Is it because of the baby?"

I honestly had no idea what he was talking about. I'd had a lot of wine, fast, but that wasn't why. "What are you talking about?"

"Our baby, the one you aborted in high school. Don't you remember that trip to Wichita? I believe it was February 1995."

I was mid-sip, and the wine went down the wrong way. I was coughing and then choking. I couldn't breathe. I had foolishly let down my guard, and now it was too late. I knew it was too late.

Buck was pounding on my back. "There, there, nothing to be alarmed about. This will all be over soon."

"You need to leave," I sputtered as soon as I could speak, although my breathing was still ragged. "You need to get out of my house *now*."

Buck calmly drank his beer, acting like nothing out of the ordinary was happening and went on. "Or is it all them other babies you murdered? I must say, I was shocked at the number, just shocked. Shame on you, Cindy Lou. Hey, that rhymes, don't it?"

"Shut up!"

"Or maybe you don't want your mama and daddy to know about all those men and what you did. Maybe you don't want them to know what your real job was, is that it? One thing I'm pretty sure about, though, is that you don't want that rich husband of yours finding out all them pesky little details about your past that you conveniently forgot to mention."

"Just shut up!" I was on my feet. I was scared enough, mortified enough, mad enough to try to drag him physically out of my house.

Buck just slowly finished his beer, softly singing *Shame on you, Cindy Lou*, over and over and over. "Or is it that other big, or should I say, *major* thing that you forgot to mention to your rich husband about your illustrious, checkered, pre-marital years? I believe you know what I'm talking about."

I willed myself not to cry. I could tell Richard that he was some lying drunk from my past. I could tell Richard that this bum was trying to extort money from me without cause. I could say that I didn't even know him. But would Richard believe me over him? I had no doubt that Buck would keep returning until he got what he was after. In the early days of our marriage, all I had to do was entice Richard into bed, and he would do or say anything I asked. But our marriage hadn't been like that in a long time. Richard no longer seemed enchanted with my charms and hadn't been for more years than I wanted to think about. I was standing on shaky ground, the fissure about to break wide open beneath my feet.

"What do you want?" But I already knew.

"I thought you'd never ask." Buck reached into his back pocket and pulled out a slip of paper. "I took the liberty of working out a payment schedule. I think you'll find it to be quite reasonable."

"What if I say *no?*"

Buck spread his arms wide. "How much do you like this big old house of yours, Cindy Lou? How much do you like your rich husband? How much do you like this high-falutin' life you got here in Scottsdale, Arizona?"

My question was: *How could everything I worked for come crashing down in a matter of minutes?* I needed time to think. I had gotten out of plenty of unsavory situations before, and this was only one more. I could find a way. "I need time to think about it."

Buck stood up. "You've got twenty-four hours. Meet me at a bar called Ernie's tomorrow at five o'clock. I won't shadow your door again unless, of course, you don't show." He started to leave, then turned back. "And I wouldn't bother calling the police if I were you. I'd get one phone call in jail, and the person I would call has a nice, fat package of information, including some juicy affidavits addressed to a Mr. Richard Stewart. The postage has been affixed."

I don't know how long I stood there after I heard him leave, but when I finally started from my shocked trance, the first thing I noticed was

Felicity's backpack in the hallway on the other side of the kitchen. Because of the music, I hadn't heard her car, and I didn't know if she had overheard any of the horrible conversation. Maybe she had gone directly up to her room. Maybe she had left the backpack there this morning.

I knew I was lying to myself.

Then I let myself cry, wondering if I was now going to be blackmailed by two people, wondering if I was about to lose everything.

NOVEMBER

7

REGGIE

It's a good question: *Would I have let things go so far if my husband had been around more?*

If I'd had Kent looking over my shoulder, seeing all the wine bottles stored first in the garage, then in our bedroom, asking questions and prying information out of me, would I have rethought what I was doing and maybe even abandoned the entire money-making scheme? Would he have been my voice of reason, my conscience, my moral arbiter? I don't feel like I have to answer any of those questions. They're rhetorical because Kent *wasn't* around. Oh, I mean, he did stop by every once in a while to ask how I was doing--how noble of him!--and to take Hayley out for dinner, which she wouldn't eat, and he did call Caleb once a week. I ask you, what kind of husband and father is that? And even if he had been around, which he WAS NOT, my husband had never, and never would be the boss of me.

After that first week passed, the period of time that Kent said he needed time to think things over, he asked if he could have even more time to think things through, that one week wasn't nearly enough time to come to any conclusions about the conflicts that had been raging inside him for so long. What was I supposed to do? I wasn't going to beg him to come back. I had never begged for anything in my life, and my dad would have turned over in his grave if he knew that I was letting the *homo*--and that's exactly what my ex-marine dad would have called Kent--back into our home.

Of course I was still hurt, but by the time our separation stretched from one week to two, to three, to four, I think I was more mad than hurt. Our monthly credit card statement showed that Kent had moved out of the Holiday Inn Express after the first week, and I presumed that he had moved in with Reed. Whatever. I was too proud to ask, and he was too chicken to tell me. But he was still having his salary from Honeywell deposited directly into our joint checking account during that early stage of the game, so I decided to let things ride for the time being. It's not like me to do that, but I felt like I had no other recourse at the time. So I let it ride.

I got on with my life. Audrey and I had plenty to do to get ready for the unveiling of our wine club, and back in the beginning, we worked extremely well together. Even if I felt like I was making all the right decisions and she was making all the wrong ones, I rarely nagged her about it. She was going through her own tough time, and I think that was what brought us so close together then. Often when she showed up on my patio with a bottle of wine, her pretty green eyes were red-rimmed, and I knew that she had been crying. I, for one, was done with my wallowing, but not her. Audrey had always been a first-class wallower, but I let that slide too. The point is that we needed each other. I suppose it could be said that our mutual need fueled us in the project's early stage of development. Well, that--and fear. When Audrey asked me for the thousandth time what we would do if our wine club didn't work, I'd finally had enough. I had my doubts too, but I wasn't going to let that stop us now. So I said to her, "Do you want to go on welfare?" That shut her up.

Keeping busy helped us get through those early weeks. And believe me, there was a lot to do. As I saw it, the first order of business was to buy the wine. It sounds easy enough, doesn't it? But even that stymied us because back in the early days, money was the big issue.

"I feel bad that we're going to buy the Two-Buck Chuck from Trader Joe's to pass off as French wine. Don't you think we should buy something a little more expensive to pass off as wine that is $20-$30 a bottle?" Audrey asked one day.

That's the price we had decided to charge for our good Éclatant French wine, but I rather agreed with her on the Two-Buck Chuck. "It does seem kind of blatantly mean."

"Let's do some pricing."

So we went to all the major chains of grocery stores and priced wine on the lower shelves, the bargain wines. We didn't go to a Total Wines or any other authentic wine shop in town because we were afraid we would be noticed if we bought in large volume. We thought this was quite clever on our part, that we were covering our tracks. This adventure took an entire afternoon as we went to each store and made lists, noting which brands were on sale at which store. We asked the various store managers if they were planning any sales in the near future, and in their opinion, what was the best cheap wine for the value. We went to twenty different stores and got twenty different answers. That was a good thing, we decided. The average layperson didn't know what he was talking about. It was simply a matter of personal preference.

When we went back home and went over our research, it was time for the big question: "How much should our initial investment be, Audrey? I was thinking $500 each?"

Audrey hesitated. "I could have $500 in two days."

"I was hoping to get the shopping done tomorrow. If it takes twenty-five minutes to steam a label off a single bottle, that's going to take some time." It was November 2, and we had planned on our first wine club meeting--actually, it was going to be a party, not a meeting--for November 17, the Saturday before Thanksgiving. We thought it would get us off to a good start if people needed a nice wine for the holiday dinner.

The color crept into Audrey's face. "I promise I'll have it in two days."

I didn't want to press her on this. She was obviously uncomfortable, so I said, "Maybe I could advance you the money this first time?"

"No!" Her voice was sharp. "We're partners, and we're going to be equal partners. I'll get the money."

I was secretly relieved that she'd said no. Kent's and my meager savings account was down to around $2000 at that point, what with one thing going wrong after another in our older house. And Hayley was getting her driver's license in a few short months. With the way she'd been acting lately, I had a sinking feeling that she was going to expect a car. According to Hayley, all the Tigerettes had cars. Yay, rah.

"It's not a big deal, Audrey. Two days is fine." I'd liked what she said about us being partners. I held out my hand. "Put her there, partner." And we shook hands on the deal. I believe that was the first time.

Anyway, we ended up buying the Two-Buck Chuck. The bottom line was this: the more inflow of cash, the better. When Audrey had the cash in hand two days later as promised, we decided to split up and hit twelve different Trader Joe's in the Valley, limiting our purchase to six bottles at each store. Again, we didn't want to attract suspicion, and people often bought wine six bottles at a time to get a discount. So if we had twenty women at our first wine party, and they each purchased three bottles of wine, we would have twelve extra. We might need all of those extra bottles to get the women tipsy enough to buy a $25 bottle of wine, or maybe someone would buy more than three bottles. At that point, we just didn't know. It was all trial and error.

Okay, we had the wine. Our next step was to affix our labels to the Two-Buck Chuck. I do have to admit that Audrey had done a beautiful job with the labels. Her chic Parisian lady looked just right, and the calligraphy she chose had exactly the right amount of curlicue embellishment, fancy but not overly pretentious. She even added a phrase in French: *Appellation d'Origine Loire Valley*, which I thought was a very nice touch. If Audrey had her way, she would have designed each label by hand, but I quickly dissuaded her of that time-consuming notion. I bought labels from Walmart, and instead of taking the finished labels to Kinko's, I sent them to the online printing company, Vistaprint. Again, we didn't want to arouse any suspicions in the local area. We were really trying to think this thing through and avoid any pitfalls that came to mind. And there were a lot.

After all our research, we were more confused than ever about French wine and regions and types of grapes, but rather than being daunted by that fact, we were going to tell our wine club ladies that this first shipment from Pierre--my mythical French cousin, the vintner at the Éclatant winery--was more of the table wine variety, designed to be sold to the novice French wine drinker. Consequently, we were going to sell what we were familiar with at our introductory meeting: chardonnay, sauvignon blanc, chablis, pinot noir, merlot, and cabernet, all from the year 2015. From there, and to keep our club going and the sales escalating, we planned to move on to select vintages and years, such as a 2004 Château Pichon Longueville Lalande or a 2004 Clos Fourtet Saint-Émilion, or anything that sounded expensive. I am not lying when I tell you that *French Wine for Dummies* became something like our bible. Even without saying it aloud, I think each of us decided that we would take one monthly meeting at a time, developing new strategies as we went along.

But back to affixing our labels to the bottles of Two-Buck Chuck. I knew it was going to take a lot of time to get the labels off seventy-two bottles of wine. We had to pick a time when our kids weren't around. Obviously, neither one of us had to worry about our husbands right then, which might be considered a blessing in disguise, but I don't think either of us thought of it that way. Time was of the essence, it was already November 5, and we still had to get our invitations out. We had decided not to do e-vites and settled on a more personal approach, which would involve more elegant calligraphy and some catchy phrase to get the women's attention.

So on that first morning of wrestling with the labels, after our kids were safely deposited at school, we were gathered in Audrey's kitchen. She had two pots of water boiling on the stove, and I was scribbling at the kitchen table. "What about 'an exploration of the wines of Loire Valley?'" I asked her.

"What about 'better than bunco?'" Audrey was watching the pot as if that would make it come to a boil faster, and she had on kitchen mitts in preparation for the scalding job. The bottles crowded every surface of her kitchen.

"Why not just say 'leave your kids at home and come and get drunk?'" She wasn't taking this seriously enough. "Come on, Audrey."

"Fine wine for serious winos?"

"Audrey," I tapped my pen on the table, "we don't have time to fool around."

"Fine. But you can be such a slave driver, Reggie." She thought about it for a moment. "*Une nuit à se souvenir.* A night to remember."

I felt a flutter of excitement. "I do believe that you just nailed it, Audrey. That's perfect." Even if I no longer mean this as a full-fledged compliment, I do have to say that Audrey has always been a very creative person.

Audrey looked at all the wine bottles and shuddered. "This is going to be a daunting task. Do you think we could put the bottles in the dishwasher? If there's any glue left on them, we could use Goo Gone. I have a bottle of it around here somewhere."

As tempted as I was by the expediency of that, I didn't think the finished product would look clean enough. "Let's just see if this method works first."

"God forbid that the internet should be wrong," she said sarcastically.

"Then put some damn bottles in the damn dishwasher." I swear, I sometimes felt that I was shouldering most of the responsibility, and I was pretty sure that Audrey needed the money even more than I did.

Without a word, she grabbed a few bottles and wedged them into the dishwasher, which was already crammed full of dirty dishes. "There."

"You're in quite a mood today." I didn't say a word about the dirty dishes. I supposed it didn't matter because the bottles were corked and sealed, but it still bothered me. Audrey looked like she was about to cry yet again, so I took pity on her. Her husband was a drunk, after all. "Did you hear something from Paul?"

"No. I told you that it's part of the program. No contact with the outside world until the family counseling session, which is next week. *Outside world.* It's like he's in prison or something."

"He'll be home soon," I soothed. I could be a good friend when I wanted to be.

"I'm starting to wonder if it's some kind of cult, you know? It all happened so fast. Like maybe Jehovah's Witnesses run Fresh Start. What if they're converting him?"

I couldn't help myself. I laughed. "Oh, Audrey. You miss your husband. That's all."

Audrey let out a sigh. "Thanks, Reggie. It helps me that we're in the same boat, not that it's a particularly good boat to be in."

"At least it's not the *Titanic*." I meant it as a lame joke. I didn't think the situations we were in were funny at all. And in truth, my boat was a lot less sea-worthy than hers. Her husband was in recovery. My husband was in the arms of another man. I refused to let my mind imagine what else he was doing with that man. It made me feel physically ill, and then I became enraged all over again. I knew I could track Kent down easily enough. I could wait in my car outside Honeywell and follow him to wherever he went at night. But my stubborn pride wouldn't let me do that. Instead, I waited at home like the long-suffering wife. The whole situation was setting my teeth on edge and keeping me up at night.

"The water's boiling." Audrey picked up the first bottle and held it over the steam.

"I'll be right there." I glanced at my phone. After four weeks, I kept expecting a text from Kent. It was just crazy. Sighing, I went over to the stove and put on my mitts.

The internet wasn't exactly right. I'll say that. Some labels seemed to come off easily enough, yet others came off in shreds, leaving glue behind. We were going to need that Goo Gone after all. We stood over our respective pots of water, sweating, and in my case, uttering the occasional expletive.

"Swearing at the bottles is not going to help, Reggie." Audrey's chestnut hair was a frizzy halo around her heart-shaped face.

"This sucks." I eyed the finished bottles, of which there were too few. At it for two hours, and we had a measly six bottles done.

"I'm going to check the dishwasher. Maybe we got lucky." She pulled out one of the bottles. The label was a soggy mess. "I guess not."

"I think we should just keep going." I couldn't think of any other solution at that point. I filled up my pot with water again and set it back on the stove.

Audrey did the same. "Let's take a break while the water comes to a boil. I'll get us some iced tea."

I sat down heavily at the kitchen table. I was exhausted. The combination of no sleep and the heat from the boiling water made me feel light-headed. However, I had no intention of quitting. In truth, the whole wine club scheme was what was keeping me going. If I didn't have that to plan and plot, I didn't know what I'd do. And there were no good choices: Fall into a deep depression or beg Kent to come home and live a lie.

Audrey set a can of AriZona ice tea in front of me and sat down. "I'm starting to think that it was a better idea to stick our label over the ones already on the bottle."

That had been our first plan, but after we discussed it, we decided that it was one more way that we could be discovered. People peeled labels off beer bottles all the time, and while we personally didn't know anyone who nervously scraped off wine bottle labels, it didn't mean that they didn't exist. The world was filled with all kinds of people, which probably included wine label peelers. Who knew? We thought that steaming off the labels was a better option, and I still think it offered a safer route. But at the rate we were progressing, we were going to spend the majority of our time standing over a pot of boiling water.

"We're going to have to wait until the bottles are completely cool before we can put on the Éclatant labels." Audrey fingered the sheets of labels in the box on the table, then she got up and went to the six finished bottles grouped on a corner of the counter. "Still warm. It's amazing how hot the bottles have to be before the label peels off . . ." Her eyes opened wide. "Oh, Reggie. I just thought of something. Doesn't heat ruin wine?"

"Oh, God." Panicked, I reached for my phone and started googling, my stomach turning cartwheels as I read: "'The same way foods transform on the stove, wine changes as it experiences high temperatures. First, tannins become more noticeable and wines take on a tangy, astringent character . . . And heat doesn't destroy bottles evenly, so it can be hard to know when a bottle is cooked.'"

"We can't know for sure that the wine is damaged then, right? I mean, this was cheap wine to begin with. Maybe its cheapness makes it immune to heat?"

Audrey was grasping at straws, and we both knew it. I could only stare at her, and I think I might have had tears in my eyes. "There's only one way to find out."

Audrey, too, looked crestfallen as she got her electric wine opener and opened the six finished bottles. We didn't even bother with glasses. We each picked up a bottle and took a slug. Audrey shuddered as she reached for the second. We didn't say anything as we sampled all six. There wasn't much to say. Two of the bottles seemed okay, but the wine was still so warm that it was hard to tell for sure. One was downright rancid, and the other three tasted slightly bitter.

"Not only is the wine cheap, but it's now just plain bad. We can't sell this."

I wanted to pick up each of those six bottles and throw them against the wall, but I didn't want to stain Audrey's old-fashioned wallpaper. I was so disappointed that I could barely breathe. What were we going to do now? I refused to scrap the entire plan.

"We are so stupid," Audrey said angrily. "How could we not have thought that we'd be cooking the wine?"

I didn't have an answer to that; we should have known. I wanted to bury my face in my hands and howl. But I wouldn't let Audrey see my mortification. There had to be a solution to this problem. It was just another roadblock, and we could expect many. We had to learn to adapt, to roll with the punches. I carried the bottles to the sink and emptied them. It was a failed experiment. That was all.

When I finished with that, I turned around. "We'll have to go back to Plan A, Audrey. We'll have to affix our labels over the ones already on the bottle. I know we thought it was too risky, but I don't see any other way."

Audrey began to nod slowly. "I'm very good with a glue gun. Let me show you just how good I am."

Audrey was true to her word--that time. I'll give her that. However, she was a perfectionist, and once again, it was slow going, mostly because she wasn't often satisfied with the finished project. Let me tell you, she agonized over each and every label, wasting way too many precious minutes trimming the Éclatant labels down to the perfect size--the labels I had bought at Walmart were too large, according to her--and then measuring and fussing and wiping off any extra glue. She was especially critical of my attempts with the glue gun. I had never professed to be an artist or a craft-oriented person, so it did hurt my feelings when she would say, "That label is on crooked," or "You can still see the corner of the Two-Buck Chuck label on that one." We had been on the project for three days by that point, and we were starting to get on each other's nerves. When she pointed out that my recent attempt looked "bubbly," I'd had enough. "This is not rocket science, Audrey."

"Do you want these labels to look professional or not?" she snapped back.

"Of course I want them to look professional, but it seems to me that we are not overly efficient here."

She dropped the glue gun and glared at me. "Number one, I am not working on an assembly line, and number two, sloppy work would make it that much easier for us to get caught."

She had a point there, and as I have said before, patience is not my strong suit, so perhaps I was rushing things a little. I couldn't help it. I had the weird sensation that someone was looking over our shoulders, watching our every action with a judging eye. Maybe it was the niggling, pesky sense of guilt that was always present, but back then I told myself that I was only being paranoid.

Audrey got up and walked to the counter where the finished bottles were. She picked up one. "Does this look right to you?"

"It looks fine."

She walked back to me and stuck the bottle right in front of my face. "Take a closer look."

I could see what she meant then. The top of the label looked like a furrowed brow. Unfortunately, that particular bottle was my handiwork.

Audrey wasn't done driving her point home. "And these." She picked up a bottle from the group and set it on the far end of the counter, then she repeated the process again and again, distastefully, as if she were picking out the rotten grapes from an otherwise perfect bunch. She separated about ten bottles in all and then turned to face me. "I'm sorry, Reggie, but these won't work. They're sloppy and unprofessional, and we can't take a chance on them."

I was pretty sure that they were all the bottles that I'd done, but I was more embarrassed than mad right then. It was me who was slowing things down, not Audrey. "I'll try to be more careful."

"I think we should leave the gluing to me. You're doing the truly hard part, running the business aspect of the operation and working on the invitations and your presentation for the first party."

She was being kind, and I appreciated it. I smiled. "I suppose we each have our strengths."

She smiled back. "That's why we make such a good team."

"I'll go buy more wine at Trader Joe's."

"Could you pick me up a container of those chocolate coconut almonds? I feel like I deserve a treat."

"Sure thing." Back then, we always did things like that for each other. It didn't really bother me that Audrey rarely paid me back for those little purchases, although the one time she asked me to pick up Jimmy's medication on a trip to Walgreens, I refused to hand it over until she grudgingly coughed up the cash. I wasn't being petty. That Vyvanse was damn expensive stuff.

I can't tell you how good it felt to get out of the house. Audrey and I had been cooped up for three days, and I was getting sick and tired of looking at her old paisley wallpaper. I ask you, who has paisley wallpaper nowadays? I am not judging her. I had those unsightly cabinets in my own house, and I knew how expensive it was to hire someone to do home repairs. People in our income brackets tended to attempt those kinds of jobs ourselves, with mixed results. And then I had a thought. Maybe our wine club would make us each enough money to afford to remodel our homes. That thought lifted my spirits considerably. I had been thinking more along the lines of being able to afford necessities with the money, but who knew? Maybe the club would really take off. Maybe I would be able to afford a decent used car for Hayley's sixteenth birthday. If Audrey and I played our cards right, the sky was the limit.

So I was feeling the happiest I had in days, perhaps weeks, when I pulled into the parking lot of Trader Joe's in north Scottsdale. It wasn't one I frequented because I was following the plan, picking stores that were not in Audrey's and my general vicinity. I had never been to this particular store in the uber upscale area of north Scottsdale, where the parking lot was positively littered with newer model BMWs, Mercedes, and Lincolns. It just figured. It was something I had gotten used to after having lived in this town for twenty years. It was annoying, yes, but it was a fact. Some people in Scottsdale had a lot of money.

I had brought my canvas wine carriers with me, and my cart was full with twelve bottles of wine when I headed for the cashier. I was almost there when I remembered Audrey's request for chocolate coconut almonds. I have to say that I was not happy about going back for the nuts. I had decided that I was going to go for a run when I got home and was suddenly anxious to do so, and Audrey needed those empty calories like she needed a hole in the head. Still, I was going to be a good friend and get the damn nuts. I found the aisle and was reaching for the plastic container when I spotted a flash of blonde hair out of the corner of my eye. I didn't think anything of it--north Scottsdale was teeming with blonde women--until I had deposited the nuts in the cart and looked up.

It couldn't be. Standing a foot away from me with a cart heaped with nothing but flowers stood Cynthia Stewart, and she was staring straight at my shopping cart heaped with nothing but Two-Buck Chuck. I tell you, if I had been wearing a jacket, I would have thrown it over those bottles, not that it would have done any good because she had already seen them. But that's how strong my sense of panic was. Audrey and I had mentioned the wine club to her in the school hallway, and now she saw all this cheap wine in my cart. Would she make the connection? Correction: Audrey was the one who had brought up the wine club. If it had been up to me, I would have kept my mouth shut. But that's Audrey for you. She simply cannot keep a secret.

"Are you having a party?" Cynthia asked mildly, eyeing the bottles.

This was going to be my first test in the lying department. And the way I saw it, I had no choice but to lie through my teeth. "My husband has invited a few business acquaintances over."

"Your husband's business acquaintances must like wine." She arched one of her perfect eyebrows. She had on these skinny jeans, no doubt designer, that hugged her perfect hips and a light blue cashmere sweater.

And some fancy heels. I ask you, who wears heels to go grocery shopping? Cynthia Stewart, that's who.

Answer a question with a question. It was Avoidance 101. "Who doesn't?"

Cynthia seemed to have to think a moment on that one. "Very true."

"If you don't mind, I have to get going. I have an appointment." I tried to push my cart past her, but it was easier said than done. She was parked right in front of me, so I would have to back up and then go around her because the aisle was so narrow. But before I could do that, Cynthia reached into my cart and pulled out a bottle of wine.

"What's this, Two-Buck Chuck? You're going to serve this at your dinner party?" I'm not exaggerating when I say her voice was dripping with disdain.

She kind of had me there. I wouldn't serve that wine at a dinner party--without the label covered up, naturally. But it was a moot question, you see. In all the years of our marriage, Kent and I hadn't had any fancy dinner parties, mainly because I am not that good of a cook. The closest we came was putting some burgers on the grill for a few friends. "I didn't say it was a dinner party," is how I got out of that one.

Cynthia acted like she didn't hear me. "Didn't you say you had a cousin who was a vintner in France?"

"Did I?" Avoidance 101 again.

"I believe you did, yes. Wouldn't a decent wine from France be more appropriate to serve at your dinner party?"

"I didn't say I was having a dinner party," I said impatiently. I was starting to feel like Cynthia had me cornered, and I didn't like it one little bit. What business was it of hers what kind of damn wine I would serve at this mythical party anyway? Who did she think she was?

"You think I'm nosy." She smiled her pretty smile.

"You bet I do." I gave my cart the slightest nudge in her direction for emphasis.

"I'm only trying to be helpful."

"I don't need your help." It became a staring contest then, and I have to give her credit. She was good at it. That wide-eyed blue gaze was mesmerizing. It was me who lost that round. "Look, if you must know, our shipment of wine from France for the wine club hasn't arrived yet."

"I see."

At her knowing nod, I felt a sharp pang of fear. What was it exactly that she thought she *saw*? I was a fraction of a second away from completely losing it--and God knew what I would say if that happened--and I had to get out of there fast. "I really do have to go." That time I did tap her cart with mine. I didn't think I was overtly aggressive. Well, maybe I was. The carts made a clanging sound.

She finally took the hint and backed up just enough for me to get around her in the narrow aisle. And then she said something completely unexpected: "I would love to be invited to your wine club."

Was she kidding? She was about the last person on earth I would want to invite. Granted, she had money and probably had friends who had money to spend, but she was not going to get an invitation to our inaugural wine club. Audrey and I hadn't worked out the kinks yet. Hell, we didn't even know if our plan would work at all. And we did not need a woman who thought she was superior to everyone else, a woman who had spent time in France and might know something about French wine, coming in and exposing us right off the bat. There was no way I would let that happen.

"The invitations haven't gone out yet." Then before she could say anything else, I added: "Aren't you supposed to be at the Tigerette practice?"

She gripped her cart tightly. "There isn't a practice today."

I knew for a fact that she was now the one who was lying. The Tigerettes practiced every single day of the week, and Hayley had told me that it was going to be an extra-long practice today. The first game of the season, on the Saturday after Thanksgiving, was just around the corner. "I *see*." And then I walked quickly to the front cashier, paid, and left. Cynthia didn't follow me.

Looking back, maybe I should have gone directly to Audrey's and told her about the run-in with Cynthia. It was my first instinct to do that, but by the time I got home and went for a cleansing, five-mile run, I had reasoned myself out of it. Audrey was jittery enough about the wine club as it was, and telling her about Cynthia might push her completely over the edge. Then I started to think that I was once again being paranoid. If Cynthia had an inkling of what was going on, she wouldn't have wanted to be invited, would she? Of course not. She didn't have a clue about Audrey's and my true motives. No one had a clue because we had the perfect cover. Who in their right mind would suspect two ordinary, middle-class housewives of concocting such a devious money-making scheme?

Did I say *devious*? No, that's not right at all. We were not trying to be devious or evil. We were only two desperate women who were trying to piece together the shambles our lives had recently become. Two desperate, sympathetic women. That's it.

Anyway, by the time I got back from my run, Kent was waiting for me at the kitchen table. I hadn't been expecting him, and he always called before dropping by, like he was some family friend or something, so it was a shock to see him sitting there in his pressed khakis and navy blue, long-sleeved shirt. It looked like he had gotten a haircut too. His blonde hair barely grazed the collar of his shirt. He looked so handsome that it took my breath away. I, on the other hand, was a sweaty mess. I knew he had seen me looking ragged like this hundreds and hundreds of times before, but now it was a completely different ballgame. I wanted to look perfectly groomed in his presence; I wanted him to desire me. I wanted him to take me back. Pathetic of me, I know, but desperation makes a jilted woman do crazy things.

Kent wasn't on a computer or reading a paper or doing anything except sitting there, and that suddenly made me very nervous. I tried to play it cool. "Hi, Kent. I didn't know you were coming over. Can I get you anything--coffee, wine?" I really wanted him to say wine.

"Thank you, no, Reggie. Do you have a minute? I think it's time that we talked."

His eyes looked so sad that it made my stomach lurch. *Oh, no.* He had come to a decision, and I wasn't going to like it. I didn't want to hear it. I could go on living in my bubble for as long as it took him to come back to his family, where he belonged. And I don't think it had truly sunk in that my bubble was bound to burst. "Let me go take a shower first, okay? And then I'll pour us some wine and we--"

"Reggie."

"No." I put my hand over my mouth to stifle the scream that was clawing at my throat to get out. "No."

But before Kent could utter another word, the garage door opened, and Hayley came in. "Hi, Daddy." She looked positively delighted to see him. She dropped her backpack and gym bag and went over to give him a hug.

"How's my girl?"

"I'm good."

He had his hands on her arms, and when she pulled away, he gave a low whistle. "Who's the boyfriend?"

Hayley then seemed anxious to get away. She laughed nervously. "I don't have a boyfriend, Daddy."

"Hayley doesn't have a boyfriend, Kent. She's been far too busy with school and the Tigerettes." I thought I would certainly know if our daughter was dating anyone. She had always confided in me. Until the Tigerettes, that is. I realized it had been a while since our last good talk. Maybe that was also a thing of the past.

Kent stood up to peer closely at Hayley's neck. "Then who gave you that hickey, Haley?"

"Hayley doesn't have--" I'd made it to the table by then and took my turn looking at my daughter's neck. There it was, the purplish bruise beginning to fade to yellow. My shaky legs forced me to sit down, hard.

My daughter's hickey was just one more thing I had missed.

8

A U D R E Y

Reggie always tended to overreact, but I guess I chose to ignore it for a long time. Take Hayley's hickey, for example. The way Reggie went on and on about it, you'd think the poor girl had committed a major felony or just announced that she was pregnant. Things were going on that she and I didn't know about, Reggie said. Hayley had refused to divulge the boy's name, and that only added insult to injury, according to Reggie. I didn't point out that Hayley probably didn't tell her the boy's name because Reggie would have called him up and reamed him out. Or worse, she would have called the boy's mother and accused her of letting her son run wild, or something equally ridiculous. So I let her rant, and to tell you the truth, my mind kept wandering off. I had bigger problems to worry about, and a fifteen-year-old's hickey didn't seem to matter much in the big scheme of things.

"Do you think I should search her room?" Reggie asked when she stopped to take a breath.

We were sitting on her patio drinking wine, which seemed to me to be a much-needed break from all the hard work we'd been doing. We had on the tall propane heater to ward off the chill. In Arizona, our wine drinking nights only followed two seasons: mister weather and heater weather. I don't know why we never varied from that routine, never decided to sit in the comfort of a family room or kitchen. Perhaps one reason was that we had more privacy outside. Perhaps a more important reason was that the darkness allowed us more freedom to say what we truly thought and felt. At the time, I genuinely believed that we thought we were totally honest with each other on those nights of comradery. I thought that we intimately knew each other. I know differently now.

I took a tired sip of the Turning Leaf cabernet and chose my words carefully. I didn't want to set Reggie off again, and I had always tried to be a good friend to her. "That might be rather extreme, Reggie. My mother used to search my room all the time, and I know that I felt that she was invasive."

I knew what I was talking about. Margot used to go through my things on what seemed like a weekly basis, and I didn't even have a cell phone or a computer, just a diary that I had the good sense to hide under a loose floorboard in the back corner of my closet. But what I didn't tell Reggie is that I not only thought it was invasive. I thought it was *hostile*. I would come home from school and find my room torn apart, drawers upended on the floor, clothes ripped from hangers. And the thing was this: She never found the diary, which actually would have given her something to be mad about. But my mother was an angry person by nature, I guess. We never had a good relationship, which did nothing to stop the immediate feeling of guilt that washed over me. I hadn't been to visit her at The Gardens since that last trip to the hospital. I hadn't called to check on her either. I promised myself I would do it soon, very soon.

Reggie sighed. "I suppose you're right. But I do want the record to reflect that I think things have changed since the girls joined the Tigerettes. There seems to be a needless cloak of secrecy about everything. That Felicity is a manipulative little bitch."

I happened to agree with Reggie. However, our girls weren't talking, and they had explained away the diaper incident as only being part of their initiation. Our girls were not doormats, and they were principled enough to stand up for themselves if they felt like they were being manipulated. I chose to believe that this was the case and that by the time basketball season finally started, Hayley and Marcy would be used to being on the squad, and things would return to normal. *Normal*, ha! I didn't even know what *normal* was anymore. I'd been a single mother for the last month, a broke single mother with a husband in rehab, a broke single mother who was gluing forged French labels onto bottles of Two-Buck Chuck. That was about as far away from being *normal* as you could get.

Reggie poured us some more wine. "Are you ready for tomorrow?"

"I don't know how to be ready." I really didn't. Tomorrow was the family counseling session at Fresh Start with Paul, and all I knew with certainty was that I was a nervous wreck. My biggest fear was that he had changed. Now that wasn't necessarily a bad thing, but I'd had a lot of time to think on those long nights in my lonely bed. It came as a shock to me that I couldn't remember a time when Paul didn't drink--and drink a lot. Even in college, back when he was a so-called rich frat boy, Paul had been the life of the party. He'd even held the record for the most beers consumed during their annual drinking contest for four years running. He'd been inordinately proud of that accomplishment back then, and absurdly, so had I. What would a sober Paul be like? I didn't have a clue.

"You'll be fine." Reggie gave me a reassuring pat on the hand. "And he'll be home soon."

I did miss him, and I did want him home. I did. But I would be lying if I didn't admit that I was worried about the problems it would cause to have him hanging around the house all day. Since my kitchen had become our workshop, our headquarters so to speak, there wasn't a chance in hell that Paul would miss what was going on. And what about all the wine bottles? If Paul was going to insist that there not be any alcohol in the house--and I could understand that--we would have to move the operation to Reggie's depressing kitchen. I hated being in her kitchen and couldn't figure out why she didn't do something with those unsightly cabinets. Plus, since she had decided to "redo" the cabinets, she kept her plates and glassware and pots and pans on the counters. There simply wasn't enough room. And one more thing: Paul would want to know what I was doing over at her house all day long. He would think I was avoiding him. It was going to be a mess.

"Kent stopped by a couple of days ago."

I immediately perked up. I had been waiting for this. I had seen his car in the driveway, but when Reggie didn't bring up the subject, neither did I. I had bided my time. I made my voice noncommittal. "Oh?"

"He wanted to talk."

"And?"

"I didn't want to," she said shortly.

I don't think Reggie realized what she was doing when she reached for the wine bottle and started to pick at the label absently. I stared at it, transfixed. That was exactly what we had counted on not happening when we glued our labels over the old ones. Reggie's nails were short, and she wasn't making much progress, but it was enough to shred part of the label.

"I know what he's going to say," she said slowly, "and I don't want to hear the words. I don't think he's ever coming back."

"You don't know that for sure." I watched her snake her nail down the label.

"He didn't stay. What does that tell you?"

I didn't want her to think that I wasn't listening, but I couldn't stand it any longer. "Look what you're doing, Reggie."

"What?" She seemed to see the bottle for the first time. "Holy shit." She pushed the bottle away as if it were burning her hands.

I started to giggle then. What we were doing was so outlandish, but it was funny too. And now we were in so deep that I couldn't see any way out. Nor did I want to. I had started to count on this project for income. I didn't have any other options. But that shredded label still struck me as funny, maybe because that was our second bottle of wine.

Reggie started to laugh too, a high-pitched crackle. "I swear, this is the first time I've ever peeled off a label. It's an isolated incident. Our wine club is going to be fine. Everything's going to be fine." She wiped a tear from her eye.

"We say that a lot, don't we?" I wanted to believe her.

"We have to." Reggie took a big swallow of wine. "Everything's going to be fine."

The morning was not getting off to a good start. First, Jimmy had awakened in a foul mood. He refused to get dressed and was sulking at the kitchen table in his pajamas while he grudgingly stirred his Froot Loops. And now my daughter was standing in front of me with a defiant look in her eye, which was not like her. Well, maybe it was more like her to act like that now that she was a blasted Tigerette, one of the so-called Top Twelve girls in the high school. But I didn't have time to dwell on that unsettling truth.

"I am not going." Marcy lifted her chin.

"Yes, you are. It is a family counseling session, and we're all required to be there." I actually didn't want to go either, and it had surprised me when I woke up that morning with an intense feeling of dread. After almost four weeks, I was finally going to see my husband, and the fact of the matter was that I didn't want to. I told myself that I didn't want to go back to that desolate, wind-blown ranch, but that wasn't the real reason. I just didn't want to go. That unwanted fact made me feel guilty, which explained my own foul mood.

"I can't miss practice. Felicity says that the only excuse for missing practice this close to the first game is if you're on your deathbed. And even that is not a good excuse."

"I am getting sick and tired of hearing what *Felicity says*. Felicity is not the boss of you, and she most definitely is not the boss of this family. Change out of your leotard and get dressed."

I was also getting sick and tired of seeing Marcy in that skin-tight black leotard that hugged her every curve. Because of her dieting, one other thing that *Felicity says*, she had lost weight, and it was disconcerting to see that my fifteen-year-old most definitely looked like a woman. And even worse, since she was constantly prancing around in that outfit, others couldn't help but notice it too. What was wrong with practicing in shorts and t-shirts? Oh, that's right. That wouldn't be appropriate for *Felicity says* attire.

"I will not miss a practice, Mom. It's too important." Marcy lifted her chin even higher. She slanted her green eyes at me as if she were daring me to contradict her.

"You are going to visit your dad." I enunciated each word. When Marcy didn't respond, didn't move a muscle, I added, "I'll write you a note. A note from your mother should be enough to excuse you from practice."

"No!"

The sharpness in her voice took me by surprise. "What do you mean *no?*"

"You are not writing me a note, and I am going to practice."

I balled up the dish towel I held in my hands and threw it in the sink behind me. I put my hands on my hips, imitating the familiar gesture of Reggie's. "Now, you listen here--"

Marcy's green eyes filled with tears, and her words came out in a panicked rush. "You can't write a note. If you write a note, the whole squad will know that my dad is a drunk! Felicity will know!"

I managed to stop my hand in midair. Honestly, I didn't even know that it had left my hip. It was out of instinct or rage or grief or disappointment- -take you pick--that I had almost become my mother, a mother who slapped her daughter. I drew in a shaky breath and put a hand on the counter for support. Marcy's eyes were round as half dollars as if she, too, couldn't believe what had almost happened. Jimmy must have been watching the whole exchange because he started to wail hysterically.

It was Marcy who went to him and put an arm around his shoulder. Marcy had always been the one who could offer the most comfort to Jimmy. She was better at it by far than I was. "It's okay, Pookie. We'll watch *Despicable Me.* It's your favorite." She murmured soothing words to him, words that I could not hear, as she led him from the room.

I didn't try to stop them. I was still too rattled by what I had almost done. When I heard the movie start in the other room, I buried my face in my hands and cried. I knew the pressure was getting to me, the pressure of being a single mother and juggling all those credit cards and the wine club. But that was no excuse for almost hitting my daughter in front of my fragile son. I had to make it up to them, but how? I don't know how much time passed before I made up my mind. I made a quick phone call, then walked into the family room.

"Jimmy, Delilah is coming to pick you up and take you over to her house." Delilah was someone I had met through Jimmy's school, an older, retired teacher who had fostered something like thirty kids with special needs and was good with Jimmy. He loved going to her house, and his face perked up for the first time that morning.

"Marcy, do you need a ride to practice?"

"No, Felicity is picking me up." She didn't look at me.

Of course. But I didn't even blink. "Good. When I get back, I'll give you a driving lesson, okay? We'll go to the mall, and I'll buy those Boyfriend jeans you've been talking about."

That got her to look up. "Sure."

And then I left. I didn't apologize because it seemed like I was doing that all the time those days, so much so that it had become meaningless. Was I bribing my kids to forgive me? You bet. However, that was the type of guilt I could live with.

Because of the events of that morning, and because I had to stop and get gas and put air in my tires--the things that Paul used to do--I was late for the meeting. I didn't like the place any better than I had four weeks before, and my shoes were dusty by the time I walked across the "campus," as they called it, and entered the building. I made my way down the hallway, trying to smile, but I could feel how it wobbled, how insincere it was going to look. I didn't know what excuse I was going to give Paul about why the kids weren't with me. Would it upset him so much that he would have a relapse? It seemed like a far-fetched notion, but I think it's shamefully obvious that I didn't have a clue what Paul was going through. However, in my defense, he didn't have a clue about how much pressure I was under either. I know that a lot of it was of my own making, the wine club scheme and the credit card juggling, and especially the mounting debt, but if you would have been in my shoes, I bet that you would have made the very same decisions.

Paul was already sitting in the room with the counselor, Delores, when I walked in. I was going to apologize immediately for being late and then launch into my story about Jimmy having a bad cold and Marcy offering to babysit him, but when Paul looked up, the words froze in my throat. What can I say? My husband looked awful. His eyes were bloodshot, and a long scratch etched down his left cheek. I guess I had expected him to look well-rested and fit and tan, more like he'd been visiting a spa than a treatment center.

"Oh, my God! Have you been in an accident?" Those were the first words I said to my husband after twenty-seven days apart.

He gave me a sheepish grin. At least that was the same. "I believe the appropriate term for it is *relapse*."

"I think a better word for it is *bender*." Delores, it would turn out, was a no-nonsense type of gal. A recovering alcoholic herself, she didn't mince words when it came to what Paul had been up to the last week. "Paul went into town for supplies--he had earned that privilege--but when he didn't return, we figured out what had happened."

"I was doing so well, Audrey. You would have been proud of me." Paul's voice broke, and it took a minute or two before he could continue. "I was going into the store to buy the supplies, but then I saw a bar across the street. It was like I couldn't help myself."

I was confused. Again, let me remind you that I was a real dunce when it came to addiction and recovery. "But surely, a drink or two . . ."

Paul took my hands and looked directly into my eyes. "It wasn't a drink or two, Audrey. I stayed drunk for a solid week. I used the money

I was supposed to buy supplies with, and I drank anything I could get my hands on."

His eyes were so bloodshot and haggard and ashamed that I wanted to look away, but I forced myself to hold his gaze. "Where did you go? And why didn't you come home?" I suppose I should have been hurt about that, but I was more curious than hurt at that point.

"I don't know where I went or what I did." He reached up to touch his cheek. "I don't know where I got this. I blacked out. I came to this morning and made my way here."

I couldn't bear to look into his eyes anymore. I turned to Delores. "Why didn't the people here go looking for him?"

"This is a voluntary facility, Audrey. We don't go chasing our patients like they were escaped prisoners." She gave a little huff. "Unfortunately, this type of thing occurs."

"But why didn't someone call me?"

Delores looked at Paul and then back to me. "When Paul signed in, he expressly asked that you not be notified if something like this happened. We honor the wishes of our patients."

I was hurt by that, believe me. I turned back to Paul. "Why did you do that? I would have come and gotten you. I wouldn't have judged you." I think that last statement was true, but I was glad that I hadn't been put to the test.

"I didn't want to disappoint you more than I already have." Paul shrugged helplessly. "This disease is something I have to conquer on my own, Audrey, which means that I can't have an enabler in my life right now."

Me, an enabler? I was stunned speechless by that. "But, but," I stammered.

"Paul thinks that your drinking prevents you from seeing the magnitude of his problem," Delores interjected.

She hadn't said that juicy tidbit in a malicious or judgmental way, simply stated it as a truth, yet I could feel the heat in my cheeks. I didn't know what Paul had been telling this woman in his counseling sessions, but he was most certainly misconstruing the facts. He was the alcoholic here, not me. I enjoyed my occasional glasses of wine, but Paul couldn't stop drinking once he'd started. I sometimes couldn't remember all the parts of the conversations I'd had with Reggie during our patio nights, but Paul drank until he blacked out. These were all huge differences between

Paul and me. This entire conversation was taking on a surreal quality. "I drink some wine," I said. "Nothing else. I am not an alcoholic."

"No one said you were," Delores said flatly. "However, Paul is. And I am, as are a lot of the other people here. Alcoholism is a disease."

"I understand that," I said. At least I think I was beginning to. "So what now?"

Paul leaned back in his chair, sighing heavily. "I signed on for another thirty days. It's the only way I can beat this thing."

Delores cleared her throat. "The program does work."

"So you're not coming home?" I know it was such an obvious thing to say, but please understand that I was shell-shocked. After all the different ways I had imagined how this family counseling session would go, this was not one of them.

Delores didn't bother answering that. She gathered her papers and stood. "I'll leave you two alone now."

"I'm sorry," Paul said when she was out the door. He slumped in his chair.

It was one more thing I was sick and tired of: *I'm sorry.* It seemed that Paul was always apologizing to me, and I was always apologizing to my kids, and my mother, and even Reggie. It seemed like I was always saying *I'm sorry* to my friend for one infraction or another. In truth, I wasn't sorry for most of the things I said and did. So why were people always making me feel so damn guilty? I was a good person; I was doing the best I could.

"How are we going to pay for this?" That terrifying thought had just occurred to me, but it hadn't to Paul. He had almost made it through his treatment, and then he had blown it, but good. Didn't he care about the kids or me? Didn't he care about anyone but himself? He was an unemployed alcoholic, and he was shirking his responsibilities. I was going to say all that to him, but he looked so broken slumped in that chair, so pathetic.

"That gold watch I got from my dad on my twenty-first birthday. Sell it."

"Oh, Paul." I knew how much that watch meant to him. It was the only thing he had left to remember his father by, the only thing he kept after they died in the plane crash and we sold off all their other belongings to pay off their gambling debts. And here I was, thinking terrible thoughts about him. I started to cry for the second time that day. Tears, another thing I was sick and tired of. Useless tears.

"Paul--" I was about to tell him how much I loved him, but I heard the faint sound of his snoring. I decided not to wake him. From the looks of him, he must have spent the past week sleeping on the hard, cold ground of the desert. I got up and kissed his forehead, and left.

It wasn't until the drive home that I realized he hadn't asked about the kids, nor had we even hugged. And there was the very real possibility that Paul had still been drunk.

The first thing I did on Monday morning was to take Paul's father's gold watch to E.D. Marshall's Jewelers, a place that bought high-end estate jewelry. It was one time that Reggie was right about something. My first thought was that I would take it to the nearest pawnshop, never mind that I had never set foot in such a place and that the prospect of doing so terrified me. But it was Reggie who pointed out that a jeweler would pay more money for the watch, which turned out to be a Rolex. Let me tell you, if I'd known all along that the watch was a Rolex, I might have already sold it. I'm ashamed to say that there had been plenty of times when I was desperate enough to do something like that. But I now had Paul's permission. I didn't feel one iota of guilt when I gave the man behind the counter the watch, and he handed back a wad of cash. I almost fainted with relief at that pile of money. It was enough to cover Paul's next month at Fresh Start and whatever legal expenses came his way while leaving me with enough to make it through another couple of months. For the first time in a long while, I felt like I could breathe.

That high I got from having cash on hand didn't last long. You see, Reggie had a vision of what our first wine party was going to be, and that vision was going to require additional funding. She had never gotten around to telling me that part of the plan, and I guess I had just assumed that we would have the party at her house. After all, the whole thing was essentially her bright idea. Common sense should have told me that it was not part of her plan.

I have described her shambles of a kitchen, and I'll even go farther right now and say that Reggie was a slovenly housekeeper. She wasn't a hoarder exactly, but she did seem to hold onto crap far past its usefulness. For example, she had piles of "how-to" books stacked around the perimeters of her family room, all for projects that she never got around to doing. That was Reggie for you. As soon as her attention waned, she abandoned the book on the nearest pile, and she bought a new book on something else. Reggie had always thought that Kent stored his golf clubs in the hall closet to protect them. The truth was that he couldn't find any other place to put them in the house or the garage because of all the clutter.

So when Reggie announced, "The wine party will be at your house, Audrey," I didn't offer up a fuss. It was going to be a lot of work to clean and scour and prepare the *hors d'œuvres*, but I didn't mind all that much. We had decided on French onion tartlets, *gougères*, and salmon *canapés*. In addition, there were going to be boxes of La Maison du Chocolat Assorted Chocolates that we had ordered from Williams-Sonoma, even though the price had made me gasp. All of that we had carefully planned.

And then Reggie proclaimed: "I found a party place where we can rent French bistro sets. Do you have room in your garage for all your furniture, or are we going to have to rent a storage shed?"

"Oh, come on, Reggie. Don't you think you're making this more complicated than it needs to be?" I knew that we had agreed that the whole evening needed to be an *experience* for these women, but come on, wasn't getting out of the house and drinking wine with friends good enough?

Reggie was on a roll, and there was no stopping her. "I found these globe string lights on Amazon. And get this," she was tapping on her phone and showed me a picture, "LED Concepts Curtain Warm White 300 LED String Icicle Lights. Wouldn't those look stunning placed around the room? We might as well buy these. We're going to need them for future parties."

I was adding up the cost in my head. "Wow," I said.

"I know! The ambiance is going to be terrific."

"Why don't we just go ahead and hire some French waiters to pass the *gougères* and *canapés*?" I meant it as a joke. I should have known better.

"That's a great idea, Audrey."

To make a long story short, we couldn't get any French waiters to work for the paltry amount we could afford to pay, which was a good thing because anyone who knew anything about French wine--or anything French, really--could expose us as the frauds that we were. We ended up hiring two male students from the drama department at ASU, who assured us they could fake a French accent. We also told them that we would buy each of them a case of beer. That was enough to seal the deal.

We worked hard, Reggie and I, getting ready for that first wine party. It took us two days to move my furniture into the garage, and when that was full, carry it over to Reggie's patio. When the bistro furniture--both low-tops and high-tops--and lights arrived, we arranged everything as we imagined a French cafe would look. Reggie was practicing her presentation constantly as we worked. She was going to speak only briefly about the Loire Valley and types of grapes, and then go into the back story of her mythical French cousin Pierre, who was also a cloistered monk and very particular about his Éclatant wines and who he sold them to. That was supposedly going to keep the women from searching for the winery or Pierre on the internet when they got home and sobered up. We set up the wine stations last, six in all, one for each varietal of wine we were trying to sell, and decorated those tables with lace tablecloths and vases of Royal French Roses, which was another expense. By the night of that first party, November 17, I do believe that we had created *une nuit à se souvenir.* A night to remember. What was really strange was that Reggie and I were starting to believe in the story ourselves.

You want to know what my children were doing during all this preparation? Marcy wasn't any problem at all. I told her that I was hosting a fancy party, and she was so absorbed in her own life as a Tigerette that she didn't bat an eye. She came home from practices exhausted, and after a meager dinner, went up to her room where I assumed she was working on her homework. She'd always been a good student and was taking advanced chemistry and algebra II that semester, so it was easy for me to explain her long hours in her room with the door closed. Jimmy, as always, was more problematic. Enter Delilah, who was a saint as far as I was concerned. I didn't have anything to worry about when Jimmy was in her care. I wasn't shirking my parental responsibilities, understand, I was on a mission to create a better life for my family. Or if not that, at least give us money for food, clothes, the mortgage, and utilities.

Reggie and I were so nervous the night of that first party! The girls and Jimmy were over at Reggie's with pizza ordered from Domino's. They had strict orders to call only in case of emergency, and I had given Jimmy an extra dose of Vyvanse, just to be on the safe side. Our two waiters had shown up and had transformed themselves readily into Antoine and Henri, with black pants, crisp white shirts, and black bow ties. They looked awfully young to me, but they were as polite as could be.

"How's your French?" Reggie asked.

"Uh, I thought you just wanted a French accent?" Antoine spoke with a twang that could make a banjo weep.

"Oh, right. Let's hear that."

The two boys tried, the poor things, but it didn't satisfy Reggie. "Okay, try to keep your mouths shut as much as possible. Just insert *oui, mademoiselle,* and *plus de vin*--which means more wine--every once in a while." Then she gave them instructions on serving the appetizers and making sure that wine glasses were full only until the open wine was gone. "Got it?" They both nodded.

Reggie and I held hands as we surveyed the beautiful scene we had created and waited for our guests to arrive. We had invited twenty women, most of them other soccer moms and a few from our neighborhood, and they were all coming. We told ourselves that it was a good sign. We had two open wine bottles on each of the six presentation tables, and we had made placards describing the grape each varietal was made from in the Loire Valley. I have to say that it looked authentic, even to me. Reggie and I each had a glass of cabernet to calm our nerves.

"We've done a good job," Reggie said, clinking her glass with mine. We'd had to rent the Waterford crystal wine glasses too, extra small ones that only held six ounces. We thought it was very French or European, something like that.

"I hope this works."

"Perception is the key."

"Then I perceive that this French wine is delicious." I am not lying that the Two-Buck Chuck did seem to taste better in the soft twinkling lights. We even had French music playing in the background. I think it was something called *Papaoutai* by Stromae. I felt like I had been transported to someplace magical.

Our guests began to arrive, and once they entered our Parisian cafe, their "oohs" and "aahs" told us that we were successful. Reggie and I ushered the women to the various tables and started pouring wine. I let Reggie do the talking, and honestly, I believed her when she talked about the Loire Valley and varietal grapes and her monk/vintner distant cousin. Meanwhile, Antoine and Henri passed the *hors d'œuvres* and smiled charmingly. From the very beginning, we had decided that we weren't going to bother with any party or drinking games. Our priority was in presenting French wine and giving these women the incentive to buy it by providing them with an experience that was different from any other party they had ever attended.

The problem was that drunk women talk, and when they talk, they drink more wine. We quickly went through the twelve bottles we had planned to let the women drink for free. And it wasn't long before I saw Judy, one of our neighbors, asking Henri to open up another bottle of wine. He looked over at me, his eyes asking the question, and I nodded. I didn't know what else to do.

I found Reggie and pulled her aside. "What are we going to do? Everyone wants more wine."

Reggie looked worried. "I know. I told Antoine and Henri to open six more bottles, but then we're cutting them off."

"It's time to start selling."

"Let's do it."

We thought we'd planned everything perfectly, and we had even developed a kind of sales pitch, something along the lines of: "Wouldn't this charming chardonnay be perfect for your Thanksgiving dinner? Or maybe you'd prefer this nice French merlot? Or maybe both? Any of these French wines would go wonderfully with your holiday meal." But when I approached the first group of women, they weren't talking about wine at all. They were bad- mouthing the president of the Mohave High School PTO. The next group was talking about some new diet, and the third group was consoling Theresa, whose husband had recently been diagnosed with prostate cancer. Don't get me wrong. I am not condemning those women. They were just tired ladies out of their houses, drinking wine, and enjoying a free night away from husbands and kids.

And no one had questioned our wine's authenticity. No one.

It was exactly what Reggie and I had hoped for, yet it wasn't. Reggie tried to get the women's attention by tapping a spoon against her wine glass, but the conversation in the room was too loud for them to hear her. She next clapped her hands together. Nada. I could see how frustrated she was becoming, and I wasn't surprised a bit when she stood on one of the bistro chairs and yelled, "Ladies!" Reggie always was one for the grand gesture.

That got their attention, and the conversation dwindled off. "Audrey and I want to remind you that we have good French wine for sale here this evening at the bargain price of $25 per bottle. It's wine you can't get anyplace else. It's French, and it's a *bargain*," she emphasized.

"I'll take a bottle of the chablis," one woman said, and a few other women followed, ordering a chardonnay, pinot noir, and some others.

Then another woman said, "How about opening more wine, Antoine?"

Still later, I could hear people murmuring about "how lovely" the evening was, how much better it was than playing bunco or cards or going to a Pampered Chef party. Reggie and I had pretty much given up by then and were drinking wine ourselves, joining in conversations and eating what appetizers were left. It had become an "if you can't beat 'em, join 'em" type of thing. And I think you could call the party a success because the last woman didn't leave until after midnight. The party had started at seven. That was five long hours of drinking our wine.

So it was no wonder that Judy, the last to leave, was quite smashed. "Lovely," she kept slurring as Reggie pointed her toward home, four houses down the block. "'S lovely."

We'd let Antoine and Henri go home two hours before, so we were the only ones left in our magical French bistro. The number of empty wine bottles covering every surface called for a trip to the recycling center tomorrow. "Well," Reggie put her hands on her hips, "I think it's safe to say that our friends and neighbors are a bunch of lushes."

"And we thought we were bad." I poured us each one more glass of wine.

"We sold a whopping twenty bottles of wine. We didn't even break even."

"Do you want to call it a failed experiment?" I sat down tiredly on one of the metal bistro chairs. It was not comfortable.

"Do you?" Reggie joined me. "Ouch. This wrought iron is murder on your back."

We looked at each other. "No," we said in unison. I took a sip of wine. Oddly enough, I had forgotten that it was Two-Buck Chuck all night long and had been offended that the women were drinking all our French wine. It was kind of funny. However, the fake wine had worked. Sure, I was disappointed that we hadn't made money, but I could not let myself dwell on that. We had already invested too much in this plan, and I needed it to work. I also had confidence we would learn from our mistakes. We only needed to tweak the plan. "I guess it's back to the drawing board."

"We need to invite women who have more money--"

"Women we don't know that well--"

"And don't particularly like," Reggie finished. "That would make it easier to be pushy."

"You know what I'm thinking, don't you?"

Reggie nodded and began to smile. "Yes."

Cynthia Stewart.

9

CYNTHIA

I suppose you want me to be honest here, so I will admit to one thing. For a period of time, I was afraid of my daughter. I have already told you that Felicity did tend to manipulate me, but I think that any kid with half a brain has that inclination when it comes to her parents and getting what she wants. I know I did. Seriously, back in the day, I could talk Sally and Dwight into anything. How do you think I got all those dance lessons that they couldn't afford? When I wanted something, they somehow found a way to provide it. Sure, I was grateful for that--even if I didn't often show it--but I also thought it was their duty to give me what I wanted. So I guess you could say that it was their fault that I was the kind of mother I was to Felicity. I inherited my parenting skills from my own parents, and everyone knows that you can't alter your DNA. Therefore, when Felicity wanted something, she usually got it. Okay, she always got it, but I refuse to think that made me a bad mother.

But yes, when I thought she might have overheard that conversation with Buck, I was afraid. I feared that she would run to Richard and ruin everything I had worked so hard for. I went straight to bed after Buck left--that's how distraught I was--and took a sleeping pill. The pill, along with the wine, knocked me out but good, so I didn't see Felicity until the next morning at breakfast. She was already there when I got to the kitchen, buried in the recesses of the refrigerator. For a girl who rarely ate, Felicity spent a lot of time looking at all the food in that overstocked appliance, but I thought nothing of that strange obsessive behavior. Louisa was already off cleaning something elsewhere in the house, and I was relieved about that. In all the years she had worked for us, she had never seen me look the way that I did that morning, still in my bathrobe, without makeup and hair done.

Neither my husband nor daughter had ever seen me look so disheveled before either. In all the years I had been married, I had always awakened before anyone else and put myself together. I liked to think of it as putting on my coat of armor. But because Buck had upset me so and because I was still feeling woozy from the wine and sleeping pill, I had gone directly downstairs in search of coffee and not bothered with the necessary and extensive regimen I usually performed to look beautiful. My coat of armor was gone, and I was defenseless. I knew it was a mistake as soon as Felicity closed the refrigerator door and got a look at me.

Her pretty eyes--she had been lucky enough to inherit the shape and color of mine--widened in surprise. "Rough night?"

I went directly to the Keurig machine, not daring to look her in the eye. "I'm not feeling well this morning," I mumbled as I inserted the K-cup.

"I think it's called a hangover."

"I think I'm coming down with the flu."

"Right."

Even with my back turned, I could feel Felicity's smirk. I was kicking myself for letting my preoccupation with Buck and his blackmail demands ruin my normal beauty routine. I was kicking myself for letting Felicity see me in my worst possible state--i.e., *au naturel.* I didn't even have on eyeliner--or a push-up bra, for that matter. That stupid Buck had thrown me for a loop. I was off my game, which made me vulnerable. It was one more thing I could hate him for, and it was already a long list.

Felicity, who was usually out the door as soon as she grabbed a yogurt, decided to settle herself at the kitchen counter. "I was going to suggest that you come to practice today, but since you're coming down with the flu . . ."

I turned around slowly, cup of coffee in hand, and licked my lips. I could feel how dry and cracked they were. I hadn't hydrated during the night because of my passed out state. And I always, always stayed hydrated. It's one of the secrets of maintaining youth. I read it in *Cosmo* once.

I somehow managed a smile. "I'm sure I'll be feeling better by then. Of course I'll come." I was supposed to meet Buck at five, but I could drop in and say hello to the girls, make an appearance.

Felicity's blonde ponytail bounced and shimmered as she shook her head. "No, Mom. I can't take the risk of exposing my team. It's too close to the first performance. And you really do look awful," she added.

I was pretty sure she was enjoying this game, and she certainly had the advantage. She looked young and beautiful, and I looked like a forty-one-year-old *hausfrau*. But she hadn't said anything about Buck, so it was in my best interest to agree with her and get her out the door before she could utter a word. Or before Richard came downstairs from his bedroom. "I suppose you're right. Have a good day."

Felicity didn't make a move to go. She slowly pulled off the top of her Voskos Greek Yogurt. "Because you were ill, you missed a great dinner last night," she said conversationally.

"Oh, what did Louisa make?" I was sipping my coffee, acting noncommittal, but willing her to go. It wasn't working.

"Daddy and I went out. He took me to that new sushi place on Thompson Peak. Delicious."

The hand holding the coffee cup started to shake, and I quickly turned back around, pretending to make another cup. I didn't want Felicity to see my fear. It had always been two against one in this household--that was nothing new--but she might have said something to Richard about the strange man talking to me in the kitchen. I couldn't remember if I'd disposed of all those beer bottles. They weren't anywhere in sight now, so where did they go and who had moved them? Fear made my empty stomach lurch.

The stream of coffee dwindled and then stopped, but I didn't dare pick up the cup with my shaking hands. "It's nice that you and Daddy spent some time together. What did you talk about?"

"Oh, this and that." I could hear the bar stool scrape against the Travertine tile. "I better go. It's getting late. Feel better. Okay, Mom?"

I nodded, but I didn't dare turn back around until I heard the door slam. I didn't realize I'd been holding my breath until it came out in a ragged *whoosh*. I sagged back against the kitchen counter. I wished I didn't feel so lousy. I wished I knew if Felicity had overheard any of the conversation, and if so, if she had mentioned it to Richard. I wished, most of all, that I hadn't let down my guard yesterday or this morning. It wasn't like me. I was a pro who wore her armor well. It was all that damn Buck's fault for bringing up a past that I thought I had obliterated. Over the years, I had almost convinced myself that it all had happened to someone else, a young, beautiful, stupid stranger.

"Good morning."

I looked up, startled. It was Richard, and my heart started to beat erratically in my chest. The look on his face when he got a load of me in all my disheveled glory revealed about a million things that I didn't want to see. And to make matters worse, he was dressed in one of his Armani suits and had a suitcase. "Where . . . where are you going?" I managed to croak out.

"New York." He eyed me up and down, and I withered beneath his gaze. "You look like hell. Felicity said you had a rough afternoon yesterday."

I couldn't read his face, but then I hadn't been able to do that in a long time, not since his trophy wife, in his eyes, became nothing more than a tarnished relic on his mantel. So what did he know? Should I tell him the truth? I wanted to tell him the truth--I truly did--but lies always had come more easily to me. "One of those ladies' lunches that went too long. A charity thing."

"Right."

He sounded just like Felicity when he said that, which made me believe that he thought I was lying. I tried my next tactic: change the subject. "Why are you going to New York?" It couldn't have been business because he'd been retired for five years now. He couldn't use that excuse anymore.

"Financial matters. Trusts, that kind of thing."

"If you give me one hour, I can get ready and go with you." Richard borrowed a friend's private plane for most of his trips. Surely, they could wait for one hour. My sense of foreboding was so strong that I could feel perspiration dripping down my sides. Richard was up to something, and I could sense that it wasn't going to be good news for me. Hadn't he said that he had changed his will? He didn't offer me any details about it either. Unfortunately, that's the way things had become between us, everything cloak and dagger and mysterious. I didn't get it.

Richard ignored that. "I'm not sure how long I'll be gone." He looked at his watch. "My limo should be here." And with that, he turned and left.

I wanted so much to run after him, and I might have done so if I didn't look like such a ragged shell of myself. And I do have my pride, you know. I value my pride almost more than anything else, so I stayed put. But that undefined sense of foreboding was awfully strong. I told myself that he'd be back. Richard always came back. I might have felt more comfort in that thought if I hadn't been stupid enough to agree to no prenup. It was Richard's selfish sons who had made sure of that, right before they walked out of the wedding chapel in Vegas. At the time, I had been desperate enough to marry Richard that I conceded to his awful sons' terms. At the time, I thought that he was so enamored with me that he would always be loving and generous. I decided it was in my best interest to keep believing in that, and so I did.

And it really was better if he was out of the picture until I could figure out a way to get rid of that damn Buck. I now had the perfect opportunity to sneak into Richard's study and get into the safe where he kept the extra cash. I hadn't had time to dwell on that problem before I conked out the night before, and now it wasn't a problem at all. Richard's decision to take one of his sudden mystery trips was a stroke of luck for me. By the time Richard returned home, I would have resolved the issue with Buck. I would make everything work out perfectly.

Later in the day, after I had told Louisa to go home early and had showered and restored myself to my normal state of attractiveness, I ventured up to Richard's study. To be honest, I did feel like I was trespassing when I opened the heavy door. Richard hadn't invited me into his inner sanctum--that's what I called it; he didn't think it was too funny--since he retired and decided to take up residence there. You see, Richard's "study" was actually the entire west wing of the upstairs. In addition to the area where he did whatever it was he did, there was a bedroom, bathroom, and a sitting room with a full bar. My bedroom was located in the far east part of the large upstairs, which might as well have been Timbuktu as far as Richard was concerned. I missed the sex a lot--or at least I did in the beginning--but I had discovered that I slept much better alone in my king-sized bed. It's funny what people can get used to during a long marriage. And everyone has his or her own quirks, don't they? I didn't think it was all that strange that we each liked our personal space.

To get to the safe, I had to press the button behind the gilt-framed Picasso, which caused a portion of the wood paneling to lift, revealing the fireproof, cast iron safe. I swear, you wouldn't even guess that a safe was hidden there. But Richard had always been a stickler for security. We even had a panic room hidden behind the wine cellar. Rather excessive, don't you think? As far as I knew, none of us ever went down there, but when

Richard saw that Jodie Foster movie called *Panic Room*, he decided that he had to have one. That was Richard for you. He never denied himself anything.

It occurred to me that Richard might have changed the combination to the safe, and I sure was relieved when I dialed the combination--Felicity's birthdate--and it opened immediately. However, I wasn't so relieved when I saw the contents in the safe. I remembered it as being full of stacks of cash and gold bars and silver coins. Now there was still some cash in it, but not nearly as much as in the picture I had in my head. I don't remember feeling especially alarmed about it at that point. I just assumed that Richard had taken most of the cash to invest, or that he had deposited it in a bank.

No, not an offshore account in the Cayman Islands. That thought never occurred to me. Why would it?

For the time being, I only needed $100,000 for the first payment to Buck. I know it sounds like a lot of money, but at the time, I was under the impression that we had so much money that Richard would never miss it. I was only worried about the first payment. Buck was demanding $500,000 total in his blackmailing scheme, paid in five installments over five months. I was never planning on giving him the full amount, even though I thought I was getting off fairly easy. That damn Buck could have asked for a cool million or something, but no, he had somehow come up with the random $500,000 number. It just showed how stupid he was. And before the next payment was due, I would have come up with a plan to get the vile man out of my life, once and for all. I'd do anything I had to, even if it meant I had to sleep with him. It's not like it would be the first time I did something like that.

I didn't count the money left in the safe. I took the money I needed and quickly closed the door and pressed the button to hide it. I wasn't feeling especially guilty about it either. It wasn't like I was stealing from my husband. Arizona was a community property state, and half of the contents in that safe were mine, fair and square. And if I had to, I could sell some jewelry and replace the cash if it came to that. It honestly never occurred to me that the money in the safe might not be Richard's either. Why would it?

It wasn't a big surprise that Ernie's was a dump, a dive bar located in the corner of a strip mall. It smelled like stale beer and sweaty men, and the floor was sticky as I made my way to Buck, who was sitting at a table in the corner. It just figured that he was the kind of man who would want to pretend that this whole sordid affair was a scene out of some low budget gangster movie. Instead of a beer in front of him, he had a bottle of Jack Daniels. It was half empty.

"You're right on time." He pushed out a chair with his foot. "Have a seat."

I have done a lot of iffy things in my life, but I had never been in this kind of situation. I wasn't exactly sure how to go about it. Did I hand him the cash over or under the table? Happy hour had started, and the bar was crowded with mostly men. I could feel their eyes on me, and I wished that I hadn't worn such a low-cut blouse, but it was too late for that. I sat down gingerly.

"Do you want a drink?" Buck had on the same shirt he had worn the day before. I think the body odor I smelled in the place was coming from him.

I wasn't going to spend more time in the dump than I had to. It wasn't likely that I'd see anyone I knew, but a gal can't be too careful. I leaned in closer. "What's it going to take for you to go away?"

"You already know."

"Seriously, you can't expect me to hand over this kind of money when I don't know whether or not you're bluffing."

Buck pulled out a manila envelope he had tucked in the waistband of his jeans under his shirt. He put it on the table. "There are some documents in here you might be interested in."

All of a sudden, I was having trouble breathing. I was pretty sure I knew what was in there.

"Go ahead. Take it. I have plenty more copies stored in my Google files. Who needs paper copies of anything these days?" He leaned back in his chair, assessing me.

"I don't want to play this game with you. I want you out of my life. I wish you'd never *been* in my life. What is it that you really want?" My words came out in short little puffs. It sounded like I was hyperventilating. "Do you want to sleep with me? Is that it?"

That vile man had the gall to laugh. "Been there, done that." He poured himself another drink. "I'm afraid I'm immune to your feminine charms, Cindy Lou. I expect payment, in full. Then maybe, just maybe, I'll go away. We'll have to wait and see, won't we?"

"You're a despicable asshole." I couldn't breathe in that stale place. The room was closing in on me, and I had to get out of there before I fainted in a heap on that sticky floor.

"You could say that," he said. "But I wouldn't say that your character is sterling either, Cindy Lou."

I couldn't bear it another second. I fished the envelope of money out of my purse and threw it on the table. My entire body was shaking, and it was difficult to stand. "I'm not paying you another dime."

"Yes, you are, Cindy Lou. You're going to pay me every red cent."

My vision was becoming blurry, and his face swam in front of my eyes. "No," I whispered.

"Same time, same place, next month."

I turned and ran. I didn't collapse until I had locked myself in the Mercedes, and the full enormity of the situation hit me. I was never going to get rid of that man. He would continue to blackmail and torment me for the rest of my life, and eventually, Richard would find out. I was stuck in a lose-lose situation.

You have to know this about me: I am a very resilient person. Like I've told you, I had been in tough scrapes before but had always managed to bounce back. This situation with Buck was not going to be any different. I was going to win. It would be ideal if he died of alcohol poisoning or in a car accident. Or even better, if the propane tank in that rickety trailer of his blew him to smithereens. At one point in time, I even considered calling some of my former boyfriends in Vegas and seeing if they could take care of the situation for me. But of course, I wouldn't do that. I'd left that all behind when I married Richard. And I really wasn't the bad person that Buck seemed to imply that I was. Youthful indiscretions are just that: youthful indiscretions. I will allow that mine might have been more grievous than most. But I like to believe that people can change. I like to believe that the past should stay there. And I like to believe that I am now a good person, no matter what other people might say or think about me.

So the first thing I needed to do was find out what kind of man I was dealing with--i.e., the kind of man Buck had become during the last two decades. I did my research, my due diligence, you might say. What I found out was that it was a pretty sad story. He'd gone from his high school glory days straight into the toilet. There were three or four arrests for drunk driving and bar fights, and he had gotten in trouble for missed child support payments, that sort of thing. Oh, and his ex-wife Mary Wilson had filed a restraining order against him. I didn't feel sorry for her, though. Anyone who would cheat me out of Homecoming Queen, a title that most definitely should have been mine, deserved her comeuppance. Other than that, he didn't seem to be a truly evil person. He seemed to be a man who had fallen on hard times. Don't get me wrong. I didn't feel sorry for him. Anyone who had been that good-looking and let himself go to pot that drastically didn't deserve my pity or my money. However, I concluded that I could handle him, and I had an entire month to figure something out.

I felt better after that and got on with my life. I had my yoga and Pilates classes, my facial, massage, mani-pedi, and hair appointments. I went to long lunches with the women I called my friends. It didn't matter that we never talked about anything important; those lunches filled up the empty time. I could keep busy, and I did as the month of November rolled by. I didn't hear anything from Richard, which was not as unusual as it sounds. When he went away on his trips, he never called, so I wasn't especially worried. It was true that the dinner hour was lonely now. Essentially, it had become the only time of day that I saw my husband, and now that Felicity was so involved with the Tigerettes, she rarely made an appearance. To tell the truth, I often took my solitary plate of food that Louisa had prepared and carried it into the family room to eat in front of the television. I'm embarrassed to admit it, but I started to look forward to that dinner on a TV tray and *Wheel of Fortune*. It could have been called the highlight of my day.

Okay, I was lonely. There, I said it. And I guess I might as well add that I was bored too. I should have been coaching the Tigerettes--we all know that now--and I should have been paying more attention. But you see, when Felicity told me she was at practice or hanging out with friends or studying, I *believed* her. I did offer to help her with her college applications but was informed that she preferred Richard's help in that department. It was kind of a relief. I didn't know the first thing about filling out a college application, but I guess the point I'm trying to make is that no one was around anymore. Most of the time, it was just me in the big, empty, echoing house.

Did I ever consider letting Louisa go and doing some of that work myself? Are you nuts?

I was feeling especially low on the day I ran into Reggie at Trader Joe's. Lacking something better to do, I dropped in to pick up some flowers. When I saw all that wine in her cart, I remembered the wine club she and Audrey were starting. With everything that was going on in my life, it had slipped my mind. But Reggie acted so strangely when she looked up and saw me. You'd think I'd caught her shoplifting or something from the guilty look on her face. I know Reggie remembers the story differently, but she's wrong. I was only trying to make friendly conversation. In truth, I hadn't talked to a single person that entire day.

I stopped my cart next to her and asked, "Are you having a party?"

Reggie's eyes were darting every which way. "My husband has invited a few business acquaintances over."

"Your husband's business acquaintances must like wine." I meant it as a joke. It's not a big deal to buy twelve bottles of wine for a dinner party. In my experience, people will always take advantage of free wine.

Reggie didn't laugh. "Who doesn't?"

"Very true." I nodded. I almost winked at her, as if we were sharing a joke.

"If you don't mind, I have to get going. I have an appointment," she said rudely.

What little I knew about Reggie back then was that she always seemed to be in a hurry. It was like she could never stand still. But I had nothing to go home to, except for an empty house, and I wanted the conversation to last a little longer. Pathetic of me, I know. So I picked up a bottle. I hadn't noticed what kind of wine it was before, and honestly, I didn't care one way or the other. "What's this, Two-Buck Chuck? You're going to serve this at your dinner party?"

I don't remember what Reggie said to that. It looked like she was going to bolt, and I was only making conversation. Then I remembered. "Didn't you say you had a cousin who was a vintner in France?"

"Did I?" Reggie's right eye was now twitching like she had a tic or something.

"I believe you did, yes. Say, wouldn't a decent wine from France be more appropriate to serve at your dinner party? Think about how much everyone would enjoy a good bottle of wine." I was only trying to make a helpful suggestion.

And then Reggie said she wasn't having a dinner party, which was ridiculous because she had just told me that she was. And I still couldn't figure out why she was acting so guilty about a cart full of cheap wine. So I smiled at her to put her at ease. "You think I'm being nosy."

"You bet I do," she snapped.

I was hurt at her tone, but then it occurred to me that Reggie was embarrassed. Maybe she could only afford cheap wine for her party. I am not one to judge about things like that--at least not to a person's face. Our carts were parked side by side, but then Reggie picked hers up by the handles and pointed it sideways. Then she hit my cart! I was shocked by that. Still, I was very nice. "I'm only trying to be helpful."

"I don't need your help." Reggie glared at me before she finally said, "Look, if you must know, our shipment of French wine for the wine club hasn't arrived yet."

"I see." I nodded at her. That kind of thing happened. But why was she replacing the late wine with a brand so cheap? I didn't know her at all then, so I was going with the theory that she could only afford cheap wine and that the wine she had been expecting from her cousin in France had been a gift.

"I really do have to go." And then Reggie *rammed* her cart into mine.

I was so stunned that I took a step backward. Granted, the aisles in that store were narrow, and it could have been an accident. Maybe it was because I was so rattled, or maybe it was because I was having a particularly bad lonely day. Whatever the reason, I blurted out: "I would love to be invited to your wine club."

Reggie looked shocked at that, but then again, most people are surprised at my actual kindness. "The invitations haven't gone out yet."

She might have said something after that, but it must not have been important enough to remember. But I left that store thinking that I might get invited to the wine club. But when the days passed and the invitation didn't show up in the mail, I decided that it was all for the best. Reggie and Audrey were not in my social or economic realm, so it was a good thing that we weren't going to be friends. And to top it off, they were exclusive and bitchy, and their daughters were lousy dancers, and they were probably going to sell lousy wine. I was even considering starting my own wine club, one more suited to my needs and the crowd of women I was associated with. If I invited them, I knew they would come.

And no, contrary to what Reggie says, I did not put two and two together on that day. I swear.

The first basketball game of the season took place on the Saturday after Thanksgiving, and I think that both Felicity and I needed it to bolster our morale. Thanksgiving Day had been a hollow celebration for the two of us as we sat at the massive dining room table picking at the feast that Louisa had prepared. It was the first major holiday that we had ever spent without Richard, and I was starting to worry about him. It didn't seem like him that he would forget to call his only daughter and wish her a happy holiday. Felicity acted rather bravely about the whole thing, and also, she had been acting nicer to me lately. She hadn't said a word about the strange man in the kitchen, and I was beginning to think that she hadn't overheard the conversation. So I could relax in her presence, and maybe that was what the difference between us was. We could bond in our mutual disappointment.

However, after Felicity went to the final practice before the big game the next day, I was so mad at Richard that I snuck into his study again. I wasn't going to snoop because I had never been a nosy wife when it came to Richard's business affairs. All I was going to do was get on his computer and see if I could find where he had made hotel reservations in New York. Short of calling every major hotel in the city, which seemed like an impossible task, I didn't know what else I could do.

I know I shouldn't have been surprised when I entered the password he had used for years--1030MGMgrand, our wedding anniversary and the place we got married--and it was incorrect. I think I was hurt more than anything. I tried a few other possibilities, with no results. Then, and only then, did I start looking through his desk. The drawers, just like the safe, were surprisingly empty. To tell the truth, I thought that my oldish husband had finally gone paperless like the rest of the world.

I didn't dwell on it. I, too, had things to do on that day to get ready for the big game. I had a hair appointment to touch up my darkening roots, and I needed to go to Saks to buy a glittery top in blue and gold, the school colors. I had tentatively suggested to Felicity that I wear a Tigerette outfit--mind you, I hadn't even seen the three new costumes yet--but she was adamant in her refusal: "It's simply not *appropriate*, Mom!"

I let it go. I was happy enough that Felicity was letting me stand on the sidelines with the team before they made their grand entrance. I was also allowed to cheer on the girls and offer encouragement as if I had been coaching them all along and not been banned by my daughter from the practices. I think it was important to Felicity that it at least *look* like I had been participating. I was grateful for that.

As I said, I hadn't seen any of the outfits yet, and so when the girls and I met in the practice room, I was relieved. Sure they were sexy, with short, short skirts and sparkly bra-like tops and sheer tummies. But they were not vulgar. As mandated by Felicity, all the girls had gotten their hair and makeup done at Pucci Salon, and they all looked gorgeous, even the two new girls, who had obviously followed Felicity's instructions to the letter. I might concede that the thigh-high white leather boots did seem a tad dominatrix, but I was probably only projecting my own past experience onto that part of the costume.

It seemed like all the Tigerette mothers were waiting outside the practice room, and since Felicity wanted to give last-minute instructions to the girls, I reluctantly went outside and joined the throng. I expected them all to be holding their breaths, waiting for the unveiling. Felicity had told all the Tigerettes to keep the costumes a secret until the game, so the women should be tingling with anticipation for this moment. But no. The topic of conversation was the wine party that Reggie and Audrey had thrown the week before. I could overhear remarks like: "magical evening," "great wine," "the lights were spectacular," "the best girls' night out ever," and "When is the next party?" Let me tell you, those women were downright giddy. You'd think they'd never been to an ordinary, middle-class drinking party before. If I started a wine club--which I was still thinking of doing--I could certainly elevate the game.

It was almost halftime, and the girls filed out. I think a few of the women gasped, but most of the women cheered. Not Audrey and Reggie, though. I happened to look over just as they were raising their eyebrows at each other. But I do believe that the majority of the mothers were impressed. Most of them didn't know the first thing about style, but it was obvious that my daughter did. I half-expected some congratulations to come my way, but it seemed like everyone in that hallway knew who was really in charge.

I couldn't help myself. I clapped my hands. "Girls! Tigerettes! I want you to go out and give the performance of your life!"

Some of the girls nodded my way--my daughter was not one of them--before they broke into a kind of march and started to chant some slogan I couldn't quite make out, pom-poms held high in the air, waving. I followed them into the packed gym, while the other mothers went and found their seats. When the performance started, I didn't cheer and encourage like I had planned because all I could do was watch, mesmerized. The girls were in perfect sync, and they danced their hearts out. When the first performance was over, they went to the middle of the gym and started the second dance, which was equally lavish and synchronized. I'm not kidding; they looked like professional dancers. And I should know.

Sure there were catcalls from the teenage boys and such. And sure, the dance was sexy, maybe even suggestive, but isn't all dancing sexy? You bet it is. And of course the "Wagon Wheel" lyrics--"So rock me mama like a wagon wheel"--could be called provocative. But you should have seen the crowd! The people just ate it up. The girls got a standing ovation when it was all over. And let me tell you, you cannot overestimate the value of a standing ovation. And I should know.

I was so proud of those girls as they marched and chanted off the gym floor. *So proud.* Their success reflected on me, or it should have anyway, and so I felt like it did that night. I don't care if that's not true. I was having a good night, the first one in a long time, and it got even better when Audrey and Reggie made their way back to the practice room after halftime. I half-expected them to start yelling at me, but they weren't going to dampen my mood. That's not what happened.

"Wow." I couldn't read Audrey's expression.

"Very . . . mature," Reggie said.

"Weren't they wonderful?" I was gushing, but the girls deserved it.

Audrey cleared her throat. "We have a question for you, Cynthia."

Well, that could have gone any number of ways, but I was in such a good mood. I smiled. "Sure."

"Why didn't you come to our wine party last week?" Reggie asked.

"I didn't get an invitation." That should have been obvious.

"Oh, no." Audrey sounded genuinely distressed.

"Can you believe it?" Reggie shook her head, disgusted. "It must have gotten lost in the mail. I told Audrey that we should have done e-vites, but she is such a talented calligrapher that it seemed like a shame to let her talents go unnoticed."

"I'm so sorry," Audrey said.

"We really wanted you to come," Reggie added.

The whole spiel sounded rehearsed to me. These women didn't know me and probably never had any intention of including me. But I really wanted to join their wine club. I don't know why I wanted it so much. It probably had something to do with my recent loneliness and the dawning recognition that Richard might be in some kind of trouble, that he might never come back. I wanted to do something that would make *me* happy.

"I'd love to join your club." I felt genuine excitement at that moment, and it felt so good. "And you know what? I'll even host it!"

Money had nothing to do with it, not then. I only wanted to belong somewhere.

DECEMBER

10

REGGIE

I didn't like the fact that we needed Cynthia Stewart to turn our wine club into a money-making venture. I had never trusted her. It wasn't only that she was beautiful and had a figure that turned most men into raving lunatics. And it wasn't because she was so wealthy, although I will admit that had made me prejudiced against her from the start. There was just something off about her that I couldn't quite put my finger on. I have always prided myself on being a good judge of character, and believe me, there was something about her that screamed *insincere!* Oh, she tried to act nice to people and all that, but when she talked to you, you got the distinct impression that she was judging you--and coming to the conclusion that she was better than you. Of course now that I know what kind of person she really is, that makes her attitude even more laughable. Really, it is funny. I would have laughed my head off about it back then, if I'd known the truth. But no, I'm not laughing now.

However, our first wine club party had proven beyond a reasonable doubt that Audrey and I needed a more affluent clientele, and Cynthia was the wealthiest person we knew. Let me tell you, it killed me to ask her to join into any aspect of our wine club, but once she volunteered to host the party, relieving Audrey and me of that financial burden, our plan seemed to finally be going in the right direction, even as it added new worries. Now I know that money does not go hand in hand with sophistication--that has become crystal clear after all this--but Audrey and I did worry that this new group of women would know more about French wine than our friends and neighbors who had guzzled the Two-Buck Chuck like cheap thirsty peasants. It was obvious that we were going to have to up the ante at the December meeting. It was back to the drawing board.

"We can't get away with telling this group of people that they're drinking French table wine," Audrey said. "With a more sophisticated audience, the wine is going to have to sound more sophisticated."

"I agree. And I don't think we can dare to glue Éclatant wine labels over the Two-Buck Chuck labels any more." Once again, we were sitting at Audrey's kitchen table, which had pretty much become my second home at that point. And it wasn't only because her kitchen had become the headquarters of our operation. The truth of the matter was that I couldn't bear to be in my empty house. Being there made me realize just how truly alone I was.

"Okay, so we've said this winery is in the Loire Valley. What are the grapes of the Loire, Reggie?"

I flipped open the copy of *The Wine Bible* that I'd ordered from Amazon, something we should have done at the beginning of our operation. It was fast becoming invaluable to our plan. "The whites are Arbois, Chardonnay, Chenin Blanc, Folle Blanche, Melon de Bourgogne, and Sauvignon Blanc. The major red grape is Cabernet Franc. Cabernet Sauvignon, Côt (Malbec), Pineau d'aunis and Pinot Meunier are minor grapes used as blending components in the red, rosé, and sparkling wines of the middle Loire. Then there are Gamay, Grolleau, and Pinot Noir."

"Wow." Audrey's eyes looked glazed.

"Here, take a look." I shoved the book under her nose.

She shook her head. "No, that's your job. Just tell me what to do."

Seriously, sometimes Audrey could be so irritating. She never wanted to take over the reins and give me a break. I was as overwhelmed as she was, and it seemed like the more I studied French wine, the more confused I became. The only comfort I could find in that was the hope that our future wealthy clients would feel the same way and have to depend on us to tell them what they were drinking. I know. The irony is not lost on me. We were trying to make people trust in our pack of lies. You don't have to keep pointing that out to me. *I know.*

I took my time answering Audrey and flipped through the book instead. To my way of thinking, we were again going to have to pick six or seven mythical varietals and redesign the labels. I turned to the page that gave an example of a French wine label, and even though Audrey had done a reasonably good job the first time around, she was going to have to up the ante in that department as well. "Here's what a French wine label is supposed to look like. Can you do that?"

"Château Latour," she read from page 117. "Premier Grand Cru Classé. Gee, I didn't know there was so much on the label. Country of origin, the estate it was bottled on, the name of the winery, classified as a first grown, region, volume in centiliters, percentage of alcohol, vintage, name of shipper, and the *Appellation d'Origine Contrôlée*. I didn't know the first time around," she said again apologetically.

I felt kind of sorry for her then. She looked so tired, the dark circles under her pretty green eyes a testament to her lack of sleep. She was having a tough time of it with Paul away for another month, and I was getting the distinct impression that she worried about money constantly. I would have offered to help her out if I hadn't been in almost as dire straights as she was. Kent had not had his last paycheck directly deposited into our joint account. I kept hoping that there had been some kind of minor delay or that the bank had made a mistake, but deep down, I knew better. He had made his final choice. And it wasn't me.

I got up abruptly to get us more coffee. I didn't want Audrey to see my eyes, which had suddenly clouded with tears. I was not going to cry over Kent anymore, and I especially wasn't going to cry in front of Audrey. I don't know if it was true or not, but I had always felt like I was the stronger person in our relationship. I would lead by example and not let her see my weakness.

When I had composed myself, I sat back down. Audrey was still poring over the label in the book. "*Château Éclatant*. I can so do this. Let's come up with the names of our varietals."

We got down to work. After we did that, we moved onto the dilemma of putting the labels on the bottles. We had learned an important lesson at the November party, and we came to the mutual conclusion that we needed to buy empty wine bottles. That meant that we would have to pour whatever wine we decided to substitute for French wine into those bottles and then somehow cork them. As usual, the internet held all the answers. We could get a pack of twelve green wine bottles for $22.32, which averaged out to $1.86 a bottle.

"That seems pricey," Audrey said. "Why don't we start saving our empties and then steam off the label?"

"We might drink quite a bit of wine, but we don't drink *that* much." I agreed that it seemed like a lot to spend on empty bottles. "Do you think we could go to a recycling center to get some?"

"We could go through our neighbor's recycling bins," Audrey suggested. "Although that seems rather tacky, doesn't it?"

"What about a restaurant?" It had just come to me, the memory of all those wine bottles that had been tossed out at the end of the night at Lindy's.

"You are an evil genius." Audrey smiled broadly.

I smiled back. "Thank you." It happened every time we sat down to work. We would eventually find our rhythm and start to click, working together like a well-oiled machine. "Now the corks. Did you know they came in different sizes? Eight-inch corks are supposed to be easier to cork than nine-inch corks. They come in packs of 100."

We had decided on a Ferrari Portuguese Double Lever Corker until I read that hand corkers are fine for a first attempt and under a dozen bottles of wine. Since we hoped our business would start growing and expanding, we elected to order a higher level corker from an online brewing supply shop. From there, we realized we were going to need shrink capsules to put over the tops of the bottles and decided on Oriental Red Pvc Heat Shrink Caps in a matte metallic finish. They went for $7.99 per hundred. This was the process: You had to soak natural corks in a pan with two quarts of warm distilled water for 20 minutes. Then you filled the clean wine bottles to one inch below where the bottom of the cork would be in the necks and placed it into the corking device. The final step was slipping the seals onto the top of the bottles and then shrinking them by rotating over steam from a kettle. Last but not least, we would apply Audrey's newly designed labels.

"More steam." Audrey shuddered. "My hair hasn't recovered from our last go-round, and now it looks like we're going to be steaming off labels and steaming on shrink caps. If we decide not to get recycled bottles, and for example, we buy 100 bottles of Two-Buck, we would be opening them, pouring the contents into a container, steaming off the label, then refilling them, corking them, and putting on the shrink caps. We'll be steaming every bottle twice."

"Maybe we should go back to buying the bottles."

"So much money going out and so little coming in," Audrey lamented.

That was the thing, you see. There was always so much to do before every wine party. Every time we thought we had found a solution to a problem, another problem popped up. We really did try to consider every angle, every possibility. We were thorough, Audrey and I, and we somehow managed to work our way through all the snags and blunders. I wish we had thought to write down how many hours we worked on forming and refining our wine club. It became a full-time job for both of us. In the end, if we took the amount of time we spent on the project and divided it by the amount of money we made, I'll bet you that Audrey and I were grossly underpaid.

"One of us is going to have to call Cynthia and ask her how many people she's going to invite to the party. Since we're having the party on December 21, the Friday before Christmas, I wouldn't be surprised if she makes a huge holiday party out of this." The worried look was back on Audrey's face.

"Don't look at me. I am not calling Miss Barbie." Even the mention of her name irritated me, and I knew that Audrey was right. I supposed if I were going to host a wine party right before Christmas that I might turn it into a festive holiday shindig, but that wasn't the point. The point was that Cynthia was the outsider in the operation, only included because of necessity. She should do the respectable thing and only invite a small group. The plastic doll knew that this was only our second party.

"I don't want to call her either, but we need to know how many people we're dealing with." Audrey drummed her fingers on the table, and I was surprised to see that the nails were bitten to the quick, a habit she'd kicked years before. "I'll text her."

Cynthia had given us her number on the night we asked her to join the club. I hadn't bothered to put it into my phone, but Audrey had. Audrey was nicer about that kind of thing than I was. To keep myself busy while she did that--I was never one to waste time--I picked up my phone just as it pinged that I had a new text message. It was from Kent, and my heart felt like it had been stabbed when I read: "You can't keep avoiding me, Reggie. We have to talk." Honestly, I hadn't been avoiding him, not exactly. I just didn't want to hear what he had to say.

Cynthia responded to Audrey's text immediately, which surprised me. I had assumed that she was getting some part of her body maintained or realigned at some appointment. Audrey's eyes widened. "She's invited fifty people, Reggie. *Fifty*."

"Shit," I muttered while I was trying to calculate how many bottles of wine that would entail. If every woman ordered three--and they might order more, who knew?--and we had to have tasting bottles, we were looking at somewhere around 200 bottles. Where were we going to store that much wine?

The worried frown was back on Audrey's face. She had also done the math. "We have a lot to do, Reggie. It makes me tired to even think about it."

"But think how much money we could make, Audrey."

I had hoped that thought would cheer her up, but she only looked tired. "There's so much to do . . . I'll probably be up all night for the next week designing the new labels."

The poor woman, I felt sorry for her; I did. However, designing the labels was her area of expertise, and I had already done my part. Fair was fair. I reached over and patted her hand with its gnawed fingernails. "This is going to work in our favor, Audrey. Trust me. We'll charge over one hundred dollars for each bottle of wine." I winked at her. "Those rich bitches are going to pay through the nose for our bottles of imported French wine."

Looking back on it now, it's clear that we were still thinking on a very small scale. But as it turned out, it was only a matter of time and experience before we moved onto the more lucrative phase of our money-making wine club. We just didn't know it then.

What did I think about the dance that the Tigerettes performed at the first basketball game of the season? Well, let me begin by saying that I was impressed. As far as my untrained eye could tell, not one of the twelve girls missed a step, but then again, my eyes were focused almost exclusively on my Hayley. I barely recognized my slightly gangly daughter as she sashayed across the floor, undulating her hips and smiling provocatively at the crowd. She looked so grown up with her hair and makeup done--yes, Felicity had won on that point too, which meant that all the mothers were shelling out an additional hundred bucks a week--and my nervousness immediately evaporated when I saw that it looked like she knew what she was doing. So I was impressed and proud of Hayley.

However, to be honest, I will admit that the first dance made me uneasy. I think it was those thigh-high white boots. They looked sharp, sure, but they also added an element of sexiness that seemed entirely inappropriate for a bunch of high school girls. Maybe I had watched too many episodes of *CSI* or something, but boots like that always made me think of hookers standing on dark street corners waiting for their next Johns. After the dance, it had been on the tip of my tongue to say to Cynthia something along the lines of: "Great dance, but the girls need to ditch the slut boots. They're teenagers. What's wrong with wearing tennis shoes?"

I didn't do it, though, for two reasons. Number one, none of the other mothers gathered in the hallway had anything negative to say about the dance or costumes, and I didn't want to look like a prude. And number two, Audrey and I had planned on asking Cynthia to join the wine club immediately after the performance, and I couldn't run the risk of alienating her right off the bat. Audrey would have killed me. So I kept my big mouth shut. Unfortunately, it was the one time I should have listened to my gut instinct and spouted off, but didn't.

I should have attended more games after the first one. I know that. I had always been the mother who went to every soccer game and sat in the bleachers, rain or shine, cheering on the team. I had never missed a school Field Day, or any other school event for that matter, and frankly, I guess I was tired of it. And come on, it wasn't like watching the Tigerettes perform was like watching an honest-to-God sporting event. Being on a pom squad was nothing like being on a field hockey team. Now that's a *real* sport. Furthermore, if I wanted to watch shaking hips and twirling skirts, I could always watch *Dancing with the Stars* on a Monday night and maybe even learn a thing or two. Not that I would do that either. If I had a choice, I would rather watch Monday night football.

Plus, Audrey and I were so very busy. We had to get all our bottling, corking, labeling, and steaming done when the kids were out of the house. We did as much as we could during the day before Audrey had to pick up Jimmy from his after-school program, but even that was not enough. I would often go to her house after ten or eleven o'clock at night when we were sure the kids were asleep. I would wait for her to call me, leave a note for Hayley in case she woke up and wondered where I was--which never happened, as far as I know--and go traipsing through the backyard over to Audrey's kitchen. I have never worked as hard in my life as I did during the months of our wine club.

Of course I missed my daughter. I missed her very much. Hayley and I had always been close, but the last three months had changed everything. And it wasn't only because of her new role as a Tigerette. Her father was no longer in the house, and her mother either acted preoccupied or pissed off. I wasn't what you would call good company during that time, and I have to give Audrey some credit for putting up with me, listening to my rages and commiserating with the hurt I felt. So I don't blame Hayley for not being there much. And it wasn't like I was overly worried about her. I knew where she was, at school or practice or a game or getting a driving lesson from her dad, who was at least helping in that small way. Let me amend that last statement: I *thought* I knew where she was. Oh, God.

That first hickey was such an obvious sign, wasn't it? I could kick myself for finally half-believing her lame excuse that some boy in the hallway at school had wanted to smell her perfume. She'd had no idea what he'd been up to, she said. It had been a dare from some of the other basketball players, she said. He had apologized to her afterward, she said. It was only a joke, and she had thought it was funny too. I can see the ridiculousness of that story now, of course, but I ached to believe her, to trust her. Also, any communication from Caleb had dwindled to practically nothing since his announcement that his dad was gay, and as you can see, I had no one. Except for Audrey and our wine club, that is.

Once the basketball season had started, it seemed only logical to me that the lengthy Tigerette practices mandated by Felicity would have tapered off. But that wasn't the case at all. According to Felicity, each dance had to be new and special and somehow better than the one before. Yadda yadda yadda. I was so sick of that Felicity shit. But I was the adult in the situation, and it wasn't like I had a right to smack some sense into a teenage girl who had such a glaringly high opinion of herself. The good news was that even if Hayley went out for the team the next year, Felicity would have graduated. There would be a new captain, and there wasn't a chance in hell that any girl who took Felicity's place would rise to the level of her conceit and vanity. It just couldn't happen.

But here's the thing: I would have all these blown-out-of-proportion thoughts about Felicity's evil manipulativeness, and just when I thought that

I really *had* to do something about it, consequences be damned, she would present herself to me. By that, I mean that she would actually come into the kitchen after dropping Hayley off from practice--she was still bringing Hayley and Marcy home from every single practice, which frankly was a godsend--and make pleasant small talk.

"Good afternoon, Mrs. Carson," she would say, that blonde ponytail of hers catching and reflecting the waning light coming in through the patio sliding doors. "Did you have a nice day?"

I'd plaster a fake smile on my face, something I've never been good at, so I'm sure it looked like I was grimacing. "Hello, Felicity."

"God, Hayley did such a good job at practice today. And it's a really hard dance."

Sickeningly, the compliment would make Hayley blush with pride. "It wasn't that hard."

"Oh, come on now. Look at how far you've come," Felicity, the mentor, the goddess, the ultimate Tigerette would say.

"It's because you're such a good coach," my brainwashed daughter would say.

"No, you have the talent, Hayley. You should know that by now."

"Oh, no, you're the one with the talent, Felicity." To my surprise, Hayley didn't bow down at Felicity's feet.

Seriously, it made me want to throw up, but I couldn't detect any malice in Felicity's tone. She stood there like a polite, almost sweet, very pretty young woman. She had this smile--exactly like her mother's--that gave meaning to the phrase, *lights up her face.* Her blue eyes looked at me directly, and she put an arm around my daughter and gave her a gentle, affectionate squeeze. Seriously, she was that good.

To stop the flow of obsequious compliments, I cleared my throat and then asked Felicity a question I already knew the answer to. "Would you like to stay for dinner, Felicity? I made chili."

Felicity didn't bat an eye, nor did she recoil in disgust, as I had hoped. "No, thank you, Mrs. Carson. My mother expects me home."

"That's too bad." I hoped my voice dripped with sarcasm. "Maybe another time."

"Sure thing, Mrs. Carson. Bye, Haley. See you at practice tomorrow. Keep up the good work." And with that, her blonde ponytail would bounce out the front door to her waiting powder blue Porsche.

"I don't smell any chili," Hayley said to me as soon as the door closed.

"That's because I haven't opened up the can of Hormel yet." I had just gotten home myself, staying later at Audrey's to finish up some more bottles while she went to pick up Jimmy.

"Oh," Hayley looked disappointed.

She hadn't eaten much in months, and chili was one of her favorites. I had honestly planned to make it for dinner, but as usual, I had run late. "I could still make it," I said desperately. "By the time you shower--"

"It's okay, Mom. I think I'll grill some chicken on the George Foreman. You don't have to worry about me."

End of scenario.

I think Felicity popped in four or five times during those months, and I even think she *timed* those events. It's like she had this sixth sense that detected when I had reached my limit on her bullshit. I would almost have to admire such talent if it still didn't make me so damn mad just thinking about it. Ultimately, it wasn't me she was trying to appease. It was my daughter who she was trying to control. If Hayley had any urge to tell me about something that had just happened, if Hayley broke the code and had the audacity or stupidity or longing to confide what was going on to her mother, Felicity's presence put a definitive stop to that. In my daughter's case, it remained a highly effective manipulative tool. Oh, God.

The day of reckoning finally arrived, as I knew it would. I had done my best to avoid Kent. I know I've made it sound like he went almost completely AWOL for two to three months, but that's not quite true. He showed up regularly to take Hayley out to dinner and to give her driving lessons, as he had with Caleb. It was a tacit agreement in our family that he be the one to instruct our children on how to operate a motor vehicle. He was the better driver. I, on the other hand, had a drawer full of unpaid speeding tickets generated by those damn radar machines located practically on every corner in Scottsdale, as well as placed in unmanned police vehicles parked along the sides of roads. I think they're illegal. I read somewhere that you don't have to pay them unless someone physically shows up at your door with a summons. I don't know if that's true or not, but I chose to believe it. I still haven't paid those tickets, which ranks right up there with the least of my worries right now.

Kent had also asked to talk to me on several occasions. He said that he didn't want to show up at my doorstep unannounced, which I suppose could be said was considerate of him. I will grudgingly concede that point. Once, he requested we meet at O'Malley's, a local bar that we had often gone to for a drink or hamburger during our happier years. He must have texted me in one of my rare better moods, and I agreed to meet him there. I had planned to go; I honestly did. I put on my newest Danskin leggings and Nike top. I had even applied a wisp of eyeshadow and lip gloss that I hadn't used in a while. I took my long, dark hair down from its usual ponytail. I was going to brush it until it gleamed, hoping it would magically remind him of the night we first met. It had been the first thing he complimented me on that night, my hair.

But when I started to brush it, I noticed a streak of gray. True, I hadn't gotten around to coloring my hair for quite some time. As a rule, I avoided hair salons and did it myself with Clairol's Nice'n Easy Permanent Color, Black 2. It was easy enough to use--the whole process only took about a half-hour--but I still hated wasting that time sitting around with goo on my hair, afraid to do anything for fear it would drip black dye all over my house. So it had been a while. Still, that streak of gray threw me for a loop. It was wide enough to remind me of the white line of fur down the back of a skunk. Even worse, it was wide enough to remind me that I was no longer young. I threw the brush across the room, fat lot of good that did, and sat down hard on the edge of the bed, staring at it. I didn't meet Kent.

But eventually, my mild-mannered, kind-hearted husband wouldn't put up with my rude avoidance tactics any longer. The text read: "I will be at the house on Saturday at seven o'clock. I'll bring food and wine. Be there. No excuses." He'd long since given up on trying to call me, knowing that I would either ignore it or hang up on him after he got a word or two out. And he knew me so well. He was bringing food--relieving me of the arduous chore of cooking something--and wine. He knew the way to my heart, absolutely. And I was foolish enough to think maybe it was a kind of date. That saying must be true: A fickle heart is the only constant in this world. Who said that--Shakespeare?

I lost track of time that Saturday. I'm not making excuses, and I'm almost positive that it wasn't because of my reluctance to sit down and have the long-overdue heart-to-heart with my husband. Okay, it wasn't reluctance. It was more like out and out fear. Even though I had started to get used to Kent's absence from my daily life by then, you must understand that I didn't want my marriage to be over. My husband might be homosexual or bisexual or whatever you want to call it, but he was still my husband. I had almost talked myself into believing that I could look the other way on that one. Anyway, I was willing to try. And believe me, I'd planned on fixing myself up. I'd even planned on wearing a dress that I'd found in the back of my closet, a dress that had been hanging there for something like ten years, still with the price tag from J.C. Penney's attached to the navy blue sleeve. I was going to try to win him back, as pathetic as that sounds.

But Audrey and I had fallen way behind schedule in bottling our wine for the Christmas party at Cynthia's. Jimmy had been home all week with a bad cold, and Audrey didn't think we should run the risk of pouring the boxed wine--the Franzia blush, merlot, cabernet, chardonnay, sauvignon blanc, and chablis--into the bottles when Jimmy was around. The kid was only eight, but he could still be a loose cannon sometimes, despite the improvement he had made on his new medication. Personally, I don't think the kid would have had a clue what we were up to, but Audrey was adamant about it. She was afraid he would say something to Paul during his weekly phone calls, that he might drop the juicy tidbit that Mommy had hundreds of wine bottles in the kitchen. I let her have her way on that one, not bothering to point out the fact that I was the one who took the finished product and stored it in my garage under a tarp or in Caleb's unused closet under a blanket.

Making us even further behind schedule was our inexperience with the wine corking machine. It had taken us a while to get the hang of that contraption, let me tell you. I mean, it was hard enough to fill the bottles that we ended up ordering on Amazon to the exact same height with the boxed wine as it was, but at times those damn corks didn't want to go into the bottles, no matter how long we soaked them in distilled water. It seemed like things were always taking longer than the time we had originally allotted to the chore. That's why we had ended up ordering the bottles from Amazon. We were spending hours trying to steam off the labels of recycled bottles from Lindy's, only to realize how many different shapes and colors wine bottles come in. Ultimately, they wouldn't do. We had to make our French wine look uniform, professional. And it was exacting, time-consuming work.

So we needed that Saturday to catch up. Jimmy was spending the night at Delilah's yet again, and Hayley and Marcy were being bussed to an away game and wouldn't be home until after ten o'clock. I know that I must have had it in the back of my mind that I needed to be home in time to change for my dinner date with Kent, but yet I let the minutes slip by in rapid succession. Plus, the passage of time was aided and abetted by the fact that Audrey and I had decided that we'd squirt some of the wine into glasses for ourselves, rather than the waiting bottles. We had to taste our product, didn't we?

We were laughing about something or other, and believe me, that felt good. It seemed like it had been ages since we laughed like that, as we used to on our wine nights on my back patio. We hadn't had one of those nights in weeks. We'd been working so hard, both of us anxious and nervous about whether or not we could pull off this scam in front of Cynthia's crowd. Oh, that's right. We were laughing about Cynthia, who had the audacity to call each of us asking extremely stupid questions. She'd asked Audrey if it would be appropriate to serve sparkling water or still with the wine, and she had asked me if I thought duck *foie gras* would pair well with the wine. She asked me about *foie gras*! Me, who tried not to prepare any food that took longer than ten minutes. Me, who didn't even know what *foie gras* was. Well, it was just too funny.

It was because we were laughing at Cynthia that neither one of us heard the back patio door slide open. Neither of us noticed he was there until Kent said, "What's going on in here? Where did all these wine bottles come from?"

"Kent!" It was the only thing that I could come up with to say. I glanced wildly at Audrey, who was standing there with a box of wine and a guilty look on her face. I'm sure that my face mirrored that expression. We were like kids who had gotten caught with their hands in the cookie jar.

Kent took another step into the room, and from that vantage point, I'm sure he could see the finished wine bottles on the table with their French labels, six varietals, all courtesy of *Château Éclatant*. I'll give credit where credit is due here. Audrey had outdone herself on the labels this time. If I didn't know better, I'd think they were real.

"What are you doing here?" I asked stupidly. Even more stupidly, I wanted to throw myself over all those wine bottles to shield them from

Kent's vision, never mind that all that would succeed in doing was knocking the bottles to the floor and shattering them.

"It's seven o'clock," Kent said quietly, eyeing the corking machine, the shrink wraps, and Audrey, who was still holding the box over a row of bottles, ready to push the button on the spout.

I had no other choice; I would lie through my teeth. "Oh, Audrey and I have taken up this hobby of pouring cheap wine into expensive-looking bottles. It's amazing how much more we enjoy drinking the wine out of pretty bottles. You wouldn't believe the amount of money we save!" I glanced hopefully at Audrey, willing her to give me some support, but all she did was roll her eyes. Subtle, right? Where was your friend's support when you really needed it?

"I'm sure there are easier ways to enjoy your wine."

I couldn't read the expression in Kent's eyes, or maybe it's that I didn't want to. My husband was an intelligent man; it was one of the first things that attracted me to him. Unfortunately, I didn't think his intelligence was going to work in my favor this time. I left the bottle I had been corking and hurried over to him. I took his arm. "Let's go home. I'm starving. What did you bring for dinner?"

"Good to see you again, Kent," Audrey called after us. Audrey was almost always unfailingly polite. It was sweet, but I would have preferred some backup when I concocted that unbelievable story.

Back at home, I decided that my best defense was offense. I waited until I had gotten plates off the counter for the deep dish Italian sausage pizza and the Kendall Jackson merlot was poured. It was very quiet in that kitchen. "Your last paycheck wasn't deposited. What's going on?" I took a big gulp of wine.

"What are you and Audrey up to?"

It made me uneasy when he used that deadly quiet voice. "Why wasn't your last paycheck deposited in our joint account?" I took another gulp of wine.

"Are you and Audrey planning on selling that wine?"

I took a large bite of pizza. It was still so hot that it burned my mouth, but I kept chewing, biding my time. We could go back and forth like this all night, volleying between paycheck and wine. My real dilemma was how much I was going to tell him. When I finally got the pizza down my constricted throat, I said, "We haven't decided yet."

Kent lifted his glass and peered into it. "If you're going to do what I think you're going to do, you are committing fraud, Reggie."

"I don't think you're the person who should be talking to me about *fraud*." I know it was a nasty thing to say, but I always lashed out when I was backed into a corner. He should have known that, and furthermore, he was the one who was pushing me. He deserved it.

He did color slightly. "Point taken."

I miserably shoved another bite of pizza into my mouth. This conversation wasn't going as I had hoped, not even close. And this was the kicker: If I had paid attention to the time, Kent wouldn't have gone looking for me over at Audrey's and seen our wine operation in all its glory. All I'd had to do was check the time, and Kent would be none the wiser. Damn.

Kent still did not touch his pizza. "I quit my job at Honeywell, Reggie. There was a change in management, and I no longer felt comfortable working there. That's why a paycheck wasn't deposited."

That utterly shocked me, and I stammered, "But . . .but why? You . . . you have a . . . family to support. You . . . you--"

Kent held up his hand. "Hear me out, Reggie. Reed wants to travel. He received some frightening news from his doctor and thinks that now is the time to travel. He's always wanted to sail the Mediterranean."

"Frightening news?" I echoed. You know that my first thought was HIV/AIDS.

"Reed has been diagnosed with colon cancer." Kent finally took a sip of wine. "I wasn't planning on accompanying him. I was going to find another job to support you and the kids."

A wave of relief washed over me. You have to remember that the wine club wasn't making any money back then, and the thought of no income was terrifying. My mind briefly flashed on Audrey, the poor woman. "Thank God."

"But now," Kent continued as if I hadn't spoken, "if you go through with this plan of selling cheap wine under the guise of fancy French labels, I have to reconsider my position."

Wow, Kent had not missed anything in that glance around the room, and I was more focused on that than what he was actually saying. "Reconsider?"

"I'm not going to continue to support you if you are doing something illegal."

"Who made you judge and jury, Kent?" I said hotly. "After what you've put all of us through these last two months, you have no right to judge me. And besides, Caleb and Hayley don't have anything to do with the wine club!"

"I'm giving you a choice, Reggie."

The nerve of him! He had taken all these weeks to try to choose between his family and his gay lover, and now he had the gall to throw this ultimatum in my face, financial support from him, or the wine club. Do you know that saying, *seeing red*? Believe me, I saw *red*.

Kent's voice was earnest. "I'm doing this for your own good, Reggie. I know how you jump into things with two feet, consequences be damned. But this wine thing you and Audrey are up to is off the charts. You can't possibly get away with it, and I don't want to see you end up in jail."

I could have told him that I didn't want to end up in jail either. I could have told him to go to hell, that he was a sanctimonious prick. The unfairness of the situation enraged me. Why was he holding all the cards, and why had I let him get away with it for weeks now? I hadn't been all that miserable without him. Furious, yes, but miserable? No. I thought I had wanted him to come back home more than anything, but now that wasn't the case. I wanted to keep the wine club going, to make it a success. It was the wine club. It was something that was mine and mine alone. Well, and Audrey's.

Unlike Kent, I could make decisions quickly. I pushed my chair back from the table. "*Bon voyage*, Kent."

11

AUDREY

You'd think that Reggie would have had the courtesy to tell me that she was expecting Kent that night, but no, courtesy was never her strong suit. I know that her excuse was that she lost track of time, but I didn't believe that for a second. Reggie was always, always aware of time. Why, she looked at that silly Fitbit on her wrist at least a hundred times a day, always acting like she was on the verge of dashing off to her next, more important appointment. It was extremely irritating, but I guess I had gotten used to it over the years, as I had so many of her other quirks. But I was bent out of shape that she had been so careless as to let Kent catch a glimpse of what we were up to. Before that, our secret had been safe, locked between the two of us, but now there was a definite crack in the operation, along with added fear, and I resented her for it.

I confronted her the first thing when she came over the next day. "Why did you let Kent come into my kitchen, and how much did he figure out?" But Reggie, as she could be when she didn't want to discuss something, was typically vague.

"He doesn't know the whole story," she said, busying herself with that stubborn corking machine.

I really didn't believe that either. I had always gotten the impression that Kent was a pretty smart man, if not overly ambitious. He had never gotten a single promotion in all the years I had known him. "What if he tells on us?" I sounded like a first grader when I said that, and I blushed.

"Who's he going to tell?"

I thought that was obvious. "The police, Reggie."

"Do you honestly think that my husband is going to turn in his own wife?" She spun around and glared at me, her hands on her boyish hips. "And isn't there some kind of law that one spouse cannot testify against the other?"

"How am I supposed to know?" I snapped back. "I'm not an expert in criminal activity."

Reggie started to laugh, almost hysterically, and pointed at all the bottles and boxes of fake French labels. "Oh, yeah?"

I guess it was kind of funny when you stopped to think about it. We had spent so many hours telling each other and ourselves that what we were doing was not all that illegal. We were only repackaging wine, making it prettier. We weren't hurting anyone. We were doing bored housewives a favor by getting them out of their houses and presenting them with a new experience. It's strange what you can convince yourself to believe, even when all evidence points to the contrary. Isn't it?

I started to chuckle too, but I was still irritated with her. Reggie was laughing so hard that tears came to her eyes. When she finally got herself under control, I said, "Are you positive Kent isn't going to go to the police?"

"Kent is going to be out of the country and otherwise preoccupied." At my questioning look, she added, "He and his gay lover are going to be sailing the Mediterranean until the gay lover croaks from cancer."

Do you see how callous she could be? "Geez, Reggie, you might want to show a little compassion."

"I do not have one ounce of sympathy for the man who broke up my marriage, Audrey. Let's get to work."

I wasn't going to argue with her on that point. God knows that we had talked about our husbands and their midlife crises until we were blue in the face. We'd joked about how lucky we were that they hadn't joined a gym, bought a convertible, and started going to the clubs in Old Town on Saturday nights to pick up twenty-somethings. That would have been so tacky, we agreed, the ultimate cliché. But we both knew that we weren't lucky. It was becoming clear that both our men were in love with someone or something else. In Kent's case, it was his college boyfriend. In Paul's case, it was the bottle.

I had my doubts that Paul was going to come home again after he finished this second stint in rehab. I hadn't seen him since that one and only depressing visit to Fresh Start, and he hadn't mentioned coming again.

But I guess he had gotten permission to call once a week. I don't know if it was because he had earned it with his progress, or if the second time around allowed more privileges, but he called faithfully every Sunday night and talked to Jimmy, Marcy, and briefly, to the abandoned wife. Those conversations were painful for me, mostly because he kept dropping hints that he wasn't ready to come home anytime soon. I guess you could say he was trying to let me down easy.

After he would tell me that he was doing fine, actually great, enjoying the physical labor, baling hay and that sort of thing, he would say something like: "I think this outdoor life suits me."

My husband, once the fledgling screenwriter, was telling me he liked mucking out stalls? I found that hard to believe. "You must be getting plenty of fresh air," I would say tersely. "You won't mind mowing the lawn anymore when you come home. Haha." Neither one of us pretended to laugh.

"The kids sound good. You're doing a great job of managing on your own, Audrey."

"I would rather have a partner here helping me," I said pointedly. Didn't he even worry about how we were managing without his income? I was beginning to think that Fresh Start demanded that its residents take a vow of poverty. I was not a fan of that vow, even though I felt like I was living it too. I was overdue on the utilities and water bills for the second month in a row. Every day I was terrified that I would wake up to no electricity or running water. And going to the grocery store felt like I was walking through a minefield, trying to find items that were on sale, searching for things that had digital coupons, trying to stretch the food budget to its maximum. I now knew way too many recipes for hamburger.

"Soon, soon," Paul said vaguely.

"Do you think you'll be home for Christmas?" I pressed.

"Uh, I don't know, Audrey. Christmas is a tough time for me."

"You love Christmas," I insisted.

"I've got to go to a meeting now, honey. Love you." Click.

I am not callous. I knew what Paul meant that Christmas would be hard for him. Christmas was the time to eat, drink, and be merry, and Paul used to embrace it fully. I guess I did too. We always bought a real Christmas tree, the biggest one that could fit in the corner of the living room with just enough room at the top to place the Christmas angel, and Paul always hung the white icicle lights, strands and strands of them that circled the perimeter of the house and hung from the top of the roof, a job that took him nearly a week. I had accumulated all sorts of Christmas trinkets that I placed around the house, everything from assorted Santa's villages to a collection of Mr. and Mrs. Santa figurines to various Christmas wreaths that I hung on all the doors, inside and out. And I baked Christmas cookies constantly so that the house always smelled like a warm, fragrant bakery. Except for writing the annual Christmas cards and Paul's dreaded job of hanging the lights, we truly loved everything about the season.

But all the accoutrements of Christmas were not what Paul was talking about. He was talking about the drinking and being merry part. Paul had always excelled in that area. Eggnog spiked with brandy was mandatory at all breakfasts during Christmas week, and Paul just kept on going from there. He moved on to mimosas before noon, and after an afternoon of beer and spiced rum, he would switch to straight Benedictine and brandy. He made it to bed most nights, but the Christmas Eve he was supposed to assemble the trampoline that Marcy and Jimmy had begged for since September, I fell asleep and didn't realize that he hadn't come to bed. I found him passed out in the backyard underneath the sagging, half-finished trampoline, curled into the fetal position, an empty bottle of brandy in his hand.

It took some effort to wake him, and when I finally roused him, I asked, "Are you all right?"

He didn't know where he was at first, which was understandable--how many times in your life do you fall asleep under a trampoline?--but he rallied fairly quickly. Paul had always been a good-natured type of guy, even when drunk or hungover, so he gave a hoarse laugh as he tried to straighten out his stiff limbs. "It's a good thing we live in Arizona, babe. Otherwise, I would have frozen to death. If we lived in Alaska, I'd be a block of ice." He looked at the empty bottle in his hand. "Just think of the cocktail you could make with a piece of ice that big. Do you think they sell giant highball glasses on Amazon?"

Do you know what? I laughed too. I thought it was funny at the time. Of course I should have taken that as one of the many, many warning signs of the seriousness of Paul's problem, but I didn't. We laughed until the tears came to our eyes. And we continued to laugh about it all day. Every time we looked at each other, we cracked up. We had to tell Jimmy, who still believed in Santa Claus, that Santa had been too busy to finish the job. He had to make all the little kids in the world happy, didn't he? Santa didn't have the time to assemble something so large, so Daddy would have to be his helper and finish putting together the trampoline very soon. The kids didn't seem too concerned about Santa's lapse. I think Jimmy was too busy playing with all the rest of his new toys.

But wait a minute; I remember now. Marcy was a different story. She glared at both Paul and me for the rest of the day. As a matter of fact, when she saw the spiked eggnog at breakfast, she stomped off to her room, and I couldn't coax her out of there until close to Christmas dinner. Oh, dear God. She knew, didn't she? How could I not have seen that?

I know now that I overlooked many of Paul's shortcomings, the missed school events and the home repairs that he always left half-finished or not done at all, the myriad excuses that he would make about not performing at work. And believe me, he was a pro at inventing excuses and blaming someone else for his failings. However, I still do not think that I could be called a classic enabler, the term that Delores so glibly accused me of being. I think that what I was doing was trying to overcompensate, trying to make the happy, loving home that I never had as a child. My father was an absentee dad, but I didn't fault him for that. He was a truck driver and spent weeks away from home. And when he was home, he rarely spoke. He would spend his time sitting in his La-Z-Boy recliner chain-smoking Marlboros. Looking back, I think he was as terrified of our mother as Aaron and I were.

I believe that I've already mentioned that my mother has always been a very angry person. Let me give you an example that demonstrates that anger, as well as why I overcompensate for Christmas. One year, I think I was around twelve and Aaron was ten, my mother actually pretended that she was going to take an interest in the holiday, something she had never done before. She even went out and bought a small silver tree. You know the kind, the ones that look like they're made out of tinsel, and you have to put the metal branches into the holes in the metal trunk, which you can still see after the tree is assembled. They're ridiculous looking things, but being twelve and usually having no Christmas tree, I thought it was beautiful. And because my mother was making the unusual effort of *trying*, Aaron and I were excited. I even dared to ask her for the dress I had seen on a mannequin in Macy's window in the mall. Mind you, my mother, who usually shopped at places like Big Lots, the Dollar Store, and flea markets, thought that Macy's was expensive, "a high falutin' place," as she called it. But I remember that she smiled at me and said, "I'll see what I can do."

You can imagine my excitement when I woke up that Christmas morning and saw that there were two gifts under that small tinsel tree, one for Aaron and one for me. It was a dress when I opened the package, just not the dress I had asked for. I didn't say a word about that, though. It was enough that she had gone out and bought us gifts. And I had learned over the years that confronting or challenging my mother was never a good thing. It wasn't like she beat us or anything, but she was a wicked slapper, and a whack across the cheek could burn for hours. She made bacon and eggs for breakfast, another rarity, and I remember that she turned on the radio to a Christmas station. Elvis Presley was singing *Blue Christmas*. I could breathe a sigh of relief. She was going to be okay that day. I should have known better, but then again, I've always been a hopeful person--even though that constantly sets me up for disappointment.

But back to the story: Aaron and I had been playing with his present, The Game of Life, for most of the afternoon, and we had been so engrossed that we didn't pay attention to the inevitable. Have I mentioned that both my parents were big drinkers? I suppose that's an important fact in this story, but I always seem to omit it in the retelling. Actually, I don't tell many people that my parents went through quarts of alcohol in a short period of time. Our trash barrel testified to that weekly. It probably is some kind of subconscious repression or whatever it is that you call it when a person refuses to remember something. Or maybe I'm simply embarrassed about it all. Here I am, a child of two raging alcoholics who went out and married another one. It's a common pattern, isn't it? Maybe I should ask Delores about it if I ever see her again.

But back to the story: While my brother and I had been playing, my parents had been drinking their cocktails, gin and tonic for her, and Jack and coke for Dad, and chain-smoking their cigarettes. It must have been going on for hours by then, but I didn't pay attention until my mother suddenly lurched out of her chair and kicked in the TV screen. It started to smoke, and she was yelling so loud that I couldn't make out what she was saying or why she was so angry. My dad just sat there, as always, not saying a word, while she then threw the silver tree against the wall and picked up my dress and ripped it in half with her bare hands.

I started to cry then--I knew I should have taken the dress to my room--which enraged her further. By the time the neighbors had called the cops and they arrived, my mother had taken the turkey out of the oven, dumped it in my father's lap, and broken all the plates in the cabinet and most of the glasses. It wasn't the first time the neighbors had called the cops, but I remember it as the most embarrassing. Christmas was supposed to be a happy time for happy families, and we clearly were not. The cops didn't haul her off to jail or anything. They never did. For reasons I have never understood, she always got away with it.

Paul broke his once-a-week-phone-call rule and called me again two days later. My panic was almost as bad as when I got phone calls from The Gardens, and I knew it was not going to be good news. Maybe Paul had gotten into an accident, run over by a tractor or fallen from the top of a barn, or maybe he had gone on another bender. I was breathless when I said, "Is something wrong?"

Paul chuckled. "How about hello?"

I breathed a sigh of relief. He sounded fine. "Sorry. I wasn't expecting another call so soon. It hasn't been a week. Did you have to get special permission?"

"I don't need permission to make a phone call, Audrey," he said quietly.

That was news. If Paul didn't need permission, then why didn't he call more often? I didn't ask the question because I wouldn't like the answer.

"I've decided not to come home for Christmas, babe. I'm sorry to disappoint you, but I don't think I'm ready to handle it yet. At this time of year, the temptation to drink would be too much for me." His words came out in a rush, as if he had rehearsed them many times.

I felt a kind of numb anger then. I know that sounds like a funny way to phrase it. I was angry, yes, that he wasn't willing to at least try to be with us for the holiday, but also numb with the new realization that Paul could call me anytime, and didn't. Had his feelings changed toward me? Would a sober Paul not love me as much as he used to? And a further realization was this: Paul had probably always been drunk when he made love to me. Would a sober Paul no longer want me? I crumpled into the nearest chair.

I must have been quiet for quite some time because Paul next said, "Audrey, are you still there?"

"I'm here," I whispered. He didn't say anything. He was expecting more of me. I finally added, and it was so low that it was practically inaudible, "I understand."

"I knew you would." Relief flooded his voice. "I truly am sorry to disappoint you, Audrey. But it is for the best if I don't come home. I've got to tell you, you really are something else. You know that, right?"

I hung up then before I could utter another word, before I could say, "If you don't want to disappoint me, then why do you do it every single time?"

I don't know how I felt about Cynthia, back in the beginning. She was exactly the kind of person Reggie and I had always agreed to dislike on principle: rich, beautiful, and with a figure that would send any woman who could afford the numerous surgeries running to the nearest plastic surgeon. Secretly, though, I was more jealous of the fact that she had *help*, this Louisa person, who cooked and cleaned and shopped for her. What I wouldn't have done to have someone like that in my life! Cynthia only had one child, after all, and a husband who was there, or so I thought in the beginning. It didn't seem at all fair in the grand scheme of things, but I still never held the animosity toward her that Reggie did. Naturally, I had some reservations about her participating in any aspect of our wine club because I was afraid that she would immediately see our club for what it was, a scam. But Reggie and I had agreed that she was a necessary evil if we wanted to make some real money. And to tell you the truth, I was secretly glad that she was hosting the December party. I was dying to see the inside of her house.

I had never planned to "go behind Reggie's back," as she now claims I did. I swear, that first time I went over to Cynthia's, it was a necessity, not an invitation. Reggie and I were in my kitchen the afternoon before the party, finishing the placards that explained each varietal. We had decided that Château Éclatant was showcasing these varietals: Savennières, Pouilly-Fumé, Sancerre, Vouvray, and Chinon. All but the last one were whites, but our research indicated that the Loire Valley specialized in whites, so in the name of authenticity--yeah, right--we were doing just that. We were finishing up when Marcy texted, saying she and Hayley needed a ride home from Felicity's because Felicity wasn't feeling well.

When I relayed this development to Reggie, she groaned. "Well, shit. I was planning on going for a run."

I didn't want to go either. Jimmy was content, planted as he so often was in front of the TV in the family room, and it only seemed logical that she be the one to go. "I have Jimmy," I pointed out.

"It's your turn to pick up the girls. I did it last time."

I didn't know whether or not that was true. It had been so long since either one of us had to make a run to get the girls. I guess we had been spoiled by Felicity's willingness to cart our girls everywhere. I felt absurdly grateful to the wretched girl for relieving me of so much taxiing. I say *absurdly* because I now know just where she was carting them *to*. But I didn't then. "Are you sure it's my turn?"

"Positive." Reggie nodded vehemently.

"Fine." I was irritated. God forbid anyone interrupted Reggie's running schedule. She said it helped her relieve stress. Well, I knew more about stress than practically anybody, didn't I? But as you probably know by now, it's not in my nature to argue, and there were strict carpooling rules. Fairness was the name of the game, so if it was my turn to go, I'd go.

I placated Jimmy with a Snickers bar--I know, I did that a lot during those months--and drove to Cynthia's house on Juniper Lane. Once I got there, I texted Marcy that I was parked in the circular driveway in front of the house. I wasn't going to go in uninvited. I hated when people did that to me, when I hadn't had a chance to pick up and tidy things, especially now since I spent most of my time bottling fake French wine. My house was starting to look almost as cluttered as Reggie's. Also, I was rather intimidated to ring the doorbell of that stately house. I think it could definitely qualify as a mansion, or maybe more of a McMansion. If I had to guess, I would say that it was in the range of ten thousand square feet. I'd grown up in south Scottsdale, with its aging bungalows and low-roofed small ranch homes, many dating back to the early 1970s. In the hierarchy that is Scottsdale, it would be accurate to say that I grew up on the wrong side of the tracks. I'd always been acutely aware of that fact.

But as I sat there, the big copper front door opened, and there stood Cynthia, beckoning to me. "Hi, Audrey. Come on in."

What was I supposed to do? I didn't want to appear rude, and I did want to see what it was like inside, so I took Jimmy by his sticky hand and walked to the door. He was in a sulky mood that day, but I generally preferred him like that. It was better than his angry, tantrum-throwing days, which thankfully, were becoming rarer. I still felt like I was constantly tip-toeing on eggshells, though.

"Marcy said that Felicity wasn't feeling well, and she needed a ride home," I said as Cynthia led me through the Great Room, the travertine tile gleaming underfoot, toward the back of the house. I could see the massive Christmas tree nestled by the fireplace, a tree that would have made the Christmas trees Paul and I used to buy look downright puny. There was a grand staircase to my left, covered with boughs of fir decorated with expensive-looking silver and gold ornaments, and everywhere I looked, there was yet another decorator-inspired Christmas decoration. I had to hold my breath to keep from gasping, vowing to myself that I would never let Cynthia into my home. I would die of embarrassment.

Cynthia's laugh sounded tinkling, like a little silver bell. "Oh, that. Felicity's feeling fine. It was just a little ruse to get you over here. I wanted to show you how I've decorated for this party."

I would later come to know that Cynthia's *little ruses* were pretty much her *modus operandi*. But I didn't then, and instead of being irritated at her for dragging me over here through rush hour traffic under false pretenses, I was overwhelmed by the beauty of her home, even more so when we reached the equally open back part of the house where she had round tables set up in the grand expanse of the family room, all covered with glittering silver and gold cloths and crystal vases just waiting for the white and red roses I could see in bunches on the gigantic center island of the kitchen. The back Nano doors opened up the entire length of the house to the flagstone patio, which also held the glittery tables. And beyond that, I could see the pool, which was crowned with a canopy made of lights. I had never seen anything like it.

"Wow," I finally said.

Jimmy was still beside me, holding my hand. "Am I in a Christmas castle?" His voice was filled with wonder. And why not? He had never seen anything this grand. Neither had I, for that matter. The poor kid had his mouth open, the sticky remnants of the candy bar staining his teeth with brown goo. He was probably now going to think he was an underprivileged kid. I couldn't blame him for that. I was feeling the same thing.

"Isn't he adorable?" Cynthia said sweetly, although she eyed him like he was some foreign object.

"This place looks amazing." I meant the compliment sincerely, even though I felt a strong wave of apprehension wash over me. How could Reggie and I get away with what we were about to do? Our Franzia boxed wine, now bottled under fancy French labels, was never going to fool people who came to parties like this.

My panicked look did not go unnoticed by Cynthia. "If there's something you don't like, I can change it."

"No, no," I stammered. "The place looks beautiful."

Cynthia surveyed her handiwork--or was it that of a party planner or decorator?--and nodded. "It gets you in the Christmas spirit, doesn't it?"

The Christmas spirit and I had not made each other's acquaintance during this particular holiday season, but I had to agree with her. "You could host quite the party in this space alone. I bet that two hundred people could fit in here easily."

"Oh," Cynthia said eagerly, "do you think I should invite more people? I know plenty more women who would be glad to come, even on this short of notice. It wouldn't be any trouble at all--"

"No, no," I interrupted again. "Fifty people is plenty." I was thinking about all the bottles that Reggie and I had scrambled to fill and label in preparation for fifty people, and all the empty Franzia boxes I had carted to the big dumpster behind Fry's grocery store. We had only finished the task this morning, which in my opinion, was cutting it way too close to showtime. That's what Reggie and I had started to call this party, *showtime*. It had become one more private joke between us, in part because we were trying to mask our fear, in part because we were usually punch drunk with exhaustion.

"What is your child doing, Audrey? I mean, he's adorable, but what is he *doing*?"

In my dazed and apprehensive state, I hadn't noticed that Jimmy had wandered over to the second majestic tree in the corner of the family room. He was standing in front of it, painstakingly removing one ornament after another and laying them gently on the tiled floor. Soon, I knew, he would start to put them back onto the tree. The poor kid. I hadn't even gotten around to getting a tree yet, and decorating it had always been one of Jimmy's favorite things to do. He did it over and over again. He was amazingly gentle with the ornaments, something that surprised me every single year. The poor kid. I had been woefully neglectful of him lately.

I blinked away the tears that came to my eyes. "I'm sorry, Cynthia. He's decorating your tree. I haven't had time to get our tree yet. Jimmy," my voice wobbled on his name, "that is not our tree. You need to come over here and stand by me." Jimmy pretended he didn't hear me and took another ornament off the tree.

My tears did not go unnoticed by Cynthia. I would come to learn that she rarely missed that kind of thing. She was downright intuitive when it came to picking up on people's vulnerabilities. "Audrey, you look like you need a glass of wine."

"Oh, I can't stay," I protested. "I have to go home and make dinner." And finish the placards and put the fake wine in the special wooden crates that we'd had to order--yet another expense I couldn't afford--with the *Château Éclatant* stamp on the top and sides. Naturally, I didn't mention that part to her.

"Just one glass," Cynthia coaxed. "Your child--Jimmy--isn't hurting anything, and he seems to be enjoying himself."

"Where are the girls?" I remembered that I was here to pick them up, but strangely, I didn't hear any high-pitched teenage giggling. The massive house was oddly quiet.

Cynthia shrugged her toned shoulders. "I think they're in the guesthouse. That's where they usually are. They're old enough that we don't have to keep tabs on them every single second, right?"

In theory, I strongly disagreed with that, and I could have pointed out that her daughter was two years older than mine, which made a huge difference in my book. But in practice, I hadn't been keeping as close of an eye on Marcy as I used to. As busy and preoccupied as I was, I had decided to trust her. She had always been a responsible girl. So I reluctantly agreed. "I suppose I have time for one glass."

"Of course you do. Who doesn't have time for a glass of wine?" Cynthia laughed her tinkling laugh again.

I gave a quick glance at Jimmy, who was still methodically removing and rehanging ornaments, and followed her over to the kitchen counter. I know I should have insisted that I had to leave, but I suddenly, desperately wanted a glass of wine. It had been such a long, trying day. One glass couldn't hurt, could it? And in a way, I justified to myself, I was doing research. I would be able to tell Reggie what kind of wine Cynthia Stewart drank. That kind of information could prove useful to us when it was time for us to up the ante on the caliber of the kind of wine we were rebottling as French vintages. Looking back, I realize it was amazing the things I could justify to myself during that time. Truly amazing. It's funny what desperation can make a person do. Well, maybe it's not funny. Maybe it's more accurate to say it was pathetic.

You can imagine my relief when Cynthia opened the wine cooler on the wall next to the refrigerator and pulled out a bottle of William Hill Napa Valley Chardonnay. Napa Valley, not French, and I knew that particular bottle went for a little over twenty dollars. So she didn't sit around sipping wine from Bordeaux or Burgundy or the Rhône that cost hundreds of dollars. That would definitely work in Reggie's and my favor. I started to relax a little after that. Maybe what Reggie and I were going to do in this very house the next night wasn't so unbelievable after all. Maybe, as Reggie kept insisting, the perception was the key. The wine we bottled certainly looked like the real thing to a person who wasn't an expert. I take full credit for that. I had spent hours and hours making those labels look authentic. And they did.

"Is this okay?" Cynthia asked. She looked hopeful, maybe a little worried.

"That's fine." I relaxed even more. She was acting like I was an expert or something--which was laughable--but I wasn't going to dissuade her of that notion.

Cynthia cleared away the roses from the center island and set a glass in front of me. "I'm so glad we're getting a chance to know each other a little better."

I smiled. Reggie would probably have a heart attack if she could see what I was doing, drinking a glass of wine with Cynthia Stewart, the enemy. She'd think I was a traitor if it wasn't for the fact that I was going to tell her every detail that happened, every bit of juicy gossip. But I have to say that Cynthia was charming that first time, even if she did talk mostly about herself, her former life as a professional dancer in two Broadway shows and all the charitable work she had done during her reign as Mrs. Arizona.

At one point, I asked her if she had grown up in Arizona, and she suddenly seemed evasive. "No," she said quickly and changed the subject. The same thing happened when I asked if her parents were still alive and lived nearby. "No," she said and poured us each more wine.

I didn't think any of it was unusual. I, for one, am reluctant to talk about my upbringing. I think I'd only ever told Reggie the entire story, so I could understand that some secrets shall remain so. I suppose I was equally evasive when she asked me what gave Reggie and me the idea to start a wine club and what my husband did for a living. That's the way most women are, you know. Initially, we're protective of our secrets and only want to reveal ourselves in the best possible light. All in all, that first encounter with Cynthia was quite pleasant. But I didn't think I'd ever sit down and talk with her again. It was clear that we had nothing in common. Plus, Reggie and I were planning on *conning* her. Getting to know her would be dangerous.

When we finished the bottle of wine, and Jimmy had redecorated her Christmas tree--the part he could reach, anyway--at least three times, I said, "This has been nice, Cynthia. Thank you for the wine, but I really have to be going now."

"It has been nice, hasn't it? I've wanted to get to know you for quite some time."

That surprised me. For one thing, I didn't know Cynthia one iota better than when we started the conversation, and secondly, I'm pretty sure that she hadn't had the foggiest notion of who I was until Marcy joined the Tigerettes. Oh, and that was another funny thing. We hadn't talked about the Tigerettes, not even once.

Then she surprised me again. "I know you and Reggie are good friends, but I don't think you should tell her about this. I know she doesn't like me."

"Oh, well. Reggie doesn't even know you. I don't know if I would go so far as to say that she doesn't like you." I stood up quickly. I know I should have vehemently defended Reggie, but I swear that there were actual tears in Cynthia's blue eyes. I couldn't hurt her feelings by telling her the truth, that Reggie disliked her on principle, which is one of the reasons we were going to scam her. I felt so guilty right then. But then again, I always felt guilty about one thing or another. I guess it's just my nature.

"Still, I would like for you not to tell her about this conversation. I don't want to get in the middle of your friendship."

Like that could happen? I tell you, it was very, very strange. "Okay, Cynthia, I won't tell her."

It sounds mean now, but I had planned on telling Reggie all about Cynthia's and my non-conversation as soon as I got home. Why wouldn't

I? She was my best friend. But when she came over later that night after the kids were in bed to finish up the placards, she was in such a foul mood. When Reggie gets in that kind of mood, you can almost see the dark storm cloud hanging over her head.

The first thing she said when she walked in and saw the still empty crates was: "God, Audrey, why isn't the wine crated yet? Have you been daydreaming and wasting time again? I sometimes feel like I'm the one doing all the work here."

Well, that just put me over the edge. I'd been working my ass off, and she knew it. "You can be such a bitch sometimes, Reggie."

"You're not exactly an angel yourself, Audrey," she snapped back.

We worked the rest of the night in silence, something that had never happened before, both of us seething with resentment. And so I didn't tell her about having wine with Cynthia. It wasn't any of Reggie's business. It hadn't been a big deal, and Reggie would blow that all out of proportion too. And besides, Cynthia had been nothing but charming.

I was such a fool.

12

CYNTHIA

Let me tell you something about Buck Boyd. I loved him. Back in high school, I had been head over heels crazy about that boy. He had been the most handsome, most popular, most athletic boy in the history of Marion High, as far as I was concerned, and when he asked me out that first time, I was absolutely stunned. I didn't think he had even noticed me. I wasn't popular, didn't have many friends, and I certainly wasn't in his top-tier crowd. I suppose it was my beauty that beckoned to him, as it would to so many men, so many times, in the years to come, but at the time I thought he must have been slightly off his rocker to ask me out. He could have any girl in the entire high school, yet he chose me. *Me*, which I came to believe, made me special by proxy.

On that very first date, we went to the town's old theater, something I rarely did. For one thing, what little money I had went to all my dancing lessons, and for another thing, it was a confirmed fact that the old Wilson theater--yes, the place was owned by that bitch Mary's mom and dad--had mice. You could be munching on your popcorn and watching a movie, and you'd feel something run across your foot. People thought it was part of the fun, those mouse sightings, but not me. However, I had no qualms about going to see a movie with Buck, who I imagined could squash one of those detestable critters with his size thirteen shoes in nothing flat.

We saw *Legends of the Fall*, and I'm not lying when I say that the incredibly sexy image of Brad Pitt as Tristan up on that screen sealed the deal for me. Maybe it was transference or something like that, or maybe the image of Brad Pitt got intermingled in my mind with the boy sitting next to me. I don't know, but either way, I was a goner by the end of that movie.

I stupidly thought that he was the person who was going to take me away from that small town and change my life. He had a scholarship, for crying out loud, and everyone knew that Buck Boyd was a young man who was going to set the world on fire. And we didn't see a single mouse during that long, long movie. Further proof that he was the one, right?

We had been together for four months when I finally admitted I was pregnant. Oh, I'd suspected that I was when I skipped that first period, but it took the second no show of the monthly blood to admit it to myself. It's frightening how much you can talk yourself into believing, even when you know you are only fooling yourself. But I was young and naive enough to believe that it would never happen to me, although the evidence in my high school proved contrary. Every year the graduating class was absent a fair number of girls who had dropped out due to pregnancy. I'd always thought those were the stupid, slutty girls who deserved it. However, I was neither stupid nor slutty. Buck, in fact, had been my first, as hard as that is to believe now, and I know several men who came after Buck who would have thought it was a hilarious joke if I told them that truth. They probably would have rolled on the floor with laughter. But I really was seventeen when I lost my virginity, and I became pregnant shortly after that.

Suffice it to say that I didn't want it. A baby would ruin all my dreams of stardom, and I had no doubt that I would be a star someday. I wasn't quite sure what I would be a star *of*, but I would be a star, nonetheless. Buck, though, was a temptation. I will admit that. He wanted me to keep the baby. He wanted to marry me.

That's what he said to me when I told him the unexpected news. "Marry me, Cindy Lou."

"But you have a scholarship to State," I protested, making him think that he was the one who would lose everything when it would be me. I had never told him that I planned to hightail it to LA the second I graduated from Marion High, leaving this podunk town and my parents behind for good.

"Married people go to college," he pointed out, his handsome chin quivering.

We were sitting in his Ford truck, and I could see his quivering chin by the light from the dashboard. We had kept the truck running for heat when we stopped at our usual spot, the spot where the very thing we were talking about had happened. That spot in the woods was never going to be the same for me. "I am not living in a dorm, Buck."

"We could get an apartment off-campus or something. People have done it before, Cindy Lou. We could work it out."

For a brief moment there, I thought that maybe it would work, that maybe I could take some college dance classes too. Those instructors would have to know more than the less than stellar teachers I'd had in this town. I could become even better with proper training. But that was a very brief moment of weakness. "How would we support ourselves and a baby? You'd need to be studying all the time, and I--" I couldn't bear to bring myself to say *taking care of a baby*. It seemed so foreign to me, unnatural even. The very thought made my stomach lurch violently.

Buck thumped the steering wheel with both hands. "Then forget college. We can have a nice life here in Marion. I can work on the farm, and we can live with my folks until we save enough for our own place."

That was the most appalling thing I had ever heard. His father liked me, and consequently, his mother did not. I could understand it. Buck's dad looked at me like he wanted to swallow me whole. "I am not living with your parents, Buck."

"Then we'll live with yours."

"Absolutely not!" If possible, that might be even more appalling than living with Mr. and Mrs. Boyd. I hadn't even told Sally and Dwight I was pregnant yet, not because they'd be mad or disappointed--instead, they'd probably be thrilled--but because I didn't think it was any of their business. I couldn't remember a time I confided in either one of my parents. That might be strange for an only child, but that's the way it had always been.

"There's a small apartment over the hardware store that people rent out. I think it's empty right now. I could give them a call."

For someone who had a scholarship to State, Buck could sometimes be thick as a brick. I think now that my love for him was dying a little more each day during those months. Maybe it was a form of self-protection. Maybe I knew, deep down inside, that if I married Buck and had this baby, I would never leave this town. Maybe I was scared to death. "I want an abortion, Buck."

"I don't." He drummed his fingers on the steering wheel. "I want us to have the baby."

"It's my body," I said. There was no dispute on that fundamental fact.

"Where are you going to get the money?"

He turned to look at me then, his blue eyes blazing, and I almost caved in that exact moment, thinking what a pretty baby the two of us could make together. But my willfulness quickly took over, as it usually does. I had grown quite used to getting my way, probably because I always had. "I thought that maybe you--"

"Nope." Buck shook his head vehemently, the honey blonde hair flopping in his eyes in the way I loved.

I didn't love it now. He was being completely unreasonable. He was the one who had gotten me into this mess. Sure, I had some money saved, but it was for my future, not for this. How would I get to LA if I didn't have that money? "This is your responsibility."

"Not doing it." He continued to shake his head. "And for your information, this is your responsibility too."

I had honestly never thought of it that way. He was the one who bought the rubbers; he was the one who put them on--had the idiot not done it right?--and he was the one who was supposed to prevent this from happening. It was his fault. I had told him at the very beginning that I was not going to go on the Pill. I'd heard it made you gain weight. I'd often wondered if that was the reason for all the fat women walking around Marion.

But I had not expected this stubbornness from Buck. At the very beginning of our still young relationship, I had been more in awe of him than he was of me. That had lasted precisely one week. I was a quick study, and it took me no time at all to figure out I was really the one in charge. He was besotted with everything about me: my hair, mouth, eyes, breasts, skin, and everything below the waist. I'm telling you, the boy couldn't get enough of it, but I'm not going to go into detail about that now. Suffice it to say that he was putty in my hands if I made the right promises. But at that moment in time, I was temporarily at a loss for what to do next.

Because I hadn't said anything, Buck thought that he had won. "So it's settled then. We'll get married and have the baby."

The tears came easily then. It was kind of amazing that I hadn't come up with that idea sooner. I am a very pretty cryer. Seriously. Some women blubber and have snot coming out their noses, and their faces scrunch up in a very ugly manner. But not me. The tears dribble out my blue eyes in a very uniform fashion and trail slowly down the dainty slopes of my cheeks. I have yet to research this phenomenon, but I do believe it is a talent. Felicity, unfortunately, inherited this talent, and it works on Richard every time. I know that if she and I had a crying contest in front of him, she would win, hands down. It's annoying.

Buck caved then. He had never seen my display before, and it caught him off guard. "Aww, come on, Cindy Lou. Don't cry."

"But I thought you would help me, Buck. You always know the right thing to do." I dabbed daintily at my eyes with the shredded tissue he had pulled from his pants pocket, willing myself not to even think of why that tissue was there in the first place or where it might have landed before.

By the time we left our parking spot, Buck had promised that he would find a way to get the money, and by the next week, I had an appointment in Wichita, far enough away that I wouldn't run into anyone I knew. He drove me to the clinic but refused to come in the door with me. I didn't mind that, though. It was enough that he had found a way to get the job done, and I hadn't had to contribute one red dime of my own money. After that, we limped through the remaining months of our relationship. Everyone still considered us to be a couple, and Buck still told me he loved me. I probably didn't say it back to him too often. I think I still did love him a little bit--he had come through for me, after all--but what I felt more was an overwhelming sense of relief. We still had sex, a lot of sex, parked in his truck in the woods, but I had learned my lesson. I put on his condoms, a skill that came in very handy over the years. On the night of graduation, I gave Buck a final kiss and left the gym and the town. I did not say goodbye, and I did not leave a forwarding address.

No, to answer your question, I did not feel any remorse about that first abortion, not then, not ever. I guess you could say that it paved the way for the others that followed, not that I dwell on that type of thing.

They say that you never forget your first love, and I suppose it's true in a way. I hadn't thought about Buck in years before the day he showed up in the front of the house in that ratty old camper of his, but I sure knew who he was the moment he opened that door, despite his aged appearance. But if the person who invented that corny saying meant that there was always a spark of tenderness remaining for your first love, then he or she is dead wrong. For me to have to set eyes on his once beautiful, wretched face made me want to hurl. I suppose, if you're being kind, you could also say that it was sad that it had come to this kind of situation. During my long nights alone eating Louisa's dinners-for-one in front of *Wheel of Fortune*, I had concluded that the man had never gotten over me. I think that was the root of the problem, not the fact that he was broke, not the fact that he had squandered his life by marrying that crown-stealing bitch Mary Wilson, and not the fact that contrary to him, I had done so well for myself. In a nutshell, Buck's unrequited love for me had led to his ruination.

But it wasn't going to lead to mine. I was supposed to meet Buck again at Ernie's. An entire month had gone by, and I hadn't figured out a way to get rid of him. I thought about hiring a private investigator, but I couldn't see the sense in that. What did I care about where Buck Boyd went or what he did while he waited for his next blackmail delivery? And it didn't do any good if I had the PI steal that packet of documents because Buck had other files on his computer and maybe even in a safe deposit box somewhere. And believe me, I had thought about not showing up or going to the cops, in spite of his warnings. But I had a gut feeling that he was going to follow through on his threats to expose some unsavory events to Richard that I wanted to remain buried in the past.

So I decided that I would pay him one more installment. It would bring the total up to $200,000, but in the grand scheme of things, that kind of money was pocket change to Richard and me. I know it does sound like a lot of money to some people, but I had always been under the impression that Richard and I were swimming in cash. I am not being a snob when I say that. I mean, look, we bought anything we wanted, anytime we wanted, and I always assumed that it would continue in that way. How was I to know that things would soon change dramatically for the worse? I was in the dark as much as everyone else about Richard's financial dealings. It's true; I've testified to that fact.

The dreaded day arrived when the second drop off was due, and I still hadn't heard a word from Richard. I still wasn't worried. Like I've said before, Richard had only been gone for a month, and he had gone to Costa Rica for much longer than that. Richard would come home when he was ready to come home, and I would be waiting with open arms. If Felicity was corresponding to her father, she certainly didn't tell me, nor had she ever confronted me about overhearing Buck's and my conversation in the kitchen a month before. I decided I was in the clear about that. If Felicity had something on a person and could use it to her advantage, she would.

I didn't fault her for that. It's human nature, isn't it? I'd done that kind of thing many times myself before I decided I would change my ways and become a good person--that is, when I married Richard.

This time when I went up to the safe in Richard's study after Felicity was off to school and Louisa was elsewhere in the house, I didn't feel like I had to be especially secretive about it. And this time, I didn't just reach in and grab. But again, I was startled by how little remained in the safe. Maybe I had been secretly hoping that the money would somehow reproduce and multiply in the month that had passed--haha!--but of course it hadn't. By the time I had counted out the money, one stack remained, and the sight of that small lonely pile made me feel decidedly uneasy. What had happened to all the rest of the bills and the coins? I guess I had never realized before that I always thought of the contents of that safe as a kind of safety net. I knew we must have loads of cash in the bank and various brokerage firms, but it was probably my small-town upbringing that made me think like that, the cash under the mattress kind of mentality. Yet it wasn't hard to convince myself that everything was still all right. We had an accountant that paid our monthly bills and credit card payments, so except for stupid Buck Boyd, why did I need cash?

I had learned my lesson and dressed for this second meeting in loose black trousers and a cashmere turtleneck sweater. Buck was sitting in the same table in the corner of Ernie's, and I noticed right away that he looked much better than he had the previous month. I knew it was due to my money that his appearance had improved. He had a better haircut, nicer jeans, and a Nike long sleeve activewear shirt on. In that dark place, I could see a glimmer of the handsome guy he used to be. It's funny, yet true, how a person with money can vastly improve his or her looks. It's also funny how Buck's improved appearance made me suddenly less nervous.

He smiled at me. "So, we meet again." And then he stood up and pulled out a chair for me.

I know. It was silly of me to think he was behaving like a gentleman. The man was blackmailing me, after all, but I think I might have smiled back. I wasn't flirting. It was just my natural instinct to smile back at someone who was smiling at me. "This is the last time I'm giving you money." I wanted to make that clear from the start.

"You will always be a fine looking woman, Cindy Lou."

You see, he was the one who was flirting with me! It also didn't help matters that I was starving for compliments. "You're looking better too." I only meant it as a statement of fact.

"Cutting back on the booze helps." He smiled again, and I was pretty sure he had gotten his teeth whitened with my money. However, it was a nice improvement, and it was only then that I noticed that he didn't have a drink in front of him. Maybe he had joined AA?

This conversation was going so much better than the last one that I let myself relax a little, which is always a mistake. "You used to be a decent guy," I said.

"I still have my moments." Then he leaned toward me. "Maybe you should give me a try, leave your old man, and I do mean *old*, and run away with me. I always knew how to treat you right, Cindy Lou."

That was true. Buck might have been my first lover, but he had remained one of the best. It's rare, I know. "Richard is very good to me," I said lightly.

He leaned back in his chair. "Then where is he?"

All of my senses shifted back into high alert. Had Buck been following me, spying on my house, tracking my comings and goings? I could not trust this man, and I was not going to bring Richard into the conversation. "Why are you doing this to me? We used to be friends."

"That's not what I would call it." So I'd been right. Buck was still in love with me and wanted to hurt me for leaving him. "Are you trying to tell me that you're still in love with me? Is that what all this is about?"

He laughed. The man actually had the audacity to *laugh* at me. "Some things will never change, Cindy Lou. You are still so full of yourself."

I bristled, but I didn't rise to the bait. I knew I was right about this. "What kind of man blackmails a woman he's still in love with?"

"What kind of woman marries a man she doesn't love?" he shot back. "Oh, that's right. She marries him for his *money*."

"I did not marry Richard for his money," I said, with as much dignity as I could muster. Buck wasn't playing fair; he was hitting too close to home. And it felt like the sticky floor beneath my chair was starting to tilt.

"Oh, come on, Cindy Lou. You can't fool me. You and I go way, way back. I know what kind of person you are."

The stupid man did not know one damn thing about me. He did not know what kind of person I had become over the last two decades. I mean, during my reign as Mrs. Arizona, I had made countless appearances at charity events and hospitals and even at a soup kitchen, which had not been a pleasant experience. But I had smiled despite the odor and the sloppily dressed people, I had played my part, and that had to count for something, didn't it?

"In fact," Buck went on in a musing tone, "you and I are very much alike, Cindy Lou."

I couldn't let that one go. "You and I are nothing alike."

Buck ignored me. "We've both always wanted more, more than we were given in life, maybe even more than we deserved. Nevertheless, wanting more has been the key for us."

I wasn't going to listen to his insane ranting anymore. I reached into my purse and grabbed the envelope with the money. I dropped it on the table as if it burned my fingers. "This is the last money you are going to get from me. And I am never going to set foot in this horrible place again."

"Shh." He put his finger over his mouth in the shushing gesture. "You're going to hurt Ernie's feelings. He's standing right behind the bar."

"Did you hear me?" I hissed. "This. Is. It."

"While we're on the subject of wanting more," Buck continued in that annoying musing tone, again ignoring me, "I've been thinking. You spend a shitload of money in the course of a day, Cindy Lou, what with your yoga and Pilates, your personal grooming and maintenance, your various shopping excursions. A shitload of money. When I walked into Cristof's and found out how much he charged for a haircut, I thought it was highway robbery. But I do have to admit that this is the best haircut I've ever had." He pointed to his hair.

I stared at him, my mouth hanging open. So not only had he been following me, but he'd gone into my salon and gotten a haircut from my stylist! That was bad enough, but now I had to agonize over what, if anything, he had said to Cristof, who was a notorious gossip. I just couldn't take it all in right now. I pushed back my chair.

Buck, damn him, looked like he was highly enjoying himself. "In light of my rumination, Cindy Lou, I have come to the conclusion that half a million bucks isn't even a stretch for you, is it? Really, there's no point to that paltry amount. Why don't we make it a cool million that you owe me for keeping your secrets safe? I think that sounds fair, don't you?"

I stood up. "I am not going to dignify that with a response."

"No need to. And don't worry. You never have to come into this horrible place again. I'll come to you." Then Buck winked at me.

I sat in the parking lot for a long time, shaking uncontrollably, too distraught to drive or pick up my phone and call an Uber. I had to think. The rules had changed in this insane, dangerous game that he had forced me into playing. The man did not only want to ruin my marriage, but he also wanted to ruin my entire life, ruin *me*. It no longer mattered what his motivation was. What mattered was that he had the ammunition to shoot me down and bury me. And he wasn't going to stop until he had accomplished that macabre goal. So there was only one thing left for me to do. Before this encounter, I had thought that getting rid of Buck would only entail getting him out of town--the out of sight, out of mind type of thing.

Now I knew that I was going to have to kill him.

The only thing that kept me going, the only thing that kept me from collapsing into complete despair or going out and buying a gun and tracking down Buck and shooting him like a dog in his ratty camper, was that I had the Christmas wine club party to plan and organize. Keeping track of the RSVPs, ordering the red and white roses from Cactus Flower, and planning the menu with Louisa kept me busy enough that I could stop my mind from dwelling on everything that was going wrong in my life. And it was a long list if I stopped long enough to let the mystery and misery of it all sink in: missing husband, dwindling cash supplies, utter and abject loneliness. Oh, and a daughter who I rarely spoke to or saw. But you see, that wasn't unusual at all, as strange as that sounds now. As I have explained, I was exactly like that as a teenager. Plus, once a teenager gets her license, it was natural that she was AWOL most of the time, or so I thought.

I know I have been accused of being a bad parent, but that wasn't the case at all. I think it would be more accurate to say that I was an *ambivalent* parent. At first, I had been happy that I gave birth to a girl. Richard already had two sons from his first and second marriages, so I had presented him with something completely new and different. I had given him a great gift, you see, and it never occurred to me that a daughter would become my rival for my husband's attention. But believe me, I found that out soon enough. Right from the start, Felicity had Richard wrapped around her tiny pink finger. All she had to do was utter a sound, and he would come running. Don't get me wrong. For a long time, there was room for the two of us in Richard's life, but as the years slowly passed and Felicity grew into her beauty, I found myself fading. Or at least that's what it had felt like. If there had been a photograph of the three of us hanging on the wall, my image would have gradually faded to sepia and then disappeared altogether. Maybe I had always instinctively known that would happen. Maybe that's why I aborted the others, to keep myself from disappearing.

I had my reasons for inviting Audrey over for the first time the day before the Christmas party. For one thing, she was nicer than Reggie back then. And for another, I had heard rumors that her husband had been sent to rehab because he had been arrested for a DUI. I don't judge people on that sort of thing. The ones who get caught are the unlucky ones because who doesn't drink and drive on occasion? Like it or not, it's true.

Anyway, I thought that Audrey, with her husband gone, might be just as lonely as me, even though she had Reggie living right next door. It never occurred to me that she would bring that strange little boy of hers. That kid gave me the creeps. It was the way he looked at you without really looking at you, kind of like he could see right through you. I got the impression that he might be one of those idiot savants, but it didn't matter because he stayed out of the way and didn't mess up the perfect placement of my ornaments too badly.

The most important reason I invited Audrey over was that I wanted her to see what I had created. Throwing the most exquisite parties had always been one of my fortes, back in the days before Richard retired and decided to become a hermit. I was something of a legend in our circle of friends. I once threw a Valentine's Party complete with a gushing Swiss chocolate fountain, Cristal champagne, and four dwarfs, dressed only in diapers, hired to play cupids, who went around shooting the guests with arrows made of spun sugar. If an arrow landed on you, you had to kiss the nearest person of the opposite gender. People loved it! Everywhere you looked, people were kissing, which made for a room full of happy people. I did hear later that some of the wives huffily suggested that I spent way too much time kissing their husbands. So what? It was my party, and kissing all those men made me feel more attractive, more desired than I had in a very long time. Richard? I don't think he even noticed all the kissing and making out. That was Richard for you.

I was almost nervous when Audrey walked into the room, but her reaction was exactly what I was hoping for. She looked like she was in awe, which was the effect I was working toward, and her compliments gave me the confidence I needed. The other thing that I needed and was hoping for was to make her my friend. I will admit this: I was jealous of her and Reggie's friendship. Have I said that before? During my lonely nights in front of the TV, I had concluded that I needed that kind of relationship. If I didn't have male companionship, I would actively seek out female companionship, and no, I do not mean that sexually. Amazingly, and despite my Vegas experiences, I have never tilted in that direction. However, Audrey and Reggie, new entrees into my social sphere, were a perfect example of what I was looking for. I was naive enough about that kind of friendship not to know that a circle of three cannot coexist equally and peacefully. Unless you're the Three Musketeers, I suppose, but I'm talking about women here. We are altogether a different species.

So I was ready for that Christmas party and more excited than I can tell you. At the last minute, I decided to wear the scarlet Oscar de la Renta dress that I had worn when I was crowned Mrs. Arizona. I hadn't worn it since the fiasco at the national pageant, but this was a festive occasion, and I was feeling festive. I did forgo the crown, which I still have--all the formers get to keep the crown as a reminder of the glory days of their reigns--thinking that it might have been overkill. The dress itself might have been overkill. I realized that when I saw the look that Audrey and Reggie exchanged when they arrived early to tote in crate after crate of *Château Éclatant*.

"That's some dress," Reggie said, not bothering to hide the sneer in her voice. She had on skin-tight black leggings and a white sweater. Reggie wasn't a stylish person, so it was no surprise.

"It's beautiful." Audrey had on a green shirtwaist dress that matched her eyes. Green was definitely her color. I was beaming at the compliment when she said, "I hope you don't get wine spilled on it." She looked to Reggie for approval.

So that was how it was going to play out with these two. Audrey had been perfectly nice to me, even friendly when we chatted over wine the day before, but with Reggie around, she was going to play it cool. If I wanted to be friends with her, I was somehow going to have to win over Reggie too. They were a pair, and I couldn't have one without the other.

But I knew Reggie was going to be problematic. Well, I'd faced tough challenges before, and if I could figure out a way to deal with Buck Boyd, I could certainly figure out a way to deal with Reggie Carson.

"Let me help you with those crates," I said to Reggie, who was lifting another crate off a dolly.

"You don't want to mess up that dress--or God forbid--your manicure."

I ignored her snotty tone and took the crate from her and set it on the counter, then reached for another. "Should I start to open these? Just tell me what you want me to do." A splinter lodged itself in my right thumb, but I didn't utter a peep.

"It's our job to set up. I mean, you went to all this trouble to decorate for the party, and Cynthia," Reggie seemed reluctant to say the next words, "it really is beautiful."

"Oh, it was my pleasure. And it's Christmas. Who doesn't expect a Christmas party to be fabulous?" I said brightly.

Reggie didn't seem to know what to do with her hands as she gazed around the room, taking it in for the first time because they'd come in the back door, through the garage, as I'd told them to do. They fluttered around her face, over the crates of wine, over the waiting crystal glasses, before settling on the counter, and I could see that they were shaking. I looked to her face and saw the worried expression in her eyes, then over to Audrey, who had a deep crease in the middle of her forehead. That's when I realized that these two women were nervous, and extremely so. Here I'd been the one thinking that I had to impress them, and they were thinking that they had to impress me. That broke the ice for me right there and then. This was my party, and I was the one in control.

"We have an hour before the guests arrive. Why don't I open a bottle of wine? We can have a glass while we get everything ready." Without waiting for them to respond, I went to the wine cooler and pulled out something that Richard had ordered from Bordeaux years before during our trip to France and had been saving for a special occasion. Well, Richard wasn't here, was he? So out of spite, or maybe out of a need to impress these two women who were bringing over their French wine, I had brought it up from the wine cellar earlier today. It was the first time I'd been down there in months because the wine cellar, just like Richard's office, was off-limits to me when Richard was around. Not that he'd ever specifically said that, but I knew that I wasn't supposed to meddle in Richard's financial affairs or his prized collection of wine. I didn't let myself dwell on the dismal fact that most of the racks in the cellar, racks that used to hold bottles and bottles of expensive wine, were now empty. Had Richard been secretly drinking the wine up in his study for the past five years? I knew it wasn't me.

"You don't have to open that expensive wine on our account," Audrey said hurriedly, nervously glancing at Reggie.

"That's right, Cynthia. We can open a bottle of ours. It's on the house." She laughed, but it sounded forced.

"Nonsense." I was already opening the wine. "Let's get this party started right, shall we?" I poured three glasses and handed one to each of them. I lifted mine. "A toast. To the best wine club party ever!"

"To the best wine club party ever," they echoed quietly.

I barely tasted the wine, which was something Richard used to accuse me of back when he was trying to educate me. "You have to savor the wine on your tongue, Cynthia," he would say reprovingly. "You don't guzzle fine wine." Well, again, Richard wasn't here, was he? All I wanted was to see the impressed look on Reggie's and Audrey's faces, and there it was. That was rewarding enough. "It's delicious, isn't it?"

Reggie looked at the bottle. "It's a very good vintage."

I beamed at them. "My Richard is a wine connoisseur. We have bottles and bottles like this down in the wine cellar." I don't know why I said that when I had just seen proof that most of the wine was gone. I guess I was still trying to impress my potential friends.

"Is your husband going to be at the party?" Audrey's voice was whispery, as if she couldn't quite catch her breath.

"Of course not! Isn't this a wine club exclusively for women?

"Right." Reggie was also drinking her wine fast. "Women only."

"That's what makes it so special, isn't it?" I gave them a conspiratorial wink.

"Right," Reggie said again, draining her glass. "Let's get things set up."

I worked right alongside them as we placed the different varietals--as they kept calling them--on separate tables. The winery they were getting their wine from was called Château Éclatant, and they were showcasing these varietals: Savennières, Pouilly-Fumé, Sancerre, Vouvray, and Chinon. Reggie explained to me that all but the Chinon were whites because the Loire Valley specialized in whites. I wasn't really paying attention to her. I was planning how I was going to help these gals sell every single bottle they had brought over. I was going to prove to them how invaluable I could be to their wine club so that they would know that I had to come to the next party, and the next, and the next. Maybe that glass of Bordeaux had gone straight to my head because I was practically giddy with excitement.

By the time the first guests arrived, I was ready. The doorbell rang, and I took one last look around the room. It was perfect. "Here we go!" I said gaily.

Audrey and Reggie looked at each other and took a deep breath. "It's showtime."

I thought that phrase was entirely appropriate. "Yes, indeed. It's showtime!"

The women arrived in rapid succession, right on time. Now I had known most of these women for years. Many of them were former Mrs. Arizona winners--we had lunch together once a month--and others were women I had met at various social functions over the years. Like I've said before, these women and I called each other friends, but we weren't what you would call close. I guess you could say we were convenient associates. Or maybe we just tolerated each other because we had nothing better to do. Whatever, the point that evening was that they all had money. Audrey and Reggie had made no bones about the fact that their wine club was *for profit*. And no, I didn't think that was tacky at all. I have always admired the entrepreneurial spirit.

I had asked Louisa to stay late that night to pass the tray of appetizers--the lemon parsley gougères, the duck pâté, the escargot on crostini, the mini ham and cheese croque monsieur puff pastry tarts, and assorted puff pastry hors d'œuvre cups--and she had enlisted the help of her nieces, Lupe and Maria. They had flatly refused to wear the Mrs. Santa costumes, but let me buy them matching red, green, and gold sheath dresses, so they felt compensated. Consequently, they were doing a good job passing food and refilling glasses. Reggie kept trying to explain the grapes for each varietal as she went from table to table, and Audrey was ready to make the receipts for the purchases, but so far, the women weren't buying much. I can't say I blamed them. I tried all the wines, but nothing grabbed me. Maybe the Bordeaux I opened earlier had ruined my palate for the evening--that's what Richard would have said--but the Éclatant wine tasted ordinary. As I walked around from group to group, I overheard conversations that agreed with my opinion.

I was going to have to do something to remedy the situation, judging from the looks of desperation that were growing on Audrey's and Reggie's faces. These women of a certain social class were used to going to charity auctions where they spent hundreds or thousands of dollars on items they didn't need, all in the name of charity. If they thought that part of this money was going to charity, it might change things. I walked to the center of the room and tapped on my glass with a spoon to get everyone's attention. "Ladies, did we not mention that ten percent of the proceeds made here tonight will go to charity?"

"That seems like a rather large omission on your part, Cynthia." It was Maeve Olson, the type of person who was dissatisfied with everything and couldn't wait to complain about it. I tell you, there's one of them in every crowd. However, she had loads of money, so she got invited to everything.

I smiled sweetly at her. "We all know it's the season of giving, Maeve."

"What charity?" someone asked, reasonably enough.

I looked to Reggie. "UNICEF," she said.

Meanwhile, a quick glance at Audrey told me she was horrified.

"Why didn't you say so?" Maeve said snootily. "In that case, I'll take twelve bottles."

"I prefer red wine," someone said, "and I'm not fond of this one."

"Next month we're going to be presenting the Elite Wines of Burgundy. Pierre, my cousin who owns Château Éclatant, is also a distributor. He knows someone at all the wineries in France."

I would later know that it was only quick thinking on Reggie's part, but on that night, I believed her, just like everyone else in the room. "Something to look forward to, isn't it, ladies? Meanwhile, we have cases of wine to buy tonight to help the starving children of the world."

The orders flowed after that. By the time everyone left, and it was well after midnight--always a sign of a good party in my book--Audrey and Reggie had sold all the remaining wine for well over one hundred dollars a bottle. I was happy for them and proud of myself. Surely, I thought, they would realize that they couldn't have been so successful if it wasn't for my help. "I'd say that was a successful night, wouldn't you?" I'd had quite a bit of wine by that point. I was drinking something white. It didn't matter what. They all tasted the same.

"It was, Cynthia. Thanks for your help. I guess I need to contact UNICEF now. We need to give them ten percent of the proceeds, but do you think that would be before or after we take out the operating costs?" The worried look was back on Audrey's tired face.

"We're not giving any of the money to charity," Reggie said. She'd started to gather the empty bottles and glasses and napkins.

"Leave that, Reggie. Louisa will take care of it in the morning."

"Oh, we can't have that poor woman cleaning up our mess. And Reggie, we are giving ten percent to charity," Audrey said adamantly.

"Those women will never know the difference," Reggie argued. "I am not callous here, Audrey. We are currently two single mothers who--" She stopped, remembering I was still there.

My ears certainly picked up on that juicy tidbit. I'd known about Audrey's husband, but what was going on with Reggie's? It would seem that we all had something in common, after all. "I don't think you need to give the money to charity, Audrey. These women all have more money than they know what to do with, and they paid for a good product, French wine. No harm done."

A strange look passed across Audrey's face, but Reggie jumped in. "Thanks, Cynthia. You were great tonight." She seemed to be really looking at me for the first time. "I mean it."

"I'll be happy to host the next wine party." A look passed between us.

"You're on," she said.

Mission accomplished. That's what I felt when I finally persuaded Reggie and Audrey to leave the mess for Louisa, and they were walking toward the back door. I had certainly helped them tonight, and surely, that counted for something on the ladder toward friendship. "I'll be talking to you soon," I said.

They were opening the back door when Audrey said in a voice that was barely above a whisper, "I can't believe we got away with it."

That's when things started to click together for me. I remembered the Two-Buck Chuck I had seen in Reggie's cart in Trader Joe's, and Audrey had mentioned operating costs. That was strange. There wouldn't be any operating costs, other than the cost of shipping, if they were getting the wine from France. Those two women were definitely up to something.

Audrey and Reggie didn't know that December night just how good my hearing was, but very soon, they would.

JANUARY

13

REGGIE

Christmas passed, and it was a dismal one with only the three of us, Caleb, Hayley, and me, gathered around the Christmas tree, and then gathered around the dinner table eating the ham I had cooked until it was as dry as sawdust. I know it's pretty damn hard to ruin a ham when all you have to do is stick it in the oven, but as I've mentioned before, I'm not much of a cook, primarily because I have no interest in it whatsoever. With the money we made from the last wine club party at Cynthia's, I was able to get each of the kids brand new Chromebooks, but even that didn't lighten the mood during the course of that long day.

New Year's Eve and Day were not any better, and it was the first time in my life that I spent that holiday totally, dismally alone. Caleb had gone back to school right after Christmas, saying he had to study, which was such a blatant lie--he was between semesters--that I didn't even try to dispute it. And Hayley went to a sleepover at another Tigerette's house. Thankfully it wasn't Felicity's house, but the fact remained that I still didn't have anyone beside me to watch the ball drop in Times Square on *Ryan Seacrest's New Year's Rockin' Eve* show. And at this point, I would like to state for the record that I still miss Dick Clark. New Year's Eve is not the same without watching Dick Clark and wondering if he used Botox to maintain that timeless face.

What made the holidays even worse--or perhaps it was the primary cause--was the fact that Audrey was still not speaking to me. We hadn't talked much on the drive home from Cynthia's after the December party because we were both so wiped out. Let me tell you, we had been tense enough when we carted our fake wine into that massive house of hers, but when I saw that she had decorated the place to look like something out of a

Hallmark Christmas movie that could have been called *Once Upon a Holiday*, my nervousness grew. Gee whiz, there should have been little fairies floating around spreading magic fairy dust and granting wishes. Audrey and I were in way over our heads. Who were we kidding? We couldn't pull off what we were about to do. And then when Cynthia pulled out that bottle of fancy French wine, I thought we were goners for sure. She was going to see right through our little scam as soon as we opened the first bottle of our Franzia wine and then announce that we were frauds in front of her expensively dressed, toned taut-faced crowd.

But surprise, surprise. It didn't turn out that way at all. Cynthia made some offhand, laughing remark that she couldn't tell a good French wine from a bottle of Two-Buck Chuck, and then she pitched right in and helped in that too fancy, over-the-top dress of hers. Of course my senses went on high alert when she mentioned Two-Buck Chuck, and my first thought--fear, actually--was that she was alluding to the time she had seen me in Trader Joe's with all those bottles in my cart when Audrey and I were getting ready for our inaugural wine club party. But the way she was acting, chatting excitedly and telling us how happy she was that we were letting her host the wine club at her house, made me think that she didn't have some ulterior motive. I wasn't sure, though. I was having a hard time getting a decent read on her. And why would I? I've never been able to read a person who is as fluid and shape-shifting as a snake. You can bet that it was part of the problem from the get-go.

I went over to Audrey's house bright and early the morning after the party at Cynthia's. Notice I didn't say Cynthia's party. It wasn't Cynthia's party. It was *ours*, mine and Audrey's. All the wine club parties were supposed to be ours. Let me be clear on that point. Anyway, I showed up excited, ready to count our loot, and what did I find? Audrey still in her bathrobe with red-rimmed eyes, looking as if she had been up all night crying. Again. I swear, that woman could cry at the drop of a hat back then. I didn't want to console her yet again about whatever had gotten her so upset, so I did what I do best in that kind of situation. I ignored the obvious.

I went directly to her coffee pot and poured a cup, and then said excitedly, "So, what's the good news, friend?"

"We walked out of there with $18,000."

I almost dropped my cup. I thought we had made a good haul, but I hadn't been sure with all the commotion and that damn Christmas music that was playing full blast, nonstop. Just for the record: If I ever hear "Holly, Jolly Christmas" again, someone can feel free to shoot me.

But back to that morning. You see, it was Audrey's job to collect the money. She had the easy part. I was doing all the real work, describing the varietals and the grapes and region they came from, trying to hawk our wares. I figured collecting the money was the least she could do, and it was the fun part, at that. "Holy shit! I knew we made a lot, but I wasn't expecting that much. That's fantastic."

"I said we *walked out* with $18,000. I didn't say we *made* it."

I knew where this was going because I knew Audrey, who always pretended to take the high road. It could be very annoying. "Audrey, we are not obliged to give ten percent to UNICEF. Those women only needed an *excuse* to spend their money." She continued to stare sullenly at me. "And it was Cynthia's idea," I added.

"You went along with it. You were the one who jumped right in and provided UNICEF as the name of the charity. You could have said that our wine club was for profit. We talked about giving part of the money to a good cause back in the beginning, but decided we were the charity. Remember?"

"We'd thought it was funny at the time." It wasn't much of a defense, I know.

"I'm not laughing now."

"Since it was Cynthia's bright idea, maybe we should call her up and tell her that she owes UNICEF $1800. How about that, Audrey?" To tell you the truth, I rather hated throwing Cynthia under the bus like that in that one particular instance. I thought the charity angle had been a brilliant idea. It had saved the party for Audrey and me. Otherwise, we would have ended up just like we had at our first party, with a bunch of women drunk on cheap wine and no money in our pockets.

"Don't you want to do the right thing, Reggie?"

"That's laughable, Audrey." But I wasn't laughing. "We're committing fraud, and you want to do the right thing? Go ahead, then. But I'd like my half right now."

Audrey reached into the pocket of her robe and pulled out a wad of cash held together with a rubber band. She handed it to me. "I knew you'd say that." She turned her back on me. "You can see yourself out, Reggie. I'm sure you know the way through my back door."

It was now January 5, and I still hadn't heard a word from her. Fifteen days had gone by, the longest period with no communication in our fourteen years of friendship. We'd had little spats before--what friends don't?--but they'd never lasted more than a day or two. And since we lived next door to each other, I'd just assumed that we'd run into each other as we were carrying in groceries, or if our daughters needed rides, but that hadn't happened, which meant that Audrey was intentionally avoiding me. That hurt. Not only had we lost all that time planning our new wine club party for January, but we had missed out on the holidays. We could have spent them together. We should have spent them together. We were both going through rough patches in our marriages, we were both inventing a money-making venture to make ends meet, and we should have been there for each other. That, perhaps, is the thing I regret most of all.

I missed my friend. I suppose it can be said that we spent so much time together, especially since the inception of the wine club, that we took each other for granted. But in her absence, I realized how much I depended upon Audrey for friendship and support. For once, I was going to take the high road, or as Audrey would say, *do the right thing*, and go over and apologize. I should have known how much reneging on a fake pledge to a real charity would bother her, especially since there had been so many witnesses, tipsy or not. I'd been thinking, in my many hours alone, that I should have piped up with a fake charity like Women Who Lunch or Christians Who Carry Guns, or something closer to home like Tigerette Daughters or Unwanted Wives. But it was too late for that. I'd already spent my share of the take on Christmas gifts and Tigerette salon appointments and the mortgage payment and a few other bills, so I couldn't offer her my share of the pledge. But I could apologize.

I didn't slide open the back door like I usually did. I knocked--that's how contrite I was. Audrey spun around, her phone to her ear, and broke into a smile. My phone rang at that moment, and I looked down at the screen: Audrey. It was my turn to break into a smile. I slid the door open and walked in. "I'm sorry."

"I am too," she said. "I overreacted."

"Can we just forget the whole thing and get back to work?"

"I'm game if you are."

"And go back to being friends," I added. It's what I probably should have said first.

"We'll always be friends," she said.

Honestly, we really didn't know anything back then, did we?

There were several things that Audrey and I learned from the December wine club party. First of all, even though the wine drinkers there weren't as sophisticated as we had feared, they certainly thought they were. And that was the key right there. We had to appeal to their sense of vanity. They had not batted an eye at spending around $100 per bottle, so we needed to present wine that was even more expensive, more exclusive. Since I'd blabbed that my French cousin was not only a vintner/monk, but also some kind of distributor--it's funny how Pierre had changed in my mind from a bald, robed monk to a stocky, grizzled, beret-wearing Frenchman--we could abandon Château Éclatant, at least temporarily, and present wine from other regions.

"You also blabbed that we were doing the Elite Wines of Burgundy at the party," Audrey reminded me.

I'd forgotten all about that, but it seemed as good of a place to start as any, so we turned to the Burgundy section in *The Wine Bible*. As valuable as that was, the knowledgeable writers of that tome didn't feel it necessary to put in any pricing. So it was back to the internet. Audrey and I went round and round about this as we researched the various Domaines, the specialized wine-producing areas in Burgundy. I wanted to include white wine from seven Domaines, and seven reds from seven other Domaines, in other words, the fourteen recommended in the book.

Audrey balked. "Do you know how long it would take me to make all those labels? I don't know if you've noticed, Reggie, but I try to be an artist about this. And that's too many varietals. Even I wouldn't want to taste fourteen so-called different wines at one time."

I suppose she had a point there, but I guess it's just in my nature to argue. "How about ten Domaines, five white and five red?"

Audrey sighed. "I know you don't like to play favorites between reds and whites, and even though that book you're so fond of quoting mentions chardonnay from Burgundy, the fact is that people associate reds with that region. Besides, at the last party--and I think we can safely assume that at least some of the people from that party will be at the next--the women seemed to prefer the red to the white. The whites were tougher to sell, and I think some of the women bought them because they didn't want to look bad in front of their peers. I vote we go primarily with red.

Since she was in charge of the sales, she would know that kind of information, so I acquiesced on that point. We finally settled on four pinot noirs from Domaine Ponsot:

Morey-St. Denis Cuvée des Alouettes 1er Cru 2014, retail $163;

Clos de la Roche Vieilles Vignes 2002, retail $495;

Clos de la Roche Vieilles Domaine 2013, retail $3200;

and Clos de la Roche 2014, retail $649.

From Domaine Romanée Conti, we selected three burgundy reds:

Romanée St. Vivant 1972, retail $1100;

Richebourg 1966, retail $2100;

and the *pièce de résistance*, Romanée Conti 1959, with a retail of a whopping $12,950. To appease me, we threw in a white: Paul Pernot Bienvenues Batard Montrachet 2015, retail $248.

By tacit agreement, neither one of us mentioned how we were *really* upping the ante this time. We were making a giant leap from $100 per bottle to a bottle that, hopefully, someone would buy for almost $13,000. I think it is safe to say that what we were doing was taking a giant leap of *faith*. I suppose we should have given a passing nod to a feeling of guilt; we were planning on duping potential buyers big-time now. But we didn't.

Audrey was taking picture after picture of each of our eight selected bottles with her phone to record every detail of those labels. When she finished, she wearily put it down. "Do you think we should knock some off on the price, not a lot, but just a little? People love to think they're getting a bargain. Before, they were supposedly getting wine that no one had ever heard of, but you can buy these bottles online. That's where we found them, after all."

"I love how your mind is working today, Audrey Maynard." And it was a wonder I hadn't thought of that myself. Sometimes Audrey could come through in a situation.

"Yeah, I'm starting to scare myself." She laughed. We had drunk so much coffee that her nail-bitten fingers were twitching with caffeine.

We devised a price list--we were going to offer every bottle at a ten percent discount--and then it was time to consider what kind of wine we were actually going to put into those fancy French bottles from Domaines in Burgundy. We went back to the list we had made when we researched the mid-to-lower shelved wines in the grocery store. I tell you, we were always researching, researching, researching before every wine party, and it was tiring and time-consuming work. I can't emphasize that point enough. Audrey and I worked *hard*. We were always trying to keep our profit margin as high as we could while trying to make our fake product as authentic as possible. I honestly don't know how professional criminals do it. It is downright exhausting trying to keep one step ahead of the people you're trying to dupe.

We finally decided that we would use Louis Jadot, Ravenswood, Barefoot, Liberty School, Castle Rock, and Mondavi as our "filler" wines, choosing the exact brands when we found out what was on sale. They were all considered to be good wines under fifteen dollars. It seemed essential that we put a different wine into all eight of the varietals this time. The last party had proven that we had come dangerously close to blowing our cover by trying to pass off the same wine as a different varietal simply because we had packaged it differently.

Audrey tossed her pen onto the table, the familiar worried look creasing her features. "This is going to cost us a fortune to get ready for this party."

"We can put everything on credit cards. When the bill becomes due, we'll have the money from the party to pay for it." At least I hoped this was true. I'd been adding up the cost too, buying the wine, the bottles, the corks, the shrinking wrap, and the labels. I felt a little queasy.

"I can't even do that, Reggie." Audrey ran her fingers through her hair. "I'm all tapped out."

"What do you mean?" But I knew what she meant. I think I was stalling for time.

Audrey shook her head and looked like she was going to start the goddamn waterworks all over again. Shit. I was so sick of watching her cry. I quickly made a suggestion. "Do you think it would be feasible for us to take out a small business loan?"

At least that got a small smile out of her.

I knew I would later regret what I was going to do next. Everyone knows that you don't loan money to friends or family, right? For some reason, it never works out. But we had to keep the wine club going. We had to.

That was what motivated me, and I reasoned it this way. If I offered to put the operating costs on my credit card this one time, and she paid me back out of her profits, it wasn't really a loan, right? So I said: "I can get the preliminary costs this time. You can pay me back out of your share of the profits, okay?"

Audrey looked relieved. "Are you sure you don't mind? I promise I'll pay you back."

I shrugged like it was nothing at all, but I was starting to feel queasy again. "Sure."

"And we need to consider something else. What are we going to do with all those wine bottles? If we buy two hundred empty and two hundred filled, that's going to be four hundred bottles. Do you know how much room that will take up?"

I was starting to get a little tired of Audrey's negativity. Couldn't she look on the positive side for once? "We'll cross that bridge when we come to it," I said impatiently. "Just leave all the heavy lifting to me while you sit and design the labels."

"What's that supposed to mean?" Audrey bristled.

I didn't want to start another fight, but Audrey seemed to think that her part of the operation was so arduous and time-consuming when all she had to do was sit at her kitchen table. I was the one who was doing all the physical labor, I was the one who was breaking a sweat, and I was the one who now had to make this next wine party a reality. So I swallowed what I was about to say and pushed back my chair.

Audrey frowned. "Where are you going?"

"I better get to work on the wine. I think I'll try Costco first. Maybe they'll have a deal on something there, and I won't have to go to thirty grocery stores. It might save some time."

I have always had a love/hate relationship with Costco, and I don't think I'm alone on this. The one that I went to in Scottsdale not only had all the usual bulk items, the coffee and the canned goods and the paper towels and toilet paper, but it was also filled with all sorts of tempting delights that you hadn't thought you needed until you got there: the jewelry, the clothes, the electronics, the furniture, the gadgets, the sporting equipment. I once walked into that store and bought a super-duper propane heater and a wrench set and a boxed set of Doris Day movies and a bicycle built for two. The only thing I'd ever actually used was the propane heater, but it was like something came over me in that store, and there were things that I simply had to have. It was like I was under a spell, but when I got home with my purchases and my empty wallet, I felt such remorse. Maybe it was shame. I am not a splurger by nature, but that store made me into one on that day. I almost wonder if they pump something into the air in that place to put people into a trance, something akin to the oxygen they pump into casinos. Don't laugh. It's entirely possible.

So I rarely went into the store after the time I made all the extravagant purchases, but it was a place where I could buy a large quantity of wine and not raise an eyebrow. So I parked my car in the always crowded parking lot, grabbed a massive cart, put on my blinders, and walked directly to the wine section in the back of the store, dodging the people who hovered like flies around the free food samples. I filled my cart with the Kenwood wines, the Costco brand, and a couple of others, and when I could buy something in a 1.5-liter container, I did. Audrey and I had been overthinking the brands of wine we were going to pass off as French. I'd just get the best deals I could and call it a day. I would be efficient, and the more wine I could buy here, the fewer stops I would have to make the next day. Audrey and I were already behind schedule, as usual. And it had to be up to me, as usual, to keep us on task and on track.

I felt like I deserved a reward after I had made my purchases and loaded all the wine into the back of my trusty old van. Seriously, there was so much wine in my car that the back end looked weighted down, like an old lady version of a low-rider. So I stopped in at a Starbucks on the way home, one that I had never frequented before. It had started to drizzle besides, and Scottsdale drivers are notoriously bad in the rain. I'm not exaggerating. Even in a light drizzle, cars slow down to a crawl, the drivers terrified of every little puddle. So I'd wait for the rush hour traffic to subside while I enjoyed my coffee. Also, sadly enough, there wasn't any reason for me to hurry home. No one would be waiting for me.

I had just settled myself into a small table in the corner, hanging my dripping hoodie on the back of the chair and pulling out my phone in the pretense of looking busy. Coffee shops are perhaps the one place that I feel comfortable in when I'm by myself. I would never go into a restaurant and get a table for one. It's not that I'm old-fashioned about it or anything like that, but I have always thought that people eating alone are sad. That might not be the case at all, but I didn't want to risk the chance that people would look at me and feel pity as I ate my salad and plate of spaghetti, as I felt like I was both conspicuous and invisible at the same time. I guess I feared that people would look at me and *know*, that they would instantly sense that I was a woman who had been dumped by her gay husband. That sounds silly--I get that--and I'm probably using avoidance as a tactic here, but my point is that a coffee shop is the one place where I was okay being alone. Consequently, as I sipped my latte and finally started to relax, I was completely unprepared for what happened next.

Kent walked in, and he wasn't alone. The man beside him was equally as tall as Kent and was so breathtakingly beautiful that he looked airbrushed. I'm not kidding. Despite the rain outside, his salt and pepper hair was perfectly groomed, and his spray-tanned skin made him look like he had just stepped out of a glossy *Vogue* ad for Calvin Klein jeans for men. I was so flabbergasted that I almost dropped my coffee right there and then. He was my competition? This was Reed, the man who had taken a wrecking ball to my marriage? Any lingering hope I may have had that my husband would return to me vanished in that instant. I could never compete with someone who looked like that, so model perfect that he might as well have been molded out of plastic. There was a palm plant next to my table, and I almost dropped to my knees and crawled behind it to hide my dripping hair and soggy sweatpants and faded Metallica t-shirt.

But I was too stunned even to do that. I was breathing in rapid, shallow gasps, and I knew I should run out of there as fast as I could, but I couldn't move. I couldn't take my eyes off of them. They were a striking couple, far more so than Kent and I had ever been, and the reality of seeing my husband with his lover felt like a slap in the face. This was *real*. It was something altogether different than hypothetically picturing my husband with another person. To actually witness Kent putting his hand on the small of Reed's back and then lean in for some comment Reed was saying turned into a physical ache that coursed throughout my body. Kent was never going to come back to me, and in a way, I couldn't blame him. Reed was gorgeous and didn't have the faint remains of stretch marks or the threat of a raging hormonal menopause on the horizon. Hell, if I didn't know Reed was gay, I would want to do him myself.

Then as I watched them order identical grande Americanos and blue-berry scones, as I watched them walk over to a table on the other side of the room, laughing about something that I couldn't hear--a joke I wasn't in on because the joke had always been on me--I started seething. The nerve of them! How dare they be happy when I had been so miserable for months. It wasn't fair that my husband traded me in for a newer, better, more attractive model. It no longer mattered to me that it was another man and not a woman. That wasn't the point. The point was that Kent and I had made *vows* to each other, in sickness and in health, for richer or poorer, till death do us part. I am not a religious person--that's probably obvious by now--but the injustice of it all made my blood start to boil.

I have been told that my temper is a wicked thing, and while I'm not denying it, I do have to say that I've always thought it came in pretty handy. When I'm mad, I think people ought to know. I suppose it goes back to my ex-marine Dad, who used to spout off at the drop of a hat. If you didn't finish your chores, you heard about it. If you didn't bring home a decent report card, you heard about it. Dad would yell, getting right in your face like that drill sergeant in *An Officer and a Gentleman*, and God forbid you backed down or even blinked. You stood there and took it. And he didn't cut me any slack because I was his only daughter. Ten minutes later, it was like it had never happened. He'd loudly expressed his displeasure, and it was time to move on. He'd loudly expressed his anger, and it was justified.

In that coffee shop, my anger was justified. Why was Kent even there in the first place when he was supposed to be cruising the Med with his sick lover? And by the way, Reed looked about as healthy as a man molded out of plastic could look. Why did Kent pick that particular coffee shop to flaunt his devotion to another in front of me? I had been there first, after all. He might have loved Reed before he even met me, he might have loved Reed even while he was married to me for two decades and fathered our two children, but I had walked into that Starbucks first, goddamnit! He had no right to be there.

I didn't mean to cause a scene; I only wanted Kent to know that I was pissed. I'd never held back when we were married, so why should it be any different now? If he'd been on a damn cruise ship like he was supposed to be, it would never have happened. So you see, it was his fault that I picked up my coffee and walked over to his table. During the course of a long marriage, spouses--or whatever we were at that time--can sense the other one coming. Kent did just that. I was halfway across the room when he looked up, the surprise turning to shock on his familiar face. Or maybe it was panic. Either way, the startled look should have been enough to satisfy me, but it wasn't. By that time, I was a spurned woman on a mission, and a spurned woman on a mission is dangerous indeed. I think we all know that by now.

The color drained from Kent's face. "What--"

"Aren't you going to introduce me?" I was shaking with rage by then.

Reed looked confused. "Who are you?"

"What, Kent? You've never shown your boyfriend a picture of me?"

"You're Reggie?"

The incredulity in Reed's voice stoked the fire on my anger. Did Mr. Beautiful think the stringy-haired woman standing beside their table was a vagrant or something? Did he think that I wasn't good enough for Kent? "You bet I am," I snapped. "I'm Kent's *wife.*"

"We're leaving," Kent said to Reed.

"I thought you already did." I think I was starting to yell at that point.

"You don't need to cause a scene, Reggie."

"I think this is the perfect place to cause a scene. You waltz in here with the man you're cheating on me with like you don't have a care in the world. What about your family? Do you remember us? We're the ones who live on Sheena in the rose-colored stucco house, by the way." Now I had everyone in the room's attention, including the barista, who had let the steamed milk overflow the cup on the latte she was filling. She let out a yelp.

"Let's take this outside, Reggie." Kent started to get up.

"But it's raining," Reed noted.

"God forbid you should get your hair wet, Reed. Or maybe you're worried the rain will ruin your spray tan. Which one is it?"

Reed dared to smile at that--damn it, even his white teeth were perfect--which just made me madder, if that was possible. I pushed Kent back in his seat. I swear, it wasn't as aggressive as everyone later said it was. But I did get right in his face like my dad used to do. "I thought you said he was sick!" A gasp went up from the room, which seemed to have grown more crowded as my tirade escalated. I guess everyone likes a good show.

Kent grabbed my wrist. "Stop it, Reggie," he hissed.

"You stop it!" I shouted. "Stop acting like the last twenty years of our life don't exist!" I wrenched my wrist from his grasp.

"You're not being fair, Reggie."

Oh, my God! The utter ridiculousness of that statement pushed me over the edge. In one swift motion, I removed the black plastic top from my latte and threw it in his face. "You fucker!" I screamed.

The rest of the exchange, if you want to call it that, is a blur. I yelled some more and called Kent every foul name I could think of. Looking back, I probably seemed like a raving madwoman. Well, I guess I was. But really, it was all Kent's fault. He was the one who walked into that coffee shop with his lover. He was the one who left me. When security escorted me out, they warned me that Kent might press charges for assault, but he never did. I suppose I have to give him some credit for that, but I give it grudgingly. Furthermore, I would like the record to reflect that the coffee was not that hot. It was not scalding, as has been reported.

I only wish that it had been.

By the time I got home, I had calmed down some, but I was still at a low simmer. When it came to my husband, I think I finally knew what I wanted. Oddly enough, it wasn't a divorce I was thinking about. It was revenge. I wanted to make Kent pay for all the unhappiness he had caused me. Maybe it would be enough if I became rich from the wine club. That would show him. He was a man who had worked for years in a middling job with no promotion and no real success. However, if I became successful in my own right, it would prove to everyone that I was the real powerhouse in our union. I was the woman who did not stand behind or beside her man, but the woman who stood in *front* of him. Take that, Tammy Wynette! I think it's safe to say that I was still one hot mess right then, but once the idea of revenge settles in your heart, it's like an intrepid, unwanted weed that keeps growing.

I needed a glass of wine, and I picked up my phone to call Audrey to come over and join me. I needed a friend, someone who would be my sounding board, someone to tell me that I hadn't made a spectacle of myself, even though I had. And on that night, I didn't want to be one of those women who drank alone. It would only add to my humiliation. But Audrey must have been watching for my car because just then she slid open my back patio door. One look at her face, and I knew it was not going to be my night to vent.

"You've got to see this." She pointed to her phone.

I had my own drama and was in no mood for another one, whatever it might be. "How about a glass of wine?" I poured two glasses without waiting for an answer.

Audrey took a big gulp of her chardonnay. "This is serious, Reggie. I don't know who posted this YouTube video, but it's appalling."

"People post all kinds of things on YouTube." There wasn't any place to sit down in my kitchen anymore--one of these days I was going to face the fact that I would never finish those cabinets and put everything back in--and the wine bottles that I had brought in from my car took up any additional space. So I walked out to the patio. Audrey followed and took her usual seat while I put on the propane heater from Costco and settled in mine.

"It's of the Tigerettes' last performance."

The dread had started to build even before I reluctantly took her phone. I stalled. "It can't be that bad. They're a bunch of high school girls."

"Just watch it." Audrey took another big gulp of wine. "It is that bad."

Watching that video was one of those rare moments in my life when I felt like time had stopped. I couldn't believe that this was the same innocent, yet sexy, pom squad that I had seen two months before. These girls were wearing outfits nothing short of bikinis as they twerked and grabbed their crotches. And then there were Marcy and Hayley, front and center, doing something that I could only describe as humping each other. The bile rose in my throat, and I chased it down with a swig of wine. I choked and couldn't catch my breath.

Audrey was pounding me on the back. "Do you need some water?"

I shook my head and threw her phone on the table like it was a hot chunk of coal. I would never want to watch that again. When I could catch my breath, I said, "We should have been going to the games."

"It's a school-sanctioned activity. It's not our responsibility to monitor those dances, right? Someone else should have been paying attention."

"But they're our daughters. How could we not have known?" I still felt like I was in a daze.

"We were so busy with the wine club that we've been negligent."

Audrey looked close to tears, and I swear that if she started bawling one more time, I was going to strangle her. Tears were useless. When was she going to realize that? We had to face the fact that we had been negligent during the past few months. We'd always trusted our daughters, but we'd allowed ourselves to overlook something that was glaringly apparent. "That damn Felicity is behind this."

"What about Cynthia? She's the one who's supposed to be coaching the team. She's the adult in this situation."

By the time that we had finished that bottle of wine and opened another, Audrey and I had concluded that it was indeed Cynthia Stewart's fault. We felt much better after we had finished the second bottle of wine and laid the blame squarely on someone else's shoulders.

14

CYNTHIA

My phone wouldn't stop ringing. In the old days, I welcomed that constant sound; it was proof of my high-in-demand popularity. It was proof that I was good at my job, and that my future, at least temporarily, was secure. But this wasn't like that at all this time. It was a few irate Tigerette mothers who wanted to know how something like this could happen, how I could have possibly condoned and supervised such a brazen show of exhibitionism. It wasn't all the mothers who called--Audrey and Reggie were not among them--but the few who did rang over and over, as if the sheer volume of calls would make me apologize or repent or whatever the hell it was they wanted me to do. I honestly had no idea. What was done was done, and in the larger scheme of things, it wasn't all that big of a deal. I actually hung up on the mother--and I'm not naming names here--who accused both Felicity and me of being tramps. Believe me, I know what a tramp looks like and how she acts, and that dance did not make the two of us, or any of the other eleven girls, tramps. It just goes to show how naive middle-class people can be. Also, I would like to make this observation: Not one single father called. What does that tell you?

Do you want to know the truth? At first, I had no idea what they were talking about. I had been to the game--I went to all the games because I was still pretending that I was coaching the girls--but I didn't watch the performance. During the last three or four games, perhaps it had been going on longer than that, I had been going into Mr. Rooney's office. It had started innocently enough, with cups of coffee and a bit of furtive fumbling, but on that particular night, Mr. Rooney had brought a thermos of gin and tonics, and well, things progressed further. Even though we were both married, I think we knew we were doing the deed for the thrill of the illicit more than anything else. I certainly wasn't attracted to him. Mr. Rooney--I insisted on calling him that because it added to the excitement for me--looked something like Jon Lovitz. And he wasn't a particularly good lover, but that didn't matter. We were in a room steps from the packed gymnasium, and I tell you, I got off on that.

So as it turned out, I didn't see the game, and neither did the principal. I didn't even go back to the practice room after the performance because I had accidentally knocked over the thermos of gin and tonics that we stupidly left on the desk, and stinky booze had gotten in my hair. I didn't want anyone seeing me look like that, incriminating evidence you might say, so I rushed out the side door before anyone could see me. It was a good thing too, or else I would have been accosted by those mothers immediately. As it turned out, I went home blissfully unaware of the so-called travesty that had just happened on the high school gym floor. Felicity, of course, when she came home sometime after midnight, didn't say a word.

I'd stayed up late that night drinking one of the last good bottles of French champagne that Richard still had in the wine cellar. I don't know why, but it had become something like a mission of mine to drink all those expensive wines before Richard returned home. I thought I was justified in doing so. I thought that it would serve him right to come home to that empty cellar after he'd left me alone for so long. He could always buy more from whomever he ordered it from in France, or I could restock it with wine from Audrey and Reggie, which would be a laugh. If their wine was fake, as I was starting to believe it was, then the joke would really be on him. Mind you, I wasn't planning on calling Audrey and Reggie out on it at that point. Sometimes a gal's gotta do what a gal's gotta do to make a buck. That's the way the world works.

So I drank that entire bottle of champagne while I tried to figure out a way to kill Buck Boyd. I spent almost an hour searching the house for the little black book from my Vegas days--the one with all my important numbers and contacts--before I remembered that I had burned it years before in a ceremonial bonfire in a trash can behind The Bellagio, right after I got Richard to say *I do*. I didn't think I'd ever need it again, or at least I hoped I would never need it again. I must have been slightly tipsy halfway through Richard's bottle of wine because I thought that was a pity.

I could have made some money off the names in that book. Never mind that it might not have been in my best interest. Talk about incriminating!

The phone calls immediately started the next morning. By the way, whoever said that you don't get a headache from good champagne is full of shit because I had to take two Advils and drink about a gallon of ginger ale before I could even function. Felicity had already left for school, so I was clueless as to what those women were talking about. But they all mentioned something about a YouTube video, so once I turned off the phone and got on the computer, I finally saw what had everyone so up in arms.

I will admit that it was a little *risqué*, but then again, aren't all good dance routines? I watched that video numerous times, and I didn't see any unmentionable body parts showing, nor did I see a pubic hair. Felicity must have made everyone get Brazilian waxes, and it was a smart move on her part. That solo dance between Hayley and Marcy was a little odd, but I didn't think it was odd because of the act they were half-heartedly trying to simulate but because it was the two of them doing it. Why would Felicity give a solo to the two new girls, the least experienced and talented on the team? I concluded that she must have had her reasons. Felicity didn't do anything that she hadn't carefully calculated.

By that afternoon, I was feeling much better and turned my phone back on. I was prepared now. I would tell everyone who called with a grievance that they were overreacting, that the dance was very much in style with all the newer rap and hip hop artists. I would tell them to get a grip and be proud that their daughters were so talented. But the next call wasn't from another mother. It was from Mr. Rooney.

"Cynthia, we have made a grievous error," he began. That's how the man spoke. He said things like a *grievous error.*

"Are you referring to the Tigerette dance or the event that took place in your office?" I asked pointedly. I didn't think I had any reason to be uncomfortable or on guard with him. After all, we were in collusion. We were co-conspirators in crime. Neither one of us had been where we were supposed to be last night.

He cleared his throat. "I suppose I am referring to both matters."

"Look, Mr. Rooney," I used the cajoling voice that he liked me to use before he attacked my breasts like they were a couple of overripe melons, "I don't think it was that big of a deal. So what if the dance was a little *risqué?* From the sounds on the video, the crowd loved it."

"However," Mr. Rooney cleared his throat again, "many of the parents did not approve of the latest Tigerette performance. I do believe the word *egregious* has come up."

"Oh, come on," I laughed. "People get worked up over the silliest things. This will all blow over by Monday."

"Be that as it may, Cynthia, it is my responsibility to bring closure to his matter."

"Okay, fine, Marvin, I'll talk to Felicity as soon as she gets home." It was the first time I had called him Marvin, and I did so in an attempt to remind him that we were supposed to be on the same side.

Mr. Rooney gulped something on the other end, probably his perpetual cup of coffee. "I have been given the impression, through numerous complaints, that most parents think it is your responsibility to keep the Tigerette dances tasteful."

"Tasteful?" If all these so-called disgruntled parents wanted to watch *tasteful* dancing, they should watch old Fred Astaire and Ginger Rogers movies. This was the twenty-first century, and *tasteful* was not a word you used to describe what these kids were doing. Didn't these parents know anything about popular culture?

"Why would you let the girls perform that dance?" Mr. Rooney asked bluntly.

Then it hit me. He had crossed to the other side to save his own hide. He was joining ranks with all those women who only wanted to see me fail. And he knew that I no longer went to the Tigerette practices. On the few days that I attempted to make an appearance before I was again shot down by my daughter, he cornered me in the hall and ogled me in my skin-tight black leotard. He had to keep his hands in his pockets to keep himself from grabbing me. Why had I even let myself believe that he would support me? He was just another typical, selfish man.

"So, you're also blaming me for this?"

The coward didn't answer my question. "I have called an assembly at four o'clock this afternoon. I will let the parents air their grievances and concerns, and then I will decide on the best course of action."

"Let me know how it goes," I said, ready to hang up.

"It is a requirement that you be there, Cynthia. You are the coach of the Tigerettes."

Oh, shit. I supposed that he had a point. And I supposed it would look even worse if I skipped the meeting. I didn't want to look like a coward in front of all those people--and I assumed it would be women--who were so jealous of me that they couldn't see straight. However, I didn't want to be the person they all hurled accusations at either. What was even more disturbing was that if I defended myself by professing my ignorance, by admitting that I was the coach of the Tigerettes in name only, I would be throwing my daughter to the wolves. Sadly, I knew that Felicity wouldn't have any qualms about pointing the finger at me. Why had I ever agreed to get involved in this high school pom squad in the first place, and why had I let the pretense go on for so long?

"I'll be there." I hung up, already trying to decide what to wear.

I dressed like it was my day in court. In other words, I put on my most conservative LBD, which by most standards, wasn't conservative at all. What can I say? Most of the items in my closet did not scream *housewife!* But I managed to conceal almost all of my cleavage with a black and white tweed Chanel jacket and a Hermes black Les Cles silk scarf. Kate Spade black pumps with a moderate heel completed the ensemble. I put up my blonde hair in a loose bun and added a Swarovski crystal comb. My makeup was neutral and minimal. I surveyed myself in my full-length mirror before walking out the door, and let me tell you. I looked damn good. If I was playing the part of the *femme fatale* in this stupid scenario, I was going to be a gorgeous one.

During the two hours I had to get ready and drive to the school, the image of what I was about to face had morphed into an angry mob that filled the gym, everyone ready to throw tomatoes and rotten eggs, or perhaps spit on me. Of course that's not how it went down at all. We were in a large classroom, and I would guess that about forty people were in attendance, and as I had suspected, there wasn't a man among them, which was a shame. A few men might have given me a fighting chance. Nevertheless, the smallish size of the crowd gave me confidence. It was a large school, and the basketball games were always packed, so if there were only forty disgruntled parents, the numbers were on my side.

I swear that I did not plan to get there late and make a grand entrance, as I have been accused of doing. I did make a quick stop at my salon to pick up a tube of Christian Louboutin velvet matte lipstick that I thought would make my lips pop a little more, but that was it. So when I finally walked into the classroom, the animated conversation stopped abruptly, and all eyes turned to me. I'm not going to lie and say that I didn't like the attention because I did. Come on, I'd been starved for attention for going on three months, and even though there wasn't a man in the audience, I would take what I could get. I couldn't be sure, but I think I heard a gasp or two erupt in the room. However, I am sure that Mr. Rooney's eyes bugged out. Good. The traitor could see what he wasn't going to get anymore.

There wasn't a chair waiting for the accused at the front of the room, which was a little disappointing now that I was there and my fear was starting to evaporate. How could all these women in their unstylish jeans and workout clothes and unkempt hair possibly threaten me? Don't get me wrong. They didn't look particularly friendly, but they weren't exactly foaming at the mouth. And I could feel that they were intimidated by me as I walked to the front of the room and took a seat in a desk that directly faced Mr. Rooney behind the lectern. I gazed around, smiling, and when I saw Audrey and Reggie sitting a couple of rows away, I waved. I wasn't particularly surprised to see them there. Their girls had been the ones who really went over the top. Maybe they'd be on my side; maybe they wouldn't. They looked at each other, hesitating a moment before they waved back. Good.

While Mr. Rooney thanked everyone for coming, I looked around. I hadn't realized it when I walked in, but the room seemed to be divided, with the parents on one side and the Tigerettes on the other. Too late, I realized that I should have sat with the squad, and if I had any doubt about that, Felicity's glare confirmed it. I wavered. Should I get up and join the team? Surely, as the team's figurehead coach, my allegiance should be with them. But the fact of the matter was that I was as clueless as the other parents. It was quite a pickle I had found myself in, and not knowing what else to do, I stayed put.

"The floor is open to questions and comments," Mr. Rooney said.

Oh, boy, I thought, *here we go.*

The first woman who got up to speak had on a gray wool skirt that might have been in style twenty years before, but outdated as it was, it matched her hair perfectly. "That dance was an affront to my Christian faith," she said angrily. She then opened a Bible and started to quote verses that she had earmarked with pink post-its.

She droned on for about ten minutes or so, and while the audience sat patiently, I spotted several women rolling their eyes. The Tigerettes were busy sending each other texts and stifling giggles. At a signal from Felicity, as one, they picked up their desks and moved ever so slightly away from the crowd of parents. *Interesting*, I thought. I looked around to see if anyone else in the crowd had noticed how Felicity was culling her herd. Or maybe Felicity was slyly, yet defiantly, asserting her dominance.

"Oh, God, I can't take it anymore." It was Reggie, whose exasperated tone sounded like a bullhorn. "Lady, I know you're not a Tigerette mother. Does your kid even go to this school? I don't recognize you."

The woman flushed. "No, but that is not the point. Vulgarity in any form--"

"Who's next?" Mr. Rooney interrupted.

And then it began as each woman stood up to state her view. Big surprise. All the views were the same. Only the invectives varied: inappropriate, tasteless, embarrassing, slutty, trampy, and yes, egregious. Frankly, it got to be a little boring, like hearing the same chorus of a song you didn't particularly like play over and over again. The Tigerettes, who were periodically standing and shuffling their desks farther away, seemed to be untouched by it all.

Just when I was beginning to think that this interminable meeting was going to wind down without any repercussions to me, Audrey stood up. She looked first at her daughter. "Marcy didn't want me to come today."

Marcy looked as startled as a deer in the headlights. "Mom," she hissed. "Would you sit down?"

That's when it hit me. All the women who had gotten up to speak before Audrey had not been Tigerette mothers, only concerned parents of other students in the school. The few who had called me that morning were not in attendance either, not that I actually knew them. Of course I should have known them. Felicity had been on the team with some of the girls for two years. I have since been told that it is a parent's responsibility to know the friends her daughter hangs out with, to at least nominally know their parents too. But it was something I had never bothered to do. I didn't see the point if those people didn't have any social relevance to me. So what was going on? Had all the other Tigerette mothers been warned to stay away by their daughters? I glanced over at Felicity, who had turned her venomous glare onto Marcy. Sure they had. I wondered how Felicity had managed that particular little trick.

Audrey took a deep, nervous breath. "I only want to say that the latest dance performed by the Tigerettes did not belong in a high school gymnasium."

"More like a strip club," Reggie piped up, which caused Hayley to slide down in her seat.

"I was embarrassed at the . . . pornographic nature of the dance my daughter performed, and I hope she is too. I hope all you girls are, especially you, Felicity," she added pointedly before sitting down. Meanwhile, the entire Tigerette team turned to Felicity for further instruction.

But before Felicity could say anything, Reggie popped up. "Ms. Stewart, as coach of the Tigerettes, how could you have allowed the girls to perform such an obscene dance?"

Pornographic? Obscene? And Reggie had called me Ms. Stewart! The two women had sat quietly, for the most part, during the entire meeting, and I was beginning to think that they were my friends. I mean, without me, their wine club party would have been a total disaster. Without me, they wouldn't have made all that money on what very well may be fake French wine. And now they had publicly attacked me.

Mr. Rooney turned to my daughter. "It looks like you have something to say, Felicity. It's time to hear the Tigerette point of view."

Felicity didn't bother to stand up. "The Tigerettes follow the instructions of the head coach, Mr. Rooney. My mother is the one who used to be a professional dancer."

I don't know why I was surprised. I knew that my daughter was capable of hurling the blame onto my shoulders. I knew her willful self-preservation trumped everything. Yet I was surprised at her nonchalance, at how easily the lie slipped from her tongue. There were eleven other girls, my possible witnesses, who knew I had not been allowed anywhere near their practices in months. But because of Felicity, they wouldn't dare come to my defense.

Naturally, Felicity's proclamation unleashed a hailstorm of accusations from the other women, exactly what I had been hoping to avoid. Believe it or not, I barely heard them. I could only stare at my daughter, who was staring back at me with a look of smug triumph on her face. Is it a terrible thing to say that I hated her at that moment? I don't care if it is. I hated her.

I stood up abruptly. "Would you excuse us for a moment, Mr. Rooney? Felicity, I want to see you outside in the hallway. Now."

I halfway expected Felicity to remain in her seat, holding court, but to my surprise, she followed me, closing the door behind her. "What do you want?"

What did I want? I turned on her, my fury making my voice shake as if it was filled with tears. Maybe it was. "Why are you lying? Why don't you say the truth for once in your goddamn, privileged little life and tell all those people that you were the one who choreographed that dance, that you won't let me near the practices, that you control every move those girls make?"

"I don't know what you're talking about."

"Don't be such a bitch, Felicity. You put those girls up to that dance, and maybe you did it so you could ultimately blame me for reasons that I can't fathom. But I want you to go in and tell the truth, and then I want you to apologize." I was breathing hard by then, and it took everything in my power not to take her by the shoulders and shake her like a ragdoll. If we'd been home rather than standing in a school hallway, I just might have done it.

"You're the one who should apologize. You're the one who drove Daddy away." Her words were sharp, biting.

I sucked in a quick intake of breath, momentarily stunned. "Don't be ridiculous. Your father is out of town on business."

"Oh, yeah? Where?"

I didn't have an answer for that, and she knew it, but I pushed on. "Believe me, Felicity, he's going to hear about how you've been acting since he left."

"And maybe he should know about your behavior, *Mother.*" She matched my stare again.

I had always thought that she had my eyes, and maybe she did in color, but it was Richard's steely resolve that I saw now. I was afraid. I didn't know if she was talking about Buck and the money or Mr. Rooney or that I was drinking all the wine in the cellar every night. Or maybe she would make up something even worse. God only knew what her manipulative, sneaky mind could concoct. It was at that moment that I realized my daughter was a psychopath. "You're evil," I spat out.

"Don't be so dramatic, Mom." Then it was like Felicity lifted a veil from her face or switched on an inner light. She smiled, revealing that she was a stunningly pretty teenager--and looking as innocent as a teenager could be. She could be a young, charming girl in an ice-cream commercial, the one who ordered a vanilla cone with rainbow sprinkles.

The instantaneous transformation threw me off guard. "What . . ."

"I'll apologize, Mom, and I think you should too. It's in both of our best interests."

She led the way in, and we both stood in front of the room and apologized for the dance. We said something like we would never let it happen again; we promised that future dances would be more appropriate to a true pom squad spirit. We guaranteed the squad's integrity. I had to hand it to the psychopath--even I believed her.

Mr. Rooney bought it too and decided that he would only suspend the team for the next two games. The school needed the Tigerette spirit, he said, for the upcoming playoffs. "These girls can help our boys go all the way to the state championship this year!" was how he closed the meeting, smugly satisfied that everyone had been appeased.

I couldn't wait to get out of there. I didn't give Mr. Rooney a second glance--the coward had gotten away with his part in the whole scenario--but I plastered a smile on my face for the other women on my way out. I could at least pretend that I was cordial and pleasant. I'm very good at that, you know.

I had almost made it to the door when I felt a tap on my shoulder. I turned, the smile so tightly affixed to my face that it hurt.

"Cynthia?" It was Audrey, and standing right next to her was Reggie. They looked something like a Mutt and Jeff version of Siamese twins.

"You're the only Tigerette mothers who showed up," I said.

"Isn't that something?" I couldn't read Reggie's tone.

"It took guts to apologize before an angry mob." Audrey laughed, but she couldn't quite pull it off.

"It did." Reggie nodded and then got right to the point. "I hope there are no hard feelings, Cynthia. We're still on for the wine club at your house, right?"

"Of course," I said brightly, feeling like my face was going to shatter from the strain. I'd truly thought these women would become my friends, but they were as willing as everyone else, including my daughter, to throw me to the wolves. They were the ones who had riled up everyone else, but they weren't the only ones who could play the game. I was a master at it. If they had a dirty little secret, I would expose it. Payback was the ultimate goal of this game. And I would win.

I opened the door for the three of us. "I'm looking forward to it."

Felicity wasn't speaking to me. I suppose she thought she was punishing me by depriving me of her valuable company, the little bitch. As observantly devious as she could be, I was surprised that she couldn't see that I didn't give a damn if she deigned to speak or not. It actually gave me great pleasure to see her struggle not to open her mouth when I put on the playlist I had compiled the night before: "You Give Love a Bad Name" by Bon Jovi, "Cry me a River" by Justin Timberlake, "Take a Bow" by Rihanna, and "You're Not Sorry" by Taylor Swift. They were all songs about betrayal, you see, and I meant them to get under her skin. What's more, I kept instructing Alexa "to turn up the volume," so much so that the house seemed to reverberate with moans of duplicity. Felicity was twitching on her stool as she spooned in her yogurt, but she followed her plan: the silent treatment. Likewise, I stuck to mine, humming along to the loud music until she picked up her backpack, stalked to the garage door, and slammed it behind her. I do have to say that I considered it my victory.

When I was sure she was gone, I turned off the music, and even though my ears were still ringing, the house was eerily quiet. Louisa had called in sick that morning, something she never did, and I was acutely aware of her absence. It was strange. It wasn't like she and I had many one-on-one conversations, and Louisa usually went out of her way to be in a different room than I was in, but with her gone, with no distant sounds of the central vac running or the thumping of her heavy footsteps, the house felt more like a mausoleum than a home. Maybe it had always been like that, and I hadn't noticed. It spooked me, so to cover the sound of silence, I turned on the kitchen TV.

I never watched the news. I found the stories depressing, the airplane crashes and wars and shootings that never seemed to end. And what's more, I thought that the newscasters, almost without exception, were wantonly self-aggrandizing. It was like they thrived on tragedy. The worse the story, the more they relished talking about it. Maybe I'm not being fair; maybe those people are only doing their jobs. But it seems to me that each person has her own tragedies and disappointments to deal with. Why should we be forced to deal with the misfortune of others? To make ourselves feel better? If so, we live in a very sick world, indeed.

What? Do you think I'm trying to minimize hurtful things I may or may not have done during the course of my colorful life? I lived in *Vegas*, remember? Furthermore, sometimes a gal's gotta do what a gal's gotta do. Period. So get off your high horse, sister. I'm only expressing my opinion.

Anyway, it wasn't like I was going to watch the news that morning either. I turned on the TV, and one of Louisa's Spanish speaking soap operas blasted forth. I wanted some noise in the house, but I didn't want *that* much noise. Louisa must have turned it up to full volume when she was in another room cleaning and I was out of the house. Or maybe, it occurred to me, Louisa was going deaf. She often didn't seem to hear me when I asked her to do something simple like scour the grout between the Travertine tiles with a toothbrush. I fumbled with the remote to turn down the volume. The soap was *La Mentira*, one of her favorites, which translated, she had told me, into *The Lie*. You will get the irony of this in just a second.

I hit the channel button instead of the volume button by mistake, and CNN filled the screen. And there was a picture of Richard, *my Richard*. It was a picture of Richard that had been taken about eighteen years before, right about the time I met him. It was Richard at his most handsome, with his too-long hair still silver instead of the white it had become, with his face carrying only the attractive age lines, those spiraling from the corners of his cornflower blue eyes. It was the Richard I had to have when I first set eyes on him in the Gentlemen's Club. I went numb. I couldn't even feel the remote in my hand as all sorts of terrible things flashed through my mind. Richard had been killed in an airplane crash. Richard was found dead of a heart attack. Richard had been hit by a bus. Richard had been sitting in a New York restaurant when a bomb went off. I thought of a lot worse things than that, but you get my drift. My first thought was that something had happened to Richard *physically*.

The picture of Richard slid to the upper corner of the TV, and it was Wolf Blitzer front and center, a serious expression on his face as he read from the sheaf of papers in his hand: "Richard Stewart, CEO of Stewart Enterprises, Inc., has been indicted on seventeen charges of racketeering, money laundering, trust fraud, and securities fraud. The financial world has not been so rocked since the Bernie Madoff scandal in 2008. A warrant has been issued for Stewart's arrest, but at this juncture in the investigation, his whereabouts remain unknown."

My first thought was that this had to be some mistake. My husband was an honest, self-made businessman who had started as a builder fifty-two years ago with nothing more than his broad shoulders and a dream. I'd heard the story hundreds of times, of how he worked sixteen to eighteen hours a day until he started to get a reputation as a quality luxury home builder. After that, he started to buy land in Scottsdale and developed strip malls and motels and commercial buildings. He was well-respected in the community and donated millions of dollars to charity. His was a true rags-to-riches, Horatio Alger story. He retired five years ago as a wealthy, successful man. Since then, he spent most of his time holed up in his study managing his vast investment portfolio . . .

The empty safe. The cleaned-out desk. The dwindling wine collection. *Oh, God.* I sank to the floor as other things started to click into place. Richard had been taking my jewelry collection, a piece at a time, to put in a safe deposit box. But if he'd actually been doing that, where was this mysterious bank? Had he been selling my diamonds and emeralds and sapphires? Also, during the last year or so, he had been taking various pieces of artwork to get them appraised, he said, for insurance purposes. He always brought the works back and hung them in their perfectly appointed places around the house, but now I wondered if he had sold those pieces and replaced them with forgeries. I wondered how much we had left. I had never had a panic attack before but knew I had one then. My heart galloped in my chest, and I couldn't get enough air in my lungs.

Maybe everything Richard had ever told me was a lie. Maybe Richard was not a self-made millionaire many times over. Maybe Richard had never loved me, but at that point, it seemed like that possibility was the lowest on my totem pole of worries. Maybe CNN was the lying entity in this scenario? According to President Trump, fake news was everywhere. Believe me when I tell you that I was one hot mess on my knees on that cold, expensive tile. My mind was racing off in a zillion directions at once as I tried to wrap my head around what was happening. For some odd reason, I still had the remote in my hand, and I pointed it at the TV and clicked. FOX, MSNBC, CNBC, and even the local news stations were all playing the same story.

My husband, Richard Stewart, had seventeen indictments against him and was wanted by the FBI. My husband, Richard Stewart, was a white-collar criminal.

It was just my luck. I'd been involved with criminals before--I am not ever going to name names on that front; it's for my own protection--but I had thought Richard was different. In other words, I had thought that he was legit. That was why I married him. He was a bona fide millionaire, not some Vegas wannabe or low-level mobster. I mean, that was *one* of the reasons I married Richard. There was the love thing too. And attraction. Definitely attraction in the early days. I guess the joke was on me. The escape/protection plan I had all figured out had backfired on me, big time. Haha.

The phone started ringing then, and it startled me. At first, I couldn't tell where the sound was coming from, and it took me a minute to locate the source. It was the landline hanging on the wall. Richard, being an old-fashioned guy--or was he?--had insisted that we keep the outdated appliance. It made its presence known now, though, loud and clear. It would ring and stop, ring and stop, ring and stop. I knew it was probably reporters trying to interview me. And honestly, it was the first time in my life that I didn't want attention. No one had yet told me to keep my mouth shut, but I knew instinctively that that is what I had to do, if for self-preservation and nothing else. Furthermore, for the second time in two days, I had been blindsided. I didn't have a clue what was really going on.

I needed to get out of the house. I needed to get away from that incessant ringing. I needed to escape once again. As I threw on some clothes, not bothering with my hair and makeup--another first--my cell started ringing too. I threw it on the bed, grabbed my Louis Vuitton bag, and dashed out to my Mercedes. I was in full-force self-preservation mode, a speed that I hadn't had to shift gears into for eighteen years. I stopped at the first Shell station I passed. I was going to fill up the tank with gas in case I needed to get out of town fast, in case I needed to flee all the dangers I had yet to understand. I swiped my card at the pump. Declined. I swiped another credit card. Declined. With rising panic, I tried all the cards in my wallet and got the same result. Yes, I was surprised. Don't ask me why. I didn't think the federal government could move that fast. I mean, we all know how long it takes Congress to get anything done, right?

The next thing I did was equally stupid. I went to the nearest bank, a Wells Fargo, and inserted my debit card into the ATM. Not only did it not give me the $1000 I had entered, but it also swallowed my card. I rushed into the bank, ignoring the stares. Normally, I would have loved the staring--it was proof of my timeless beauty--but I knew that wasn't the case in this instance. I looked like a frightened rabbit, my hair still disheveled from sleep, and traces of yesterday's eyeliner and mascara ringing my eyes.

I pushed my way to the front of the line and slapped my hands on the counter. "Your damn ATM ate my card!"

The teller looked a little frightened. "What's your account number?" She poised her hands over the keyboard.

"I don't know my account number! Who knows her own account number?" I turned to the people behind me. "Do you know your damn account numbers?" They backed away. Maybe they thought I had a gun. I don't know.

I finally gave the teller my name. She typed, typed. "I'll show you to the manager's office."

The manager looked like he was about twelve. He sat me down and did his fair share of typing before announcing: "Mrs. Stewart, I'm afraid your assets at this bank have been frozen."

I didn't wait to hear any more. I had left my phone on the bed, and now I raced back home to get it, running two red lights and seeing the flash from the cameras. Ha! You could bet your ass I wasn't going to pay those speeding tickets! I parked my Mercedes haphazardly in the front of the house and raced up the stairs. I had our lawyer, Gerald Busby, in my contact list. Richard had thought I might need his number sometime. Thoughtful of him, wasn't it?

Gerald Busby answered after the first ring. "I sent you an email early this morning, Cynthia, as soon as I heard. I'm afraid that the federal government has frozen all of your assets until this matter is resolved. You don't happen to know where Richard is, do you?" he asked pointedly.

"I don't know where my fucking husband is! I don't know a goddamn thing!" Little did I know that *I don't know a goddamn thing* would be my mantra for quite some time.

I didn't know what else to do, so I went downstairs to the wine cellar and got the most expensive bottle of wine that Richard had left. I knew it was the most expensive because he kept it in a glass case. Well, I'd show him; I knew where the key was! I carried it upstairs and poured myself a hefty glass to ward off another panic attack that was threateningly close to the surface. What was I going to do? How would I live? Maybe they would find Richard soon, and he would send me a message in a secret code, a message that told me where he had hidden money, buried it in the backyard maybe, or sewn it into the mattress. I know. I was grasping at straws, and they were turning to sawdust in my hands.

I was pouring my second glass of burgundy when the back door flew open, and Felicity came running into the kitchen. Funny, but I hadn't given a thought to Felicity since I turned on the news. I hadn't even considered that the kids at school would be talking, that they would see the news on their phones and start to whisper and point. I guess it's more sad than funny that I hadn't stopped to think about Felicity. But Felicity and I were in the middle of a major fight, remember?

Felicity did the most surprising thing. She flung herself into my arms and sobbed into my chest. "What is happening to us, Mom? What are we going to do?"

The wine glass was still in my hand, and I tried not to slosh any on her glossy hair. She was more pathetic than I had ever seen her. My baby girl was suffering. I honestly didn't think she had it in her, and I felt a small tug at my heart.

I reluctantly put the wine glass down and awkwardly patted her head. "We'll be all right, honey. Your mother will figure something out. I always do."

15

AUDREY

I saw the story about Richard Stewart on the news, of course. Who didn't? It was *everywhere*. I mean, the guy was some kind of major scam artist, wasn't he? The press kept comparing his crime to Bernie Madoff's, who I didn't know that much about. But I got the crux of what they were saying. Richard Stewart had been a very naughty boy indeed. I suppose I felt a little sorry for the investors that he had bilked millions of dollars from, but when you're talking about that kind of money, it's hard to work up sympathy for people who have it. I'm not being callous here. I simply cannot wrap my head around that many zeros. I was struggling to put food on the table, while millionaires had lost millions. It was probably a drop in the bucket to most of those people. So really, what was the big deal?

Did I feel sorry for Cynthia? Are you kidding me? I was still a little angry at her for allowing the Tigerettes to perform that obscene dance. I was all ready to forgive her if she acted like she was truly sorry about the whole thing, but the way she waltzed into that parents' meeting put an end to that. Number one, she was late, and number two, she was dressed to the nines in an outfit that would have fed my family for about six months. And she didn't act like she was sorry at all for putting my daughter in such a compromising position. Instead, she acted like she owned the room, smiling that condescending smile of hers, like she was a queen or something. I know that she and Felicity apologized at the end of that long meeting, but I could tell that they didn't mean it. It just didn't sound sincere or heartfelt. But as Reggie pointed out to me, we needed Cynthia to make the wine club a success, so we had to play nice. *Play nice.* Those were Reggie's words, not mine.

Reggie, on the other hand, was absolutely enamored by the scandal. Seriously, she ate up every single salacious detail. She even brought over a small TV from her house that we set on the kitchen table--there wasn't any room on the counter or center island because of all the wine bottles--and turned it on so we could watch the unfolding news while we bottled, corked, and labeled our wine. "Can you believe this?" she asked on that first day that the story broke. She had her face right up to that small screen.

"It certainly explains why Cynthia spends money like it was water." I was still peeved over the outfit Cynthia had worn to the meeting. I couldn't get it out of mind. Most of the parents were sitting there in jeans and t-shirts, myself included, and she had dressed for a ladies' luncheon at the Beverly Hills Wilshire Hotel, for crying out loud.

"Poor Cynthia," Reggie said in a fake sympathetic voice, "her husband is a crook, and now he's going to jail."

"If they can find him." I was steaming on a shrink cap and wanted Reggie to turn off the stupid TV and get to work. We still had way too much to do before the wine party, and she wasn't pulling her share of the weight. I'd been averaging about four hours of sleep a night for weeks by then. Sometimes even after Reggie left for the evening, I continued to work. The whole operation was set up in my kitchen, after all, and I didn't have the luxury of escaping it the way that Reggie did. I was beginning to wonder why we hadn't set up our business in Reggie's crappy kitchen since her idea of cooking was putting a Lean Cuisine in the microwave. I made meals for my family and had to put all the equipment away each day when they were due home and drag it out late at night, then put it away and drag it all out the next morning. It wasn't fair.

Reggie continued to gloat. "It serves Miss High and Mighty right. Cynthia can't act like she owns the world now, can she? Do you think she'll visit old Dick in prison for the monthly conjugal visit?"

I smiled at that, despite myself. "Good old Dick might have himself a heart attack when he gets a load of the prison food. It ain't going to be Châteaubriand."

Reggie laughed and then turned back to the TV. After she'd wasted more precious minutes, she said, "Do you think Cynthia was in on it? Do you think she knew what her husband was doing?"

That thought had not crossed my mind. Both Reggie and I knew firsthand, unfortunately, that your husband could be up to something that you didn't have a clue about. As it was, I currently didn't even know where Paul was. He should have been home by now, and even his weekly phone calls had stopped. But you know what the weird thing was? I didn't mind all that much. I was too busy to dwell on it anymore, and by that time, the kids and I had settled into the routine of being a family of three. Jimmy didn't cry himself to sleep every night over Paul by then, and I didn't know if I should be happy or sad about it. I finished shrink wrapping one bottle and automatically reached for another. That's pretty much how I went through my days--on autopilot.

"If Cynthia did know," Reggie went on, "then she'll go to jail too, won't she?"

"Then I hope she didn't know. Where would we have our wine parties?" Maybe it was selfish of me to think about the wine club first, but that's the way I thought back then. If I couldn't make some money with this plan, I didn't know what I'd do. I didn't know if I'd even be able to drag myself out of bed in the morning. And I wondered about this more than once: Did poor houses still exist?

"Shit, you have a point there. But I sure would like to see Cynthia in an *Orange is the New Black* jumpsuit, wouldn't you?"

"Unfortunately, she'd probably look good even in that." I reached for another wine bottle.

"Would you let me enjoy my fantasy, Audrey?" Reggie still wasn't budging from the TV. "Boy, that Richard," Reggie marveled. "He makes our little scam look like pocket change."

"Should I feel noble now? Richard stole millions, and we're only stealing a few thousand. Wow, we're not crooks at all, if you look at it that way." I didn't disguise the snippiness from my voice.

Reggie turned to look at me. "What's gotten into you, Audrey? Did something happen that I don't know about?"

"No, you are currently up to date on all the sordid details of my life, Reggie." Well, that wasn't exactly true. I had never told Reggie the extent of my credit card debt. I had paid a couple hundred on each card after our last wine club party, but with the exorbitant interest rates, that paltry amount hadn't even made a small dent. It was another unsavory thing that I didn't dwell on much anymore. As fatigued as I was, it took all my energy to get through the motions of each day.

Reggie, uncharacteristically, didn't take offense at my foul mood. "Look, sister, it's my job to be the crabby one. You're stealing my thunder."

That coaxed another tiny smile from me. "Duly noted."

Reggie reluctantly pulled herself away from the TV then and picked up a label. I had to bite my tongue to keep from yelling at her to stop. Reggie wasn't as exact with the gluing on of the labels as I was. She still hadn't mastered the knack of the glue gun; she didn't have the patience for it. "You take over the shrink wrapping, and I'll start gluing, okay?" I pulled off the oven mitts and handed them to her. I was tired of standing over the steam anyway. My hair never looked good during those days.

Our conversation turned to our girls, a topic that was frustrating to us both right then. Instead of being chagrined or embarrassed by the commotion the last Tigerette dance routine had caused, our girls were blatantly unapologetic. Hayley and Marcy had actually had the nerve to reprimand Reggie and me for being the only two Tigerette parents who attended that farce of a disciplinary meeting. I think her exact words had been: "I told you not to come, Mom. Do you know how embarrassed I was?"

I'm sure my mouth gaped open. "You were embarrassed by my attendance at a public meeting and not by your simulated lesbian sex act in front of God knows how many people now that it has aired on YouTube?"

Marcy rolled her eyes. "That's how the dance was choreographed, Mom. Felicity said it was artistic."

It was my turn to roll my eyes. "Well, then. In a world ruled and sanctioned by Felicity Stewart, the dance is perfectly acceptable. Is that what you're saying, Marcy?"

Marcy shrugged. "I thought it was a good dance. And Hayley and I had the two solos. Don't you know how important that is?"

I was stunned into silence by my daughter's cavalier attitude about the obscene dance and the YouTube video. Absolutely stunned. The whole sordid event made me want to throw up. I felt the bile rise in the back of my throat and had to choke it down. Reggie and I had confronted our girls at the same time, hoping to find strength by banding together, but even that didn't seem to get through to the two of them, as thoroughly brainwashed by Felicity as they were. Or maybe *poisoned* is a better word. Still, I felt that Marcy needed to be punished somehow, if for no other reason but that she would have a glimmer of realization that her behavior had been unacceptable. I couldn't ground her--I needed her out of the house to do the wine business--so I settled on "punishing" her by insisting that she donate ten hours of her time to working at a soup kitchen for the homeless downtown. She'd rolled her eyes at that one too.

"The season is going to be over soon," Reggie said next. "And Felicity is going to graduate in May. Then she'll be out of our daughters' lives."

"I guess that's something to look forward to," I said grimly.

A thoughtful expression crossed Reggie's face. "You know, if I ever found myself in a dark room alone with Felicity, I don't know what I'd do."

I smiled for the third and last time that morning. "Now that's a fantasy I can enjoy. Would you strangle her?"

"No, I'd have a gun. Did I not mention that?"

"You can be such a mean bitch, dear friend." I felt almost happy for the first time in days, maybe weeks.

"You got that right, sister," Reggie cackled.

My phone rang then, and under normal circumstances, I wouldn't answer it when we had found the rhythm to our work as we had then. But I had sent Jimmy to school that morning, even though he said he had a sore throat. I know. It was a rotten thing to do to my child, but Reggie and I needed to make progress on our bottling and labeling that day. I believe that I have already mentioned that I wasn't a very attentive mother during that time, especially to my son. I was bribing him with Snickers bars and planting him in front of mindless TV shows regularly then. And on that day, I sent him to school sick. I am so ashamed when I think of it now, but I wasn't back then. Well, perhaps I did feel a shred of shame, but it was all for a good cause, the wine club. The wine club trumped everything, even my children and my faltering marriage. Or so I thought.

When I picked up my phone, I saw that it wasn't Jimmy's school calling. It was The Gardens' number flashing on my screen, and I felt the familiar dread and guilt wash over me in one big wave. I hadn't been to see Margot in weeks. I just couldn't deal with her right then. She'd always been such a difficult, angry person, but now she was a *caged* difficult, angry person. You'd think it would make dealing with her easier in a way, but it didn't. In that small, cluttered room of hers that always smelled faintly of urine in spite of the Lysol, her fury seemed magnified, not diminished. I know. It's not a good excuse for not visiting her, but it's the only one I've got.

I listened to Gail's crisp British voice with a growing sense of detached horror. I could hear her voice, but it wasn't connecting with me. It was as if she was speaking about someone else. When Gail finished with her spiel, I stupidly asked, "So do you think I need to go see her?"

Gail's tone was abrupt, dismissive. "My dear, I do believe you know what the proper thing to do is, don't you?"

Reggie was right by my side when the phone slid from my numb hands. "You look like you need to sit down, honey." She led me to a kitchen chair and brought me a glass of water. "What's wrong, Audrey? What do you need me to do?"

It's funny, but I had forgotten how compassionate Reggie was that morning until just now. I've been mad at her for so long that I guess it's hard to remember the times that she was there for me when I needed her.

Don't you think that's strange?

I'd heard what Gail said over the phone, but I still wasn't prepared for what greeted me at Osborn hospital. My mother, the bane of my existence for my entire life, had been stricken by a massive stroke. She was unconscious when I arrived at her hospital room, hooked up to various machines that further seemed to dwarf her small covered figure. Had she always been that small, or had she shrunk in the months I had been absent? Or maybe my fear of her had made her seem larger than life? Whatever the case, it was a tiny, frail old woman lying under the blanket now, unmoving and silent. Which made me almost believe that it wasn't my mother at all. My mother would be rip-roaring mad, yanking out the tubes and swearing at anyone who came into the room.

So that's why I turned to the nurse who was adjusting some knobs and said, "Are you sure this is Margot Keller?"

The nurse gave me a strange look, but she bent over the wristband on the patient's arm. "Yes, this is her."

"Is she going to wake up soon?" I asked. If that were the case, I felt the need to warn the young woman to stay out of her way. Margot would be mad as hell and likely try to take a swing at her, which was why I was keeping my distance.

"The doctor will be in soon with the prognosis." She walked briskly out of the room.

I wished I could follow her. The idea of being alone in this room with my comatose mother terrified me. I'm not sure exactly why. It was true that I disliked being in hospitals in general, and it was also true that I was afraid that if she woke up, she would still find some way to blame her predicament on me. She'd probably say something like: "If you hadn't been such an ungrateful bitch of a daughter, leaving me trapped in a nursing home, this wouldn't have happened to me."

But really, it was more than both of those. Strangely enough, all the times that I had daydreamed about Margot finally gone from my life, I had never once wished her dead. Furthermore, I guess that I had never actually *imagined* her being dead. Maybe I had always pictured her as a being who would perpetually hover over me like a malevolent angel I would never escape.

And now this. I finally dared to creep closer to the bed, and I could see that her mouth was twisted around the ventilator, and the right side of her face drooped. But those things didn't shock me nearly as much as her hair. What was left was white and sparse. I could see her scalp in more than one place, and that made me sadder than anything. I had never seen Margot without her flaming red wig. I don't remember at what point in her life she began to wear it--in her early forties, maybe--but she was never seen without it. On the rare occasions when I would drop by her house announced, and later on the nursing home, she always had it on. I was convinced she slept in it, and maybe even showered with it on. But now the wig was gone, and with it, my mother's last bit of armor against the world.

I started to sniffle and reached into my purse for a tissue. It was so sad, yet my reaction surprised me. I hadn't even liked the woman, but could it be that I had somehow loved her? I started to cry harder when the feeling of loneliness washed over me. I was going to lose her, if not now, probably soon, and my husband should be standing by my side. Or perhaps I had already lost him too, not when he got his DUI and went to Fresh Start, but years before when drinking became his reason for living. I started to cry harder at that point, and though the tears were probably more for myself than my mother, they were real.

I had composed myself before the doctor finally arrived. That's the thing about hospital time, you know? The minutes drip by, and you lose all sense of time, so I don't know how long I stood there staring at my mother before Dr. Coogan walked in. He didn't tell me anything that I hadn't already looked up on my phone. He said it was difficult to determine how much oxygen had been deprived to the brain tissue, and then he went on to give the list of possible complications that occur if and when my mother came out of her coma: paralysis, difficulty swallowing or talking, balance problems, memory loss, difficulty controlling emotions, depression, pain.

"Her advanced age will be a factor in her recovery," he concluded as if that summed up everything.

"But physical therapy would help, wouldn't it?" I asked.

He rubbed the bridge of his nose with his forefinger and thumb. "If she does come out of her coma, it is a possibility that she will need full-time care."

"Yes." I had already considered that possibility. "The Gardens also has a skilled nursing section adjacent to the assisted living quarters." It was a dismal place with residents strapped into wheelchairs and propped up in front of a TV set with dazed expressions on their faces. (Much like I was doing to my son, I bleakly realized.) The cost of that kind of treatment was almost twice as much as Margot was paying now, and I didn't know if her insurance would cover the cost. And hiring a private nurse in addition to that was out of the question as far as finances were concerned.

"I'm talking 24/7 care," he said gently. "It's hard to say how long treatment would be necessary."

What? Wait a minute. Was he implying that it was my duty as her daughter to bring her to my home and care for her? That would be impossible. I had two children to care for, a household to run, and now I was operating a business out of my kitchen. And I didn't care if it was selfish or not. I was not going to take care of Margot for days, or months, or years when the woman had never done anything nice for me in my entire life. She hadn't even come to my wedding to Paul, let alone offer to contribute a dime, because she was mad that Paul's rich parents wouldn't pay for her dress. The idea of physically caring for my mother--feeding her, bathing her, dressing her--was repellent to me. And maddening. Why should I make sacrifices for her when she had never sacrificed one damn thing for me?

"Do you have other family members who could help in this situation?" Dr. Coogan looked at his watch. My time was up.

"Yeah, right." Aaron would prefer it if I called him after Margot was dead and cremated, her ashes spread not in some meaningful place, but rather, flushed down a toilet.

"Very well, then." Dr. Coogan glanced at his watch again.

"Thank you for your time." As far as I was concerned, he was welcome to go and pursue other causes that weren't as lost as this one.

Two days later, Margot was still in a coma, being kept alive by the marvels of medicine on the taxpayers' dime. The more I thought about it, the madder I got. I'd felt sympathetic toward her at the beginning, but enough was enough already. I'd even gone to see her on both days, sparing what moments I could of my precious time, and stood by her bedside, willing her to die. Before you judge me, consider this: If Margot did regain consciousness, the chances that she would have any viable life were looking dimmer and grimmer. The MRI scan detected minimal brain activity, so what was the point? Why were they keeping her alive? But I wasn't God, and I wasn't going to play God, so I willed myself to be patient and threw myself into my work.

It was three o'clock the day before the January wine club party, and Reggie and I were finished. I had just put the last label on the fake Romanée Conti 1959, the one with a retail price of $12,950 that we were offering at a ten percent discount. Because of the astronomical price and because we wanted to present it as exclusive, we had only labeled seven of the Ravenswood pinot noir as that vintage. It was our jewel offering of the party, and Reggie and I were both seeing dollar signs dancing before our eyes. Since we usually finished preparing for a wine party in the wee hours of the morning the day of the party, cutting it right down to the wire, we were feeling giddy with relief.

"I think I'll go for a run to celebrate and think about the piles of money we're going to make." Reggie was already stretching.

Since Reggie lived in athletic wear, she was always taking off for a run at the drop of a hat, which frankly, got on my nerves most of the time. We'd be in the middle of something, and she'd announce that she was going to run to "clear her head," leaving me to finish the task. I guess I should have been used to it by then--Reggie could be so inconsiderate about things like that--but it still rankled. However, on that day, I told her sure, go for a run, and we'd have a glass of wine when she got back. But for some reason, I didn't wait. We had a couple of bottles of the Kenwood cabernet left over, and I decided to pour myself a glass. I didn't usually do that in the middle of the afternoon, not when I had to pick up Jimmy from Delilah's later, but after the week I'd had, I felt like I deserved it. Besides, one glass wouldn't hurt.

I had settled myself in a kitchen chair, propped my feet on the one opposite, and taken that first blissful sip. I closed my eyes at the sensation of the wine on my tongue, just for a second or two, and when I opened them, there stood Paul, staring at me through the glass sliding door. I was so surprised that I almost dropped the glass. I'm not going to lie: It was a hefty glass in a big domed goblet. "Paul!" I'd say it looked like I had seen a ghost, but that was far from the truth. He had on jeans and a flannel shirt, his face was tanned a golden brown beneath a cowboy hat, and he looked more handsome than he ever had before.

He slid the door open and stepped in, his happy smile suddenly gone. "You're drinking in the middle of the afternoon?" Those were the first words he said to me: *You're drinking in the middle of the afternoon?* After weeks of silence, those were his first words.

I immediately felt the need to defend myself, but it wasn't like I could tell him the truth, that Reggie and I had just finished bottling close to three hundred bottles of fake French wine, and I was celebrating. So my first words to him after weeks of silence were: "What are you doing here?"

"I live here." He stuck his arm out the door and motioned to someone. "She's in here." And then *someone* appeared, a brunette waif-like creature with dark eyes so big and round that they looked like that old cartoon picture of Betty Boop.

If it had been a month before, I would have thrown myself into his arms, but not now. The unexpected sight of him unnerved me, and his little friend was not helping me get my bearings. "I . . I wasn't . . . expecting you," I stammered.

"I wanted to surprise you. And I rang the front doorbell because I didn't want to barge in and scare the hell out of you."

"The front doorbell is broken." Among other things. Since Paul had been gone, and even though he had been the worst handyman in the world, no one had attempted to fix the bell or the garbage disposal or the broken latch on the garage door. I guess I'd naively thought that when Paul finally came home all clean and sober and shiny new, he'd get right to those things.

Paul opened up his arms wide. "Come here, babe, and give me a hug."

I finally set down my wine glass and lumbered to my feet. We hugged awkwardly. Oh, his arms and the feel of his chest against my body were the same, but still, it was awkward, clumsy. "I wish I knew you were coming. I could have bought something special for dinner--" I trailed off as the waif surveyed my kitchen. There were still two crates of wine that Reggie and I hadn't lugged out to the garage yet, the open bottle of wine on the counter, and of course, my incriminating mega glass of cabernet.

"Is there always this much alcohol in the house?" the waif asked disapprovingly.

"No, there is not," I said icily, not bothering to add that there was usually five times as much, if not more. "Who are you?"

"My bad." Paul chuckled unconvincingly. He, too, was looking around. "This is Sondra, my life coach."

The Paul I knew didn't say stupid things like *my bad*. It must be the influence of his prepubescent, alleged *life coach*. "Why do you need a life coach?" I eyed her suspiciously. She did not look like a life coach, not that I would know what one looked like.

"The program at Fresh Start recommends a life coach at this point in my treatment."

"You're not done with your treatment yet?" I was incredulous. Was my husband such an incorrigible drunk that he had to go through rehab four or five times--*in a row*? I'd never heard of such a thing. Even the movie stars you heard about going to rehab didn't repeat the program over and over again consecutively. I was beginning to smell a rat, and that rat looked like Sondra.

"Treatment is an ongoing process," Sondra piped up.

"So I've been told," I snapped at her. "Say, Sondra, why don't you go snoop around the rest of my house while I talk to my husband *alone*."

Sondra gave Paul a protective look as if she didn't know if she could trust me not to pour that glass of wine down his throat. She waited for his nod. "I'll be right in the next room." Then she scooted into the family room. I could tell she was dying to open drawers and closets. She probably had a nose on her like a K2 dog.

"What's really going on, Paul?"

Paul wouldn't quite meet my eyes. "I'm done with the program, but I still don't trust myself, Audrey. And I like it there in Wickenburg. They've hired me as a kind of handyman/caretaker on the property. The pay isn't much . . ."

I couldn't stand it one more second. "How dare you! How long are you going to continue to ignore your family and responsibilities? How long are you going to continue to ignore me? I'm having a tough time putting food on the table, and you're mucking out stalls and doing God knows what with Miss Snoop Dogg in there. Tell me the truth, damn it! Are you ever coming back, Paul?"

His blue eyes looked pained in his tanned, handsome face. He swept his arms around the room. "That's just it. Being here, trying to provide for you and the kids, the responsibilities. They're what made me drink in the first place, Audrey. Can't you understand that?"

"What I understand," I said through gritted teeth, "is that you were, and always will be, a spoiled, pampered rich boy who doesn't know how to grow up. You were a big drinker when I married you, the life of the party. It's not me, and it's not the kids, and it's not this house that drive you to drink. You just don't want to do anything that isn't *fun!*"

Paul had the audacity to look surprised, then hurt. "I thought you'd understand, Audrey. You've always been so supportive of me, and I don't know why this has to be any different. In another two or three months--"

"I think you need to leave now." I'd been gritting my teeth so hard that my jaw ached. Why hadn't I seen this man for what he truly was? How could I have been so blind? Even if Paul did conquer his addiction, he wasn't going to change.

Snoop Dogg came back in the room then. "The only alcohol in the house is in here, but I still think it's too much of a temptation for you right now, Paul."

The stupid girl hadn't even looked in the garage. I stuck my hands on my hips, imitating Reggie's pose, and I do have to say that it made me feel more powerful, more aggressive. I needed that. "I agree."

Paul shook his head sadly. "Something's gotten into you, Audrey. I don't get it."

"That's right. You don't."

By the time Reggie returned from her run, I was on my second mega glass of wine and facing an entirely new future. And for once, I wasn't crying.

What do you want me to say about the January wine club party? It changed everything.

Okay, first of all, it was a success beyond Reggie's and my wildest dreams. I know that Cynthia, to this day, takes all the credit for that, but it isn't true. I've already told you how hard Reggie and I worked to get ready for the party, starting from when we decided to branch out of the Éclatant brand in the Loire Valley and move onto the other regions in France. We were the ones who did all the research and selected the vintages and then bought cheap wine and bottled, corked, and labeled it. I have burn marks on my hands from all that steam--when I was too tired or too tipsy to put on those oven mitts--to prove it. You can bet your sweet ass that Cynthia doesn't have burn marks. Hell, she probably doesn't have stretch marks either, but I guess that's beside the point. And the point is that Cynthia never did any of the hard work, never even labored over the details of the operation, yet she still felt entitled to her piece of the pie. Oh, I know she thinks she did her part by providing the rich clients, but Reggie and I probably would have gotten around to that eventually. Maybe. Anyway, what I'm saying is that I still don't think it was fair.

The party was held on January 27th. Reggie and I both wondered what kind of decorating scheme Cynthia would create with no major holiday in sight. But she didn't disappoint. She created a kind of winter won-derland in that large family room of hers that stretched across the back of her house. She'd hung twinkling silver lights and even had fake snow that should have looked cheesy but didn't. She'd also covered the pool in back with a sheet of glass so that it looked like a skating rink. Honestly, when you walked into the back of that house, you forgot that you were in the Arizona desert. I think she'd even turned down the temperature because it was chilly in that room before the guests arrived. So chilly, in fact, that I wished I could settle in on that oversized couch of hers in my pajamas, pull a blanket up to my chin, and wrap my cold hands around a mug of hot chocolate.

Again, Reggie and I were extremely nervous before that party. We'd seriously upped the price of the wine and further embellished the story about that distant French cousin who was a monk and a vintner, who now miraculously had become a world-class distributor of French wine with access to all of the exclusive wineries in France. But you know what? Not one person at that party or the parties to come ever questioned that outlandish story. To this day, I still can't believe it that not one of those supposedly sophisticated women didn't see right through that lie like it was a moth-eaten wool sweater. But those women, dressed in their designer dresses and shoes and diamonds, bought it without question. They glugged down bottle after bottle like they were entitled to it. It just goes to prove that people really do believe what they *choose* to believe. I will grudgingly admit that Reggie was right on that one observation, not on a lot of other things, but on that score, yes.

Reggie and I were also kind of nervous about how to address Cynthia's current predicament. I thought we should act like we didn't know anything about it, but Reggie thought that was ridiculous. "It's all over the news, Audrey. How could we not know? Let's not bring it up unless she does."

We didn't have to wait long. We had lugged the last crate of wine into the kitchen--and let the record reflect that Cynthia did not help with that--when Cynthia said, without preamble: "The media has blown the story about Richard all out of proportion. Some of his disgruntled clients and competitors are just talking trash. Richard is clearing everything up as we speak. So let's not talk anymore about it tonight." She smiled that dazzling smile of hers. And I've got to say, she looked fantastic, in a silver metallic clingy dress and matching sky-high heels. She didn't look like a woman who was losing any sleep over her husband's scandal.

"Sure, Cynthia." Reggie opened a crate. "But I'm sure that a lot of other women will be bringing up the subject. A financial scandal like this is major news."

I wanted to reach over and pinch that sinewy arm of hers. Reggie couldn't let it go, couldn't wait to get in that little dig. As I said, Reggie was gobbling up The Fall of the House of Stewart, as she liked to call it, like it was a pint of Ben & Jerry's. If I didn't stop her, she'd be pressing for more details and asking Cynthia what prison she hoped the FBI would send Richard to. So I said, "I'm sure the whole story will blow over soon." I shot a warning glance at Reggie. "Let's get ready for the party."

"No, let's get the party started." Cynthia walked over to her wine cooler and pulled out a bottle of 1982 Château Lafite Rothschild.

I heard Reggie gasp beside me, and I think my mouth hung open. From our research, we knew that particular vintage went for over $3300. "Wow," I said. "Are you sure you want to open that before the party? I mean, we have all this wine here." Sadly, it was wine that would dim in comparison to this elite bottle. She'd done this at the last party too, whipped out a genuinely expensive bottle of wine from that little cooler of hers. I think that's when I began to suspect that Cynthia had something up her sleeve.

"This is Richard's last bottle from the wine cellar, and we're going to drink it." She giggled mischievously, sounding like she was already a little drunk. "Let's make it a tradition that we toast before every wine club party." She poured three glasses and passed them out. She lifted hers in the air and waited for us to do the same. "To the three of us. May we be successful."

Reggie scowled. "What do you mean, Cynthia? Are you talking about the party, or life in general, or--"

Cynthia waved her hand, dismissively. "It's just an expression, Reggie. Salut!" She tapped her glass against ours and drank.

There was no other choice but to do the same. And let me tell you, I almost swooned at that first sip. I had never tasted a wine that good before. Actually, I'd never tasted a wine over twenty dollars, but even I knew that this was an exceptional vintage. I looked at Reggie, and even though the scowl was still on her face, I could tell that she was blown away by the wine too.

There was no time to savor the wine then because we only had about twenty minutes to set up for the party. Reggie and I busied ourselves putting wine bottles and labels and glasses on the table, and Cynthia started to take out plates of prepared hors d'oeuvres from her massive Sub-zero and placing them on a big center table in the middle of the room. That's when I realized that Louisa and her nieces weren't there. "Where's Louisa?"

"The flu," Cynthia said shortly. "But I think this arrangement is better. When people get the munchies, they can get the food for themselves. I made all these from scratch."

Yeah, right. Later that evening when I went to throw away some napkins, I saw the plastic containers from Costco. All Cynthia had done was transfer those appetizers onto fancy plates. But I didn't know that then, and as soon as the guests arrived, the party swung into action. There wasn't any charity--real or fake--that we had to resort to for this party. The women seemed impressed by the selection, and I kept thinking to myself how smart Reggie and I had been to put different wines in the bottles this time because now the varietals did taste distinctly different. I could hear women comparing them, acting like they knew what they were talking about, while Reggie went into her presentation on the different grapes and soils in the various domains. Cynthia kept circulating, urging people to buy, and very soon I was marking down each bottle sold with its price and putting the money into a metal cash box that I had covered with the various labels I had designed for each type of wine. I didn't know how much money we were making, but I knew it was a lot. I couldn't wait until Reggie and I got home and counted our bounty.

Reggie was excited too, and when the party wound down, she was anxious to scoot out the door and go home with our fabulous ill-gotten gain. But I didn't think it would be very nice of us to leave Cynthia alone to clean up the mess. It's not in my nature to leave a mess I helped create in a person's house, to eat and run, you might say. So we washed the crystal wine glasses by hand and put the rest of the food away, that kind of thing. Reggie grumbled under her breath the whole time. Understandable when you consider that she didn't even clean up the messes in her own kitchen, but it wouldn't have been right not to do it. I don't remember talking very much during the cleanup. We were all tired.

Reggie and I were finally ready to head out the door, I had the cash box under my arm, when Cynthia said, "Ladies, you haven't finished your Château Lafite. It's too good to go to waste."

Even Reggie had to concede that she had a point. So we dutifully gathered around Cynthia's granite kitchen island once again and sipped our wine, talking about how successful the party had been. We'd sold five of the seven fake Romanée Conti 1959, which was the real triumph of the night, and we'd sold almost all the wine. Out of over two hundred bottles of wine, we only had twelve left. As we talked, I realized I still had the cash box under my arm--kind of like I was protecting it, I suppose--so I set it carefully on the counter. When I looked up, Cynthia's eyes were on that box.

"How much money did we make?" Cynthia raised her eyes to mine, and calmly took a sip of wine.

Surely, I'd misheard her. "Excuse me?"

"What do you mean by *we*?" Reggie's voice was suspicious.

Cynthia had been drinking wine with the guests all night--to help sales, she said--but she was stone-cold sober. She spoke slowly and distinctly, enunciating every word. "By *we*, I mean Audrey, Reggie, and Cynthia. So let me ask the question again: How much money did we make?"

I was too flabbergasted to speak, but Reggie, of course, was not. "There are two people in this partnership, Audrey and me. You are not our partner, Cynthia."

"I beg to differ, Reggie. The three of us are in this together now."

Cynthia's blue eyes were cold, and frankly, she was scaring me a little. "You can't be serious, Cynthia. You have all the money you need, and Reggie and I started this wine club together. We've done all the work, and all you've done is host two parties."

"Do you know how much it costs to host one of these parties?" When we didn't answer because we knew she must have spent a lot, she said, "Which reminds me. I want to be reimbursed for the parties' expenses before we divide up the money." She sounded like a bandit in an old western who had just robbed a stagecoach and was divvying up the loot with his shifty partners.

"Fine." Reggie's simmering was reaching a boil. "You won't be hosting any more parties. You're out, Cynthia."

Cynthia's smile was tight. "Your wine club won't survive without my influence and my guests."

"We'll see about that!" Reggie huffed.

"No, I don't believe we will." Cynthia set down her wine glass. "We'll divide the money three ways now, minus my expenses. Open the cash box, Audrey."

"You will get one-third of this money over my dead body." Reggie glared at her. She was always so overly dramatic that it was embarrassing.

I looked from one to the other. If it came to a catfight between them--and they both looked like they were aching to take a swing at each other--I thought that Reggie would win by sheer strength. But I wouldn't discount Cynthia doing something underhanded, like gouging out Reggie's eyes. I cleared my throat. "Let's be reasonable here. Cynthia, you've done a wonderful job hosting the last two parties, and we will reimburse you for your expenses. However, Reggie and I started this wine club, and we don't want a third partner." I picked up the cash box, tucked it under my arm, and took Reggie's arm. "Let's go."

"Wait a minute." Cynthia hadn't moved, but the determination in her voice halted us. "I want you both to remember that you forced my hand. I have been nothing but nice to the two of you." She picked up her wine glass again and took a sip. "You are going to let me be a partner in your wine club, or I will expose your dirty little secret. French wine? I don't think so."

FEBRUARY

16

CYNTHIA

I would like to clear up something once and for all. I was not menacing or mean when I informed Audrey and Reggie that I was going to be a third partner in their phony wine club. I merely *suggested* that it would be in their best interest to cut me in on the deal. I mean, come on. After all my hard work, it was only fair that I participated in profit sharing. Without my magnificent house, my exquisite decorating, and my wealthy friends, the wine club wouldn't have survived past that first podunk, amateur party they threw back in November. Those two women had no business sense at all. I had understood that important fact right away, so when I saw my opportunity after the January wine club, I grabbed it. There was just over $90,000 in cash and checks in that crummy little metal box that Audrey stored it in. Seriously, it looked like she was a sixth-grader hoarding her allowance, and it took all my willpower not to rip it out of her hands and tell them that I was now the one in charge. But I didn't do that. No, I was perfectly nice about the whole thing. And it's only justified that a person gets paid for services rendered, right? That's the lesson I took away from my years in Vegas. Trust me when I say that I learned that lesson well.

It might be true that I wouldn't have *horned in* on their little scheme--as Reggie persists in calling it--if I hadn't desperately needed money. When your assets are frozen, you're caught between a rock and a hard place, and my husband was making no move to contact me to tell me it had all been a mistake, that he had not bilked millions out of investors and ruined everything. I might have been in the dark about his whole operation and naive about the consequences, but that didn't stop me from daydreaming that I would get some message from Richard that he had a secret bank account in Switzerland and would be sending a private jet for me.

And Felicity too, I suppose. It's funny, but I rarely gave a thought to Felicity during that time. I'd told her that I would think of something to help us get through the unpleasant ordeal when she had cried in my arms, but instead of forming any meaningful connection with me, she had gone on about her merry, selfish way, asking me for money for gas and Pucci salon visits and trips to the mall after they cut off her credit card. She didn't give a damn where the money was coming from and continued to act as if it grew on trees. In no time at all, I had quickly gone through the rest of the money in the safe and had no idea what I was going to do next.

I hadn't been so broke since my short-lived dancing career in LA, and I had truly forgotten how miserable it was. Let me correct that. When you're used to having money and don't give a second thought to dropping a couple grand at a day spa or Saks, the lack of money is twice as devastating. In no time at all, I was reduced to doing my own hair and nails, which doesn't sound like a big deal to most people, but when you're a former Mrs. Arizona and have a reputation to uphold, it is a big deal. So I didn't go out much during those days. It wasn't vanity or the lack of money that kept me from my usual haunts, my long luncheons with my so-called friends, my Pilates and yoga classes, my hair salon. I couldn't bear how people would look at me. Believe me, there was no compassion when the mighty have fallen. Rather, there was a smug delight, and people would look at me like: "Serves you right. Now you're one of us." But this was the thing: I wasn't like one of them. I was an innocent victim. How could they not see that?

On the night of the January wine club party, I was feeling pretty low. I'd had to let Louisa go, not that she was surprised by that announcement--even she watched the news--and I'm pretty sure she had a knowing smirk on her face when I told her I no longer required her services. I didn't come right out and say that I couldn't afford her anymore, but I'm pretty sure she knew, judging from that smirk. It was strange. I didn't think it would be as great of sacrifice as it turned out to be. We'd rarely had a conversation that lasted more than a minute, due mostly to the fact that I couldn't understand her Spanglish, and she pretended not to understand my perfectly spoken English. So I was surprised at how much I missed her, yet I did miss those lumbering, echoing footsteps and the knowledge that she was somewhere in the house pretending to work, but instead, watching her soaps. The house was too big, too quiet. It really did start to feel more like a mausoleum than a home, especially when dust started to appear on every surface. I halfway expected to turn a corner and see a petrified mummy walking towards me, arms outstretched. It was scary.

I guess what I'm trying to say is that my decision to go into partnership with Audrey and Reggie was not as premeditated as they would like you to believe. There was something about the way that Audrey guarded that cash box that made things click into place for me. Those two thought nothing of waltzing into my home and selling their fake wine and then waltzing right back out again with all the loot, not bothering to clean up the mess they'd made. I ask you, is that fair? No, it is not. And I was the one who told them that they needed better cheap wine to put into those fancy fake bottles of theirs. They would have been caught early in the game if they'd continued on their original path. So I think that you could safely say that I was the one who truly figured out how to make their scheme work. After I got involved, the money started rolling in. I take full credit for that.

I'm not going to lie. I knew that neither one of those women was initially happy to have me as a partner. They made that clear right away. They were standing in my kitchen, drinking that exorbitantly expensive 1982 Château Lafite Rothschild--which neither one of them thanked me for, by the way--and they looked shocked when I informed them I was now their partner. I mean, how dense could they be? From the beginning, all roads had been leading up to this.

Reggie, as usual, spoke first. "How long have you known that the wine isn't French?"

"I've had my suspicions ever since you rammed your cart full of Two-Buck Chuck into mine at Trader Joe's, Reggie." I don't think I suspected anything then, but saying so made my position stronger and my story better.

Reggie's face darkened. "Shit."

"What is she talking about, Reggie? When did this happen, and why didn't you tell me?" Audrey looked at her accusingly.

"I didn't think it was that big of deal--"

"Of course it's a big deal, Reggie!" Audrey snapped. "We're partners, and we're supposed to tell each other things like that. I would never have agreed to let Cynthia host the Christmas party if you'd told me--" She stopped suddenly, remembering I was standing right across from her.

"I was going to tell you, and then I just . . . didn't." Reggie shrugged. She didn't look at all apologetic.

Audrey glared at her. "If you'd told me, it would have changed everything."

Aha, I was thinking. *There is a chink in their armor.* That was good news for me and information that I could work with. This whole scheme wasn't going to work well for me if it was always two against one. I was smiling when I said, "It doesn't matter now, Audrey. I know about the scam, I'm your partner, and it's time to count the money."

I knew that Audrey had been raking in the dough all night, but even I was surprised by the amount. The problem was that a large amount of it was in checks, which wasn't an optimal situation. Checks can be traced, and it was an issue I was going to have to address very soon. "I'll take the checks to the bank tomorrow and cash them. Then we can all meet back here tomorrow afternoon and open a bottle of wine and celebrate." I think it's perfectly clear that I was being friendly.

"Over my dead body." Reggie said that kind of thing a lot.

I was slightly offended by that. Not overly surprised, but still offended. "What's the matter, Reggie? Don't you trust me?"

Before Reggie could open her mouth, Audrey said hurriedly, "It's not that, Cynthia. It's just that it's always been my job to cash the checks."

"Who said it was your job, Audrey?" Reggie asked snidely. "I mean, for all I know, you've been pocketing some money before you give me my share."

"Damn it, Reggie. Don't be ridiculous. I would never do such a thing." However, Audrey's face was flaming red.

"Ladies," I interjected, "why don't we all go to the bank together tomorrow?" The biggest checks were for the five bottles of Romanée Conti 1959. Five large checks and three partners. There was no way we could divide that equitably. And I, for one, wasn't going to take one check and give them each two. From the looks on their faces, I could tell they were thinking the same thing.

Reggie nodded sullenly. "I guess that's the only way. I guess the question now is, who's going to take the cash box overnight?"

I could tell that it was Audrey's turn to be offended, but she was always more diplomatic than Reggie--at least in the beginning. "I'll take the box and leave the key with Cynthia."

She produced a tiny, flimsy key from the pocket of her gray slacks. What did I say about acting like a sixth-grader? It was one of those miniature little keys that looked like the kind you would use to lock a diary you didn't want your mother to read. It was kind of laughable. But we weren't laughing. We were talking about a lot of money, and as it turned out, three desperate women.

"We'll meet at the Chase Bank on Thunderbird," Reggie instructed. "No one banks there, right?" After Audrey and I shook our heads, she added, "At nine o'clock sharp." She looked at me pointedly, as if I wouldn't be bothered to be there early in the morning instead of in the afternoon. While that might have been true in the past, it wasn't anymore.

I'd be waiting at the bank before either of them showed up. And I had the key.

Do you know how hard it is to cash a check at a bank where you don't have an account? Well, neither did I until Audrey, Reggie, and I had to go to four different banks before we found one that would cash a couple of the checks. And then we had to go to five other banks to cash the remaining ones. This was the thing. We couldn't divide up the checks and go our separate ways, as I suggested because all the checks were made out to Audrey Maynard. Not only was this news to me, but it was also news to Reggie.

"Why didn't you tell me that you had all the checks made out to you, Audrey?" Reggie was so disgusted by that point that she couldn't stop pacing.

"Who else was I supposed to have those women make the checks out to?" Audrey seemed genuinely bewildered by the whole thing. "It seemed like all the women were crowding around me at once, and what could I do, have them make it out to Éclatant Wines? You never did set up a company on LegalZoom, Reggie. You were supposed to do that, but you never got around to it. You'd rather go for a run than sit down in front of your computer." It was her turn to stare angrily at her friend.

"How about Cash, Audrey? They could have made out the checks to *Cash*."

Of course I was enjoying their bickering, but the more pressing concern to me was that those two were still thinking on such a small level. They hadn't even begun to see the big picture. We were standing in the parking lot of the last bank after spending all morning running around town like chickens with their heads cut off. It was so amateur hour, and it only proved how much these two women needed my skills. It wasn't like I was particularly savvy about running a business, but I had been self-employed at one time. Not that those customers would pay in anything but cash. However, you get my point. I was smarter than these two when it came to getting a successful business off the ground.

I pulled out my phone and started to type. "The way I see it, we have two options. We could open up a joint account at one bank, or we could get a credit card machine. Merchant One is one of the top five small business card processors."

Reggie actually looked impressed. "I like the idea of getting a credit card machine, like one of those portable ones they use in beauty shops and some restaurants."

"I like the idea of a joint bank account. We'd all get checkbooks and ATM cards, right?"

"Why don't we do both?" If we were going to make as much money as I hoped to make, both seemed essential. After both Reggie and Audrey nodded, I said, "Let's go to another bank and set up an account under the name Éclatant Wine." I was feeling pretty proud of myself. I'd been a partner for less than twenty-four hours and was already contributing excellent ideas.

But Reggie was one step ahead of me. "We can't do that. We'd need a tax ID number, and I, for one, don't want to pay taxes on this money. Do you?" She arched her eyebrows at me.

I didn't know if the question was a trap or a test. Did Reggie want me to say that I thought I should pay taxes on my share--which is something I didn't want to do--or that I was on board with the club, the legal ramifications be damned? It was a conundrum. My husband was currently under indictment for all kinds of federal crimes, and I honestly couldn't remember if tax evasion was on that long list. Yet if I wanted to partake of the earnings of this club, which I did, we should all agree on the tax issue.

"I'd rather not pay the taxes." I looked to Audrey.

She shrugged but looked nervous. "What's one more broken law at this point?"

Let me tell you, that Reggie was a sly one because next, she said, "I don't think we can set up an account in our names either."

I had a suggestion for that. "We could continue cashing checks made out to Cash, and we could keep the money in Richard's safe. It's hidden in our wall and fireproof--"

Audrey was already shaking her head. "That would be rather inconvenient for Reggie and me, wouldn't it?"

Reggie snapped her fingers. "I've got it. We could open a college account in our daughters' names. How about that?"

I had no idea if that would work either, but if our daughters' didn't pay taxes on it, what was the harm? "The Felicity, Marcy, Hayley Account. I like it."

"I like FHM Account better, the initials placed alphabetically."

I conceded on that point.

"I don't know." Audrey had the perpetual nervous look on her face. "I always wanted to set up a college account for Marcy, but we didn't have the extra money. And now to do it as a cover for a fraudulent wine company seems unfair to her. And to Hayley and to . . . Felicity, I guess."

I didn't like the way she hesitated over Felicity's name, but then again, Felicity probably wasn't going to need college money once Richard straightened out his monetary problems. And who was I kidding? There was no love lost between my daughter and me and hadn't been for a long time. As far as I was concerned, Felicity could fend for herself. At this point in the game, I needed the money a lot more than she did.

"But Audrey, it *is* a college fund. We're going to make so much money that there will be plenty for our daughters to use toward college. It's a great idea."

Audrey managed a smile. "Well, Reggie, if you put it that way, I guess I'm in."

So it was settled. After we all went home and got our daughters' social security numbers, we met at a Harris Bank on Scottsdale Road. It wasn't difficult to persuade the woman behind the desk to open the account when we told her that the three girls were close cousins and all wanted to go to the same university. Again, that was Reggie's idea, and I was beginning to marvel at what a smooth talker she was. I was good, but she was damn close. Notice that I didn't say *liar.* I didn't think of it as lying, not then. We were just three business partners trying to make a go of it. That was all.

When we finished at the bank, I thought something had changed between the three of us, that being partners in crime had brought us closer together in a very brief period. I suggested that we go out to lunch at a cute little French bistro I frequented that was down the street. "We need to celebrate." I guess I said that a lot, back in the beginning.

"Isn't that place expensive?" Audrey asked.

"It doesn't matter, Audrey. We need to get home and start to brainstorm our next wine club party." Reggie took her by the arm.

The restaurant was expensive, and I almost offered to treat them before I realized that I could no longer afford to eat there either. "We could go somewhere else, like Chili's." I shuddered inwardly.

Audrey looked torn. "I do like that Awesome Blossom of theirs."

Reggie took hold of her arm possessively. "Audrey, we have a lot of work to do."

I suddenly, desperately did not want to go home to that big, cold, empty house. "I have a couple of hours free right now. I'd be happy to help you."

"That's not necessary, Cynthia. But thanks anyway," Reggie added as an afterthought.

"Why not, Reggie? Having another person do the work would be really helpful."

"We don't need her help in that part of the operation." Reggie could be so stubborn. Have I mentioned that?

"Okay, maybe not now, but in another week or two when we start all that bottling, corking, and labeling, it would be nice to have another pair of hands."

"It gets so crowded in your kitchen, Audrey, that we'd be stepping all over each other."

For crying out loud, you know? I was not only extending an olive branch, but I was also offering to help them. Under normal circumstances, I would be happy to leave the dirty work to them, but my circumstances were no longer normal. I was playing a waiting game, waiting for the other shoe to drop, so to speak. And I was lonely.

But I have never, ever been a beggar. "That's fine." I plastered my prettiest smile on my face. "But maybe when you get to that bottling stage, you could move the operation to my house. I have a very large kitchen, as you know."

Audrey brightened. "That sounds like a great idea--"

Reggie interrupted before Audrey could finish. "We'll think about it, Cynthia."

They should have taken that olive branch. Things might have turned out differently if they had.

There was another thing I missed about Louisa. She had multiple brothers and sisters and a large extended family that I had called upon from time to time. For example, if I needed the palm trees around the pool trimmed, I would have Louisa call her brother Jose. If I needed extra help at all the parties I used to throw, I called upon her nieces to help serve, just like I did at the Christmas wine club party. Her mother, Guadalupe, was a great seamstress who had done alterations on my fancy ball gowns from time to time. And her nephew Eduardo would come over with his long ladder and change the lightbulbs on my twenty-foot high ceilings when one went out, and move various pieces of furniture from room to room when I got bored. Altogether, Louisa's family was very useful to me, and they worked for dirt cheap. Sometimes I even got away with paying Jose or Eduardo or Guadalupe with a case of beer. It had been a very satisfying relationship.

But it was her cousins, Pepe and Angel, who had really come in handy in the last couple of months. You see, I am getting back to the story of Buck Boyd and what had been going on with him during the months of December and January when I was supposed to pay him another installment on the blackmail money--that he had now jacked up to one million dollars. Since I no longer had the money or the contacts to hire a hitman to put the bead on Buck, I had to come up with another plan.

You do not have to look at me that way. When I said that I wanted Buck Boyd dead, I didn't mean *dead* dead. I just meant dead to me. He needed to go away. Now that Richard was out of the picture--I assumed temporarily--you would think that it didn't matter if Buck sent him the incriminating packet of information he had on me. I mean, the FBI didn't know where Richard was, so how could a lowlife like Buck Boyd possibly know where to send his trash, right? However, Buck knew something else about me that I never wanted to see the light of day, an act that I'm pretty sure didn't have a statute of limitations. You've probably figured out what I'm talking about now, haven't you?

Anyway, Pepe and Angel were burly guys. Taller than most Mexicans and broad-shouldered with bulging biceps, they were exactly what I needed to keep Buck Boyd away. So I'd hired them to be my security guards, so to speak. Or maybe they were more like bouncers. The first time that Buck pulled up to my front door to collect another installment of money at the end of December, Pepe, or maybe it was Angel--I had a hard time telling them apart--ended up picking up Buck by the seat of his pants and throwing him back into that ratty camper of his. I was watching from the front window, hiding behind the curtain when that happened, and I cannot tell you how much satisfaction it gave me to see Buck getting tossed into the front seat headfirst. I'm pretty sure he banged his head on the steering wheel. The second time he showed up, about a week or so later, he came armed with a baseball bat. However, Pepe and Angel were quick on their feet, and in no time at all, they had wrestled the bat from his hands and chased him across the front yard. It took a couple of hours before Buck returned, his hands held up in surrender, to retrieve his truck.

I suppose you could say that next to watching *Wheel of Fortune*, it was my major form of entertainment during the months of December and January. I didn't doubt that Buck would not give up easily, and he didn't. He tried approaching the house in a UPS van once--he even wore that ugly brown uniform--and made it to the front door before Pepe and Angel caught onto him. And boy, did they let him have it then! Fists went flying before Buck was successfully tossed back into his vehicle. I gave Pepe and Angel each a case of beer that time. Buck kept trying, though. For his next attempt, he donned a business suit and drove a black Lincoln Town Car, like he was picking me up to take me to the airport or something. He had a cap pulled low over his forehead and had on a fake mustache. It was only after he rang the bell and Pepe and Angel could hear me screaming through the locked front door *it's him, it's him* that they tackled him to the ground.

Meanwhile, Buck was using other methods to get under my skin. He kept leaving threatening messages on my phone. As a rule, I don't answer my phone when I don't recognize the number, but Buck was tricky. He must have spent a small fortune on those burner phones you can get from Walmart, probably because he didn't want those messages traced back to him, which was smart. I guess I do have to give him that. And he was smart enough not to leave a trail of emails that could be linked back to him too. But he made sure to make his presence known. He left a package addressed to Richard in the mailbox. Naturally, I had been expecting that, and naturally, I didn't read any of the papers inside. I knew what was in them. I went directly up to Richard's office and ran all the documents through the shredder. Two more identical packages that followed suffered the same fate. I theorized that Buck was trying to make clear to me that the evidence would always be around. Point taken.

Did I mention that he followed me? I would be driving to an appointment, and I'd look in my rearview mirror and see that ramshackle camper of his about twenty feet behind me. Now he never overtly approached me in public--maybe he was again protecting himself, who knows?--but he made sure I knew that he was there. I almost got used to seeing that camper parked down my street or in the parking lot of my hair salon. Even when I didn't see that camper, I still *expected* to see it, which was almost worse.

Now don't get me wrong. It wasn't that I was afraid of Buck Boyd, not exactly. I knew his mama and his daddy and the house he had grown up in. I even knew that his brother had an IQ of about 60 and hadn't made it past the sixth grade. So rather than being afraid of him, it was more like I was *unnerved* by his utter devotion to his cause: his desire to ruin me.

But ultimately, I knew that Buck Boyd was a coward. I mean, he hadn't even made it through college on a football scholarship before he hightailed it back to Marion, where he thought he was a big fish in a small pond. He probably couldn't hack the big league. Then he had been stupid enough to marry Mary Wilson, the girl who stole the homecoming queen crown from me. That alone showed that he had no vision or imagination. Which was also proven by the fact that he was still driving that stupid old camper. I had just given the man $200,000, so why hadn't he gone out and bought a decent car? That's the first thing that most people did when they came into a windfall. They'd go out and buy a new car, the more expensive, the better. So why hadn't Buck gone out and bought a BMW or a Lexus, considered his job with me done, and gone back home? Do you see what I mean? The man had zip when it came to thinking outside the box.

It's hard to say how long things with Buck would have continued in the same vein if Richard hadn't gotten caught and left me in such a financial shambles. I am not lying when I say I harbored the hope that Buck would have seen the news and realized that he was trying to get blood from a turnip. He hadn't come around in a while, so maybe that was what had happened. Or maybe Pepe and Angel had finally scared him off. I didn't know, but it was now February, and I had no protection. When Louisa went, she took her entire family with her, which seemed rather vindictive on her part, if you ask me. I had been nothing but nice to that family, and now even they didn't want anything to do with me.

I always want to start this part of the story with: "It was a dark and stormy night . . ." Stories like that always set the right ominous tone. But it wasn't dark and stormy, and it wasn't even night. It was a February afternoon in Arizona, one of the best times of the year to be in Scottsdale. The daily temperature can reach the mid-70s, and tourists flock to town for the Waste Management Golf Open, the Barrett Jackson car auction, and the beginning of spring training. All in all, it's a festive time of year, and even I had caught a bit of spring fever on that warm and sunny afternoon. I had turned off the air conditioning, opened the Nano doors in the back of the house, and was thinking about putting on my bikini and sunning myself by the pool, something I never did because nothing ages a beautiful woman faster than baking in the hot Arizona sun. I guess what I'm trying to say is that I wasn't acting like my normal self on that particular day.

It was around three o'clock in the afternoon, and although I wanted a glass of wine, it was much too early to do so. I didn't want to become one of those women who sat alone and drank all day, tempting as it was. So as a compromise, I'd gone out to the guesthouse and found a wine cooler, which doesn't even really count as alcohol in my book. I hadn't been in the guesthouse in months and had no idea who had stocked the refrigerator with the six-pack of Seagram's Escapes. My guess was Felicity, but it was one more thing I wouldn't confront her with. The girl was only a couple months away from turning eighteen, so what did I care? It was such a small matter in the big scheme of things. I settled myself on a chaise lounge on the patio, out of the sun, and sipped the cooler. It was such a beautiful day that it even made my troubles seem less dark. I closed my eyes.

The next thing I knew, someone was tapping me on the shoulder. "Wake up, sleepyhead. We have some business to attend to."

It is always a bad thing to be caught off guard. I knew that, yet for some inexplicable reason, I had totally let down all my defenses on that ill-fated afternoon. I was drinking in the middle of the day, and I had not only unlocked a door of the house but also left it wide open. I knew who it was, of course, even before I opened my eyes. I could smell his beer breath; I could sense his heaviness. In the brief moment before I opened my eyes to face the man, the only thing I could be thankful for was that I wasn't in a bikini. My defenses were down, but at least I wasn't almost naked.

"It looks like you were expecting me."

I was in his shadow as Buck Boyd leaned over me. "I wasn't."

"Don't you hate to drink alone?"

"I'll get you a beer." It sounds funny that I would offer a drink to my mortal enemy, but I needed a quick excuse to get up from the chaise. I was at a distinct disadvantage with him looming over me. Plus, if Buck drank, he might get sloppy, and he might be more manageable. He followed me into the house, as I knew he would. I got a beer from the Sub-Zero, and after a moment of hesitation, I reached for Richard's expensive Johnny Walker Blue Label blended scotch whiskey. Scotch would get the job done faster than beer, so I poured a hefty glass of that too.

"I do believe that you've been avoiding me, Cindy Lou. You hurt my feelings." Buck eyed the scotch, then reached for it.

"I hope I hurt more than that," I said.

Buck laughed good-naturedly. "Yeah, what happened to the Mexican henchmen? They could throw a mean punch."

"Didn't you get the message? I don't want you here." My voice came out level, but I was quaking inside. It probably wasn't one of my better ideas, but I got a bottle of Sauvignon Blanc out of the refrigerator and poured a glass. It was a good thing it had a screw top. I could never have managed a corkscrew right then, although it did occur to me that it might come in handy as a weapon.

"Yeah, I got that loud and clear." Buck drained his glass. "But this is the thing, Cindy Lou. You and me had an agreement."

Without a word, I placed the bottle of scotch in front of him. All this time, mind you, my mind was working, considering and rejecting means of escape and methods to get the man out of my house, or preferably, out of my life.

"According to my calculations, you still owe me $800,000." He poured another glass.

"I already gave you $200,000, Buck. That seems fair to me. Say, why don't you buy yourself a new car and go back home?" I eyed him over the rim of my glass as I took a tentative sip. Despite the circumstances, it tasted astonishingly refreshing. I took a larger swallow. Liquid courage, I guess you could say.

"Aww, Cindy Lou, don't be like that." He smiled, and it was the same boyish grin he had in high school. It pained me to recognize that he was still a good-looking man.

I set down my glass. "Look, Buck. I'm tired of this game. It's time for you to go."

"I thought I made my position clear to you, Cindy Lou. I don't have a home to go back to. Besides, I kind of like it here. I've got my eye on a condo not too far from here. Wouldn't that be something if we were neighbors, Cindy Lou?"

The first thing I thought of was, *so that's what he's spending my money on.* Then the horror of it came back all over again, along with the truth I'd been pushing away for the last two months, the truth I hadn't let myself dwell on anymore. But it hadn't gone away. The awful truth was that Buck was *never* going to leave me alone.

Buck didn't take his eyes off me, even as he refilled his glass. "That husband of yours has got himself into quite the situation."

"That's none of your business." I picked up my wine and drank.

"Oh, I think it's everybody's business now, Cindy Lou. Just ask CNN and Fox News. I figure the next thing you're going to tell me is that you don't have any money to pay me what is rightfully mine."

It infuriated me that he would even think that he deserved any of my hard-earned money. Well, Richard's hard-earned money, perhaps, but I had paid my dues to get my share. Still, I thought that the best tactic right then would be to agree. "I don't have any money. You were always so bright, Buck. Why, you nailed that one right on the head. Now finish your drink and leave. Our so-called *agreement*--and I never agreed to anything--is over."

"I've been pondering this problem." It would seem that Buck always pretended not to hear me. "And I do believe that you have some saleable items around this great big house of yours. Isn't that right, Cindy Lou?"

I was more surprised at this suggestion than I should have been. Years of being out of the racket had definitely dulled my game. So I stalled. "The FBI has frozen my assets."

"What the FBI doesn't know doesn't count. Have you made a full inventory of your assets yet, Cindy Lou?"

I wondered how he knew I was supposed to do that but hadn't gotten around to it yet. "What kind of saleable items did you have in mind?" I used my best bitch voice for that one.

"Oh," Buck looked around the kitchen and pointed to the crystal wine glasses hanging from a rack, "like those. Baccarat, are they?"

I shrugged my shoulders. "Fine. Take them."

Buck looked surprised, then amused. "Nah, that was too easy. They must not be worth much." His eyes seized upon my hand. "That ring of yours should bring a nice chunk of change. How about that for a start?" He looked satisfied with himself.

"What? This?" I held up my hand; then I pretended to start to pull it off. "You can have this." I moved the ring ever so slowly toward my knuckle. "But you do know it's fake, right?"

"Aww, come on, Cindy Lou. You're joshing me."

"Nope. Haven't you done your research, Buck? All of us rich ladies wear our fake jewels in public, while the real ones are hidden in our safes. Why, that's just common knowledge. We want to protect ourselves against *thieves*." My ring, of course, was real, but there was no way in hell that I was letting Buck Boyd get his hands on it. I'm not talking about sentimental value. I'm talking about monetary value. It was the most valuable asset I had.

Buck looked torn as he finished his third glass of scotch. He scratched his head, then seemed to come to a decision. "All right then, Cindy Lou. Show me your safe. I bet there're all kinds of items in there that could help settle your debt to your old friend. And don't be telling me that you don't know the combination to that safe."

I'd been about to do just that, the words had been on the tip of my tongue, but Buck beating me to the punch gave me the idea that I'd been searching for ever since he walked into the backyard. I sighed dramatically. "Okay, you win. It's this way."

I didn't lead him up to Richard's study, although I would have loved to see the look on his face when I opened the door and revealed that it was empty. You see, I had decided at the last minute to put my share of the wine club money in a shoebox in my vast closet because I didn't trust Felicity, who might have figured out the combination. However, that plan would not have gotten rid of Buck Boyd. So instead, I led him down the back stairs to the basement. I opened the door to the wine cellar and led him through.

"Why is this wine cellar empty?" he asked as he saw all the empty shelves and coolers.

"I drank it all."

Buck laughed, the last laugh he would have in quite a while.

I led him to the back of the wine cellar and pushed the hidden button behind the last cooler, and the soundproof door slid open. I reached in and switched on the overhead light and stepped inside the small room. "Come on." I motioned to Buck. "You have to see this. The safe is in the back."

"I never would have thought of looking for it here." Buck actually sounded impressed.

"That's the point."

As soon as he was fully into the room, I pushed him with all my might and lunged for the door. I pressed the button once again. Just as the door was sliding shut, Buck turned around, and I could see the look of surprised dismay on his face.

I am not going to lie. Locking Buck Boyd in Richard's panic room was one of the most satisfying moments of my life.

17

AUDREY

I know.

What I should have done with my take of the money from the January wine club was pay off some of my astronomical credit card debt. That would have been the sensible thing to do, wouldn't it? Well, I didn't do the sensible thing. It was the first time I had that much solid cash in my hands, and I guess it went straight to my head. The best way to explain it is to say that it was like I sat down and polished off an entire bottle of wine on an empty stomach. It was such a heady, euphoric feeling with no possibility of a hangover, or so I thought. You must remember that I grew up in a household where any extra money meant another trip to the nearest liquor store for my parents, and even during my long marriage to Paul, we had always been strapped for cash by the end of the month. We had never even gotten far enough ahead in our debts to start saving for that mythical "rainy day." So for me to have that much surplus of cash in my possession made me feel like I'd just won the lottery.

Don't get me wrong. I didn't just go out and blow it, at least not to my way of thinking. After Paul and his life coach--yeah, right--stopped by my house, I finally realized that I should not count on him coming home anytime soon. As a matter of fact, I wasn't sure I wanted him back. I hate to admit it, but I was becoming more like Reggie in that department. On some days, I would wake up so angry with him that I couldn't see straight. Why was it that some men, when they reached their mid-forties, suddenly decided that they weren't happy? They were no longer satisfied with the life they led, the cards they'd been dealt, which included their jobs, their homes, their wives, and their children. Did some giant gong suddenly go off in their heads when they woke up one fateful morning, a gong that signaled it was time to go on a futile search for greener pastures? It must be a real affliction because you hear about it all the time.

But my question is this: Why don't women do the same damn thing, just up and leave? Why are we the ones who are always left holding the bag?

I'm sorry; I didn't mean to rant. I'll return to the subject at hand. What I did with a large chunk of that money was buy a car for Marcy. My windfall occurred two weeks before her sixteenth birthday on February 10th, and even though she had quit nagging me about a car for her Sweet Sixteen, I bought her one anyway. Well, I didn't buy it; I leased it. It had been so long since I bought a new car--and I wanted her to have a new car with an extended warranty, given that Paul would not be around to help with any minor repairs or changing the oil--that I was shocked at the price of new vehicles. So leasing seemed like the best option. It was only one more monthly payment. Furthermore, it would really help me out to have Marcy run errands for me and pick up Jimmy, that sort of thing. It was, in fact, very practical for me to get my sixteen-year-old daughter a car.

Okay, it might have been a bribe. Ever since Marcy joined the Tigerettes, I had felt the distance growing between us. We didn't sit down and have our long talks anymore, and the more time she was spending with Felicity and her privileged group, the more the chasm deepened. While she never did apologize for that raunchy dance she and Hayley performed at the January basketball game, she had, possibly to make amends, started to spend more time with Jimmy. She was the one who helped him with his baths and put him to bed on all the nights I was too tired to get up from a kitchen chair because I had worked on my feet all day over a pot of boiling water--and was soon going to have to get up and repeat the process until well past midnight. She had become more helpful, and I wanted to reward her for that. Maybe I was trying to make up for her absent father too. Maybe I wanted her to love me again.

So on the morning of her sixteenth birthday, I had the car parked in the driveway, a big red bow on top, like the kind you see in Christmas commercials. I was so excited that I was shaking as I made her favorite French toast for breakfast and waited for her to come downstairs. It was a Saturday, and my plan was to take her to get her driver's license in the new car. Reggie was probably going to be mad at me because I wasn't going to work designing the new labels that day, but I didn't care. This day was going to be for my daughter, and it was long overdue. I knew that she would pass the test. Kent had been kind enough to include her in the lessons he gave to Hayley, which was something that further irked Reggie because she liked to bitch and moan that her husband didn't contribute anything during that time. But he did come around a lot more than she let on. That's Reggie for you. The glass was always half-empty.

When Marcy finally came down the stairs, no doubt lured by the aroma of the French toast, she didn't mention that there weren't any presents waiting for her on the kitchen table like there usually were on birthday mornings. "That smells good, Mom." Marcy, who hadn't eaten much in months, looked appropriately hungry.

"Happy birthday, honey!" I put a plate of French toast in front of her and kissed her cheek. "What are your plans for the day?"

Jimmy, who had already been planted in front of the TV, straggled in at the sound of her voice. He'd made a necklace out of painted elbow macaroni that he shyly gave to her. "Happy birthday, Marcy!"

"I love it!" Marcy promptly put on the necklace and gave Jimmy a big hug. She was the only one who could do that without him trying to squirm out of the embrace.

I felt such love as I gazed at my two children. They had been such troopers during Paul's absence, even while they'd been stuck with me. All in all, I thought the three of us had done a good job of navigating the choppy waters. Marcy hadn't answered my question about her plans, and I was too excited to hold in my big surprise any longer. At that point, I wasn't very good at keeping secrets. That was yet to come.

"Don't you want to know where your present is?" I was practically hopping from foot to foot.

"That's okay, Mom. I know money's been tight. You've had to spend a lot on the Tigerette stuff."

Well, that about broke my heart. For one thing, I didn't think she had appreciated all the money I'd spent, and for another, the fact that she hadn't been expecting anything from me brought tears to my eyes. I was all choked up, but I said, "You might want to look out the front window. Something is waiting for you."

She looked at me, her green eyes wide. "Are you saying what I think you're saying, Mom?"

"Could be."

She dropped her fork and ran to the front door, Jimmy behind her. I could hear her whoop of joy as she bounded out the front door. The entire neighborhood heard it too. By the time I reached the driveway, a few neighbors had come outside to investigate. My neighbors on Sheena were an incredibly snoopy bunch, but on that particular morning, I didn't care. I wanted everyone to see my daughter's joy.

Marcy opened the driver's side door. She was kind enough to let Jimmy crawl in first, but I guess it also gave her time to text. I was so used to seeing the phone in Marcy's hand it hadn't registered that she had run out of the house with it. In two seconds flat, Hayley came running out of her house next door, and with a squeal, she jumped in. "OMG! How'd you swing it, Marcy?"

"Can you believe it?" Marcy squealed over the honking horn. That was Jimmy, naturally.

Reggie came up beside me. I hadn't told her a thing about the car, and the look on her face told me she was just as surprised as my daughter. "What did you do, Audrey?"

"What does it look like, Reggie? I got my daughter a car for her birthday."

"I can see that," she said drily. "But did it have to be a Lexus?"

"A 2018 Lexus GS 300," I happily confirmed.

"What are the neighbors going to think?" Reggie's whisper in my ear was more like a hiss. "Don't you think they'll wonder where you suddenly got this kind of money? Everyone knows your husband has been . . . out of work for a while."

"What do I care what they think?" I said defensively. "Besides, it's leased."

"They don't know that."

Leave it to Reggie to try to spoil my happiness. "It's none of their business, Reggie, or yours."

"I thought we agreed that we weren't going to be showy with the wine club money, that we would lay low for a while."

We had done no such thing, and I told her so. "We did not discuss how we would each spend our share of the money."

"I'm sure that we did. The whole idea was not to arouse any suspicion, including making expensive, splashy purchases." Reggie glared at the car, then at me. "A Lexus? Holy shit, Audrey."

I'll admit it. Reggie was truly starting to irritate me. We had been best friends for so long that I had gotten used to her bossy ways and opinionated assertions. But why did she feel the need to spoil my happiness on my daughter's sixteenth birthday? That was going too far. I needed to take her down a peg or two. "What's the matter, Reggie, are you afraid I'm making you look cheap? When Hayley's birthday rolls around next month, I guarantee you that she's going to expect a new car too. What are you going to do then?"

"Goddamnit," Reggie muttered as she turned and stomped away.

The sound of her front door slamming made me smile. I felt like I had won that round, which was rare enough in our relationship. Maybe having so much money empowered me because I suddenly felt like the table between Reggie and me had turned full circle. I did not have to do every single thing that Reggie dictated. I was just as important to the wine club as she was, and I could do what I wanted with my own money, money that I had earned through hard work and creativity. Like, present my lovely daughter with a lovely car on her sixteenth birthday.

I was feeling happier than I had in a long time when I walked over to the car with the keys to the Lexus dangling from my hand. "I'm going to drive you to the DMV, young lady, but you are the one who is going to drive home with her brand new license."

A funny look came over Marcy's face, and it wasn't a happy one. "Uh, Mom?"

Just like that, my short-lived happiness vanished. "What's the matter? Don't you like the car?"

"I love the car, Mom, but--" Marcy looked to Hayley for support, but Hayley was suddenly engrossed in her phone.

My heart felt like it was sinking to my knees. "Don't tell me that you're having Felicity take you, Marcy." I couldn't believe it. Was that little bitch going to take this away from me too?

"No, Mom," Marcy said hurriedly. "It's just that I talked to Dad last night, and he said he wanted to take me. I told him he could."

"Oh."

That was the only thing I said to her. Did I want to rail against the injustice of it all? You bet I did, but I did not. The man who had been absent from our lives was going to share this momentous occasion with our daughter, and I, the parent who had supported, fed, and loved her during all that time, was now *persona non grata* It made my eyes burn, not with anger, mind you, but with tears.

It was like Marcy's utterance of *Dad* magically conjured up Paul because, in the next few seconds, he pulled into the driveway. To be more accurate, Betty Boop was the one driving the Toyota that pulled into my driveway, and Paul occupied the passenger seat. I was thinking that Betty Boop was not only a life coach--yeah, right--but also a chauffeur. I was about to say something to that effect when it hit me: Paul's license was still suspended.

Paul bounded out of the car, the boyish grin that I had once found so charming on his face. "Nice set of wheels, birthday girl! Did you borrow it from that rich friend of yours?"

"Nope. It's all mine." Marcy had opened the car door as soon as Paul went over to her, and Jimmy had immediately crawled over her to get to Paul. He was too big to jump into his father's arms, but he did it anyway. The little traitor.

Paul looked over Jimmy's head at me, a questioning look on his face.

"It's leased." I didn't say it loud enough for Marcy to hear. For some reason, I didn't want her to know, preferring that she think that I had bought it outright for her.

"Oh." Paul nodded knowingly as if that explained everything.

If you'll remember, I have already mentioned that my husband had absolutely no sense at all when it came to money. Growing up with trust fund parents, he hadn't had to worry over every nickel and dime. Until his parents died in the plane crash, I think that Paul thought that money somehow reproduced itself into a never-ending supply. It was "an ask and you shall receive" kind of arrangement. Then when we got married, I was the one who handled our finances, paying our bills and refinancing our mortgage and other loans when lower interest rates became available. Paul never asked questions--which was coming in pretty darn handy on that particular morning--and I had always appreciated the fact that he trusted me to take care of things. That is, until the last few months. After Paul told me to sell his Rolex, he had never once asked how I was managing to support his children in his absence. I mean, come on! Was that total naiveté on his part or just plain ignorance? I was starting to lean toward the latter option.

Paul was still holding Jimmy, whose legs were dangling to Paul's knees. "She's a beaut, Marcy. My little girl is going to go to the DMV in style. Are you ready?"

"I'm so-o-o ready, Dad." Marcy had already gotten back in her new car. "Let's go!"

I tapped Paul on the shoulder. "Aren't you forgetting something, Paul?"

Paul finally set Jimmy down. "I don't think so, Audrey."

Then I played my trump card. "Your license is still suspended."

"I know that, babe," he said with exaggerated patience. "That's why Sondra's going too." He motioned to the waif, who promptly got out of the car and walked over.

"That's ridiculous, Paul." I was trying very hard not to lose control in front of Betty Boop, who already thought I was some kind of wino enabler to my husband. It shouldn't have mattered to me, but I would be lying if I didn't say that it made me feel somehow unworthy. "I'm her mother, I'm the one with the license, and I should be the one to take her." Please note that I didn't add that I was also the one who had bought--leased--the car for our daughter.

"Come on, babe," Paul cajoled. "You get to see our daughter every day, and I haven't seen her in months. Please let me do this with her."

I'm pretty sure that Betty Boop could see clear to my tonsils in my gaping mouth. "You are the one who has chosen to stay away," I stuttered when I could finally speak.

"He's been in *treatment*," Betty Boop piped up.

"Yeah," Paul parrotted, "I've been in *treatment*. I've been working so hard, babe. Please let me have this day with my daughter."

It's very difficult to argue with a person whose stance is pure bullshit, especially when said person has been used to charming his way out of unpleasant situations his entire life. The presence of Betty Boop didn't help either. However, I would have gotten into that shiny white Lexus despite all that if my daughter had asked me to go with them. But she didn't. I looked over at her, but her face was turned away, saying something to Hayley as she got out of the car to go back to her house. I willed her to look my way, but she didn't.

"Okay." My voice sounded like I was underwater. "You can take her."

"I knew you'd understand, babe." Paul kissed my cheek. "Come on, partner," he said to Jimmy, "you're coming too. We'll make a day out of it."

Reggie didn't come over after my entire family--plus Betty Boop--had driven away without me. That surprised me. I was sure that she had been watching the entire scene from her front window, but for once, she seemed to have had the good sense to leave me alone to wallow in silence--which is what I had done. By the time my family had come home, I had watched seven episodes of *Snapped* on Oxygen. In case you've never seen it, that show is about women from all walks of life who suddenly get fed up with their husbands and murder them--i.e., they *snap*. I know how awful that sounds, and it wasn't like I was watching episode after episode as research that I could then apply to Paul. I still had a faint lingering hope that Paul would somehow come to his senses and return home, even if that faint hope was nothing more than a nebulous shadow in my soul. Plus, murdering someone was something I had never consciously planned to do. Please remember that.

So, Reggie came over the following Monday after the kids were in school, and she was ready to get to work. The wine club party for that month was scheduled to take place on February 24, and as usual, we were behind on our production, mostly because it had taken us a while to decide which region we were going to produce fake wine from next. We'd had such great success the previous month with the expensive wines that we wanted to repeat it. But this was the thing: When you were seriously looking for outlandishly expensive French wine, it wasn't that easy to find. So it was back to *The Wine Bible* again and the expert advice of Karen MacNeil.

We finally settled on the tiniest of all the major Bordeaux wine regions, the Pomerol appellation, and we further narrowed it down to Château Pétrus, a small wine estate of about twenty-eight acres that was widely regarded as the outstanding wine of the appellation. The estate produced a red wine entirely from merlot grapes and was one of Bordeaux's most expensive and sought-after wines. A 750ml bottle of Pétrus wine was priced at an average of $2,630. After Reggie found all that out, she said, "This is the one. It's right up our alley. We are really going to rake it in this time."

I have to admit that focusing on one estate made my job much easier that time around. I didn't have to design seven or eight completely different labels. With all the wine coming from one estate, the labels would basically be the same, with only the year changing. It was back to the internet, and we narrowed our chosen wines to these Château Pétrus vintages:

a 2003 for $3,000;

a 1987 for $2,500;

a 2005 Château Pétrus Pomerol for $4,500;

and a 1953 Pétrus 1.5 L Magnum for $16,000.

I know. The prices were already astronomical by that point, and it made me nervous. It was like we kept upping the ante by about one thousand percent with each wine party. It was like we were a snowball turning into an avalanche as it rolled crazily down the mountain. To try to contain things a little, I thought we should include a bottle of more moderately priced wine--relatively speaking--that came in at around $900, just so we didn't look so *greedy*, I guess you could say.

But Reggie was having none of that. "It's all about keeping up with the Joneses for those women, Audrey. We've seen how quickly they jump on the bandwagon after the first couple of women decide to buy." She laughed. "It's like taking candy from a baby."

"I don't think you should get too cocky about this, Reggie. The higher the stakes, the more the risk."

"You are such a worrywart," Reggie sniffed.

"Someone has to be."

"Why don't we ask our *partner* Cynthia Stewart what she thinks?"

It made my skin crawl when Reggie used that sarcastic tone. It's not like I was happy that Cynthia barged her way into our club by threatening to expose us--which is exactly what she did, no matter what she says--but she had come up with a good idea or two, like opening a joint bank account. We had each put in $10,000 of our January earnings into the account, and I felt like it was a kind of safety net for me. It sounds weird to say that now after everything that has happened. But in February, it was time to buy supplies again, and instead of taking out more money on my overloaded credit cards, I could use the FHM card for the account. We each had a card and checkbook, mind you. We *each* had one.

"Let's not start talking about Cynthia now, okay? We need to focus on what cheap wine we're going to use for our filler wine this time around."

We still wanted to keep the profit margin as high as possible, but it had to be pretty good wine. So we ended up settling on Kendall Jackson, a wine that I had always considered to be my special occasion wine. At about twelve dollars a bottle on sale, which it was at the grocery store right then, we could still make a lot of money, and no one was going to turn up her nose at a glass of KJ cabernet, pinot noir, or red wine blend. For the

1953 Magnum, we would go with the KJ merlot vintner's reserve, which was a little more expensive, but when you're talking about asking $16,000 a pop, it was a good choice. Since we were going to fill the Château Pétrus wine bottles with a highly regarded wine in its own right, I started to feel like we might get away with it once again.

After that, we got right to work, me copying the labels and Reggie ordering new bottles and corks and shrink caps on the internet. We'd had a pleasant enough day so far, but it was like Reggie couldn't let things well enough alone. She hadn't said a word about Marcy's new car or Paul showing up, but I guess she couldn't hold it in any longer. I guess she just couldn't keep her big mouth shut. "Why did you let Paul take Marcy to get her driver's license? I mean, he hasn't been around for months, and then he shows up and gets to participate in the momentous occasion."

"I didn't want to cause a scene." I didn't look up from my work.

Reggie sighed dramatically. "Oh, Audrey, you can't be Paul's doormat forever."

That got my goat; it truly did. I threw my marker across the room, which I guess was being a little dramatic on my part too, but Reggie was the one who started it, as she always was. "First, you call me a worrywart, and now you call me a doormat. Tell me, Reggie, which term do you think describes me more precisely?"

I seriously think that Reggie thought I would keep taking her abuse forever because the look on her face was one of total surprise. "I'm not calling you names, Audrey."

"You most certainly are. And frankly, Reggie, I'm tired of it."

"I'm not calling you names, Audrey," Reggie repeated slowly. "As your friend, I'm only trying to give you helpful advice."

"You are in no position to give me advice, Reggie. You're the one who keeps telling me we're in the same boat, remember? Both of our husbands have deserted us, and both our daughters have become stuck up Tigerettes, who don't lower themselves to speak to us anymore. So please believe me when I say that I don't think your advice is necessary or helpful *at all*." Let me tell you, I was on a roll.

Most people would apologize at that point, or at least feel bad for hurting a friend's feelings. But not Reggie. She geared up for the attack. She angrily pushed her chair away from the table and stood up, her hands on her hips, her dark eyes flashing. "Saturday morning was sickening, Audrey, just sickening. You go out and buy your daughter an expensive car--"

"It's *leased!*"

Reggie railroaded right over that. "And then when your husband pulls up with his nymphet, you actually let him and his girlfriend take your daughter to get her driver's license. It was *sickening*."

"I believe you mentioned that," I snapped back at her. I could feel the heat rising to my face as I returned a jab of my own. "And while we're on the subject, your husband is not making any secret of his affair with a *man* either. Didn't you say he was all over his lover when you saw him in Starbucks, that the PDA was, to use your choice word of the day, *sickening*? And did you honestly believe that story about Reed being sick and the Mediterranean cruise? Ha! You're more of a fool than I am."

"Your husband's a drunk!" Reggie bellowed. "Everyone but you knew that for years."

"Your husband's gay!" I yelled right back at her. "And the person who should have known that was *you!*"

Reggie reached over and slammed down the lid on her computer, and for a moment I thought she was going to throw it at me. I think she thought about it--I really do--but what she ended up doing was scooping up the computer and stalking out the patio door. I was both surprised and relieved that she was the one who chose to abandon the biggest, ugliest fight of our friendship. We'd had skirmishes before, but that exchange was a first. We had never tried to intentionally hurt each other in all the years of our friendship, and the fact that those barbed words had come out so effortlessly for both of us frightened me. It was as if we had crossed some line that we had always carefully toed before, and I didn't know if we would ever be able to go back to the way things used to be. I didn't even know if I wanted that to happen.

I was shaking like a leaf. I absolutely hate confrontation of any kind, yet I had jumped into that one with both feet. And the surprising thing was that I wasn't sorry. Well, maybe I was a little bit sorry, but the truth of the matter was that I was still mad. Reggie had been flat-out wrong. It simply wasn't true that everyone knew--such hyperbole on her part!--that Paul had been an alcoholic but me. He had always been the life of the party, sure, but he had held onto a steady job and been a good parent, which is more than I can say about my mother and father. Now they were seriously a couple of prize-winning alcoholics. But Paul? He hadn't been anywhere near that bad, and he had always been a happy drunk. Can happy drunks still be considered alcoholics? I mean, I know that they can be--Delores, I am sure, would attest to that--but this is the big difference in my book. With a happy drunk, you don't have to worry about flying fists and smashed TVs and neighbors calling the cops. They only fall asleep under half-assembled trampolines and find the whole thing funny when they ruin Christmas for their kids.

I was still shaking and mulling all this over when I received the phone call. I figured that it must be Reggie calling to continue the fight or apologize, which was the more doubtful of the two options. But it wasn't Reggie. It was Maeve Olson, probably the snootiest of all Cynthia's friends, but she was the one who usually got the ball rolling at the wine club parties by making the first hefty purchase. I didn't dislike her--I didn't even know her--and even though she was intimidating with her sable trimmed jackets and family heirloom pearls, she was vital to the success of our operation.

"I hope you don't mind that I called you at home," Maeve began, sounding like she didn't give a damn if I minded or not, "but I've found myself in a bit of a jam. My husband has some important clients coming over for dinner tomorrow night, and since there will be eight of us, I need two more bottles of the Romanée Conti 1959. Do you have two bottles, and if so, are they available for purchase?"

My heart started to pound then. I had precisely two bottles of the fake Romanée Conti 1959 bottles left in my garage where we stored the leftover wine and empty filler wine bottles because Reggie was too lazy to finish cleaning out her garage, let alone a closet. So it made perfect sense that I was in charge of the storage of bottles until Reggie and I drank them on her patio late at night, pretending that the wine was the real thing and laughing until tears came to our eyes about what we were doing and how we were getting away with it. And do you know what? That wine tasted better than any other wine we'd ever had.

I was not thinking about the ramifications of my actions when I told her that I had two bottles available for purchase. When Maeve asked if she should pick them up at Cynthia's or my place of residence--that's how she said it--I told her that I would personally deliver the wine to her door, which I did the following day. Maeve paid me in cash. Can you imagine that? I mean, who has over $20,000 in cash around the house? I guess the answer to that is Maeve Olson.

I didn't ask Maeve how she had gotten my number. I should have.

My mother was a tough old bird. Any sane person would have to give her credit for that, and I did--albeit grudgingly. She was in a coma for twenty-two days before she woke up. I hadn't been back to visit her since the first couple of days after her massive stroke, but I didn't even feel guilty about it. I mean, what was the point? She wouldn't even know I was there, and if she had been conscious, she wouldn't have given a damn one way or the other. I will admit that I had allowed myself the luxury of thinking that she wouldn't wake up at all, that I would eventually get a call from Osborn Hospital that Medicare was no longer going to cover the expenses to keep a lost cause alive, that it was time to pull the plug. Then as far as Margot Keller was concerned, all of my problems would have been solved. I wasn't even planning on any funeral service. For the life of me, I couldn't think of anyone who had crossed paths with Margot during her long life who would be the least bit interested in mourning her. I would simply have the body cremated and then unceremoniously dump her ashes in the parking lot of the nearest liquor store. Believe me when I say that would have been an entirely appropriate farewell to Margot Keller.

But the tough old bitch fought her way to consciousness, and the staff at Osborn was anxious to get rid of her. I can't say that I blame them. My mother was paralyzed on her right side, but that didn't prevent her from swiping food from her tray onto the floor with her left. She did other things with her left hand as well, most noticeably, flipping the bird to every person who walked into her hospital room. She couldn't speak, but the guttural gibberish that she did manage to spew forth left no doubt in any person's mind that she was calling you every filthy expletive known to mankind. She was like an ancient, withered parrot trapped in a cage, and she was mad as hell about it. And now it was my problem to find a place that would take her. She needed more care than The Gardens' skilled nursing center could provide, and I'm positive that Gail was happy to have Margot off her watch. She emailed me a list of possible specialty care nursing facilities.

I didn't go and visit the six or seven places on the list, as I probably should have. Instead, I called each one and settled on the cheapest. Don't misunderstand me. Every single place costs more money than you can imagine, and while Medicare would cover some of the expenses, there would still be out-of-pocket costs. Margot had been paying those extra expenses at The Gardens from her savings, so I wasn't overly worried--until I got another phone call from Gail, the phone call that put a new perspective on the whole situation.

"Audrey, dear, when you come to retrieve your mother's possessions, please stop by my office to settle up her account."

"What do you mean? Don't you require payment on the first of the month, and wouldn't that mean that you owe Margot for the time she was at the hospital?"

Gail cleared her throat as if she had a sour taste in her mouth. "That is quite correct, Audrey, but in your mother's case, she is in arrears for the last two months. She guaranteed me that you would cover the expenses, dear, I did not want to bother you while your mother was going through such a trauma. However, now that she is out of danger and will be moving out of our facility, this debt needs to be accounted for."

I thought about not paying it. I mean, what were the bill collectors going to do? Harass an old stroke victim who couldn't even speak? Ruin her credit rating? And I thought about not even returning to The Gardens to collect Margot's possessions, thus avoiding the situation altogether. But Gail had my phone number and address in Margot's contact information, and in the end, it just didn't seem right not to pay the bill. They had put up with my mother for two years, which said a lot about their patience and endurance. I was sure that they had suffered a lot of abuse from Margot in that time--everyone who came in contact with her suffered abuse--and in my book, that deserved compensation. So I paid the bill out of my wine club money. More specifically, I ended up paying the bill with the money from Maeve Olson.

Do you see what I'm getting at here? I had fretted about that outstanding bill of my mother's for days, my resentment growing. I had finally come into some cash, and now I had to spend it on that woman? Not only had she been a terrible mother to me, but she was also now costing me my hard-earned money. It was like adding insult to injury. Where were the gods of justice in this scenario? Was the world going to keep bitch-slapping me every time I turned around? I was really getting tired of it. And then, *voilà!* I got that call from Maeve.

No, I didn't share any of my worries with Reggie about any of the stuff that was going on with my mother, and I'm still not sure why. She now thinks it was an intentional plan all along, but it was not. She might even now think that I made the whole thing up, which is absolutely not true. Everything that I'm telling you is true. All that happened was that I had a large unexpected expense and then came into a large amount of unexpected money. Tit for tat, yin for yang. It seemed fated; it seemed justified. That's my explanation.

18

REGGIE

That stupid Lexus. I had always suspected that Audrey lacked in the common sense department, but going out and getting that car for Marcy's sixteenth birthday was over the top. She should have figured that one out. Our neighbors gossip a lot, and I knew, even if Audrey didn't, that she and I were the main topic of conversation during those months. What's better to gossip about than scandal, right? Both of our husbands had flown the coop, and I'm almost positive that Mrs. Simpson, who lived directly across the street from us, was taking notes on the two jilted ladies' comings and goings. That's why I had to take all those empty wine bottles out of Audrey's garage and transport them to the recycling bin behind Lindy's in the dead of night. Otherwise, Mrs. Simpson would grandly announce to the entire neighborhood that Audrey and I were drowning our sorrows in vast quantities of wine. Which was not entirely untrue. We could put away three bottles of wine on my patio or in her kitchen after a long day's work. However, we always got up in the mornings and went about our ever-growing business of bottling fake expensive French wine.

Things were starting to click for the wine club by February, despite Cynthia barging her way into the operation, and then Audrey had to go out and buy that outrageously expensive car and plop it down in the middle of our Honda/Toyota/Kia neighborhood. We had a major argument about it, and we said things to each other that good friends often don't--that is, the truth. But seriously, how could she not have known how blatant Paul's drinking problem was? I saw him pretending to fix the tiles on their roof one time, and he was so drunk that he kept missing the nail with the hammer, then he'd slip down the slope of the eave and laugh hysterically. He did it time after time, and it was like watching the same thirty seconds of a *Three Stooges* tape over and over. I think Kent finally went over and talked him down before he fell off and broke his neck.

However, my point is that while I was yelling the obvious truth at Audrey, I later regretted hurting her feelings. Maybe she didn't regret the argument as much as I did. I certainly can't make assumptions about her feelings anymore. To tell you the truth, I'm starting to wonder if I ever really knew her at all.

Audrey had the annoying habit of stretching out tasks way past their due date, while I was much more efficient in my work for the club. Consequently, she acted like she was constantly busy, that worried crease deepening between her green eyes, and I found myself with time on my hands, even after I bought all those cases of Kendall Jackson wine for the February party at grocery stores across the valley, which took more time than you can imagine. I started to make out an expense report at that point because a lot of money was coming out of my pocket, and I was paying for gas traveling from store to store, plus putting miles and miles on my car. I also figured the wear and tear on my car into my report, and so I started to write out a monthly check from the FHM account to myself. It was perfectly legitimate. Every company reimburses its employees for travel expenses. It adds up, you know?

Back to the question of who apologized first. Me. Yes, once again, just like I had in January, I took the high road. If I wasn't over at her house working on the wine club, I had a hard time finding something to fill my time. I am a restless person by nature, but even I can only run so many miles before I need to turn my attention to something else. I suppose I could have worked on those stupid tweaker cabinets, but I had grown used to them. When I walked into my kitchen, I saw them, but I didn't *see* them. So that wasn't even an option I considered. Plus, I was anxious to get back to the routine of Audrey's and my days where I actually felt like I was accomplishing something. And I was lonely. Audrey might be able to fill time by dragging out every chore to its painful death, but I was ready to get corking again. Literally. So I walked over two days later and went back to work.

We didn't fall immediately back into our old comradery. We were cordial enough with each other, overly polite and rather stiff until I steered the conversation to Cynthia. She was kind of a Switzerland topic, neutral because of our mutual dislike and mistrust of her and her motives. I know that Audrey says now that she never actively disliked Cynthia, which is blatantly untrue. We enjoyed talking behind her back and making fun of her, especially since Richard was still in the news, mostly because he still hadn't been caught. It was good to see Audrey laugh again, even though she stated that she hated to gloat at another's misfortune. Yeah, right. I didn't buy that do-gooder speech for a second, but I went along with it to get our friendship back on an even keel, listening to her and keeping mum until I had the perfect opportunity to drop my bombshell. I had some news, all right.

I had started to drive by Cynthia's house every other day or so. I swear I wasn't stalking her or spying on her. Not yet. You see, initially, I was only interested in the case against Richard and wanted to see how many reporters camped out in her front yard, but those fickle reporter types didn't last all that long because Cynthia refused to come out and give an in-depth interview. That surprised me, given that she was such an attention hog. I mean, you should have seen what she wore to that disgruntled parents meeting after the sickening Tigerette performance. Sheesh! Did she think she was going to a film premiere in Cannes?

Anyway, Audrey thought that Cynthia didn't make an appearance outside her house, or anywhere for that matter because she had a good lawyer. I, on the other hand, thought it was because she had been in on Richard's Ponzi scheme all along. Every time she publicly denied the allegation, her eyes shifted from side to side and her shoulders tensed up. Body language doesn't lie. She knew something.

Consequently, even after the reporters had gone, I kept driving by. It became something of a late afternoon routine for me. I started running in a park near her home and only had to make a slight detour to get to her street. It was such a pretty street, all the grand houses and palm trees and long curving driveways. It was weird. While driving down the street made me green with envy, it also calmed me. It was *tranquil*, I guess you could say.

Being convinced that Cynthia had been in on Richard's crime, I had also developed this fantasy that she had money buried in her yard or something. The Feds had frozen all of Richard's offshore accounts and whatnot, but people do leave money in secret hiding spots around the house. I know that I was doing that very thing since the last wine club party had been so profitable. Of course there was also the possibility that Cynthia had tons of money in that safe of Richard's that she had mentioned. However, if she had something valuable in that safe, I doubt that she would have offered its use to the wine club. Audrey and I would have wanted to see the exact location of the safe, and I would have demanded that she share the combination and practiced opening it myself. Hence, the buried treasure in the backyard theory evolved. Talking about it now makes the whole theory--and me--sound strange. I don't know. Maybe I just got bored during that hour of the day.

However, the buried treasure fantasy was not the bombshell I was ready to drop on Audrey that February morning. "I was driving by Cynthia's house the other day, and I saw the strangest thing."

"Why would you be driving by Cynthia's house? It's got to be a good eight miles to her house from here, maybe more. And it's out of the way to any store you go to." It was Audrey's turn to stand over the steam to put on the shrinking caps. She complained about this task to high heaven, but I think she liked to think it was helping her complexion, like a facial or something.

"I've been running in a park over there. It's got one of the best running tracks in town." The park didn't have a running track, but Audrey didn't need to know that detail. It wasn't pertinent to the story.

"It still seems weird that you'd be driving by her house for no reason." Audrey's eyebrows were arched when she looked at me over her shoulder.

I tamped down my impatience because we were still on such tender terms and took a deep breath. "Audrey, do you want to hear this or not? It's juicy."

"Oh, all right. I suppose you're going to tell me that Cynthia's been seeing someone who is obviously not her husband because no one knows where he is."

"Damn it."

Audrey gave that low throaty chuckle of hers. "Sorry to have knocked the wind out of your sails, Reggie. Go on, though. I'm interested."

Her apology, whether she meant it or not, appeased me, so I went on. The story was too juicy not to share with someone. "Well, this guy pulled up to her house in this old camper." I saw that Audrey was about to say something, but I beat her to the punch. "No, it wasn't some repairman or cable guy or pool guy or Uber driver or Amazon delivery. There wasn't any logo on his truck, and he didn't have any uniform on. He looked kind of sketchy too. He was looking over his shoulder and kind of squirrely about the whole thing."

"Like he was casing the joint?"

I had to laugh at that one. "Are you staying up late at night watching old cops and robbers movies, Audrey? *Casing the joint?*"

"You know what I'm doing late at night, and it's not watching TV. What I meant is that he sounds like he was some thief or something. Why didn't you call Cynthia immediately? That's what I would have done."

"Right, Audrey. I should have called Cynthia and told her there was a strange man outside her house, and I knew that because I was also parked outside her house in the middle of the day for no good reason." I hoped that my voice dripped with sarcasm.

"Let's get back to that. Why were you parked outside Cynthia's house in the middle of the afternoon? Is there something going on that I don't know about?"

"Of course not!" I said, startled. "Do you think Cynthia and I have some side deal going on or something like that? That's horseshit, and you know it, Audrey. I would never go behind your back like that!"

"That's not what I meant," Audrey said hurriedly. "I know you wouldn't do that kind of thing to me, Reggie. Now get back to your story. I won't interrupt again."

I didn't return to the gossip about Cynthia right away. For a long time, I just stared at her, wondering if Paul was the cause of Audrey's sudden mistrust of people. I couldn't blame her for that because I'd been feeling the same way since my husband's revelation that our marriage had been a big, fat lie. I didn't like that she would insinuate that I was capable of making a secret deal with Cynthia, of all people, but we were still in the process of getting over our last major fight. And at least she wasn't crying. Come to think of it, I hadn't seen her cry in two or three weeks. I would take that as a good sign and go on with my story. You see, I took the high road once again.

"So this guy is looking around the place like he's seeing if the coast is clear. Then he walks around to the side of the house, maybe thinking he can make it to the back, but there's that tall stucco wall that divides the front yard from the back. He acted confused for a second or two, and then he retreated about twenty feet, turned around, and ran at the wall. Right before he smacked headlong into it, he made this leap and caught the top with both hands, then pulled himself over."

I had Audrey's rapt attention now. She'd stopped steaming shrink caps and was leaning against the kitchen counter. "What do you make of all this?"

"My hunch is that he used to be some kind of athlete. He has that build that a lot of high school football players have. His shoulders were still broad, but he had a beer gut on him. Still, he made it over that wall."

"No, I mean, why do you think he wanted to get over that wall so badly?"

I didn't want to embarrass myself by sharing my weird theory about the buried treasure with Audrey, so I shrugged my shoulders. "Beats me. But here's the strangest thing: He never came back to his camper. By the time I finished my run, a tow truck was hauling the camper away, and he wasn't inside."

"Maybe it broke down, and he called a cab."

"Maybe," I said slowly, "or maybe he's still inside the house."

Audrey grinned. "Maybe Cynthia has a sex slave."

I grinned back. "Don't you think that she'd prefer to have a sex slave who drove a Mercedes or a BMW?"

"I'd be deliriously happy with a sex slave who also cooked and cleaned house."

"And paid the bills."

The conversation got even sillier after that. We weren't making fun of Cynthia, not exactly, and it's not like we had to worry about her safety. She'd started to group text every morning, and that morning's message had said that we could expect sixty guests to this wine party, which meant that Audrey and I had to bottle at least forty to sixty more bottles of wine for the February club meeting. It meant more money, sure, but we were working our asses off, and if Cynthia kept increasing the size of the parties, we were going to have to hire help, or as a last resort, move the operation to Cynthia's massive kitchen. Audrey kept hinting about moving the operation out of her cramped space, but I was still resistant to the idea. I liked Audrey's and my routine, and I had a gut feeling that if we moved Control Center to Cynthia's, she would assert more and more power. I refused to let that happen.

Audrey and I put our supplies away that afternoon and went home to our dinners and our family time, such as it was. Hayley preferred to spend her time at home squirreled up in her room, and I returned to Audrey's around ten o'clock for phase two of that workday. We worked until a little past midnight. I was tired, but I felt like it had been a good day. Audrey and I seemed to be back on the right track. What's more, we had each other's backs--or so I thought.

"How about a glass of wine before I head home?" I said.

"I would love a glass of wine." Audrey sank heavily into a kitchen chair. The dark circles under her eyes were almost purple.

"I'll go into the garage and get a bottle." Then I had an idea. I was in a celebratory mood, after all, and on a lark, I said, "Why don't I bring in one of these bottles of Romanée Conti 1959? We can toast to a good day."

Audrey immediately sat straight up in her chair. "We don't have any of those left, do we? Didn't we drink them sometime last week?"

I didn't have any recollection of that. We'd bring out one of our wine club bottles from time to time and pretend like we were drinking the real thing. It always made us laugh, and both of us gushed over the wine, saying how marvelous it was to savor such a rare vintage on our tongues. Let me tell you, it was a hoot. "I don't think we did. Come on. It'll be fun after such a long day. Just tell me where you think it is in the garage, and I'll get it. You don't have to do a thing."

Audrey shook her head vehemently. "No, Reggie. I'm sure we drank it. I'll get a bottle of our Romanée St. Vivant 1972. I know where I put a bottle of that." She was out of her chair before I could stop her and returned with that particular fake vintage. "This is just as good, isn't it?"

"Audrey, we're talking about fake French wine, remember? This one is a Liberty Creek instead of a Ravenswood, I think, not a French vintage at all. And right now, anything sounds good. Start pouring, sister."

"Absolutely." Audrey busied herself opening the bottle. "Friends drinking wine together. That's the important thing."

I honestly did not think anything was strange about those missing bottles of wine that night. It's only when I look back on drinking wine that night that I can see the guilty look in Audrey's eyes as she peered at me over the rim of her glass.

There was another reason why I kept cruising around Cynthia's area of Scottsdale. There was a park, and I did run it on occasion, but it also happened that Reed Sylvester owned a deluxe condo two blocks from the park. How did I know that? I am not a fan of Facebook, although I did look up Reed to see that his picture confirmed the fact that he was every bit as gorgeous as I remembered from that ill-fated encounter in Starbucks. However, to my great relief, he had not posted any pictures of him and Kent, no smiling poses in front of the Grand Canyon or sunbathing by a pool. Which only confirmed my suspicion that his tan was a spray-on and not real. Which is neither here nor there in the big scheme of things.

I got Reed's address from Caleb. Hayley had flatly refused to give it to me, saying that she respected her father's privacy, but it appeared that I could still nag Caleb into compliance if I was persistent enough, if I bombarded him with texts and phone calls until he finally relented, saying: "Don't do anything stupid, Mom." I would like the record to reflect that I didn't make that promise.

Don't get me wrong. I had no intention of repeating the Starbucks incident, nor did I want a confrontation with Kent of any kind. I might have tended to be combative when provoked, but I wasn't looking for a fight. All I wanted was to see my husband. I missed him. After all the wrong he had done to me, I still missed his presence at the dinner table and in my bed. I missed his subtle sense of humor and his genuine niceness. Now that he was gone, I realized that Kent had been the equalizer to my more aggressive personality. It was like I had lost my partner on the seesaw of life, and when I let my temper get out of control, I didn't have Kent there to rub my tense shoulders and murmur, "Take it easy, Reg." Consequently, I felt like I was a tightly wound wire coil that could detonate at any minute. Did I blame him for that? I suppose that I did, on some level.

Still, I did not mean my husband any harm, even though I will admit that I seethed with jealousy every time I saw Kent and Reed come out of their house. I mean, they acted like an old married couple when they carried in the groceries from Reed's fancy car or when they puttered around their little yard or strolled through their neighborhood. It wasn't like I parked across the street and spied on them, just like I wasn't spying on Cynthia. I only wanted a glimpse of what Kent's life was like without me. Unfortunately, by my eyewitness account, it looked like he was perfectly happy *sans Reggie*, perhaps happier than he had ever been. That hurt my feelings more than I can tell you, and it forced me to relive our years of marriage, turning the pages of the well-worn memories as I tried to find what had been missing, what I had done wrong. And I can honestly tell you that I couldn't come up with anything, which led me to only one conclusion: The fault for our failed marriage fell squarely on Kent's shoulders.

Do you want to know what the worst part of spending time in Kent's new neighborhood was? It was the newfound knowledge that Hayley spent a lot of time at Kent's place. How did I not know that? I knew that Kent gave her driving lessons, and I knew that he was giving her money that I wasn't supposed to know about, but I had no idea that she spent a couple of late afternoons a week at his condo. Hayley had been telling me for months that the Tigerette practices often ran late, and I had accepted that as truth. But now my eyes were telling me a new version of the story.

I couldn't believe it on that first Tuesday afternoon when I saw Felicity's powder blue Porsche pull into the driveway. Hayley got out of Felicity's car and walked to the front door. She fished a key out of her backpack, went in, then came back out to wave to the others in the car. In addition to Felicity and Marcy, I recognized two other Tigerettes as they trooped in the door. A few minutes later, another car pulled up, and by the looks of their letter jackets, I surmised that the five boys who got out of the car were on the basketball team. I knew that Kent, who had gotten another job at Intel, and Reed, who also worked there, weren't home. Alarm bells? You better believe they were ringing loud and clear.

I rolled down my window and could hear the faint sound of music and high-pitched teenage laughter. Were they having a party? Were they drinking? Were they smoking pot or doing drugs? Maybe it was because I was still naive, or maybe it was because it was five o'clock in the afternoon and still light outside that I ruled out that possibility. Even I knew that when high school kids in Arizona wanted to party without the threat of parents barging in, they drove out to the desert after it got dark outside. I remembered quite a few parties I attended where we all drank Coronas around a roaring bonfire. At least this was safer than that. I didn't have to worry about my daughter getting pushed into a fire or stung by a scorpion.

But I did have to worry about Felicity, who probably posed far more danger than a bonfire and scorpion combined. Was this all her doing? However, that didn't make sense either. Felicity could have easily had a party in the guesthouse at the back of her property any time she wanted to. Look at that first Tigerette sleepover. Audrey had told me that Marcy had admitted that they'd had some wine. That didn't bother me nearly as much as when Hayley admitted to me that the sleepover had been entirely unchaperoned. That lazy Cynthia didn't have the good sense to walk back there and check on the girls from time to time. What had she been doing in that great big house of hers, reading *Cosmo* and painting her talons? In my book, that had been another strike against her, both as a parent and as a person.

You must understand two things. First of all, I know that teenagers party, whether the parents try to stop them or not. But secondly and more importantly, this was the first time I had faced the dilemma. Caleb, as I have mentioned, was not outgoing or popular in high school. His idea of a fun Friday night was playing video games and eating a movie box of Sour Patch Kids. Oddly enough, I had encouraged him to seek out more outgoing friends, who likely tended to party. But he'd rolled his eyes and returned to Dungeons & Dragons. Hayley, however, was an entirely different story. Becoming a Tigerette had propelled her into the higher echelon of high school society, and now she had a group of friends that I knew nothing about. Before the Tigerettes, I had known every single kid she hung out with, plus their parents. I had made sure that she didn't get in with the wrong crowd. For example, in third grade, Hayley had a friend whose mother worked at Hooters. I'd thought that was scandalous at the time and had told Hayley to say goodbye to that friend. I feel kind of bad about that now. The friend had been a nice little girl with curly blonde pigtails.

I was in a quandary as I let the minutes tick by. Under normal circumstances, I would have marched right up to that front door and demanded to know everyone's names and their purpose for being in my husband's lover's condo. But this was not a normal circumstance. I wasn't supposed to be anywhere near Reed's condo because Kent had threatened to get a restraining order after I inadvertently ran over Reed's cat. I swear it was an *accident*. Reed had this fluffy Persian cat that was black as coal, which is why I didn't see it on the road that night. I mean, I don't particularly like cats--I think they're the bitchiest animals on the planet--but the cat was on the *road*, for Pete's sake, not on the sidewalk as Kent has claimed. I suppose it didn't help matters that I'd had a little wine before I decided to take a midnight drive. Thank God Reed talked Kent out of calling the cops because I don't think I would have aced a sobriety test.

But back to my quandary. I decided to call Caleb to see what he thought about his not-quite-sixteen-year-old sister partying in the afternoon in his father's new residence. The call went straight to voicemail, probably intentionally. Caleb was still peeved at me for ignoring his warning not to do anything stupid and *accidentally* running over Reed's nasty cat. I knew I should drive away and confront Hayley when she got home. I would further alienate her if I barged in and made a big scene in front of her friends. She would accuse me of being an *embarrassment*, which seemed to be her new catchall word lately. Besides, Kent and Reed--they even drove together to work, as sickening as that is--got home around 6:05. It was now 5:45. How raucous could an after-school party be if it only lasted an hour? And maybe in my naiveté, I was being ridiculous about the whole thing. The kids were probably watching a movie and eating potato chips. You know, kid stuff. They weren't guzzling Grey Goose vodka straight from the bottle. Of course not.

I had just turned my key in the ignition when the front door of the condo opened, and the boys tumbled out, roughhousing, pushing, cackling, and patting each other on the back. They jumped into their Jeep and took off way too fast down the residential street. The girls were coming out of the house when Reed and Kent's car pulled in. I had parked three houses down the block, but I still slunk further down into my seat, pretending to be invisible, which was a crazy thing to do since Kent and I had owned this van for almost ten years. If he saw me, my goose was cooked. However, the two men didn't look my way as they greeted the girls, not acting at all surprised to see them coming out of the condo. I could hear them greet each girl by name, which was more than I could do, sad to say. I took that to mean that Kent must have known that the kids hung out there, that he must have given his approval. This had to be the new hangout spot for the popular kids, and Hayley was undoubtedly glowing with pride. It was one more thing I hadn't known was happening in my own daughter's life.

But oh, there was soon to be more, much more.

"How much did this set you back, Cynthia?" I asked as I surveyed the hundreds of red roses and exquisite lace tablecloths. Cynthia had even filled her pool with roses, and the petals glistened as they bobbed on the top of the water. It was total overkill, but her house and yard were magically beautiful yet again. And thankfully, she hadn't chosen a Valentine theme, which would have set my teeth on edge. Valentine's Day had come and gone. Good riddance. I have always hated that manufactured holiday and all the romantic bullshit it's supposed to represent.

Cynthia shrugged. "Four, five thousand?"

I was shocked at the amount and irritated that she was so blithe about that much money. "That's the wine club money you're spending now, Cynthia. The more you spend on decorations, the more you cut into our profits."

"I'm spending money to make money, Reggie. I'm sure you can understand that concept." She took a sip of wine from the pre-party bottle she had opened. "And I don't see you skimping on your new expense report. Wear and tear on your car, Reggie? You're charging the wine club more than your car is worth."

"Stop it, you two. Let's set up for the party." Audrey's face looked even whiter than usual, and the set of her mouth was grim. "How many bottles of wine for the tasting, Reggie? We've got ten more guests this time around."

"I'll start opening bottles." I edged closer to Audrey and whispered: "Are you feeling all right?"

Audrey shook her head. "It's nothing for you to worry about, Reggie."

Earlier, as I was bringing in the cases of wine, Cynthia had cornered Audrey. They were in a far corner of the dining room while Cynthia spoke in a low voice, her blue eyes boring into Audrey's green ones. They hadn't invited me into the conversation, which bothered me, but what could I do? There wasn't any time to confront them before the party, so I tried to convince myself that it wasn't anything important. They were probably talking about napkins or the appetizers. However, Cynthia had been more animated since that corner talk, while Audrey had seemed to retreat into herself, like a turtle tucking its head under its shell.

One of the things I remember most about that party was that it was loud. I couldn't tell if any of the guests could even hear my spiel on the four Château Pétrus Bordeaux wines that Audrey and I had chosen to present. Sixty women drinking and talking can cause quite the commotion, and when I looked at all those well-dressed women, the thing that came to mind was that they were like an overly excited gaggle of geese.

Mind you, I'm not complaining. It was like they couldn't wait to get their hands on the exorbitantly expensive Château Pétrus vintages, and I swear that when I presented the 1953 Pétrus 1.5 L Magnum for $16,000, the ten new members of the group practically trampled all over each other to be the first to buy.

"They're new money," Cynthia explained after the party finally wound down, and a parade of Ubers had driven away some very drunk women.

"I have no idea what that means, Cynthia," I said irritably. Cynthia had spent a small fortune on the decorations but hadn't bothered to hire anyone to cater or clean up. That was so typical of her. She loved the show aspect of each party but couldn't be bothered with the gritty aftermath. While she pretended to carry wine glasses into the kitchen, Audrey and I were wiping and washing. I hate to clean, which made me irritable enough, but it was compounded by the headache that had grown exponentially as the party got louder and louder. I was surprised that no else could hear the pounding in my head.

"They don't come from family money, which means that they have to try harder to fit in." Cynthia stopped the pretense of carrying in wine glasses altogether and perched herself on a barstool. She reached for the nearest bottle, and lacking a clean glass, drank directly from it. Believe me when I say that the gesture didn't look any classier on her than it did on a wino straddling a park bench, despite the Marc Jacobs dress and a rock the size of Gibraltar on her ring finger.

I was dying to point out that she didn't come from family money either, that she had married into it, at least as far as I knew, but Audrey said something more compelling. "Let's count the money. That way everyone will know exactly how much we made tonight and how much her share is." She looked directly at Cynthia when she said that.

Cynthia either didn't see the look or intentionally ignored it. "Good idea."

Tallying up the total took about thirty seconds since most of the purchases had been by credit card on our new machine. Do you want to take a guess at the grand total? Remember that in addition to the 1953 Pétrus 1.5 L Magnum for $16,000, we had a 2003 for $3,000, a 1987 for $2,500, and a 2005 Château Pétrus Pomerol for $4,500. We hadn't offered any discounts this time because the real wine was so sought after that Audrey and I hadn't thought it was necessary. Another factor to consider is that people seem willing to purchase more with a credit card. For one thing, it's not as painful as paying cash. You don't even have to think about it for a month. Okay, I won't keep you in suspense any longer. I'll tell you. Our grand total for the night was just over $300,000. *$300,000.* We had definitely been called up to the Majors.

"Holy shit," I said.

"We're rich." Audrey looked like she was in shock.

"I'm calling my personal shopper at Saks," Cynthia said.

"It would take my husband a year to make this kind of money." Audrey could not tear her eyes away from the total on the machine.

Cynthia laughed gaily. "Who needs husbands?"

"We don't." I took the bottle from Cynthia's hand and took a swig myself.

I think that moment was the happiest the three of us had ever been or ever would be together. We were grinning at each other like idiots, like we had the world by the balls and the sky was the limit. The only thing spoiling my complete contentment was that blasted headache. The swig of wine I had traveled straight to my head like a missile to a target. It exploded on impact. "Audrey, do you have some Advil in your purse? My head is killing me."

Audrey dutifully got up and rummaged in her purse. "I'm afraid not, Reggie."

"Check the medicine cabinet in the powder room. I think there's a bottle in there." Cynthia was swaying ever so slightly on the barstool.

The powder room in the front hallway looked like a bathroom in a Frat house after a party: towels and toilet paper littering the floor, lipstick smears in the sink, and more than one red wine splotch on the walls. And I smelled the unmistakable odor of vomit. Cynthia's fancy friends might dress the part, but they weren't going to win any prizes for holding their liquor. I wasn't going to mention the disgusting state of the room to Cynthia, though, because she would undoubtedly cajole Audrey and me to clean it up. And Audrey probably would. I held my breath and did a quick search of the medicine cabinet. No Advil, Tylenol, or Bayer.

I passed by the grand curved staircase, heading back to the kitchen, then stopped short. Maybe Cynthia had some tablets upstairs. Earlier in the evening, she had given the ten new wine club members a tour of the house, so she probably had the upstairs in as excellent condition as the downstairs and didn't mind people viewing it. The women had come back down after the tour gushing about how beautiful her bedroom was with its canopied bed and Monet paintings on the walls. Audrey and I had exchanged looks over that. We'd been in Cynthia's house several times by then, yet Cynthia had never once given us a tour of the upstairs rooms. What were we, second class citizens or something? However, it wasn't curiosity that drove me upstairs that night. It was pain. I honestly didn't think I was going to be able to drive home unless I had at least the promise that the headache would lessen. I climbed the stairs.

At the top of the stairs, I had two choices, left or right. All the doors lining the hallway were closed and offered no clue as to what was behind them. So I blindly chose right and walked to the end of the hall of the west wing. I opened the door and gasped involuntarily. It wasn't Cynthia's room but Richard's, and let me tell you, it looked like something out of a movie, with that heavy mahogany desk and crown molding and a big bar on one side, trimmed in brass with crystal decanters lining the top. Beyond that, I could see a bedroom and another room that looked like a sitting room. Richard's space was probably more square feet than my entire house. I swear, I was backing out of the room, I was planning to close the door quietly and try another room, but then I remembered that Cynthia said that Richard had a safe in his study. What was it she had said? Then it came back: *It's hidden in our wall and fireproof.*

I couldn't help myself. It was like being in a movie where the actor is looking for the secret button or fake brick that opens the hidden door. So I turned on the light, walked over to the paneled wall and started to feel around. Did I feel silly doing it? Oh, yeah. But I'd been daydreaming about Cynthia's secret stash of money for days, and while I was convinced it was buried somewhere in the backyard, I was still very curious about that safe. Only people with tons of money or a lot of valuables would need a secret, fireproof safe. I was curious. Period. If I found the safe, I'd take a picture of it with my phone and show it to Audrey later, saying something like: "Get a load of this, sister. This is how rich people live."

I was feeling sillier by the second as I felt up that wall, but as it turned out, Richard was a lot more clever than I was. I didn't find the magic button or whatever it was, and Audrey and Cynthia were going to start wondering what was taking me so long to get a simple pain relief tablet. I was going to have to admit defeat about that safe and drive home with a blistering headache as my penance. I walked back to the door I had come in and reached for the light switch, but my hand stopped in mid-air. There must have been twenty different switches on that panel, and I had no idea how I had found the one that turned on the light. It had been dark, and I had simply reached by the side of the door frame and flipped a switch, just like I did at home. I'd lucked out, all right, and now I had no idea what to do.

I thought about leaving the light on and going downstairs. Maybe Cynthia would think she'd accidentally left it on when she gave the tour to the new wine club members, although I hadn't heard any women on the tour mention this room. Cynthia must not have shown it to them. I was going to have to figure this out. Logically, I told myself, the light switch would be the one nearest the door. I held my breath as I tentatively touched the button closest to the door. I sincerely hoped it wasn't some sound system that would start blasting Vivaldi. I don't know why I pictured Richard as an opera lover. I guess the classy, opulent room gave me that vibe.

I had found the secret button. A small panel slid open on the wall next to the switches, but it didn't reveal a hidden safe. It looked like a miniature TV screen, and I was thinking that it was an odd place to put a TV. You couldn't see it from Richard's desk, and even if you pulled up a chair to watch your favorite program, you'd be sitting too low to see the screen. It didn't make any sense at all. Then I peered closer.

I could see a man on the black and white screen. He looked vaguely familiar to me as he sat in a small room. There were beer cans all around him and boxes that looked like they had supplies of some kind. The guy seemed to be sleeping, his head nodding. I leaned even closer to the screen, and all of a sudden, it was like he could sense my presence. He jumped up, throwing the blanket to the floor, and started dancing around like he was crazy or drunk or both. It looked like he was yelling something. I could see his lips moving, but I couldn't make out the words. All I knew was that he was directing his diatribe at me.

It was only when the man started to take off his clothes and throw them in my direction that I recognized him as the man who had scaled Cynthia's fence and never came back out. He was in a room with a camera somewhere in this house.

And Cynthia could watch his every move because he was her prisoner.

MARCH

19

AUDREY

"So," Cynthia said when she cornered me right before the February wine club party began, "did you get a phone call from Maeve Olson?"

"Why would Maeve call me?" I tried to act innocent, but the truth of the matter is that I'm not a very good liar. Well, I guess it's more accurate to say that I was still in the process of becoming a person who knew how to bend the truth, avoid the truth, or out and out deny the truth. I was a work in progress, you might say.

"She called me to ask for your number. I believe she was under the mistaken impression that you were in charge of wine sales." Cynthia's eyes were as cold and hard as blue ice.

"Well, she never called me." I tried to push past her, but Cynthia grabbed my arm.

"Don't bullshit me, Audrey. Did you sell her the last two bottles of Romanée Conti 1959? She told me she was having a dinner party and wanted to buy those last two bottles. She *told* me she was going to call you."

I couldn't look her straight in the eye and tried to push past her again. "She must have changed her mind."

Cynthia's grip on my arm tightened. "This is the deal. I want half the money you got from Maeve. In exchange, I won't tell Reggie how you've gone behind our backs and stolen our share of almost $26,000. That sounds fair, doesn't it?"

I was so scared that my legs had turned to jelly and I had to lean against the wall for support. But the funny thing was that I would be more scared--terrified, in fact--if Reggie found out. She would never forget my one transgression and would make my life miserable. I'd probably have to move to another state to get away from her scathing, recriminating glare. I'm not exaggerating. I thought Reggie was terrifying when you got on her bad side. "It's a deal," I said, just as Reggie came in with a crate of wine and glanced over at us. "Don't tell Reggie."

My next major worry on that evening was that Maeve would show up and somehow let the cat out of the bag that I had sold her the wine on the sly. But guess what? For one measly, lousy time in my life, luck was on my side. I kept watching the door until the party started, but Maeve never showed up. Cynthia noticed that too, of course, and after the party had started, she sidled up to me and whispered that Maeve had called to say that she wasn't feeling well. She winked at me--I guess because she thought that we now shared a secret--but I was wondering if she had somehow gotten to Maeve and poisoned her. Even then, I wouldn't have put something like that past Cynthia.

I did pay Cynthia that time, although I resented doing so. She acted like she was as pressed for cash as Reggie and me, but that couldn't have been even remotely true. If she was desperate for money, as she claimed, why hadn't she sold that enormous diamond ring of hers? Or maybe some of that fancy artwork hanging on the walls or her Mercedes? Cynthia's husband might be a fugitive and her assets might be frozen, but Cynthia didn't seem to be cutting any corners in her lavish lifestyle. However, I did recognize that I had done a bad thing, even if I had used a big chunk of that money to pay off the nursing home debt of my refusing-to-die mother. If something like that happened again--and I somehow knew that it would--I would figure out some way to keep Cynthia from finding out.

But by the end of that highly profitable February wine club party, I was feeling much better. We had made so much money that I could swallow the loss of the $13,000 that I had slipped to Cynthia when Reggie went to the bathroom to find an aspirin for her headache. She was gone for a long time, but Cynthia and I weren't stilted at all as we drank some wine and talked about what we were going to do with the money. Cynthia was going to head to Saks, which I thought was a waste, but I was thinking that it was my turn to get a new car. Don't misunderstand. I was limping along in a 2004 Suburban that had so many miles on the broken odometer that, in dog years, it would have been the biblical age of Methuselah. So it would not be a frivolous purchase at all. I was talking necessity, not extravagance.

When Reggie finally appeared, she had this weird smile on her face. "What took you so long?" I asked.

"I got lost."

Cynthia gave that tinkling laugh of hers that sounded so fake. "It is a very big house."

"It is a very *interesting* house." Reggie could not wipe that silly grin off her face.

Cynthia didn't flinch, nor did her expression change. "What do you mean, Reggie?"

"I only meant that it has a lot of rooms. One of these days, you're going to have to give Audrey and me a tour."

Cynthia set her wine glass down carefully. "Another one? I'm sure I did that back in December. I distinctly remember showing you my bedroom."

"Nope." Reggie shook her head, still grinning. "She hasn't given us a tour yet, has she, Audrey?"

I wasn't sure what was going on, if anything. Sure it was a big house, but I didn't particularly want a tour. What was the point--to emphasize the vast differences between the haves and have nots? No, thank you. And I especially didn't want a tour tonight. All I wanted to do was get home and have another glass of wine. "I don't think we want a tour, Reggie. It's time we headed home."

"I agree with Audrey. It's late. Maybe some other time, Reggie."

"I'm going to hold you to that, Cynthia. And I'll look forward to it."

On the way home, I asked Reggie, "What was that all about?"

"Nothing, Audrey. I was toying with her."

"For crying out loud, Reggie, why did you need to do that? The tensions between the three of us are high enough without you antagonizing her."

Do you see? That was a perfect example of Reggie being unnecessarily mean for no reason. I was no fan of Cynthia's either, especially after she had recently robbed me of $13,000, but when it came to the wine club parties, we worked pretty well as a team during those five hours. She should have left it at that. But no, not Reggie.

Reggie turned onto Sheena. "Can I let you in on a little secret, Audrey?" She didn't wait for a response. "That powder room looked like a disaster area. I only wanted to see Cynthia's face when she got a load of that. Her hoity-toity friends do not respect personal property. And they seem to throw up a lot."

I had to admit that it would have been interesting to see the look on Cynthia's face, even though it wasn't nice of us to leave her with that mess to clean up. But hey, she could hire back Louisa with the money she had extorted from me. It was not my problem. I had other, better things to think about. "What are you going to buy with your newfound wealth, Reggie?"

"I'm going to get a new car. My old van is too conspicuous." Reggie pulled into her driveway.

"What do you mean by it being *conspicuous?*"

Reggie turned off the ignition and gave a tired sigh. "I'll tell you in a day or two. I'm still mulling over a plan."

That was our way. We told each other difficult things that were going on in our lives when we were good and ready. So I didn't object. "I'm going to get a new car too."

"Just promise me one thing, will you, Audrey?" Reggie's fingers were drumming the steering wheel. "Don't buy anything too flashy, okay? The Lexus was bad enough, but if you buy another expensive car, the neighbors will really get suspicious. Old Mrs. Simpson will think we're running a drug cartel and call the cops. You know how she is."

"Don't tell me how to spend my money, Reggie," I warned. "We've already been through this." Our last big fight was still too near the surface, and I felt the heat rise to my face. I had only been thinking of a soccer-mom-nice SUV, but it still wasn't any of her business.

"Fine." Reggie put up her hands in mock surrender. "I'm just stating the obvious."

"Good night, Reggie." I got out of the car, slamming the door behind me. I no longer wanted to share a glass of wine with her and talk about our most recent success. That was the first time we didn't celebrate together after a wine club party.

"I've been doing surveillance on the girls. They're having parties at Reed's condo on Tuesday and Thursday afternoons," Reggie told me one day in early March. "I don't think it's anything to worry about, but I thought you should know."

We were at our usual positions around my kitchen table, trying to come up with an idea for the March wine club party. I dropped the pen

I'd been doodling with and stared at her. She said it so matter-of-factly, even as I could see the worry in her eyes. But that wasn't what appalled me. What appalled me was that she had kept this news concerning our daughters from me. "How long have you known this?"

Reggie shrugged evasively, "A couple of weeks, I guess."

"Damn it, Reggie, we have always protected our daughters together! How could you not have told me immediately? Instead, you drop this bombshell on me two weeks after the fact!" Let me tell you, I was mad.

Reggie held up her hand like she was a traffic cop warning me to stop before I crossed a busy street. "Before you blow your top, Audrey, hear me out. The parties last about an hour in the late afternoon, and I've never seen a kid come back out looking like he's drunk or stoned. Kent seems to know that the kids are using his place."

"What kids?" I said through gritted teeth.

"It's always Marcy, Hayley, Felicity, and a couple of the other Tigerettes." She swallowed. "And five of the boys from the basketball team. I think they're watching TV and eating snacks. You know, kids just hanging out after school."

"Or they could be having sex, Reggie. Didn't you think of that?" I was fuming at the multiple possibilities running through my head.

Reggie immediately became defensive. "I asked Hayley, and she confirmed that it was all perfectly innocent. Then she accused me of spying on her and threatened to tell Kent."

"So what if she told Kent? You're her mother, Reggie. You have a right to be concerned about her whereabouts." I couldn't believe that the woman I had regarded as my best friend for so many years could be so dense. I couldn't believe that she hadn't told me about the after school parties sooner.

"Kent has a restraining order against me," Reggie said quietly. "I'm not supposed to be on his street at all."

"God Almighty!" I exploded, sounding for all the world like Scarlett O'Hara. "Who haven't you been spying on lately?"

"It's a small list, Audrey."

She wanted me to smile at that, which is why I didn't.

"It's what kids do, Audrey. You know that."

I did know that, which was why I was worried. Margot had had good reason to tear my room apart looking for my teenage diary. I was not what you would have called an angelic teenager. I'd had some boyfriends, a couple of them older, and dabbled in some drugs. However, I didn't want my daughter to fall into that same trap, a trap that was born out of peer pressure or a need to rebel or low self-esteem. In my case, it had been all three. It had taken years for me to figure that out.

"I went snooping through Hayley's room," Reggie admitted next. "I couldn't find anything that seemed abnormal for a teenage girl. Of course it could be that she has secret Twitter and Instagram accounts, or it could be that I'm incredibly stupid. Please don't judge me for that. I know how you felt about your mother snooping through your stuff at that age."

I still did resent my mother for that, or perhaps I just resented her for the nasty person she had been. And still was. Now she was the nasty person who refused to die and was going to cost me a small fortune for no good reason that I could fathom. But that hadn't stopped me from doing my own search of my daughter's room. "I've snooped through Marcy's room too. On more than one occasion. I even looked through her purse." Like Reggie, I had wondered if my daughter was too technically savvy for me, or if I was so out of touch that I didn't know where to look. Or if I didn't know what to look for. That was a distinct possibility.

"It will all be over soon." Reggie didn't mean to sound ominous, but she did. "It's the state championship game, and win or lose, Felicity's reign as evil queen of the Tigerettes will be over for good."

"Maybe our daughters' changes in personality are not entirely Felicity's fault," I said sadly. "We've been preoccupied with the wine club for months now. We are not the mothers we used to be."

Reggie shook her head vehemently. "Bullshit, Audrey. Felicity is a manipulating, controlling young woman who knows how to get her way, to force people to her will. All we've been doing is trying to support our families and keep the roofs over our heads. We are not bad mothers."

I disagreed with Reggie on that point because I knew how negligent I had been with both my son and daughter since Paul left. But I was getting tired of going around in circles about the disturbing topic of Felicity. "We've only had this very same discussion for months now, Reggie. Yet we never do anything about it. If we think she's so evil, why haven't we *done something*?"

While we both knew that Cynthia wouldn't be any help at all in the matter--she seemed to be just as cowed by her daughter as everyone else--and while Mr. Rooney also seemed to be under Felicity's spell as he had demonstrated at that farce of a disciplinary meeting, we might have tried the school board, or called up the other Tigerette mothers to get their take on the situation. Something. Instead, we threw ourselves into the dream of the wine club and let everything else go.

Reggie must have been thinking along the same lines. "Because we don't have any proof that she's actually done anything wrong. While I'm positive she has brainwashed our daughters, I can't prove that it was against their will. In fact, they seem to be quite happy--other than when they're with us." She smiled ruefully. "However, I'd still like to get her alone in a dark room."

Reggie was always one for hyperbole, and it wasn't the first time she'd mentioned this fantasy. "Right. You might strangle her with your bare hands, or didn't you add that you might have a gun?"

Reggie had turned back to her computer. "I've taken the gun out of the scenario. If I were ever going to murder someone, I wouldn't waste my one shot on that little bitch."

I knew she was kidding, or just being Reggie, or whatever, but I let out a little gasp. "Reggie!"

"Relax, Audrey. You know me better than that."

I wasn't so sure anymore, but I kept my mouth shut. We got back to work.

Two days later, I took Jimmy to the state championship game, the Mohave Tigers versus the Saguaro Sabres. And I dragged Reggie along with us, kicking and screaming, you might say. While she would readily admit that basketball was a sport, Reggie had this spiel that watching the Tigerettes dance was not a sporting event, and therefore irrelevant to her as an avid sports fan. For years she had spouted on and on about her glory years as a field hockey superstar in high school and college, and even after I told her that I didn't care to know what that sport was, she would, during patio nights, reminisce about winning plays and matches won during the pouring rain. Or maybe it was sleet. I honestly don't know because I wasn't paying any attention. But on the final game of the basketball season, I told Reggie that we needed to go. We had only attended a handful of games since November, which was shameful, so I got adamant about it and told

Reggie it was our duty as parents to attend the final one. Hence, Reggie's kicking and screaming.

To be more precise, I meant that it would be the final game for Marcy. I hadn't even told Reggie about this decision because I didn't care whether or not she would let Hayley try out next year. My decision was final. Marcy did not know this yet either, and I fully expected a knock-down, drag-out fight when she was told that her career as a Mohave Tigerette was finished. I wasn't going to be mean about it. I would wait until the final glow of the final performance had worn off, and then I would politely, lovingly tell her that she would be a Tigerette for another year over my dead body.

I had been toying with this act of parental control for some time, but it didn't come to a head for me until the last time I went snooping in Marcy's room. I opened that closet door of hers and saw the row of sequinned, shimmering, short, short uniforms, the stripper, thigh-high white boots, the blue and gold pom-poms, and for some reason, I just lost it. I sobbed. It wasn't all the money that I had spent on those barely-there outfits--although God knew it had been a small fortune--but it was as if all the Tigerette shiny adornments represented the loss of my daughter's innocence. I hadn't cried for weeks, but I sobbed brokenheartedly for a solid twenty minutes as I stared into that closet. Call it my mother's intuition that arrived too late.

I hated crowds, so consequently, my mood was not much better than Reggie's when we squeezed into the packed bleachers on game night. Being in a crowded place got Jimmy overly excited, and it wasn't long before I let him loose, allowing him to slither down between the slats of the bleachers and play among the discarded candy boxes and popcorn bags with all the other unsupervised children. I felt guilty about all the germs and gross ickiness down there, but I was not the only parent who allowed her child to wallow under the bleachers. It didn't stop Reggie, though, from shaking her head disapprovingly. She, the mother whose relationship with her son seemed to grow more distant with each passing week.

"I'm in hell," Reggie said once the game got underway.

It was hard to disagree with that. The gym was suffocatingly hot and smelled like buttered sweat and old tennis shoes. The guy next to me, the one who was hogging my space, must have been a heavy smoker, so that was added into the dizzying mix of odors. But it had been my idea, you know, so I had to grin and bear it. "Suck it up, Reggie," I said to her.

"I would gladly suck it up, Audrey, if I could breathe at all."

Her saying that only made my lightheadedness worse. She was such a spoilsport. If Reggie wasn't happy with the way things were going, she could ruin the mood for everyone. "We only have to stay until the girls perform, and then we can leave."

So Reggie sat stone-like beside me, albeit a sweating stone, seething with resentment, and I did the same. In the old days, she and I would have been uncomfortable, sure, but we would have had fun making snide remarks about the other parents, gossiping about this and that, until we were both laughing. While that made me sad on one level, it made me resent her all the more on another. Reggie couldn't stand not being in charge, not calling the shots. I ignored her while I kept bending down to peek under the bleachers, trying to make out Jimmy, but it was like a blur of scurrying rats down there. It was hard telling what Jimmy might be eating off that filthy floor. In short, as if I haven't made this clear enough, we were both miserable.

The whistle blew for halftime, and shortly after that, the Tigerettes marched in, followed by their head coach--yeah, right--Cynthia. And God Almighty!--I'm sorry that I keep channeling Scarlett O'Hara--if she didn't have on the same tiny blue and gold number the girls were wearing. The outfits didn't leave much to the imagination, short of seeing the outlines of actual nipples or crotches, and they seemed to accentuate every girl's curve. And Cynthia's, who out-curved them all, times ten.

"What the hell?" Reggie said.

"Unbelievable." I could only stare. The weird thing was that all the girls looked good, including Marcy, who had lost quite a bit of weight this year. She was sixteen, a young woman, but I didn't particularly want others to see her like that yet. But it was obviously too late for that. The crowd was on its feet, cheering and whistling. They'd noticed.

It wasn't like the dance was raunchy, certainly not like the video that went viral on YouTube. And it wasn't like you could say that the blue and gold outfits were exactly vulgar--more like over the top. The Tigerettes executed a flawless routine to Queen's "We Will Rock You" that climaxed in the girls lining up, arms around each other, kicking in unison like the Rockettes at Radio City Music Hall. All in all, the whole thing seemed like a performance you would see in a showroom at Caesars Palace. It was glitzy, sexy, polished. Cynthia, standing on the sidelines at the back of the girls, followed the routine. She might have been at the back, but you couldn't miss her. The crowd ate it up.

"This has got to be Cynthia's doing," Reggie yelled over the crowd.

Once again, I couldn't disagree. The thing that disturbed me the most wasn't the fact that the dance was sexy, even provocative. The dances that I had seen all season had been of that caliber, so I shouldn't have been surprised. And I wasn't. Felicity was good at giving the crowd what they wanted. What disturbed me the most was that the girls, my daughter included, had seemed to transform during the course of the season into seasoned showgirls. It was like they were now accomplished professionals. It was like they would be waiting for the men to line up at their dressing room doors when the show had finished, and those men would want to unwrap the entire package. Maybe I was overly protective at this late stage in the game, but that was the image I couldn't shake from my mind.

I felt slightly sick to my stomach, so I didn't object when Reggie said we were leaving. I had planned on going back to the practice room after the show and giving Marcy the box of Godiva chocolates I had bought to celebrate the end of her career, the end she didn't know about yet. But now that seemed entirely inappropriate. I was already envisioning my daughter as a showgirl for hire. I didn't need to add the startling picture of Lady Godiva riding naked on a horse through town into the mix.

I had to crawl under the bleachers to locate my son, and it was as disgusting as I had feared. He started to bellow as I grabbed his hand and pulled him from the carnage, and he continued to do so all the way home. I didn't blame Reggie when she declined my offer of a glass of wine, saying that she had a headache. If I were her, I would want to go home to an empty house right about now after the chaos of the gym and the spectacle we had just witnessed. I intended to give Jimmy a mild sedative in a cup of chocolate pudding and settle him in front of the TV until he got sleepy enough for bed. He was filthy, but bath time was always a struggle, so I decided it could wait until tomorrow.

Don't judge me. Have you ever cared for a child with disabilities? Ultimately, the goal is to keep them calm, to try to make them happy, and when necessary, to use substances that have been medically prescribed.

I had just opened the door when I heard Paul call out, "Don't be alarmed, babe. I'm in the kitchen. I guarantee you that I am not an intruder." He appeared around the corner of the kitchen with his hands up, grinning.

"Daddy," Jimmy stopped whimpering and ran into his arms, naturally. The traitor.

"Hey, buddy, good to see you." He sniffed. "Did you turn into a fish when I was gone because I sure do smell something stinky."

Jimmy giggled. "I am not a fish."

"But you do like water, right?"

Jimmy liked water; he just didn't particularly like baths these days. But he nodded obediently. The traitor.

"How about we go upstairs and get a bath before your bedtime snack? We'll play submarine with that boat of yours." Paul raised his eyes at me, and I nodded. He kept talking in a soothing voice as he took Jimmy by the hand and led him upstairs.

I was relieved. It was a luxury to be excused from one parental responsibility after months of going it alone. And Paul was Jimmy's father. I debated about a nanosecond before I poured a glass of wine. The life coach--yeah, right--wasn't around, and I needed a glass of wine. Paul was the alcoholic, not me. Let him deal with it.

When Paul came down a glass of wine later--I had just poured my second--he wasn't in the same jovial mood. "You shouldn't have let Jimmy crawl under the bleachers during the game. He could've gotten lice."

That was so preposterous that I laughed. "That's not how a kid gets lice, Paul."

"I was at the game." Paul pulled out a kitchen chair and sat down next to me.

That surprised me. I'd figured Jimmy had told him about the bleachers. "What'd you think?"

"I felt like I was in a titty bar." Paul eyed my glass of wine, then went and got a diet Coke, acting as if he knew exactly where everything was. Which he did. I hadn't changed a thing in the refrigerator since he left. Hadn't even cleaned it, truth be told.

"Welcome to the Tigerettes." I took a sip of wine.

"I guess I would have enjoyed it if I had been drunk. But I'm not. I told you that she should quit back in the beginning when you were worried about the money."

"But you didn't tell her that, and I didn't have the heart to because she wanted it so much. And then you left." I fingered the stem of my wine glass. "Besides, it's a moot point now. The season is over."

Paul sat back down, but he wasn't relaxed. "How have you managed since I went to treatment?"

That was the first time he'd asked me that question. But it was his turn to be too late. I wasn't going to tell him a damn thing; he didn't deserve it. I changed the subject. "Where's the life coach? I thought you couldn't make a move without her."

The new Paul could stay on the conversational track. "First the Lexus, now there's a shiny new Lincoln MKX parked in the driveway. Did you win the lottery, babe?" His smile was weak.

I guess I forgot to mention that the car I decided on was not the nice-soccer-mom car that Reggie had strongly suggested that I get. And it was because of her bossiness that I decided on another expensive car. "It's also leased," I said by way of explanation, which was not an explanation at all.

"Babe, you know what I'm getting at here. Where is all the money coming from?"

My mind whirred until I seized on an almost forgotten fact. "You told me to sell your Rolex, remember?"

"Right." Paul pondered that for a moment.

I was counting on Paul's complete ignorance about money to help me out. "It was worth more than you think." That was, of course, a blatant lie.

"That's good." Paul leaned back in his chair, studying me. "Did you get a job, Audrey? That's why I wasn't worried when I left. I knew that you could always go back to teaching."

I felt like he had handed me a present. "That's right. I got a job." The way I looked at it, it wasn't necessarily a lie. The wine club was a full-time job, even if it wasn't the type of employment Paul had in mind.

"Good for you. What school?"

"Where are you living?" I countered. "Surely, you're done with your *treatment* for the third--or is it fourth?--time."

Paul's face turned pink. "I've been living in an apartment over on Thunderbird for the last two weeks."

"You what?" I was so stunned that I wanted to throw my glass of wine in his face, Reggie-style, but I drained it instead. I needed it too much to waste it on a dramatic gesture.

Paul reached for my hand, and his voice was earnest. "You see, babe, I'm in the process of transitioning. Sondra thinks I need to live on my own for a while in the 'real world'--Paul put air quotes around those words--before I can return to my 'normal'--air quotes again--life."

"Is Sondra living with you?"

Paul's face was now bright red. "Yes, but it's not what you think."

My voice was icy when I said, "And what exactly am I thinking?"

"She's my life coach, Audrey. I need her."

"I was your life partner. I needed you."

"Needed?" Paul had the audacity to look surprised.

I was totally fed up with Paul and his self-centeredness. I suppose I should have been fed up with him and his bullshit years ago, but I guess you could call me a late bloomer when it came to matters of the heart. I blame my mother for that too.

I slammed my hands down on the table. "You are such a piece of shit, Paul! You left me high and dry with two kids to support while you took your own sweet time deciding whether or not you wanted to come back. Well, don't come back. We're doing fine without you."

Paul's jaw tightened. "You've changed, Audrey. You are sitting here and lying to my face. I know you don't have a teaching job. Jimmy told me you spend all your time cooking in the kitchen. What are you cooking, Audrey?"

"I'm running a meth lab out of this very kitchen, Paul." At the shocked look on his face, I started to laugh. And once I started, I couldn't stop. The image of Reggie's unfinished cabinets, the tweaker group as she called them, popped into my head. I laughed until the tears were rolling down my face.

When Paul could get a word in edgewise, he said, "You are putting my children in danger, Audrey. If you are running an illegal operation--"

That set me off again. My word, he was a stupid man. He'd known me for years, and he thought I'd be cooking meth in my kitchen? Granted, I was doing something illegal, but a meth lab? Give me a break. "Oh, Paul," I gasped, "you are such a ninny."

I could tell that he was getting mad by the way his eyes turned from light blue to navy, by the way his cheek billowed in and out as his jaw clenched. I didn't care if I'd riled him up. In the old days when I saw such a mood coming on, I would have gone out of my way to console him, to retreat into myself, but those days were gone. After all these months, he finally showed an inkling of concern about his family's welfare. But his so-called concern started about the time I got the Lexus for Marcy. That's when it hit me. Paul hadn't mentioned having a job or even looking for one. Sondra might be currently footing the bills, but sooner or later, she would grow tired of it, as any sane woman would. So Paul, trust fund baby that he was, a man used to be taken care of, a man cocooned in his vast web of narcissism, needed money, and he was coming to me. It was unbelievable.

Yet before I could tell him all that, Marcy burst through the front door. I'd expected tears of grief for the end of the basketball season, but that wasn't the case at all. She was all smiles. "Guess what? Felicity has decided that the Tigerettes are going to continue. We're such a good squad that she's entered us into competitions!"

I groaned inwardly, while Paul, the piece of shit, congratulated her on this new development and raved about her performance that evening, not mentioning that he had thought he was in a titty bar when he watched the girls dance. Big surprise. Marcy babbled on happily until Jimmy came down for his goodnight kisses. When Paul offered to tuck him in and read him a story, I readily agreed. I didn't suspect a thing. It was only after he left that I thought to check my underwear drawer, the safe place I'd been keeping my wine club cash.

Big surprise. My money was gone.

I was still angry and upset when I went to visit my mother the next day at Belmont Skilled Nursing. It was not my choice to go and see her, but a call from the director of this facility, Jean, summoned me to the ranch-style brick building. Margot had been more agitated than usual, she told me, and she thought that a visit from a family member might help calm her down. Yeah, right. A visit from me would be the last thing Margot needed to soothe her agitation and overall nastiness. I hadn't been to see Margot once since I placed her in the facility, and you would think that would give Jean a clue about how my family operated. But no. Jean sweetly, yet persistently told me that a visit from a loved one brightened the day of each and every resident. Yeah, right.

But I went. I figured that if I didn't find something to occupy my time, I might have spent the day tearing out my hair and raging against the injustice of marrying such a loser as Paul. Or I might have spent hours driving up and down Thunderbird, stopping at every apartment complex, looking for Paul and loudly demanding my money back. Or I might have seen Sondra's Toyota in one of the parking lots and rammed my brand new Lincoln into the passenger side door. Still yet, I might have called the police and had them track down Paul, which would have undoubtedly opened a whole new can of worms. What if the cops wanted to know how it came to be that a middle-class, suburban mom had so much cash hidden in her underwear drawer, a drawer filled with decidedly unsexy cotton panties? Would I have to make up a story about an unexpected inheritance, or would I have told them that I was now in the private escort business? Oh, God, would I have told them the truth?

Belmont was a facility filled with people waiting to die, some forgotten, others neglected by those who were unwilling or unable to care for them. It was another depressing place that ignited a flare of guilt to anyone who walked through the door. It made The Gardens look like a paradise, and yes, I admit that I felt guilty when I had to go to the front desk and ask which room Margot Keller was in. I'd hired movers to move Margot's things from The Gardens to her new room at Belmont, and now the much smaller room was crammed full of Margot's old desk and chair and couch and bureau. I had to squeeze into the space.

Despite the crowded room, I could immediately see the signs of Margot's agitation when I reluctantly took a deep breath and entered. The side table that slid under her hospital bed was overturned, and her pillows had been thrown to the floor. Those were probably the only items she could reach. She was awake, propped against the bare headboard, her white hair standing on end. Her paralyzed arm, the right, was crossed over her small frame like a broken wing. She looked tired, and frankly, more than a little pathetic. If she were someone else's aged mother, I might have felt sorry for her, but she was my mother, the non-nurturing soul who'd had the misfortune to produce children. And had never stopped being pissed off about it.

"I heard you've been acting like a pill today, Mother." I tried to smile at her, but her belligerent gaze bored into my heart. "The people here are only trying to take care of you."

She garbled something indistinguishable.

"Why can't you just be nice?" Without looking into those watery green eyes, I righted the table, picked up the sippy cup of water, the comb, a magazine, the TV remote. I found her glasses underneath the bureau. She must have ripped them off and thrown them, and I wondered who had been the target. Maybe several people had been in today to try to calm the old woman down, but if so, it looked like they had given up and left her alone. I didn't blame them.

"How have you been?" I asked conversationally, not knowing what else to say. I wondered if she was aware that I hadn't visited before.

I picked up the two pillows from the floor, but I have to tell you that I was reluctant to move closer. The way the hospital bed was pushed against the wall left her good side, the left, free. Believe it or not, after all these years, I was still afraid of those flying fists. My mother was left-handed, and she might have been over eighty, but I knew that one left fist could still pack a wallop.

"Is there anything you need?"

Through the gibberish coming from her twisted mouth, I would swear that I could make out *fuck you.*

"Right back at you, Margot." I was being childish. I knew that, so I took the plunge and moved close enough to the bed to tuck a pillow behind her head. She shook her head furiously, and unbelievably, she snarled at me like a rabid dog.

"Damn it, Margot," my voice was heated, "you have always been such a bitch."

Her left hand came down on my wrist like a vise, and she twisted. It hurt. It hurt more than you think it would. I wrenched it away. "Why don't you die?"

The *fuck you* was louder that time, and when I looked down at my red wrist, I saw her claw-like hand slowly give the finger. After everything I had done for her, the woman still hated me. I knew from an early age that my mother didn't love me, but over the years her dislike had turned to open hostility. Why was she still here, and why was I the one who had to take care of her? Why did she continue to extract a toll from me, both emotionally and financially? *Why?*

I leaned down and whispered in her ear. "Why didn't you ever love me? I tried my best." I still had one pillow in my hands, and I lifted it in front of her face. "You should have loved me."

The pillow was moving toward her face in slow motion, drawing nearer, nearer . . .

Margot's eyes were wide, and for the first and last time in my life, I saw her fear.

20

REGGIE

Audrey bailed on me. There is no other way to put it. I don't care what she says, and I don't care what excuses she still tries to make. She left me high and dry, with virtually no options. She *bailed*.

It was mid-March, and we were in the usual throes of choosing the wines, designing the labels, buying filler wines, ordering bottles and shrink caps, etc. Because the Château Pétrus estate from the Pomerol wine region of France had been so popular and profitable in February, we had chosen an equally elite wine estate for March: Château Lafite Rothschild. Lafite was one of four wine-producing châteaux of Bordeaux originally awarded First Growth status in the 1855 Classification. That would mean nothing to our clients when I mentioned it in my presentation, but believe me, it is a big deal in the French wine-drinking world. We chose four vintages:

Château Lafite Rothschild Pauillac 2006 for $1,200;

Pauillac Château Lafite Rothschild 1 L Cru 2010--Domaines Barons de Rothschild for $2600;

Château Lafite Rothschild Pauillac Red Bordeaux Blend 2000 1.5L for $5,500;

and Château Latour Grand Vin de Château Latour Pauillac Red Bordeaux Blend 1961 1.5L for $13,500.

I was confident that this would be our most profitable party yet. I mean, you hear the name Rothschild, and you think money, money, money--right?

So I went over to Audrey's house one beautiful Monday morning, raring to go to work as usual, but when I slid open the back patio door to her kitchen, she wasn't bringing in empty bottles from her garage, and there weren't any pots of water boiling on the stove. Nope. She stood right by the kitchen island, a cup of coffee in her hand and a suitcase at her feet. This was so out of the ordinary that my first thought was that something terrible had happened. But Audrey didn't look particularly stressed out--at least no more than usual--so I tried to make a joke: "Are you running away from home, sister?"

"Nope. I've decided to take the kids to San Diego. Do you want a cup of coffee?"

I had already been on my way to the coffee machine, but I stopped in my tracks. "What?"

"San Diego. The kids. It's spring break, Reggie."

"I know that. Hayley's still in bed, but--"

"What did you think I was going to do with Jimmy all week? We can't have all the tools of our trade hanging around while he's in the next room watching TV."

To tell the truth, I hadn't thought much about it. I guess I had assumed that she would pawn off Jimmy to Delilah yet again. That poor kid. Audrey passed him off like a football every chance she got. He was probably starting to wonder where he actually lived and which woman was his mother. But San Diego? That was extreme. "Why can't Marcy keep him occupied during the day?"

Audrey shook her head. "My mind's made up, Reggie. I'm taking the kids on vacation. They deserve one, and I do too. We'll be home on Sunday." She set her empty coffee cup in the sink. "It's been a rough few months. Surely, you can understand how nice it would be to get away for a few days."

I wasn't mad at her, not yet. I was confused. "I don't understand how you can just up and leave with no warning. We've got so much work to do."

"There's always work to do, Reggie. This being my kitchen and all, I'm glaringly aware of that fact every time I walk in. I'm starting to feel that I should be steaming a shrink cap or corking a bottle instead of cooking dinner or having a cup of coffee. But that's beside the point. The point is that I've decided to take my kids on a much-deserved vacation, and I'm going."

"Does this have something to do with your mother?" Audrey had been acting strangely ever since she got the phone call from the director at Belmont. Not only did she not want to talk about her mother's passing, but she also didn't plan any funeral or memorial service. I offered to help her with that task, but she shut me down completely with an: "I don't want you ever to mention her again. I mean it, Reggie."

I'd goofed, and Audrey's green eyes blazed. "Damn it, Reggie. This has nothing to do with that woman. I'm going on a vacation like normal people do. It's not that big of a deal."

But it was for me. The two of us had a hard enough time getting the bottles of wine ready for the growing number of clients we had coming to the parties. I knew I couldn't do it alone. "How in the hell do you think I'm going to get everything done by myself?"

"If you quit spending so much time driving around spying on people, you could accomplish a lot more."

That was hitting below the belt. I spent as much time, if not more, than Audrey getting ready for the parties. And I should never have told her about that goddamn restraining order that Kent finally got after I called him and accused him of condoning unsupervised parties in his condo. He'd gotten good and mad about that. Unnecessarily so. He said that Hayley had asked him if she could have friends over after school, and he'd agreed. He said they cleaned up after their snacks and never left any mess. He said that she was his daughter too, and I had no business spying on her or him. Then he accused me again of running over Reed's nasty cat on purpose. He'd had enough. Oh, and then he'd added that I was acting like a crazy person and should seek professional counseling.

I was starting to get a little steamed. "You know very well that I carry my weight in this operation. But the fact of the matter is that it's a two-person job. You know that. If you take off for a week, I don't know if we can possibly get everything done before the party on the 24th."

"The party has been moved to the 31st. I talked to Cynthia, and she agreed."

I couldn't believe it. "You went behind my back and talked to Cynthia? First, you abandon ship, and then you collaborate with the enemy."

Audrey sighed tiredly. "Damn it, Reggie. I knew you'd overreact like this. I'm going on a much-needed vacation with my kids. And I had to call Cynthia because it's her house. She's our partner, not the enemy. If you don't think we can get the wine ready because I'm taking off for one lousy week, call Cynthia. Tell her it's her turn to help. Which it is, by the way."

I totally agreed that Cynthia didn't carry her weight in the operation. She'd muscled her way in with threats of exposure, and now all she did was host a party and rake in the dough. But that wasn't the point here. The point was that Audrey was abandoning me during the hardest part of our month, the bottling and corking. She hadn't even given me the courtesy of a heads up. "Tell me, Audrey, how would you feel if I took off and left you holding the bag?"

When Audrey lifted her head from the cup she was rinsing to put in the dishwasher, her eyes were tragically sad. "I already know that feeling well, Reggie."

I knew she meant Paul. At least I thought she was referring to his extended absence and not to my work in the wine club. If she was implying that I didn't carry my weight, she was dead wrong. And I was not about to feel sorry for her. She was supposed to tell me about things like this. Had she been planning this vacation for weeks, or was it a last-minute deal? Our wine club was gaining a reputation as *the* place to go and get wine in Scottsdale. The wine club should be our first priority. How could she possibly jeopardize that at such a critical time in its evolution? I would never do that to her.

Audrey called to her kids to hurry up and then turned to me. "We'll be staying at the Catamaran on Mission Bay. Only call me if it's an emergency, okay? I need to spend some time with my kids." She should have left it at that, but she didn't. "Maybe you should also use this time to spend with Hayley."

Goddamnit. Was she now insulting my parenting skills? How many low blows could she work into one conversation? "Are you insinuating that I--"

"Call Cynthia. Instead of spending so much time driving by her house, you might be able to go inside and find whatever it is you're looking for."

Her kids trooped down the stairs then, suitcases bumping behind them, and Audrey started to go around the house, checking all the doors and windows. It was her blatant hint that I needed to leave, and I did so by fuming and stomping out the patio door.

I hadn't gotten around to telling Audrey that I had seen the man on a monitor in Richard's study, and I suspected that he was indeed inside a room in that big house of Cynthia's with a camera watching his every move. It would have given me great pleasure to prove to Audrey that I had been right to suspect that something had happened to the man who scaled the backyard wall. The reason I hadn't told her is that I didn't know what I was going to do with that information yet. My gut told me that Cynthia had secrets that I had only begun to tap. My gut also told me that it would be very valuable to have information I could use against a woman like Cynthia Stewart. Not that I was planning to blackmail her or anything outlandish like that, but you just never knew.

I *am* getting to the part about how I spent some of my newfound wealth. First, it was a giddy feeling to possess that much extra cash for the first time in my life. I did not grow up in a household that had much money. My dad George, the ex-marine, worked as a land surveyor for the state. His salary wasn't anything to write home about, but the benefits were good. I overheard my parents talking about that a lot, the *good benefits*. It took me a long time to figure out what that meant, but as a little kid, the glowing reference to the *good benefits* made me feel safe. My mom Cheryl worked as a receptionist in a dentist's office, which is probably the reason why I have such good teeth--along with the good benefits, that is. She also did nails on the side in our house at the kitchen table. She was a walking advertisement for those nails, my mom, and always had perfect hair and makeup too. Her one regret might have been that her only daughter did not turn out to be a girly girl. Don't get me wrong. That's only a hunch. She never said anything like that to me. My dad yelled a lot, as I have already mentioned, but all in all, my brothers and I had a very happy childhood. Don't believe what anyone else says on that subject. We were happy, and while not remotely rich, we were comfortable. We had those *good benefits*, you know.

What I am getting at here is that I was not raised to be extravagant, and during my marriage to Kent, money always seemed to go out at a greater velocity than it came in. I worried about our financial situation a lot because we could never manage to establish any safety net. On the rare occasions when Kent got a Christmas bonus, something catastrophic would invariably occur: a broken furnace, a transmission problem, a property tax bill, the damn Tigerettes. I thought we'd never pay off both my kids' orthodontia work because they did not, unfortunately, inherit my good teeth. Needless to say, we didn't own a second home or a boat or take airplanes to exotic destinations. What I am saying is that I was used to it. I might have complained from time to time, but we were all happy. I guess I didn't scratch too far beneath the surface on that one, did I?

The money. I had to think carefully about how I was going to spend it. Not being used to having that kind of unencumbered cash, I wasn't quite sure what to do with it. To tell you the truth, that stack of bills frightened me a little. You read all these stories of rich people who spend, spend, spend on foreign cars and mansions and private jets. And then they end up with nothing, like some professional football players or child actors who never had any talent to sustain a career. I didn't want to be frivolous with my newfound money, unlike those other two so-called partners. Cynthia always talked about shopping or going to a salon--in my opinion, entirely worthless pursuits. And Audrey. Well. She was downright stupid with her money, buying cars and taking vacations. When you stop to think about it, Audrey became the poster girl for everything that a newly rich dumb person does. She was like a person who had just hit a casino jackpot on the slots and then went and blew it all on roulette. It still makes me mad to think about it.

I did buy a car for Hayley's sixteenth birthday. Yes, I let peer pressure get to me. I didn't have a choice because Audrey had gone out and gotten a new car for Marcy. However, it was a far cry from a Lexus. Instead, I bought Hayley a used car on CARFAX, a 2016 Nissan Altima. It was a perfectly good, safe car; I did my research on that model and year. My daughter, now the spoiled Tigerette, dared to grumble about it until I threatened to take it away from her and drive it myself. It would have been a mean thing to do, but it would have served the ungrateful child right. And I would have done it. However, she quit grumbling about it when she realized that the used car got her from Point A to Point B just like a Lexus or BMW would. I did notice, though, that she and Marcy usually took Marcy's car when they drove off together.

After careful consideration of all my options, I decided the smartest thing to do would be to invest the money. I liked the whole concept of "the rich keep getting richer." And how did they do that? They invested their money wisely. Which then became the problem. I didn't have a clue how the stock market operated or what stocks or mutual funds or bonds or US treasury notes to buy. That became abundantly clear to me after I made an appointment with a financial advisor at Fidelity. After about an hour of looking at the clean-cut young man's pie charts and graphs and listening to his spiel about long-term growth versus less conservative returns, I was more confused than ever.

When he finally got around to asking me how much money I wanted to invest--a question he should have asked first, in my opinion, I said, "I have forty-five thousand, in cash." I reached into my purse and pulled out the stack of bills that were held together by a rubber band.

He looked vaguely disappointed, and after a moment's hesitation, said, "We don't take cash here. I need a check or a cashier's check."

I thought that was ridiculous. "You're a bank, aren't you?"

"We are an investment brokerage firm," he corrected.

I was so embarrassed. I think I mumbled an apology--I might have told him to fuck off; I don't remember--and left. There had been an accident on Scottsdale Road, and the traffic was so congested that I decided to make an immediate left and take a detour through Scottsdale Airpark. It wasn't a shortcut to my house, but I would rather be moving in the wrong direction than stuck in traffic, so I drove through the industrial park with its large office buildings with hangars in the back. As luck would have it, I saw a For Sale sign on one of the buildings, and that's when it hit me. *Property.* What better investment could there be? I immediately pulled over and called the number on the sign. The realtor told me all about the property. Then he named the price. It was way too rich for my blood, so I thanked him, told him I would think about it, and drove home.

Were my hopes dashed? Not for a minute. If I couldn't afford an industrial property, there was no reason why I couldn't buy another house. Another house would have a kitchen, and wasn't Audrey always complaining about having the winemaking aspect of the business--and I use the term *winemaking* loosely--in her kitchen? If I bought another house, we could move the entire business there. We wouldn't have to put everything away when we finished working for the day, only to drag it all out again. We wouldn't have to worry about any kids or husbands walking in unannounced. We wouldn't even have to constantly clean up after ourselves, as Audrey always insisted we do, despite my grumblings. And our business would have its own address, which somehow made it more legitimate.

You don't have to point out the irony of that; I get it. The point here is that I was not only making an investment, but I was also thinking of the wine club first and foremost. I thought it was going to continue to grow, and we would definitely need more space. It was a win-win situation all around.

Location, location, location. The top three criteria for buying a house, as the saying goes. I took that to heart and spent the next week or so driving up and down streets no more than a mile away from Audrey's and my houses on Sheena. I figured that if we were going to start commuting to work every day, we would want our travel time to be no more than five minutes. Honestly, I was thinking more of Audrey when I planned that. She was the one who had more time restrictions on her day, with a small kid who needed to be driven to and picked up from places.

I, on the other hand, was mercifully past that phase of my life now that Hayley had her driver's license, and I decided that once I found the house, I would start to run to and from work every day. Even during the summer months when the temperature soared above 110 degrees, I could always take a shower at the new place after an especially sweaty workout. We could even furnish the place with living room furniture and bedroom sets and a TV. The new house would not only be our place of business, but we could also make it a home away from home. It would be perfect.

I had three or four places picked out and took one Saturday to go to open houses. I would like the record to reflect that I went on a *Saturday*, a day when Audrey and I couldn't work on the wine club because she had Jimmy to deal with. I did not, in any way, skirt my responsibilities when I went house hunting. And I wasn't secretive about it either. I just didn't mention it to her. Or to Cynthia. Why in the hell would I have told Cynthia anyway? She wasn't my friend. I didn't even particularly like her. Even if she was a so-called partner in the wine business, she didn't need to know how I spent my free time or my money. And this is the most important fact: The business I was conducting was all for the good of the wine club. First and foremost, I was thinking about the wine club.

I can tell you what I hate about going to open houses. Every single time I would walk into a house for sale, there would immediately be a realtor hovering over me, asking questions and offering to give me a tour of the home to point out the various "amenities." I was probably rather rude to those people when I would grab the printed sheet with the home's description and price and tell them to mind their own business. I didn't need someone telling me what I wanted. I knew what I wanted. And the last house on my list, a four-bedroom ranch house on an acre property on Cholla was exactly it. It sat back from the road, which provided even more privacy, and had desert landscaping, which didn't require much maintenance. It also had a pool in the back that was green with algae, a carport instead of a garage, a swamp cooler instead of air conditioning, and a kitchen that boasted appliances from the 1970s. In short, it was a fixer-upper. But it was vacant, which made it perfect. I made an offer on the spot.

I know now that I should have made an offer ten percent below the asking price, but it had been two decades since I'd been in the market for a house. Maybe I was a little out of practice. However, even after the appraisal revealed that the house needed new wiring and had termites, I felt like I had gotten a good deal for the $600,000 price. Even when the appraiser told me that the house was basically a teardown, I was happy with my investment. Finding an acre lot in the middle of Scottsdale was like finding a needle in a haystack, and I had all the confidence in the world that the land alone was worth the price and would continue to increase in value. Besides, I hadn't been looking for my dream house. I had been looking for a place to house a business. And 68993 E. Cholla had a lot of space. The back patio alone could probably store a hundred cases of wine. Hell, Audrey and I could build a big shed in the backyard to store equipment and bottles of wine when our club went global. And I was confident that our wine club would go global. So you see, the house was indeed perfect.

The next part is where it gets a little bit tricky. To get the best possible mortgage rate, I needed to put ten percent down on the house. With the cash I had on hand, I needed $15,000 more. After the February party, Audrey, Cynthia, and I had each kept half in cash and deposited the rest. Of course we had all gone to the bank together a couple of days after the party to make sure that everyone was following the rules.

Was it a matter of trust? You bet it was. I didn't trust Cynthia farther than I could throw her, and I wasn't confident anymore that Audrey would do the right thing. She'd been acting so squirrely lately, moody and bitchy and unpredictable. So, I had the $15,000 in the FHM joint account, and I whipped out my checkbook and wrote the check. I also decided--and this was at the last minute--to have the mortgage payments paid directly out of that account too. Very soon, Audrey and Cynthia would see the benefits of having our business in another building. And since the house was for the benefit of the wine club, it was a wine club expense. It didn't take a rocket scientist to figure that one out.

Yes, I put the title in my name. It was my idea in the first place, and I'm the one who found the house and made the down payment. Yes, it was expensive to immediately repair the wiring and the plumbing and the pool pump and the crack in the foundation. But I was thinking ahead. If the building was going to house a business, it had to be up to code. Naturally, it was the wine club's responsibility to cover those expenses. I made sure of that.

First of all, Cynthia should have never been a partner in the wine club. She hadn't been there at the inception of the plan, she hadn't been there when Audrey and I developed our business model, and she hadn't had to agonize over whether or not people would actually fall for our scheme. All she had done was find out our secret, and to this day, I don't think she would have ever figured it out if I hadn't run into her at Trader Joe's that day. And I would like the record to reflect that it wasn't my fault that I was in the wrong place at the wrong time. It's Audrey's. If I hadn't had to go back down the aisles in search of her damn chocolate coconut almonds, I would have already been through the checkout line and out of the store.

I would also like to point out that Audrey never did pay me back for those empty calories that she needed like a hole in the head, nor did she ever pay me back her half of the expenses for the January party. I realize now that has always been her style. She would ask someone for a favor and then never pay them back. If you ask me, that is not how friendship is supposed to work. True friends help each other out--I am completely on board with that--but when it comes to money, you don't ever stiff a friend.

Okay, I wanted to keep Cynthia's involvement in the wine club to a minimum. She could host the parties and take her unearned third of the profits, but the day-to-day part of the business was Audrey's and mine. In that way, I could still think of us as the controlling partners. In Audrey's kitchen, she and I were like a couple of ballet dancers as we moved from task to task. We had the rhythm down pat, and Cynthia would have only gotten in the way. Plus, if I were to be totally honest, I thought that I was the controlling partner. I was the one who always chose the wine regions and did all the research. Anyone in her right mind would tell you that selecting the regions and vintages were the keys to a successful party. Neither Audrey nor Cynthia could be bothered to pore over Karen

MacNeil's *The Wine Bible.* They simply sat back and expected me to make the right choices. And I always did. So in that way, I do consider myself to be the brains of the operation.

But when Audrey decided that she would abandon ship and take her kids on vacation, I was facing a dilemma. There was no way that I could get everything done by myself. Believe me, I know because I tried. After Audrey and the kids left on that Monday morning, I went into her house and tried to do it by myself. I was not breaking in. I knew that she kept a spare house key in a fake rock in the planter in front of the house, just as she knew that I kept my spare key taped to the underside of my mailbox. So it wasn't even remotely like breaking and entering. I was only carrying on like a good soldier would. Even though Audrey and Cynthia had gone behind my back and made the decision to change the date of the party, I got it in my head that I would prove to Audrey that I didn't need her to get the job done.

I couldn't do it. I started by trying to put the few Château Lafite Rothschild labels that Audrey had gotten done on the boxes of bottles that we had ordered. During the weeks of the business, I had not gotten any better with the glue gun, so I abandoned that practice and moved onto filling the bottles with the Carlo Rossi, Yellow Tail, and Château Ste. Michelle that we had decided to use. I didn't have the patience for that job either. I wasn't getting the levels right, and I kept pouring the wine back into the big bowl that we used, putting the funnel back in the top of the bottle, and starting over. I was getting nowhere fast because my forte was corking, and I had become something of an expert in that area. And packing the bottles into crates; I was good at that. When it became clear that the only thing I was accomplishing was a mounting frustration, I knew what I had to do.

I had always said that I would enlist help from Cynthia when hell freezes over, but it looked like hell had just grown a little chillier on that Monday. You can bet that I didn't want to make the call. Spending hours with the woman would take all the patience I possessed, which wasn't much to begin with. What in the world would we talk about? Her glory years as Mrs. Arizona? Seriously, just the thought made me almost break out in hives. However, I did make the call. For the good of the wine club, I did it. Well, that plus the fact that I wanted to see if Cynthia's prisoner was still in the house. It made me feel better about the whole thing if I thought of it that way, as a mission to see what Cynthia was really doing.

Cynthia didn't seem surprised at all when I called, which pissed me off, but I went over the next day anyway. Let me tell you, that was a pain in the ass. It took four trips to get all of our stuff over there, and I was getting madder and madder at Audrey with each trip. She'd really messed up when she decided to go to San Diego. Furthermore, did Cynthia offer to help with all the heavy lifting? Are you kidding? When I told her that she needed to get a kettle of water boiling, she found two in her cabinet, filled them, put them on the stove, and stood there and watched. *She watched water boil* as I lugged in boxes of bottles and wine and shrink caps and all the other crap.

"I'll do anything you need me to do," she said as she watched the water. "All you have to do is tell me."

"Haven't you heard that a watched pot never boils?" I snapped at her as I started unscrewing the 4-liter jugs of Carlo Rossi Paisano that were going to go into the 2000 Château Lafite Rothschild Pauillac Red Bordeaux Blend bottles.

Cynthia gave that tinkling laugh of hers. "That's so true. This reminds me of my dancing days when I'd be so hungry after practice that I'd stand in front of the hot plate and watch the Ramen noodles. It seemed like it took forever for them to boil."

"It's hard to imagine you eating Ramen. I always pictured you eating caviar at some fancy New York restaurant during your days dancing on Broadway."

Cynthia walked over to the center island and started to imitate what I was doing. "Oh, there was that too. But dancing doesn't pay very much, and New York is an expensive place to live."

It was going about how I had expected. The main topic of conversation would be Cynthia Stewart. I wasn't having any of that. "Where's Felicity?" Cynthia had assured me during the phone call the day before that Felicity was out of town.

"She's at a spa in Tucson. It's her birthday present."

I was wondering how much that cost. Between Audrey and her, they were cornering the market on stupid ways to spend money. "A spa retreat is a fancy graduation present."

"It's not a retreat. Felicity's getting a boob job."

"Are you kidding?" I laughed. I mean, how ridiculous could this woman get?

Cynthia shrugged. "It's what she wanted. Now explain this process to me. I want to get it right."

So I explained the order in which Audrey and I did things, and do you want to know what the funny thing was? Cynthia took to it like a fish to water. Audrey complained all the time about how hard it was to get the levels exactly right and how time-consuming it was to stand over a kettle of boiling water to put on a shrink cap. But Cynthia didn't complain once. *Not once.* In her large kitchen, we didn't get in each other's way, and unlike Audrey, she did everything I told her to do as soon as I told her. Together, Cynthia and I were much more efficient than Audrey and me. And she didn't babble or complain. Let me tell you, it was a revelation. Despite myself, I felt a little bit of admiration for her.

"You're good at this," I admitted when we decided to call it quits for the day at about four o'clock that afternoon.

"I'm glad I finally got to help with this part of the operation." Cynthia reached into her wine cooler and held up a bottle of Simi Chardonnay, questioning. I nodded.

She continued to talk as she poured. "If we continue to grow the business, we might want to look into a bottling company because three women can only do so much. I've been doing some research, and there's a place in Temecula, CA, called Mission Wine Bottling. We could pour all this cheaper wine into barrels to make it look authentic, and then ship it to them. They'd bottle it and send it back, and then no one has to work in a kitchen all day."

I thought it was a brilliant idea Not so much the bottling company--I, too, had thought of that part--but I hadn't thought of putting the cheap wine into barrels that wouldn't arouse the suspicions of the bottlers. However, I didn't want to gush all over the idea and give Cynthia too much credit. "How much would something like that cost?"

"I haven't checked into the pricing yet, but if we go global, we'll make so much money that it won't matter. Plus, what about the cost of pain and suffering?" Again that tinkling laugh.

"I want to go global too!" You could have knocked me over with a feather. That's how surprised I was. Cynthia had been thinking along the same lines as me, unlike Audrey, who fretted because the wine parties were growing larger. Audrey didn't see the big picture; Cynthia did. I almost told her about the house then. I swear I almost did, but even though Cynthia had been great today, I still couldn't trust her yet. However, God help me, I do admit that I was beginning to wonder if I had misjudged her.

"Great minds think alike." Cynthia clinked her wine glass to mine. "I'm going to need the money. It would seem that my loving husband didn't leave me with much of anything."

"I don't get it. You've got this house and everything in it. Couldn't you sell some of that stuff? Or jewelry?" I couldn't help myself. I stared pointedly at her ring.

"Richard mortgaged the house to the hilt, so even if I could sell it, I wouldn't get any money out of it. But I can't sell it, or anything else in the house. Thanks to Richard, all of our assets are frozen, remember? I'm what you could call cash poor at the moment."

Well, there went my theory about there being some buried treasure in the backyard. I was watching Cynthia closely, and it seemed like she was telling the truth. "My husband left me high and dry too. And he left me for another man."

"Tell me about it."

And so I did. We talked about deadbeat husbands for a while, and really, there's something about trash-talking husbands that bonds women together. I'd never heard Cynthia say a bad word about Richard--although the conniving criminal certainly deserved it--but she was letting it all hang out that afternoon. She even cried. Her performance was so convincing that I didn't suspect that they were crocodile tears. Cynthia should have been an actress. Seriously, she's that good. But you probably know that by now.

Cynthia opened the second bottle of wine and poured us each a glass. "Now about that house tour? Would you like to do it now?"

That's how sucked in I got that afternoon. I had completely forgotten about the man that Cynthia was holding prisoner and my mission to find him. "That would be great."

Cynthia led me upstairs and showed me her room, then Felicity's that looked so much like a pink princess palace that it was sickening, and finally to Richard's study. Cynthia led me directly to the opposite wall and reached behind a painting that she said was a Picasso. A panel slid open, and there was the safe I had tried to find.

Cynthia fiddled with the combination lock, and the safe door opened. "This is the safe I told you about. It used to have a lot more in it than it does now," she laughed. "In fact, it's empty. Before the wine club, I had to clean it out just so Felicity and I could live."

I was getting an entirely new impression of Cynthia on that afternoon. Scarily enough, it was almost like she somehow knew all the treacherous and sneaky things I had theorized about her. And she was now dispelling those myths, one by one. I took a quick glance toward the wall by the door.

Cynthia either noticed it or had already planned to show me the monitor as the next part of her demonstration. She flicked the appropriate switch, and another panel slid open. "This is the window to the panic room, as Richard always called it. He saw the *Panic Room* movie, the one with Jodie Foster, and he decided we had to have one. It was a ridiculous expense. We've never even used the darn thing. It's filled with supplies for Armageddon, and they just sit there. I suppose I should check the expiration dates on those." She was giggling as she stepped to the side. I could see that the camera panned an empty room.

The wine talked before I could stop it. "But I saw a man in there when I was looking for Advil at the last wine party. I'm so sorry. I came in here by mistake, and the monitor was on." That, of course, wasn't true, but I had to save face somehow. I was blushing--and I never blush--because I felt guilty for being where I wasn't supposed to be. "I wasn't trying to be nosy or anything, Cynthia," I quickly added. "It was a mistake."

"Oh, you saw Graham then. I said that we've never used the panic room, and we haven't, but an old friend came two or three weeks ago and wanted a huge favor. Graham is a very old and dear friend from my New York days who got hooked on heroin. He didn't want to go to a rehab center because he is quite a well-known playwright in New York, mostly off-Broadway. He didn't want the exposure, so he asked if I would help him detox. I didn't want to do it, naturally, but how can you turn down an old friend?"

"But it looked like he was yelling, and he started to strip. He looked like he was in distress." Staring at the empty screen, I could still see it vividly. The man had not been happy to be in that room. He had been irate.

Cynthia shook her head sadly. "It was a very rough two weeks. Poor Graham. Of course I had a doctor check on him four times a day. I guess you saw him after the doctor took the straight jacket off. It wasn't pretty, was it?"

I shuddered involuntarily. "No, it was horrible."

"There is a happy ending, though," Cynthia said brightly. "He completed his withdrawal and went back to New York. He hasn't done a drug since."

I was feeling more foolish by the second. Here I'd been thinking the absolute worst about Cynthia and her motives, and all she had been doing was helping a friend. Still, I had to clear up one more thing. "I was driving by your house one day--only because my husband lives a couple of blocks over--and saw the man, Graham, scaling the fence. I didn't know what was going on." My face was burning with shame at that point.

"I didn't want to put him in the panic room at first, but he wouldn't take *no* for an answer. He did climb that fence because he wanted help so badly. However, it is a lot to ask of a friend, don't you think?"

"Yes. But you know what?" I laughed nervously. I had drunk too much wine and was losing control of both my mouth and common sense. "I thought what a good solution it was to lock up a man you wanted to get even with. I was even wondering if I could ask to put Kent in there. Out of sight, out of mind, you know?" Again that stupid, nervous laugh.

Thankfully, Cynthia laughed too. "Oh, Reggie, you really are too much. Keeping a man prisoner in your own home? Can you imagine how hard that would be?" She started to walk out the door. "Come on. I'll show you the actual panic room." She looked back over her shoulder. "Just to put your mind at ease."

Cynthia led me down to the lower level of the house, showing me the large workout/dance space, the depleted wine cellar that she laughed about, saying, "I had a ball cleaning that out," and the empty panic room. It was well-lit and fully stocked, and there was even a small TV, a small refrigerator, and a double bed that was probably more comfortable than the one I had at home. I had been such a complete and utter fool. Maybe Kent had a point. Maybe I was going off the deep end, but my *perception* of what I had seen had been so real.

We went back upstairs and finished the second bottle of wine. Cynthia agreed with me that Audrey had left me in a lurch. "She shouldn't have done that to you, Reggie, especially without warning. It wasn't fair."

"It was a shitty thing for her to do."

Cynthia nodded. "That's not what good friends do."

"No, it's not." Cynthia had gotten it exactly right, and I was happy that she was on my side in the matter. By the end of the week, if things went as well as they had today, Cynthia and I might come to the conclusion that we didn't need Audrey at all.

21

CYNTHIA

Don't be silly.

I knew that I couldn't keep Buck Boyd in the panic room forever. That was never my plan. When I locked him in the room, it had been a split-second decision. But once he was in that room, I realized the brilliance of my quick thinking. I was safe. I didn't have to worry about him following me or trying to blackmail me anymore. If you want to know the truth, days went by when I didn't think of Buck at all. Every once in a while, I would watch him from the monitor in Richard's room. You know, just for kicks. I turned on the sound once--I guess Reggie didn't figure that part out when she went snooping in Richard's study, the nosy bitch--but Buck was so nasty to me that I quickly turned it back off. You'd think that a man in his captive position would figure out that he should be nice to his jailer, but Buck was stupid enough to call me every vile name in the book. He even had the audacity to tell me that when he got out of the *hell hole*, as he called it, he was going to go directly to the authorities. It was not a smart move on his part, but then again, Buck Boyd had never excelled in the common sense department.

Let me emphasize this point: My initial plan was to keep Buck safely ensconced in that sealed, soundproof room only until I could think of another plan. Unfortunately, another brilliant plan did not magically come to me, which was unusual. I have always considered myself to be a master at getting out of scrapes and coming up with solutions, but as the days, then the weeks passed by, I couldn't think of a better place to put him.

Do you remember when I said that I wanted Buck dead? It was still true, but I didn't want to be the one who did it. While it might not have been the first time I had blood on my hands, I found the idea of killing him in my own home distasteful. Even if I did it in a bloodless way--say poisoning or figuring out a way to pump carbon monoxide into the room--I would still have to figure out how to dispose of the body. And a woman with my petite bone structure wouldn't have a prayer of being able to lift the body of a two hundred pound man, especially if that body was dead weight. No pun intended.

So for the first month, maybe it was a little longer, Buck stayed where he was with little or no thought from me. I knew there were enough provisions stocked down there to provide for a family of three for four weeks. With only one person in the room, the provisions would last a little longer, perhaps another couple of weeks. Everything was good until Reggie decided to snoop that night of the February wine party.

How did I know that she'd been in Richard's study? Well, it was pretty easy to figure out when I saw that the monitor was on the next day. She probably thought she turned it off, but like everything else in the house that Richard designed, it was unnecessarily complicated. That's when it all came together for me. Reggie had been gone a long time in search of Advil for her fake headache and then she had asked why I had never given her and Audrey a tour of the house. Reggie had seen Buck on the monitor. Believe me when I tell you that it was an *oh, shit* moment for me.

With the monitor already on, I couldn't help but watch Buck. It wasn't a pretty picture. He had taken off all his clothes, and his beer belly was as white as snow. I don't want to talk about his penis, other to say that you couldn't miss the dangling appendage. From the look of things, Buck had gone through all the alcohol first, judging by the beer cans and bottles of wine and vodka and expensive scotch. Then once the booze was gone, he had torn through the food like a ravenous bear. Wrappers and cartons littered the floor. Truthfully, it looked like he was sitting in a sea of garbage. That was something I hadn't considered-- how to get rid of the trash. The room had a toilet behind a small screen in the corner, thank goodness for that, but why wasn't there a trash chute or holding receptacle for food containers and bottles and cans? Evidently, my brilliant husband wasn't as brilliant as he had always thought he was. No place for trash in the panic room was a major omission, thanks to Richard. There was also the glaring fact that Richard had gotten *caught* by the feds for about a zillion crimes. Brilliant? I don't think so.

Staring at the monitor, I knew that the situation in the panic room had reached a crisis point. Buck was acting like a caged animal, pacing and scratching himself like a baboon in the zoo. That didn't concern me as much as the shelves. They had been full of supplies and were now almost completely empty. I couldn't let him starve, could I? I mean, I could have let him starve, but that brought me once again to the problem of a dead body and how to get rid of it. What made the situation even worse was that Reggie had seen this dismal scene. I couldn't stand it anymore and turned off the monitor. I stood there, thinking. I was going to have to somehow get Buck out of the room for a short time to get it cleaned and restocked, and I was going to have to convince Reggie that what she saw on the screen wasn't what she thought it was. It was going to have to be one humdinger of a story.

Drugs. It came to me all of a sudden. I smiled. I could tell Reggie that Buck was an old friend of mine who was going through withdrawal and had asked for my help. Drug story number one. And I could drug Buck, knock him unconscious and tie him up and move him to another location while I had the panic room cleaned and restocked. Drug story number two. And there was a bonus to this. While Buck was temporarily out of the room, I could give Reggie the tour. It wouldn't be the tour she wanted, though, if she was looking for dirt on me. No, she was going to see that any suspicions she had about me were completely unfounded. It was such a perfect plan that it sent tingles down my spine.

Sure, there were a couple of minor snafus, like how I was going to get some drugs and then administer them. The only thing I knew for certain right then was that I wasn't going to be the one who gave the drugs to Buck. Can you imagine what he would do to me if I opened the door to that room? Even in his nuttier-than-a-fruitcake state, he would overpower me in about two seconds flat, and then he would either beat the living daylights out of me or try to strangle me. Maybe he would do both. Then he would escape and go directly to the police with his packet of information that described my very colorful Vegas past. It still wasn't a hollow threat. I mean, I no longer cared what Richard would do to me if he learned about some of the things I'd done. Seriously, that would be like calling the kettle black, wouldn't it? And what was there left to take away from me? Richard had already ruined everything. But what I was really concerned about was the possibility of going to jail. There is no statute of limitations on murder.

The next thing I did was walk into Richard's bathroom. I had just remembered that he had been on Oxycontin after his hip replacement surgery two years before. He hadn't liked taking it because he said it made his head fuzzy and being the arrogant man that Richard was, he thought he needed to be in control at all times. He'd been such a big baby after that surgery--like most men are when they get sick--and when I couldn't stand fetching him one more cup of tea or slice of buttered toast, I had hired a private nurse to care for Richard 24/7. I'm pretty sure that Richard developed a crush on that young woman. We kept her on long after Richard was up and walking around again. Who knows? Maybe it was mutual. She certainly didn't object when Richard bought her an all-expense-paid trip to the Bahamas. Come to think of it, I'm pretty sure that Richard left on a business trip that coincided with the young woman's trip to Nassau. Oh, well. It's water under the bridge now.

Sure enough, there was an almost full bottle of Oxy in the medicine cabinet. That was the best news I'd had that day. I counted out the pills and carefully put them back into the bottle. I also noticed on the label that there was still one refill left on the prescription. That was good to know. If all this worked out, I might keep Buck drugged all the time. It would be the humane thing to do, wouldn't it? He might then be content to get high and play solitaire all day long. And as an added plus, a drugged-out Buck might not eat so much damn food. Seriously, have you ever seen a fat drug addict? I had recently watched a documentary on the meth epidemic in America's heartland, and those tweakers are skinny, skinny people. While it's certainly not the best diet in the world, I suppose the loss of appetite could be considered one of the better side effects of drug addiction.

However, I had to wonder if the pills were going to be enough to knock out a big man like Buck. He would have to be restrained and forced to take the pills. I would have to throw in a bottle of whiskey for good measure. That should do the job. Now I just had to figure out who I was going to hire to give the drugs to him. It would have to be more than one man, and they would have to be discreet and people I could trust. You've probably already guessed who came immediately to mind. That's right. Pepe and Angel. I had already told them that Buck was a very, very bad man, and they hadn't given a second thought to beating him up. It was only logical that they wouldn't have any problem binding him, drugging him, gagging him, and taking him to a secure location. Rest assured that I was going to pay them well. If I have learned nothing else in this life, I have learned this: Every man has his price. Every woman too. There is nothing sexist about that reality.

The next day my money talked, and Pepe and Angel were on board. They drove a much harder bargain than I had anticipated, but I didn't begrudge them that. Secrecy always comes with an exorbitantly high price tag. I hired back Louisa too, even though she was kind of snippy about it and wouldn't agree until I doubled her salary and shortened her work schedule to two days a week, Monday and Friday. I had to pay her more for catering wine club parties too, along with her nieces. I hated to part with that much cash, but I was tired of TV dinners and my toilet was beginning to look rather nasty. Louisa Sanchez wasn't the best house cleaner in the world, but I had missed hearing her lumbering gait and her Spanish soap operas. I was glad to have her back in my life. She was a person I could truly trust. Or so I thought.

Oh, I talked a good game. I've always had that skill, and I have always used it well. When Audrey, Reggie, and I would drink wine and discuss what we were going to spend our money on after the wine club meetings, I never told them the truth. I always said I was going to go shopping or to my salon, all the things I used to do and all the things they still expected me to do. But I was throwing them off the track. I had a plan for that money. It was going to be an investment in my future. So I was trying to squirrel away as much of it as possible. Which turned out to be much, much harder than I expected.

Hiring back the Sanchez family took a big chunk of my cash, but I considered it to be a necessary expense. And heaven knows that I had enough expenses as it was. When my accountant informed me that he was no longer authorized to pay the monthly bills, I was unhappy, sure, but there was nothing I could do about it. Frozen assets are frozen assets. I was confident I could handle things by myself. I mean, how much did it cost to run a household? It turned out that big houses cost a lot to maintain. I'm not going to tell you how much my monthly APS bill was because it will literally make you sick to your stomach. Add to that the water and gas payments, the cable and phone bills, gas, groceries, pool and yard maintenance. And as for the cost of insurance? Forget about it.

It was the first thing to go. Of course that meant that I no longer had the option of setting my own house on fire to collect the insurance money, but I'll save that story for another time.

So my plan was to sock away as much money as I could get my hands on. I could be noble about what I was doing and tell you that I was saving up the money for Richard's bail if he ever got caught by the feds. I could be noble and tell you that I was saving for Felicity's college education. But I would be lying to you, and I'm telling the truth here. You might say that it is only my version of the truth, but that wouldn't be correct. I am telling the *real* truth, and the truth about the money was that I was saving it for *me*. It was my getaway plan. If Richard could seemingly disappear off the face of the earth, then so could I. There was no doubt in my mind that Richard was living the high life in Argentina or Brazil, seducing pretty senoritas and drinking gallons of Fernet. The more I pictured that scenario, the madder I got. Why should Richard, the egomaniac who had gone and ruined everything because of his greed, get to be the one having all the fun?

Two could play at that game. If Richard could live out his fantasy in some tropical location, so could I. And let me make this perfectly clear: It was never my intention to try to find Richard. I value my pride almost more than I do anything, and I was not about to hunt him down and throw myself at him, begging him to love me the way he used to. I'd already played the beautiful, adoring wifey-wifey bit for far too many years. I even sacrificed my career for that man, and if I hadn't decided to marry Richard, I'm sure that I would have been a Vegas headliner by now. It made me incredibly sad to realize that lost opportunity, and it made me incredibly sad to acknowledge that Richard and I hadn't been happy for years. Even before his retirement five years ago, we'd been leading separate lives that hardly ever intersected. And I think it's clear by now that I had no idea what he'd been up to. I am not a stupid person, but Richard pulled the wool over my eyes, just like he did to everyone else. Now he was gone, and the more time that passed, the more certain I was that I would never hear from him again. Surprisingly, it didn't hurt as much as I thought it would.

So instead of planning to reunite with my long-lost crook of a husband, my first idea was to take a bunch of money and head to a villa somewhere in the Tuscan countryside, preferably a villa that had its own vineyard, or better yet, its own winery. But after a while that daydream got a little boring. What do people do in the countryside anyway? Did they sit around and watch the grapes grow? There probably wasn't much nightlife, and I highly doubted that there would be a mall nearby. Plus, I'd have to learn Italian, which sounded tedious, and there would probably be a bunch of paperwork involved in getting an extended visa. All those were reasons why the daydream lost its appeal for me. I might have grown up in a small town, but I was definitely not a country girl. So I shifted direction and was leaning toward Miami. The Villa Casa Casuarina, Versace's mansion on Ocean Drive, was now a glamorous boutique hotel at the center of the Art Deco District, a two-minute walk from South Beach. Now that was the kind of place that had my name all over it. Miami was at the top of my list.

Felicity? No, I didn't have any intention of taking her with me. You would think that Richard's spectacular fall from grace in the financial world, and his subsequent cowardly flight, would have brought us closer together, but that didn't happen. It wasn't my fault. Even after my conniving bitch of a daughter threw me under the bus at the disciplinary meeting at Mohave High School, I still offered to take her out to dinner once a week or so--an offer she always declined--and I would ask how her day had been because that was what a parent was supposed to do.

Also, I paid for *everything* for that kid. But did she ever thank me for my financial contributions to her well-being? No, she did not. She'd always been a secretive little brat, but during the months of Richard's absence, the secrecy had grown worse. Every single time I would walk into a room and see her on the phone, she would say a hurried, "I'll call you back," and hang up. I strongly suspected that she was talking to Richard, but when I would ask her who was on the phone, I got the proverbial "nobody." Felicity talked to "nobody" a lot. When she graduated from high school in a couple of months, I was leaving it up to "nobody" to take care of her. I was done.

As I was saying, I needed money for my final getaway plan. My wine club earnings were a decent start, but it wasn't nearly enough. Technically, my assets were still frozen. Every single day I woke up expecting some black-suited feds to show up and start hauling off paintings and furniture, and then they would tell me that I needed to vacate the premises. But they didn't come. I guess they were waiting until they caught Richard, and I guess I should have been grateful for that. But not one damn person I tried to talk to, including our accountant and family lawyer, seemed willing to give me answers to any of my questions. You better believe that living in limbo can drive a person up a wall. Would you like to wake up each morning wondering if it was going to be the last day you spent in your home? Would you like to wake up each morning scared to death that some dumpy female FBI agent was going to rifle through your closet and steal your best clothes? I think not.

I took matters into my own hands. Obviously, I couldn't sell my house right under the noses of the feds. They were still watching the house, waiting for Richard to come home--I hoped they weren't holding their breath on that one--but not as frequently as they had in the beginning. I only saw their black sedans cruise by the house twice a week or so. It was nothing compared to the number of times I saw that old gray van of Reggie's driving up and down my street. It was bad enough that I'd had first Buck and then the feds watching my every move, but that Reggie! It was creepy. I couldn't figure out what she thought was so fascinating about my house or my life. Granted, I'm sure she knew that my life and business were way more interesting and important than hers, but still. I think that's when I knew, really knew, that something was seriously wrong with the woman.

So while I couldn't sell the actual house, I didn't see why I couldn't sell the *contents* of the house. Sure, I knew I wasn't supposed to do that either, but it didn't seem right to me that the federal government could seize all of my property. With a crime, just like in a marriage, shouldn't there be due consideration to community property? Shouldn't I be properly compensated for everything that I had given to my marriage, my husband, and my daughter for *years*? You bet I should. So I called an appraiser from a well-respected estate auction service in Scottsdale. Mind you, I was supposed to make a list for the feds months ago of all the assets that Richard and I had acquired during our marriage. And I was finally doing it, sort of. When you looked at it that way, I was actually doing the federal government a favor.

When the three appraisers arrived from Hoffman Estate Auctions, they immediately went to work, going from room to room. One of them was jotting down notes on the furniture, one of them was looking at the paintings, and one of them wanted to see my jewelry.

"Right this way," I said as I led him to my upstairs bedroom. I believe I've mentioned that Richard had taken most of my jewelry to a safe deposit box in some bank. I was now almost one hundred percent sure that neither the safe deposit box nor the bank existed. However, I still had a diamond tennis bracelet, an emerald necklace, a string of pearls, and some sapphire earrings. I got them out of my tall jewelry box and laid them on the king-sized bed's white duvet. The jewelry looked so puny against that massive bed that I was downright embarrassed.

"I have more in a safety deposit box . . . somewhere." I don't know why I needed to defend my meager selection of jewelry that was left, but I did.

The appraiser murmured something I couldn't hear as he got out a precision microscope and digital caliper from his bag. It took him a whopping sixty seconds before he looked up at me and said, "These are very good representations."

"Excuse me?" I had no idea what he was talking about.

"These are high-end crystals and cubic zirconia, not sapphires, pearls, emeralds, or diamonds."

I don't think you can begin to fathom the level of mortification I felt coursing through my entire body. Had that stupid Richard taken all my good jewelry and replaced it with fakes? I hadn't seen him take these particular pieces out of my jewelry box, but that didn't mean he didn't do it. "Are you sure?"

He nodded. "Quite sure."

I don't remember twisting off the diamond ring from my left ring finger. But it was suddenly in the palm of my hand, and I was holding it out to the appraiser. "What about this one?"

I knew for a fact that Richard had never had this four-carat diamond ring in his possession. I knew that because I never took it off, not even in the shower. In many ways, that ring symbolized my success, and also, to me, my inherent value. Richard had bestowed this ring upon me on our wedding day, and the sheer enormity of it brought tears of joy to my eyes. I had made it! Richard, a successful businessman, a strikingly handsome older gentleman, had given the very valuable ring to me, a struggling Vegas dancer. The ring made me worthy. The ring was my last hope.

That last hope flickered and died as the appraiser shook his head. "High-end cubic zirconia, Mrs. Stewart."

I couldn't quite wrap my head around it. The only time the ring came off my finger was when I cleaned it, and I sometimes left it on even then as I took the special brush I had ordered online and rubbed it across the sparkling diamond--which had been fake all along. Even when Richard put that ring on my finger, he knew that he wasn't giving me the real thing.

I don't remember walking down the stairs, but I do remember that I went into the kitchen and poured myself a large glass of chardonnay. It was ten o'clock in the morning as I sipped that wine and held back the tears waiting for the appraisers to finish their assessment of my furniture, antiques, fine rugs, and paintings. I sipped that cold wine as I waited for what I knew was inevitable.

Everything in the house was fake, and Richard had known it all along.

Do you know what the funny thing was? On the day that Buck Boyd scaled my stucco fence and trespassed onto my property, he had eyed my diamond ring like it was the ultimate prize in the bottom of a Crackerjack box. I had told him it was fake to throw him off the track. That seemed absolutely hysterical to me after the appraisers had come and gone. Because the ring actually had been fake and not my most valuable asset. If I'd known that then, I would have given it to Buck Boyd and sent him on his way. Buck would have found out the truth when he tried to sell the worthless piece of crap, but it would have bought me more time to figure out how to make him disappear. Then he wouldn't have been in the panic room; he wouldn't have still been a burden to me. And he wouldn't have still been costing me money. Just the cost of restocking the panic room was enormous. I stocked it up but good, with a two-month supply of food, toilet paper, and booze. I even bought a small TV to put in there, but that was for Reggie's benefit when I showed her the temporarily empty room. The panic room didn't have any cable hookup, so the blank TV would sit there to taunt Buck and remind him of his mind-numbing boredom after Pepe and Angel removed him from the trunk of my Mercedes. I thought it was a nice touch on my part.

I was never going to forgive Richard for knowingly giving me a fake diamond ring on our wedding day. Do you know that saying--you can forgive but not forget? I wasn't going to do either one. Richard was an SOB for doing that to me, an impressionable young girl, and it was probably a good thing that he didn't try to get in contact with me any time soon because I would have let him have it. Verbally, I mean. If you'll remember, I no longer had my little black book with all those useful, if not entirely legal, contacts from Vegas. But I would be lying if I denied fantasizing once or twice about ways to get even with Richard. A particularly satisfying scenario involved locking Richard in the panic room with Buck. Buck might be a drunk, but Richard was old, and I'm sure that Buck could beat the crap out of him. I would have been very happy to watch that scene on the monitor in Richard's study while I sipped his most expensive cognac. Then I would have turned off the monitor one last time and forgotten the fact that either one of them had ever existed.

But back to my more pressing problem. I no longer had any valuable assets to sell, so the wine club was going to have to be my ticket out of my old life. I was going to have to work hard to make it even more successful. I did think that Audrey, Reggie, and I could start raking in some serious dough if we worked together and they listened to me. I had all kinds of great ideas. We could go global, offering rare and expensive varietals online. Or we could even go back to their original Écalant wine, which seemed to have the cheapest production costs, and start an online wine club. And we could start hiring an outside company for the bottling and labeling of the wine. There was no need for the partners in the club to do the grind work. We needed to delegate. I only had to convince my small-minded business associates to think outside the box.

I mean, really. Do you know how podunk and archaic that kitchen operation of Audrey and Reggie's was? It was ridiculous. They had been complaining for months about how they did all the work and how time-consuming it was. Now I knew why. They had made the whole bottling and labeling and corking as difficult as possible. And it wasn't hard at all! I have always been a very fast learner, and once Reggie told me what to do, I was on it. I was efficient. Reggie and I accomplished more in three days than she and Audrey accomplished in two weeks because I was so good at it. We also didn't waste time talking or taking coffee or wine breaks. What would we have talked about anyway? I had nothing to say to Reggie and had only wanted to know what went on in the day-to-day part of the operation. I planned on taking over the whole club someday soon, and I needed to know every aspect. My goal was to impress Reggie and drive the wedge between her and Audrey in just a little deeper. So I kept my mouth shut and let her boss me around. However, I feel the need to mention that Reggie is not a pleasant person to be around. Please note that I'm being kind here. I didn't call her a bitch.

The March wine club was on the last day of the month. I was especially proud of my decorating skills for that party. Easter was the next day, and I had decorated the entire place with pastels: light blues and pinks and yellows. The flowers I chose were lilacs, and the entire place smelled heavenly. I hired one of the best catering businesses in town too, and I don't mind telling you that when I wrote a reimbursement check from the FHM account, I did pad it just a little bit. I mean, why not? You should have seen how much Reggie charged the wine club for the wear and tear on her old van. Give me a break. I could have rented a Lincoln town car and gone and gotten the wine myself for cheaper than that.

Besides, what Reggie and Audrey didn't know wouldn't hurt them. I had gone to the bank by myself a few days earlier and told the very nice manager that since the account was a college fund, the three of us only needed a yearly, not a monthly, electronic statement. The manager wanted to have all three signatures to do that, and I told him, sure, I would take care of it, and returned the next day with Audrey's and Reggie's signatures. Well, the signatures certainly *looked* real.

As you know, the wine club parties kept increasing in size, and the March meeting was no exception. There were eighty guests. It's not like I had that many friends--I didn't have any--but word of mouth is a powerful sales tool. People I didn't know kept calling me up and asking for an invitation, and I didn't turn anyone away. In retrospect, it is obvious that I should have vetted the guests more carefully, but the more guests, the more money. That was my motto. And honestly? My wine club parties had become *the* monthly place to see and be seen, and I loved it. I felt like I was the reigning Mrs. Arizona once again. Sure, I realized that my notoriety, thanks to Richard, probably had something to do with it. But I really think it had more to do with my prowess as a hostess. I knew how to throw a party.

The four vintages of Château Lafite Rothschild were selling like hotcakes, and Audrey was running credit card after credit card on our little portable machine. I saw Maeve sidle up to her and whisper something in Audrey's ear. I was instantly on guard. I had made it very clear to Audrey that if Maeve wanted to buy any wine on the side, she had to share it with me. But how could I know for sure that something like that was going on? I looked over to see Reggie, who was deep in conversation with one of the new guests, and I swear that I saw Reggie hand the woman a bottle of the

1961 Château Latour Grand Vin de Château Latour Pauillac Red Bordeaux Blend, the one that went for $13,500. I'm also sure I saw her mouth the words, *You can pay me for this in cash tomorrow.* Reggie might deny this until she's blue in the face, but I know what I saw.

Believe me, that got my dander up. My two so-called business partners were making side deals, or selling wine under the table, or whatever you wanted to call it. How could they? Was everyone in my life cheating me out of what was rightfully mine? But the next question that popped into my mind was: *Why hadn't I thought of it first?* I was the one who had all the contact information for our guests. Reggie and Audrey didn't. So it would not be out of the realm of possibility to make a few phone calls tomorrow, especially to the newcomers who were at the party for the first time. Once I established who was in charge, all those people would come to me, not to the other two, if they decided after the party that they needed more wine for a special occasion. Or if they found out that one of their friends spent more money than they had and didn't want to look cheap. That was a good angle to use on most of these women; it could definitely work.

I heard someone calling my name over the din and looked over and saw that Audrey was waving frantically at me. My wine glass was empty, and she was near the tasting table, so I walked over, my pink chiffon Versace dress swishing gracefully around my ankles. Did I mention how good I looked that night? Seriously, I looked stunning. If someone didn't know me, they wouldn't suspect that I had gotten dumped by my husband, the criminal, or that my high school boyfriend, the extortionist, was drunk and drugged in the secret panic room downstairs. I was as coolly elegant as Princess Grace of Monaco in her glory years.

"I've run out of paper for the credit card machine," Audrey said apologetically. "I didn't think we'd sell this much wine. But it's a good thing, right?"

It was so like Audrey to not come prepared. Ever since her trip to San Diego, she was even spacier than usual. "Do these women really need receipts?"

Audrey's voice was a little too loud when she said, "We're running a *business* here, Cynthia. Of course these women want receipts. They're spending a lot of money."

I hated to leave my own party. No good hostess does that, but the queued women were looking at me expectantly. I, of course, had been the one who ordered the machine, which is why I still had the box it had come in. I was pretty sure there was another roll of paper in there. It was in the closet in the guesthouse where I put all the things that I didn't think I should throw away but didn't know what to do with. "I'll be right back," I said. I smiled brightly at the women. "Buy a lot of wine, ladies."

One of the ladies that I'd never seen before in my life said, "This is a great party, Cynthia. It's everything I heard it was going to be."

I kept smiling. It *was* a great party.

The backyard, as always, had lights strung around the pool, so I had no trouble making my way to the guesthouse at the far end of the property. As I drew closer, I noticed a light coming from the small kitchen alcove. That was strange. I thought that Felicity was either out or upstairs, as she usually was. I didn't even try to keep tabs on her anymore. When I was her age, I had considered myself to be a fully grown woman and resented any meddling questions from my parents. So I generally left her alone, believing that to be the right way to deal with a teenage daughter. Also, being around Felicity gave me a headache.

The walkway to the front door passed right by that alcove, and I could see that it was indeed Felicity sitting at the kitchen table, intently staring at her computer and on her phone at the same time. Her back was to me, and I could clearly see what was on the screen.

Porn. My daughter was watching porn.

Honestly? I didn't think it was that big of a deal. It was graphic, though, and the close-ups of the woman on the screen were *close-ups*. Then the camera moved, and I could see more of the room. There was another woman there, and more men. And then I could make out the faces of the two women.

They weren't women. They were girls.

And then I knew how Felicity had initiated the two girls she didn't think deserved to be Tigerettes.

APRIL

22

AUDREY

Matricide. You don't have to tell me the name. Believe me. I know. But I truly don't remember doing it. I mean, I know I was in that cramped room that smelled of old flesh and old food and dying dreams. I remember hunting for Mother's glasses and finding them under the bureau. I remember picking up that pillow from the floor and holding it out to her. Other memories crowd in too: the look of pure rage on her face, a look that I had associated with her for as long as I could remember. It is a look that I swear I remember from my infancy when I was lying in a crib, and she peered over that insurmountable railing with nothing but resentment seething from her every pore. Margot's rage was a pungent, tangible force. It was there, in that room, on that day. Yes, I remember that.

But the next part is where it gets surreal. When the pillow started to creep closer to Mother's face, the hands were not mine. I know that because I was watching the whole thing from a different vantage point in the room, farther away from the bed. Everything was moving in slow motion, but I could see the entire scenario clearly. I held my breath as the pillow moved closer, closer, closer to the face of that old woman. I continued to hold my breath as the ancient, vengeful woman struggled. And she did struggle. For a partially paralyzed, fragile-boned octogenarian, that woman fought valiantly to breathe as those white hands pressed down on the pillow with a force that was perhaps harsh, but necessary.

As I watched from my safe distance, I recall thinking that this wasn't the way things were supposed to be. A daughter did not do that kind of thing to her mother. It was unthinkable! And yet that struggling woman was the person who had always chosen cruelty over kindness, a person who resented and victimized her children. A woman, who in her dying days, bedridden and at the mercy of others, refused to bend her will, refused to admit to her multitude of sins and ask forgiveness, a woman who was incapable of even being remotely *nice* to another living soul. Somehow the atrocious act happening before my very eyes seemed justified. Margot Keller's existence had long since ceased to be necessary on this earth. It was a good thing.

I helped after that. I smoothed the sheets and pulled down Margot's dressing gown that had become obscenely twisted during her futile struggle. I plumped up the two pillows and put them comfortably behind her head before I pulled the blanket up and folded her hands across her chest. When I couldn't find her flaming red wig, I combed her white hair, trying to smooth down the patches that stuck straight up, trying to conceal the bald patches on her skull. I closed her eyes, forever concealing that wild look of fear. Or was it still the rage that I saw? Whatever. With those pale green eyes closed, she looked more peaceful than I had ever known her to be. It was a good thing.

I closed the door softly behind me as I walked out. The hallway seemed much longer than it had before, and I averted my eyes from the open doors where patients lay on beds, much like my mother's. Most of them looked quite peaceful, too, much like my mother. On my way out, I stopped by the director's office and peeked my head inside the door. "Jean, Mother's finally sleeping peacefully. I gave her the meds on the table. I don't think it should be necessary to disturb her for a while, do you?"

Jean gave me a practiced, recycled smile. "Didn't I tell you that a visit from a loved one often does the trick?"

"You were right," I said. "I'll try to visit more often."

"I'm sure your mother would enjoy that."

I drove home and immediately fell asleep. I didn't even make it up the stairs but collapsed on the couch and slept soundly. I didn't ever want to wake up, to swim to consciousness, but the hand shaking my shoulder and the voice were persistent.

"Mom? Mom? Are you okay? Why won't you wake up?"

When I could finally pry open my eyes--and they were so heavy!--I saw Marcy's face leaning over me, a worried expression creasing her forehead. "What time is it?"

"It's almost six. I picked up Jimmy like you asked, and he says he's hungry." She leaned closer, and even though she was trying to be sly about it, I knew what she was doing.

"I haven't been drinking wine, Marcy." I sat up on the couch. "The dentist gave me something for the pain I've been having in my tooth. I guess it knocked me out." Oh, the lies were starting to come so easily.

"Can we order a pizza for dinner?"

"Absolutely."

The Domino's pepperoni pizza made for two happy kids. I managed to get down a part of a slice as I waited for the phone to ring. Looking at the two of them, I wondered how it could be that a mother would not love her children with complete and utter devotion. It was something that I simply couldn't fathom. I needed to do something nice for them, something that showed, tangibly, how much I loved them. I was wondering what that could be when my phone rang.

It was, of course, Jean. "I'm so sorry to tell you this, Audrey dear, but your mother has passed on."

"Excuse me?" I don't know why, but her words sent a shock of surprise up my spine.

"Your mother, dear, she's passed. Mercifully, it was in her sleep."

Her voice contained such genuine sympathy that I started to cry. Jean had probably conveyed this very message to hundreds of people before, but I felt like she really cared about me, about my loss. I could barely hear the rest of what she said in her professional--yet still touching--voice of condolence, something about how these things were a shock but not unexpected. Something about the circle of life. Something about the funeral home they generally sent the bodies to and if she wanted me to call them to pick up my mother.

I said yes and yes. Yes, yes, it was a shock, but certainly not unexpected. It was so true but still so sad. So grateful I was the last to see her alive. We planned to cremate the body immediately, so there would be no funeral service. I thanked her for her kindness.

Matricide? I prefer not to think of it that way.

I was definitely the third wheel at the March wine club party. It was not unexpected, and I knew I was taking the risk of being left out of our three-way wine club partnership--and I use the word *partnership* loosely--when I decided to take my kids to San Diego for spring break. However, there are some things more important than money, you know? My kids and I had gone through a lot in the last few months, and we needed a break, if only to reward ourselves for managing to keep it all together after Paul decided to turn his disease into a weird form of midlife crisis. Also, I needed time to reflect on what I was going to say or do to Paul about stealing my money. Blatantly stealing my money. I mean, how stupid could he be to think I wouldn't know it was him? Did he think I let people roam my house at will? Did he think I had lovers who went rummaging through my bureau drawers when I went into the bathroom to change into something sexy? Ha! That was a laugh.

The other reason I wanted to go to San Diego was that I wanted time away from the whole wine club bottling operation that had overtaken my kitchen. I'd wanted to move the daily operation to Cynthia's for a while by then because *I wanted my kitchen back.* Even a seasoned wine drinker/ lover like me can get sick of being constantly bombarded by the sight and smell of wine. No matter how much we cleaned--well, I cleaned; Reggie was such a slob in that department--I would find red sticky splotches of wine on my floor or stains running down the cabinets from overfilled bottles. It is possible to get sick of the smell of wine, and my kitchen reeked of it. Seriously, it makes you feel like you have a constant hangover.

Reggie, not surprisingly, didn't understand any of that. Her kitchen sometimes smelled of cat food--which was strange because she didn't have a cat--so why would she even notice how my kitchen smelled? That was Reggie for you, unobservant and inconsiderate. All rolled into one. I know that her take on the whole thing is that I abandoned her, which is flatly wrong. Reggie didn't like the fact that she wouldn't have me as her lackey for an entire week.

But after due consideration, I decided that taking a vacation would be just the ticket for getting my family back together again. Initially, the kids weren't overly excited by the idea, if you can believe that. What kid didn't want to go hang out on a beach or rent a little sailboat on Mission Bay? But I cajoled and promised paddleboard lessons to Jimmy--a good way for him to work off steam--and a new bikini for Marcy so she could tan her now svelte body. We drove over to Mission Bay in my new Lincoln, me talking the whole way about how much fun we were going to have while the kids stayed glued to their various devices.

By the time we got there, I knew that the vacation was going to be a big, fat bust, and it was. Two days into it and Marcy was complaining that she was missing Tigerette practices, and Jimmy was complaining that he missed Delilah and her dog. I made them stick it out, though. Number one, I wasn't going to admit defeat to Reggie, and number two, I'd had to borrow money from the FHM account for the trip because Paul had stolen all my cash. Don't get me wrong. I *planned* on paying that money back. I'd already contacted Maeve Olson, and she was interested in buying more wine from me. Soon, I hoped I would have a steady source of income.

On the night of the March wine club party on the 31st, I acted like nothing was out of the ordinary when Reggie and Cynthia acted like they were best buds. Well, okay, not that. They were cordial to each other, which was a big improvement, but Reggie didn't make any secret of letting me know she knew where everything in Cynthia's kitchen was. No surprise there. I'd heard Reggie brag about how well she and Cynthia had worked together as a team and about how they had accomplished more in three days than we did in two weeks. She didn't get a rise out of me, though, because I refused. I'd only say, "Oh, that's great, Reggie. Now I have time to spring clean my house and catch up on yard work."

Which, of course, she didn't get. To be fair, she had asked me about my trip, and I'd lied and told her that the kids and I had a fabulous time, and I asked what else she'd been doing, and she told me she'd done some running and catching up on her reading. We were both full of shit, and we both knew it. But that's the kind of friends we had become by that point. The lying kind.

There were eighty guests at that party, eighty thirsty, clamoring women who couldn't drink fast enough, couldn't buy our wine fast enough. I was still the one in charge of the sales, and while I could no longer remember how I had gotten that job in the first place, I was a seasoned pro at it by then. When our small credit card machine ran out of paper, though, I panicked. It had never occurred to me that that kind of thing could happen, and those women were an impatient lot, crowding around my table like a well-dressed, cackling brood of hens. Cynthia acted all put out when I asked her for a spare roll, but she went and got it and returned to the party. Eventually. She seemed to be gone for a long time searching for that paper, and when she handed it to me, she had the strangest look on her face.

Now it is no secret that Cynthia is a very beautiful woman, so beautiful that I had never seen her look anything less than perfect. But at that moment, as she handed me the roll of paper, her face was ashen, her blue eyes vacant, and her hair looked like she had raked her well-manicured fingers through it. It was startling. "Are you okay, Cynthia? Maybe you should go lie down or something."

She seemed to snap out of her trance then. She straightened her shoulders. "I'm fine. I need a glass of wine."

She drifted off, her pink chiffon dress swishing gracefully around her long, slender legs, but she still looked distracted. Honestly, she looked like a person who had just received some shocking news, and I thought that maybe she had just gotten a call from her cowardly, fugitive husband. Now while my husband was a yellow-bellied wimp, no question about it, Richard was a coward on an international scale. You'd think that Cynthia and I might have commiserated on that miserable commonality, but we didn't. We weren't that kind of friends--if we could even be called friends.

I looked over at Reggie, who was talking a mile a minute to a group of ladies and wondered if she and I could still be called friends. We hadn't even driven over to this party together like we usually did. And right at that moment, Reggie was acting more animated than I had ever seen her before. It was like she was putting on some kind of show, and I had no idea why that would be. Was she trying to impress these ladies or something? In the old days, we would have driven home together and talked about all the phony-fake women here tonight. We would have made up names for them and laughed. It's snarky behavior; I know that. But that's how Reggie and I used to be. I'm sure that she was the one who started it most of the time. But I have to admit that I found it very entertaining. And it was harmless.

In reality, we were probably more cowed by this type of woman than anything else. In reality, we were probably jealous. I now had more money coming in than I ever had before, yet I knew I would never fit in with a crowd like this. I guess what Margot had always yelled at me when I was in high school, dressing for a date in torn jeans and a crop top, was true: I had no sense of style. She took it a step farther and called me a tramp.

She, the woman who bought her clothes at Walmart. Go figure that one out, would you?

After the party ended, Cynthia didn't offer Reggie and me a glass of wine, which was another unwelcome first. She brushed us off with: "I'm the one who has a headache this time. Let's see how much we made and call it a day. Louisa and her nieces can clean up."

One of the things Cynthia had spent her money on was hiring back Louisa. I had never understood Cynthia's bond with her maid. Louisa was heavy, surly, with a constant scowl on her face. She didn't speak much English, but I'm positive that she understood everything that was said to her, even if she pretended that she didn't. To be honest, she scared me a little. But Cynthia, on the other hand, seemed to have a great affection for her. I could understand the dependence she had on Louisa, I suppose--not that I would know about a maid/employer relationship firsthand--but Cynthia also genuinely seemed to care for her. It was something to watch them interact. Cynthia would ask Louisa to do something, Louisa would scowl, disappear for a while, but eventually come back and do it. It was certainly a weird dance they had together.

I no longer brought my little metal cash box with me to the wine club parties. Both Reggie and Cynthia had bullied me into submission on that point, saying that my box was too small, unprofessional, and tacky. I now kept the money in Richard's old English walnut cigar box, which made the cash smell like tobacco, but none of us complained. We all started to count the money, then we counted it again, silently. I think all of us were shocked by the amount. I'd wondered if we could ever top the March party, but we certainly had. Thanks to the number of guests and the price tag of $13,500 on the 1961 Château Latour Grand Vin de Château Latour Pauillac Red Bordeaux Blend, we had made almost $500,000. *$500,000.* Most of it wasn't in cash, but just the number dancing in my head made me dizzy.

"Holy shit!" Reggie said.

"We're talking serious money now." Even Cynthia looked duly impressed.

"Don't you think we should open up a bottle of wine and celebrate?" Reggie must have wanted a glass as much as I did.

Cynthia pointed to her temple. "Headache."

Reggie and I took that as her not subtle hint to get out of there, so we began to gather up our things. "Cynthia," I addressed Cynthia because

Reggie had been studiously avoiding me all night, "what time should we meet at the bank tomorrow. I was thinking--" But Cynthia's face had again contorted into something almost unrecognizable. There was rage flitting across her features--oh, I knew that look well--but also fear. I thought it was fear. I followed her gaze and saw that Felicity had walked in the open back door.

"Hi, Mrs. Maynard, Mrs. Carson," Felicity bubbled.

It surprised me every time. I'd conjure up this picture in my head of Felicity being the Wicked Witch of the East, but then I would see her in person: a stunningly pretty teenage girl with a sunny smile and dewy skin. It was hard to reconcile the two, the image and the reality. Maybe if I hadn't listened to Reggie spout on and on about how evil the girl was, I would have thought about her differently. However, as much as I hate to admit it, in this case, Reggie, God help us, had been right all along.

"I told you to stay in the guesthouse." Cynthia's voice aimed for sternness but wobbled. "We need to talk, and I instructed you to stay there until the party was over."

"I came to get a diet Coke. We're all out in the guesthouse." Felicity smiled sweetly.

"Damn it, Felicity! I told you to stay put!" Cynthia's eyes were now flashing daggers at her pretty daughter.

"Don't be mad, Mom. All I want is a simple diet Coke." She looked around at all the empty wine bottles and dirty glasses. "It's not like I'm drinking *alcohol*, right?"

I was suddenly glad I didn't have a wine glass in front of me. As comforting as it was to know that Cynthia and her daughter had the same kind of exchanges that I had with Marcy, I was feeling more uncomfortable by the second. The tension between the two was palpable, simmering, threatening to erupt. "Mrs. Carson and I will be gone in about five minutes." But for some reason, I didn't move. Neither did Reggie.

"If you were ever going to listen to me once in your life, Felicity, let it be *now*."

"Sure thing, Mom. I'll just get my diet Coke, and I'll go back to studying. Finals are coming up, you know." Much like Louisa behaved when Cynthia told her to do something, Felicity took her time going to the Sub-Zero and getting out the drink.

Cynthia waited, never taking her eyes off Felicity until the girl was again facing us. "Studying? Is that what you were doing in the guesthouse, Felicity? I don't think so."

"Why are moms always so suspicious?" Felicity had turned to Reggie and me, her eyes imploring. "I mean, I could be out doing all kinds of things on a Saturday night, but I'm not. I'm at home. Does that look suspicious to you?"

I thought that she had made a valid point, but I somehow knew--call it instinct, if you will--that Felicity had something up her sleeve. If she had waited five minutes longer, Reggie and I would have left. The door was wide open, and Felicity would have known when we were gone. Something more was going on here.

Cynthia's hands clenched into fists, and I swear, I thought she was going to hit her daughter. But then she slowly lowered her fists to her side. "Okay, Felicity, have it your way. Why don't you tell Mrs. Maynard and Mrs. Carson what you were *really* doing in the guesthouse? I'm sure they'd be interested in knowing."

"I think Mrs. Carson and I will be going." I was suddenly desperate to get out of there. My stomach had started to churn uncomfortably, and I had a bad taste in my mouth. I looked at Reggie. "Let's take the stuff out to our cars."

Reggie, though, seemed fascinated by the spectacle. "I would like to know what Felicity was doing. What does a pretty teenage girl, one who doesn't have a date, do on a Saturday night at home? Post on Facebook or Instagram? Tweet or text? Listen to music? Watch videos? I'm very interested, Felicity."

Reggie must have been hitting below the belt with the dateless comment because Felicity's eyes flared momentarily. But it was brief before her features settled back into neutral, benign territory. "All of the above." The contrived sweetness was back in her voice.

"Why don't you be more specific, Felicity, *honey*? What type of videos were you watching?" Cynthia's eyes bored right into Felicity's.

Felicity's uncertainty was again brief, and it was almost as if I could see her switch mental gears before deciding which one to settle on. A sheepish smile spread over her face. "I wasn't supposed to tell you, Mom. But Dad called."

"What?" Cynthia grabbed onto the counter for support. She was suddenly weaving back and forth. "When? Where is he? We're going to have to let the FBI know--"

"Whoa, Mom. Hold your horses. He just called to wish me an early happy birthday."

"Where is he?" Cynthia demanded again.

"Like he would tell me that, Mom? Are you serious?"

"We still need to let the FBI know. They could put a tracer on your phone."

Felicity rolled her eyes. "Get real, Mom. He used a burner phone. Obviously," she added as if only an idiot wouldn't have figured that one out.

Cynthia narrowed her eyes at her daughter. Then she let go of the counter and straightened her shoulders. "I don't believe you, Felicity."

Felicity shrugged. "Suit yourself, Mom."

Cynthia had another stare-down with her daughter; neither one of them broke the gaze. "Let's go back to the videos you were watching on a dateless Saturday night, shall we?"

"Right, the videos." Without taking her eyes from her mother's, Felicity took a long sip of her diet Coke, then: "The videos. That reminds me. Do you remember that old VCR player that Dad refused to get rid of? We used to make fun of him, but he wouldn't get rid of it, would he? But you know what? I need it now. I've decided I'm going to use it for my final art project. I'm calling it *The Past: Rewound*. Catchy title, isn't it? Anyway, I think he put it in the panic room. I'm going to go down and look for it, okay? I promise I'll let you see it when I'm finished. It's going to be really good."

Cynthia finally broke the gaze in their staring match and looked up at the ceiling, taking deep breaths. When she spoke, her voice was weary. "Go to the guesthouse, Felicity. Now."

I seemed to detect a note of defeat in her voice, and for probably the first and only time, I felt sorry for her. There was something very off about her daughter, but the disconcerting thing was that you couldn't put your finger on it. Outwardly, she couldn't have been any more perfect, but she was as hard to pin down as a Monarch butterfly. Or maybe a dragonfly would be a more appropriate insect when it came to Felicity.

I looked over at Cynthia, who was staring after her daughter, a thoughtful look on her face. "We're going now." I picked up a crate of empty wine bottles.

Surprisingly, Reggie followed suit without interjecting anything inappropriate about the scene we had just witnessed. "Great party, ladies. Be at the bank at nine."

Reggie and I loaded our respective cars, and it was only as I was about to get into my Lincoln that Reggie walked over to me. It was the first time she had spoken directly to me all night. "What do you make of that scene in there?" she asked, leaning against the top of my rolled-up window.

"Believe it or not, I felt kind of sorry for Cynthia. Marcy has her difficult moments, but that Felicity takes the cake."

It was Reggie's turn to wear a thoughtful expression. "You and I have both known that something has been going on with the Tigerettes all season, and now we have proof."

I was confused. We had witnessed a tense scene between a mother and a daughter. That was it. "We don't have proof."

Reggie straightened up, and that determined frown that I was all too familiar with came into play. "Oh, we have proof, all right, Audrey. And I'm going to get to the bottom of it."

Without another word, she turned and walked to her car. I left, and then she left. Neither one of us suggested sharing a bottle of wine when we got home.

Please don't look at me that way.

Of course I once again asked Marcy if anything strange was going on with the Tigerettes or if anything happened at their afternoon get-togethers at Kent's new condo. I probably wouldn't have even done that if Reggie hadn't been so insistent that the mother-daughter tiff that we had witnessed between Cynthia and Felicity had convinced her that indeed something sinister was going on with the Tigerettes, her insistence that the strange fight was somehow proof of that. As I mentioned before, I had snooped through Marcy's room more than once in the last few months and hadn't found one single shred of evidence that my daughter was engaging in anything horrible. But I hated searching through her things, knowing as I did exactly how it felt to have a mother search your room like you were some errant inmate, and she was the warden looking for illegal contraband. But I still did it, and each time I did, I felt guilty, almost dirty. After Margot passed on, I couldn't even do that without the self-loathing becoming so unbearable that I would rush downstairs and pour myself a glass of wine. I'd stand at the kitchen counter and gulp it down, trying to cleanse my mind, my guilt, my soul. The wine didn't help much.

But I did ask Marcy one day in early April. I guess you could say it was to ease my conscience more than anything. I had been wearing blinders for so long that ignoring the changes in my daughter or placating my son with Snickers bars and mindless TV had become second nature. But I did ask her. And Marcy, who had been eating fat-free vanilla yogurt out of the container, calmly put down her spoon. She sounded exactly like Felicity when she said, "Why in the world would you think that?"

I fumbled the ball right there and then. "Well, your dances are provocative, and surely, you can't be practicing all the time like you say you are, and Felicity was watching some videos the other night, which seemed to upset her mother . . ." I trailed off, at a loss for how to continue.

Marcy then looked at me like I had suddenly sprouted horns on my forehead and said, "God, Mom! We're a pom squad. It's not a *cult*."

I blushed, too embarrassed to take offense at that. But I didn't let it drop just yet. "All I'm saying is that you've changed a lot this year, Marcy. I don't feel like we talk anymore. I don't feel like I know what's going on in your life."

Marcy's contrived smile and sweetness were again all Felicity. "Oh, Mom, I've grown up. That's all."

I should have vehemently argued that point, telling her that she was nowhere near an adult as far as I was concerned, but it seemed like we had been having this same argument for months now. It never led anywhere. "I just want to make sure you're okay," I said, lamely.

"Oh, Mom, you worry too much." Marcy rinsed off her spoon and then kissed me on her way out the door. And that was that.

Those first few days of April were unseasonably warm, with the temperature hovering near one hundred degrees, a sure sign that the relentless Arizona summer was coming soon. Maybe it was only my imagination, but it seemed to me that the sudden early heat put everyone a little on edge. I'm afraid that I didn't keep my edginess entirely under wraps on the three days a week I had to go over to Cynthia's to work on our next wine party. It was kind of funny. I had been complaining for months about doing all the work in my kitchen, but now that I had to physically drive over to Cynthia's to do the labels and bottling and corking, I resented it. With three people and plenty of room, the work hummed along. The three of us talked some, but we didn't talk about anything important. Rather, each of us seemed to be on guard and wary of the others. In short, preparing for the next wine party wasn't fun anymore, not like it had been when it was only Reggie and me.

That was another thing that surprised me, how much I missed my former best friend. I missed her sliding open my patio door as soon as all the kids were off at school. I missed her going directly to the coffee machine, talking all the time about something she had seen on TV or read. Or about other people. Reggie had always been a great mimic, and when she would meanly imitate someone we both knew, I would be rolling on the floor. Of course the person Reggie had imitated the most and the person we had gossiped about the most was standing in the kitchen with us. So there was none of that now in Cynthia's house. Instead, Reggie seemed preoccupied most of the time, maybe even angry, but surprisingly, she was keeping it in check. I guessed that something was going on with Kent, but I didn't ask her. It seemed to be understood among the three of us that we weren't talking about our husbands. The unwritten rule suited me just fine.

Yes, I'm getting to Paul. During the lousy family vacation to San Diego, I had decided that I wasn't going to find his apartment on Thunderbird, bang on the door, and demand my money back. There were a few reasons for that decision. Number one, I am not by nature a confrontational person. Secondly, I did not want to find him in a compromising position with Betty Boop. That thought, even after all the time that had passed, made me feel physically ill. Betty Boop was young, waiflike, and in all probability, didn't have stretch marks or heavy, sagging boobs. The comparison between us would only serve to point out my shortcomings. But perhaps the most outstanding reason for my refusal to bring Paul to justice was that it seemed downright ludicrous to demand that he give me back the money he had stolen because it was my stolen money in the first place. Do you see what I mean?

There was yet another reason too. Knowing Paul as I did, I was sure that he had already spent my stolen cash. Paul didn't have a lick of sense about money and probably never would. To understand Paul, that point has to be emphasized. What's more, I was convinced that he would spend the money on something stupid or extravagant. Paul was always big on the grand, impractical gesture. I do not mean that in a derogatory way. Paul, in his foolishness, always tried to be generous.

For example, the year that I turned forty, Paul decided that a perfect gift for me would be a hot air balloon ride. I am terrified of heights, and he knew that or should have known it, but Paul thought it was perfect. He put it this way: "You've always said you want to see more of the country, babe." Yeah, right. I'd been thinking more along the lines of an Amtrak ride to DC, not a damn balloon over the Arizona desert. But I went to make him happy. I spent the entire trip, eyes closed, huddled in a corner of the little basket that was the only thing that separated me from life and death. I didn't see a thing.

I am truly sorry to report that I was right on the money--haha--about what Paul would do with my stolen $45,000 that he stole. I just didn't know that it would be quite so extravagant and stupid. Paul showed up one morning, grinning from ear to ear. "I have a surprise for you."

"What would be the best surprise is if you gave me back my money." I wasn't happy to see him. I'd been on my way out the door to Cynthia's, and I was already running late. The last thing I needed was to give those other two some time to talk about me when I wasn't there to defend myself.

"Oh, babe, don't be like that. The way I figured it is that your money is still my money, and my money is still yours. We are still married, you know." He was standing framed in the kitchen doorway, his hands stretched out on the frame, and he looked, unfortunately, more handsome than ever with a tan that made his blue eyes look three shades darker.

I couldn't argue with the being married part. The strange thing was that in the months of our separation, neither one of us had mentioned the word *divorce*. I don't know why that was. Maybe in a very strange way, we still loved each other, although I'd certainly been trying to box up my feelings for this man for a while now. "Where's Betty Boop?"

Paul straightened his shoulders, a move I knew meant he was feeling on the defensive. "I no longer need a life coach, Audrey. I'm done with all that."

"Or maybe Betty Boop got tired of you freeloading off her?" I knew it wasn't a kind thing to say, but I also knew it was the truth.

"Oh, babe, don't be that way. I'm a changed man, new and improved."

I knew what he was going to say before he said it, and I felt my knees wobble. All I could think was: *I'm not ready yet. I might not ever be ready.*

"Yep." Paul nodded. "I'm moving back in. We can pick up right where we left off--without the booze, of course."

"No." The word came out as a whisper, but Paul heard.

"Come on, babe. I'll make everything up to you. I'll start looking for a job first thing tomorrow morning. I'm thinking something in graphic design."

I could only shake my head at that. It was simply ludicrous. Paul didn't have any training in the field, but it was so typical of him. New and improved? I didn't think so.

"Come on, babe. This was the plan all along, wasn't it? I'd get better, get my disease under control, and come back home." Paul's voice had turned more desperate. "This is my home too, Audrey."

"Maybe you should have been thinking more about your home during all the months you were gone." I could see the edge of Paul's suitcase, the one he had taken to rehab, just beyond the door, and dread filled me.

"Babe, I don't have anyplace else to go."

That didn't make me melt either.

"If you want me to get on my knees and beg you, I will." And he did, right there and then. He clasped his hands. "Please, let me come home, Audrey."

What was I supposed to do? Legally, we were still married, and legally, we owned the house together. Yet I still would have said *no* if I was operating the wine club business out of my kitchen. But I didn't have all the wine bottles in my kitchen anymore. And my poor, neglected son certainly needed his father around. "You have to sleep in the den," I said then, making the no-win decision. If I could keep Paul at arm's length for a while, I could figure out what to do. But right now I was late for work.

"You are the best." Paul leaped off the floor, picked me up, and twirled me around. "Now for the surprise. Come with me."

Paul didn't seem to notice how stiff I was in his arms or how I dragged my feet as he led me outside and showed me the surprise. I was too stunned even to speak.

"Isn't she a beauty? We are going to have such adventures on her." He took me to the end of the driveway to show me the back. "I named her after you."

A sailboat. Paul had spent my money on a sailboat and a trailer to haul it here and park it right in my driveway. My first thought was that I couldn't get my car out of the garage, and my second was that buying this sailboat said everything there needed to be said about Paul, who was not a sailor, didn't have his license back yet, and as far as I knew, had never even been on a sailboat. *A sailboat.* God help me.

"What do you think, babe?" Paul was running his hand lovingly over the hull of the *Audrey.*

What I was thinking was *escape.* I had to get out of there before I started to pummel Paul with my fists, before I started screaming in frustration, knowing that if I began to scream, I would never be able to stop. "I have to make a phone call."

I ran to my kitchen. I was going to call Reggie to tell her and Cynthia that I would be very late today, but I was shaking so hard that I dropped my phone and it skittered across the floor, landing next to the trash can. I was too mad to even cry at that point, but when I bent down to pick up my phone, I noticed a scrap of paper on the floor, one that had probably missed the can when Marcy emptied the small pink waste paper can in her bathroom into the kitchen one this morning. I realized it was trash day, and I hadn't remembered to take out the trash, so it was still in the kitchen--and so was the paper.

It was a receipt from CVS, and there was only one item on it: First Response, $14.99.

I knew what that was, and I knew who had bought the pregnancy test. That's when I did start to scream.

23

CYNTHIA

I don't know what came over me.

There I was, walking down the aisles of Fry's grocery store. I was supposed to be shopping for food, which is not even remotely my favorite shopping excursion. Just give me a credit card with no limit and a couple of hours at Saks, and I can shop the heck out of that store. But Fry's? Forget about it. The food shopping used to be Louisa's job, and I thought she would take it over again when I hired her back. No such luck there. Unbelievably, Louisa flatly refused to do my grocery shopping anymore, or cook meals, or wash laundry, or do much of anything else, for that matter. I had doubled her salary and cut her days down to two a week, and still, she treated me like that.

You're asking me why I didn't fire her again? That's a loaded question, honey, and the best reason I can come up with is that odd as it sounds, I considered Louisa--and Pepe and Angel too--to be the closest thing to family I had left. I know that sounds pathetic, but it is one hundred percent true. And just like family members related by blood, they could be moody and bitchy and sometimes spiteful. So the reason I was in Fry's on that day was because Louisa was being mean to me again.

I had decided to make the best of it, though, and had dressed in what I thought was appropriate attire for a full-fledged grocery shopping expedition. I wore my red Louboutins and a short, black leather skirt designed by Yves Saint Laurent. People were staring at me. Granted, that is my standard effect on people, and one that I usually welcome, even promote. But it wasn't working so well that day. Instead, I felt like a fish out of water as I cluelessly walked up and down those crowded, cramped aisles, pulling items from the shelf and putting them in my cart, then changing my mind and putting them back. I was getting more unsettled and flustered by the minute at the sight of the stacked cans of food, the frozen food laid out in freezers, the piled fruits and vegetables that threatened to tumble down, the sheer number of choices I had to make. I had always thought of myself as a person with great self-control, a person who could keep her emotions in check and her head held high in almost any situation. But on that day, I blew it, big time.

I don't know what came over me, but all of a sudden, I was starving. I'm not talking about the hunger you feel when you've skipped breakfast or lunch. And I'm not talking about the hunger you feel when you're on a low-carb diet. I'm talking about a ravenous, gnawing ache that came out of nowhere and seemed to take over my entire body. *I was starving.* I was in the bakery section at the time, and I reached for a loaf of French bread. I didn't even take it out of the brown paper bag as I brought it to my mouth and started to tear off chunks of warm bread with my teeth. I probably hadn't had a piece of bread in fifteen years, and while that bread was delicious, crunchy on the outside and moist in the center, it wasn't enough. It wasn't right. The ache did not go away.

The cakes were lined up in a cooler by the counter, and they looked heavenly. I pushed my cart over and opened the plastic lid of the first one and took a bite, scooping it out with my fingers. German chocolate. Tasty. The next was a carrot cake with cream cheese icing. Not bad. One by one, I opened the lids and took a bite of each cake in turn: angel food, chiffon, red velvet, black forest, coconut, devil's food. From the corner of my eye, I saw a lady behind the counter. She was approaching me, frowning. I hurriedly closed all the lids and put my sticky fingers on the handle of my cart. "Just looking," I said, and rushed off to find something else that would satisfy my hunger.

I passed the raw meat counter next, and while the T-bones and chops didn't look half bad, I zeroed in on the hamburger, punching a hole in the cellophane wrapper and taking a scoop out of one, two, three, four packages. It wasn't awful, but the ground-up meat somehow reminded me of Buck Boyd's face after the last time I had asked Pepe and Angel to restrain and drug him. I gagged. A little boy was pointing at me, tugging on his mother's shirt. "Mama, mama, look at that lady. She's eating *raw hamburger.*" The woman, who was deeply engrossed in the conversation she was having on her phone, told him to stop pointing. It wasn't polite, she said.

I desperately needed to get the taste of raw meat out of my mouth, so when I looked up and saw the aisle with Snacks, I made a beeline there and started to reach for the bags, ripping open the tops. I dug in with both hands and started stuffing the salty goodness into my mouth. I was moving very fast by then and tried every bag I could get my hands on. I did not discriminate; nothing was taboo or off-limits. Ruffles, Lays, Poore Brothers--so many yummy flavors: barbecue, french onion, jalapeno, salt and vinegar!--Doritos, Fritos, tortilla chips, pretzels, pita chips, pork rinds. I did not discriminate. When I left that aisle, a salty rainbow littered the floor. And I was still starving.

I was starting to perspire by then as I headed down the aisle that contained packaged cookies on one side, crackers on the other. The cookies were first. Again I started ripping open packages and cramming cookies into my mouth. I could barely breathe around the mouthful of Milanos and Oreos and Chips Ahoy. I wasn't even really aware of what I was doing anymore. All I knew was that I had to make that gnawing hunger, that awful ache, go away. I didn't know if it was rivulets of sweat or tears running down my face by the time I destroyed the boxes of Ritz, Wheat Thins, Saltine, and graham crackers. And I didn't care. All I knew was that I couldn't stop. And it still hurt.

I was running blindly through that very large grocery store after that. I could hear someone over the loudspeaker call for cleanup up on aisle 2, then 4, then 6, then 10. Someone was calling for security as I reached the candy and nut aisle and started in on all the delicacies that the store offered: the gummy bears, the Hershey's bars, the Almond Joy's, the Twizzlers. My jaws ached from chewing; my throat burned from swallowing. But I couldn't stop, even knowing that all the food in the store would not ease the pain, nor would it ever make the pain go away.

Because everything that I had ever done in my life--all my past choices and decisions, the bad, the sordid, and every sorry detail of them, coupled with the illusion of everything I thought I had accomplished or become--came crashing down on me. There was no escape.

And it hurt.

While acknowledging that my binge eating spree in Fry's grocery store was not one of my finer moments, I would also like the record to reflect that I made full recompense for my actions. I would also like the record to note that the Fry's on Tatum and Shea had some very nice, understanding people working there that day. I had chosen that particular store because it was far enough away from my home that I didn't think I'd run into anyone I knew, which turned out to be smart thinking on my part.

The security guard who finally calmed me down and escorted me to the manager's office was a retired guy in his late seventies, and the manager also seemed instantly wowed by my charms. Not that they were in full view that day, mind you, given that I had perspired off most of my makeup, my hair looked like I had been caught in a windstorm, and I had stains dribbling down my pink silk shirt. But his wife must have been un-attractive enough that I looked pretty good to him because the manager said he would bend over backward to be fair about the whole incident. I apologized profusely and paid the astronomical amount that they said my destruction had caused. I swear I didn't know that groceries cost that much, but I guess it adds up when you rip open that many packages of food. Who knew?

Once I pulled myself together after that spectacle, and I'm not going to lie, it took a solid two days, the thing I regretted most was how much money the whole thing had set me back. My escape money, the money I was going to use for a luxurious lifestyle in Miami, couldn't seem to grow. It was like every time I got a little ahead, something would come up. It was frustrating how that worked. It sometimes seemed to me that everyone in the whole wide world had his hand out. Services like utilities and the internet had to be paid for, people had to be paid for their work, and if you were dealing with the Sanchez family, it would seem that some people expected to be paid even if they didn't work.

What I'm trying to say here is that I was having trouble getting ahead in the game. For the first time, if only for a fleeting moment, I had a glimpse of what had happened to Richard and what he had gone through. He probably thought the money would always continue to roll in, and when it stopped, when he got in over his head, he was in a real pickle. However, that still didn't explain why he had given me a lousy fake diamond when he married me.

So after the night I found out what Felicity had been up to during the Tigerette season, I decided that it was time to pack up and go, to make my escape permanent and final. If I took out the rest of the money in the FHM account, I might be able to swing it. Of course now I was probably looking at a dinky apartment in Ft. Lauderdale rather than the Versace mansion, but the point was to get away, leave everything behind and start again. I had done it three times in my life: when I moved to LA, when I moved to Vegas, and when I married Richard. I was good at starting over and forgetting about the past. I was good at reinventing myself, and believe me, I was anxious to get on with something new. It was my turn to be the star of my own life.

I know that probably sounds awful, but let me explain. Things had really gotten out of hand, and I didn't want to deal with them anymore. That doesn't sound any better when I put it that way, but please, put yourself in my position. First I'll start with the wine club. Initially, I'd wanted to be friends with Audrey and Reggie. I'd been jealous of how close they were, back at the beginning of the school year. While they seemed to be at odds now, it was no skin off my nose because I no longer wanted to have that kind of friendship with either of them. They weren't that likable. They were small-minded, narrow, and didn't see the big picture.

At this stage in the game, we should have had an internet wine club going, and we should have had an outside source bottling our wine, and we should have also expanded the number of parties, maybe by renting out the ballroom in the Four Seasons a couple of times a month. We needed to hire more employees too. In short, Reggie and Audrey were a couple of dipshits to work with. Neither one of them had any vision, and I would be better off going out and starting a better wine club on my own. Like in Florida. I could make a lot more money without having to share the profits with either of those two.

And there was Richard, who could be taken out of the equation easily enough. The way I saw it, I was never going to see him again. Either he was never found, or he went to jail. Months had gone by, and he hadn't once tried to contact me. He had gifted me with fake jewelry and put me in a house full of equally phony shit. And I was eventually going to be evicted from the house anyway. It was only a matter of time. That didn't bother me nearly as much as the fact that I had wasted my youth, my peak years, on that man. Thanks to Richard, I wasn't getting any younger, and at forty-one, the time was now or never to get out there and start making things happen with other attractive, eligible, wealthy men. If I waited another year or two, I was going to have to start considering plastic surgery on my face, which was a scary prospect. I mean, have you seen those shiny-faced women who go under the knife? They all look pretty much alike, with only two variations on the same theme: they either look like cats or apes. It makes me shudder to think about it and trust me. I've thought a lot about it.

I hate to bring up the subject of Buck Boyd, but I suppose I have to, given the fact that he still resided in the panic room in my basement. I suppose that *existed* would be a more appropriate word. In truth, Buck Boyd was looking a little peaked by that time. He hadn't seen the light of day in something like two months, but his lack of vitamin D was not the major issue. He wasn't eating, even though I had Pepe or Angel--I still couldn't tell them apart--take down a basket of oranges and bananas and peaches. I'd even gone out and gotten McDonald's for Buck once or twice, which my boys delivered to Buck, but he didn't even taste a french fry. I'd check in on Buck on Richard's office monitor every other day or so, but his deteriorating physical appearance was starting to depress me. I don't like to be depressed.

It wasn't my fault. The first time that Pepe and Angel were supposed to move Buck, the time I had to prove to nosy Reggie that nobody was in the panic room, they had scoffed when I showed them the bottle of Oxy and said, "If you grind these up in a shot of whiskey, I think it'll do the trick."

One of them, laughing, said, "That no work."

"Yes, it will," I answered, even though I had no idea. You'd think that my years in Vegas would have taught me a thing or two about drugs, right? Didn't happen. Wine is okay for you, but serious drugs can cause serious damage to your looks. I'd seen it happen to tons of dancers I used to kind of know.

The other said, "We need heroin."

It was my turn to scoff. "I don't know anybody who sells heroin. The ladies I lunch with aren't in the market for that particular product."

He nodded sagely. "I know a guy. But it's going to cost you, Miz Stewart."

Boy, they weren't kidding about that. The heroin became another sinkhole into which my money disappeared. I suspected that Pepe and

Angel might have been padding the price and putting a sizable chunk in their own pockets, but I didn't look up the price of heroin on the internet to check it out. When the day finally arrived, when Buck was magically gone because a brilliant plan had finally come to me, I didn't want to leave any evidence that he had been in that room if the time ever came that I was questioned about him. Deny, deny, deny, and don't leave a paper or internet trail. Everyone knows that.

Believe me when I say that Buck was not feeling any pain during that time. At least I didn't think so. Pepe and Angel did like to rough him up every chance they got, which perhaps further contributed to his deteriorating overall physical appearance. But at least he wasn't ranting and raving anymore, which was a good thing, right? Mostly he just curled into a ball on the small couch and stared at the blank TV. So I suppose a case could be made that Buck was reasonably content, considering the circumstances. When I left town, I was going to give Pepe and Angel some more money--they wouldn't do anything at all unless they were paid upfront--and have them take Buck to someplace miles into Mexico, preferably a place without any phone communication, and then let him go. However, I was also going to *strongly* suggest that if they didn't want to travel that far, if there was a problem with their immigration status, they might consider an old boarded up mine shaft in the Bisbee area in southern Arizona. It wouldn't take too much effort to pry off a couple of boards and shove Buck inside.

That brings me to Felicity. While I have explained my complicated feelings about my daughter--I might have loved her, in a rather distant, distracted way, but I certainly didn't like her--I knew I was going to have to figure out some way to get her out of this recent mess. She'd gone over the top with the sex videos. I am not a prude by any stretch of the imagination, but even I knew that what Felicity had done was atrociously wrong. When she'd marched herself back into the house after the March wine club party--after I had expressly told her to stay in the guesthouse until I had time to think about the best way to handle the sticky situation we were now embroiled in--I wanted her to tell Reggie and Audrey what she had been up to, what she had, in all likelihood, insisted that Hayley and Marcy do to become accepted by Felicity as Tigerettes. I almost *insisted* that she tell those two women. It would have served my little witch right.

But what did my conniving daughter do? She turned the tables on me and blackmailed me. So much time had passed since the first day that Buck had shown up on my doorstep that I thought Felicity hadn't seen him sitting at the kitchen counter. My mistake. I should never have underestimated such a sophisticated player, and between Richard and me, Felicity had learned from the best.

It is a valid point to ask why I didn't tell Reggie and Audrey myself what Felicity had been up to on that March night. I do have a very good reason. I saw the graphic images of those two young girls and countless boys, but I hadn't actually seen my daughter in any of the videos. I thought I heard her voice once or twice, but I wasn't sure. I suspected that Felicity was the one taping the performance, but I wasn't one hundred percent sure of that either. You see, I still held out hope that Felicity had not stooped that low. And as I poured myself a hefty glass of fake Château Lafite Rothschild after Reggie and Audrey finally left, I even halfway convinced myself that was indeed the case. The videographer seemed like a person who knew what he was doing with a camera. In other words, the snippet of the porn tape I had seen looked like it had been done by a professional, not by a teenage girl. So *voilà!* Felicity was not the culprit.

I poured another hefty glass of wine to give me the courage I needed to go out to the guesthouse and confront my daughter on that night. I cannot tell you how much I dreaded that conversation. First of all, I was on shaky ground. Obviously, it was illegal to tape underage girls having sex. But Felicity was also underage at the time of the video, so if she, in fact, had been the one who taped the whole thing, would she go to jail or juvie or some detention center? Would she not be allowed to graduate from Mohave High School next month? That was a terrible prospect. I had been counting the days until Felicity turned eighteen, which was one week away, and then graduated. As far as I was concerned, once Felicity graduated my responsibility to her was done. The thought that she might be hanging around longer if she got into trouble did not make me happy.

It would seem that there was not enough wine in the world to give me courage when it came to Felicity because when she eventually came back into the house, I was still standing by the kitchen island with a large wine glass in my hand. I hadn't moved one inch toward that guesthouse. In truth, I guess I was aiming to drink myself into a stupor and avoid the conversation altogether, but now it was too late for that.

Felicity, looking wide awake at that late hour, settled herself on a bar-stool and folded her arms over her chest. "I got tired of waiting for you out there."

"So you came to me," I said, stalling for time. You'd think that I would have come up with some line of approach to this conversation as I was drinking my wine, but sadly I did not. I had instead spent a lot of that time dwelling on the second catastrophe of the evening, discovering that Felicity knew that Buck Boyd was in the panic room. If I had sometimes been afraid of my daughter in the past, I was now completely terrified at how much power she had over me. All she had to do was make one phone call, and I was history.

Felicity, of course, was prepared. "How much did you see?"

"Enough."

"It's not what you think."

"It is exactly what I think." Thankfully, the wine started to kick in then, and I felt what I should have felt all along--anger. I set my glass on the table. "Why did you do such a terrible thing, Felicity?"

"I wasn't the one holding the camera."

"Filming underage girls having sex is illegal, Felicity."

Felicity shrugged. "Teenagers do this all the time, Mom. Haven't you ever heard of sexting?"

"Also illegal."

"So is keeping a man in the panic room against his will."

I drew in a sharp intake of breath. "We're not going there right now, Felicity. I want to know why you did this, who else knows about it, and how many people are involved. This was your idea, wasn't it?" I knew this to be true, so I didn't wait for an answer. "Did you do this to Hayley and Marcy because you were mad that they were chosen for the team?"

Felicity remained unruffled. "As usual, Mom, you're missing the point. This is simply part of the Tigerette *initiation*. If you're a part of the Top Twelve, you have to do this."

I didn't succeed in hiding my confusion. "What's the Top Twelve?"

"The Tigerettes, and therefore, the most popular girls in school."

"I thought the Tigerettes were a pom squad, not a porn group."

"The Top Twelve are sexually active girls."

"Sexually active with *whom*?"

"The basketball players, for starters."

"For starters?"

Felicity shrugged again. "They're only boys. There might be some other people involved too. There might be some teachers."

I had to grab onto the counter for support as the magnitude of what my daughter was saying sunk in. "So this is like a . . . sex ring with the Tigerettes, basketball players, and some of the teachers?"

"I wouldn't call it a sex ring," Felicity said.

"What would you call it?" I was having trouble breathing.

"It's more like a club. We have viewing parties, that kind of thing. It's very exclusive. We only invite members. And it's not like we send the videos out on the internet. I'm not that stupid."

"Is this how you were initiated into the Tigerettes?" I had assumed that my daughter was sexually active, without ever once asking for details. And I always thought I would be slightly disappointed if she was still a virgin when she graduated from high school. But what she was describing was wrong on so many levels, on *all* levels.

Felicity's little smile looked smug. "No, I developed the idea. It's new this year."

I stared at her, finally getting it. Felicity did start this club to get back at the two new girls. She came up with the most demeaning thing she could think of too. "You are evil," I hissed at her.

"The apple doesn't fall far from the tree, Mom."

"You need to be punished for this." My voice was shaking, and I was still holding onto the counter for dear life. "I'm going to call Mr. Rooney and have him deal with what is going on in his school."

"Mr. Rooney already knows."

I tasted bile in the back of my throat and had to swallow hard to keep from vomiting. "Then I will call the police."

"If you call the cops, Mom, I'm going to tell them about the man in the panic room. It's your turn to talk."

Felicity had settled back on her stool and crossed her arms again, the smug smile returning to her face. She seemed to think she had won that round, and unfortunately, she probably had. I looked at her long and hard. "How do you know there's a man in the panic room?"

"I wasn't sure--until just now. But I think it was the McDonald's bag that tipped me off. That, and the locked door. The door never used to be locked. I'm not stupid, Mom."

No, my bitch of a daughter was not stupid. She was cunning, conniving, and terrifying. Furthermore, she didn't seem at all appalled by the notion that I was holding a man captive against his will. It was unsettling. I stared into her shrewd eyes, and I had a sinking feeling that she was lying to me, not about the Top Twelve, but about Buck. She had known he was in the room. She'd probably even talked to him. How much had he told her in his effort to enlist her help for his escape? I felt like the wind had been knocked out of me, and I couldn't get enough air into my lungs.

"You look beat." Felicity slid off the barstool. "I think we should call a truce, don't you? If you don't tell, I won't tell."

Felicity didn't wait for an answer as she, unbelievably, skipped off to bed.

I tried to convince myself that the awful knowledge of what Felicity had been up to for the entire school year could work to my advantage. As mean and depraved as it was, creating sex videos of those two underage girls could force Felicity to finally, for the first time in her life, receive the punishment that she deserved. If I told the cops and she was arrested or detained, or even better, put into a psychiatric facility, she would have to face the terrible consequences of her terrible actions. It would serve the little bitch right, wouldn't it? And as a bonus, my daughter would be out of my hair for good. If she ever got out of whatever facility detained her, and if she ever tried to find me--which was as likely as drawing all six Powerball numbers--I would be long, long gone. I would be living under an assumed name and dating all the wealthy, eligible men in Miami or Ft. Lauderdale. Maybe I would have even made it over to Europe and gotten some royal duke or earl so enthralled with my charms that he would have married me and given me a title. I have to admit that I've always secretly wanted to be a duchess.

However, that meant that I had to clean up my own mess before I called the authorities. There was no doubt in my mind that the first thing that Felicity would say once they slapped the handcuffs on her was: "You think I'm the bad guy here? Why don't you look in the panic room?" Then it would be my turn to have the cuffs slapped on while Felicity smirked. Yes, Felicity and I would be quite the pair, mother/daughter criminals, tried, judged, and convicted by juries of our peers. And it would be just my luck that I'd wind up in the same prison as her. I couldn't even begin to wrap my mind around that nightmare.

So I finally had to get rid of Buck Boyd. While I wasn't naive enough to think it would be easy, I was not prepared for the flat-out resistance from Pepe and Angel. I mean, they'd seemed to enjoy roughing up Buck for weeks, but when I nonchalantly suggested that it was time to remove Buck from the panic room and take him to an abandoned mine shaft in Bisbee--I'd decided to cut right to the chase and skip the whole Mexico idea because I was pretty sure that Pepe and Angel were illegals--they both seemed highly offended.

"We don't kill nobody," Pepe said sternly.

"There is the possibility that he could survive the fall." Desperate times call for desperate measures, but even I knew that was a far-fetched thing to say.

"You call Mexican mafia for that." Angel put in his two cents.

I almost said, sure, just give me the number, but the way they were looking at me stopped me cold. I could see in their eyes that I had crossed some line. Beating up a drugged-out guy was okay in their book, but pushing him down an abandoned mine shaft to certain death was a whole new ballgame. I think that was the first time I realized that Pepe and Angel--and perhaps even Louisa--could also use incriminating evidence against me. I had banked on the notion that they wouldn't go to the cops because of their immigration status, but now I wasn't so sure. Looking at the two burly guys, I knew then just how fragile my position was with the Sanchez family.

I quickly gave them one of my dazzling smiles and changed the subject. "Don't you know I'm kidding you? I've been talking to Buck, and he's apologized for treating me so horribly. I'm going to let him go soon."

"We could drive him to the desert," Pepe offered, perhaps trying to prolong his employment.

"That won't be necessary. I'm going to drive Buck to the bus station myself and buy him a ticket back home."

"No work?" Angel's dark eyes bored into mine.

Even those two words from Angel suddenly seemed menacing. "It's a vacation," I said nervously. When their expressions didn't soften, I added, "A *paid* vacation. You'll still get your money."

That elicited half-smiles from them, which did nothing to soothe my growing uneasiness. After nicely asking Pepe and Angel to make sure that Buck got two shots of heroin before they left for the evening because he had been "sleeping poorly," I locked the door behind them and leaned against it, breathing heavily. You better believe that I was kicking myself right about then. How could I have been so stupid as to trust those two when all they wanted was my money? I didn't have their loyalty, nor could I trust them to keep the whereabouts of Buck a secret. What the whole thing proved to me was that I needed to get rid of Buck that night. If they turned on me, it was going to be their word against mine. I was pretty sure I was going to come out on top of that situation, but I didn't want to take any chances. The whole exchange had rattled me. That's my only excuse for not turning on the alarm.

Felicity had a dance competition at Shadow Mountain High School that evening. The only reason I knew that was because she had sent me a text. Since our so-called pact to not rat each other out, she had been sickeningly sweet towards me. I supposed she had decided that she needed to change her behavior to cover her tracks too. Or maybe she was actually starting to feel guilty about all her rotten behavior over the past year. I had no idea. I couldn't read the girl. She was so much like how I'd been at her age that it scared me to death. I guess I deserved it, in some karma sense of justice, but I didn't have to like it.

Do you want to know what my plan was? I honestly didn't have one. Even after I checked the monitor in Richard's study and saw that Buck was curled into his usual fetal position on the couch and seemed to be totally zonked out, I paced around for a while, trying to come up with the best way to move his body out of that room, across the wine cellar, up seven steps, across the kitchen to the garage, through the garage, and then how to lift him into the trunk. I was hoping that adrenaline would kick in, and I would be magically infused with superhuman strength. After that, I was going to drive him out to the desert. The desert was always the best way to dispose of bodies; it was a lesson I knew well from my Vegas days. In all probability, I didn't think that Buck would survive the night. He was obviously in bad shape, and once the sun came up--it had been unseasonably hot--it would bear down on him with an intensity I didn't think he could stand without food or water. There were plenty of animals in the desert too, javelinas and wolves and vultures and bobcats. All nature had to do was take Her course.

The stench hit me immediately as I tentatively opened the door. My goodness, the man must not have bathed in weeks, and the strong odors of sweat and fear were overwhelming. I gagged, but I determinedly moved closer. I had a large kitchen knife in my hands, just in case, even as I knew there was a remote possibility that Buck might rear up and attack. He didn't, and as I crept closer, closer, he didn't budge. He didn't move a muscle. He didn't even seem to be breathing. Had that extra shot of heroin been too much? Had he overdosed? While that scenario would be a perfect solution, I did feel a little bad about that. Truly, I did.

Buck was breathing, but it was very, very shallow. He'd lost so much weight that his bruised cheekbones stood out in sharp relief, and I swear I could see the outline of his ribs underneath the thin cotton of his now gray t-shirt. He looked like a homeless, drug-addicted, battered, shattered man, and unexpectedly, tears welled up in my eyes. I had done this to him, and it was disgraceful. *But he would have ruined me!* I had to keep focusing on that thought to get through what I had to do. And I did have to do it. If Buck was not permanently out of the picture, he would torment me for the rest of my life. I knew that for a fact.

I was about to touch him, to take a deep breath, hold it, and slip two arms under his arms and begin the dragging process. But I heard a sound. It was muffled, but in that large house, I knew exactly what the sound was. I'd heard it plenty of times when I was down in the wine room and Louisa was overhead in the kitchen. It was the sound of footsteps, and I could tell that those footsteps were crossing the kitchen, getting closer to the stairs. Someone had broken into my house! I hadn't turned on the alarm, and now, on this of all nights, someone had broken in.

Well, I wasn't going to stay in the panic room with that near-dead body. Given my chances with Buck or a would-be rapist, I chose the rapist. I do not mean any disrespect to victimized women, of course. I just mean that my chances were better if I was out of that foul-smelling room with the deteriorating creature of my own making. I ran out, planning to ram my attacker with my body, planning to use the knife that I still clutched in my hand, planning to scream for all I was worth, planning to survive anything the guy would try to do with me. I was a raging dynamo.

But I stopped dead in my tracks just inside the wine cellar, the knife falling from my uplifted hand, the scream dying on my lips.

It was a thief, all right.

It was Richard.

24

REGGIE

Okay, I admit it.

That house I bought on 68993 E. Cholla Street was a big, fat lemon. Did I listen when the appraiser told me that it was a teardown? Of course not! So I guess I wasn't all that surprised when the house needed more than new wiring and treatment for termites. It also needed new plumbing, new insulation, new windows, a new pool, and something had to be done about the massive crack in the foundation. Do you see what I'm getting at here? In the end, I had to gut the house and start building it again from scratch. I don't mean me personally, obviously, but let me tell you, I was there every day to oversee the contractors and the construction workers. You would be amazed at how unscrupulous some of those people in the building industry can be. I caught one guy trying to walk off with a box containing one of my brand new toilets. If I hadn't been on top of things every single second, it's hard telling how much they would have ripped me off. *Goddamnit, I know.* I get the irony. Enough already.

But if you know anything at all about me by now, you know that I would only give up on the project over my dead body. Despite all the setbacks, despite all the checks I kept writing out of the FHM account, I was going to keep going on that house until it was built to perfection. I guess you could say that the house became an obsession of mine during that time. I'm not sure exactly why. I sure didn't give a rat's ass about the condition of the house I lived in, but for some reason, that house became extremely important to me. I think that in the back of my mind, I hoped that when the house was finally completed, everything in my life would miraculously fall into place. It would house a very successful business, and now I had it in my head that I would move there too. My brand new life would start in that almost-new house.

Weirdly enough, I had this idea that maybe Audrey would move in with me. Don't get me wrong. I was still mad as hell at her for all kinds of things. She'd abandoned the wine club and me when we both needed her most, and worst of all, she was once more acting like Paul's doormat. I couldn't believe it when I saw that ridiculous boat parked in their drive-way. Number one, it was a gigantic waste of money, and number two, it was proof that Paul was back and acting as stupid as he always had. I'd always thought that Audrey could do better than someone like him, a guy who thought he was way more charming than he actually was. Seriously, the guy didn't know the definition of *work ethic*. He thought he'd give you one of his goofy smiles, and everything would be just hunky-dory. Give me a break! If Audrey ever came to her senses, I was going to give her the opportunity to move in with me. Which proves beyond a reasonable doubt that I was always a good friend to that woman. No matter what she says.

So, my house on Cholla was a money pit and was depleting all my resources. And no, I didn't feel all that guilty about writing out checks from the FHM account. After I called the bank to request that the state-ments be sent out annually and was informed that since it was a savings account, it was already set up that way, I could relax. By the time the other two figured out what I had been up to, the house would be finished and operational, and they would see that I was the only one who had the good sense to invest in the future of the wine club, in *our* future. Well, I was hoping that when we had traveled that far down the road, say another six months or so, Cynthia would have already decided she was bored with the whole thing and reverted to her Lunch with the Ladies lifestyle.

Because of my situation with the money pit, I jumped all over the idea Cynthia had for the next wine club party. Believe me when I tell you that I had initially planned to veto any suggestions she made about the club, just out of principle. She shouldn't have been in the wine club in the first place--I believe I've mentioned that once or twice--but the fact of the mat-ter was that it was a good one. Champagne.

We'd been sitting around Cynthia's kitchen island brainstorming ideas. The previous Pétrus and Rothschild wine selections had been so profitable that I was already on my computer looking up châteaux that specialized in producing wines that had achieved *Premier cru*, or first growth, status in the Bordeaux Classification of 1855. Audrey was doodling, as she always did at that stage of the game, and Cynthia was pacing around and around the island. Frankly, she was making me nervous as she stomped around. It was like she was trying to squash bugs on the floor with every step she took. She'd been acting jumpy all morning. But she stopped suddenly and said, "I've got it! People always think that French champagne is exorbitantly expensive, so let's show them how expensive it can be."

Audrey looked up from her doodling. "Like Dom Pérignon?"

"Exactly." Cynthia nodded.

I got right on it and soon found the most profitable bottles to suit our purposes:

NV Moët & Chandon Nectar Imperial Rose at $1,550;

Dom Pérignon Oenotheque Rose Champagne Magnum at $7,000;

Armand de Brignac Brut Rose Champagne at $9,800;

and Armand de Brignac Brut Gold Champagne at $17,000.

I read them aloud to the others.

"Those are so expensive!" Audrey, the naysayer, said.

"They're perfect." Cynthia looked over my shoulder at my computer screen.

Audrey refused to join us and was looking at her phone instead. "The brut gold champagne has a very distinctive gold bottle with a leaf. And it comes in a box. How are we going to get ahold of those things?"

I rolled my eyes. "You worry too much, Audrey."

"Reggie, we need to make these look authentic. You know that." Her green eyes flared at me.

Before I could say something back, Cynthia interrupted. "She's right, Reggie. Try Amazon."

I found some gold wine bottle centerpieces that came close to the designs of the brut gold champagne bottles. "These could work. All you have to do is paint on the leaf. The boxes should be easy to find too."

"The brut rose champagne bottles are pink, and the labels look like embossed foil, maybe metal. It's a very intricate design." Audrey put her phone down. "Maybe we should do champagne with bottles that aren't quite so distinctive."

Truth be told, I also thought that maybe these particular bottles were out of our reach. Audrey and I had always strived to be as authentic as possible in our work, but Cynthia refused to be fazed. "Look, these women don't know the difference. If we come close to the originals, what's the harm? And the bottles we're talking about are the most expensive. I say we go for it. We're talking tens of thousands of dollars here."

I was torn. While I hated taking such a big risk, the money was very, very tempting. I was thinking about all the upgrades I could make in my house with that kind of money. Maybe I could even start buying other fixer-uppers and start renovating them as well. It would be a whole other business opportunity for me, but with this new venture, I wasn't going to have any partners. I had all kinds of wild ideas around that time, as you well know. Dollar signs can hypnotize even the most level-headed of gals right out of her common sense. "I vote with Cynthia," I said.

"And what if I'm the only dissenting vote?" Audrey's eyes flared again.

"Majority rules," I said. "We'll do the gold and brut champagnes."

"You don't have to be in on this particular wine party if you don't want to be, Audrey. It's up to you."

Even I was surprised at the dismissive anger in Cynthia's voice. But I would be lying if I didn't say that I considered, for about a nanosecond, how much more money that would mean for me. But I couldn't let Cynthia call all the shots. So what if she'd had one good idea? It was still my wine club--and Audrey's, kind of. So I used my most persuasive tone--note, it was *not* bullying--when I turned to Audrey. "Like it or not, the three of us are in this together. Come on, Audrey. You can do those labels, can't you?"

"Of course I can do the labels!" she snapped.

I ignored her snappishness. "Good. It's settled. Now we need to decide on our filler wines. We have a lot of work to do."

Audrey wasn't exactly what you would call surly the rest of the afternoon, but she sure as heck made it known that she was displeased. Cynthia and I pretended not to notice as we chose Widow Clicquot at $15 per bottle for the gold brut, and Korbel Sweet Rose ($12), Wedding Favor Mini Champagne Rose ($7) and Barefoot Bubbly Pink Moscato ($9) for the three other champagnes. When we were finished for that day, Audrey packed up her things and said she'd be back tomorrow with a draft of the labels. She didn't slam the door on her way out or anything like that, but she was upset. I could tell.

That's why I knocked on her patio door later that evening, to see if she was still upset, not because I was curious about why Paul was back and why he'd bought a stupid boat. Well, okay, maybe I was curious a little bit, but really, I went over as a friend, not as a nosy bitch. I only hoped she saw it that way. That's why when I saw her standing at the kitchen sink doing dishes, I pushed the door open a crack after knocking again and said, "I come in peace." I held up the wine bottle I had in my hand, a $24 bottle of Graef chardonnay, one of the nicer bottles that I'd started to buy recently. "And I come bearing gifts."

It seemed like it took a long time for the small smile to appear at the corners of Audrey's mouth. "We'll have to drink it on your patio." She stuck her head in the family room. "I'm going next door." Then she followed me back to my house.

I'd like to say it was like old times, sitting there on my patio with the citronella candle burning between our two wine glasses. But it wasn't. We were both tense, and it was like we didn't know where to start. I had about a million questions I wanted to ask her, but she'd become so touchy over the last few months that I honestly thought she would bite my head off if I said the wrong thing. Which had never stopped me before and didn't stop me that night either, I'm afraid to say. So the first words out of my mouth were: "A boat, Audrey?"

She sighed. "Yep. A goddamn boat. Paul's back in town."

"Where'd he get the money?" It was a reasonable question. Paul had never made all that much money to begin with, and he hadn't held a real job since his DUI.

Audrey hesitated only a moment before answering. "He stole it from me."

"Oh, for Pete's sake!" I exploded, and I didn't hold anything back. "What a scumbag! Why didn't you report him to the police?"

"How was I going to explain where I got the money in the first place? It's not exactly normal for a middle-class suburban woman to have that much cash laying around."

I could see her point, but still, I was incensed, for her sake. "Paul still shouldn't get away with it."

"I'm not planning on letting him get away with it."

I was intrigued and leaned a little closer. "What do you mean?"

Audrey shrugged. "I haven't decided yet. For the time being, he's sleeping on the couch in the den and taking care of Jimmy." Before I could get another question out, Audrey deftly changed the subject. "What's new with Kent?"

"Well, I haven't run over any more cats yet, if that's what you're asking." That coaxed another small smile out of her. "But I might have chopped down those two rose bushes that he now seems so fond of. *Seemed* fond of."

"You didn't!"

I nodded. "I'm afraid so. But the man provoked me."

I briefly filled her in on the story, not that there was all that much to tell. Kent had called me up and said we needed to talk in person. I told him I was too busy to meet with him, and then he just spilled it over the phone: He wanted a divorce. He had finally made his decision, and the person he wanted to be with was not me. By the time I drove by his house that night--and I was only driving by during the darkest hours because of the stupid restraining order--I had worked up a righteous rage.

I had come prepared, having bought a small hatchet at Home Depot on the way over there. The rose bushes bloomed on either side of the front door, but by the time I finished my work, only the stumps remained. I worked with a devilish fever, my anger stoked by the audacity and coward-ice of the man, who had dropped the divorce bombshell over the *phone*. It didn't matter that I had told him that I was too busy to meet with him. He still owed me the courtesy of a direct confrontation. It was only after I got into the car that I realized my hands were bleeding. I'd been so mad at the man for so long that I didn't even feel the pain of the thorns cutting into the flesh of my palms.

Audrey looked thoughtful as she poured more wine into each of our glasses. "So, you're still driving by the condo?"

"Not during the daylight hours."

"After the last wine party, when we witnessed that awkward scene be-tween Cynthia and Felicity, you seemed convinced that we now had proof that the Tigerettes were up to something. I thought for sure you had been spying on Hayley and Marcy after school. I was counting on it."

I was glad it was dark because I could feel my face flush with guilt. I had become so busy with the endless things that were going wrong with my new house that I had dropped the ball on that one. That was the moment to come clean with Audrey, to tell her how I was now spending the majority of my free time. But do you know what? I didn't. The house wasn't ready yet. It probably wasn't even technically a house at that point, gutted as it was, with tarps and sawhorses as its only furniture. If I told Audrey about it and she decided to take a look, she would think that I was foolish, maybe even insane. It was something I sometimes wondered about myself. Was I slowly losing my mind? Would I eventually slip into dementia, as my father had? As I roamed about in the darkest hours of the night, I did feel as if my grip on reality was tenuous, at best.

I took a quick sip of wine. "I'm sorry to disappoint you, Audrey, but you know, the restraining order."

"The restraining order didn't stop you from chopping down the rose bushes," she unnecessarily pointed out.

She was starting to get my hackles up. I was being nothing but nice to her, and she was deliberately provoking me. "What do you want me to do, Audrey? Peek in the windows of the condo at five o'clock in the afternoon when anyone driving by could accuse me of being a peeping Tom?"

"Yes," she said, looking at me over the rim of her wine glass. "That's exactly what I want you to do."

"Why don't you do it?" I said, exasperated.

"It's more of your thing."

"So you're saying that trespassing and spying are crimes that I would be more likely to commit?" I was really on the verge of telling her to go home. I'd finish the bottle of wine by myself, which would be infinitely preferable to her company.

"Just get off your high horse, Reggie." Audrey calmly took another sip of wine. "I'm merely suggesting that you do something that you're already inclined to do because I found a receipt for a pregnancy test on the floor of my kitchen. I need to know what's going on."

"What?" I felt like someone had punched me in the gut, and let me tell you, I toppled right down from that high horse. "Is Marcy pregnant?"

"She said it wasn't hers, that she bought it for one of the other Tigerettes."

"I don't buy that."

Audrey shook her head. "Neither did I. So I bought another pregnancy test and made Marcy take it. I watched my daughter urinate on an EPT stick, Reggie. Even as I watched her peeing on that stick--and she was throwing a fit, crying and sobbing uncontrollably--I couldn't believe that I was that kind of mother. It was only when I saw that the test was negative that I believed her."

"Holy shit," I gasped, and then realization struck. I could barely utter my daughter's name. "Hayley?"

"I don't know." But when Audrey saw the stricken look on my face, she softened. "What Marcy said was that I didn't know the girl."

My heart was hammering in my chest. "Do you believe that?"

Audrey shrugged. "I don't know what to believe anymore."

"If Hayley was in trouble, she'd come to me. I know my daughter and . . ." I couldn't even begin to convince myself of that anymore. If my daughter was scared or worried these days, she would most likely turn to Marcy first, maybe even the detestable Felicity. Maybe she would even go to Kent before she went to me.

"Why don't you ask her?"

I resented the taunt, but I took the bait. I pushed myself back from the table and went inside, up the stairs, and didn't even knock before I flung open the door to the dark room. I could see my daughter's form huddled under the covers--I hadn't realized how late it was--as I flipped on the overhead light. "Wake up, Hayley."

Hayley blinked against the light. She saw the look on my face and scrambled to sit up. "What's the matter, Mom? Has something happened? Did Caleb or Daddy get in a car accident? Mom? Mom! Say something! You're scaring me!"

I knew that I looked a fright, wild-eyed and ready to pounce. I gulped in air, trying to calm myself. I only wanted the truth from my daughter; I didn't mean to terrorize her. Still, my voice, when I found it, came out about a hundred decibels too loud. "Audrey found the receipt for an EPT test. Marcy said it wasn't hers, that she bought it for someone else. Are you that someone else? Are you pregnant, Hayley?"

Hayley let out a whoosh of air. I didn't know if it was a large sigh of relief or an attempt to gather her thoughts together. It seemed like an eternity before she answered my question. "No, Mom, I'm not pregnant. I don't even have a boyfriend, remember?"

"I remember a hickey."

"That was just a guy fooling around to impress his buddies. I told you all that."

I was finding it difficult to absorb what she was saying because my relief made me feel so light-headed that I was dizzy. My daughter's dark hair hung around her shoulders like a cape, and her dark eyes were wide and innocent. She looked so young right at that moment that I wanted to snatch back the words I had just spoken. How could I have thought that this young daughter of mine could be pregnant? She wasn't even sexually active, for Pete's sake! I was almost as bad as Audrey who had watched her daughter pee on the stick of an EPT test.

"I'm sorry I woke you up," I said, instead of an actual apology.

"You scared me to death, Mom," Hayley accused. She was wide awake now.

"The thought of you being pregnant scared *me* to death, Hayley. You're sixteen years old, only a sophomore in high school."

"Well, I'm not pregnant, so as usual, you overreacted."

The fact that I barged into her room in the middle of the night, wild-eyed and loud, prevented me from refuting her statement. "You're my daughter, I love you, and I was worried," I said in my defense.

Hayley sighed again and snuggled back under the covers. "I love you too, Mom. Would you turn off the light on your way out? I have a chem test first thing in the morning."

That statement made me feel guilty, as it was designed to do. And all in all, I was feeling pretty stupid for thinking the worst of my daughter. She'd always been such a good kid. "Sure thing, honey," I said sheepishly. I reached for the light switch, then stopped because another important question had popped into my mind. "I just want to know one more thing before I go. Who did Marcy buy the EPT test for?"

"You don't know her." Hayley's voice was muffled beneath her covers.

"Just give me a name."

"I'm not going to tell on her, Mom. It's her business, not yours."

"Fine. Give me a description of her--short, tall, blonde, brunette, that kind of thing." I was trying to picture the Tigerettes in my head, but I had been to so few ballgames that I wasn't coming up with any specifics. Plus, I was usually focused on my daughter and holding my breath, hoping that she didn't make a mistake or that a boob didn't fall out of her skimpy costume.

"God, Mom! It's none of your *business*."

"Don't use that tone on me, Hayley." I had been telling her that for how many months now? And each time, as I heard my own mother's voice in my head, I cringed. Which should have been enough to stop me from saying it so much. That, and the fact that it didn't do one bit of good.

"Sorry," came out from under the covers, and Hayley yawned loudly.

I turned out the light and went back out to the patio. I had gotten the information I needed, hadn't I? And really, what did I care who the might-be-pregnant girl was? As long as it wasn't my daughter, it was no concern of mine, as my daughter had pointed out.

Audrey gave me a questioning look as I sat back down at the patio table and took a big slug of wine. "It's not Hayley, thank God. But she wouldn't tell me who it was either."

"Maybe it's Felicity?" Audrey said.

"Now there's a happy thought."

"How do you think Cynthia would take the news?"

"Granny Cynthia would not be a happy camper." I grinned at her, and for a moment, I caught a glimpse of the way things used to be between Audrey and me.

But Audrey dropped the ball on that exchange and instead stared into her wine glass. After a minute or two, she said, "I'm getting sick and tired of all the secrets."

I was on guard immediately. She was addressing that barb at me; I could just feel it. Had she found out about the house on Cholla, or did she know that I had secretly sold a bottle of Château Latour Grand Vin de Château Latour Pauillac Red Bordeaux Blend the day after the last wine club party to one of the new women in the club? Believe me when I say that I only planned on doing something like that one time. I needed a little extra cash to cover the new windows in the Cholla house, and that extra $13,500 came in mighty handy. All three of us had made so much money from that wine club party that I honestly didn't think it was a big deal.

Audrey snapped out of her reverie then and gave her throaty chuckle. But it wasn't convincing. "Oh, you know, the Tigerette stuff and Paul's whereabouts for the last two months. It's all so emotionally draining."

So maybe she wasn't addressing the snarky remark to me? But I wasn't sure. I'd have to be careful about what we talked about next. "Have a little more wine, Audrey." I reached for the bottle.

"Oh, Reggie, I can't tonight. I'm beat." Audrey put her hand over the top of her empty glass. "I've got two loads of laundry to fold before I can even think about going to bed."

Maybe it was silly of me, but it dinged my feelings that Audrey was going to put folding her stupid laundry ahead of spending time with me. "If you've gotta go, you've gotta go." I probably sounded peevish when I said that.

"I'll see you tomorrow at Cynthia's." Audrey started toward the fence in the stucco wall that separated our backyards. She turned back, though, as she opened it. "If you do decide to drive by Kent's condo in the light of day, and if you do see Felicity's car parked in front, it might not be a bad idea to check it out."

"I'll think about it," I said coolly and busied myself pouring another glass of wine. When I looked up, Audrey had disappeared.

Goddamnit. Audrey had planted a burr under my skin, just as she had intended. I couldn't stop thinking about what she had said, and it was tearing me up inside. I should have marched up to Kent's doorstep and pounded on the door two months ago, the very first time I saw the girls, and then the boys, go into the condo. Yet I'd slunk down in my seat like a coward. I am not a coward, and maybe if I hadn't run over Reed's stupid cat, things would have turned out differently. Maybe if I hadn't bought the house on Cholla and had more time on my hands, things would have turned out differently. And by *differently*, I mean that the whole sordid scheme of Felicity's would not have been allowed to go so far for so long.

However, I refuse to take all the blame. If anyone should shoulder most of the blame, it is Cynthia. She was the mother of that evil girl, and she should have known what Felicity was capable of. Knowing now what kind of person Cynthia actually is, it wouldn't surprise me a bit if she didn't plant the seed in Felicity's head in the first place. And then there's Audrey, who has always acted like a big, fat chicken, too scared of her own shadow to take the initiative in any matter. And then there's Kent, who should have had the presence of mind to find out what unsupervised teenagers were doing in his condo. And then there's Paul, who is absolutely oblivious to *everything*. And then there's me, who let a dinky restraining order get in the way of my better judgment. What a sorry group of parents we all turned out to be.

But even though I strongly suspected that I had made a mistake by not getting to the bottom of the mysterious after school activities going on in Kent's condo back in February, I didn't resume my spying right away. Why? Because Audrey had asked me to do it. That's the reason. She wanted answers, but she didn't want to put herself in any compromising position to get them. No, she wanted me to be the fall guy, the one who took all the risks. She wanted me to be the one who looked like an idiot if all our suspicions were unfounded. It was a lot to ask a friend to do, although I suppose we weren't really friends by that stage of the game, at least to Audrey's way of thinking. I just didn't know it yet.

Audrey tried to bring up the subject once or twice during those last two busy weeks of April, but I brushed her off, saying something like: "Who has time to do anything else but get ready for the champagne party? Do you know how hard it is to find magnum champagne bottles in this town, Audrey? Do you?"

She backed off immediately. I think that she knew that she wasn't pulling her weight to get ready for this party. She was always leaving work early from Cynthia's, saying that she had to pick up Jimmy, or she had to take Paul to a counseling session or a job interview. Once, she even had the nerve to say that she was leaving early to take Paul to a golf outing with his friends. I know she saw me roll my eyes at that one because she quickly embellished the story with: "The golf course is a great place for Paul to network."

Give me a break. The man didn't have any skills to network *with*. All her loser husband wanted was to play a round of golf, and very possibly, sneak a couple of beers at the halfway house. Yet Audrey was oblivious to what was going on right in front of her nose, and once again, she was letting Paul walk all over her. It was sickening to watch, just sickening.

I can't say that Cynthia was much better during those weeks. Back in March when Audrey abandoned me, and Cynthia and I were forced to work together to bottle the wine, Cynthia had been fast and efficient. I'd almost come to respect her a little. I should have known better. This time around, Cynthia seemed distracted and jittery, and her eyes looked swollen and dazed. What was worse was that she kept dropping those hard-to-find magnum bottles. And boy, did I resent the hell out of that. I'd had to drive all over town to find them, and now I was going to have to go out and repeat the process. That is, I had to go running from liquor store to liquor store after the three of us cleaned up all the glass, and let me tell you, those large bottles created a lot of shards when they smashed against a travertine floor.

I got so fed up at one point that I asked her, "Are you on drugs, Cynthia--valium, oxy, Vicodin?"

She stared at me with a wild look in her eye. "No." She swept up some shards of glass. "Why? Do you have some?" I swear, she sounded almost hopeful.

I think it's safe to say that none of the three partners were in great shape for that party, and by the time the April date finally arrived, I didn't care if I ever saw another champagne bottle in my life. To make matters worse, Cynthia enlisted Audrey's and my help in decorating for that party. She had us hanging lights and polishing champagne flutes and ironing tablecloths. Well, okay, Audrey did the actual ironing, but I was the one who was lugging the crates of champagne to our different tasting areas. I kept waiting for Louisa to show up and help, but that didn't happen, and when I asked Cynthia why Louisa wasn't there, she almost bit my head off. "Louisa is not your concern, Reggie!" she shouted at me. I responded to that by *accidentally* dropping a tray of canapés.

Yes, you might say that we were acting childish by that point in time. You might say it, but I wish you wouldn't.

There were almost one hundred guests at that party. I assumed that they were all still acquaintances of Cynthia's, but that turned out not to be the case. The parties were becoming so popular through word of mouth, Cynthia said, and when a woman called her up and asked for an invitation, Cynthia complied. But I think that at this particular party we had women who had been driving by and decided to stop by to see what was going on. I guess what I'm trying to say is that it was not the well-heeled group that the original parties had attracted. I actually thought some of the younger women were dressed like hookers, and I distinctly heard one young blonde woman, dressed in an obscenely short, obscenely tight red spandex dress, say to her equally blonde friend that once they got a little tipsy here, they should bail this boring party and head out to the clubs in Old Town.

I wouldn't have cared how the women dressed if they were buying our champagne. Most of them were not. Naturally, I was trying to push the Armand de Brignac Brut Gold Champagne at $17,000 a bottle, but I was met mostly with incredulous stares. One woman, who already seemed to be a little drunk, elbowed her friend and said, "That's just *insane*. Isn't it insane, Jenny?" Jenny agreed that it was indeed insane.

I overheard other negative comments too, and it was making me uneasy. These women were the loudest, most obnoxious group yet, and they didn't seem happy with the four varietals of champagne that we were offering. Yet they continued to drink it, a lot of it, even as they dismissed it as inferior. I decided that something needed to be done and rounded up Audrey and Cynthia. We conferred in a corner of the kitchen. "We need to do something. This is not going well."

"Who are these people?" Audrey asked, the worried crease prominent between her green eyes. "We can't keep giving them free champagne."

That's when Cynthia admitted the truth. "I don't know who they are."

"Great," I said disgustedly. "It's confirmed. We have a bunch of free-loaders at this party."

For once, Audrey had a reasonable suggestion. "Why don't we offer the champagne at half price? It might hurry things along. And we're out of canapés." She looked at me then, as if it was my fault that I *accidentally* dropped that tray before the party started.

"I don't have any more food," Cynthia said. "Haven't these women ever heard of *dieting*?" She saw something over my shoulder then and gasped. "These women are roaming all over my house! What if they steal something? What if they--"

Cynthia pushed me aside and tried to yell over the deafening crowd. "Those rooms are off-limits! No one goes upstairs, and no one goes down-stairs! Everyone needs to stay in this area!" Cynthia frantically tried to corral the errant women, but she was about as effective as a gnat on a herd of oxen.

Audrey pulled out her phone. "Maybe we should call the cops?"

"Audrey, what are we going to tell them--that these women have crashed our fake wine party?" I heard the smashing of glass then and looked over to see that one woman had pushed another into the display of Dom Pérignon Oenotheque Rose Champagne Magnums. A few of the bottles exploded on impact with the floor, and champagne arced through the air, fizzing.

The woman who had been pushed into the Dom Pérignon display came up fighting, and it was only a matter of time before we had a free-for-all on our hands. Elsewhere in that large, crowded room, I heard glasses shatter-ing. I took a quick look out the open Nano doors and saw that three or four women had jumped fully clothed into the pool. I had never seen anything like it. "Where did these women come from, the nearest trailer park?"

"I'm thinking they escaped from Estrella Women's Jail," Audrey said. "We need to stop them."

I'll be honest with you. If these women totally trashed Cynthia's house, it was no skin off my nose. Since she was the one in charge of the guest lists for the parties, the debacle of this one was her fault because, in her greed, she had forgotten that these parties were supposed to be exclusively for women who could afford our fake French wine. However, I knew that Cynthia was going to take any damages out of the wine club earnings, which at this rate could drain any profits. It's what I would do if it were my house getting trashed, so unfortunately, I couldn't hold that against her.

I jumped onto the kitchen island and started to yell. I have been told that I have an extremely loud voice--some have even said that it is grating--but you better believe that it came in handy in that situation. "Everyone out now! We've called the cops, and they're on their way!" That was an idle threat, but they didn't know it.

Then I couldn't help but add, mostly for my wicked pleasure, "If you are in violation of your parole, ladies, you best consider a hasty departure."

I looked over at Audrey and had the pleasure of seeing her laugh. I hadn't seen that in way too long. It spurred me on, and I'm not sure exactly what else I started to yell--I wouldn't be surprised if it was pretty raunchy stuff; I was on a roll--but ten minutes later the house was cleared out.

The strange women were gone, but the debris remained. I didn't think the Ice Queen could cry because I had never seen her do so, but Cynthia looked close to it now. "This was a disaster."

"I don't think we profited from the champagne," I said, surveying the mess.

Audrey, to her credit, didn't say *I told you so.* "We sold a few bottles of the cheapest stuff, but I don't think it's going to cover our costs."

"That's all?" It wasn't like I was surprised. It was more like the disappointment hit home right then. In my mind, I had already spent my money on landscaping and walnut floors and a new sump pump. Unfortunately, I had put down sizable down payments on all those things. We had to wait an entire month for a new party, and I was already overextended. What was I going to do?

Cynthia picked up a shard of glass from the floor. "My house is in shambles."

"We'll help you clean up," Audrey offered.

I groaned inwardly. Why was Audrey always offering to do that? I mean, come on, it was Cynthia's fault those women were at the party, and

I didn't think it was necessary for me to clean up her mess. But I didn't want to look like a total ogre in front of the other two, so I got out the broom from the pantry. It was a sad fact that I knew exactly where it was located after having used it too many times in the last two weeks. I went to work, moving as quickly as I could, hurrying the other two along. All I wanted to do was go home and pour myself a glass of wine. I didn't care if it was red or white, a cheap bottle or an expensive one.

All I cared about was that it wasn't champagne.

MAY

25

CYNTHIA

"Where's my daughter?"

Those were the first words my lying, thieving husband said to me after a five-month absence. *Where's my daughter?* Not "I've come back for you," or "I'm sorry to have made such a mess of things." Nope. *Where's my daughter?* I guess that tells you right there where Richard's priorities were. He had not returned for me, as I had fantasized about for months. He had not sent a private jet to whisk me away to Switzerland or Argentina. In all probability, he'd never given me a second thought once he walked out our door back in November. But he had come back for his daughter. She had always been the one he truly loved.

I wasn't all that surprised. Richard and Felicity had always been thick as thieves--that pun is intended--and seemed to have an understanding between them that I could never quite grasp. But what about *me?* Had I been nothing more than an accessory to Richard, and when he grew tired of me, he discarded me like an outdated Gucci handbag? The nerve of him! I had stood loyally by my husband for years. I might not have been as loyal as some wives, and I suppose I shouldn't have slept with the pool guy once or twice, or that homely man who came to install our state-of-the-art sound system. But if you looked at the big picture, I was more loyal than unfaithful, damn it. It seemed to me that should count for something.

The kitchen knife clattered to the tiled floor of the wine cellar, and I stood gaping at the man. I don't know how I immediately recognized him because he didn't look at all like the tall, broad-shouldered man in a custom Armani suit who had left five months before. Richard's silver hair had grown past his shoulders, and his normally clean-shaven face was covered in a scraggly beard that was more gray than silver. It was odd. Richard had always been so vain about his chiseled jaw and fastidious in his grooming. Now his shoulders looked stooped, and he was wearing baggy pants and a flannel shirt that the old Richard wouldn't have been caught dead in. As he stood before me now, he looked every bit of his seventy years.

My first words to him were, "Where the hell have you been?"

"Where haven't I been?" he said cryptically.

"Why . . . why are you here?" I stammered.

"I missed my daughter."

"And what about me?" I couldn't take my eyes off his face. The light was dim in the wine cellar, but I could still see that his eyes looked worn, bloodshot.

Richard sighed. "I knew you could take care of yourself, Cynthia. You're a survivor."

Was I supposed to be flattered by those words? I wasn't. "You really fucked up, Richard. And you left me holding the bag."

"Come on, Cynthia. You knew exactly what I was doing. You knew very well where all the money was coming from, and you didn't seem to mind spending it."

I took a step backward, feeling as if the air had been squeezed out of my lungs. Was Richard going to try to implicate me in his Ponzi scheme? Was he too much of a coward to take the full brunt of the blame? "I don't know what you're talking about!"

"You signed documents too, so don't play coy. It does not suit you."

It was true that Richard would stick documents under my nose from time to time and tell me to sign them. I was sure that he had told me they were for our lawyer. "I might have signed some papers, but I didn't read them."

"You should always read a document before you sign it, Cynthia. Didn't I at least teach you that much?"

"You are such a piece of shit, Richard." My teeth had started to chatter, but it wasn't cold in the wine cellar.

"You wouldn't have thought so if I hadn't gotten caught."

Unfortunately, that had a ring of truth to it. So I ignored it. "How did you get back into the country?"

"I never left the country."

"I . . I don't understand." Again I was stammering. It was like my mind could not keep up with the words Richard was speaking.

"There's such a thing as hiding in plain sight."

I looked at Richard closely in the dim light, his scraggly beard and mismatched clothing. Was he saying what I thought he was saying? "Have you been hiding out in a homeless shelter, Richard?"

"It's better if you don't know, Cynthia."

Richard had always been maddeningly evasive, but he couldn't just disappear, leaving his family in financial ruin, and then show up unannounced and not expect to answer any questions. I had so many. I chose the one that had been burning foremost in my mind. "Did you ever love me?"

I could see Richard's smile in the half-light. "When I met you, Cynthia, I thought you were the most beautiful, sexiest woman I had ever met."

That didn't exactly answer my question, but Richard knew me too well. I have always been a sucker for compliments, especially as they pertain to my beauty. But I wasn't going to let that deter me. "Then why--"

"And I still do."

He was cunningly sly. I had to give him that. It was part of the reason he had been such a successful businessman. I mean, a successful *thief* for so long. "You gave me a fake diamond on our wedding day."

"True," he said, nodding. "The cost of insuring a real diamond of that size would have been exorbitant."

"So," I said slowly, "you gave me a fake diamond because of *insurance* reasons?" I couldn't decide if that was even more insulting than the phony rock.

"Do you think that's the real issue here, Cynthia?"

I absolutely hated it when Richard adopted his superior tone. "No," I snapped. "The real issue is that you stole millions of dollars, disappeared off the face of the earth for five months, and now you're back. Which seems to be a stupid move on your part. You are a fugitive, Richard. Don't you know that the feds have been watching the house since you left?"

"The feds think I'm in Lucerne."

"Why do they think that?"

"It's better if you don't know, Cynthia."

"I don't think I know anything at this point. And I'm beginning to wonder if I ever knew you at all." Richard was rattling me. He knew all the right buttons to push.

"Where's Felicity?"

"Your daughter doesn't want anything to do with you," I lied. It's what I do when I feel trapped. I lie.

"She knew that I was coming sometime this week."

I'd known there was a definite possibility that Richard and Felicity were communicating, but the truth hit me like a sucker punch to the gut. I had always been the odd man out when it came to those two. I always would be. "Why didn't you ever try to get in contact with me? Were you willing to risk it for your daughter but not your wife?"

Richard had always been prone to only answering the questions he chose to answer. He gestured at the empty shelves in the wine cellar. "Where did all my wine go?"

"I drank it." Unbelievably, I felt a stab of guilt.

"What about the Château Lafite Rothschild?"

"It was delicious."

"Is that why you're down here at eight o'clock in the evening, searching for another bottle of my wine?"

"Oh." I looked around at the empty shelves. It occurred to me then that Richard might think it odd that I was down here, rather than up watching TV or in my bedroom. And at the sight of Richard, I had completely forgotten my mission for the evening. I had a drugged-out man in the panic room just a few feet away, and at that moment, I thought I heard a faint moan. My heart seized up in my chest.

"I always knew the panic room would come in handy," Richard said then.

The panic room? Again my heart seized. "Is that why you're here, to hide out in the panic room?"

"Hiding in plain sight. It's an art I've perfected."

"How long are you planning to stay?" I glanced nervously over my shoulder. I needed to stall Richard.

"Felicity graduates soon, and I am going to attend. Undercover, of course. She's my only daughter, Cynthia."

"And then? What happens after Felicity graduates?" My mind was whirring, and I knew I heard a low moan from Buck. Was it possible that the last syringe of heroin was wearing off? How was I going to get him out to the desert if Richard was in my house? The fact of the matter was that I couldn't. For that evening, I was going to have to abort my mission to get rid of Buck once and for all. And I was going to have to get the door sealed again before Buck gave everything away. I was also going to have to get Richard out of the basement and as far away as possible from the panic room. Maybe I could offer him a glass of wine? I had one of the fake Château Lafite bottles from the March wine party upstairs. I could hope that Richard's sensitive wine palate wasn't as refined as it used to be.

"New York."

I was so preoccupied with Buck in the next room that I thought I hadn't heard Richard correctly. "New York?"

"Felicity wants to study fashion design at the Pratt Institute. I'm going to make sure that it happens."

Can you imagine how shocked I was to hear that? I didn't know that my daughter was interested in anything other than the Tigerettes and asserting her dominance over people. Once again she had been scheming behind my back, but this time it was with her father. He was willing to take her away and fulfill her dreams, leaving me in the dust. Never mind that I had been planning on running away myself. That didn't even figure into my outrage. I don't think I had ever been as mad as I was right then.

"And how are you going to accomplish that? She's a spoiled brat, and you're a fucking fugitive! Also, we don't have any money for an expensive school like that!" I was yelling, and for just the tiniest of moments, I thought about picking up the knife from the floor and running it straight through Richard's darkly corrupted heart.

"I have my resources."

"I bet you do!" I shrieked. "You probably have all kinds of secret bank accounts, and you two will live in style while I'm left homeless and broke!"

"You've always been overly interested in creature comforts." Richard's superior tone was maddeningly calm.

It was just too much. Richard was the one who had wanted this massive house, filled at one time with all the best art and carpets and furniture that money could buy. It hadn't been me. Sure, I liked to be surrounded by nice things, but I also knew what it was like to struggle for a living and to suffer for your dreams. I was not a prima donna by any stretch of the imagination. Richard and Felicity were the divas, *not me.*

I was perspiring with anger, my makeup ruined, and I was panting. "If you take Felicity to New York, I'm going to call the FBI."

"Do you think it's in your best interest to have the FBI know of your involvement in our investments?"

I could see how it had been Richard's plan all along, this trump card of his. I didn't know anything about his crooked dealings, and he knew it. But would the FBI see it that way, or had Richard somehow always planned to frame me? Maybe he'd juggled the books even more than I thought, or maybe he had forged my signature on documents that I hadn't seen. But this was the gist of the situation: Yet another man was attempting to blackmail me. I stared at him in abject fury.

"So my plan is this, Cynthia. I'm going to lay low in the panic room until Felicity graduates. You can pretend like I'm not even here if that is your preference."

"My preference is that you rot in jail. Or hell," I said through gritted teeth. I turned my head at the sound. The moan was unmistakable this time.

"What's that noise?" Richard made a move toward the panic room.

"You don't want to go in there."

"Do you have an animal in there?"

"The panic room is off-limits for the time being."

Richard ignored me, and he should not have done that. It would be the last time. The sound was growing louder. "Who or what is in that room?" He brushed by me and stepped into the darkened space.

Would you believe me if I told you that I tried to stop him from entering the panic room, that I tried to block the opening with my body? I guess it doesn't matter now, does it? Richard was in the room with Buck, and I was outside the door, right by the secret button that sealed the room. My survival instinct took over.

I pressed the button.

You don't have to tell me. After I pressed that secret button, I was in one doozy of a situation. Now I didn't have one man held captive in the panic room; I had *two*. I would imagine that Richard was not too worried at first, though. He'd designed the hidden room for safety, not captivity, and of course, he knew where the other secret button was, the one on the inside of the room, the one designed to let the owner of the house out once the coast was clear and danger had passed, the one hidden in the floor in the northwest corner behind the toilet. The smug man probably thought he had all the time in the world to figure out why there was a strange drugged-out man already occupying the couch. In his bogus benevolence, Richard probably thought he could actually help the poor soul, maybe offer him a sip of water or a saltine. Then he would calmly saunter over to the toilet, unscrew that small tile on the floor, press the button, and *voilà*. He had heroically saved them both from the evil clutches of the she-devil.

Or maybe Richard imagined it this way. He had decided that his plan of action was to "hide in plain sight" in his own home, but he hadn't taken into account that he might get lonely in the solitude of the panic room. But now he magically had company. Richard would be thinking that it might be nice to have someone to talk to, to share a can of Chef Boyardee with while they played Mah Jongg. Maybe they would play poker or gin rummy or double solitaire to pass the time. But the real entertainment would happen when they turned on the elaborate camera system inside the room, the camera that was programmed to view every single room of the house. Together, as they kept track of my comings and goings, my long baths and TV dinners, they would conclude that I was quite entertaining. They might decide that I was much more fascinating to watch than Jerry Springer or the Kardashians. Life in Richard's panic room would be very sweet indeed.

And really, Richard wouldn't be worried about a thing because, you see, there was also a special phone down in the panic room. It would be more accurate to call it a two-way radio. To be even more precise, it was a professional DMR digital handheld radio. Without a doubt, Richard had thought of everything when he designed that room, including the possibility that there would be no cell phone service, or that a thief would cut wires, or that there might be some other man-made emergency or natural disaster. Yes, indeed, Richard was a meticulous planner, or perhaps he preferred to think of himself as more of a visionary. He would never consider himself a control freak, but if the shoe fits, right? Anyway, the point is that Richard had prepared. That room was ready if he ever needed to take up temporary residence. He even had a timing mechanism that would automatically open that sealed door after a set amount of time, say, two or three days. So nothing would hinder his escape from the room when he decided it was time to leave. Nothing.

But poor, poor Richard. He didn't take *me* into consideration. I would call that a huge mistake on his part, wouldn't you?

Disabling the button that opened the door from the inside, the timer mechanism, and the camera system were the easy parts. I did that as soon as Buck was safely ensconced in there. Okay, maybe the entire disabling action wasn't all that easy. Since I couldn't call the company that had installed the system because I didn't want to raise any suspicions, it was up to me. I pored over the instruction manual that came with the system for a couple of hours before I figured it out. However, I didn't dare go down there and get the two-way radio. If you will remember, Buck did not take kindly to being locked up. He ranted and raved and was an all-around complete asshole. I worried about that radio constantly, but Richard had designed a secret place in the wall for it--is it becoming clear that Richard liked secrets?--and I could only hope that Buck wasn't bright enough to find it. He wasn't. So when I had him drugged for the first time and went down to restock the panic room, I was able to get it. All problems solved.

And now that Richard had taken up residence down there, the two men who had dared to blackmail me were taken care of, right? Out of sight, out of mind, and all that jazz. End of story, case closed. I wish. I had a guy who was about to go through one hell of a heroin withdrawal, and a fugitive from the law who was about a million times smarter than Buck Boyd would ever be. When Buck became coherent--if he ever became coherent--he would spill his guts to Richard about my fabled past in Vegas, and Richard, no doubt, would give him an earful of my so-called wrongdoings since then. It had always hurt my feelings when people talked about me in unflattering terms. But so be it. There was nothing I could do about it now. Since Buck hadn't eaten in weeks, there was still plenty of food and water down there. They could entertain themselves with stories of how rotten I was for the next two weeks or so. I could only hope that when they figured a way out of there--and I had a sinking feeling that Richard would--I would be long gone.

The April wine club party dashed all hope for an immediate escape from the hell I had found myself in. I know people have accused me of orchestrating, creating, or masterminding that hell, but trust me, they are flat-out wrong. I was provoked into taking matters into my own hands by both of those men. If either one of them had treated me with one ounce of respect, things might have turned out differently. But they didn't. So they got what they deserved. All's fair in love and war. And you know very well that I am not making up that saying. I think someone famous said it once.

As you know, the champagne wine club was a fiasco. Serving expensive French champagne was a brilliant idea, if I do say so myself, but news of the party got into the hands of the wrong class of people. It was not my fault that happened. I kept getting phone calls from people who said they knew so and so, who had told them about these brilliant wine club parties. Even if I hadn't exactly heard of the woman who supposedly referred them to the party, the women seeking an invitation all sounded quite sincere. And of course, once the women started to show up at the party, I couldn't rescind the invitations. It was too late, and most of the women who showed up were skanks. Believe me, I know what a skank is, and those women fit the definition to a T. I had to wonder if some of them had flown down from Vegas to crash the party. I'm not kidding; it was that bad.

They practically destroyed my house, and the cost of getting the stains out of the furniture and the rugs and replacing the broken glasses and dishware ate away the entire profit from that party--and then some. Louisa grumbled so much about the mess that I had to hire a professional cleaning service to come in and get the job done. It goes without saying that I used the FHM account to cover the rest of the expenses. All of the destruction was bad enough, but then some of those women had the nerve to start wandering around my house. I caught three or four of them trying to head downstairs to check out the wine cellar to find a better wine to drink. That was laughable because those women wouldn't know the difference between a glass of piss and a nice glass of Cristal. But I wasn't laughing. Right next to the wine cellar was the panic room, and I think we all know what I didn't want them to find in there. Granted, the chance of discovery was slim, but you just never knew.

Audrey, and especially Reggie, acted like the whole thing was funny. They didn't seem disturbed at all that strangers were vandalizing my personal property. Reggie jumped up on the kitchen island and was laughing and yelling out these raunchy comments. She was egging the drunk skanks on, and believe me when I tell you that those women didn't need much egging. I was so mad and disappointed when my so-called partners finally left that I seriously considered dropping out of the wine club altogether. I now knew the entire operation inside and out, and if I could enlist Louisa and her nieces to help with the day to day grunge work, I knew for a fact that we could get the job done better and more professionally than Audrey and Reggie ever could. Audrey was too slow, and Reggie was too sloppy. Okay, maybe I wasn't that serious about quitting the wine club because I now needed money more than ever. Between all my household expenses and the leaching Sanchez family and the heroin habit I was fostering, I was pretty much broke. Again.

I was going to have to participate in another wine club party, and it was going to have to be the most lucrative of all. I would see to it.

Richard did tell the truth about one thing. Felicity was definitely expecting him. Richard took up residence in the panic room during the last week of April, and as the first week of May came to a close, Felicity began to find excuses to stick around the house more. Felicity, who usually seemed so jaded and bored about everything, suddenly had an air of excited anticipation about her. Her blue eyes shone, and she brushed that blonde ponytail of hers until it gleamed. She would sit at the kitchen island after she got home from Tigerette practice, doing her homework, she said, but she kept looking to the front door. Every time she heard a car pull into the circular driveway, she was out of her seat and throwing open the door, only to be disappointed at the sight of the landscaper's truck or an Amazon delivery. It was pathetic, in a way. Did she actually think that her father was going to drive up and then walk through the front door in broad daylight? Did she not realize how big of a crook he was? If I didn't know her so well, I would have almost felt sorry for her.

But I did know her, and I didn't feel sorry for her. Graduation was less than two weeks away, and she planned to run away to New York with her daddy, who she still seemed to view as some kind of knight in shining armor. She wasn't planning on giving a thought to me; she would never look back. I know, I know. I have mentioned on more than one occasion that I couldn't wait until my daughter was gone. That's very true. But it's only because she had been shutting me out for so long. A perfect example was her secret plan to go to Pratt and study fashion design. Why wouldn't she tell me something like that? Wouldn't I be the perfect person to help her with that career choice? I have always been known for my fashion sense;

you can ask anybody. But did my daughter even consider coming to me for advice or tips? No, she did not. Fashion was one thing I was exceedingly good at, yet my daughter did not even acknowledge that obvious truth.

I held my tongue for as long as I could, but one day after she must have run to the front door at least four times, I said to her, "Are you expecting someone?"

She wiped the disappointed look off her face in an instant and shrugged. "Not really."

"So," I said conversationally, settling myself on another barstool, "graduation is just around the corner, and I don't know anything about your plans." It was legitimately happy hour, 5:30, so I was drinking a glass of wine. "You haven't mentioned any colleges you're interested in lately."

"I'm still trying to make up my mind. I'll probably end up going to U of A. A lot of the kids in my class are going there."

"That's a good choice." I didn't know whether it was or not. I didn't know anything about how one went about applying to colleges, not having bothered with it myself. "I wouldn't know, though," I added. "I went straight to work."

"Right." Felicity looked up from her book. I hadn't seen her turn a single page during the hour she'd been sitting there. "You were a dancer."

She gave a sarcastic emphasis on *dancer,* but I ignored it. "And a personal stylist, remember? I've always been interested in fashion. You know that." Was I goading her? You better believe it. It might have been my second or third glass of chardonnay, or else I would have known better.

Felicity cocked her head to one side, appraising. "Are you getting at something, Mom?"

Why did I always ignore how smart she was--conniving smart, like Richard? I took a sip of wine. "Of course not, honey. I'm just interested in what you're up to." I took another sip of wine. It might have been my fourth glass. It was one of those days that worry--and yes, guilt--had me all tied up in knots, so I wasn't as focused as I could have been. Which explains what came out of my mouth next: "You're not still making movies of those girls, are you?"

Her eyes narrowed. "No. Are you still holding a man prisoner in the panic room?"

I narrowed my eyes back at her. "No." I didn't know whether or not she was lying, but I was not. I was holding *two* men prisoner in the panic room, not one.

We heard a car pull up outside, and Felicity couldn't help herself. She walked quickly to the front door, a smile on her face. When she opened it, a middle-aged man handed her a package. That one was probably the knock-off Gucci belt I had ordered. The nights were so long and unbearably lonely that I had turned to Amazon for company. I was probably somewhat addicted to shopping there. Amazon always had something to offer that could cheer me up.

Felicity didn't even try to hide her disappointment as she walked back to the kitchen and handed me the brown package. She blinked rapidly, and with a start, I realized she was holding back tears. I hadn't seen the girl cry in years, and she was trying so hard not to now, that I, unbelievably, felt a rush of true pity for her. She was waiting for a man who would never come, and she didn't even know it. Maybe, just maybe, I owed it to her to do something nice, and the idea popped into my head immediately.

"For your graduation present, why don't I send you back to that spa in Tucson? You had such a good time there, and this time you can relax. You won't be recovering from a boob job so you could get facials and massages. And maybe you could take an Uber over to U of A to check it out."

I felt a rush of exhilaration. This sudden idea of mine was truly inspired. If I could convince Felicity to leave immediately after graduation, I could get Richard and Buck out of the house, permanently. Richard would have been in the panic room for about a month by then, and with all the food down there, he should still be in pretty good shape. Buck would have been down there for . . . Well, over three months. Maybe it would be closer to four? Whatever. I wasn't particularly worried. In my ideal fantasy world, Richard would have nursed him back to health, and they would just be happy to be free. They would just be happy to be alive. So happy, in fact, that all would be forgiven.

I know what you must be thinking: I must have drunk a lot of wine that afternoon. Unfortunately, I cannot dispute that claim.

"I'll think about it." Felicity returned to her history book. She twirled nervously at her ponytail as she kept glancing at the door.

"You do that, honey. But trust me on this. It's a good idea. Graduating from high school is a big accomplishment, and you deserve to be rewarded."

Granted, Felicity didn't sound overly enthused, but I had confidence in my ability to persuade her. Once she realized that Richard was not coming to get her, she didn't have many options, at least not ones that I knew about. I know that's not saying a lot. I obviously didn't know much of anything about my daughter, other than she was a first-class mean girl.

I went upstairs after that, and I cannot tell you how exuberant I felt right then. Finally, after months of waiting, inspiration had struck. I now had a plan. I would call the spa in Tucson and book a one-week stay for my daughter. Then I would arrange for a car to pick her up immediately after the graduation party that was being held in the school gym. I thought the party was supposed to go to midnight, but I didn't fret about that detail. Meanwhile, I'd persuade Audrey and Reggie to move up the wine party to three days after graduation. I'd have money then, and by the time Felicity got back, if she ever came back, I would be gone.

Hold your horses. I'm getting to that part. I, of course, had a plan in mind for Richard and Buck. I am not completely heartless, you know. I had finally come to the conclusion that I couldn't enlist the help of Pepe and Angel anymore. They'd come sniffing around once or twice, asking if I needed their help, but I had graciously declined and gotten rid of them as soon as possible. I now felt like there was something sinister about those two. They had shifty eyes and always smelled of beer and seemed overly anxious to get back inside the house. I couldn't figure out what it was that they wanted. I mean, I had asked them to kill a man, and they had declined. I was still paying them, and they weren't doing one damn thing for me. I couldn't trust them anymore, and they were beginning to scare me. They were another reason I needed to leave. And Louisa too. She was getting surlier and grumpier by the day.

So I had come up with another plan for Richard and Buck. It was brilliant--if I do say so myself. And it was humane. It was so obvious that I was kicking myself for not coming up with it earlier. I was going to have to somehow re-enable the timing device on the security system in the panic room in such a way that the door would slide open four days after my departure. The men would be sitting in the room when suddenly, magically, the door silently disappeared into the wall, and they would be free, just like that. The house would be empty, or maybe Felicity would be home by then, but the point is that I would be long gone. I was the one who was finally wonderfully free. *Brilliant.*

I went upstairs then, and for the first time since I had entombed Richard in the panic room, I felt the need to turn on the monitor in his old study and see for myself what those two men were up to. I knew it wasn't going to be pretty. Without his daily heroin fix, Buck would be wretched, sweaty, and I could picture vomit stains on his shirt, on the floor. Richard would be equally unkempt, and he hadn't looked so hot when he went in there. His scraggly beard would be longer, as would Buck's, and Richard would have torn the place apart, looking for the two-way radio or some other communication tool. Perhaps he would be trying to fashion some kind of weapon, just like prison inmates did, something ingenious made out of the plastic tubing from the shelves or the sharp lid of some can. Richard might not have been the genius I had thought he was for so long, but he certainly was *ingenious.*

It was going to be very hard to watch those two men down in that room. It's not like I wanted to see them suffer--well, maybe a small part of me did--but I was curious more than anything. Now that I had a solid plan, I could take it. I opened the panel to reveal the monitor and turned on the knob that brought the room into focus. I was holding my breath as I did that, curious, yet filled with trepidation, but nothing happened, no picture emerged onto the screen. I'd had quite a bit of wine, so I thought I must have turned the wrong knob. I tried others, but the screen remained dark. I stared at it for a long time before I let the realization fully sink in: The camera wasn't working, and someone had turned it off.

My first thought was that Felicity had been up here messing around, but I had to discard that immediately. I didn't think she even knew this monitor existed. Otherwise, she would have seen her father and let him out two weeks ago. Then I thought of Reggie, who knew where this monitor was because she had stumbled upon it, and then I had to prove to her that no one appeared to be in the panic room anymore by bringing her back up here. But I hadn't let her out of my sight any of the times she had been over since, so she was out as a suspect. Louisa? That was a possibility, especially if she thought it was a hidden TV and she had a sudden urge to watch her Spanish soaps, but Louisa, thanks to Pepe and Angel, probably already knew there was a man imprisoned down there and had done nothing about it--except extort more money from me.

That left only one person, the one I didn't want to acknowledge. Richard. He must have figured out a way to turn it off from inside the panic room, or he had always known that a way existed. The possibility of deprogramming the camera from the inside was something I had missed, something I hadn't thought to do in the hours it took me to disable the functions that I could. The implications of this made the bile rise in my throat. It tasted like sour wine, and I gagged. Richard had turned off that camera so I would have no idea what they were up to down there. Richard had designed every aspect of that room, and he would know every intricacy of the system, every trick in the book. The room, after all, was designed to protect the people in it, not to hold them captive. There were probably secret backup plans in case of electrical malfunctions or power outages. Maybe there was a secret tunnel?

Maybe they weren't in the room at all.

I stumbled down the stairs and made my way to the kitchen. I wasn't sure what I was going to do next. My mind was fuzzy with shock and fear. Should I go downstairs and check the room? Should I tell Felicity the truth? Should I get in my car and drive?

Felicity was still sitting at the island. She took one look at my face and said, "God, Mom, what's the matter?"

I shook my head. I couldn't speak.

For once, Felicity took pity and brought me a glass of water. "Drink this, Mom. Tell me what's going on."

I drank the glass thirstily. I would tell her everything. "Felicity--"

The doorbell rang then, and Felicity was still young and naive enough to look hopeful. "I'll get it."

I recognized the two agents Felicity brought back to the kitchen. They had been over several times. But why were they here now? They looked like they meant business, but the man and woman in their dark, nondescript suits always looked like that. Had someone called them with new information? I looked at Felicity, stricken, my face a question.

Felicity understood and shook her head *no*. She raised her perfectly arched brows at me, asking the same question.

I shook my head *no*.

Felicity also knew who they were. "The FBI is making its weekly courtesy call," she said, stone-faced. She sounded just like Richard.

26

AUDREY

Watching my daughter pee on that pregnancy test stick was one of the worst moments of my life, and lately, I'd had quite a few. But I believe that one took first prize. I felt like a monster as I watched my sobbing daughter cower over the toilet seat. She was mortified. I was mortified but still convinced myself that it was necessary. I didn't believe her when she said she bought the pregnancy test for someone else. By that point in time, I no longer believed anything anyone told me. You see, I had surrounded myself with liars. I had become a liar too, so much so that I wouldn't know the truth if it slapped me in the face. So I made my daughter humiliate herself in front of me while I watched with cold detachment. It was now officially true: I had become a monster.

Also, I was a hypocrite. I had lost my virginity at fifteen to a senior at my high school. It was because of a dare. Don't get me wrong. I was not the one who was being dared; he was. I barely knew the boy, other than from passing him in the hallway between classes, but that didn't stop me from saying *yes* when he asked if I wanted to go to the movies with him on Friday night. And it didn't stop me that I knew it was a dare. Some of his buddies had dared him to bag a freshman before he graduated. I guess you could say that I was the perfect candidate. Everyone knew that I would make out with almost anybody, and I advertised my full chest shamelessly with low-cut, tight tops. I knew all that, yet I still went. I was curious, more than anything else. I wanted to see what all the fuss was about.

We went to the drive-in on Hayden and McKellips. I don't remember what was playing, other than it was some horror movie, because I was only pretending to watch the big screen. I wasn't nervous, but I didn't have to be. His nervousness made up for both of us, and I began to suspect that he was also a virgin. He couldn't stop fidgeting and kept glancing in his rearview mirror, which made me wonder if someone was supposed to watch--or witness--the conquest. About halfway through the movie, he made his move. He kissed me, and his tongue tasted like Juicy Fruit gum. I appreciated that. It seemed like a thoughtful gesture.

He must have borrowed his parents' car for the occasion. It was a big sedan of some kind, and the passenger seat reclined flat. He was quite tall, though, and couldn't seem to maneuver himself over me properly. He kept shifting his weight, and his knees bumped the floor. He started to sweat. His armpit was in my face, and it smelled funky, which only contributed to the awkwardness. When he suggested that we move to the back seat, I didn't object. I wanted him to look at me when he took my virginity.

But he didn't look at my face. After we hurriedly removed the necessary clothing, he gave scant attention to my lips or breasts and went straight for his target. His eyes were closed as soon as he entered me, and they remained closed. The whole thing took about two minutes, and it hurt. I had been expecting that. Everything I had read said that happened the first time, but I hadn't expected how bad the pain would be. I bled, and the boy handed me a wad of tissues, asking me not to get any blood on the seat. His parents would kill him, he said. I did the best that I could and stuffed another wad of tissues in my panties. We climbed back in the front seat and left immediately. He didn't try to kiss me goodnight.

Honestly, I don't even remember his name.

I had just turned fifteen years old when I lost my virginity so a boy could win a dare. Yet I was appalled that my daughter, who had just turned sixteen, might be sexually active, might even be pregnant. I can't count how many pregnancy scares I had in high school, or the number of pregnancy tests I bought. But still, the monster in me forced my daughter to humiliate herself to prove her innocence while I watched. It was exactly like something Margot would have done to me, which meant only one thing.

I was a hypocrite, a monstrous hypocrite, just like my mother.

I do believe that Reggie went kind of crazy right about then. She had always been a bundle of frenetic, nervous energy, and I had often wondered if the woman even knew what it meant to *sit still*. But those weeks in May saw Reggie reach a new zenith in her hectic hyperactivity. She was up at the crack of dawn and spent a good portion of her day jumping in her van, running some errand or other, only to return home and lug box after box of God knew what into her house. Then she would jump back in her van and start the process all over again; she was a constant blur of motion. It wasn't like I was spying on her or anything. We lived next door to each other, and I couldn't help but hear her old van cough to life before she peeled out of her driveway. I had known Reggie long enough to know that she was up to something, and I didn't have a good feeling about it.

No, I didn't come right out and ask her. By that point, we were barely speaking to each other when we weren't working on wine club business at Cynthia's. It is in my nature to avoid confrontation if at all possible, and I knew that if I asked Reggie what the hell she was doing with all those boxes, she'd get her hackles up and somehow turn the tables on me and make me feel bad. As you've gathered by now, Reggie thrived on confrontation, and she was good at it. She would go on the attack, and I certainly didn't want her to start asking me questions about why Paul was back living in my house. I didn't doubt that she would once again accuse me of being a doormat. And you know what? It would hurt because it was kind of true.

I say *kind of true* because while it was a fact that Paul was living in the house, I wasn't making his life easy. He was still sleeping on the couch in the den at my insistence, and I didn't cave when he complained about how lumpy and uncomfortable it was. And I flatly refused to do his laundry. You should have seen the unbelieving look on his face the first time he sauntered into the laundry room with an armload of dirty clothes, saying, "I'm out of clean underwear, babe."

"That's too bad," I said. I was transferring a load from the washer to the dryer, and sure, I could have taken the laundry out of his hands and thrown it in, but I didn't.

Paul looked uncertain, standing there with his dirty laundry. "Should I put these on the floor, or do you want them somewhere else?"

I slammed the dryer door shut and then pointed at the washer. "There's the washing machine. Help yourself."

"You're not going to wash these for me?" Really, the look on his face was priceless.

"Nope. You're a grown man. You can do your own damn laundry, *babe*." And I stepped around him and left the room.

Let me tell you, it felt so good not to cave, not to give in to the man as I had done for so many years. Granted, the laundry was a tiny issue, but I did savor the small victory for about five minutes before he tracked down Marcy and had her do his damn laundry. What a baby, right? And yes, I still cooked for him, but that was only because I was already cooking for the kids, and it would have been cruel of me to tell him that he couldn't sit down at the dinner table with us. The kids seemed happy to have him back, the traitors, and I had to grit my teeth during those meals while Paul told his funny stories and entertained the kids. I concluded that in a perfect world, my husband would have been a standup comedian. I'm thinking Don Rickles. You know, someone who might be a little funny but is not a particularly likable person.

But do you want to know what irritated me the most about Paul? It was the way that he just assumed that everything would return to normal now that he was home. He didn't seem to get it that he had left us for months, lived with another woman--yeah, right, his life coach--and neglected every single one of his responsibilities. He didn't seem to get it that his leaving had been devastating for me and left his family in a desperate situation. In his view, his being home was enough to make everything hunky-dory again. Never mind that he still hadn't gotten a job, although if you asked him, he would probably have the nerve to say that his *recovery* was his job. Never mind that he watched me go to work at Cynthia's three days a week while he sat in front of the TV in his pajamas. Never mind that he was another mouth to feed. He was home, and he thought that was enough. He probably also thought that everyone should stand up and give him a round of applause too. The prodigal husband had returned. It was maddening.

I'd had to tell Paul about the wine club, but I sure didn't go into any specifics, such as the fact that we were putting cheap wine into expensive-looking French wine bottles. Such as the fact that I was engaged in an illegal enterprise. But do you want to know what he said to me when I told him about the wine club? He said, and I quote: "It saddens me that you're making money from alcohol."

Can you believe that? I was so steamed that I opened a bottle of wine right in front of him and poured myself a nice big glass. His face darkened as the level in the glass grew higher, and he ended up stomping off to the TV again. I ask you: Was it my fault that he had no self-control? I know, I know. My husband had a *disease*, but frankly, I was getting a little tired of hearing about it. I drank the entire bottle and then left the empty bottle on the kitchen counter as evidence--or sad but true--maybe it was more of a taunt. I don't like to dwell on that.

Paul had gotten his driver's license back by then, so no one can blame me for not taking him to his AA meetings. I'm not sure when he stopped attending the meetings at the church on Shea. In the beginning, he went two, sometimes three times a day. Then he stopped. I didn't have a clue that he was no longer going to the meetings. I also can't pinpoint the exact day that he started drinking again either. We were living under the same roof, but other than having dinner together, we were leading separate lives. I didn't keep tabs on him every time he walked out of the house, and I was under the impression that he spent most of his time at home in front of the TV. Plus, I didn't think that it was my responsibility to check up on him all the time when he holed up in his den. What was he, my third child? And for crying out loud, weren't three stints in rehab enough? I mean, come on.

All I know with certainty is the first time I saw him drunk. I had just put dinner on the table. I had made a chicken and white bean stew, and it smelled heavenly. I called for the kids to come to dinner, and then I called to Paul. The kids came to the table, but Paul didn't. "Has anyone seen Dad?" I asked Marcy and Jimmy.

"I think Daddy's sleeping again," Jimmy said as he picked up his spoon. "He's been taking a lot of naps."

I didn't even get it then. No, my first thought was that maybe Paul was depressed, and I was thinking, *oh, great, now I have that to deal with too.* I stomped down the hallway to the den, fully expecting to see him sprawled out on the fold-out couch. But he wasn't there. I checked all the bedrooms upstairs next, with no luck. You have to understand that I was getting madder by the second. Not only did I do all the shopping and cleaning and cooking while Paul did nothing, but now he didn't even have the decency to show up at the dinner table on time. No, he had the luxury of taking naps while I did all the work.

I returned to the dinner table. "We're going to eat dinner without Dad tonight." I pulled out my chair.

But before I could sit, Marcy piped up. "Did you check the boat, Mom?"

"Why would I check the boat?"

Marcy shrugged. "Dad's been spending time out there. Haven't you noticed, Mom?"

Well, no, I hadn't noticed. I hated even thinking about that damn boat. It was still parked in our driveway on its trailer. It was an eyesore, and every time I saw it, I felt a fresh wave of anger. Paul had taken forty grand and wasted it on a godforsaken boat that he didn't even know the first thing about sailing. It hadn't moved an inch since it was delivered, and it took all my willpower not to back into it when I pulled out of the driveway. The only reason I didn't was that it would dent my new Lincoln, and after the fiasco of the last wine club party, I didn't have the money to repair a car. Or a damn, useless boat.

"You should check the boat, Mom."

Marcy's voice had a definite tinge of accusation now, and I think that's when the realization started to sink in. However, since I made her pee on the stick while I watched, Marcy's voice always, on the few occasions when she addressed me directly, had a tinge of accusation. I really didn't want to go out and check the boat. Out of some misguided principle, I hadn't even given Paul the satisfaction of setting foot on it. I don't know what I was trying to prove. In hindsight, it seems pretty silly, but at the time, I thought I was making a point of my displeasure. Why did the idiot go out and buy a boat?

It was hot below deck, and as soon as I crawled down the narrow stairs, the stench hit me, a combination of alcohol and perspiration and perhaps something else. I could see Paul on the narrow bunk bed, and I tripped over a bottle as I inched closer. There was a lantern on the center table, and I reached for it.

The clattering of the bottle must have awakened Paul. "Don't turn on the light, Audrey. I don't want you to see me like this." His voice was only slightly slurred.

"What have you done?" It was a needless question--the answer was obvious--but I was thinking about all the money and time he had wasted on rehab, only to come back to where he had started.

"I. Am. Drunk."

"Why?" I wish I could say that I felt sympathy towards my husband right then, but I didn't.

"It's just too much."

"What is?"

"All of it. Everything."

"That is such a loser thing to say." I could not keep the exasperation out of my voice. Didn't he know that everyone felt overwhelmed at times? Did he think he was the only person who found it difficult to cope? At that moment, I wanted to take him by the shoulders and shake him, hard.

"Yes," he agreed. "I am a loser."

"Do you want me to call your AA sponsor?" I thought that was the right thing to do, but more than that, I didn't relish the thought of cleaning him up myself. Paul had been shit-faced drunk many times during our marriage, but he had always been a happy drunk. This was just pathetic.

"No." His voice was soft in the darkness. "Call Sondra."

I couldn't believe it. Paul wanted me to call Betty Boop? "Not a chance," I said, my voice heated. "I'm not calling your girlfriend."

Paul didn't dispute that. "Please. My phone . . . is . . . in . . . the den. She'll know what to do."

What choice did I have? I couldn't see his face, but Paul sounded awful. Maybe I should say that it sounded more like he was *broken*. The kids would be wondering what was going on by now, and I didn't want them to come out and see their father like this. I had too many memories of finding my father and mother passed out in their matching La-Z-Boy chairs on too many mornings after. And I didn't want my kids to feel the shame and revulsion that I had felt. In the past, I had always tried to protect the kids from their father's drunkenness. I was going to do it one more time.

I found Paul's phone in the den, and I found Betty Boop's contact information. I called her. "Paul is drunk in the boat, and he's asking for you," I said shortly as soon as she answered the phone. I didn't introduce myself.

"How much has he had to drink?"

"I don't know." I'd knocked over one bottle, but there could have been others.

"I'll be right there." She didn't ask any more questions.

It was only natural that I looked at their chain of texts next. I suppose I was looking for proof of an affair or expressions of undying devotion. I didn't find anything explicit like that, but the texts proved that Paul and Sondra cared about each other. They had nicknames for each other, Squirt and Cowboy. It was uncomfortable reading those, and it was also uncomfortable to see how Paul had grown more and more depressed and unhappy as the days at home went by.

One text popped out at me, and I unexpectedly felt the sting of tears. It was the last text from the night before, and it said: Why doesn't she love me anymore, Squirt? *Why doesn't Audrey love me?*

"That's just plain stupid," Reggie spouted. She was pacing around Cynthia's center island, her computer opened in her hands. "We have always had the wine club parties on weekend nights, not a Monday. Who wants to go out on a Monday night?"

Cynthia, for some unknown reason, was rearranging the glassware in her cabinet. "It is not stupid at all, Reggie. School gets out early this year, on May 18th. Many families pack up and leave shortly after that to go to their summer homes in Flagstaff or Coronado."

Reggie barked a snide laugh. "How silly of me not to take into consideration the plans of our clients to go to their *summer* homes. When are you planning to leave for your *summer* home, Audrey?"

"Cut it out, Reggie. Cynthia does have a point. If we wait much longer than that, people will have packed up and left for the summer." I never wanted to take sides when the two of them bickered, but I always had to give in. I guess you could say that I was generally the swing vote, which meant that I was always the bad guy in the eyes of one or the other.

Cynthia gave a triumphant smile. "Two against one, Reggie. Majority rules. We'll have the party on the 21st."

"Thanks a lot, Audrey." Reggie's voice dripped sarcasm. "We're going to have to work our asses off to pull off this party so soon."

"Do you have something better to do, Reggie?" I asked mildly. I was not going to let her get under my skin, and I had every right to voice an opinion. In this case, though, I voted with Cynthia, not because of her reasoning, but because I was desperately strapped for cash. Maeve Olson no longer seemed interested in buying wine from me--she wasn't returning my calls--and obviously, my husband was no help financially at all. My family was back to living on hamburger again, and I was behind on the mortgage payment. After I found Paul drunk on the sailboat and Betty Boop whisked him away, I immediately put the eyesore up for sale on Craigslist, hoping to get back at least some of the forty grand. There'd been no takers yet, and I was starting to panic.

Reggie wasn't about to let Cynthia win on any point. "If what you're saying is true, Cynthia--and I do think you overestimate the number of families in this town with summer homes--what are we going to do for the months of June, July, and August? Put the wine club on summer hiatus?"

"Why don't we cross that bridge when we come to it?" Cynthia said cryptically, glancing yet again at the door off the kitchen that led down to the wine cellar.

Reggie slammed her computer down on the counter. "If you want out of the wine club, Cynthia, just say it. It's certainly not going to break my heart when I cry all the way to the bank."

For the briefest of seconds, I hoped that Reggie would look my way and say something about how she and I would be happy to take back full control of the wine club again, that we could go back to how it was in the beginning. But Reggie kept glaring at Cynthia.

"You are so dramatic, Reggie. I'm not leaving the wine club. I'm only pointing out that we will have to reconsider our business model during the summer months." Cynthia was now the one pacing with her computer in her hands.

Cynthia had been almost as bad as Reggie in terms of nervous energy ever since I arrived. It was wearing me out to watch the two of them scurry around like blind mice. All that energy and we had not accomplished one damn thing this morning. I was so tired, physically and emotionally, but we had to get the ball rolling or we would never make any money. "Can we please get to work?"

But that damn Reggie. She had a burr under her skin, all right. "In a minute, Audrey. I have something I want to ask Cynthia out of genuine curiosity. Tell me, Cynthia, what in the world will poor Felicity do now that she isn't the queen of the Tigerettes?"

I gasped in spite of myself. Not only did the three of us not talk about our husbands when we worked on the wine club, but we also didn't talk about our daughters and the Tigerettes. I wasn't sure why this second hot topic had become taboo, but it had. It wasn't natural. When most women got together, they talked about their children, especially if the children were in the same sports or school activities. But the three of us, all moth-ers of a member of the Mohave High School Tigerette pom squad, never did. It was like we all secretly knew that the subject of the Tigerettes would divide us into our separate camps and bring up all kinds of resentments and accusations. It would also cause the end of our wine club. And none of us could afford that. But leave it to Reggie to open the smelliest can of worms.

"She was the captain, not the queen, Reggie." Cynthia was back to rearranging glasses.

"You could have fooled me," Reggie said. "And according to Hayley, Felicity cried like it was the end of the world after the last competition."

"Marcy said the same thing," I added. I couldn't help myself, and I'm not sorry to say that the idea of Felicity bawling her eyes out had given me great satisfaction. Marcy had cried too, naturally, bemoaning the fact that the Tigerettes would never be the same without Felicity. But my heart was singing. Unbeknownst to anyone but myself, I had already started to look into a couple of charter schools for Marcy to finish her high school education, away from the Tigerettes and everything the snobby Scottsdale school represented. She could focus on her grades again, and in effect, start all over.

I know, I know. The irony is not lost on me. If only I had enacted the plan months sooner, things would have been different. Could you please hand me that box of tissues? I'll blow my nose and then get back to the events of that morning. Thanks. That's better. Now, where was I? Oh, right.

Reggie had just taunted Cynthia about Felicity, and Cynthia snapped back at her: "They won the competition, didn't they?"

"What does that have to do with anything?" Reggie looked genuinely bewildered.

I'm pretty sure that Cynthia was imitating Reggie's warrior pose when she put her hands on her hips and matched Reggie's steely glare. "Isn't winning the point?"

"I'm not sure."

"Come on, Reggie, you were a high school and college jock, weren't you? So you tell me. Isn't winning the point?"

"Goddamnit, Cynthia." Reggie picked up her computer and started pacing again.

Cynthia smiled and quit fiddling with her glassware. She came and sat on a barstool. "Let's get to work."

At first, I thought that Cynthia had won that round, and I wasn't sure how I felt about it. I was so mad at Reggie, and I felt so wounded by her, but it was kind of like the world as I had known it had shifted. Reggie always got the last word. Always. And I guess I always, as much as I hated to admit it, respected that.

I shouldn't have underestimated her. Reggie's voice was low and so controlled it was scary when she said, "All I'm saying, Cynthia, is that if I ever find out that Felicity has done anything to hurt my daughter, in any way, shape, or form, I will get even."

Cynthia's eyes narrowed to slits. "Are you threatening my daughter, or are you threatening me, Reggie?"

"Let's just call it a general announcement." Reggie finally sat down then. "Now let's get to work."

Paul came back home. After being gone for a whopping two days, he was back home, sheepish and subdued, but home. Was I supposed to be happy about that? Because I wasn't. Wherever Betty Boop had taken him to detox--and I didn't know because I didn't ask--the doctor or PA or psychiatrist had prescribed Disulfiram, which Paul was stupidly gobbling like candy. At almost $600 a bottle, it was expensive candy. He also now seemed to crave sweets in general: mint chocolate chip ice cream, candy bars, cake and cookies. I saw him go through an entire package of Oreos during an episode of *Criminal Minds,* and then he went into the kitchen to get the brand new gallon of ice cream, followed by a bag of marshmallows that had to be at least two years old. I kept telling myself that he was trying, that anything was better than him drinking himself into oblivion. But I had become like an overly wrung washcloth. I couldn't squeeze out one more drop of sympathy or compassion or understanding.

So between Jimmy's and Paul's medications and food and all the other due bills, I was standing on quicksand and sinking fast. And get this, the Tigerettes had decided that they wanted to give Felicity a going-away present that she would remember, a trip to Disneyland, and everyone had agreed that it was perfectly acceptable to chip in one hundred dollars. I mean, that was just insane. Yet Marcy thought I was the one who was insane--and/or an ogre--when I threw a fit about it. She claimed that she would be the only one who didn't contribute toward the extravagant gift if I didn't give her the money. I told her that she was going to get a summer job, and then she had to work part-time during the school year. She had a brand new car, and there was no reason why she couldn't at least find a babysitting job. She would have to pay me back. It did not go over well, and I shuddered to think how it was going to be when I told her that she wasn't going back to Mohave or the Tigerettes in the fall. I decided once again that I would tell her later, back when I still naively thought there was such a concept as *later*.

The bids for the *Audrey* were nonexistent. Evidently, Arizona was not a boating capital of the world. Big surprise there, right? Something needed to be done, and I decided to turn once again to Maeve. Even though she was not returning my calls, I decided that I might be able to entice her in person with our May wine selections. The April champagne wine club had been such a disaster that Reggie, Cynthia, and I were unanimous in our decision--a very rare occurrence indeed--to go back to an established, well-respected château. We chose Château Margaux, a wine estate in Bordeaux that produced one of the four wines to achieve *Premier Cru* status. These were the wines we decided to "produce" for the May wine club party:

Château Margaux Premier Grand Cru Classé 2005, $1000;

Château Margaux 2010, $1,100;

Château Margaux 2015, $1800;

And Château Margaux Premier Grand Cru Classé Red Bordeaux Blend 2009 (6000ml), $17,000.

After Reggie and Cynthia's verbal sparring--and trust me, Reggie had definitely been threatening Felicity and Cynthia during that go round--we all worked together quickly and silently. The wine was ready to go two days before Felicity's graduation, which was a victory for Cynthia, and she didn't hesitate to let Reggie hear about it. Those two women acted like petulant children when they got together, and it was draining me. Like I needed one more thing to sap my energy at that point in my life. I hope I don't sound like a big whiner because I do not, in general, whine, nor do I relish being the guest of honor at my solitary pity party. But things were definitely reaching a crisis point, or maybe it is more accurate to say that things were spiraling out of control, and I had no idea how to reign in the chaos. I might have been drinking too much too, or maybe it just seemed like it because I was now drinking alone every night. I don't know.

It didn't help that I wasn't sleeping either. As exhausted as I was, as much as I willed sleep to come, as hard as I tried to bribe slumber with wine, it wasn't happening. Every time I closed my eyes, every time I felt the beginning of sleep start to erode the edge of consciousness, I snapped awake, sweating and panic-stricken. It was her face I saw. Every night I saw my mother's face. It was not the angry face she had worn throughout my childhood, with her mouth a thin line of disapproval and her tousled red wig looking like it had just erupted in flames. And it wasn't the peaceful old woman lying in a bed in a nursing home with her hands neatly crossed over her chest as if she were in prayer. It was that final image of Margot alive when she lay almost bald, her sparse white hair in stringy clumps, her right side paralyzed, her hand a claw, when she lay vulnerable while the pillow came closer to smother out her life. And when the raw fear opened her eyes to the coming terror of death. That was the face that haunted me every single night.

I was not looking or acting my best at that time, so it was no wonder that Maeve looked startled, perhaps even a little frightened when I showed up on her doorstep the evening before the last wine club party. "Oh, dear, Audrey, have you been ill?" she asked.

"I have been a little under the weather lately, Maeve." Trust me, that was not a lie. But when she took a quick step back from the door, I added, "It's nothing contagious. Allergies." Okay, that was a lie, but it was necessary.

I hurried on with the speech I had prepared. "I'm here to offer you a discount on the wine that we are offering to our clients tomorrow night. You have been such a loyal customer, and I wanted to reward you with these." I lifted the two large bottles of Château Margaux Premier Grand Cru Classé Red Bordeaux Blend 2009. "These are going for $17,000 tomorrow night, but I'm going to offer them to you at $15,000 each."

Maeve did not look delighted by the offer. "I am planning to attend the party tomorrow night. My cousin is in town, and Cynthia told me it was fine to bring--"

My desperation was so strong that I rudely interrupted her. "What about a twenty percent discount? We can call it an Early Bird Special. Haha." I smiled wanly.

Maeve looked at me closely. "Cynthia told me that all wine must now be purchased directly through the wine club."

"Yes, well . . . but that doesn't apply to our most loyal customers . . ." I was floundering, and she knew it.

"I think I'll buy my wine at the party tomorrow, Audrey." She glanced at her gold watch. "If you'll excuse me, I'm late for an appointment." Maeve closed the door with a little more force than was necessary.

My face burned. I had just gotten the royal brush off from Maeve because Cynthia, the bitch, had gone behind my back and cut me off, probably to put more money in her own pocket. *The bitch.* I was mad, sure, but I was more embarrassed than anything else. It could be possible that Cynthia was trying to make things more above board with the wine purchases, but I highly doubted it. However, to confront her about it would only prove that I had been doing something sneaky again. I was screwed either way. It just figured.

I don't want to talk about the horrible May wine club party that ruined everything. May 21, the night that will live on in infamy in the minds of all those who were involved was shocking. It was chaotic. It was a disaster.

It was the end.

I left that wine club party in a daze. I know that Reggie and Cynthia say I slipped out the back door, that I was a coward trying to escape, but that is not the way I saw it at all. I prefer to say that I was in shock, and I'm pretty sure that I was. It was so loud, and it seemed like everything was happening all at once. In all the commotion and confusion, no one was paying attention to me, and rightly so. The worst perpetrators by far were Reggie and Cynthia, no doubt about it. While the house the three of us had built together was already teetering on shifting ground, simply waiting for the inevitable earthquake that was to come, both of those women were the ones who hurried the process along by planting bombs. And the house came tumbling down.

I don't remember driving home, which supports the theory that I was in shock, doesn't it? All I remember is walking out the open back door of Cynthia's house, and the next thing I knew, I was sitting in my parked car in my driveway staring at the *Audrey*. I hated that boat with a passion. You might even say that hating that boat had become the only thing I was truly passionate about anymore. So I just sat there, staring at the boat. I supposed that an objective observer could say that it was a pretty boat, blue and white, very nautical looking for a boat that had never left dry land. Perhaps another family might have created beautiful memories on a boat like that, but it was too late for my falling-apart family to be those lucky parents and children. As of that night, there wouldn't ever be the possibility of beautiful memories.

As I sat in my car, hypnotized by that boat, all I could think about was how that boat had become the emblem of everything that had gone wrong in my life. My alcoholic husband, who had disappeared for months on end, had stolen my money to buy that boat. Those were accurate facts. What is not so clear is how I got to the point that night where the damn *Audrey* became a symbol of my neglected son and daughter. It even became emblematic of the despicable Tigerettes and the horrible, manipulative Felicity. I could also see the now failed wine club in the reflection of its shiny side. The way the streetlight shone on its hull made the gleaming images flash by, one after the other. And of course Margot's terrifying face took its proper place in the menagerie of injuries and transgressions. It was hypnotizing.

I don't know what time it was when I started to think about the three gallon jugs of gasoline we kept in the garage. There weren't any lights on in my house, nor Reggie's. She hadn't returned yet from Cynthia's--that is, if she would return at all. The entire block was dark except for the intermittent streetlights. We kept the gas in the garage for the lawn-mower and in case of emergencies. In the past when Paul didn't want to go to work, he would conveniently be out of gas. I solved that problem by stocking up on gas when I went to fill up my car at the Shell. It solved the problem of that one feeble excuse of Paul's, but he developed many more over the years. Still, out of habit, I kept the extra gasoline on hand. For some strange reason, it made me feel like I at least had that aspect of my life under control. Even more strangely, having those gallons of gas in the garage made me feel safe.

If only someone on our street had been awake, maybe they could have stopped me. I like to think that would have been possible, but deep down, I don't think I could have been stopped. By the time I had doused the boat with gasoline, I was filled with a single-minded purpose: I was going to get rid of that damn eyesore. That was my sole focus. I wasn't thinking about how close the boat was to the house where my children slept; I wasn't thinking about Paul. I wasn't thinking rational thoughts at all. All I wanted to do was make that damn boat, and everything it stood for, go away. I had candles in the garage too, and I lit one after the other and threw them onto the deck of the boat, the captain's chair, the padded benches. Finally, the boat caught fire.

As I watched the fire catch and sputter and slowly spread, it never once occurred to me that Paul might be passed out on the bunk in the lower cabin again. I swear.

27

REGGIE

I drove by Kent's new love nest--I think I started to call it that to further enrage myself--on a Tuesday, the same day of the week I had first seen the kids go inside. And believe me when I tell you that I was as prepared as I knew how to be. Thinking ahead, I had rented a Buick, just a regular sedan, you know, so that it wouldn't arouse any suspicions in that neighborhood. I had found Caleb's old bird watching binoculars in the hall closet. I didn't know if I would need them, but almost every TV show I'd watched about spying had the spy looking through a pair of binoculars. I packed a large water bottle, an apple, and a turkey and swiss sandwich. I think I made the sandwich because it gave me something to do to occupy my time leading up to the expedition. I'd woken up nervous that day, knowing what I was about to do. Or maybe my nervousness stemmed from the strong sense of foreboding that festered like a boil in the pit of my stomach. It was like I wanted to know what my daughter was up to, but then again, I didn't want to know because I had a sinking feeling that it would be heartbreaking. I somehow knew that things would never be the same again.

Felicity's powder blue Porsche pulled up around five o'clock, just as it had before. It was the same drill. Hayley went up and unlocked the door, went in, came back out, and motioned for the others to follow. This time only Marcy and Felicity got out of the car. Less than five minutes later, the car with the boys pulled up. It was too hot for them to wear their letterman jackets, but given their height, I assumed they were basketball players. I couldn't tell if it was the same group of five boys as the first time, not that it mattered. What sent a cold chill down my spine was that the boys outnumbered the girls. There was something about the unevenness of the sexes that disturbed me. Again I could hear high-pitched laughter and the faint sound of music.

I sat in the hot car parked across the street from the condo for another fifteen minutes or so. I had two choices: either I knocked on the front door or I peeked through the windows. The condo had one large window in the front. The living room, I presumed. Being an end unit, I could see that it had two larger windows and one smaller window on the north side. The small window was high, so it was probably the bathroom, while I figured that the larger windows were the two bedrooms. The kitchen would probably be in the back of the unit, and I would know for sure if I would get out of the damn car, but it was like my legs suddenly felt like they weighed a hundred pounds each, and I, the runner, was having a hard time catching my breath. I felt woozy, like I was coming down with the flu. Me, the woman with the constitution of a horse, felt like she was going to throw up.

I decided to call Hayley. If she answered and I heard the sound of the TV and kids in the background, I would know she was all right, that she was just a normal teenager hanging out with a group of friends. There is nothing wrong with a mother calling her daughter on a typical day, you know, so there is no need to remind me that I was procrastinating. I knew I was procrastinating, but when you're afraid, the mind can throw up all kinds of roadblocks and make you think they're good ideas.

Surprisingly, Hayley answered on the second or third ring. "What's up, Mom?"

I was dumbstruck and mumbled something almost unintelligible. "Just, just calling to . . . say hi?"

"That's weird, Mom."

It was weird. I never called Hayley in the middle of the afternoon for no reason, yet I fumbled along. "What are you up to this afternoon?"

"I'm just hanging out with some friends at Dad's. I thought you knew I did that on most Tuesdays."

"Yeah, right, sure. Be home in time for dinner, okay?" I quickly hung up. I felt like such a fool, but things were about to get unfortunately dicier. At that exact moment, Reed's car turned onto the street and headed for the house, and there I was like a sitting duck. Even though I was not in my old van, I'm sure that Kent could see me clearly through the rolled-down-window of the sedan, my phone in one hand and the binoculars circling my neck like a cumbersome necklace. I had no time to slouch down in the seat or drive off unnoticed. *Goddamnit.* Why in the hell were he and Reed home early?

After Reed parked his fancy car--what was he, Kent's chauffeur?--Kent lost no time in crossing the street and leaning in my window. "I'm fresh out of rose bushes for you to chop down, Reggie. What are you doing here? You know perfectly well the restraining order is still in effect."

Kent hadn't said a word about the rose bushes to me, and I'd rather hoped that he thought the culprit was some neighborhood juvenile delinquent or something, but no such luck. However, he had just handed me the perfect excuse. "The rose bushes are why I'm here, Kent. I've been feeling kind of bad about that, and I came to apologize." I reached for my purse. "Let me reimburse you for the plants." I found my wallet. "How much do those things cost?"

"What's with the binoculars, Reggie?" Kent said evenly.

He wouldn't believe it for a heartbeat if I told him I was bird watching. He knew that I didn't have the patience for that kind of thing. "Oh, I found these in the hall closet and thought I'd take them to a lens shop and have them refurbished. Then I could give them to Caleb the next time he comes home." It was such a flimsy lie that I flushed.

"Reggie, why are you here? Your shenanigans have really upset Reed."

"My *shenanigans*? God, Kent, when did you get so fussy?" I knew that I shouldn't have said that as soon as the words popped out of my mouth, but the man should have known not to back me into a corner.

Kent shook his head sadly. "Work with me here, Reggie. Reed has not been feeling well lately, and all we need is peace and quiet. Is that too much to ask?"

Then I felt like a heel as I suddenly remembered that long ago conversation when Kent had told me that Reed had cancer. But since they hadn't gone on a cruise, I thought he'd been lying. Maybe they hadn't gone on the cruise because they didn't have the money, and *that* I could understand. "I sincerely apologize, Kent. I'm not here to cause you harm, and look, if it makes things better, I can buy Reed a new cat too." A small shudder convulsed my shoulders; I hoped he didn't see.

He did, and he smiled a little. "You're here spying on Hayley, aren't you?"

"I plead the Fifth." My word, it was hot in that small car. I was sweating like I'd just finished a ten-mile run. And the mention of our daughter reminded me that I needed to leave before she saw me lurking out here. She would not be happy to see me. Furthermore, my cover would be blown, and the kids might be looking out for me next time. "I better get going."

"Not so fast." Kent reached in and took the key out of the ignition. "Since you are here and since you won't return my phone calls, let's talk about the divorce."

"I'd rather not," I said sulkily. Why did he think I hadn't answered his calls or texts? Wasn't it obvious that I didn't want to talk about the divorce? Stupidly, I suppose that a small part deep inside my soul hoped that Kent would change his mind. Rationally, I knew that would never happen. But hope burns eternal, as that saying goes. It's such a stupid saying. Letting the candle of hope burn eternally makes a person chase after a lost cause way past its expiration date.

"I want this to be as amicable as possible, Reggie, so I've taken the liberty of hiring a divorce mediator. We won't need to hire expensive lawyers to represent us. We don't need to make this divorce contentious or confrontational."

"What if I want to hire a lawyer? What if I want to be confrontational?" I don't know why I said that. In all honesty, I thought a divorce mediator was a good idea. I also didn't want to sully the memory of the good years of our marriage with an ugly, nasty divorce. But of course I let the words slip out before I gave them thought. I swear, I sometimes wished that someone would sew my mouth shut.

Kent sighed, a sound with which I was all too familiar. It meant that I was being difficult, while he was Patience personified. He took a few moments before he said, "I am going to be fair with you, Reggie. You can have the house, and I'll pay child and spousal support. I don't make as much money as I used to, but I will still support my family."

"How noble of you." *Goddamnit.* Where was a person with a needle and thread when you needed one? And here's the thing: Kent had been sending me checks from time to time in the months we had been separated. I didn't mention it before because I hadn't cashed them. My pride instead drove me to tear up the checks into tiny pieces and send them back to him in blank envelopes. And my pride wouldn't let me acknowledge the truth, that the man I had married was truly a kind and decent human being.

Kent stuffed his hands in his pockets--another familiar gesture--and said quietly, "I didn't mean for this to happen, Reggie. I'm sorry."

"I know," I said quietly. "I'm sorry too. I know I can be a bitch sometimes." If I didn't get out of there soon, I was going to start blubbering and probably beg him to reconsider. I didn't want him to see me being so pathetic, even though I recognized that I was indeed pitiful. I extended my hand for the car key.

"So, we'll handle this with a mediation?"

"You don't need to worry, Kent. I won't make the divorce difficult. I promise." I meant to keep that promise, even if I had to enroll in an anger management course. Sure, I still felt incredibly sad too. Kent deserved to be happy, but I was not the one who could truly fulfill him. And I never had been.

Kent handed back the key. "Sixty bucks for the rose bushes," he said, smiling.

I managed a wan smile. "Can I write you a check?"

"Sure thing. You can mail it to me."

I started the car, and I was seconds away from escaping undetected when the front door of the condo opened, and the kids poured out. I could hear Hayley's *God, Mom!* from across the street and read her disgusted expression loud and clear. So close and yet so far from my getaway. My cover was blown, and I was going to have to come up with Plan B.

I leased the blue Buick for another two weeks and started to follow Felicity. Once I came up with Plan B, I wanted to kick myself for not thinking of it sooner. If I was ever going to get to the bottom of what was going on with the Tigerettes, I needed to go to the source. Which was Felicity, the star and coach and self-crowned queen of the Tigerettes. Felicity, the manipulative puppeteer of young girls' lives. Felicity, that conniving, self-serving, startlingly pretty little piece of shit. Even now, I can't think of her without automatically balling up my fists.

By following Felicity's powder blue Porsche, I learned a thing or two about that girl. First of all, she was her mother's daughter. For a teenager who was pretty, Felicity spent a lot of time and money making herself look good. I supposed that Cynthia had taught her that as I followed her to the stylist to the salon to the gym and to Fashion Square shopping mall.

Getting out of the car and trailing her on foot took some effort, let me tell you. That girl moved *fast* through Nordstrom and Saks and Anthropologie and Abercrombie and Fitch. It was obvious that she knew her way around those stores, and most of the clerks addressed her by name. I had on an oversized hat and sunglasses, which didn't make me particularly conspicuous in a shopping mall full of women who had just had a facelift or Botox or an eyelift or a jaw restructuring. At Lululemon alone, the girl dropped over four hundred dollars on workout wear, which made me briefly consider once again if Cynthia had a secret stash of money, or even more egregious, was embezzling money from the FHM account. Even more than I was, I mean.

It was at Kate Spade New York that I overheard a very, very valuable piece of information. While the store clerk wrapped up Felicity's newly purchased $250 handbag, she asked Felicity what her plans were after graduation. Felicity was maddeningly vague about her long-term goals and aspirations, but very specific about her immediate plans. "My mom has hired a car and driver to pick me up at the gym after the lockdown graduation party. I'm going directly to Canyon Ranch Spa in Tucson for a week. Facials, massages, the whole nine yards. Isn't that great?" The young salesclerk agreed that it was indeed great, while I was thinking: *Who sends an eighteen-year-old girl to a spa for graduation? Who are these people?*

Naturally, Felicity spent a good chunk of her time with the Tigerettes, my daughter included. The amount of time was probably not as extensive as it was during the interminable basketball season and the following competition tour, but it was still two or three hours every day. They did the usual things, the mall and Jamba Juice and California Pizza Kitchen and Harkins Theaters. But oddly enough, the only times that I saw boys included were the afternoons spent at Kent and Reed's condo. It seemed very strange to me that Felicity didn't have a boyfriend, and I began to wonder if she was gay. It could have been that I had homosexuality on the brain, given my recent history, but it still seemed odd. And I've got to tell you that I was starting to wonder if I'd just imagined that the Tigerettes were up to no good. I wasn't finding any evidence to suggest that these kids were into drugs or alcohol or fucking like bunnies. Believe me, that girl knew how to cover her tracks.

I was missing something, something crucial. I knew that, but I couldn't put my finger on what was so out of whack in Felicity's life. On the surface, it seemed like she was a normal teenager, but all of my instincts screamed that she was up to no good. She made my daughter wear diapers, for crying out loud! I didn't care if it was some hazing ritual; it was still humiliating to the diaper wearer. What's more, it was obvious that Felicity had the power to cast some kind of spell over all the Tigerettes, Hayley and Marcy in particular. All she had to do was snap her fingers, and they came running. What was up with that? Was she a witch or sorceress? I will admit that I came up with all kinds of outlandish theories about Felicity during those long, tedious hours of surveillance. The witch theory was probably the most bizarre. In all probability, Felicity was probably no more than a rich spoiled brat, the truest definition of a *mean girl* that I'd ever had the misfortune to meet.

I was sitting outside of Cynthia and Felicity's house one evening, mostly because I didn't have anything better to do. It was well past midnight, and Felicity had come home hours before. Yet I still sat there thinking, wondering what, if anything, I was missing. That's when I remembered the night after the March wine party when Felicity had walked in from the guesthouse in back. I'd known it was there. The entire back of the house was windows, and you could see it from the kitchen and family room. However, I hadn't had any idea that Felicity had been in there all night. It had its own entrance that you couldn't see from the main house and was far enough away from the house that a teenager could get away with a lot--if she was devious and her mother was an oblivious dipshit. Well, Felicity was devious, and Cynthia was an oblivious dipshit when it came to her daughter. Then there had been that tense mysterious exchange between them. Cynthia had been upset about something, and it definitely concerned her daughter.

But here was the question: Could a person get into the guesthouse without passing through the main house? I remembered the mystery man who had scaled the wall that one February afternoon and never come back out. Granted, he could have come out the front door after I left my surveillance post for the day, but I was 99.9 percent sure that I had seen the same man on that video camera in Richard's office. I didn't buy Cynthia's explanation that the man was an old friend who was going through detox. That smelled as fishy as a koi pond. However, that was neither here nor there at this juncture. The point was that the man had gotten over the fence undetected by Cynthia, and I had no doubt that young kids--say tall basketball players used to jumping--could do the same. So that was one possible way to get to the guesthouse if you didn't want someone in the primary residence to know what you were doing.

The other way would be a door somewhere along the perimeter of the stucco fence. Shortly after Audrey and I became friends, we had both chipped in and hired a guy to bash a hole in the shared stucco wall that separated our backyards. He'd installed a wooden door with a simple latch, and we had used that door as the primary way to get to each other's houses for over a decade. Audrey and I hadn't thought it necessary to get a keypad or a padlock because we were such good pals--how naive of us!--but if Richard had built this house and put in a door, there would surely be some kind of security code or something. And I had no doubt that Felicity would know the code.

That's when I got out of my car and circled that imposing-looking fence. Cynthia's property was so large--I would guess a couple of acres--that she didn't share her fence with any neighbor. I was still nervous about it, though. I supposed that I wasn't technically trespassing because I was outside the fence, but it was the middle of the night, and I certainly felt like the sneak that I was. Unlike my street, there weren't streetlights in this neighborhood, and I had to use my phone as a flashlight. I made slow progress because of the prickly pear cacti and large rocks next to the fence, but finally, at the very back of the house where there was a path, I found the door. It wasn't a flimsy wooden thing like Audrey's and mine. This door was made out of heavy-duty aluminum or steel. Next to the door was an electronic keypad. As I waved my phone over the ground, I could see that the path ran the length of the back of the fence. If a teenager wanted to enter, all he or she would have to do was park a few houses to the north and walk down this path right to the door. And punch in the code that Felicity had provided.

Okay, so if Felicity was doing something naughty in the guesthouse, the question was: *What was it?* Felicity would be graduating in two days, a Friday, and time was running out to get to the bottom of the situation. That's why I didn't have any qualms about breaking into Felicity's car the very next day. Come on. It's not as bad as it sounds. I mean, Felicity didn't even lock her car most of the time, being as she was a protected young millennial who was too naive to think anything bad could ever happen to her. Oh, it was easy enough. Felicity had parked her car to go in and pick up her massive amount of weekly dry cleaning. They always had the order waiting for her, so she just parked in front and ran in, leaving her Porsche running. I already knew all of this about her from my surveillance, so I was ready, parked two cars away. She went into the dry cleaners, and I was out of my car and peering in her car windows in two seconds flat. I saw something that looked like a small suitcase on the backseat, so I reached in and grabbed it and was already backing out of my parking space when Felicity came out carrying her load. Seriously, all my years of running paid off in spades that day.

Or did it? I suppose that's the real question here. As you've probably already surmised, the suitcase was a video camera case. I sometimes wish I had never stolen that camera, watched the nauseating videos, and solved the mystery of what Felicity, in her warped psyche, commanded my daughter to do so that she would be accepted as a goddamn Tigerette. Those videos of Hayley and Marcy and all those boys were sickening and heartbreaking. They weren't as graphic as some of the pornographic films I'd seen over the years because the videographer was too amateurish. And I did not doubt that the videographer was Felicity. However, as I forced myself to watch those degrading videos, alternately chugging wine and blubbering and puking my guts out, what I ultimately saw was not the clumsy sex and blow jobs, but the loss of my daughter's innocence. From the comments I could hear in the background--Felicity's voice--it was also clear that she relished every moment of my daughter's humiliation. At one point, she said, "Do you think you have what it takes to be a Tigerette now, Hayley?"

I was enraged.

I agree that I am a vengeful person, and I had never wanted to get revenge on anyone like I did Felicity Stewart. I know she was a minor when she made those videos, but she wasn't a minor when I kidnapped her. I guess you could say that all those months of spying on people had made me something of an expert in scheming. So after I spent that Thursday night watching my daughter prostitute herself to be accepted by Felicity's crowd, I had everything planned out perfectly when I picked up Felicity after the lockdown graduation party the next night.

I was meticulous. I turned in my leased Buick and rented a limo, then I went to Party Time and rented a chauffeur's costume, even going so far as to add a fake mustache. I also had a sign printed up with her name on it and was holding it up as Felicity tumbled out of the building with all the other new graduates. They were sobbing melodramatically and promising to keep in touch through the years. Many of them were holding their newly distributed yearbooks. A few of them looked a little wobbly on their feet, and as I had hoped, someone must have snuck in some forbidden alcohol. Felicity was one of the wobbliest. That was a very, very good thing.

I grabbed Felicity immediately and escorted her into the waiting limo before her real driver caught on. Felicity tumbled into the roomy backseat. "I love limos," she said drunkenly.

"Good evening, miss. I will be your driver to Tucson." I even typed the spa's address into the GPS. I was playing a part, remember? "Your mother provided a bottle of champagne. It's in the ice bucket."

"Oh, goodie!" Felicity clapped her hands.

Did I melt a little at Felicity's unexpected childish giddiness? No, I did not. I had a plan, and I was sticking to it. I looked at Felicity in the rearview mirror. She was drinking the champagne straight from the bottle and tapping furiously at her phone. I had to get that phone away from her at the soonest possible moment. All of my hair tucked painfully beneath my chauffeur's cap was starting to give me a headache, but it was of no consequence. I was going to do this.

"I'm afraid there's been an accident on route 10, miss. There's no need for us to sit in stalled traffic. I'm going to drive around for a while until it's cleared. Enjoy your champagne."

"Whatever," Felicity said. She was still tapping at her phone.

I certainly knew that all kinds of things could go wrong with my plan. Felicity might have said that she had forgotten something and needed to stop by her house and get it. She might also change her mind altogether if she was invited to another party. Or she might text Cynthia and thank her for the limo, and Cynthia would say, "What limo? I ordered a town car." But the stars aligned for my plan that fateful night, and none of those things happened. After about thirty minutes or so of driving aimlessly through Phoenix, Felicity fell asleep, her mouth hanging open, her legs sprawled. And *goddamnit*, she still looked pretty.

"I'm going to stop and get some gas," I said, even though she seemed to be passed out. I pulled over on a dark street, reached back, and took her phone from her limp hand. I threw it out of the window and drove to our true destination.

The house on Cholla had made some progress. It had actual doors and walls and windows installed now, even though it was still pretty much bare bones on the inside--concrete floors, no insulation, no electricity or running water. No matter. I had prepared the small bedroom in the back of the house, the room farthest from the street, for Felicity's arrival. It was not as barbaric as some people have claimed. It did have a blowup air mattress on the floor, a blanket, a bucket for bathroom use, a jug of water, and some granola bars and beef jerky to sustain her for the short term. Mind you, I was only thinking of Felicity's punishment for the short term. I don't think I ever planned to keep her for more than a couple of days. I will admit that the chains that I had bolted into the wall looked somewhat medieval, but they were necessary. I had not scheduled any workmen for the next week, so the duct tape I had on hand to put over Felicity's mouth might not have been totally necessary, but I wasn't taking any chances.

I parked in back of the house and carried Felicity in. She was much heavier than I had anticipated, but I did it with ease, fueled as I was with adrenaline--and perhaps a touch of madness. She was starting to stir, though, by the time I got her into the room and clasped the manacles around her wrists behind her back. I had manacles for her ankles too, but that suddenly seemed rather cruel. She was still like a rag doll as I propped her on the air mattress. I was starting to unwind the duct tape, which I was going to take off when I came to check on her each day so she could eat and drink--please remember that--when Felicity's eyes flew open. The coldness of the manacles must have awakened her.

"Where am I?"

"It doesn't matter where you are, Felicity. You're going to be here a while, at least until I think you've been adequately punished." I had taken off my cap, and my long, dark hair flowed down my back.

Even in the dimness, Felicity knew who I was. "Mrs. Carson, what do you think you're doing?" There was no slur to her voice now, just the beginning of panic. Felicity searched around her frantically, probably looking for her phone.

"Your phone isn't here," I said calmly.

"You can't get away with this! My mother will report that I'm missing, and she'll call the cops. This is kidnapping!"

"Do you really think your mother is going to call the spa and check up on you? As far as she's concerned, you're safely in Tucson until she sees you next. I figure that gives me a week or so."

Felicity rattled her chains in response. "You are so fucked up! You will never get away with this!"

"I saw the videos." I was still talking in that dead-calm voice. "You humiliated my daughter, and now it's your turn. I want you to know what it feels like to be humiliated, Felicity."

"You!" Felicity shrieked. "You're the one who stole my camera! You had no right!"

"*You*, you're the one who forced my daughter to have sex with those boys. I don't know how you did it, you conniving little bitch, but I am going to teach you a lesson. You cannot get away with the kind of shit you've been shoveling all your life. Do you hear me?"

"Fuck you, Reggie Carson."

The menace in her voice was chilling. You'd think that someone in her position would be saying they were sorry, or sobbing, or begging to be freed, promising never to do a horribly evil act again. But not Felicity. She was all hellfire and fury. I almost respected her a little for that. But not quite.

I tore off a piece of duct tape and advanced toward her. She started kicking, naturally, and squirming away as far as the chains would allow. She was panting like an animal and surprisingly strong. I finally tackled her to the air mattress and straddled her. But something had been gnawing at me since the beginning of the whole Tigerette nightmare, and I wanted answers. "Tell me, Felicity, how do you bend people to your will? How do you always get your way? How did you coerce Hayley into having sex with all those boys? *How do you do it?*"

"You stupid cunt, like mother, like daughter! Hayley and Marcy should never have made the team. They're not good enough. And the bitches wanted to do it. They're stupid cunts!" Then she spat into my face.

That was the first time I hit her.

Why didn't I immediately confront Hayley about the videos?

That's a good question, but I'm not sure how to answer it. Maybe I thought that verbalizing the situation would make it more real, and I definitely didn't want it to be real, despite the evidence to the contrary. Unfortunately, maybe this seems more plausible: I had crossed the line into a kind of temporary madness by that point. I mean, I had a kidnapped teenager chained to the wall of an abandoned house, and I'm pretty damn sure that no one in the world would call that sane. When you look at what the three of us had become by that May--Audrey, Cynthia, and me--I'd say that we exhibited in graphic detail every character flaw known to womankind. No, I am not trying to make an excuse now. I'm telling the truth. The three partners of the wine club--maybe because of the wine club, maybe not--were all fucking nuts.

I have often wondered if all three of us subconsciously knew that the wine club was coming to an end and that the May party would be our last. For one thing, we were getting very sloppy. We worked feverishly to pour those boxes and boxes of Black Box wine into the four differently labeled Château Margaux bottles, not even bothering to differentiate the kind of wine in the four varietals we were going to offer. It was a mistake we had already made, and we should have known better. And contrary to how we usually operated, we bottled and corked half of the wine into the extra-large 6000 ml Château Margaux Premier Grand Cru Classé Red Bordeaux Blend 2009, the one going for $17,000. We usually only made a few of the big-ticket item of the night, but we were all fiercely driven by money at that point. Mind you, as we worked silently and fast in Cynthia's kitchen, we didn't know each other's money woes. We were each enamored with our own need for cash, so much so that no one batted an eye when someone--I think it was Cynthia--suggested that half our bottles be the most expensive fake French wine. In fact, we all thought it was an excellent idea. We all wanted more money.

For that last wine club party, Cynthia had gone back to her original guest list, the fifty friends and acquaintances of hers that we knew had money to spend. Cynthia had even hired a catering service, and black-clad waiters floated trays of canapés around the room. I was doing what I always did, trying to launch each wine tasting with a description of the château and the type of grape that had been grown for each vintage. It was really kind of funny when I think about it now. I had become quite knowledgeable about French wine, and I'd only tasted it the one time Cynthia brought out one of Richard's bottles! It was strange, too, how I could almost convince myself during those parties that the wine we were selling was real.

Maeve Olson arrived last. She had been absent from the last couple of parties--I now know why obviously--but I wasn't particularly happy to see her. She was a snob in the truest sense of the word, and it was because of her that Audrey and I got in such a huge fight after the December wine club party when she forced me to say that we were donating part of the proceeds to charity. But that wasn't the worst part of her arrival. The worst part was that she had brought a guest, her cousin from New York, who just happened to be a man.

Cynthia always fawned all over Maeve for no reason that I could figure out, and she swooped right in that night, saying, "Why, Maeve, you didn't tell me your cousin was such a handsome man."

Tyrone Jenkins was not in the least bit attractive, with his beaked nose and hooded eyes and thin face. He looked prissy to me. And gay. Not that I would know a gay man when I saw one. As you well know, my track record is not exemplary in that area. I married a gay man, for Pete's sake, and didn't even know until my son told me.

Anyway, the presence of a man at our women-only party set me off from the get-go. These parties were supposed to be for *women* to get together and forget all about their men and children and jobs while they got slightly tipsy and had a good time in the process. So as soon as Cynthia finished with her fawning, I grabbed her and Audrey and corralled them into the kitchen. "Men are not allowed at these parties, Cynthia. You know that. Tell Maude that Tyrone has got to go."

"That's rude, Reggie." Audrey looked bewildered, an expression she wore almost constantly those days. It drove me crazy.

"I'm not going to make a scene and tell a guest in my home that he has to leave. If he leaves, Maeve will leave, then half the party will follow her out the door like a bunch of baby chicks following their hen." Cynthia glanced over at Maeve and Tyrone. "Besides, he looks harmless enough. And maybe he has some money to spend. What's the big deal?"

So I was outnumbered again. "Fine," I huffed, "but I have a bad feeling about this."

"Just get back to your presentation, Reggie. And push the Premier Grand Cru Classé Red Bordeaux Blend. We need this party to be a success."

Like she needed to tell me how to do my job. However, each of us, for our own reasons, did need this party to be a success. And maybe she did have a point about not causing a commotion, but I still had a bad feeling in the pit of my stomach. "I don't like it," I emphasized one more time before we each went back to our posts.

I had just taken my place by the Premier Grand Cru Classé Red Bordeaux Blend when Maeve walked up to me, her cousin and about half the guests in tow. "Reggie, maybe you should let Tyrone take over the presentation," she said. I swear that she had a wicked look in her eye.

"Why would I do that? Is Tyrone some wine expert?" Goddamnit, I was falling right into the witch's trap.

Maeve smiled sinisterly. "As a matter of fact, Reggie, he is. Tyrone is a Master Sommelier."

"Maeve, you weren't supposed to bring that up," Tyrone demurred, but he was preening.

"It is so hard to pass the Master Sommelier Exam that only about two hundred and thirty people worldwide have passed the test in its forty-five-year history," Maeve went on. "It is a grueling three-part test. First, an applicant must pass an oral test of wine theory, knowing wine-growing regions and styles. Then they have to pass a service portion of the test, and then there's the notorious part of the test, the blind tasting, in which each applicant must identify three red and three white wines based on flavor and appearance alone. Most people who take the exam each year fail it, but not Tyrone."

"It took me three tries," Tyrone admitted, then added: "But that's normal."

As I stood there uselessly, holding that giant bottle of fake French wine, my heart pounding, and my mouth so dry that I couldn't even swallow, I looked frantically around the room for my partners. Audrey was sitting at her table with the credit card machine, the bewildered look on her face magnified by ten, and Cynthia looked as frozen in time as a porcelain statue.

As always, it was up to me to take the lead. "Tyrone is out here on vacation, isn't he, Maeve? I don't think we need to bother him with tasting our wine. What does a Master Sommelier do on vacation? He drinks beer!" No one laughed at my feeble joke.

When it comes to saving her own hide, Cynthia can act quickly. I grudgingly concede that. She was at Tyrone's side in a matter of seconds. "Reggie is right, Tyrone. You're a guest in my home, and I haven't even shown you our wine cellar yet. Come with me, and I'll give you the grand tour."

Now Cynthia had told me that there wasn't any wine left in Richard's wine cellar, and I had no idea what she planned to do with him once she got him down there to show him the empty shelves. Hell, she could seduce him for all I cared. But the longer we could keep him from tasting our wine, the more time I had to come up with a way to save this party, the wine club, and our reputations.

Tyrone wasn't impressed by Cynthia's offer. "I would love to taste the 2009 Cru Classé Blend. It's one of my favorites."

I was watching a nightmare, and I wasn't going to wake up anytime soon. Furthermore, I couldn't do one damn thing about it. I watched, horrified, as Tyrone reached for an already poured tasting glass and took a sip. I don't think it was only me. I think the entire room was holding its collective breath as Tyrone swirled and sniffed and then sipped.

His lips curled in distaste. "Why, this is nothing more than ordinary table wine, a cabernet from Chile."

"I knew it!" Maeve exclaimed triumphantly. "These women have been scamming us for months!"

Other women started to clamor. "I want my money back!" and "Someone call the police!"

But before I had a chance to defend myself--if that was at all possible--and before anyone could do anything, there was a commotion from the back patio, and two bearded, scruffy men rushed into the room, brandishing what appeared to be pool sticks. They looked so unkempt and wild that they reminded me of the outnumbered Scotsmen warriors in *Braveheart*. I didn't recognize them then as Richard and what would turn out to be Buck Boyd, the man on the video. I thought they were intruders or those crazed crystal meth zombies that go on killing sprees. Women started to scatter and shriek.

"Let me at the bitch!" one of the disheveled men shouted.

I heard a helicopter coming closer outside just as the front door burst open, and a SWAT team in protective gear with pointed guns ran into the room. I had never before been in the midst of such confusion and mayhem. The shattering glasses and the women screaming and crying and cowering made the April champagne party look like child's play. People were tripping and falling and stomping all over each other, trying to get to safety. But where could they go? We were caught in the middle of two men smashing bottles and glasses and furniture with pool sticks and a small army of muscled men with guns. And I was still standing there, holding that giant bottle of fake French wine that had proved our undoing at the hands of a Master Sommelier.

The SWAT team, who had been joined by some official-looking people in black suits, approached the bearded men, and I looked over to see where Audrey sat. She wasn't there. I searched the room for Cynthia as I started to move through the crowd but couldn't see her either. When I became blocked by all those shrieking women caught in the middle of men with weapons, I dropped to the floor and crawled. I butted my head against knees and crawled over people and slithered on my belly to get to the garage door.

Then I stood, opened it, and ran.

28

CYNTHIA

Do you want to know the truth about that last wine club party? All three of us--Reggie, Audrey, and I--ran away. I know that Reggie likes to say that we were all three big, fat cowards. But I disagree vehemently with that assessment, and everyone knows by know that Reggie is an extraordinarily gifted exaggerator. Reggie can speak for herself on that point, but I know that I was not, and have never been, a coward. I ask you: If you are running to save your life, does that make you a coward? You cannot look me in the eye and tell me that it does because it *does not*. It takes courage to get the hell out of Dodge when the going gets tough. I ought to know; I'm an expert on the subject.

By the night of the wine club on May 21, my life had become unbearable. I'd been waiting for the other shoe to drop for about two weeks by then, and I could barely make myself get up in the morning for fear of what the day would bring. The reason for all my inner turmoil was that the two men I had imprisoned in my panic room were no longer there, and it seemed like Richard and Buck had simply vanished off the face of the earth. They were no longer in that room, so where in the hell were they? As many times as I wished that they had not provoked me until I had no other alternative but to lock them in that small room and throw away the key, to find out that they were no longer there was even more alarming. Every single minute of every single day, I expected one or both of them to break into my house and let me have it. I don't want to go into the graphic details of what I imagined they would do to me. Suffice it to say that I doubted that I would still be beautiful. Consequently, I was in a constant state of terror.

I found out the hard way that Richard and Buck were no longer my guests on the evening that the two FBI agents made their weekly unannounced visit. Minutes before, I had just discovered that I could no longer view the banes of my existence on the monitor in Richard's office, but I was drunk enough--I will admit that--to think that it must have been my error. I was still reeling from that when the two agents, Woodfred and Prentiss, showed up and announced that they had a search warrant and were going to search the house. That was a first. They'd looked suspiciously around the property before, of course, but they had never had a warrant. Now they were going to be looking into every nook and cranny.

Felicity, still waiting in the kitchen for a daddy who would not show, pretending to study, was the defiant one. "I want to see the warrant."

The woman agent, Prentiss, showed it to her.

Felicity glanced at it like she'd seen a hundred search warrants before and handed it back. "Why are you searching the house *now?*"

"We have new evidence to suggest that Mr. Stewart is in the immediate area," Woodfred said.

Felicity opened her mouth to speak, but I had found my voice. "That's ridiculous. Richard would certainly be out of the country." My hand was amazingly steady as I lifted the wine glass I still held in my phony-ringed hand to my lips. "And if my husband was in town, which he is not, he has not made an appearance here."

"We would like to verify that," Prentiss said.

"This is an invasion of privacy!" Felicity yelled.

"Why, miss? Do you have something to hide?" Woodfred's voice was gruff.

For the briefest of moments, I thought my daughter might be trying to protect me, but that was dashed immediately when she arched her brow at me and said, "Of course not. Knock yourselves out. Be sure to show them the panic room, Mom. If someone were going to hide in the house, wouldn't that be a perfect place?"

That got the agents' attention, all right. "Where is the panic room, Mrs. Stewart?" Prentiss said. "Why don't you lead the way?"

What was I supposed to do? I had no choice at that point, and as I led the two agents down the stairs, I felt like a condemned woman being led to the gallows. I would slide open that heavy door and expose the two haggard-looking, smelly men. I would slide open that heavy door and expose what I had done. The fear at what I was about to do, for some reason, made me start to babble. "Richard installed the panic room when we built this house. I thought it was a frivolous expense at the time, and I still do. Honestly, the room has never been used. It was meant to keep our family safe, not harbor criminals."

We got to the door, and the two agents drew their guns. "Please open the door, Mrs. Stewart."

I really thought my life was over as I pressed that button, and the door slid slowly open. The opening door would automatically trigger the lights and the room would blaze into view, so I closed my eyes. I couldn't bear to look. Now I did realize that both men, when caught, would very likely go directly to jail, Richard because of the zillion indictments against him and Buck because of his attempt at extortion. However, they would bring me down too. I didn't doubt that. Buck held all the sordid secrets of my past like trump cards, and Richard would claim that I had been in on his Ponzi scheme. They might want to throw in a few good punches too. Neither one of them were gentlemen; neither one would have any qualms about hitting a lady.

"Clear," agent Prentiss said after stepping in and making a quick sweep of the room. "No one's here."

What? I dared to open my eyes and couldn't believe what I saw. Or rather, what I didn't see. Not only was the room empty, but it was also extremely neat. The blanket was carefully folded on the couch, and there wasn't a scrap of litter in sight. Even more surprising, it didn't smell like two unwashed men had occupied the room. Richard must have expected that the FBI would eventually trail him to this space, and he had covered his tracks well. Inadvertently or not, he had also covered mine.

I didn't realize I had been holding my breath until it came out in a strangled whoosh. I was safe, for now. "As you can see, agents, there's no one here."

"We can see that." Disappointment was written all over Woodfred's pockmarked face.

The agents did a thorough search of the rest of the house and the guesthouse and left empty-handed. I didn't feel giddy with relief, however, because I knew what all this meant. It meant that my purgatory, at least in Richard's mind, had begun. He would show up when it was most inappropriate, most embarrassing, most appalling, and most damaging.

And I had no idea of when that might be. I also had no idea where they could have gone, and all I could do was wait, always wondering: *But where are they now?*

By the night of the last wine club party, I was a frazzled mess, but I also had at least a partial answer to my question. It took me hours to find the trap door to the secret tunnel leading out of the panic room. *Hours.* I took a crowbar and pried off the tiles on the floor. I invested in a metal detector to run over every surface in the room to try to locate a steel door or latch. It was only when I tried to think like Richard that the answer came to me. Richard would never want to go down to escape; Richard would go up. I dragged a ladder down the stairs and started searching there, and sure enough, there was an almost seamless trap door in the far corner of the room. I pulled it down, and its ladder unfolded, and once you climbed up, it led to a crawl space between the floors of the house. I had to screw up my courage to go back up there with a flashlight and peer around about ten minutes later, and for about the thousandth time in the last few months, I wished I owned a gun.

The space was only big enough for one person to go through at a time, and I had to crawl it army-style like I was in the trenches. The tunnel snaked under the kitchen and family room, and only then did it go underground, under the patio and through the backyard. It was made of concrete, so it wasn't like a person would get terribly dirty crawling through the thing--thoughtful of Richard, wasn't it?--but it did take some time. I don't think I ever truly understood how big my house and property were until I crawled through that tunnel. And do you know where it eventually came out? The linen closet in the guesthouse, which was in the hallway between the bedroom and the kitchen. I don't think I'd ever realized there was a linen closet there until I popped open the door at the bottom and crawled onto the beige carpeting, panting. The crawl had taken me twenty-five minutes.

So I didn't know where Richard and Buck were, and I didn't know when they had escaped, but at least I knew how. I planned to use that information. The more I thought about it, the more certain I was that Richard would want to make his appearance in a crowd, rather than trying to corner me in my bedroom one night and beat the crap out of me. Richard, always one for the grand gesture, would prefer to have an audience witness my ultimate humiliation. He was probably watching the house, but the FBI agents were also watching the house. Would Richard risk making a scene knowing that the FBI would likely be following close behind?

I guessed that he would. He hated me enough now that he wanted revenge. Richard had always been a vengeful person. But that wasn't really it. The only thing that mattered to him, maybe the only thing that had ever mattered to him was Felicity. As far as Richard knew, she was still waiting for her daddy to take her to New York. Maybe he knew that he was going to be captured eventually, but it could very well be true that Richard wanted to go out with a bang, and by doing so, he would prove to his daughter that he wasn't a coward. It would be a misguided attempt on his part, but it was certainly Richard's style, which made me certain that Richard was going to make his Last Stand at the May wine club. It all made sense in the warped worldview of Richard Stewart.

As nervous and frazzled as I was on the night of the wine party, I was ready. I had packed a bag and had it waiting in the guesthouse, and I packed frugally, for me. I hated the thought of leaving my closetful of beautiful clothes, about the only thing I had left in the world, but such was my determination. I was going to buy an airplane ticket in cash, but when I went to the bank to withdraw money from the FHM account, I was informed by a prim, thin-lipped woman that the account was overdrawn. I was furious at Reggie and Audrey. I mean, I had been withdrawing money from the account too, but I didn't think I had taken out that much. That meant that my so-called partners had been embezzling money! I was so mad that I almost drove directly over to their pitiful little houses and let them have it, but ultimately, I couldn't see the point. It was too late. That's when I decided that I would take the cashbox from the party when I made my escape. Fair was fair, right?

I honestly didn't know that Maeve's cousin was a Master Sommelier. If I had known that, I wouldn't have let Maeve bring him, period. But that Maeve was a conniving bitch, and after buying all that expensive fake wine from Audrey, I guess she thought she deserved to get even. And in doing so, by causing that scene of outrage and inciting the mob, she actually did me a huge favor. Those women were absolutely furious with us, and you should have seen the looks on Reggie's and Audrey's faces! It was hysterical. They acted genuinely surprised, as if they thought they could get away with this little scam forever. I mean, come on, even the best schemes eventually get exposed, and the clock had been ticking on this one for months.

I saw Richard and Buck running across the yard before they even made it to the patio. Did I know my husband, or what? He was barely recognizable--and I guessed that was on purpose--but what surprised me was that he was still with Buck. Buck was a big, fat loser, and Richard? Never mind. I guess Richard was now a loser too. And I'm pretty sure they were both drunk, which only meant that Buck's stupidity was also rubbing off on Richard. They entered the house with weapons made out of metal pipes, and that was my cue.

Before anyone could get a grip on what was going on, I grabbed the cashbox and hightailed it for the basement stairs. I was shaking as I crawled up onto the back of the couch to push open the seamless door, wondering if anyone had followed me. And do you want to know what my biggest fear was? That someone would come and close the panic room metal door behind me, and I would suffer the same fate I had bestowed on Richard and Buck. It sounded like a barroom brawl was going on upstairs, and I made it to the crawl space without detection. I crawled about halfway in the tunnel and waited. I waited for hours until I felt it was safe enough to crawl the rest of the way and walk to the grade school parking lot where my Mercedes was parked, filled with enough gas to get me four hundred miles out of this town and out of this life.

Did I give any thought to Felicity as I waited in that damp, claustro-phobic tunnel? No, why would I?

29

AUDREY

I'm going to tell you the saddest part now. At least I think it's the saddest, although the whole story is pretty sad, isn't it? What was it I told you about being a pity party of one, that I was sick of it? It's still true. But I have to tell you this part of the tale, if for no other reason than to clear my conscience. Yeah, right. Like that would ever happen.

On the night after the last wine club party, I was mesmerized by the flames as they crackled and grew, beginning their destruction of the *Audrey* and everything she stood for. The fire was a thing of beauty to behold, reminding me as it did of a camping trip that Paul and I had taken the kids on four years before. We had seen the Grand Canyon that day and settled for the night in a campground just outside of Flagstaff. It had been unseasonably chilly that June night in the mountains, and Paul and I stayed up much later than the kids, cuddling under a blanket by a cozy fire and looking up at the stars. We passed a flask of Jack Daniels back and forth, which was why we dared to make love out there, with the kids sleeping in a tent only ten feet away. But as I stood rooted to the spot in my driveway, watching that hated boat burn, burn, burn, I wondered if that long-ago camping trip was the last time I had felt truly happy. It was a very sad thought.

Sad, too, was the fact that my nosy neighbors were streaming out their doors and onto the street in front of my house and shouting, ruining my lovely memory. Carl, who lived four houses down the block, was pulling frantically at my arm. "Audrey, get away from the fire! You're going to get burned!"

I tried to resist, but he was too strong for me. "Can't you let me watch this in peace?" I cried out as he pulled me toward the street.

"Are the kids inside?" someone asked. There was quite a crowd gathered in the street by then. "That boat is awfully close to the house."

My kids. How strange it was that I hadn't given a thought to them until that moment. They were always, constantly on my mind, night and day. I felt the familiar panic, but I couldn't move. The crowd had hemmed me in, or maybe it was that my legs had turned to stone. I couldn't move; I had become a statue.

"Someone go inside and get my kids!" I screamed. Maybe I only thought I screamed because no one seemed to have heard me over the roar of the fire. And the sirens. Now I heard sirens drawing closer and closer. Who had called the fire department, and why? This horrible boat was meeting its proper death. I didn't need any firemen putting a stop to what I had rightfully started. I would tell them that when they got here. I would tell them this fire was none of their business. It was mine.

I heard screams then, and the screams did not belong to me. I wasn't alone. The crowd around me was starting to panic.

"Did you hear that?"

"Dear God, is someone in the boat?"

"Someone call for help! Do something, *goddamnit!*"

I thought the voice was Reggie's, but when I turned toward the speaker, it wasn't her. So where was she anyway? Reggie would get a big kick out of watching this boat burn. I knew she'd think I had done the right thing. And she would understand why I had to do it. I wished she would get here soon. She was missing a good show.

Marcy and Jimmy were running from the house, and Marcy was screaming and crying as she pulled her brother along. "My dad is in that boat! Someone has to help my dad!"

The sight of my children broke the spell I was under, and I ran toward them and fell to my knees, pressing them against my chest. "Everything is going to be fine," I said rotely. It was what I always told my children: everything would be fine; everything would work out. I told them this even when I knew it wasn't true, like now. Do you see? I lied to everyone, including my own children.

"Mom! Dad is in the boat!" Marcy shrieked.

She'd said that before, hadn't she? "No, Marcy, your dad is in--"

"The boat!" Marcy covered her face with her hands and sobbed.

I turned to the boat. The flame had grown magnificently once it lost my rapt attention. Paul couldn't be in the boat, could he? He was asleep in the den. That's where he slept now, on the couch in the den. But he wasn't out here with our children. He was a sound sleeper, but surely, the cacophony of voices out here would have awakened him. Unless he was passed out, drunk again . . .

Oh, my God! Paul was in the boat.

I ran to the boat then, elbowing people out of my way and shrieking like a madwoman. Someone had brought a fire extinguisher and was futilely trying to fight the flame with its foam. "I have to get my husband out!" I screamed, lunging at the burning hull. But strong arms pulled me back once again from the flames that were mine. I was crying then, and it wasn't only for Paul. And the tears weren't only for my poor children. They were for everything, including my mother. I had snuffed out her life like a candle. And now I was burning my husband alive, like a human sacrifice. I retched, but nothing came up. I hadn't eaten all day. I was empty.

The firemen pulled up then, and people were shouting at them, telling them that someone was in the boat. The events happening in front of me were moving across my vision in slow motion. It seemed to take an eternity for the firemen to unfurl their hose, to attach it to the hydrant, to point the nozzle at the burning boat, and spray. One of the men in his bright yellow jacket and boots crawled into the smoldering boat and disappeared down the hole. He was shouting something to his comrades that I couldn't make out. And there were more sirens. The paramedics had arrived and were carrying a stretcher onto the boat.

The crowd of nosy neighbors had grown eerily quiet. I stared at the smoldering boat, an arm around each child. They clung to me, and I was grateful. I didn't know how much longer I would have that beautiful luxury. Every so often we would hear voices from the boat: inhalation

injuries, soot in the airways, second and third-degree burns. I heard coughing, and I wondered if it was Paul or another person on board. I prayed that it was Paul.

When another eternity had passed, the stretcher was hoisted into view. "Stay here," I said to my children before I ran to the boat. They didn't listen; they followed close.

"Is he alive?" I asked one of the people carefully bringing the stretcher off the boat. My voice was a whisper, and I had to repeat the awful question. "Is my husband alive?" I couldn't tell by looking at him. His entire body, except for his face, was covered in white sterile gauze. His face was red, angry-looking, his eyelashes and eyebrows gone. My husband's face would never be handsome again.

"Audrey." Paul's voice sounded hoarse, parched.

"Oh, Paul, I'm so sorry." I reached out to touch him, but the paramedic stopped me. I could cause an infection by touching his open wounds. But I already knew that. All you had to do was look at what I'd done. All you had to do was see what kind of person I had become. I was diseased.

Marcy, Jimmy, and I followed the ambulance to the hospital, where we waited for another eternity in the ER waiting room. I drank cup after cup of bitter coffee and the kids stared listlessly at the TV. Sometime during that night, I was questioned by some man--a police officer, a fireman, a doctor? I'm not sure--about the origins of the fire. The lie was immediately on my lips. I would tell them about the old and very dangerous kerosene lamp that Paul used below deck for light. I would tell them that it was a fire hazard from the beginning. That old kerosene lamp started the fire.

But then I looked at my son and my daughter, their infinitely sad faces, and the final lie died on my lips. "I did it," I said. "I set the boat on fire."

30

REGGIE

You can bet your sweet ass we were all cowards that night. All three of us. I have been accused of climbing up on my high horse from time to time, but that Cynthia takes the cake. She was scared shitless that night, just like Audrey and me. You could see it in her face, her eyes, and if I'd caught a glimpse of her belly, it would have been as yellow as mine and Audrey's. Let me give you an example that proves Cynthia was scared. Cynthia was always so meticulous about the way she looked--she's a narcissist if ever there was one--but on that night, her blonde hair stuck up like a poof ball on one side, and she had lipstick on her teeth. She would have been mortified if someone had pointed out those imperfections to her, so believe me when I tell you I was tempted. However, she looked so un-put-together for a change that I let it ride. Let other people see that the former Mrs. Arizona was *so* not perfect. On any other night, Cynthia's slide into imperfection would have been one of the highlights for me. But as I've said, the place erupted all at once, so Cynthia's appearance was the least of my concerns.

I ran. Once I had slithered on my belly like a reptile through the sea of high heels and the fallen Chanel suits, once I had gotten to the garage door, I opened it and ran. I ran past my car parked in the driveway outside the garage. I noticed that Audrey's car was already gone, but I didn't give that a second thought. When I am really stressed out or when I'm angry--which pretty much means all the time--I run. Once I get the adrenaline pumping, I can think more clearly. There was a myriad of official-looking cars parked outside and more men with guns, but their attention seemed to be riveted on the house. They didn't notice a long-legged, middle-aged woman in black pants and black shirt and black ballet flats kicking up her heels and hightailing it through the next-door neighbor's yard. I wondered how Audrey had made her escape with Cynthia's house surrounded like it was. Maybe she had given herself up and was already being escorted to jail. It was no concern of mine.

Wait a minute. Yes, it was a very big concern of mine. What if Audrey was spilling her guts to the cops that very minute and throwing me to the wolves? What if she was saying that I was the mastermind behind our entire scam and that she had been nothing more than an innocent employee trying to make a couple of bucks while her alcoholic husband was drying out for the hundredth time? I mean, I *was* the mastermind of the wine club, but Audrey and Cynthia had been just as greedy and culpable as me. We had divided the profits from our sales equally, and even though I had always thought that was inherently unfair, that I should have gotten more than them simply because it was my idea, I went along with the plan without complaining. Well, okay, I probably complained loudly once or twice, but I got over it. The thought of Audrey misconstruing the truth made me run faster, harder.

I had a couple of immediate problems to contend with. The first one was my shoes. I could feel every rock and pebble through their thin soles as I took to the street a couple of blocks away. How I longed for my Nike Air Zoom Pegasus 35 running shoes! I could run a marathon with no problem in those babies, but they were at home in the laundry room where I'd left them. And I knew better than to go home. Wouldn't that be the first place the cops would try to find me? I decided that I should stop by Kent's condo first and borrow a pair of his running shoes. It was a sad but true fact that my soon-to-be-ex-husband and I wore the same size shoe. We had been on pretty good terms since I'd agreed to use a mediator for the divorce. I had also quit driving by his house and destroying his property. So maybe I'd get lucky, and he wouldn't ask any questions when he handed over his running shoes.

My second problem was much bigger. I had no place to run *to*. You have to remember that at that time I had no idea that one of the bearded men who had crashed our wine club party was Richard Stewart and that he was the focus of the FBI raid. I actually thought the whole thing with Maeve's cousin, the Master Sommelier, had been a set-up or something, maybe by Maeve herself. I thought that Audrey, Cynthia, and I were the focus of the raid, and believe me, that had me running scared.

Too late, I realized that the three of us should have had an escape plan in case we ever got caught. It wasn't like we had to have a plan to run away together to a cabin up north or down to Mexico. Shit, that was an awful thought, having to spend time in a cramped hideout with those two. But we should have at least gotten our story straight, you know, what we would divulge and what we wouldn't. But again, too late. And I, the most pragmatic of the group, hadn't even thought far enough ahead to figure out a good escape plan for myself. I suppose I had always known, deep down, that we wouldn't get away with our scam forever, so it was out of character for me. Shit, shit, shit.

I ran up Kent and Reed's sidewalk and pounded on the door. I was already sweating hard, and Kent didn't live that far from Cynthia. I was in great shape, so it must have been fear. I pounded on the door again and was mid-pound when Kent opened it. I didn't waste any time. "I need to borrow your running shoes," I panted.

From the look on his face, I could tell I looked pretty awful. "What's going on?" He peered over my shoulder, probably looking for our old van.

"No time. I need your shoes."

He folded his arms over his chest. "Not until you tell me what's going on."

I didn't have anything to lose at that point, so I told him the truth. "Our wine club got raided by the FBI tonight, Kent. I'm on the run, and I can't run in these damn shoes." I lifted my foot to show him the thin tread on the bottom of the ballet flat. "Ballerinas obviously do not run on rocky asphalt."

Kent's face fell. "I can't believe you're still doing that, Reggie," he said, aggrieved. "I told you months ago to stop. Selling wine under false pretenses is illegal."

"Save the lecture, Kent. All I want is your shoes."

"You're asking a lot of me, Reggie. I don't want to be involved in this. You should turn yourself in."

Kent could be so maddeningly *moral*. "Please, Kent, give me your god-damn shoes. I promise it will be the last thing I ever ask of you." I think we both knew that wasn't true, but Kent went back into the house. I didn't know if he was calling the cops or telling Reed or watching TV or getting the damn shoes. He returned with the shoes. "Thank you."

Kent shut the door without another word.

Kent's shoes felt so much better--marvelous, actually--and I was back on the road, running. I disposed of the useless ballet flats in someone's garbage can that was perched at the curb waiting for trash pickup the next day. I had a twenty-dollar bill in my back pants pocket for emergencies, something I had done since it was my dad's parting advice before I went to college: "Always keep a twenty in your pocket, Regina, in case a date goes wrong or you get stranded. A twenty is all you need." That twenty was the only thing I had. I'd left my purse at Cynthia's, along with my car. And unfortunately, I don't think my dad had ever counted on inflation. I didn't even know if I could buy a bus ticket with only twenty dollars.

In the end, there was only one place to go, one choice. I headed west toward Cholla. My house there was about a ten-mile run from Kent's, an easy enough distance for me. I had a spare key hidden under a rock in the front of the house that the contractor used to get in. Trust me when I say that I didn't relish spending any more time with Felicity than I had to. It was Monday night, and she had been chained to the wall since the wee hours of Saturday. I didn't think it was all that much time. I read a story once about a man who kept a sex slave in a box under his bed for something like five years. I don't remember if the man's wife knew about the sex slave or not, but the point I'm making here is that the enslaved woman survived. While I wouldn't go so far as to say that Felicity was thriving in her present circumstances, she didn't have it as bad as some captives who were tortured. I would have liked to torture her, but I didn't. I might have slapped her a few times, but it was only because she was such a mouthy little bitch.

Excuse me? Did I enjoy hitting Felicity Stewart? I'm pleading the Fifth on that one.

Anyway, I had been going over to check on Felicity a couple of times a day, mostly because I had to. I had to take off the duct tape so she could drink and eat, not that she was doing either. After Felicity's ranting the first night, she now exhibited a controlled fury when I took off the duct tape. She no longer tried to scream. The first time she screamed, I did hit her, but only to make a point. Most of the time, I talked to her. Or maybe I should say that I questioned her. I still wanted to know why she had made those sex tapes of Hayley and Marcy, but other than saying that they weren't good enough to be Tigerettes, there wasn't a satisfying answer that came from Felicity's poisoned mouth. I was beginning to think she did it just to see if she could get away with it.

I let myself into the house and found the flashlight I kept by the front door. I'd check on Felicity first to get it out of the way, but I didn't plan on keeping her company that night. I planned on spending most of the night by myself, trying to figure out a way to get a cell phone to contact Hayley and Caleb to let them know I was all right. I was sure they'd be mad at me too, once word got out what their mother had been up to for the last seven months, but once they heard my side of the story, I hoped I could convince them that I had done what I had done for the good of our family. School was out for the year now, and I wanted to convince Hayley that she needed to go with me when I decided on my final destination. Caleb had elected to stay in Tucson for summer school. I was pretty sure my son didn't like me much anymore. It was going to take some effort to get him to see my point of view.

I shined the light on Felicity as she huddled against the wall. She didn't look so hot. Her hair was stringy, and the room she was in wasn't the cleanest of places, so she was covered with a gray film of dust. I probably used more force than necessary to take off the duct tape, but you know. I put a bottle of water to her lips. "Drink some water, Felicity."

She shook her head while she glared at me.

Honestly, it gave me the creeps. That girl could spit venom from her eyes, as well as her tongue. During our time together, Felicity's answers to my questions were curt and cunning, often ambiguous. And what struck me most was that Felicity showed no remorse for anything she had done. Seriously, she didn't express even a *shred* of compassion. For example, when I asked her if she loved her mother, her answer was: "What is there to love?"

"How's my little psychopath doing tonight?" That's what I had started to call her. And I didn't mean it as an endearment. I had come to the conclusion that the girl was indeed a psychopath.

"When are you going to let me go?"

"I haven't decided yet." It sounded like a taunt, which it was, but it was also the truth. Now that I had Felicity where I wanted her, I wasn't quite sure what to do with her. The workmen would return to the house at the end of the week, and she needed to be gone by then. But what was I going to do? Unchain her, drive her home, deposit her on Cynthia's doorstep, and say *here*?

"I'm sorry," Felicity said.

"Excuse me?"

"I'm sorry I was mean to Hayley and Marcy. They're nice girls, and I took advantage of them. I'll apologize to them too if you want me to."

I didn't really believe her, but oh, did I want to! I wanted her to be accountable for her actions. I wanted her to *know* that she had taken my daughter's innocence and exploited her. "Nice try, Felicity," I said. "But I'm not buying the shit you're peddling."

She looked pathetic, squatting there on the mattress, sniffling, her hair a mess and a couple of bruises on her cheeks. *Dear God, had I done that?* I swear, I didn't think I'd hit her that hard. I didn't know about her, but I felt genuine remorse. What was I trying to prove by chaining up a teenager?

I studied her for a moment. "Why don't I take off your chains for a few minutes so you can stretch?" She had orchestrated a moment of weakness in my conscience, but I didn't see the harm in letting her walk around the small room. I had a flashlight and--God forbid--I could use it for a weapon if I had to.

"Thank you," she sniffled, her head downcast.

While I was unlocking the manacles, a sudden wave of exhaustion hit me like a tsunami. The wine club was now a thing of the past, I had just run ten miles trying to evade the FBI, and I had reduced a teenager to an animal. That's what was going through my head. That's why my guard was down.

The next thing I knew, Felicity had thrown her vengeful weight on me and knocked me to the ground. I was reeling from the blow to my head when I felt the explosive pain in my ribs.

31

AUDREY

There we were, all three of us in the holding cell in the Scottsdale jail, and even then we couldn't agree on anything. We'd all been brought in at roughly the same time, me from the hospital, Cynthia from a school parking lot where she was trying to wrestle an oversized suitcase into the trunk of her Mercedes, and Reggie from some vacant house on Cholla that she apparently owned. I figured we must have been under surveillance all night, maybe even before that, and it was a sting operation designed to round us all up at the same time, but I didn't dare ask. We were all exhausted and shell-shocked from being arrested, but after each of us were led away and separately questioned by police before being returned to the cell, it was like the Band-Aids had been ripped off, exposing the ugly wounds beneath. We felt betrayed by one another, and we were all as mad as tired, scared, and desperate women could be. It had been a mistake for the deputies to put us in the same cell, and there was no doubt in my mind they would soon regret it. We could be a pretty shrill group when we got going.

I knew the truth about the Tigerettes now, but the magnitude of what those girls had done had not fully sunk in yet. While my husband was fighting for his life in the ER, my daughter decided it was the perfect time to cleanse her soul. Believe me, it wasn't, but I had no idea what she was going to divulge when she asked me if she could tell me something, something important. So I'd said, "Sure, honey," and took both of her hands in mine.

"Felicity was so mean to Hayley and me at those first practices, Mom. She even made us wear diapers because we were the newbies. But you already know that part because you were peeking in the window. Boy, did that make Felicity mad."

That seemed so long ago and so innocuous now that I wondered why I had been so outraged at the time. "Go on," I urged Marcy. "Tell me about that raunchy dance that went viral. Who's idea was that?" I asked the question even though I knew the answer. I wanted to hear Marcy say it.

"Well, Felicity choreographed the dance, but she made it into a competition. The two girls who scored the highest got the two solos. It was a big deal, Mom. Really, it was."

Just thinking about that dance got me incensed all over again. "That dance put you and Hayley on display and caused an uproar among the parents--"

"Mom," Marcy interrupted, "I can't tell you what happened if you go off the deep end at every little thing. This is hard enough as it is." She sniffled and wiped a hand across her nose, just as she had when she was a little girl confessing some crime she thought she had committed. The "crime" usually consisted of her not brushing her teeth before bed or of her stealing a piece of Jimmy's candy.

However, I knew that I wasn't going to be so lucky this time. I promised not to interject until she finished. "Unless you tell me something really bad."

"It's pretty bad."

I added another jolt of fear to the ragged ache that had steadily grown all night long. "Please tell me, Marcy."

Marcy took a deep breath. "Felicity really pumped Hayley and me up after that dance. The parents might have thought the dance was too sexy, but the kids at school loved it, especially the guys on the basketball team. Felicity started telling everyone that Hayley and I were the real stars of the Tigerettes now, and they started hanging around our lockers. We were popular, Mom, and we liked it. For the first time in my life, I felt pretty."

I couldn't help myself. "You've always been pretty, Marcy." She rolled her pretty green eyes at that one, and I squeezed her hand. "Go on with the story. But I do have one question. Why didn't any of these boys ask you out on dates? Why didn't I meet any of them?"

"Mom," Marcy didn't successfully hide the exasperation in her voice. "People in high school don't date anymore. We hang out in groups."

That was news to me, but I nodded an assent.

Marcy took another deep breath. "So a group of us started to hang out." At my questioning look, she furnished, "Tigerettes and basketball players. We just did the normal stuff, you know, watched movies and kidded around. Then one night one of the guys brought over a porno tape, an old DVD, you know, that he'd taken from his mom and dad's bedroom or something, and--"

"Wait!" I was not keeping my promise, and at Marcy's look, I retreated. "Sorry."

"So we watched it, and it was kind of funny, and it kind of made me uncomfortable, but everyone else seemed to be into it, so I played along. When the movie was over, Felicity said, 'I bet we could make our own porno movie, and it'd be better than that one.'"

Marcy waited for me to interject, but I was too stunned to speak, so she rushed on. "So Felicity took a vote about who should be in the movies, and the guys voted for Hayley and me. We didn't want to do it at first, but everyone was like, 'hey, we're all friends here' and stuff like that."

Marcy's head was down now, and her voice was lower. "Felicity told Hayley and me that we didn't have to do it, but that the guys were totally into us. And to keep them interested, she said, we were going to show them how hot we really were. She said we could do it in her guesthouse because we'd be more comfortable there, and she'd steal some of her mom's wine and valium, and she'd get the protection . . ." Marcy's voice dwindled to nothing.

My voice, when I found it, wasn't much louder. "You did it?" At Marcy's nod, I gulped down a ball of sorrow that was forming in the back of my throat. "How many videos?"

"Four or five."

"Who watched the videos?"

"Only the Tigerettes and basketball players. They didn't go viral if that's what you're asking. Felicity used a real video camera. No one videotaped the . . . the *stuff* on their phones."

I didn't want to ask *anything*. I didn't want to know any more of this horrible story. But I had to. "So who was the EPT test for?"

Marcy went even paler than she already was. "That was for me. Garrett's rubber broke, and I was afraid . . . but I wasn't, you know?"

It was strange. My mind felt blank, but a line of questions kept running across it like an old fashioned ticker tape. It had to be some kind of self-preservation. If not for that ticker tape to focus on, I would lose it completely. "Where are the videos now?"

"That's just it. I don't know. Someone stole Felicity's video camera out of the back of her car, and we just don't know."

"Now, they will go viral."

"That's what I'm afraid of."

I couldn't do one damn thing to ease her concerns about that, nor did I want to. Felicity might have run the show, but my daughter didn't have to be a willing participant. She was certainly not blameless in all this, she who craved attention so badly that she would resort to making porno films. Had she craved all that attention because she wasn't getting it at home? Both Paul and I had been AWOL as parents for the last seven months.

"Why . . . why were you and Hayley the only two girls who did this? Why didn't Felicity participate instead, since it was her idea?" I was getting mad at the little witch all over again. As usual, she kept herself just above the fray. She'd put my daughter in a lewd, compromising situation for her own enjoyment, and she needed to be punished.

"Felicity was the camera person," Marcy whispered. "And besides, she couldn't because she's in love with someone."

"Who, who is Felicity in love with?" The girl had never had an actual date on any weekend night that I had been over at the house. Oh, that's right. Teenagers didn't date anymore. The rules had changed.

"She won't say who he is, but he's older, much older, she said. And way more sophisticated than the high school boys. She's going to run away with him after she graduates. But don't tell anyone I told you that, okay, Mom? It's supposed to be a secret."

"She's in love with a teacher?" I murmured.

"Oh, God, no." Marcy shuddered dramatically, a gesture that reeked of Felicity. "Have you seen the male teachers at Mohave? I don't think so."

It was only later, when I had a lot of time on my hands, that I would ponder the true nature of Felicity's love interest, and it was then that I shuddered dramatically. But at that time, I was only thinking of my daughter. I didn't know if I would be able to save my husband, the man who would require multiple surgeries and more care than I could give him--if he survived what I had done to him. But perhaps I could still save my daughter and my son.

"You're not trying out for the Tigerettes next year, Marcy. In fact, you are never going to set foot in Mojave High School again." She started to protest, the tears welling, as I had expected. "I'm going to make a phone call."

I stepped out into the hallway and called my brother Aaron in Oregon. It was a phone call that was long overdue, and I began without preamble. "Mother's dead, Aaron."

There was a long silence at the other end before he said. "Would you think I'm a bad person if I said I'm glad?"

"Would you think I'm a bad person if I said I killed her? I put her in a skilled nursing facility after her stroke, and she was still as mean as ever, and I didn't really know what I was doing, and I'm sorry--"

Aaron interrupted. "Don't beat yourself up about putting the old lady in a nursing home that couldn't handle her. No one could, not even Dad. And I'm the one who should be apologizing, Audrey. I left you holding the bag on that one. What did you do with her ashes? Flush her?"

I started laughing then, hysterically, and it took me a while to pull myself together. Aaron waited patiently; he was always a patient soul. He would be a good, stable influence on Jimmy and Marcy. After the year we'd had and what was still to come, they were going to need it. "I have a huge favor to ask of you, Aaron, really huge." Then I asked him.

I was ready when the detectives came shortly after that. If you want to know the truth, I think I was relieved. Or maybe I was still in shock. The whole chain of events is quite fuzzy in my memory, almost surreal, very much like the day in the nursing home when I watched those hands put the pillow over my mother's face. Being questioned by the detectives at the station didn't help my confusion either. They were throwing out charges for selling fraudulent wine and then wire fraud. Who knew that taking credit cards as a means of payment could cause so much trouble because it meant that money was wired across state lines? Which meant that the FBI would be called in too.

Then the detectives started threatening prison sentences: two years, five, ten. All of that was meant to shock me into submission. It was kind of funny. I was already in shock, so after a while, all I was hearing was blah blah blah. I did hear this: Originally, it was Maeve who tipped off the cop about the wine club's nefarious dealings. Then they received phone calls from the Sanchez family, Louisa, Pepe, and Angel. Even the bank that held the FHM account notified the authorities that there was suspicious activity--i.e., copious withdrawals on an account that was set up as a college savings fund. I told them my side of the story, what I could remember of it, and then I was led back to the cell. All I wanted at that point was peace and quiet, relatively speaking, but that was not to be. We were going to have it out in that jail cell once and for all, just as the deputies who put us there had planned all along.

32

REGGIE

"**G**oddamnit, Audrey, you are not going to plead guilty. All three of us are going to plead innocent. We're going to say that we didn't know that my French cousin, the monk/vintner, sold us fake wine."

"Tone it down, Reggie. They can hear us. Don't you have any sense at all? Don't you think you can control yourself just this one damn time?" Cynthia still had on the blue chiffon dress she had worn to the wine club party, but it now looked like it had been through a shredder.

She was probably right about that. Why else would the nincompoops have put all three of us in the same holding cell? Besides, yelling at the top of my lungs made the wound in my side ache even more. The detectives that picked me up decided that the puncture wasn't deep enough to warrant medical attention. I told them that the fact that it was a *rusty nail* ought to be motivation enough to take me to the hospital. Unfortunately, though, I'd had to admit that I'd had a tetanus shot two months ago after I cut myself while sawing on a ceiling beam at the Cholla house.

"We *are* all guilty, Reggie. Why would we plead otherwise?" Audrey's voice sounded weird, like she could only speak in a low monotone.

Believe me when I tell you that Audrey looked like absolute shit. Her green eyes were bloodshot, her face smeared with soot, and she absolutely reeked of smoke. I know that I didn't smell like a bed of roses either, given the fact that I'd run ten miles and then wrestled on the dirty floor of a partially renovated house with a psychopathic teenager.

Let me tell you about that. I was winning. After Felicity attempted to stab me with that rusty nail, I was so enraged that I found a strength I didn't know I possessed. I managed to flip her over and was straddling her. We were both slapping and scratching and grunting like animals. But I somehow managed to wrest the rusty nail out of her hand and was seriously considering giving her a dose of her own medicine when the cops burst through the door and pulled me off her. I would have kept at her indefinitely, I think. A sound ass-whooping was probably the least of what the girl deserved after what she had put my daughter through. And let me repeat this important fact: I was winning. It didn't work to the girl's advantage that she'd had very little to eat or drink for the past three days, of course, but still. She was a worthy adversary. I'll give her that much.

When the cops, who seemed surprised--perhaps *mortified* is a better word--to discover a teenager had been chained to a wall in the house, began to question Felicity, she turned on the waterworks. Man, oh man, that girl could cry a river, and she did. "That woman kidnapped me," Felicity cried to the cops, "and she starved me and beat me. And I don't know why! I want to go home!"

"Knock it off, Felicity! You are a compulsive liar!" I yelled at her while the cops were yanking my hands behind my back to put on those plastic cuffs that look like the zip ties you would put on a bag of garbage. "You made sex tapes of my underaged daughter! Arrest that conniving little bitch, officers!"

Instead, they put a blanket around her thin shoulders and led her to a different car than I was led to. I'm pretty sure the cops were initially on her side. I couldn't blame them. The situation didn't look good if you looked at it objectively. Those chains dangling from the wall certainly had a medieval, dungeon-like look to them. Which is probably why the cops refused to take me to the hospital. They seemed to think I was the bad guy in the situation. Or maybe they thought I would run if they took me to the ER. If so, it was smart thinking on their part. I would definitely have tried to make a run for it.

Cynthia, who had been pacing the small cell, spoke next. "Did they offer you a plea deal, Audrey?"

"I don't even know what that is," Audrey said in her monotone voice.

"Snap out of it, Audrey. We need to come up with a plan, and it makes sense for us all to plead the same." I'd walked over to where she was slumped on the bench and could smell the acrid smoke. "What is wrong with you, and why do you smell so bad?"

"I burned the boat. I didn't know Paul was sleeping below deck." Audrey stared at the wall over my shoulder.

Well, that knocked me for a loop. It really did. "Is Paul okay?"

"No. He was still in emergency surgery when I was arrested."

"Oh, God, Audrey." I was ready to sit down next to her and put my arms around her, but the third wheel in our operation interrupted and messed everything up like she always did.

"I wouldn't be talking if I were you, Reggie. You smell like a locker room. What were you doing when you got arrested?" Cynthia pinched her nose between her thumb and forefinger.

There was nothing left to lose at that point, was there? So I told her. "I was wrestling with your daughter, who I kidnapped after her graduation party. Do you know what your daughter has been up to, Cynthia? She's been making porno tapes of our daughters with various basketball players." I glanced at Audrey, not knowing if she knew, but she nodded. *Goddamnit.* How long had she known, and why didn't she tell me?"

Cynthia stopped pacing. "You kidnapped my daughter?"

"Yep. And I chained her to a wall. I was trying to teach her a lesson."

Audrey burst out into this kind of hyena, out-of-control laughter. "You chained Felicity to a wall, Reggie? That's hysterical!" Then Audrey was coughing and gasping for air.

"How dare you, Reggie!"

That was the thing about Cynthia's reaction. She was faking outrage, but I swear I saw a slight smile play around the corners of her mouth before she went into her fake *how dare you* mode. And please note that Cynthia didn't even ask if Felicity was all right. What does that say about her? Maybe I didn't need to say what I said next, but it seemed like we were way past trying to be civil towards each other. "How could you not have known what your daughter was up to, Cynthia? You really suck at motherhood. Do you know that?"

"Right back at you, Reggie. How could *you* not know what *your* daughter was up to?"

It was a valid point, but I ignored it because it stung too much. "*Your* daughter was the one who manipulated *my* daughter. She's *awful*, Cynthia. Even you can't deny that, can you?"

"The Tigerettes." Audrey's voice was back to the creepy monotone. "Everything started because of the Tigerettes. Felicity wanted all the girls to buy those slutty boots and new outfits for every dance and get their hair done. All of that extravagance takes a lot of money. A lot of money."

"Maybe your daughters didn't *deserve* to be Tigerettes. Have you thought about that, Audrey?" Cynthia's blue eyes flared at that, and she looked and sounded so much like Felicity at that moment that I almost lunged at her. Almost.

"They made the team because they worked hard, Cynthia. The judges were fair."

I was glad to see that Audrey was getting a little bit of life back in her, but I wasn't going to hold my breath on that one. Audrey always caved. Just look at how she let her husband walk all over her. He left her, telling her he was going to rehab, which I highly doubted. Who goes through rehab for that long? And then he lived with another woman, and still, she took him back. She was a doormat when it came to that man. I still stand by that. I might have been blind to my husband's true nature, but no one could ever call me a doormat. I stand by that too.

"Those judges were a bunch of dowdy fuddy-duddys," Cynthia sniffed. "They didn't know the first thing about dancing. Back in my Vegas days--"

That got my attention. "What Vegas days, Cynthia? I thought you were a dancer in New York."

Audrey raised her eyebrows. "You were a showgirl, Cynthia?"

"I'd put my money on a pole dancer in a strip club." And looking at Cynthia right then, I could imagine her slithering around a greased pole, discarding one item of clothing after another. It would all make sense, the way she carried herself in that too sexy of manner, the seductive way she dressed, the way she flirted with men and seemed to crave their attention, the rich older husband. Yep, Cynthia had been a stripper.

"My past is none of your concern!" Cynthia snapped. "And I was not a stripper. I was a professional dancer. The two of you have led such drab little lives that you wouldn't know the first thing about being on stage."

Yep, Cynthia had been a stripper. It was the happiest realization of my night, let me tell you.

Cynthia, naturally, changed the subject. "You both know very well that the wine club would not have been a success if I hadn't gotten involved. I think we can all agree on that."

"Audrey and I could have made a success of it on our own. We might not have made as much money, but--"

"We all would have made more money if Audrey hadn't been selling our most expensive bottles of wine on the side to Maeve."

"What?" I turned to face Audrey.

"You took some of that money too, Cynthia," Audrey accused.

"What?" I was really, truly blindsided by that revelation. Okay, I sold one bottle on the side, but it was just one bottle, one time. What punched me in the gut, though, was the fact that it was Audrey who had been selling wine outside the club and pocketing the money. I couldn't believe that Audrey would do such a thing. I couldn't believe she had it in her.

Cynthia was on a roll now. "And guess what, gals? The FHM account is not only depleted, but it's also overdrawn. You two have been stealing money from the company account. That's called embezzlement."

I hazarded a guess then. "I'm sure you've been dipping into the company account too, Cynthia. Admit it."

Sure, I'd been taking money from the account--I wouldn't know how astronomical the amount was until later--but it was all for the good of the wine club, wasn't it? At least I thought of it that way. But the other two? What did they need the money for? Audrey's frivolous vacation to San Diego? Cynthia's shopping habit? I'd seen the piles of Amazon boxes on her front doorstep. The woman had a serious problem. But it was still stunning that nothing was left.

Cynthia didn't admit it. "I'm thinking of suing you two for embezzlement."

I assumed my warrior pose then, hands on my hips, my shoulders squared. I'm pretty sure I was also flaring my nostrils. "Then I'll countersue, Cynthia. And by the way, you can't sue someone for embezzling when you were doing the same thing."

"You don't know that," Cynthia flared her nostrils right back at me.

She had me there, but I wasn't going to admit it. "Just try me."

"I admit I took money from the FHM account," Audrey interjected. You could see her flush, despite the soot on her face.

"*Goddamnit*, Audrey, stop admitting to everything. You're not supposed to say anything until your lawyer shows up. Haven't you watched enough *Law & Order* episodes to know that?"

I'd had the good sense to refuse to answer the cops' questions until my lawyer showed up, which for me, was going to have to be a court-appointed public defender. He or she hadn't shown up yet. I took it as a bad sign.

"For once, Reggie is right, Audrey. Not a word until your lawyer shows up." Cynthia had finally stopped pacing and was holding onto the bars of our cage as if she were checking how secure they were.

"Did your lawyer show up when the detectives were questioning you, Cynthia?" I asked. I had a very stupid moment of hope right then. If all of us refused to talk, maybe we could still get out of this mess with only a slap on the wrist or something like that. I know. I know. It was illogical. But desperation, fueled by fear, can make you hallucinate. Trust me on that.

"Apparently, our family attorney is busy defending Richard right now," Cynthia said angrily.

"That's going to take a while, isn't it, Cynthia? How many indictments does Richard have against him?" I knew I was rubbing salt into the wound. That's why I did it. "It looks like you're in the same boat as Audrey and me. You're going to have to use a court-appointed public defender too."

Cynthia pushed away from the bars and turned to face me. "Would you just *shut up*, Reggie? Part of the reason I wanted to be in your stupid wine club in the first place is that I wanted to be friends with you and Audrey. You seemed like you had something special going on. Ha! I guess the joke's on me. Because look at the two of you now. You've been at each other's throats for months, going behind each other's backs and behaving more like enemies than friends. Maybe that's because you, Reggie, are the most disagreeable person I've ever met."

"You're going to have to try harder than that to hurt my feelings, Cynthia." My voice sounded choked as I had to force the words out around the lump in my throat. I looked over at Audrey. Maybe I should finally apologize to her. Maybe we could still salvage our friendship out of this whole debacle.

But Audrey was holding her head in her hands. "I'm so tired of listening to the two of you. I'm just so tired. Besides, it doesn't matter. Everything is ruined. Everything is gone."

She sounded so sad and hopeless that the tears sprang immediately to my eyes. I brushed them away with the back of my dirty hand. "Don't say that, Audrey. We still might be able to salvage--"

Audrey looked up with those beautiful, sad, weary eyes of hers. "I didn't wait for a lawyer. I told the cops everything they wanted to know, I think. I confessed."

Cynthia groaned. "We are so screwed."

Wondering if Audrey had just ruined everything, I said through gritted teeth, "*Goddamnit,* Audrey."

33

CYNTHIA

I don't know how long I waited in that secret tunnel. I don't wear a watch, and I didn't have my phone because I knew that the cops could track me with that. You see, I thought I had considered every angle. But it was frighteningly claustrophobic in that damp, concrete escape tunnel, and I started to get anxious. That's always been the thing about me: I don't like being alone with my thoughts. And in that tunnel, as I waited, I thought about all the things I could have done differently, all the things I wish I'd never done. I am not prone to introspection, but that tunnel seemed to demand it. Finally, I couldn't stand it any longer. That's when I got careless. I didn't care if I had waited for ten minutes or ten hours. I just wanted out, out of the tunnel, out of that house, out of that town, out of my life.

I could see by the clock on the stove in the guesthouse that I had only been in the tunnel for four hours. It was barely past midnight, but I decided to grab my bag and make my getaway. I had packed lightly for me, but I would guess that my Louis Vuitton suitcase weighed well over fifty pounds. It slowed me down. Of course it didn't help that I still had on my Jimmy Choo heels, but I'm the kind of gal who would never be caught dead in tennis shoes in public unless I was on my way to the gym. So I limped along the four blocks to the grade school where I had parked my Mercedes. I didn't see another car in sight, and I felt a surge of hope. I was going to make it! All I had to do was get in my car and drive, drive, drive. I'd even taken the Mercedes to the mechanic's and had the oil changed, the tires rotated--and the GPS system turned off. Do you see? I was sincerely dedicated to my plan.

I was having trouble getting my suitcase into the trunk of the car, and no, I didn't for one second think of leaving it in that parking lot. I had selected my clothes--my armor--carefully for my new life in Florida, and I needed everything in that suitcase. So I was straining to get the damn thing in my trunk when a lone police car pulled into the school parking lot. I figured the guy was on his nightly security patrol or something, so I wasn't too worried. One car, one guy, and I knew I could talk my way out of anything with those odds.

"Do you need some help, ma'am?"

The officer was young, maybe in his early thirties, with short hair and a friendly smile. No problem. "That would be lovely," I said. "I have a plane to catch, and I'm going to be late if I don't hurry."

"Funny place to park your car if you're on your way to the airport," the young officer remarked as he easily hefted the heavy suitcase into the trunk.

"Not really." I smiled my beauty queen smile. "I just live across the street." I pointed at the houses in that general direction. "I had company tonight, a bon voyage party, you might say, and I needed the parking space in my driveway for my guests." Oh, yes, the lies were dripping off my tongue like maple syrup.

The young officer slammed down the trunk and paused. He was studying the license plate. "Hold on a second, would you, ma'am?" He walked hurriedly, purposefully to his car.

"Sure thing." My voice might have been light, but my heart had started to flip flop like a caught fish. I knew he was going for his radio, and I knew that there was a distinct possibility that there might be an APB out on this car, or me, or both. As soon as he ducked inside his sedan, I rushed to my own driver's side door. I didn't have time to wait around while he called in what he had found.

It was too bad that there hadn't been an old guy on duty that night, one who had eaten too many donuts or had arthritis or a hip replacement. Because that young guy was fast. I had no sooner started my car than he was at my window. Mr. Nice Guy was gone, and instead of greeting me with a smile, he had his gun pointed directly at my head.

"Step out of the car, Mrs. Stewart."

I didn't have a choice, did I? I didn't want to go to jail, but I didn't want to be dead even more. It wasn't long before backup appeared, and in a matter of minutes, the parking lot was swarming with cop cars and black sedans. They hadn't had far to travel. Most of them had probably been four blocks away at my house when they received the call. I sat in my car, sweating and fretting, as I saw all my dreams swirl down the drain.

It was totally devastating to realize that I had never had a chance of escaping on this night. I had missed my window. I had waited too long because I needed money to fund my new life. And it was all Richard's fault. If he hadn't made such a mess of things, I would never have had to rely on the wine club for money. If he had at least bought me a real damn ring instead of one made of cubic zirconia, I would have had something to sell. But no. Richard had left me with nothing. I didn't want to go to jail, but I did want Richard to rot in jail for the rest of his life. I hoped they would send him to the same prison as Bernie Madoff. Then the two old disgraced codgers could fight it out for top dog. The winner would be the one who had ruined the most lives.

It was easy enough to figure out why the cops put the three of us in the same holding cell. I wondered if they had it bugged, but that probably didn't matter too much because Reggie's voice carried like she was speaking through a bullhorn. Seriously, that woman never did have any volume control. Anyway, I'm sure the cops wanted us to turn on each other, to rat each other out. I have to admit it was a good plan on their part. It's like they already knew who they were dealing with. Or like they wanted us to torture ourselves with each other's company. Mission accomplished. It was a long, torturous night.

Oddly enough, I had never been arrested before. I know it's hard to believe, given my storied past, but it's true. It's just as nerve-wracking as you would expect. Any time one of us had to go to the bathroom, we had to knock on the cell bars and scream bloody murder to be let out. Well, maybe we didn't have to go that far, but we did. After a while, Audrey and I gave that job to Reggie. We had her bellowing like a moose when we needed water or had to pee or wanted a blanket. The cops were accommodating enough. I don't know if it was because they didn't usually have three Scottsdale housewives in the cell at one time, or if news of what we had been up to for the last several months had gotten out, and each cop wanted to take a look at the women who had pulled the wine club con. Maybe they wanted to look at me, the former Mrs. Arizona. I bet it's not every day that they had a beauty queen locked behind those bars. It was unfortunate that I did not look my best on that night.

It went on and on, that night. We traded barbs and insults that were useless, meaningless. We had gotten caught, and it was over. But it was like we couldn't get enough of goading each other. At one point, and she kept coming back to this subject all night long, Reggie said to me: "You don't seem too concerned that I kidnapped your daughter, Cynthia. You didn't even ask if she was all right."

It had not occurred to me to do so, but I said rotely, "Is Felicity all right?"

"She's alive, in case you're interested." Boy, Reggie could be so nasty.

"Well, I guess you can't be accused of murder, Reggie. Isn't that something--" I couldn't continue because the word *murder* made my blood run cold.

"You always said you wanted to get that girl alone in a dark room," Audrey said from her corner of the cell. "I didn't think you'd actually do it."

"She deserved to be punished for what she did," Reggie went on belligerently. "It wasn't like her mother would ever punish her."

"Shut up, Reggie. You know she'll press even more charges against you," I said tiredly, turning my face to the wall.

"I don't give a rat's ass. It was worth it, and I'd do it again." Reggie banged her fist against the wall for emphasis.

"Oh, Reggie," Audrey said with what sounded like genuine sympathy. But who can say for sure?

The truth? I was glad that Reggie kidnapped Felicity and held her hostage for three days. Being captive for that short period wouldn't seriously hurt her physically, but it just might have taught that ungrateful girl a lesson. Reggie had done something I had always been too chicken to do--i.e., punish my daughter. Years ago when Felicity's Terrible Twos lasted until she was about eight, Richard forbade me from even putting her in Time Out. Instead, he let Felicity--and then I let Felicity--get away with anything her vicious, demanding heart desired. Of course Reggie went too far, as always. I would soon discover that Reggie had slapped Felicity around some--something Reggie conveniently forgot to mention during that long night--and that Felicity had marks on her face. Now *that* was going too far. Felicity might be the world's greatest teenage bitch, but she was stunningly beautiful. And she was going to need those good looks to get her through life. She might be awful to people in the future, but she would look good being awful.

Shortly before dawn, the three of us settled down. We were all exhausted, but I don't think any of us slept at all. We would be arraigned in a few hours, and the process would begin. At least that's how they did it on TV, so I assumed that those cop shows at least tried to make things look realistic. I knew for a certainty that I was not going to get our family attorney, Gerald Busby, to represent me. Richard would tie him up, and then he would probably need Busby to represent Felicity too. Given that everyone was a minor during those videotaped sessions, I didn't know what would happen. I didn't let it concern me too much, though. As far as I was concerned, Felicity was on her own. After everything that had happened, I highly doubted that I'd ever speak to my daughter again.

I was more concerned about my own future. Don't look at me that way. It's true that I had the most to lose in this situation. It was only a matter of time before I was questioned about that long-ago night in Vegas. Surely, Buck had gone to the police by now. That is, if he wasn't arrested along with Richard, or passed out drunk in some dive bar. The story was finally going to come out, one way or the other.

I was twenty-two when I started dating Rico Giambatta. I knew he was connected to the mob, as did everyone else up and down the Strip. Now it's true that I dated several guys simultaneously. I preferred to call it *dating*, even though everyone else up and down the Strip knew I would sometimes take money for those dates. It was a common practice among the dancing girls I hung around with, so it wasn't like you could call it prostitution or anything like that. And it wasn't one of those escort services that you see in flyers all over Vegas. Some of the other girls and I showed men a good time, and they liked to reward us for our efforts. It was as simple as that.

Anyway, back to Rico. Maybe I thought I loved him back then. I was still dating a lot of different men, but he was certainly my number one guy. He was extremely handsome in that way of Italian men: dark hair, dark eyes, olive skin, and a manner about him that just screamed *sex!* We had been dating for something like four months when he asked me to do him a favor. I didn't hesitate. Everyone knew that when you did Rico a favor, he rewarded you handsomely for it. I'd seen a diamond tennis bracelet in the gift shop in Caesar's and had promised myself that I would own it. Rico agreed to my terms.

I was supposed to go on a date with a business associate of his, Salvatore Russo. I knew what that meant. There would be a nice, expensive dinner, maybe a show, and then we would go back to his room at whatever high dollar casino he was staying at. But Rico made it clear to me that it wasn't going to go down like that. He wanted me to ask Rico to take a drive out to the desert after dinner.

Now everyone knows what it means when Italians in Vegas with mob connections talk about taking a drive out into the desert. The desert outside Vegas conceals a multitude of sins. Everyone knows that. "Wouldn't that look suspicious to Salvatore?" I asked Rico, right before I left his apartment to go on the date.

"You're going to have to be especially persuasive tonight, Cindy. If anyone can do it, it's you. I know you're the right girl for the job."

What can I say? I was flattered, but still. "This is going to cost you more than a diamond tennis bracelet," I said.

"Anything your heart desires, baby, you name it."

Rico always did know how to push my buttons, so I agreed, and everything went according to plan. I am not going to tell you--or anyone, ever--what I had to do with and for that man to get him to agree to go for a midnight drive in the desert. But I do have a way with men--you can carve that fact in stone, honey--so I did what he asked, and we went for a drive.

The man was insatiable, and I was still doing my job, crouched down on the floor of the car when the shot came. I hadn't been expecting the shot. I mean, I knew something like that would probably happen, but I guess I didn't want to let myself actually think about it. I was in shock, I think, as his dick went limp in my mouth and the blood rained down. There was so much blood. Blood everywhere. I couldn't get out of that car fast enough, and there was Rico, waiting to whisk me away in another black car, just as he promised, while his underlings torched the car with the dead body.

So there were no fingerprints of mine at the scene, but eyewitnesses saw Salvatore and me leaving the casino. And this is the truth: Someone will always talk. Sooner or later, someone who knows something will talk. It might be a passing, drunken conversation in a bar, it might be in confidence to a friend, or it might be someone earning bragging rights in prison. But I was young and not worried. I had to lay low for a while, and it was the only time in my life I was a brunette. Rico was arrested a month or two later, but he didn't give me up.

Enough time passed that I thought I was safe. Weeks and then months would go by without me even thinking about that night and how I was an accessory to murder. And then Buck Boyd showed up out of nowhere. I thought I'd loved Buck at one time too, but then I didn't anymore. The same goes for Richard. I thought I might have loved him also, but now I'm not so sure. Maybe the truth goes something like this: I have been with a lot of men in my life. I have been temporarily infatuated with a select few. But love? I don't think I've ever truly been in love with anyone.

Isn't that sad?

AUGUST

34

AUDREY

What is today's date?

It's August 28th? Unbelievable.

I guess that means we've been talking--or rather, I've been talking and you've been recording the conversation and taking notes--for going on three months now. I lose track of time in here, but I guess that's not such a bad thing. It's not like I have anywhere else to go, right? But mind you, I'm not complaining. In fact, for the first time in as long as I can remember, I'm getting enough rest. I know it's probably from the drugs they give me, but I'm all right with that too. Going to bed is the one thing I can look forward to. For eight hours out of each long day, I don't have to think about anything at all.

I pled guilty, despite the enormous pressure from Reggie and Cynthia during that night in the holding cell. I did not cave. I want the record to reflect that. I pled guilty not only because I was, but also because I wanted to do the right thing for the sake of my children. Marcy and Jimmy might go through the rest of their lives with the stigma of having a mother in jail hanging over their heads, but at least they would know that I owned up to my crimes, in the end. That has to count for something, doesn't it? I pray to God that it counts for something.

I'm pretty sure that I walked into that arraignment the morning of May 22nd looking like a ravaged, homeless, disaster victim. I was still covered in gray ash, and my hair smelled like it had been singed. I had stood awfully close to that fire, but it wasn't like I was being vain about burned hair. No, I was more concerned that the people in the courtroom would know that I stank. Reggie had already told me that I smelled--she could still get under my skin like no one else--and I had become fixated on that. It was like my fiery body odor was emblematic of the charred person I was inside. Now everyone would know what kind of hellish person I had become. For a woman who had always been acutely aware of what others thought about her, it distressed me greatly.

I'd met my attorney, a young woman fresh out of ASU law school, about five minutes before I walked into that courtroom. It was obvious she was nervous. She kept dropping her papers and clearing her throat. And fidgeting. Young Ms. Bramlett was a fidgeter, even more so than Jimmy. I, on the other hand, felt quite calm. Well, I guess it would be more accurate to say that I felt *numb*. I'd torched a boat with my husband aboard, gotten arrested, and spent an agonizing night in a holding cell in the last twenty-four hours, and I couldn't quite wrap my head around all that had happened. Likewise, the memory of being called in front of the judge, of standing and walking to the front of the room, is hazy.

"How does the defendant plead?" the black-robed judge asked.

"Guilty." I distinctly remember saying that word.

And then everything gets fuzzy again. It was like saying that word *guilty* opened up the floodgates of all my transgressions, and they came pouring out. I started to babble about wine labels and Carlo Rossi and Cynthia's parties and my alcoholic husband who was no longer handsome because I had set him on fire and the white pillow covering my mother's face. All the words got jumbled together, and then I was crying. I hadn't cried in weeks, mostly because Reggie had accused me of being a crybaby, so I had plenty, *plenty* of tears stored up. Ms. Bramlett told me later that I had been inconsolable. She'd had to search in her big bag for a wadded up tissue to staunch the flow. It didn't begin to do the job, and I had to wipe my nose on the sleeve of my shirt over and over again. What kind of person does that?

Evidently, judging by where I am now, not a completely sane person. This psych ward at the Arizona Department of Corrections is not a bad place to be. There are the drugs that help me sleep and make me so calm that I don't recognize myself. For some reason, they also make me bloated, but that's not really something I have to worry about any more. It's actually kind of funny now to think back on how appalled I was when I gained a few pounds. For years I gained and lost the same ten pounds, and now I simply don't care. It's not like I have to worry about fitting into my clothes anymore. The jumpsuits here are of the one-size-fits-all variety. It's comforting.

And there are the daily counseling sessions, which I also find comforting. I think of the gray-haired lady, Lois, as the mother I never had. She's very kind, and she listens intently. I trusted her immediately, which I guess is why I told her about my mother. I thought I told her the truth about what happened during Margot's last day in the nursing home, but I don't think she believed me. I kept returning to the subject, trying to absolve my guilt, so much so that Lois eventually called Belmont and talked to Jean, the director. Lois said that Jean told her that Margot Keller died of natural causes, that I did not suffocate her with a snowy white pillow.

"No, I put that pillow over her face," I insisted.

"Audrey," Lois said gently, "you are not responsible for the death of your mother."

Oh, but I am, aren't I? I think. I'm so confused. Maybe I just imagined that I put that pillow over her face. I honestly don't know anymore. My mother's ashes are still in my closet, on the shelf next to my one good pair of black pumps. When the house is finally sold, I wonder what will become of them.

I see the look on your face, but don't worry. I have not told Lois nearly as much as I've told you. You are my primary confidante, without a doubt. Lois is trying to help me feel better and work through my tangled, complicated feelings, but you are going to serve a higher purpose. People will learn from my mistakes because of you and the book you are writing on the power of forgiveness. And I greatly appreciate that; it helps me.

To pass more time, I write daily letters to my children. I don't have a lot of news to report because every day here is pretty much like the next, so I talk about the past. I bring up memories of former Christmases and birthday celebrations and camping trips, you know, the happy family memories, back when our family was happy. At least I think they were happy times, but I'm not sure now. Sometimes other memories creep in while I write, the times when Paul was too drunk to assemble the trampoline or too drunk to remember to go to Marcy and Jimmy's soccer matches or pick them up from school. In those reimagined memories, Paul's face is not as it was then. It is not handsome. It is charred black and frightening. When that happens, I have to stop writing and ask the nurse if I can have another pill.

Marcy and Jimmy write once a week, and I imagine that Hannah, Aaron's wife, makes them do it. She probably stands over their shoulders and supervises every word. They seem like they are getting on well enough, although Aaron wrote me that he knows it will take them time to adjust. I don't know what that means. In Marcy's letter, it was clear that she was not happy that she would not be going back to Mohave High School this fall, that she would not be able to try out for the Tigerettes. I expected as much, but I don't regret my decision to send her as far away from that place and its nefarious pom squad as I could. Wasn't it the infamous Tigerettes that started the avalanche that destroyed everything? I think it was.

I wrote Aaron to suggest that he put both my children into counseling, but he wrote back that he can't afford that kind of thing, doesn't believe in it either. You cannot believe the guilt I felt on that score. If only I hadn't been so foolish with all that money we made from the wine club. If only I had squirreled some away for the proverbial rainy day, I could have paid for counseling for my children. But I didn't. The only defense I can think of when it comes to that money is that I did use a lot of it for household expenses. But it isn't much of a defense, and it wasn't how I spent most of the money. I should have thought ahead. I should have known that catastrophe lurks around every corner, but I refused to recognize its dark shadow. And now it's raining cats and dogs, and I can't do one damn thing about it. I don't even have an umbrella.

I write letters to Paul too. They are much more difficult to write than the ones I write to my children. Some I send, and some I just compose in my head. Do they read them to him at the acute burn facility he is recuperating in? I don't know. I can only hope they do because I pour my heart and soul into those letters. I rewrite our history together, glossing over all the bad times and focusing on the good. I tell him I miss him and that I'm sorry. I do not tell him that I love him because I'm not sure if I do anymore. I burned his body by mistake, but he seared my heart on purpose. That's a big difference. I am his next of kin, though, so the authorities at the facility notify me from time to time of his condition. I have been told that he is now blind. "Love is blind," I said to the woman who told me this over the phone. It is so obvious, yet she seemed stunned by the truth.

Poor Cynthia. I can feel pity for her now. She was a woman who seemed to have it all: money, beauty, glamor, a popular kid, a magnificent house.

She seemed to glory in all that, but I don't know why now. She was in as much trouble as Reggie and me. Why didn't she say so? Why didn't we? I was always intimidated by her, but I guess I have a low feeling of self-worth. It is because of my mother, Lois says. My mother never *validated* me. But is that why I was such a promiscuous girl until I met Paul, who I thought was my savior?

Did my daughter prostitute herself because I didn't *validate* her?

Is that why Cynthia did the same thing in her younger years in Vegas?

You've actually made me feel better by enlightening me about Cynthia's past. I didn't dislike her as much as Reggie did, but I'm not quite so intimidated by her now. And I do know this too: I was always envious of her. As I was bottling wine in her kitchen, I wished it was my own. The meals I could have cooked in that kitchen would have been stupendous. Meanwhile, while I was preoccupied, my daughter was having sex with boys she didn't love because she was seeking popularity or approval or acceptance or *validation*.

I was bottling fake French wine and selling it to rich women, so I guess you could say I was doing the same thing as my daughter, seeking all of the above.

I should hate Reggie, but I don't. I miss her terribly. I'm isolated in this ward--you've got to lock up the crazy women, right?--but there is a view of the outdoor area, including the running track, out the sunroom window. It's from a distance, but I know it's her. She is allowed her time outside at precisely three o'clock every afternoon. She is focused, frenetic energy, running with long-legged strides, around and around that track. Her black hair has turned partially gray now, and it looks magnificent as it flows out behind her.

She runs, while I look forward to that nightly dose of medication, handed to me in a white paper cup. I look forward to those tablets almost as much as I used to look forward to those nightly glasses of wine. And do you know what? Those patio nights with Reggie are the things I miss the most. I miss the talking, laughing, confiding.

Oddly enough, I miss the wine club too. But mostly, I miss drinking wine with my best friend.

35

CYNTHIA

I know I look completely different with short hair, but it was something that I had to do before one of the other women in my cell block decided to chop it off while I slept. I'm not kidding. I overheard a couple of them saying that I was so vain about my hair that they should do something about it. So I beat them to the punch. I went to what they call the beauty shop here and asked the dyke in charge of the place to cut it. She's no Cristof, as you can see for yourself. It's a little ragged around the edges, but I wasn't going to complain when she was finished. She still had the scissors in her hands, and they had come mighty close to my eyes while she sheared off my hair. But I didn't flinch. No, I did not. When she finally set down those scissors, I gathered my gorgeous blonde hair off the floor and told her that I was donating it to Locks of Love. She thought I was being funny, but I was dead serious. One bald woman in the world is probably feeling pretty damn lucky right now to have a wig made out of my lustrous blonde hair.

I try to keep to myself as much as possible in here. It's not because I'm scared of the other women. Well, okay, I might be a little scared. For the most part, they are a terrifying group. In my cell block alone, we have four murderers, five prostitutes, and about a hundred others in here for drug-related charges. If you recall, I saw that show about meth addiction in the Midwest a few months back, but I had no idea how rampant drug use and abuse and addiction are in this country. The druggies in here have all lost their looks, and some of them have even lost their teeth. I just don't understand how a woman can let herself go like that. Where is her pride? And get this: One toothless woman in here actually sold her baby to buy a couple grams of cocaine. Can you imagine that? Talk about poor parenting.

Don't look at me like that, okay? I never said I wanted to be Mother of the Year, so you can wipe that smirk off your ridiculously young face and *stop judging me*!

And I didn't know that Reggie had kidnapped my daughter! Felicity was supposed to be at a spa in Tucson. The driver I'd hired to take her there after the graduation party did call and tell me that Felicity was already gone by the time he arrived at the school. I didn't think anything of it because I thought Felicity might have taken it into her head to persuade some of her underlings to drive her there. She would want an audience to witness her entrance into that exclusive resort and spa. It was just up her alley to do something like that. Besides, the girl was eighteen, a high school graduate, and on her own as far as I was concerned. So what if she got slapped around a little by Reggie? She had it coming. And no, I have not heard a word from Felicity since I've been in here.

Let's talk about something else.

Richard. The guy lawyered up, just as you would expect, but in the end he agreed to some kind of plea deal. I saw on the news the other night that he was waiting for his sentencing in one of the country club federal prisons. He probably plays golf every day and has his meals brought to him on a silver tray. Hell, he probably has a bidet in his cell so he can keep his ass squeaky clean. It makes me so mad just to think of it. I was really hoping that he'd end up being some guy's bitch in a prison overrun by heavy duty criminals. It used to be a favorite daydream of mine, but that is not how the story unfolded. The only commendable act that Richard did during this whole ordeal was not rat me out for holding him hostage. He didn't even mention it. However, I guess I wasn't really holding him hostage if he knew how to get out all along, right?

Which brings me to the sorry subject of Buck Boyd. The guy was a bigger con artist than me and a blackmailer on top of that, but do you think he's in prison? No, he is not. Oh, he was initially arrested at the last wine club party for breaking and entering or trespassing--you know, one of the lesser crimes--but the police let him go after questioning him. But not before he told the police all about how I had imprisoned him in my panic room. The police had no idea that Buck had been blackmailing me for months because they only heard his side of the story, which is that

I locked him in the panic room for no good reason, then proceeded to drug him, etc. I'll probably get more years tacked on for that juicy piece of information, while Buck is undoubtedly already back in Marion, Kansas, living in his ratty camper and drinking beer.

That damn Buck Boyd. Shortly after I was arrested for wire fraud and all the other stuff associated with the wine club, an anonymous person- -yeah, right--sent a thick packet of documents to the police department and the FBI. I had always half-hoped that Buck was bluffing on that part, but he was not. Consequently, I have since been questioned repeatedly about the disappearance of a guy named Salvatore Russo and will soon be extradited back to Nevada. I act like I have never heard that name, and I never change the expression on my face. I have to be a good actress because my public defender is totally worthless. He wears a bola tie and keeps a tin of Skoal in the front pocket of his suit. As far as I can tell, he hasn't done one damn thing in my defense. I know he thinks I'm guilty as sin, but it's not his job to judge me, is it?

Speaking of acting, have you decided yet who's going to play me in the movie you're writing about all this?

You haven't? Say, are you sure you're not an actress yourself? Over the last three months, I have sometimes had the feeling that you're studying me, that you might be writing the starring role for yourself. It's not a bad idea, you know. If you went to Cristof, he could give you a makeover that would knock your socks off. I'm not kidding. You could be really pretty if you put a little bit of effort into it.

However, I have been doing a lot of thinking on who should play me in the movie. She has to be beautiful, obviously, and smart. And she has to be a good dancer. It's too bad that Goldie Hawn and Meryl Streep have gotten so old because either one would have been perfect if she was about forty years younger. Scarlett Johansson would be a good choice, as would Blake Lively. Reese Witherspoon is another one I've had on my mind, along with Cameron Diaz. Is she still acting these days?

You're going to have to get a character actress to portray Reggie, some- one like Allison Janney or Joan Cusack. When you stop to think about it, Reggie really does resemble Joan Cusack. Connie Britton would be a perfect Audrey. Can't you just picture it? I can. Promise you'll keep me posted when the movie goes into production.

Yes, I know that both Audrey and Reggie are also in this prison. The word around here is that Audrey had some kind of nervous breakdown during her court hearing. I have to hand it to her. It was a brilliant move on her part. I wish I would have thought about blubbering and crying in front of the judge myself. Maybe I could have even pulled off acting so crazy that I was deemed unfit to stand trial by a court appointed psychiatrist. Then I wouldn't have to endure this endless waiting, which is pure agony. I swear, the legal process moves at a snail's pace. One of the women in here has been waiting for her trial for almost three years. If I have to wait that long, I'm probably going to forget which of my crimes I'm standing trial for. That might work to my advantage, though. If I can't remember the crime, it will be that much easier to convince a jury that I'm innocent.

Since Audrey is locked up in the insane asylum part of the prison, I haven't seen her, but I've seen Reggie a couple of times. Her exercise time is at three, and mine is at two, so I saw her when I was going in, and she was coming out. The first time she looked right through me. I'm not kidding. She acted like she had never seen me before in her life. Let me tell you, it hurt my feelings. After all we have been through together, you'd think that she would at least have the courtesy to say *hi*. But then I realized that she didn't recognize me because of my hair. Not only is it cut very short, but it's also not really blonde anymore, as you can plainly see. On the outside, I had my roots touched up at the salon every two weeks. Plus, I've put on a few pounds in here, but I don't want to talk about that either.

So the second time I passed her in the yard, I said, "Reggie, it's me, Cynthia."

Reggie's eyes grew wide when she heard me, and then a big grin appeared. It was definitely what you would call a shit-kicking grin. "Holy shit," she said. "You've just made my day, Cynthia."

I am not stupid. I knew that she didn't mean that as a compliment. For one thing, orange is not my best color. But I gave her my loveliest beauty queen smile. "I'm glad to have made you happy, Reggie."

"Oh, you have," she chuckled, before she hit the track and started to run for all she was worth.

Maybe I should start to run during exercise period too, instead of sitting on a bench and trying to keep the sun off my skin. But then it would look like I was copying Reggie, or maybe that I even respected the fact that she was so dedicated and in excellent physical condition. But I don't want anyone to think that I respect anything that woman does. I don't have much left in this world, but I do have my pride. More than almost anything, I value my pride.

No, I did not fill out that final questionnaire you gave me. I didn't see the point. I've told you my story, and I've told you the honest truth. Although that last question--Do you have any regrets about the wine club?--intrigued me. I guess the answer is yes and no. I would join the wine club again in a heartbeat, but I would do it my way. I'd have an online presence, and I would definitely hire people to do all the grind work. Audrey and Reggie never had the vision that I did. They thought inside the box, not outside, while I would have taken the wine club to a global level. And I wouldn't have gotten caught. You can trust me on that one.

Oh, before you go, I have one more favor to ask you. Do you have any cigarettes?

Goodness no, I haven't taken up smoking! Do you know how much smoking ages a woman's skin? I want the cigarettes for bartering. I'm not kidding. They're like gold around here.

36

REGGIE

I run to preserve my sanity--what's left of it anyway.

I swear, I'm not taking a jab at Audrey. Her nervous breakdown is not a laughing matter, and while I feel sorry for her, I can't say that I was all that surprised. She'd been acting kind of dazed and confused for months. It was like when you looked into her pretty green eyes, you could see that the light was on, but no one was home. Do you know what I mean? At one point I wondered if Audrey was suffering from PTSD, triggered by Paul's abandonment. She should have been jumping up and down with joy because that loser husband of hers was gone, but Audrey was always too romantic, too soft-hearted for her own good. However, she did set Paul on fire, so I guess she kind of snapped out of it, right? I'm sure she didn't torch that stupid boat with Paul inside on purpose. But a small part of me wishes that she did. Don't tell her I said that, okay?

And I still run to try to control my anger. However, for that to truly work, I'd have to be running a hell of a lot more than one lousy hour a day. And do you want to know who my anger is directed at these days? Felicity. It's still that conniving little bitch who can set me off like no other. The anger begins to simmer when I think about how Felicity ended up getting away with making sex videos of my daughter. I knew she was smart, but I still underestimated her. As soon as the girl was released from the hospital--can you believe they thought she needed medical treatment for a couple of bruises?--she broke into my house and stole back her camera and the disgusting videos. And then she destroyed the evidence. Since the videos had never been on the internet and had only been circulated among the Tigerettes and boys' basketball team, there was no longer proof of the crime. There was only my word against Felicity's, and since I tend to come across as a ranting, crazy person, who do you think the cops believed? That's right. Felicity.

What's more--and now I'm reaching a low boil--none of the Tigerettes would fess up to the crime either, including my and Audrey's daughters. And forget about the boys on the basketball team. They'd had their fun and hadn't gotten into trouble, so no one there felt the need to tell the truth. It was unbelievable. I begged Hayley to tell the cops what had happened, but she would not relent. She said she didn't want to be embarrassed in front of the entire school, but I still think that Felicity cast some kind of evil spell over the entire squad of Tigerettes. Or maybe she made them sign a loyalty oath or something. Whatever. It worked. No one talked, and Felicity remained above reproach. If I ever get out of here and have the opportunity to kidnap Felicity again, you can bet your sweet ass I will do it.

And now I'm getting to the roiling boil part. When Felicity got out of the hospital, the poor little rich girl had no place to go. Her daddy and mommy were both in prison, and the house had been seized by the FBI. And whoops! Felicity wasn't rich anymore. Daddy and Mommy had squandered their wealth, and even her powder blue Porsche was repossessed. So guess what happened next? *Felicity was invited by my daughter and almost ex-husband to move in with them.* It was unbelievable.

When Kent gave me the news during the one time he visited me here, I would have shoved the table over in my fury if it hadn't been bolted to the floor of the visitors' room. "Are you kidding me?" I screamed at him. "That girl is a psychopath!"

"She's a perfectly nice girl," Kent said calmly. "And she's Hayley's best friend."

Believe me, I rolled my eyes at that one. "Marcy is Hayley's best friend, Kent." Had he been blind all those years? The girl lived next door, for crying out loud. The two had been inseparable for years.

"Marcy and Jimmy have gone to live with their uncle in Oregon."

That was news to me, of course, but I had to give some bonus points to Audrey. She'd figured out a way to get her daughter away from the terrible Tigerettes. But now the most terrible Tigerette of all was going to be living under the same roof as my daughter. "I do not want Felicity anywhere near my daughter." I was so mad that spit flew.

Kent calmly took a handkerchief from his pocket and wiped the spittle from his chin. "Don't you think that giving her a temporary home is the least I can do? You kidnapped her and hit her and chained her to a wall like an animal, Reggie. The poor girl is struggling, and at least part of it is due directly to you. You're just lucky that she decided not to press charges against you."

"Lucky!" I exploded. "She's not pressing charges because she's desperate for a place to live, and you're the sucker who's falling for it."

While I didn't need extra charges tacking on more years to my sentence--if I am convicted--it still infuriated me that Felicity took the high road. And I know why. If she didn't press charges, it was like it never happened. It was like I never came up with the ingenious plan of kidnapping her and teaching her a lesson. So in the end, Felicity had not learned anything at all. And she *had* been scared of me when I had her chained up; I just know it. I saw her fear, but now it's like it was a bad dream.

"I think you may have misjudged the girl," Kent said quietly.

"No, no, no, no, *no*. That girl made sex tapes of our daughter with multiple partners, *multiple* partners, Kent. I saw them myself, and they were the most disgusting thing I ever watched. You've got to believe me. Why would I make up such a terrible thing?" But I could tell before he spoke that Kent did not believe me.

"You were under a lot of stress for months, Reggie, and you were engaging in criminal activity. Perhaps your recollection of events has been affected by all that. You were not acting like yourself at that time. You ran over Reed's cat on purpose, and you destroyed some of our property. You were not in your right mind, Reggie," he added in a gentler voice.

"Would you shut up about the fucking cat?" I screamed. "I'm afraid for our daughter's safety and well-being, and you're bringing up dead cats and mangled rose bushes! I don't want that manipulative bitch living with my daughter!"

I was escorted back to my cell shortly after that and lost my exercise privileges for a week. And I'm pretty sure I scared Kent off for good. I mean, that man had to put up with a lot being married to me all those years, but did he have to invite that little bitch into his home the minute I got locked up? How had Felicity so easily pulled the wool over his eyes too? And then I was forced to consider the possibility that everyone in my life was crazy except for me, and of course, the alternative: that everyone else was sane, and I was the crazy one.

Goddamnit.

I do not like being confined in a cage. It goes against my restless nature, and I sometimes feel like I could chew through the steel bars with my teeth. However, and this is kind of weird, I do like the routine here. Everything happens at precisely the same time every single day: our meals, our showers, our outdoor time, our bedtime. It kind of reminds me of my childhood. My father ran a strict boot camp when I was a kid, and my brothers and I thrived on it. Nobody told Dad that it was stupid or unreasonable to raise his kids like they were marines-in-training. So we all accepted his strict rules and the regimented routine as normal. I think it made all of his kids tougher too, even me, the only girl.

That toughness has its benefits around here. All the women on my cell block know that I don't take shit from anybody. If I'm in here long enough, I could definitely become the Head Bitch. I just made up that name, but there is a definite hierarchy here, and the woman who seems to be Head Bitch is a foul-mouthed Latina woman who's in here for a gang-related murder. We have a wary mutual respect for one another.

I do not want my son and daughter to visit me in here. I suppose I am embarrassed about being inmate 26893, but that's not the only reason. If they came and I actually was forced to see myself through their eyes, I might just fall apart. Looking through the mirror of their eyes, I would see that I am, in fact, a failure, a loser, a criminal. While all those things are most likely true, I don't want to be forced to confront the worst aspects of my nature--at least not yet. So I'll continue to stew in my anger and blame everyone else for the mistakes that were made. I blame Audrey for being too slow and too chicken and Cynthia for being too careless and too vain. Blaming others and not taking responsibility can't go on forever, but it's keeping me going for now.

I know, I know. It's juvenile. But fantasies are hard to come by in here.

And then there's always the hope that when I finally do go to trial, I will be found innocent. The jurors will understand that we weren't actually hurting anyone by selling them fake French wine. The jurors will understand that those women had money to burn, and I was only trying to make some money because my gay husband left me for a man. I was a single mother who was forced to find a way to make a living, or I would find myself out on the streets, homeless and penniless. Mind you, I'm not holding my breath on that one, but it's part of the prison mentality. If someone in here asks you what crime you committed, you're supposed to say, "I'm innocent." Everyone does it. I think it has something to do with the idea that if you say it often enough, sooner or later you begin to believe it. I haven't gotten to that point yet.

I am a survivor, and I know I will make it through all this. I'm not so sure about the other two, though. I got a load of Cynthia the other day, and it's not pretty. She has this frowsy-looking butch haircut now, and she's gained a lot of weight. I wouldn't have recognized her if she hadn't called out my name. And I'm not going to start lying to you now. It made me inordinately happy to see her like that. It just proves the theory that I had all along. Anyone can look pretty if she has enough time and money to spend on herself. Which Cynthia definitely did, for years. She's got the time now--ha ha--but she certainly doesn't have the money, does she? She just looks like a normal person these days, and I don't know, maybe if I met her for the first time now, I might actually like her because she's not so pretty. It's doubtful, but I'll give her the benefit of the doubt because she looks so plain Jane.

Who am I kidding? I still wouldn't like her. She had no business horning in on our wine club, and now I'm glad she's fallen from her mighty self-imagined throne. I wonder if the FBI will auction off her beauty queen crown, along with the rest of the trappings in that big house that used to be hers. This prison is a gossipy place, and I heard that she's going to be extradited to Nevada for another crime. I'm not surprised at all by that. Cynthia always did have a sneaky way about her. I think that's where Felicity gets it. But then there's Richard's less than sterling qualities to consider too. I guess Felicity's DNA didn't come from the best stock.

Hell, no, I don't feel sorry for Felicity! And now she's living under the same roof as my daughter! *Goddamnit!*

Sorry. I'm composed now. Just don't bring up that girl's name again, okay? You should know by now how much it riles me up.

I'm not completely heartless because I do worry about Audrey. In a way, I'm glad she's locked up in the psych ward because I don't think she could handle day-to-day prison life. It's a tough crowd, and it's in everyone's best interests to fend for herself. I have no problem with that, but Audrey would shatter like a crystal vase under the pressure of always having to watch her back. I think I saw her one time, looking out the window while I was running the track. She was pretty far away, but I recognized her auburn hair and the heart shape of her face. I think I saw her lift her hand as she stared out that window, like she was going to wave at me, but then she was gone. I don't know. Maybe I imagined the whole thing. I have been accused of making things up lately, but still. It gave me a pang. I miss her.

And I miss the nights we used to spend on my patio drinking wine and talking. That's how I came up with the idea of the wine club, over that bottle of Meiomi pinot noir the night after our daughters made the Mohave Tigerette pom squad. It seems like such a long time ago now when Audrey and I were best friends and nothing more than suburban housewives worrying about ordinary things like our husbands, our kids, and money. We were so naive about a lot of things when we started our business, but I still think that the wine club was a good idea. Brilliant, maybe. For a time there, we were making money, and we were making people happy. It really does all go back to people's *perception* of something. People think that wine is supposed to taste better if it's in a fancy bottle and if it's supposedly French. And no one can dispute the fact that it took a Master Sommelier to expose our scam.

I know, I know. And since this is our final interview session, I'll finally admit it too. All three of us, Audrey, Cynthia, and myself included, were the ones who really caused the wine club to fall apart. We turned into the worst versions of ourselves. We were not kind to each other. I'll go even further and say that we were downright mean to and distrustful of one another, all because each of us wanted more, and then more, and then more money. We were all driven by the mighty dollar and motivated by greed.

You can quote me on that. Actually, you should use it to end your story on *American Greed.* I don't care what Audrey and Cynthia have told you. You have to use that line to end the episode when it airs on CNBC. And I'll tell you why. The wine club was my idea, I was the brains of the operation, and I always get the last word. Always.

Wait a minute. Why are you suddenly in such a big rush to get out of here?

Wait a minute. You've never actually showed me your credentials, or did you? I'm not quite sure. You flashed some kind of badge in front of my face three months ago and said I could trust you, that you wanted to hear my side of the story. And I told you everything. I told you the truth because I did trust you. You seem kind of young to be a producer at CNBC, but you've been very nice, very accomodating, very professional. And now you can't wait to get out of here. It's like you finally have all the information you need. And for what?

You're smirking at me.

Wait a minute. Did you or did you not tell me you were a producer at CNBC, or was that simply my perception of a woman dressed as a young professional? Goddamnit, are you wearing a disguise?

Come back here and sit down. It's your turn to answer some questions, starting with: Who the fuck are you?

Don't you dare walk out that door.

Don't you dare.

T O   M Y   R E A D E R S :

Thank you for reading *The Wine Club.* I have completed seven additional novels, each a distinct and interesting story with great characters. If you liked *The Wine Club,* I believe you would like my other novels as well, and of course, I would love for you to read them.

Please visit the Library page on my website at LaurieLisa.com for more details on each of the other completed novels and their upcoming release on Amazon:

- *Across the Street*
- *The Light Tower*
- *Hollister McClane*
- *"star-cross'd lovers"*
- *David's Women*
- *Family Mythology*
- *Queen of Hearts*

You can also join my Reader's List at LaurieLisa.com to receive updates on the pre-orders and release dates for my novels. Feel free to make personal requests to me directly or ask questions about my books.

I look forward to hearing from you!

Laurie.

Printed in Great Britain
by Amazon

79477485R00294